HIS TO ERASE

SARAH J POULSEN

WARNING:

This is a dark romance.

It contains mature themes, graphic sexual content, violence, and emotionally triggering subject matter. This book is not intended for sensitive readers or anyone under the age of 18.

Please read with care and check the list below before continuing.

His to Erase explores themes of obsession, revenge, trauma, survival, and psychological unraveling. It is intense, emotional, and raw. The characters are messy, broken, and sometimes cruel. But their journey is meant to wreck you—in the best way.

Content warnings include:

- Emotional abuse
- Gaslighting and manipulation
- Stalking and non-consensual tracking
- Flashbacks, PTSD, and memory loss
- Trauma-induced dissociation
- Kidnapping and captivity

- Physical assault and threats
- Obsessive, possessive love interests
- Death, murder, and mafia/organized crime violence
- Dubious consent (consent is present but emotionally complicated)
- Rough, explicit sex with dom/sub, praise, and degradation elements
- Blood, bruises, and knifeplay (light)
- Forced proximity, control dynamics, and internalized shame
- References to past sexual exploitation (non-graphic)
- Torture and revenge (graphic later in story)
- Language, violence, and adult themes throughout

This book is for the readers who crave stories that **bite**, characters who break, and love that burns everything in its path.

If you're still here—you've been warned.

And you're exactly who this book was written for

PLAYLIST

CONTROL - HALSEY
NFWMB - HOZIER
HEAVEN AND BACK - CHASE ATLANTIC
EAT ME - DEMI LOVATO
TRAIN WRECK - JAMES ARTHUR
VISCIOUS - TATE MCRAE
DEAD MAN'S ARMS - BISHOP BRIGGS
FEATHER - SABRINA CARPENTER
YOU BROKE ME FIRST - TATE MCRAE
PLEASE PLEASE PLEASE - SABRINA CARPENTER
GREEDY - TATE MCRAE
DON'T BLAME ME - TAYLOR SWIFT
HAPPIER THAN EVER - BILLIE EILISH
LOOK WHAT YOU MADE ME DO - TAYLOR SWIFT
WE CAN'T STOP - MILEY CYRUS
BEST FRIEND - SAWEETIE, DOJA CAT
BAD AT LOVE - HALSEY
YOU SHOULD SEE ME IN A CROWN - BILLIE EILISH
MALE FANTASY - BILLIE EILISH
ALL THE GOOD GIRLS - BILLIE EILISH
ORDINARY - ALEX WARREN
SLOW IT DOWN - BENSON BOONE
GOOD LUCK, BABE - CHAPPEL ROAN

LUNCH - BILLIE EILISH
OBSESSED - OLIVIA RODRIGO
RISK - GRACIE ABRAMS
PAINT THE TOWN RED - DOJA CAT
NIGHTMARE - HALSEY
VAMPIRE - OLIVIA RODRIGO
ABCDEFU - GAYLE
UH OH - TATE MCRAE
ALWAYS BEEN YOU - JESSIE MURPH
OXYTOCIN - BILLIE EILISH
TOUCH ME LIKE A GANGSTER - JESSE MURPH

Authors notes:

This book wouldn't exist without you. And let's be real—you knew it was about you the second he put a hand around her throat and said, mine.

You've been through more than most people could survive—and you did it with your head high, your heart guarded, and your middle finger up. I watched you fall apart and still show up. For me. For everyone. For yourself, even when you didn't want to.

You love your dark romance—feral, filthy, and unhinged in the best way. So I gave you obsession. I gave you chaos. I gave you survival that looks like a mouthy grin, a don't-fuck-with-me stare, and a soft heart buried under too much armor. I wrote the kind of love that doesn't show up to save you—it drags you through the fire and dares you to save yourself.

This book isn't just for the readers. It's for the girl who lived it. For the woman who came out the other side louder, softer, meaner, kinder, and realer than ever.

Thanks for being my ride or die. Thank you for letting me write this story. Thank you for trusting me with the hard parts. And thank you for still choosing me.

Authors notes:

You're the reason this book has teeth. And I hope when you read it, you feel seen. Loudly.

I had so much fun writing this book, and I've never been more excited about where this journey is taking me. I knew I'd struck gold the second I decided to start writing women their own stories. So to everyone who's been a part of this ride...I AM SO GRATEFUL YOU'RE HERE!

Let's fucking go.

Sarah J. Poulsen

PROLOGUE

5 years ago

The phone vibrates against the table, an unwelcome intrusion. I glance at the screen, my jaw locking the second I see the name. No way I'm answering that.

I let it ring out, watching as the screen goes dark. A second later, it lights up again—this time with a text.

> Stop ignoring me. Pick up.

My fingers flex, a slow inhale filling my lungs. The phone buzzes again, and this time I answer. "You've got ten seconds."

The voice on the other end is a ghost from a past I buried. "We need you for one last job."

I exhale slowly, forcing control into every muscle. "I'm retired. You already told me the last three were my last ones."

"I know," his tone edged with something I don't like. "But you're going to want this one. It's Calissi."

The air shifts. My grip tightens around the phone, but I don't move.

"He's in Colorado," he continues. "Figured you'd want to settle the score."

Calissi. The unfinished job. The mistake I never should have made.

I lean back, trying to steady my pulse. I should say no. A bigger

1

man would let it go. Instead, I hear myself say, "I'll think about it." Then I hang up.

The silence in the room is suffocating. My pulse is slow and even, but my mind is already there.

Calissi's on his knees. Sweat drips from his temple, mixing with the blood running down his face, but the bastard still smiles. Like he's not seconds away from dying. Like he knows something I don't.

I tighten my grip on the gun, aiming between his eyes. I have him. Finally. After months of tracking, weeks of picking off his men one by one, of circling each other in the dark like animals. Every single step has led me here. To this.

The barrel of my gun is pressed to his skull.

He spits blood onto the warehouse floor, grinning like a man who still thinks he's got the upper hand like this is all a big joke. Like he's untouchable.

"You look like shit, Stevie." His voice is all smug amusement, despite the split lip, and the bruises already forming on his face. "What, been losing sleep over me?"

I cock the gun with a steady grip. "Not anymore."

He chuckles. "You really think this is how it ends?"

"Yeah." I flick the safety off. "I do."

A muffled cry cuts through the space and I freeze.

No.

I turn, slowly. Please, no.

Why is she here?

One of his men has her in a chokehold, dragging her forward, her eyes are wide and filled with something I've never seen on her face before—fear. Her wrists are bound, and her mouth is taped. Her body jerks as she struggles, but it's useless.

Calissi sighs, tilting his head like this is some minor inconvenience. "Had a feeling you'd come sniffing around eventually. Figured I should keep a little insurance, just in case."

My heart pounds like a war drum.

"You fucking touch her," I warn, keeping my voice low, "and I will—"

He just laughs.

"You'll what?" His voice drips in mockery. "Shoot me? Please. Let's be real, I own this town." His eyes flick to her. "But, hey, I'm a reasonable guy. Drop the gun, and she walks."

I know it's a lie.

I know it down to my goddamn bones. But she's staring at me, silently pleading, and my hands feel like iron around the gun.

I drop it.

The second it hits the ground, he moves.

My eyes are on her, so I don't see his guy come up behind me. A fist slams into my ribs, hard and unrelenting.

Another cracks across my jaw, snapping my head to the side. Pain detonates, and stars burst behind my eyes.

I barely get my footing before he's right in front of me. His knee drives into my gut and I double over. A boot slams into my ribs, and my body hits the ground.

The taste of blood floods my mouth as he crouches next to me, grabbing a fistful of my hair and yanking my head back, forcing me to look at him. His breath is hot against my face, his smirk dripping with amusement. I know there's nothing I can do to fight back, or he'll kill her.

"You stupid, stupid motherfucker." He clicks his tongue, feigning disappointment. "Dropped your gun over her? Really? Thought you were smarter than that."

I don't answer. I can't. My lungs are barely able to drag in air. He sighs like this is all so tedious.

"And here I thought you'd be a challenge."

Then I hear a gunshot, and I feel the next one fired off as white-hot agony tears through me as my body seizes.

Above me, he shakes his head, wiping the blood from his mouth. "This could've been so much easier," he muses, stepping back. "But hey—I love a good tragedy."

The world is slipping. My pulse is a dull, slow drum, while blood is pooling around me.

I force my head up, jaw tightening against the pain. And then I spit right on his polished shoes.

He stills. For the first time, his smirk twitches. I can see his mask slip for a second. Then he laughs. A deep, smug chuckle, shaking his head like I'm the dumbest son of a bitch he's ever met.

"You should've just shot me when you had the chance," he says, almost disappointed. "Now look at you."

He lifts his boot, walking away.

And then—darkness.

I

"ALWAYS WATCH THE ALLEY."
(THAT'S WHERE PEOPLE BLEED, BEG, OR GET FOUND.)

Ani

I should've walked away. I should've just let someone else find him bleeding out in that alley, letting fate decide whether he lived or died, but I didn't.

Obviously, because I'm not a monster.

Now, months later, I'm standing behind the bar, wiping down a glass like it's going to confess something to me if I rub hard enough, pretending he's not watching me like I'm the most fascinating thing in the room.

We're... seeing each other, I guess?

He's pursuing me, that much is obvious, but I never committed to anything, nor will I, but he keeps showing up. He's all charm, slow smiles and expensive whiskey poured like a promise.

But I'm still undecided.

Not because he isn't attractive—he is. In that curated, dangerous way that makes girls mistake danger for depth. But I've learned that interest isn't the same thing as safety and attention isn't the same thing as caring.

So I let him chase me, and keep pretending I'm not deciding whether I'll run or let him catch me.

Frank *looks* like the kind of man who gets what he wants, whenever he wants it.

7

Hell he *acts* like the kind of man who always gets what he wants. There's nothing casual about the way he looks tonight.

He's wearing another dark, expensive suit—the kind you only wear if you've got the money to make dry cleaning someone else's problem. The fabric clings in all the right places, accentuating the kind of body that's used to being looked at. Not overly muscled but not lean—just powerful. Controlled. Just like everything else about him.

His hair's a little too long, slicked back in a way that should read sleazy—as in *mobster with a God complex*—but on Frank, it doesn't. Not quite. No, on him it looks... deliberate. Calculated. Not a single strand out of place. Just like the rest of him.

He's already smiling when I look up. Enough to suggest that he knows I'm watching. Or worse, that he planned for me to be.

It's the kind of smile that makes people trust him too quickly.

And sure—he's attractive. I'm not blind. He's tall, well-dressed, and objectively handsome in that magazine-spread, secret-sociopath kind of way. He's the kind of man women rewrite their morals for, and are willing to ruin their lives for.

Not me.

I've seen what that smile does to people.

He smiles like a gentleman, but there's something behind it—something slick, dark and dangerous.

I know I'm supposed to be flattered by his attention, but when his eyes rake over me—slow and greedy, like he's trying to memorize me by inch. All it does is make my stomach twist and my skin crawl. It makes me want to bolt for the door and not look back.

At least, that's what I tell myself.

"You've been quiet tonight, doll," his voice is smooth like aged whiskey and just as dangerous. There's a weight beneath it—something coiled and unreadable. "That pretty little head of yours thinking too much again?"

I smile and set my glass down with all the elegance of someone who's pretending they haven't already fantasized about stabbing him with a stir stick.

"Just counting all the red flags I've been ignoring," I say sweetly, like we're flirting and not circling a battlefield.

His grin spreads, like he knows exactly how much damage he can do with it.

That's the problem with men like Frank. They don't just walk into rooms—they own them. Or at least, they like to pretend they do. Maybe he thinks he owns me too.

The thought sours fast, but I don't let it show. I've spent years surviving men who thought their power made them invincible. Who saw girls like me as soft things to mold.

I've been here before. Standing too close to the fire, letting my guard slip one calculated inch at a time. Pretending I'm not already cataloguing the exits, every time he leans just a little too far into my space.

I know what happens when men like him think you're theirs, and I'm not naïve enough to think I'm still untouchable.

Not anymore.

And if I'm not careful, Frank DeLuca might just be the mistake that finally gets me killed.

He taps his fingers against the bar, slow and rhythmic, like a man who's entirely too pleased with himself. "You know, Ani, it's been months since I got out of the hospital."

I arch a brow, unimpressed. "And you're just now realizing that? Must've been a rough recovery."

He chuckles, shaking his head. "Nah. Just figured now's a good time to finally thank you properly."

I lean forward, resting my elbows on the bar, pretending to be interested. "Most people just say thank you and move on, maybe send a fruit basket if they're feelin' a little spicy."

"Right, but I'm not most people."

Unfortunately.

He smirks. "So, how about dinner?"

I huff a laugh, wiping down the counter between us, the same one I've scrubbed three times already tonight. Mostly out of spite.

"That's the third time you've asked me out this week, Frank. You must be a masochist... or desperate. Neither are a good look."

He leans in, close enough that I catch the sharp hit of his cologne. It's expensive—probably imported—but he's wearing too much of it.

"Just persistent."

I roll my eyes so hard I almost see last year. "It's not happening."

"Yet," he says smoothly. "I'll just keep coming back. Sooner or later, you're gonna get sick of saying no."

I tilt my head like I'm thinking about it. I'm not. But the performance helps me feel like I'm in control of something.

"Or," I say sweetly, "I'll just start charging you a fee every time you walk through the door. Win-win. That might actually pay my rent."

His grin spreads, slow and satisfied. The kind of grin that says I always get what I want, and you just haven't realized it yet.

"I'll pay whatever you want me to, love. As long as you let me sit at your bar."

Of course he would say that. The man turns obsession into flirtation like it's a love language.

I don't answer.

Not out loud.

Because this is the dance we do—him, charming and cocky, me, unimpressed and pretending I don't wonder what it would feel like to let my guard down for half a second.

Spoiler: I'm not going to. But he doesn't need to know that yet.

I've outrun worse.

I don't even know this man. Not really. I mean, sure—I technically saved his life a few months ago. Mistakes were made. And ever since, he's apparently decided I'm the prize in some long-con romance novel he's acting out in his head.

He's been asking me out nonstop ever since. He clearly doesn't know how to take no for an answer. Or he does, and he's just refusing to accept that I mean it.

I know two things about Frank. One, he either has money or really wants people to think he does. And two, he enjoys the sound of his own voice almost as much as he enjoys seeing me pretend not to be interested.

Either way—not my problem.

But maybe...just maybe...dinner wouldn't kill me.

A free meal and a little attention I don't have to reciprocate? That's not the worst thing in the world. I've suffered through worse in cheaper shoes.

I shake my head to clear the thought, but before I can throw another verbal punch his way, the door swings open behind him, and a gust of night air follows the next customer inside—cool and sharp and laced with something that makes the hair on my neck stand up.

Frank just sips his drink, eyes still on me as I slip back into autopilot. Smile. Move. Glass. Pour.

I keep my hands busy so my thoughts don't start asking questions I don't want answers to, but I can feel his gaze follow me with every step I take.

"One day, Ani," he murmurs. "You'll say yes."

I glance at him, unimpressed. "Or maybe one day you'll learn to take a hint."

He grins, unfazed, sliding off the stool. "Not likely."

He's a picture of confidence as he strolls toward the door. I watch him go, shaking my head as I turn back to work. I should find that more irritating than I do. Instead, I find it intriguing.

The night drags, and by the time my shift is nearly over, my patience is hanging on by a thread. The bar is mostly cleared out—

just a few stragglers nursing drinks, waiting for last call. I drop off a check for one of them and start wiping down the counter when I feel eyes on me.

I glance up, and sure enough—there is. Table twelve. Alone. Overconfident. The kind of man who doesn't ask so much as hover like you're on display.

His gaze drags down my body slow enough to be deliberate, like I'm a meal and he's deciding where to start.

"You got a name, baby?"

I blink once, keeping my expression neutral and polite, but I'm already fighting the urge to dump his drink in his lap.

"Yeah," I say. "It's No."

He chuckles like I just flirted with him. I've been here a hundred times before—it's just another night, and another man who mistakes disinterest for challenge.

"Feisty," he grins, like he thinks he's original. "I like that."

I don't.

I don't like that he's still staring, his eyes haven't left my chest once. I really don't like that familiar pressure behind my ribs—that quiet alarm that's always right.

"Bar's closing soon," I say, keeping my tone flat. "Which means you should finish your drink and leave."

There's a long enough pause for me to glance at the door, clocking who's left. Counting how many more minutes I'll have to pretend for. I don't keep pepper spray taped under the register for nothing.

"Not before I get your number."

I meet his eyes, letting my expression drop into something cold and bored. "You think I give my number out to drunk men? Let alone ones who can't take a hint?"

He blinks, trying to process, but I don't wait for a reply. I grab his glass, dump the contents into the sink, and slap his check down in front of him.

"Last call," I say, my voice sickly sweet. "Pay up."

The man glares at me but pulls out his wallet. I don't move until he drops a few bills on the counter, stumbling slightly before making his way out.

I don't breathe until the door swings shut behind him.

By the time I finally step outside, the night air is sharp as it creeps beneath my jacket. The streets are quiet, just the occasional car rolling by, headlights cutting through the dark. I pull out my phone and glance at the text from Frank.

If you need a ride, just let me know.

No thanks.

The last thing I need is another favor I didn't ask for. I walk fast, my boots hitting the pavement in steady, measured steps, but something feels... off.

Not *normal-girl-walking-alone-at-night* off. Not even *city-level-caution* off.

It's the kind of off that makes the hairs on the back of my neck stand up like they've been personally briefed on incoming danger.

I glance over my shoulder, but the street's empty. Every instinct I have is screaming. Not whispering. Not nudging. Screaming.

I know what it feels like to be followed. I know the difference between anxiety and experience. But it's not paranoia if it's happened before, right?

My keys are already in my hand by the time I turn the corner. I don't look back again, because looking back makes it real.

My heart's hammering by the time I reach my building. The entrance is half in shadow, and the flickering light above the door is doing that lovely horror-movie thing where it buzzes once, then goes dark.

Perfect.

I shove the key into the lock, twist, and duck inside like the door might disappear behind me. Then I slam it shut and lock it, pressing my back to it, just for good measure.

I don't hear anything.

No footsteps.

No breathing.

No horror-movie reveal.

Just silence.

The only thing I hear is the quiet sound of my own pulse trying to climb into my throat. I pause, taking a deep breath. *Okay, maybe that was nothing and I was being paranoid.*

I drop my keys onto the counter and exhale. The worst part about running from your past isn't the running itself. It's the way you never stop looking over your shoulder, waiting for the moment it finally catches up.

I take off my boots and let them crash against the wall, one bouncing off at an angle like even they're tired of holding it together.

My jacket follows, sliding off my shoulders, it hits the floor with a damp thud. I should hang it up, but I don't.

The air in here is stale—cold in that weird, bone-deep way that sticks around no matter how many times I mess with the heater. Like the apartment itself has just... given up.

The couch is older than my trauma, sagging like it's seen some shit and decided it no longer has the strength to care. There's a tear in the armrest that I keep pretending isn't growing and like most things in my life, it came damaged and I took it anyway.

The kitchen's more of a suggestion than a functional space. The fridge hums like it's threatening to quit. It's loud and a little too passive-aggressive. The cabinet holds a mismatched graveyard of mugs and takeout containers I swear I'll recycle someday. There's no art on the walls. No warm lights. No fake plants. No half-assed attempts to convince anyone—including myself—that this is a place someone lives in, not just crashes in between jobs.

Just the essentials. Just enough to survive another day.

The only exception is my books.

They're everywhere. Piled on the floor. Stacked on chairs. Stuffed into the one rickety shelf I drug home after a thrift store haul. It holds all my leather-bound classics, poetry anthologies, and stories about monsters, villains, and happy endings.

It's a far cry from the life I used to have.

Once upon a time, my apartment had matching furniture. A real couch. A full set of dishes. Shelves that weren't collapsing under the weight of bad decisions and trauma bonding with paperback spines.

The place felt warm, and lived in. Safe.

I had space, a bathroom door that locked without a prayer, and a bed that didn't scream in protest every time I turned over. I also didn't used to fall asleep wondering if someone was watching me from across the street—or if the next knock on the door was going to unravel whatever sanity I had left.

But sure. I'm thriving.

I rub a hand over my face trying to shake it off. There's no use romanticizing what's already gone.

That life? That girl? She didn't make it.

I make my way to the bathroom, flipping on the light, and I meet my reflection like I'm checking in with a stranger who owes me answers.

The mirror above the sink is cracked in the corner like a spiderweb of glass, spreading like a warning.

My dark eyes are rimmed with exhaustion, and my hair is falling out of the braid I threw together twenty minutes before my shift. This girl looks like she's seen some shit.

I peel off my work clothes one layer at a time, swapping them for sweatpants and the oversized hoodie that knows all my secrets. This part's all routine.

Change.

Eat.

Try to sleep.

Wake up.

Repeat.

It's not a life, but it's working for now. And sometimes, that's all survival really is.

I head into the kitchen and yank open the fridge door. It groans like it hates me, and the bulb flickers revealing the depressing inventory of a woman with commitment issues and no interest in grocery shopping.

There's half a carton of milk, a takeout container that might be from last week—or last month, honestly, it's a gamble—and a half-eaten roll of cookie dough I've been pretending is breakfast.

I slam the door shut and reach for the mac and cheese in the cabinet instead. The blue box kind. The one that doesn't ask questions or require emotional investment.

Filling a pot with water, I set it on the stove and crank the burner until the gas hisses and finally catches with a flickering flame that looks just as exhausted as I feel.

Minimal effort. Minimal thinking. It's all I have the energy for tonight.

As I wait for the water to boil, I lean against the counter and cross my arms like that's going to keep the thoughts in.

I'm all auto pilot right now. I stir the noodles, drain them, then dump in the powdered cheese and the splash of milk that may or may not be flirting with its expiration date. It mixes into a color that shouldn't exist in nature as the smell hits the air.

I take a bite straight from the pot, and naturally it's too hot, and burns my tongue, but I barely flinch.

My mind drifts—uninvited, like it always does when things get quiet. And I let it. Because fighting it takes more energy than I have tonight.

It's almost been a year since I got here.

Long enough that the nightmares have changed shape, and long enough that the bruises have faded.

It's been almost as long since I found Frank bleeding out in that alley, slumped against a wall like he had all the time in the world. Five months since I hesitated when I should have just called for help and walked away.

I didn't even plan on going down the alley.

Sarah, my just as unhinged best friend was the one who was supposed to take out the trash before she left—basic end-of-shift protocol. But does she ever actually finish a shift without getting distracted by something shiny or flirty?

Of course not.

She bailed early—again—probably climbed onto the back of some guy's motorcycle while I got stuck doing her closing duties. Best friend of the year. Truly.

So there I was, grumbling to myself, dragging out the trash and mentally writing her obituary—when I saw him.

At first, I thought he was just another drunk guy slumped against the wall, breathing through whatever bad decisions landed him there.

I was going to leave him. I swear I was. But then I saw the blood and heard the gasp.

"Help."

Just that. Barely a whisper. But it landed like a punch. And now I can't shake him.

Sighing, I toss the spoon into the sink with more force than necessary, and drag myself to the couch, sinking into the worn cushions like they might swallow me whole if I ask nicely.

I grab my phone out of habit—not because I want to be online, but because the silence is louder without the glow of distraction.

I swipe the screen, scrolling through meaningless updates, vacation photos, engagement announcements, and baby bumps. There's an occasional post from someone I used to know—people who have no idea where I am. People who think I just disappeared.

Which, to be fair, I did.

I left everything behind. Burned the trail, and slammed the door, locking it from the other side.

But no matter how far I run, no matter how many nights I spend staring at this same cracked ceiling in a city where no one says my name—it never feels far enough.

I open the message thread with the lunatic I call my best friend.

Me: In case you're wondering, I'm still alive.

I made boxed mac and cheese and only cried a little.

I'm calling it a win. You'd be proud.

AND I didn't set anything on fire.

Sarah: YET. Proud doesn't even cover it. This is growth. Boxed carbs and emotionally suppressed tears? You're basically thriving.

Do I send flowers or a fire extinguisher?

Me: Whichever one comes with wine.

Sarah: Noted. Care package incoming. But you don't drink? Did we start? Also, don't think I won't show up and drag your emotionally unavailable ass home if you go dark again for another week.

THE DAYS BLEND TOGETHER. WORK. SLEEP. REPEAT.

Every couple of nights, like clockwork, Frank strolls into the bar, slides onto the same damn stool, and watches me with that smirk—the one that says he knows exactly how our conversation will go.

"How about dinner, Ani?"

"No thanks."

"You're breaking my heart, doll."

"Good. Maybe it'll make you stop asking."

But he never does. He keeps coming back, keeps watching me, and keeps acting like he knows something I don't.

Tonight's no different.

He settles in like he owns the place, fingers drumming an easy rhythm against the counter, patience stitched into his every movement.

"You know," he muses, tilting his head slightly, "some would call this playing hard to get. You don't even text me back anymore."

I don't bother looking up as I dry a glass, keeping my voice flat. "And some would call this not interested."

"Hmm." He takes a slow sip of his drink, like he's actually considering that. "See, that's where I'm struggling. If you were really not interested, you'd have thrown me out by now."

I let out a slow breath, setting the glass down with a deliberate clink. He's not wrong, and that pisses me off more than I want to admit.

"Trust me, Frank, it's something I think about daily."

His grin is dripping with something unreadable. "That right?"

"Absolutely."

"And yet," he leans in slightly, lowering his voice just enough that the words curl into something smug, "here I am."

I narrow my eyes, watching as he signals for another drink like he doesn't have a care in the world. I pour it without a word, setting it down with a little more force than necessary, so it sloshes on the counter.

He doesn't even break eye contact. He just lifts the glass and takes a slow sip.

"You know what I like about you, baby girl?"

"That I don't like you?" I deadpan, already moving to clean up an empty glass left behind next to him.

He chuckles, shaking his head. "The fact that you're a terrible liar."

My stomach tightens, but I keep my face neutral. He's wrong. I'm an excellent liar. It's why I'm still alive.

I turn away from him, busying myself with stacking the clean glasses, but he's still there, his presence pressing against me even without him moving an inch.

"You could make this easy," he says after a moment. "One date. One dinner. Then, if you still don't like me, I'll leave you alone."

I glance at him, unimpressed. "You really expect me to believe that?"

He places a hand over his heart, trying his hardest to look offended. "You wound me."

"Good," I mutter, brushing past him to grab another bottle from the wall. "Maybe it'll finally make you stop harassing me."

His smirk doesn't falter. If anything, it deepens—like I just confirmed he's winning whatever game we're playing. Like rejection's just foreplay to him.

"That's what you said last time."

"And yet you're still here."

"Exactly," he says, all smooth arrogance and way too much eye contact. "Which means you're doing something wrong."

God, he's relentless.

I scan the room for a lifeline—someone who needs a refill, someone vomiting on a barstool, literally anything to save me from this conversation. But there's nothing.

"Or you just have a problem with rejection."

I say it like I'm commenting on the weather. I've said no to him so many times it's practically my job title at this point, but he just grins like I handed him another reason to stay. Maybe that's the problem, maybe guys like him don't hear "no." Maybe they hear "not yet."

Maybe they're always looking for the crack in your armor instead of respecting the fact that it's there for a reason.

But, I don't say any of that.

I just keep pouring drinks and pretending he doesn't make my skin itch in a way that feels too familiar.

He watches me while his fingers trace patterns against the counter, and I know what he's doing. "You call it rejection, I call it persistence."

I shake my head, biting back a smirk that's more reflex than amusement. I still don't know what his angle is. Maybe he just likes the chase. Or he sees something in me he can't quite name—some crack in the foundation he wants to dig his hands into. Or maybe he just gets off on watching me squirm.

Wouldn't be the first.

Either way—I don't trust him. Not with his smile, not with his persistence, and definitely not with the way his eyes linger. But I'd be lying if I said I didn't like the distraction.

I exhale through my nose, setting down the last clean glass and grip the edge of the counter like it might have the answers I don't. Because I know what's coming. He's not going to stop asking. He's going to keep showing up and pushing. Keep circling until he either gets what he wants—or I finally break character.

So maybe it's time to end the game. Maybe I will say yes. Just once. Just enough to remind myself why I don't say yes in the first place.

I turn, leveling him with a look. "One date."

Frank stills. It's brief—so quick I almost miss it—but it's there. That flicker of something behind his eyes, something sharp and knowing, like he was just waiting for me to break first.

His smirk curves slowly. "You sure, sweetheart? Hate to think you're giving in already."

I cross my arms. "Don't flatter yourself. The sooner this happens, the sooner you stop asking."

He lifts his glass, tilting it toward me in a slow, lazy toast before taking a sip. "We'll see."

I roll my eyes, already regretting this. "Pick a time and place, and I'll meet you there."

He sets his glass down with a quiet clink, standing with that same practiced ease, adjusting the cuffs of his suit like he knew this was inevitable.

Smug bastard.

"Smart decision."

I scoff. "It's a pity date—don't get ahead of yourself."

2

"BAD DECISIONS START IN DARK CORNERS.**"**
(THAT'S WHERE **I'**D WAIT TOO**)**

Ani

For the first time in weeks, I actually had a night off. And I wasted it saying yes to this date.

Sarah and I were supposed to hang out—vegging on pizza in our sweatpants, watching something stupid on TV. I was looking forward to it. She even promised to bring wine this time, which means I was definitely robbed.

At least we have part of the day.

I'm sitting cross-legged on a bench with a towel around my shoulders and bleach fumes burning my nose while Sarah mixes toner like she's doing God's work. *Okay, she is. Bleaching my hair is not for the weak.* She's wearing an old band shirt, socks pulled halfway up her calves, and her Ipad is balanced on the sink playing The Big Bang Theory.

I'm trying not to gag at the smell.

She's squinting at the back of my head like it personally offended her. "This section is so thick, I'm pretty sure it just gave me attitude."

I smile into my coffee. "They're tired of your abuse."

She scoffs, parting another piece with the brush. "Please. I'm the best thing that's ever happened to your scalp."

I hum. "That's what my last therapist said, too."

25

"Ha. Not me being more consistent than your therapist."

"Honestly? That tracks."

She leans closer, brushing toner down to the ends while humming something vaguely threatening while I try not to move.

"I still can't believe you're going on this date," she says, shifting to the other side. "I thought we agreed he gives red flag energy."

I lift a brow in the mirror. "You agreed. I just nodded because you had foils in."

She tilts her head so I can't see her face but I know she's glaring. "You're emotionally compromised."

"Says the girl who's been flirting with catfish."

She glares. "He's not a catfish. He's keeping the suspense alive. It's foreplay—with a moral code that definitely includes choking."

I nearly spit my coffee. "Jesus Christ. You're going to get baby snatched one day."

"No way." she says innocently. "Communication is hot. So is choking. Ideally at the same time."

I snort, biting the inside of my cheek. "Remind me why I let you near chemicals?"

"Because I don't trust anyone else not to turn your blonde into a cautionary tale."

Fair.

She was one of the first people I saw when I moved here—grinning behind the bar with this wild, unbothered energy like nothing could shake her. I hadn't even said a word yet, and she handed me a shot and told me I looked like I needed it.

Something about us just clicked after that. No weird in-between stage of pretending to be normal. Just full-send chaos and honesty from the start.

We've been like this ever since.

You know when you find that one person you can say literally anything to—like there's no filter, no judgment, just instant understanding? That's her.

My disaster twin.

"You're sure you wanna go?" she asks after a pause. "You don't have to say yes just to prove you're not still wrecked by what happened."

She knows me too well sometimes.

"I don't know," I admit, quietly. "Maybe I just want to feel something that doesn't come with a memory attached."

Sarah sets the brush down and meets my eyes in the mirror. "You're allowed to feel good without punishing yourself for it."

God, if only it were that simple.

She moves behind me again, gently massaging toner into the ends.

"Besides," she smirks, "if he's a letdown, at least your hair's out here making up for it."

I roll my eyes. "Wow. Truly the support I needed."

"Don't blame me—your tits showed up dressed for applause."

"You're only saying that because I let you bleach me."

"That, and because I'm not blind."

I snort, pretending that any part of our conversations are normal. While she rinses the last bit of toner into the sink, she says, "So what's your plan if the date goes well?"

I blink. "Define 'well.'"

She shrugs. "Like, you don't immediately plot his death."

"Oh. Then yeah, I guess that'd be new."

Sarah hands me a towel and starts wiping her hands. "You're allowed to want shit, Ani."

I glance up at her.

"You know. Mutual obsession, light emotional damage, and a good dicking. The essentials."

I snort. "That last one was a stretch."

"I said what I said."

I love our friendship. I don't say it out loud, but I think she hears it anyway. Because when I stand up and pull her into a hug, bleach stains and all, she just wraps her arms around me and says,

"I'm just saying—if God has favorites, you're definitely top five. Bare minimum."

And somehow, that's exactly what I needed to hear.

Once my hair's done, we migrate to the kitchen like we always do when we're avoiding the fact that time is passing, and she throws a pizza in the oven.

"Okay," she says, cracking open a can of Sprite like we're about to get serious. "You never actually told me what this man did to earn your attention. Aside from existing and having abs," she adds, wiggling her eyebrows.

I groan, dragging both hands down my face. "That was taken out of context."

"You called him a walking red flag with dick-slinging energy. Don't backpedal now."

"Okay, that one I might've said."

We keep going like that—her poking, me deflecting, and of us pretending we're not circling the fact that I said yes to a man I probably shouldn't trust. What I really want is this—cheap comfort and snarky commentary from someone who gets me without needing the full rundown of why I flinch when people touch me too suddenly, or why I don't talk about my ex.

Luckily, she never pushes. She just... gets it.

We were halfway through a YouTube rabbit hole of worst-date horror stories when her phone dinged.

She glances at it, then immediately shoves it under her thigh.

I raise a brow. "Oh no. That's your I-did-something-face."

She stays suspiciously still. "It's nothing."

"Sarah."

She sighs, pulling the phone back out with the guilt of someone who just texted an ex. "Okay. So. You know how I said I blocked Kaleb?"

"No."

"Well, I did. Emotionally."

"Jesus Christ."

She winces. "He just messaged me, saying he was in town."

"Please tell me you didn't reply."

"I didn't! Yet." She bites her lip, then mutters, "I may have heart-reacted."

"Sarah."

"It was a reflex!"

I try to stop a laugh from coming out, but I can't. "So let me get this straight. The man who ghosted you for six weeks and then reappeared with a new girlfriend and a motivational podcast is now back in town—and your first instinct is heart emoji?"

She groans, dropping her head into her hands. "I know. I have a disease. It's called attention whore."

I try to glare, but she looks genuinely tortured that I mostly just wanted to throw my hairbrush at her. "What does he even want?"

She looks at me. "Dinner."

"No."

"I said maybe."

"Sarah!"

"Okay, god," she laughs, standing up and grabbing her bag. "You're right. I'll cancel. Probably. Eventually. But I do need to get out of here before I cave and text something worse. Then I'll be late for work."

I narrow my eyes. "Define worse."

She smiles sweetly. "A selfie."

"Oh my god."

"Don't worry, I won't actually do it," she calls over her shoulder. "Not unless he double-texts."

She's already halfway to the door, waving her phone in the air like a white flag of slutty surrender.

She just had to go pick up a shift, so naturally, I said yes to the date. I don't even know why, I'm capable of sitting at home alone for one night.

Maybe I thought it'd finally shut him up.

I'm just tired of him hovering like he already knew I'd cave eventually. Maybe I wanted to prove—to him or myself, I don't even know at this point—that he's not as unshakable as he pretends to be.

Whatever the reason, it was a mistake.

I should be in my sweats, curled up and eating something unhealthy. Not standing in front of my closet trying to figure out how to look like someone not going on a date with a man I already don't trust.

Eventually, I settle on my usual—black on black. Obviously. I end up in a fitted crop top with a neckline dipping just enough to cause problems, but not enough to be an open invitation.

It says I showed up, not that I'm interested.

I pair that with high-waisted jeans—also black, and ripped—that hug every inch of me like they were personally tailored by the gods of emotional damage and good decisions made late at night.

Not that I'm dressing for him, this is for me. That way I look like I can throw a punch and walk away without smudging my mascara.

It's a look that says, I could ruin your life, but I don't feel like it tonight.

I lace up my combat boots, knowing they're still comfortable enough to walk home in if I decide to ghost halfway through this disaster. Which, let's be honest, is already feeling like a strong possibility.

The Uber's waiting at the curb, and I'm already questioning every decision that led to this moment.

The ride is quiet, giving my brain time to spiral as the city blurs past in neon streaks and glowing streetlights. The closer we get, the heavier the regret sits in my stomach.

By the time we pull up, I'm already planning my exit. The restaurant doesn't look like a restaurant, it looks like a threat with marble stairs, and gold-trimmed doors.

Jesus Christ.

I sigh, slipping out of the car before I can talk myself into staying inside. The air is cool against my skin and the sounds of the city are muffled under the weight of too much money and exclusivity.

I spot Frank standing outside the entrance with his hands in his pockets, watching me with that same smug confidence—like he knew I wouldn't back out.

His suit is dark and effortlessly tailored, the kind of cut that makes expensive look easy. Even under the streetlight, he looks polished—clean-shaven jaw, long hair pushed back like he stepped out of a magazine shoot. He doesn't belong on a quiet sidewalk.

His eyes find mine, and he holds my gaze. There's a glint in them that looks like either mischief or arrogance, I'm never quite sure which.

I feel a quiet hum under my skin. The one that always stirs when he looks at me like that. But want and trust aren't the same thing, so I keep walking. I've noticed the way his mouth tilts when he watches me approach, and the closer I get, the stronger I can smell him.

"You clean up nice," he says, while his eyes drag over my outfit with something unreadable.

"So do you," I deadpan. "Shame it's wasted on this place."

He chuckles, shaking his head. "And here I thought you were starting to like me."

I tilt my head. "Not even a little."

His grin widens, like he sees right through me. He steps closer, offering his arm. "Shall we?"

I don't take it, but I do follow him inside.

The restaurant is too much.

It's all dark wood, gold accents, and chandeliers dripping with crystals. It's the kind of place where the wine costs more than my rent and the silverware probably has a better pedigree than I do. A quiet hum of conversation fills the space, broken only by the occasional chime of glass meeting glass.

Frank definitely belongs here.

The moment we step through the doors, heads turn. Not because he demands attention, but because he wears power like a second skin.

He just places a hand at the small of my back, and mutters something about reservations to the hostess who's currently drooling over him.

She just nods, grabbing two menus, and leads us through the maze of white tablecloths and expensive conversation.

I slide into my seat, stretching out my legs like I don't care about the stares we're getting. Which I'm sure are due to my outfit choice. If I knew I had to go prom dress shopping to eat here, I would have definitely found a way out of tonight.

Frank watches me, amused, as he settles into his own seat. "What?"

I prop my chin in my hand, tapping my fingers against my cheek. "Nothing. Just wondering how many threats it took to get a table like this."

His smirk curves, slow and lazy. "What makes you think I had to threaten anyone?"

I arch a brow. "Because men like you don't ask for things. They take."

His expression doesn't change, but something shifts behind his eyes. "And yet, here you are. Voluntarily."

I scoff, reaching for the menu. "We'll see how voluntary it feels by the end of the night."

He laughs, and I hate that the first thing I notice is how good he is at this. Not just the date—though, yeah, he's excellent at that—but the way he reads people, adjusts, and plays the role perfectly.

"Tell me something true about you," he says at one point, watching me over the rim of his glass.

I smirk. "I think most rich people are deeply miserable."

He grins, unfazed. "That's a cop-out. Tell me something real."

I tilt my head, pretending to think about it. "Alright. I like thunderstorms. The louder, the better."

He nods, like I just revealed a profound secret about my soul. "Good answer."

I resist the urge to roll my eyes so hard they detach. What is this, a game show? Cool, Frank. Would you have sent me home if I'd said sunshine and puppies?

"Your turn," I say instead, leaning back and pretending I'm not already questioning all my life choices that led me to this table. Again.

He leans back in his chair, swirling the wine in his glass. "I don't make promises I can't keep."

Something about the way he says it makes my skin prickle and not in a good way, but also, not in a bad way.

I take a slow sip of my drink, letting the silence sit between us for a beat too long. "That supposed to impress me?"

His mouth curves just enough to count as a smirk. "Just letting you know what kind of man I am."

Oh, good. A warning. Like I haven't heard that one before. He's charming, witty, and smooth in ways that should set off every internal alarm I've got hardwired into my spine. But somehow... it doesn't.

Dinner lasts longer than I expect, but I laugh more than I should. So I guess that's a win. And somewhere between the second glass of wine and the third story about his supposedly tragic childhood, *which may or may not be real—I haven't decided,* I forget to keep my guard up.

When he walks me outside, the city buzzes softly around us like it's in on something I'm not. I realize—I actually had a good time. And I hate that.

I should've hated every second of it, or found a reason to leave halfway through. Hell, I should've rolled my eyes and made some excuse about an early shift or a sick cat or literally anything else.

But instead, I'm standing on the sidewalk in front of a restaurant I never would've chosen, staring at him in the soft glow of a streetlight, and I don't feel like leaving. And he knows it.

He's watching me with that smug, satisfied look like I'm the prize. Or maybe he's hoping I've stopped resisting.

He steps closer, tilting his head slightly as he watches me. "I was right, wasn't I?"

I raise a brow. "About what?"

His smirk is lazy, and smug. "You like me."

I snort, shaking my head. "You're tolerable at best."

His eyes flick over me, slowly. "That's a step up from last week."

I roll my eyes, already reaching for my phone to see how close the Uber is. "You're exhausting."

He grins like that was exactly the answer he was expecting. "You may have agreed to one night, but I don't think you realize how patient I am."

He leans in closer, brushing a kiss against my cheek. "I'm just glad I found you when I did."

The Uber pulls up and I take a step toward the door, barely resisting the urge to sprint, because as much as I like Frank, I'm not sure I want to kiss him. Behind me, he's still standing there with that same self-satisfied smirk—the one that's been tattooed onto his face since the moment he decided I was worth chasing. Or collecting. I still haven't decided which.

I grip the door handle, already crafting the perfect non-goodbye in my head. Something neutral and dismissive, but cold enough to make a point.

He opens his mouth to say something—probably clever, but definitely unwanted. I don't give him the satisfaction, I just slide into the car, dead silent, and let the door slam shut between us like a punctuation mark.

When I'm not at the bar, I work at the library. It's quiet, predictable, and full of stories that aren't mine.

I like it that way.

Most people here don't talk, and if they do, it's in whispers. No forced small talk. No fake smiles. No one asking what I'm doing later or if they can buy me a drink.

It's just shelves and silence and the comforting hum of old HVAC and the smell of old books.

I push a cart of returns through the aisles, the scent of dust, paper, and worn leather curling around me like a weighted blanket I actually want. The library is nearly empty—exactly how I like it. A few regulars hover in their usual corners, and there's a pair of students whispering over a laptop. At one table there's always this one retired guy who smells like peppermint and sadness, and then there's the occasional lost soul flipping through pages like they're looking for something they can't name.

I shelve a few books, fingers trailing over familiar spines as I move through the stacks. There's something grounding about this place. About the fact that it doesn't ask anything of me.

Here, I don't have to be the bartender with the forced smile, swatting off attention I didn't invite. I don't have to be the girl looking over her shoulder, pretending she's not still waiting for the other shoe to drop.

I can just... be.

Occasionally, Sarah shows up with coffee and chaos energy, pretending to browse while whisper-yelling at me from across the aisle like she's physically incapable of respecting the sacred quiet.

We close the bar together most nights—so naturally, she knows all my secrets and exactly how many shots it takes before I start making death threats or bad decisions. Sometimes both.

She's the only one who gets a pass and she knows it.

I slide another book into place, then pause when my eyes catch the next one in the pile.

The Art of War.

A little on the nose, but fitting.

I smirk and shelve it anyway. If nothing else, the universe has a twisted sense of humor.

"You always look like you're plotting something when you're in here," a voice says behind me.

It's a low, deep kind that hums along your spine before your brain can catch up. And just like that, I'm on alert.

Every survival instinct I've ever developed clicks into place as I turn my head. I've spent years perfecting the art of the blank stare. The casual, don't-fuck-with-me deadpan. I'm already prepping to tell whoever it is to mind their own business and choke on a dictionary. And then I see him.

Oh.

Well.

Shit.

He's tall.

Like... tall.

Which, okay—not hard to accomplish when you're five-foot-one on a good day with boots and vengeance.

But this guy?

This guy would feel like a giant even if I were standing on a chair with a weapon.

It's not just the height. It's the way he holds himself. He doesn't just take up space—he owns it.

I'm 100% certain the air bends around him and the walls asked permission to still be standing.

He's all muscle and menace wrapped in an exhale of total control. He doesn't move. Doesn't smile. Doesn't flirt. He just exists like a problem I haven't solved yet. That should be my first red flag.

A big, neon, flashing red flag.

But instead, my brain short-circuits and my body does that annoying thing where it forgets I'm not supposed to feel anything right now.

I cross my arms. Mostly to keep from folding and partially to remind myself that I've been through worse than whatever this walking testosterone ad is selling.

I know I'm staring, but he has perfect hair, that's dark and messy—thick enough to grip, and careless in the kind of way that says he ran a hand through it once, then let the rest burn.

There's black ink curling up his arms that coil like smoke, disappearing beneath the sleeves of his fitted black shirt like sin dressed up as art. And it's the worst kind of ink—the kind that looks personal. The kind that makes you want to ask questions you have no business knowing the answers to.

More ink licks at his knuckles, trailing over his fingers—veins made of violence and precision. It's all so intricate and brutal. It's beautiful in the way a loaded gun is beautiful. It shouldn't be sexy. Yet, it is anyway.

And then there's his jawline.

Jesus.

It's a crime scene.

It's cut from something cruel, ancient and holy, shadowed with just enough scruff to make him look like the reason your mother warned you to never leave the house in short skirts.

All I can think—because of course I can't stop thinking—is how it would feel between my thighs.

Hot. Rough. And unforgiving.

And yeah, maybe I need therapy. But this? This is definitely not the cure.

My stomach clenches. *Jesus Christ, Anianne. Pull it together.*

This is not a swooning situation, but the way his smooth, golden skin looks is making me drool. It has nothing to do with sun exposure and everything to do with the kind of genetics that should be illegal.

And then—there are his eyes.

God.

His eyes.

They're the kind of dark that swallows light and doesn't apologize. Like a goddamn threat.

His lashes are criminally long, just to add insult to injury. All soft edges wrapped around sharp intention.

He looks like the kind of man who clocks exits, memorizes weaknesses, and has already mentally figured out what people to remove from the equation in case shit goes sideways.

And yet—they settle on me. And stay there.

Like I'm the one he's already decided is going to ruin his night. Or maybe he's going to ruin mine. He's giving off that vibe—the I-could-kill-everyone-in-this-building-and-still-be-home-by-midnight vibe.

The kind of energy that should send me running. And the worst part is, I hate that it works on me. Because it shouldn't. It should terrify me. But instead, I'm standing here wondering how those hands would feel pressed against my throat. Which is exactly the kind of thought that makes me question every life decision I've ever made.

Everything about him screams, don't ask questions you don't want answers to. And yet, here he is. In a fucking library, like he belongs here. He's without a doubt the most dangerous fucking thing in this entire building.

I shouldn't be memorizing the details, shouldn't be imagining what the ink beneath his shirt looks like, where it stops, how far it goes, how much of him is covered in it.

But I am.

And when my gaze flicks back up to his face, those black eyes are waiting. The tilt at the corner of his mouth suggests he caught every second of my mental detour into why-is-this-stranger-the-hottest-walking-danger-sign-I've-ever-seen territory.

It's not quite a smirk, but not quite a glare either. It's just a quiet, pointed look that says, *are you going to answer my question— or just keep staring?*

Shit.

I blink once—maybe twice—then force my face into something neutral.

Unbothered.

I'm going to pretend I didn't just get caught undressing him with my eyes while my brain short-circuited over his murder vibes and bone structure.

Totally casual.

I clear my throat, praying that too much time didn't pass. Because if he's the type to keep score, I just lost the first round.

"That's an interesting assumption."

At least my voice is steady. Thank fuck. Because nothing else about me is.

He watches me, and he's giving me the kind of look that should make me nervous, only it doesn't.

"Am I wrong?"

No hesitation. No shift in tone. Just a quiet, confident push.

My fingers tighten slightly around the book I forgot I was still holding.

"No comment."

The corner of his mouth twitches like I amused him, but it's gone almost instantly. Replaced with something cool and direct.

"I'm looking for a book."

Cool. Me too. Preferably one that explains what the hell is happening to my pulse.

I cross my arms and lean a hip against the cart, pretending I'm not bracing for whatever comes next.

"Funny. That is what libraries are for."

His brows lift slightly. Which is rich, considering the man radiates brooding antihero energy with a side of 'I bury bodies for fun.'

"You always this helpful?"

I tilt my head, my smile all teeth.

"Only with people who say please."

He exhales through his nose, slow and even, before tilting his head slightly. "Where's your philosophy section?"

Philosophy? Really?

"You don't look like the type to be in here searching for ancient wisdom."

Which is code for, *You look like the type to punch someone in a bar, not quote Plato in a library aisle.*

He doesn't answer right away. He just stares at me with that same calm, unreadable intensity like he's letting me talk myself into a corner—then deciding whether he wants to follow me in and set the place on fire.

Finally, with zero inflection and absolutely no remorse, he says, "And you don't look like the type to judge people by their covers."

Touché.

Fucking ouch.

I exhale through my nose and reach for the cart, mostly so I don't say something stupid like *wanna elaborate, Socrates?*

"Come on," I mutter, turning. "I'll show you."

I lead him through the aisles, trying to focus on my steps and not the ridiculous awareness prickling along my spine like he's following too close.

He isn't. I checked.

But his presence is too much. Too intense for a room that's usually filled with nothing but whispers and the occasional rustle of pages.

I stop at the end of the row and gesture to the shelf.

"Here. All the wisdom of the ages at your disposal."

He steps forward, hands in his pockets like he's not a threat at all. Which is exactly what makes him one as he scans the titles—sharp and unhurried, like he's committing them to memory instead of actually reading.

He nods once. "Thanks."

Just lethal calm dressed up as casual interest.

I exhale, like maybe I've been holding my breath this whole damn time, and push the cart forward without looking back. Whatever that was, I'm not unpacking it. Not today.

I finish the rest of my shift like nothing happened.

Or at least, I try to.

Because an hour later, he's still here—tucked into one of the deep leather chairs by the windows like he's a regular or something.

He's got a book in hand, with his legs stretched out, and his posture is casual in the way that screams deliberate. Like someone who wants to look relaxed.

There's a sharpness to him.

A coiled stillness.

I tell myself I don't care. I repeat it like a chant. Maybe if I say it enough, I'll believe it.

It's none of my business if some heavily tattooed, vaguely divine-looking stranger decides to spend his afternoon pretending to read a book he hasn't looked at since I showed him the damn shelf.

It's not weird.

Not weird that he hasn't turned a page or moved in an hour.

Definitely not my problem.

And yet—when I push the empty cart back toward the front desk and pass by his chair again, I look. And there he is. Same chair. Same book. Same unreadable expression.

His posture is all bored disinterest—but his eyes are moving. Too slow to be skimming, but too fast to be reading.

I frown.

Now I know what I'm looking for. He's not reading at all, he's waiting. But I have no idea who he's waiting for, or what.

Something about him doesn't add up. There's no way he's actually here for the philosophy section. Hell, he's probably not here for the books at all.

Again, not my problem.

I force my gaze forward and shove down whatever weird, crawling instinct is trying to claw its way up the back of my spine like a warning.

He's just some guy with tattoos and too much presence. He's not the first, and he won't be the last.

I keep pushing the cart through the nonfiction section like I'm not seconds away from glancing back again like a crazy person. When I finally loop back around, he's gone.

The chair is empty and the space he took up now feels too quiet. Like something was ripped out of it.

The book he wasn't reading is still there—abandoned on the side table, spine cracked but untouched. Like it's been sitting there collecting dust for years instead of the last two hours.

There's no sign of him.

No evidence he was even real.

I stare at the space for a beat too long, then shake my head and move on.

Shift change is seamless, I trade the quiet, book-dust air of the library for the smoky, whiskey-laced hum of the bar. The low murmur of conversation is already picking up speed—punctuated by the sharp clink of glasses, the hiss of a soda gun, and the occasional scrape of chairs against concrete floors.

All the usual signs that tonight's going to be loud and full of people who want attention they haven't earned.

I tie my apron at the waist, rolling my shoulders back, and brace for another round of bullshit with a forced smile and zero patience —especially since Sarah took the night off for a date and left me to fend off the circus alone.

My gaze happens to flick toward the door every few minutes, scanning for a certain too-tall, too-inked stranger with those black hole eyes and a silence I haven't stopped thinking about all day. I know the chance of him coming in here is practically none, but I don't care. I'd sell my right ovary to see him again.

Only, he doesn't show. But the second I step behind the bar, the real problem of the night makes himself known.

Frank.

He strolls in like he's the damn headliner. His swagger just shy of a parody, grin already cocked like he knows I'm going to be annoyed and likes it.

Which—he's not wrong.

Honestly, the only thing more persistent than Frank is my desire to hit him with a bottle and get away with it.

He slides onto his usual stool—far too comfortably—and smirks like he's been waiting all day for this moment.

Spoiler... I haven't.

He taps his fingers against the bar, steady and rhythmic, like he thinks it's charming. I still don't know what he does for work. Every time I ask, he gives me a different answer—some vague one-liner about consulting or investments or "owning things."

Totally normal. Definitely not suspicious.

Yet, here he is again. Same stool, same cologne, and the same look that says you'll give in eventually.

I don't plan to, but the universe has a twisted sense of humor lately.

"You look like you missed me."

I grab a glass, already reaching for the whiskey. "You look delusional."

He chuckles, settling into his seat like he has nowhere else to be. "That's not a no."

I arch a brow, pouring his drink. "It's not a yes, either. It's a go away."

His grin is easy, like he enjoys being told no just to prove it doesn't matter. "You'd be bored without me."

I slide the glass across the bar, unimpressed. "I'd be thriving without you."

Frank lifts his drink, taking a slow sip, watching me over the rim. "We both know that's a lie."

I roll my eyes, setting another order on the counter for the server. "You're awfully smug for someone who hasn't won a damn thing."

He tilts his head, that same slow, infuriatingly confident smirk playing at his lips. "Haven't I?"

I cross my arms. "Nope. You're still here, still asking and still convinced this is going somewhere."

He takes a sip of his drink, watching me over the rim of his glass. "You'd miss me if I stopped showing up."

I snort. "Like I'd miss food poisoning."

His chuckle is deep and unbothered. "Well, lucky for you, I'll be gone for a bit. I have to go out of town for a few weeks."

I blink. Surprised. Not that he's leaving—just that I didn't hear about it until now. He loves talking about himself.

I school my face into relief, placing a hand dramatically over my chest. "A Christmas miracle. I knew if I prayed hard enough, the universe would answer."

Frank just shakes his head, tipping his glass in my direction. "Try not to be too heartbroken, sweetheart."

I flash him a deadpan look. "Oh, don't worry. I plan on celebrating."

His smirk doesn't fade. If anything, it deepens. Something a little too knowing flickers behind his eyes as he sets his drink down with an easy, practiced grace. "You enjoy it while it lasts. Because when I get back, I'm taking my girl on another date."

My girl?

I blink, a slow burn of irritation crawling up my spine.

Not because of the way he says it—like it's fact, like this is already a done deal—but because some part of me expected it.

Of course he can't just accept the fact that I haven't done or said anything after our first date to lead him to believe I wanted another one. I mean, yeah I had a good time, but I'm not convinced he's boyfriend material.

I cross my arms, tilting my head. "Bold of you to assume I'll still be here."

He just hums, pushing up from his seat, stretching like he has all the time in the world. "Oh, you'll be here."

The confidence in his voice grates against my nerves like he knows something I don't. Like he's already seen how this plays out, and he's just waiting for me to catch up.

I huff, reaching for a glass to clean, forcing my focus anywhere but on him. "Well, I hate to break it to you, but I don't do repeats."

Frank leans in slightly, voice dropping to something just low enough to be dangerous. "We both know that's a lie."

My stomach tightens.

I grip the glass a little too hard, rolling my eyes. This conversation needs to be over before I start questioning things I shouldn't. "You gonna drink that or just sit here making grand declarations about a future that doesn't exist?"

He chuckles, standing to his full height. "Keep telling yourself that, sweetheart."

And then, with one last cocky smirk, he downs the rest of his whiskey, sets the glass down with a deliberate slowness, and strides around the bar like he owns it.

A few heads turn as he passes—women watching him like he's something worth chasing. *Maybe he is and I'm just immune to him.*

Before I can react, before I can even process what he's about to do, he leans in. His hand brushes my waist with a light, passing touch, before he presses a slow, infuriatingly confident kiss to my cheek.

My breath catches—just for a second—before my brain catches up, and I jerk back.

He just chuckles, standing to his full height, completely unbothered by the way I glare up at him.

His eyes flick over me, satisfied, before he murmurs, "See you in a few weeks, baby."

Baby?

My fingers curl into fists, heat prickling at my skin—and not from the kiss, but from the audacity.

I hate how smoothly he says it. The bar door swings shut behind him and I exhale, trying to force my pulse back to normal.

3

"Don't trust a girl who keeps her hands steady around blood."

(She's already seen too much)

Ani

After last night's shift, my body aches in that used up, still vibrating from noise and people kind of way. My brain floats somewhere between consciousness and denial—half-asleep, and half-reluctant to wake up at all.

Today is mine.

No bar. No library. No drunk flirtations. No fake smiles. No smug, cocky men walking in like they own the air.

Just me. My bed. And no plans.

The first real full day off I've had in—I don't even know how long.

I stretch slowly, blinking at the ceiling, letting the weight of silence press into me. It's almost nice enough to pretend things are normal.

Today I'm supposed to start looking at buildings.

The thought should make me feel excited and hopeful, like I'm finally moving toward the thing I swore I wanted.

But instead, it knots in my chest—tight and sharp and way too familiar. This was always the dream, wasn't it?

A little bookshop. Nothing flashy. Just... safe. And mine.

Somewhere quiet, somewhere new. Somewhere that smells like pages and paper instead of spilled beer and cigarette breath. Somewhere I could breathe, and start over. And now that it's actually here—on the edge of becoming real—I don't know what to do with it.

It's hard to chase a dream when you're still trying to convince yourself you deserve one.

It's also hard to have your dream life when you're still looking over your shoulder.

It's been over six months. Surely, no one's after me anymore. Surely, I'm safe to actually start living again.

Right?

I exhale, rolling onto my side and reaching blindly for my phone on the nightstand. Maybe I'll check some new listings. See what's out there. See if this dream still fits or if I've outgrown it without realizing.

Maybe I'll even text Sarah—see if she wants to come with. I didn't get to see her at the bar last night, and she's not on the schedule tonight either.

I tap the screen, and I have one new message.

> Sarah: Babe. I wanted to hang today, I swear. But I've been puking my guts out for like three hours straight. Pretty sure my insides are staging a coup, so I don't get laid.

I stare at her message, thumb hovering over the screen. But then my phone buzzes again.

> Sarah: Also I think I'm dying.

> If I don't make it, you can have my vibrator and my collection of emotionally unavailable fictional men.

I snort.

> Me: Wow. A whole legacy. Should I give your eulogy or just read your search history out loud?

> Sarah: Just scatter my ashes in the bar bathroom where I peaked socially. Tell the cute guy from Tuesday I loved him.

> Me: He asked if ranch comes on the side, Sarah. You're better than that.

> Sarah: Am I though?

Before I can fire back, another message pops up—and this one wipes the grin right off my face.

> Boss: Need you tonight. Taylor already told me you'd cover. Thanks.

I blink at the screen. *What the actual fuck.* Taylor is the new girl, and I already don't like her.

Ugh.

I groan, letting my head drop back against the pillow, staring at the ceiling.

I stare up at it, silently daring my boss to change his mind through sheer force of will. *Yeah. That'll happen. Right after men learn how to tip.*

So instead of spending my one sacred, mythical day off scoping out potential bookshop locations like a functioning adult with dreams and ambition, I get to spend it dodging drunk idiots and pouring top-shelf whiskey for men who think a "nice smile" is a tip.

I sigh like the world has wronged me—which, honestly, it has— and shove the blankets off, swinging my legs over the side of the bed with the enthusiasm of a woman headed to her own funeral.

Fine.

If I have to go, I'm at least doing it with decent eyeliner and a soundtrack. Music first. Sanity second. Murder third.

I grab my phone and flick through the only playlist worth having when the world feels like a headache wrapped in a work shift.

Billie Eilish.

Just the right amount of don't talk to me energy wrapped in velvet vocals and barely concealed rage.

I hit play and let the first notes roll in like fog, the kind of sound that settles into your bones before you even realize it's there. They crawl up the walls, soak into the floor, and lodge somewhere behind my ribs.

It's a vibe.

My vibe.

One I apparently needed like air.

Some people meditate. I let Billie haunt the room until I feel like a person again.

I twist my hair up, letting the strands fall where they want. It's the kind of effortless that takes ten minutes and a handful of cuss words. A swipe of eyeliner sharp enough to warn people. And a touch of highlighter I'll pretend is accidental.

Just bold enough to say don't even think about it.

Then comes the outfit.

I don't reinvent the wheel—I just stick to black.

I land on a fitted top that hugs in all the right places but says I dare you more than look at me. High-waisted shorts. Sheer black tights. Topped off with my favorite boots, the ones with thick soles and bad decisions stitched into the seams.

They add an extra inch, but more importantly—they'll let me put someone through a wall if it comes to that.

THE SHIFT STARTS FINE ENOUGH. ANNOYING BUT manageable. It's the usual crowd.

And then—of course—two drunk idiots decide to ruin everyone's night by taking their half-assed testosterone contest from slurred insults to swinging fists.

When I round the bar, glasses are shattering, chairs are screeching against the concrete, and one of them's got the other in a chokehold so weak it's mostly just aggressive cuddling.

I sigh, cracking my neck.

Why is it always the dumbest ones who want to fight in public?

"Alright, idiots," I call out, like I'm already bored. "Take it outside before I throw you both out myself."

The bigger one turns toward me, red-faced, sweaty, and way too full of false confidence.

"Mind your business, sweetheart."

Oh.

Oh, honey.

He really picked the wrong girl for this conversation. Especially tonight of all nights. Please, fuck around and find out.

I don't give him the chance to finish his next word. I grab the back of his collar and yank—hard. And there's a beat where his brain short-circuits, his feet stumble, and his expression goes from cocky to confused in the span of half a second.

Good.

I don't wait for him to recover. Don't give him the dignity of catching up before I shove him straight toward the door with the kind of force that's been building in my chest all fucking night.

His friend stumbles after him, arms flailing like a cartoon idiot, barely catching himself before I decide to make him my next project.

"Out," I snap, the word sharp enough to draw blood. "Before I call the cops, or better—before I stop holding back."

The whole bar's watching now, but I don't care. Let them remember what happens when you mistake short for soft.

"And don't come back," I add as the door slams shut behind them. "Ever."

I turn back toward the bar, pulse hammering, hair stuck to the back of my neck, and absolutely zero regrets.

Not even two minutes later, some idiot decides to test my patience again. Because apparently, tonight is Let's See How Far We Can Push the Bartender night.

A hand is suddenly, inappropriately low on my waist, fingers curling like they belong there. Then it slides lower.

The laugh that follows is low and slurred with cheap liquor and an overinflated ego.

I don't think. I react.

My fingers wrap around his wrist in a flash, twisting it back hard and fast—not enough to break it, but enough to make a point.

He gasps, and the sound is choked and ugly, like the realization is just catching up to him mid-breath.

His whole body jerks, stumbling toward me as his eyes go wide.

"Don't," I growl, "ever touch me like that again."

He tries to say something—some drunk defense, some pathetic plea—but I give his wrist a little more pressure, just enough to cut the words off before they can crawl out of his throat.

I should stop there. I know I should, but logic never wins with me. Because for one dark, flickering second, I want to feel it.

The shift. The snap. The break.

I want to feel bones give under my grip. I want to hear that sharp, unmistakable crack—the kind of sound you don't forget.

A reminder that girls like me aren't here for your amusement. That the next time he reaches for someone, he'll think twice—and maybe the time after that, he won't reach at all.

I hate the way the thought coils in my chest like it belongs there.

Instead, I shove him. Hard. Right toward the bouncers, my teeth clenched so tight my jaw pops.

His face goes red—humiliation flushed across his skin like a slap —rage simmering just below the surface, but I don't care.

The bouncer grabs him without ceremony, yanking him toward the exit like he's trash that stayed too long at the party.

He stumbles, sputtering, but doesn't say a word. Not with my eyes on him. And not with everyone watching.

Another problem solved.

Another impulse buried.

I take a slow breath, exhaling through my nose, trying to shake off the heat crawling beneath my skin.

Ever since the incident—the one I don't let myself name—these thoughts come too fast and I hate it.

I hate that violence feels like muscle memory now. That my first instinct is no longer to flinch—but to fight.

I exhale again, this time slower. Letting the pulse in my throat finally settle.

My hand finds the bottle of whiskey without looking, already halfway through pouring myself a drink that isn't technically allowed but is absolutely earned. Then I turn back to the bar—and I freeze.

There's a guy tucked in the farthest corner, just outside the reach of the bar lights. I can't see much of him, just his broad shoulders, long legs, and the kind of stillness that feels intentional.

My stomach flips before my brain has a chance to play catch-up. If danger had a favorite seat, it's definitely the one he's in.

He's not drinking, or I would've been over there by now.

I can't tell if his eyes are on me or the door or nothing at all— but I feel it. That prickle. That old, familiar whisper of instinct that says you're not alone.

Whatever. Not my problem. If he wants a drink, he'll come ask for one like everyone else. I shove the thought away and turn back to the bar, forcing myself to focus. I pour drinks, take orders, and pretend the exhaustion dragging claws down my spine isn't winning.

A familiar buzz rattles against my thigh, so I pull out my phone when no one's watching and glance at the screen.

Sarah: Still dying, thanks for asking. Send whiskey and forgiveness. Preferably in that order.

Me: You're the worst coworker I've ever had. And I've worked with a guy who used to put pickles in his pockets.

Sarah: Hot. What's happening? Anyone cute? Any murders?

I glance at the far corner, feeling the weight of his stare, and I don't know why, but I bet that man would be a good time just based on his energy alone.

Me: One possible shadow-dwelling psycho in the corner. Jury's out. Could be hot. Could be a hallucination.

Sarah: DO NOT BANG A HAUNTED MAN, HOE.

I tuck my phone away with a smile tugging at the corner of my mouth, but it fades quickly, because when I look back up—the table is empty. And yet... I feel it. The air thickens with gravity that wasn't there a second ago.

I feel it before I see it and my pulse kicks up. *Traitor.*

It's him.

Tattoo man.

Library guy.

Mr. Philosophy with murder eyes and a jawline that belongs in a museum I wouldn't survive.

He's all dark gaze, broad shoulders and carved-from-trouble energy wrapped in bad decisions. And somehow—some-fucking-how—he looks better than I remember. Which should be illegal. Or at least taxed.

Let's be honest—I didn't do him justice.

Not even close.

He steps up to the bar, placing both hands on the counter like he owns it. The ink on his knuckles stands out against his skin, intricate and brutal—a warning dressed as art. He doesn't smile, he doesn't need to.

"Whiskey. Neat," he says.

His voice is exactly how I remember it—low, deliberate, and smooth enough to be velvet but threaded with something darker. It's a punch straight to my pussy.

I take a slow breath, willing my pulse to stop doing that stupid fluttering thing it's been doing since he walked in.

"Well, well. If it isn't the great philosopher himself," I murmur, reaching for the bottle. "You here to discuss Nietzsche over cocktails?"

He doesn't react.

"Just the whiskey."

I tilt my head, letting a smile tug at my mouth.

"Shame. You don't strike me as a light reader."

One corner of his mouth twitches—barely—but it's enough to register. Then it's gone. Buried under that unreadable, coiled stillness again.

"And you don't strike me as a bartender."

My brow arches. "No?"

"No."

His gaze drags over me slowly, and way too effectively.

"You look like trouble."

I pour the drink as steady as I can manage, even though my

insides aren't.

"That's funny. I was just about to say the same about you."

He doesn't answer. Not right away. He just watches me as he takes the glass from my hand, and his fingers brush mine. Just for a second, but it was long enough.

A flicker of heat that rushes straight through me. I have to bite the inside of my cheek and keep my expression neutral.

Or I try to.

He lifts the drink to his mouth, slow and unhurried—like he's doing it for show and knows I'm watching.

Because I am.

He sets the glass back down, eyes dipping—not just to my chest, but lower, like he's giving me time to catch him.

"You should be careful who you flirt with, bartender." His tone is mild, but his gaze is anything but.

I lean against the bar, meeting it head-on.

"And you should be careful who you underestimate."

This time, he smirks. A slow, crooked curve of his mouth that feels more like a threat than a compliment.

And my pulse spikes again.

His fingers tap once against the glass, then he lifts it again, and sips like he has all the time in the world.

My eyes track every movement, helpless against the pull—how his fingers wrap around the glass, how his mouth barely parts, how the amber liquid slips past his lips.

I hate the way my body reacts. The way my pulse kicks up, and the way my skin heats under the weight of his stare like I'm already losing a game I didn't agree to play.

I roll my shoulders back, forcing my spine straight, as I arch a brow. "So, what, you only read when I'm around? Or do you just haunt libraries for fun?"

A flicker of amusement passes through his expression, but it's gone before I can grab onto it. "You were watching me."

I scoff. "You were the one pretending to read."

He hums, low in his throat, the sound lazy and dangerous, like he's amused.

When he sets his glass down like he's got all the time in the world to play whatever game he's started, I can't help but drool a little.

"Was I pretending?"

My pulse skips—a full traitorous stutter.

I narrow my eyes, leaning in just slightly, refusing to let him see how much that one line got to me.

"You tell me."

The corner of his mouth lifts. Just a fraction. And then he leans in, slow and intentional, like he's doing it to prove a point. The scent of whiskey curls off his breath, laced with something darker.

God, he's infuriating.

And hot.

But mostly infuriating.

I shift my weight, pretending to straighten a bottle behind the bar just to break eye contact.

"I think," he murmurs, voice like a velvet noose, "you're just looking for excuses to be near me."

My jaw tightens.

Oh, fuck you.

I don't say it out loud, but I think it hard enough that I'm sure he hears it. His eyes don't leave mine. He just lets the words hang there like a challenge.

A line I haven't decided whether to cross—or set on fire.

My fingers twitch against the bar and I roll my eyes with a little more force than necessary. "You've got a real problem with misreading people, huh?"

He tilts his head, studying me with the kind of focus that makes your skin feel too tight. He's peeling back layers with his eyes and not even pretending to be subtle about it.

"I don't misread anything, sweetheart."

Sweetheart?

Yeah, no. The way he says it—it's not sweet, it's a threat dressed as affection. A dare.

Heat prickles up the back of my neck, curling low at the base of my spine and I know without a doubt, it's a warning I should listen to.

But don't.

Then it spreads, pooling right where I don't want it to. God, I hate the way my body betrays me sometimes. I press both palms against the bar, grounding myself against the cool surface.

"I'm not your sweetheart."

The words snap out sharper than I intend, but he only smirks—wider this time.

"You keep telling yourself that."

He takes another slow sip of whiskey, mouth curling around the rim of the glass like he knows exactly what he's doing.

His eyes stay locked on mine—steady, and impossible to read.

"Let's see how long you believe it."

Fuck. Him.

I glare, refusing to acknowledge the way my thighs are pressing tighter together under the bar. Or the fact that his voice could probably be classified as a lethal weapon with the way it goes straight to my currently aching pussy.

I hate him.

I hate the way he talks. I also hate how badly I want to climb across this counter and see if his mouth is as good as it was in my imagination.

But instead I ask, dry as ever, "Do you always try to flirt like this, or am I just lucky?"

He sets the glass down, his fingers dragging along the rim with slow, deliberate strokes. Then he leans in again, this time close enough that I can feel his breath brush the space between us.

"Who said I was flirting?"

My skin prickles, and God, I hate that I'm this wet for a man who hasn't even touched me. He hasn't even laid a single fucking finger on me—and still, I'm one breath away from unraveling.

His voice is too smooth. It doesn't need to rise above a whisper to dominate the air. It's the kind of sound that wraps around you like silk and steel, equal parts luxury and restraint. A quiet threat, and a promise I'm not sure I'd survive.

This guy hasn't done anything but sit there, sip whiskey, and look at me like I'm already his. And apparently, my body couldn't get on board fast enough.

I can feel the slick between my thighs like he's already been there, wrecked me, and left the memory behind.

And for what? A smirk? A voice that sounds like sin learning how to purr?

Jesus fucking Christ.

I tighten my grip on the edge of the bar, willing my expression into something smug, like I'm not seconds from saying something reckless.

"Then why are you still here?"

He doesn't answer right away. He just watches me like he's already undressed me in his mind and is now deciding what to do with the mess he made when he lifts his glass in a lazy toast—like we're both in on some unspoken joke—and the smirk returns, cocky and unbothered, like he never left.

"Because I like watching you pretend you don't want me to be."

My stomach drops.

Not the fluttery kind. The violent, molten kind. The kind that shoots straight through my core and leaves a dull, aching throb in its wake.

I open my mouth, ready to claw back some ground, throw something sharp and mean—something that'll make me feel in control again, but a hand slaps against the bar before I can speak, dragging me back to reality with all the grace of a brick to the head.

I blink, pivoting toward the new problem of the night. A half-drunk asshole waving his empty glass at me like I'm his personal barmaid.

"Hey, baby, let's move it along, yeah?"

He rattles the ice like it's a fucking dog whistle, but I don't move. Neither does Tattoo Man.

But I feel the shift in him.

His posture doesn't change, not really. Just a flicker in his eyes —barely a breath—but it's enough.

I lift my chin breaking the stare first and reach for the bottle with the kind of slow, deliberate calm that doesn't feel natural.

"You're gonna need to learn some patience," I say coolly, pouring the drink just slow enough to piss him off.

My blood is buzzing.

The drunk guy snatches his glass like I owe him something, muttering a barely coherent thanks before stumbling off toward a booth, already forgetting I exist.

Must be nice.

I exhale and press my fingers into the wood, trying to reset and while I'm at it, I try to shake off the heat crawling up my spine and the awareness still coiled tight between my thighs like a loaded weapon.

This is fine. Totally normal.

A tattooed deviant lurking at the bar like he wants to eat me alive, and I'm... What, exactly?

Flattered?

Irritated?

Soaked?

All three.

Unfortunately.

Apparently, I'm into brooding men who look like they strangle people for sport and flirt like it's foreplay for murder. Add that to the list of things to talk about in therapy.

I glance back—and he's still there.

Still watching.

Still carved from shadows and sin.

His arms are folded across his chest, and those dark eyes—God, those eyes—they haven't left me once. That mouth twitches like he knows exactly what he's doing to me, and it's making me want to agree to really bad things.

I need to walk away and ignore him. Especially considering the type of men lately who come here and stare at me. I mean I know it's a bar, but I'm not sure what the fuck is going on lately. Whatever, let him stew in whatever smug, cryptic bullshit he's clearly enjoying.

I grab a glass and pour, going slow on purpose. The liquid slides down the glass like honey, catching the light just right. I know he's watching. I can feel it.

That stare of his presses into my skin, and it should piss me off. Instead, my pulse stutters.

I keep my face bored and unreadable, even as heat creeps up my neck. I slide the glass across the counter with a flick of my wrist. "Try not to look so impressed."

He doesn't touch it or even glance down. He just drags one finger slowly along the rim.

"Should I be?" he murmurs.

My thighs press together before I can stop them, as a slow burn curls low in my stomach, and I swear I feel it spread.

I arch a brow, holding onto sarcasm like it's the only thing keeping me upright.

"What, never had a woman pour you a drink before? Or are your standards just that tragically low?"

It comes out smoother than I feel. I'm about two seconds away from combusting under the weight of his stare. But his expression doesn't shift. If anything, that mouth of his twitches again—like he's just pacing himself.

"I've had drinks poured," he says, voice calm—almost bored. "Just not by someone who makes me wonder what else those hands could fit around."

Heat flares immediately and I can feel it go straight to my cheeks.

Asshole.

I roll my eyes, crossing my arms. More to hold myself together than to shut him out.

"Do lines like that actually work for you?"

He takes a slow sip of his whiskey, then sets the glass down and leans in just enough for his voice to roughen.

"Do you feel like walking away right now?"

God, I want to punch him.

I hate that my brain doesn't fire back with something sharp and clever—just that quiet, immediate *no* that lands low in my stomach.

But that's not an answer I'll ever say out loud, so I keep my expression neutral.

"You're awfully cocky for someone who just drinks whiskey and broods over philosophy books."

I let it hang there, just long enough to feel the stretch.

"What's your deal, anyway? You make a habit of eye-fucking bartenders until they collapse out of sheer confusion—or do your pick up lines usually get them naked?"

His eyes flicker—but there's not a single crack in his composure.

"Only the ones who pretend they don't like it."

My panties are now *ruined.*

I should remind him that I don't play these games. That men like him—men who move with deliberate confidence, who make you feel like they could ruin you just for fun—are exactly the type I swore I'd never fall for again.

This time when he leans in, it's close enough that I catch the warmth of his breath against my skin. He's now close enough that if I moved just a little, I'd be in dangerous territory.

I don't move, but God help me, do I think about it.

And then—just as I think he might actually fucking touch me—he pulls back. Which irritates me more than it should.

I scowl as he slides a few bills onto the counter. "Keep the change, sweetheart."

My jaw locks. "I told you not to call me that."

His smirk is infuriating, all patience and power.

"And yet," he says, lifting his glass to his lips, "you still answered to it."

I open my mouth—to say what, I don't know. But before I can find something sharp enough to throw back at him, he's already standing, already turning toward the door, already leaving me behind.

I watch him go, pulse hammering, with heat simmering beneath my skin like a slow-building fire.

He never touched me, and yet, I feel wrecked.

And that pisses me off.

4

"Some nights aren't accidents…"
(They're invitations)

Ani

After back-to-back shifts all week—library all morning, bar all night—my body's a tangled mess of exhaustion, and my muscles ache in ways that only come from being on my feet for too long, dealing with too many people, and pretending I don't want to strangle half of them.

And yet—I'm still awake.

I'm laying in bed, staring at the ceiling, too wired, too restless, and far too distracted for something like sleep to take me.

I've seen him twice this week.

Tattoo Man. Still nameless. Still unreadable.

He's made himself comfortable in the bar—showing up late, lingering even later, ordering whiskey and watching me like I'm something worth figuring out.

We talk, if you can call it that. Mostly, it's arguing in the kind of way that makes my pulse do things I pretend not to notice.

Tonight, he showed up with takeout from my favorite place—the hole-in-the-wall spot around the corner. It's the kind of place you guard with your life so it doesn't get popular, but still feel morally obligated to brag about like a well-earned personality trait.

And this fucker walks in holding a take-out container like it's no big deal. With a twice-baked potato.

He brought *my* order.

Something about that pissed me off more than it should have, because what are the chances?

Then he took a bite.

And fuck me if it wasn't downright disrespectful how hot it was watching him.

That's *my* comfort food and this motherfucker had the audacity to take two bites and push the container away like he was bored. Like my holy grail of post-shitty-day indulgence was a mild inconvenience.

I wanted to stab him.

Twice.

He offered it to me and I could've strangled him then too. Or dropped to my knees and let him feed it to me in a way that would've made everyone else in here extremely uncomfortable.

Honestly, it could've gone either way.

Later, when I passed his table to offer a refill, he barely looked up from his phone.

"You sure you don't want it?" He asked, I'm sure just to prove a point.

I was starving and bitter that he was wasting the best potato in the city.

Rude.

By then, I was crashing and hangry—my stomach was hollow, my nerves were fried, and at that point, I was just trying to survive on caffeine and stubbornness, so I gave in and ate the damn thing.

I nearly moaned when I took the first bite, it was that good.

Zero regrets.

He didn't say a word after either. He didn't watch me, didn't make it weird. Nothing.

Then, when the bar thinned out and the night started closing in, he stood, dropped a hundred-dollar bill on the counter, and walked out. Like it was nothing.

But here I am, still thinking about it. Thinking about him.

About what he was wearing...and how he looked wearing it. Not to mention watching him take those few bites of the potato will live rent free in my mind for a while.

Fuck.

I squeeze my thighs together, rolling onto my stomach, hating myself for this. Because it wasn't just what he did tonight—it was how he looked doing it.

The loose black Henley, with the sleeves pushed up just enough to expose his inked forearms, those thick wrists, and his strong hands. I fantasize for a solid two minutes about those hands and what they could do.

And don't even get me started on the gray sweatpants... Who wears sweats to a bar?

That was just cruel.

Goddammit.

I need to stop thinking about him.

That's my last thought before sleep finally drags me under. But the past has never been kind enough to let me rest.

The first crack of thunder doesn't wake me. Neither does the rain—rattling against the windows like it's trying to get in. Not even the wind, screaming down the alley like something feral clawing at the walls can wake me.

But the screaming does.

I jolt upright, gasping—my body tearing itself out of the dream like a man drowning, breaking the surface just to breathe.

I don't know if the scream came out of me or it was just in my head. No one comes knocking, and there's no concerned voices, no neighbor pounding on the wall asking if I'm okay.

So either I was silent or they just didn't care. And I honestly don't know which one makes me feel more pathetic.

My breath shudders out, sharp and uneven as sweat clings to my skin, soaking into the sheets like a second suffocating layer of everything I keep trying to outrun.

I press the heels of my palms into my eyes—hard—but the

images are still there, burned into the inside of my skull. I don't know how long I can keep shoving those memories down before they catch up to me.

It's too hot in here, it feels like the kind of heat that seeps into your lungs and makes it impossible to breathe. The walls feel closer than they should, and the shadows stretch in the corners like they've been waiting for me to break.

"You think you can just leave?"

The voice slices through the thick air, sharp and familiar, curling under my skin like it never left.

"You're nothing without me."

They echo louder and I gasp as the pieces slam back into place like shrapnel burrowing beneath my skin.

The words don't hurt, not anymore. But the memory of his hands do. My spine hits a wall, the breath leaving my lungs in a silent gasp. Sometimes I wonder if running was the right choice, and then I have these moments where I remember certain things, and I know I made the right call.

Thunder rolls, shaking the world beneath me or maybe that's just my pulse.

"I should kill you for this."

My skull was slammed against drywall, I remember the impact sending a sharp crack of lightning through my vision, and the world tilted.

The bus is the next thing I remember.

I don't remember buying the ticket, and I don't remember getting on, but I knew that Denver was my final destination based on the ticket in my pocket.

I just remember sitting there, staring out the window as the city blurred into nothing but streaks of light and darkness.

And here we are, months later, and I'm laying in this bed, in this apartment that still doesn't feel like mine, surrounded by a life I haven't let myself settle into.

I press my fingers into my thighs, forcing myself to breathe, to move, to exist in the present.

If there's one thing I learned that night—one thing that carved itself into who I am—It's that I will never be trapped again.

It's getting worse. I wake up knowing I was running, and everything else is a blur. Fuzzy edges. Static. Fragments I can't place, like someone tore up the picture and left me to guess what it used to be.

The full story never comes. Just slivers. And the second I try to hold onto them, they vanish. Slipping through my fingers like they were never mine to begin with.

The fact that I don't remember—should terrify me.

What scares me is what I *do* remember. Not in perfect detail, not in a way I can lay out step by step—but in a way that lingers. The way my muscles still tense if someone raises their voice too loud, or that I still flinch at shadows that move too fast, in spaces that are too small.

I rub a hand down my face and exhale, trying to force the tension out of my shoulders.

It's 4:13 AM. Which means it's way too early to be awake, but too late to go back to sleep.

Not that I could if I tried.

I already know how this day's going to go, like something's pressing into my skin and won't let up until I do something about it.

I think about calling Sarah, but it's too early, and she'll just tell me to go back to bed—which we both know isn't happening.

So instead, I get up, shoving off the covers, and let muscle memory do the rest.

Lately, my newest obsession is the gym. It started as a distraction, a way to stay out of my head whenever I couldn't go back to sleep. Now, it's more than that. It's control.

But control never lasts long.

By the time I'm starting my shift at the library, my mood is already sliding.

Too little sleep. Too much caffeine. And far too many ghosts pressing in behind my eyes.

I shelve another book harder than necessary, while silently apologizing to it.

I don't even hear him approach.

"You for sure always look like you're plotting something when you're in here."

His voice cuts through the quiet like smoke curling under a locked door—soft, amused, and dangerous in all the ways I wish I didn't recognize.

I go still while my fingers pause mid-reach, curled around the spine of a book. My pulse trips, but I don't look. Not yet.

Not him.

Not now, when I can barely breathe through the anxiety coiled in my chest like barbed wire. I exhale through my nose, like maybe that'll keep the emotion out of my face.

Tattoo Man.

Library Guy.

Bar Guy.

The man who cracked my ribcage open with a look and hasn't stopped pulling pieces of me out since.

He's leaning against the end of the aisle like the shelves were built to hold his weight. All calm menace and unbothered dominance, like he could ruin me without even raising his voice.

His long sleeves are pushed to the elbow, showing off those gloriously flexed forearms. His ink is peeking out like it's taunting me—just enough to make my brain short-circuit, but not enough to be useful.

And the worst part is, he looks completely unbothered. Like he didn't just light my whole body on fire by breathing in my vicinity.

Heat crawls up my spine, unwelcome and immediate. And yeah—I hate that I notice how the fabric clings to him. How he looks like he was carved from something dangerous.

And fuck me, I want him to touch me with those hands I've shamelessly fantasized about more than once.

His hands stay shoved in his pockets like he's not a threat at all—while those dark eyes drag over me in slow, clinical passes like he's tracking every breath, and every tick in my pulse I didn't give him permission to notice.

I arch a brow, because if he's expecting a warm welcome, he's about to get lit on fire instead. I'm not in the fucking mood.

"Maybe I am plotting something. You should be worried."

His lips twitch slightly, like I confirmed whatever he came here already believing.

"Should I?"

His voice is pure arrogance.

I turn back to the shelf and shove a book into place with more force than any book should have to be put through.

"That depends. You planning on pissing me off?"

He hums, stepping closer. His presence wraps around me, consuming me, like heat and danger and something I shouldn't want but definitely do.

He lowers his voice, dipping his head slightly. "Seems like someone already beat me to it."

I stiffen, trying not to look at him or react.

"You think you know me now?" I ask, forcing the words out through clenched teeth.

He doesn't answer right away—just watches me with those dark, unreadable eyes like he's trying to decide how hard he wants to push.

"Didn't take you for the type to be tied down."

My body reacts before my brain catches up. Every nerve goes electric—like I just walked into a war zone with no armor and a target painted on my chest.

And my pussy? A fucking traitor. She's throbbing with all the things I'm picturing and shouldn't be. *Like exactly how it would feel being tied down for this man.*

But also—How. Dare. He.

I turn my head just enough to glare at him.

"Excuse me?"

His mouth curves, like he can already feel the fire in my blood, and he knows exactly where my mind went. His dark eyes flicker down—just for a second, but enough to call me out without a single word.

Then, with that maddening, smug amusement curling in his voice, he says,

"Not what I meant, dear."

He tilts his head slightly—like a predator enjoying the squirm.

"A boyfriend... who pissed you off?" A pause. "Or just left you needing to put your hands on something?"

He lets it hang a little too long. Then adds, low and unbothered —"Hard."

I blink.

It takes a full second for my brain to switch tracks, to process what he's really asking, and when I do, annoyance flares.

I huff a breath, slamming another book onto the shelf beside me. "No. No boyfriend. Not now, not ever."

His brow lifts. "Tell me how you really feel?"

I smirk, crossing my arms, refusing to let him pull me under his spell again. "I'm not exactly the commitment type."

His smile widens, as if he's just heard something deeply amusing. "I don't believe that for a second."

I scoff, grabbing another book, and shoving it into place like it personally offended me.

"Not my problem."

"Mm."

He leans against the shelf beside me, arms still in his pockets— But there's nothing casual about the way he watches me.

"What's your type, then?"

"You mean besides not you?"

His eyes gleam, dark and unreadable.

"Careful, sweetheart."

There's something in his tone that tightens the air—like the moment before a storm. I should shut up and be smart. Instead, I smile—because apparently, I want to get wrecked today.

"Why?" I tilt my head, all sweet venom. "Scared I'll hurt your feelings?"

The second the words leave my mouth, his energy shifts, and something darker slips in under the surface.

He moves.

Fast.

I take a step back without thinking—only for the bookshelf to stop me cold as solid wood hits my spine.

What I should do and what I actually do, are two wildly different things I'll shame-spiral about later.

He shifts closer, enough that I have to tilt my chin up to keep our eyes locked. To hold my ground.

"You like playing with fire, I see?"

The words are a dark murmur slipping under my skin like smoke. Stoking something hot and reckless. Soaking me in seconds.

A rational person would be careful here, and choose their words wisely, then back away.

Not me.

I blame it on the mood I woke up in, on the lack of sleep, or on the way his voice slides between my legs like a sin I'll confess to later.

I smirk, letting my gaze drag over the sharp line of his jaw, those dark eyes, and the mouth that's probably ruined women for life.

Instead, I feed the fire.

"You think you're the fire?"My voice is all syrup and venom. "That's cute."

His eyes darken and my pulse stutters. Before I can breathe, his fingers grip my chin with just enough pressure to send a violent, traitorous shiver ripping down my spine.

And just like that—I'm fucking gone.

Fuck him.

Fuck him for looking like that and standing there like he already owns me. Like he knows exactly how bad I want him, and how hard I'm fighting not to show it.

My jaw tightens and I grit my teeth, clinging to the last threads of control, trying to force down the heat pooling between my legs, and the need crawling up my spine like a live wire.

I know he sees it by the smirk that deepens, turning dark.

The space between us vanishes like it was never there. His mouth crashes onto mine but it's not a kiss—it's a goddamn wildfire. His fingers twist into my hair, yanking just hard enough to make me gasp—and he swallows it like it's his fucking favorite sound.

Then he pulls back, just enough to breathe against my lips.

"Wonder if he knows how easy you break."

The words scrape at something raw inside me. I should ask what the hell that means. Who he's talking about, but I don't.

I don't even pull away. Instead, I kiss him back—hard and desperate.

Whatever it meant—I don't care. Not right now.

The voice of reason tries to surface with all the reasons this is a terrible idea. Every red flag, every line he's already crossed. But I shove that voice way down. Right next to the one that said I shouldn't let him touch me in the first place.

His hands slide down, gripping my thighs—and suddenly, I'm airborne. He lifts me like I weigh nothing, setting me on a nearby rolling ladder I didn't even notice. Pinning me there with the full weight of his body, the scent of him wraps around me like smoke and heat and destruction.

Who the fuck is this man?

Heat coils low in my stomach. My fingers dig into his shoulders as soon as he starts to roll me down the aisle like we're on rails to hell—right into the far corner, deep in the shadows.

I expect him to keep kissing me and finish what he started. I want him to press his mouth to mine until we both forget our names, but he doesn't.

"Climb."

I blink. "What? No."

His fingers tighten against my thighs—tight enough to warn me that he's serious.

"You heard me."

I really should remind him I don't follow orders—especially from men who wear control like cologne. But I don't. Because apparently, my body didn't get the memo. It's already leaning into him.

My jaw clenches as defiance coils tight in my gut like barbed wire.

Fine. I'll climb, but not how he wants me to.

I smile, and keep my front to him as I take the first step. Then another. Slow, and deliberate enough to taunt.

If he thought I was going to give him the satisfaction of watching me obey—he can choke on it.

I feel his hands, sliding beneath my skirt as his fingertips ghost up my thighs. It's so light it's almost cruel.

My breath catches as heat lashes through me, sharp and twisted and impossible to ignore.

God, I hate this, or maybe I just hate how much I don't. Because I still don't stop him or tell him no.

"Turn around."

His eyes lock on mine like they never left and everything in me goes still.

I grip the ladder tighter, and for lord knows what reason, I do. Slowly.

His gaze drags over me, and for the briefest moment something dark flickers there, something thrumming with amusement.

"You like taking orders, don't you?"

His voice is silk-wrapped sin. I force a laugh—but it's breathless and weak. And it's a betrayal I can't hide.

"You wish."

His grip tightens on my hips enough to remind me I'm not in control anymore.

When his mouth brushes the inside of my thigh, just under the hem of my skirt, it melts my ability to think.

A sharp sound rips from my throat, caught between a gasp and a warning I'll never say out loud.

My fingers claw at the ladder, my nails are scraping metal like I'm trying to anchor myself to anything but him.

"You sure?"

That voice—It's a fucking dare dressed as a question. I want to say no, I want to roll my eyes and tell him to fuck off, shoving his smug mouth back where it came from.

But my body has other plans because I'm soaked and throbbing. Everything in me is surrendering without permission.

I know he knows too, because I feel it in the slow curve of his mouth against my skin. In the way he doesn't even bother looking up before his teeth scrape me again, only harder this time.

A growl bursts low in my throat.

God, I hate him.

I hate that I'm letting this happen, and that I'm wet for this man I don't even know. I haven't had a man touch me like this in... God, I don't even know how long.

Every cell in my body is screaming yes while my pride dies a quiet, painful death. But I still don't stop him.

And he doesn't wait.

His fingers hook the side of my panties—dragging them aside slowly. He wants me to feel every second of it.

"What do you think you're doing?"

The words come out sharper than I expect. A last-ditch flare of pride.

His mouth brushes higher, and his lips are maddeningly close to where I'm already dripping for him.

Then he says, dark and commanding. "Hold still, and be quiet."

The first slow drag across my slit sends a jolt through my entire body, my legs threatening to give out where I stand.

A strangled sound tears from my throat before I can even try to hold it in. It's pathetic, and it echoes louder than it should in the empty library.

God, I hope no one's over here. And more importantly what the fuck am I doing?

He groans against me. *Groans.* Like he's been starved for this and I'm his reward.

My thighs twitch, and I can feel the ladder digging into my palms the tighter I hold on, every muscle in my body is pulled tight.

It feels so fucking good, yet nowhere near enough.

My mind scrambles for something to focus on. The books. The chill in the air. The flickering overhead light. Anything but the way his tongue just circled my clit like he knew exactly what would make my knees go weak.

I can feel the slow, filthy flick of his tongue tasting the exact moment I lose every ounce of self control.

This is insane. What am I doing?

His hands are holding me open now—spreading my thighs like I belong to him.

And the way he's licking me?

God.

Every flick of his tongue is a brand. Every slow, punishing stroke is him saying mine without needing to speak.

And I am fucking here for it. I hate how much I love it, and I hate the way my hips rock forward, chasing every flicker of pressure like I'm starving for it. He's wrecked me with nothing but his mouth.

Then he pulls back. Just for a breath, long enough to blow against my soaked cunt and I nearly come undone.

"Already shaking," he murmurs, voice dark and wrecked and way too fucking satisfied.

"I've barely even started."

I'm going to kill him. *Right after I come.*

I grit my teeth, my pulse pounding in my ears. "Then maybe get on with it and stop narrating."

The bastard chuckles like this is a game and watching me unravel is the whole fucking point. I'll have to analyze that later, when I can think clearly.

"Shh."

It's barely a whisper. But his grip tightens, then he licks—a slow, maddening slide up my thigh that makes every nerve in my body seize like I've been set on fire.

"You should be watching the door, sweetheart."

His voice is dark, pure fucking arrogance, laced with something even worse—certainty. As if he knows I'm about to open my mouth and say something, he cuts off my thoughts.

"You don't want anyone catching you like this, do you?"

Heat floods my veins, a violent mix of rage, desire, and humiliation.

I bite down on my lip, hard, pulse hammering, but even just that thought of someone walking by has my eyes snapping toward the end of the aisle and locked on the door.

A slow hum of satisfaction rolls from his chest, vibrating against my core, his tongue dragging exactly where I need it.

"Good girl."

No, fuck him. What was that, and why did my entire existence just melt for him with two words.

He keeps me pinned and helpless beneath the weight of his hands. I'm gone as soon as his tongue drags across my cunt with a slow, deliberate stroke from my clit to my entrance. It's fucking devastating.

His grip on my thighs tightens, forcing them wider, pressing bruises into my skin as he dives back in.

No hesitation. No teasing. Just filthy, raw fucking hunger.

I gasp, dropping my head back onto who knows what. My fingers claw at the rungs of the ladder as he devours me, as his tongue laps through my arousal, circling my clit in a way that makes my knees shake.

I don't even realize I'm grinding against his mouth until his hands slide further up, gripping my hips, pinning me down like he's keeping me exactly where he fucking wants me.

"I knew you'd taste like this," he growls against my pussy, voice hoarse.

I whimper, hating the way heat licks through me like wildfire at his words. His tongue is punishing me for something, sending sharp, electric pleasure down my spine.

My body shudders, completely at his mercy. My eyes drift closed, as the tension builds.

"The door."

The order is a growl, low and devastating, while his fingers dig into my thighs like a warning.

I suck in a sharp breath, rage curling into something just as dark, and just as dangerous.

Without hesitation he presses one finger into my entrance, making me feel every inch of him.

Then comes the second finger, his knuckles flush against me before I even have the chance to catch my breath.

A sharp, aching stretch, as my body pulses around him, struggling to stay still.

I have no time to think. No time to fight the way my body reacts instantly, greedily, taking what he gives like it was made for this. For the unbearable sensation of being pried open, and claimed. His touch branding me like a tattoo.

When he curls his fingers, brushing against the spot that has my breath shattering—I swear he smiles as he adds another finger.

I can only whimper—a raw sound I barely recognize as my own.

"Fuck, you're tight."

My body clenches around him, involuntary and desperate. I need more friction.

His fingers press deeper, pumping in and out in a slow rhythm. "Bet you'd let me ruin you right here."

A silent curse spills from my lips, while my body is being ripped apart at the seams. *Yes, yes sir, I almost certainly would.*

"You're fucking soaked, for me sweetheart," he growls against my skin, the heat of his breath sending a fresh wave of humiliation and desire rolling through me.

I hate him.

Or I just hate that he's still fucking teasing me, drawing slow, torturous circles with his tongue, drinking in every reaction like I belong to him.

And I hate that in this moment, I do.

A strangled sound slips from my throat as he flicks his tongue against my clit, and it's fucking devastating. I jerk against him, help-less to the way my body spirals under his mouth, his hands, his fucking dominance.

"That's it."

His voice is low and taunting, dripping with dark amusement, he's so fucking cocky it makes my pussy throb. Clearly, she's just been neglected for too long.

My thighs shake against his grip, his tongue is relentless. His lips seal around my clit, sucking just enough to make my pulse stutter violently.

Fuck.

A wrecked, helpless moan spills from my throat, loud and needy. His fingers dig into my skin, keeping me right where he wants me.

I bow, my back arching, my hips pushing into his mouth as pleasure crashes through me like a fucking tidal wave.

It's too much and not enough at the same time.

My entire body clenches, my pussy pulses as my orgasm slams into me, consuming me.

I gasp, my vision turns hazy as the world tilts. My knees threaten to give out, and the way his hands are digging into my thighs tells me it's the only thing keeping me upright.

And still—he doesn't stop.

"Fuck—"

His teeth scrape, his tongue flicks, dragging me through it, pushing me higher, stretching my release into something unbearable, something violent.

Another moan rips free and his hand snaps up, one clamping over my mouth as he keeps fucking devouring me, the other still knuckle deep in my pussy, pumping in and out, keeping me locked in place.

"Be quiet."

The command slices through the haze, but his palm stays clamped over my mouth as I shatter against him—every ragged sob of pleasure swallowed by his hand.

He groans against me like I'm his favorite fucking meal, his tongue is relentless as he wrings every last drop of release from me, licking me through it like he's savoring a goddamn victory.

It's not until I'm shaking apart, ruined and breathless, does he finally pull back. But he doesn't go far.

His breath ghosts over my overstimulated pussy, like he's wondering if he can break me completely—just because he fucking can. And at this point I'm not sure I'd stop him.

Clearly, I'm not in my right mind.

He chuckles, low and smug, soaked in satisfaction.

"Told you."

His fingers drag up the inside of my thighs, slow and possessive, spreading the mess he made of me across my skin like a fucking brand.

"You like playing with fire."

Then, with his eyes still locked on mine, he licks his fingers clean.

The bastard doesn't even blink.

My skin still tingles where his mouth was.

I should feel used.

Instead, I feel cracked open. And he didn't even have to try.

5

"If your power goes out, the dark won't hide you."
(It exposes who's already watching)

Ani

By the time I get home, my body's vibrating with exhaustion. Every step feels like it's dragging through wet concrete.

I don't even bother with the lights.

The glow from the streetlamp outside spills enough light through the blinds to make out the shapes of my furniture.

I drop my bag with a thud, pull off my boots, and collapse into the corner of the couch like it's muscle memory.

The silence swells around me.

No music. No voices. No bar chatter or clinking glasses or the steady hum of the espresso machine from the library.

Just stillness.

I lean my head back, close my eyes, and try not to drift right back to the library. *I can't believe I fucking did that.*

Who hooks up with some mysterious, tattooed God in the middle of a public library—on a damn ladder, no less.

What the hell is wrong with me?

I've gone over it a thousand times, replaying every second in my head like I'm trying to study the scene of a crime. And maybe I am. It felt like I blacked out, like some reckless, unhinged version of myself shoved all the caution and survival instincts aside and decided, *yeah, let's ride this stranger's face next to a goddamn copy of War and Peace.*

I'm not even going to lie—that was one of the hottest things I've ever done. It should scare me. What he did—what I let happen. But all I feel is this sick, dizzy hum under my skin. Like I want him to do it again. The danger doesn't register until it's already touching me...and that's what really terrifies me. That's the part of me that liked it.

My body still tingles when I think about the way he moved his tongue, and the way he looked at me like I was the only thing he'd ever wanted. The way he moaned against my cunt was like he was getting drunk off it.

It's been days since I've seen him. Since he touched me. He ruined me with his mouth and left like he hadn't just taken a piece of me with him.

I can't stop thinking about him.

About how he stood there after—all smug like he hadn't just turned my world inside out. *Like...what the actual fuck?*

He licked his fingers right there in front of me, making sure I saw every second. Then he looked up at me with that sinful mouth and had the audacity to say—"Next time, I won't stop until your legs give out and you beg me to keep going anyway."

Next time?

I stood there for a full minute after, trying to remember how to breathe.

He's a dangerous, walking red flag. The kind of man who smells like sex, secrets and bad fucking decisions.

I keep telling myself I should be relieved that I haven't seen him again. That this was a one-time thing.

But the truth is, I don't feel relieved.

I feel restless and on edge. Like something unfinished is coiling under my skin, waiting to strike.

The worst part is, I don't even know his name. *Which is prob-*

ably for the best, a reminder to the logical part of my brain that this is why we don't do these things.

He's just some stranger who stepped out of the shadows and somehow saw all the way through me. And now I'm haunted by the memory of his mouth.

I force myself up off the couch, dragging my body toward the kitchen. I haven't eaten all day, unless you count coffee and a bite of someone's leftover fries.

As soon as I open the fridge to find something to eat, everything goes black. The lights vanish, and the hum of the fridge dies. I blink, frozen for a second, waiting for it to turn right back on like it usually does. Only nothing happens. I listen to see if I can hear anything, but all I hear is silence.

My fingers brush the edge of the drawer where I keep the flashlight, my pulse is a steady war drum in my ears as I try not to go straight to panic mode. I pull it open, slowly, like I'm waiting for something to jump out, grabbing the flashlight. Of course, it's dead.

I set it on the counter, reaching for my phone to use the flashlight, only to realize I don't actually know where I put it.

It's too quiet.

I exhale through my nose, trying to slow my breathing, and turn toward the hallway.

The knock hits so hard and fast it sends me stumbling back. The edge of the coffee table catches my shin as pain flares, sharp and immediate, but I barely register it through the jolt of fear flooding my system. A strangled yelp claws its way up my throat, and I slap a hand over my mouth before it can escape.

I cautiously move toward the door, every step weighted with the kind of dread you only feel when something is deeply wrong. My breath slows, and I press my eye to the peephole. No one's on the other side.

Then it happens again.

Three sharp, deliberate raps. Only this time... it's coming from the window.

Everything inside me locks up. My chest tightens, and the blood drains from my face, leaving me cold and weightless all at once. That window leads to the fire escape three stories up. It's rusted and old—barely anyone uses it. No one should be out there.

I don't move at first, I just stand there with my pulse hammering, and my heartrate climbing higher with every second that ticks by in silence.

Then—like an idiot—I walk toward it.

My legs feel disconnected from the rest of me, like they're being dragged by something that doesn't care if I make it back. The closer I get, the louder my heartbeat becomes.

I reach for the curtain, fingertips trembling, and tug it back— just enough to see that the landing is empty. The metal rails glint faintly in the ambient light from the alley, and the wind creaks through the frame like it's breathing, but there's no shadow. No movement. No one waiting in the dark.

I let out a breath I hadn't realized I was holding, it's shaky and uneven, like the fear's still trapped somewhere in my chest.

Maybe it was debris, or maybe I imagined the whole thing. I slide the curtain back into place and turn away from the window, forcing the air back into my lungs. Which honestly, takes everything in me.

I grab my phone, which is now at 2% battery—and the charger from the floor. Then I open the drawer next to the microwave and take out the knife I've only ever used when I feel like it might help.

I like the weight of it in my hand. It makes me feel like I'd stand a chance if someone came through that door.

The whole building feels like it's holding its breath as I crawl into bed fully clothed with the knife tucked under my pillow.

The moonlight filters through the window, casting long, thin shadows across the ceiling. They stretch and shift with every gust of wind.

I need sleep, tomorrow's a double—library in the morning, then

I close the bar. That's twelve hours of pretending I'm fine and smiling when I have to.

At least Sarah will be there with me, which means I'll get to pretend less and swear more.

Small mercies.

If I sleep now, I might survive it. But my eyes won't close, that would be too convenient.

My thoughts won't stop because something about tonight feels familiar, and that's what scares me the most.

I roll onto my side, tucking the blanket under my chin and force myself to breathe slowly.

"Don't act like you didn't ask for this."

The words hit like a bullet, ripping through whatever fragile peace I managed to scrape together.

I flinch—but I don't move. I try to speak, but my mouth won't open. My voice is gone.

"You think anyone's going to care? After what you did?"

His voice is louder now, closer.

And suddenly—I'm not in bed anymore. I'm on my hands and knees, covered in blood. The floor's cold beneath me, sticky with something I don't want to name. I look up and see myself in a broken mirror. My mascara's streaked, and my eyes are haunted.

There's a ringing in my ears, and something sticky clings to the side of my face.

And then I wake up.

A gasp rips out of me as the knife clatters to the floor, breaking the silence like a gunshot. I lurch upright, heart slamming against my ribs like it's trying to claw its way out.

I'm soaked in sweat, shaking, and breathing way too fast. I press the heels of my hands into my eyes.

Breathe, Ani.

Breathe.

I wish I could remember.

Or maybe I wish I could forget.

I just wish these dreams would stop hunting me in the dark like they know I won't fight back.

I REACH FOR THE KEYBOARD, FINGERS HOVERING FOR A BEAT before I type one word into the search bar: *missing*. I hesitate, then add: *Woman*. Nothing specific. Just enough to test the waters. I don't know what I'm looking for. An obituary. A name. A story that explains why my nightmares are getting worse.

Or maybe... I want to know if he's still out there.

The man I haven't talked about out loud in over six months. The one whose voice still crawls through my skull when I close my eyes.

I delete the words, my pulse suddenly hammering like I did something wrong just by typing them. What if he's not dead? What if he's looking for me? Watching? Waiting?

What if... he's already found me?

I lean back, the chair groaning under me as I push away from the desk, rubbing my eyes. I just need a second. Just one second to close my eyes and reset before the bar.

I jolt awake to the sound of someone snapping gum way too close to my ear.

"Jesus, Ani. If you're gonna nap on the job, at least leave me a note so I don't think you're dead."

I blink against the harsh overhead light, groaning as I lift my head off the desk. My cheek's stuck to the surface and my spine feels like it's been rearranged by a drunk chiropractor.

Sloane's standing there, library lanyard slung around her neck, and her oversized hoodie swallowing her frame. Her blonde curls are piled on top of her head like she lost a brawl with a scrunchie and just walked away from the scene.

She's smiling, but there's concern in her eyes.

"Rough night?" she asks, tossing a stack of books onto the return cart.

"You could say that." I rub at the knot forming in my neck. "How long was I out?"

"Long enough that I started planning your funeral playlist."

"Make sure it's depressing," I mumble. "No Dancing Queen bullshit."

She snorts. "Bold of you to assume I'll honor your last wishes."

My body's not just tired—it's empty. I feel like I've been holding on too tight to something for too long, and now I'm just... frayed.

Sloane leans on the desk, narrowing her eyes. "Seriously, girl. Are you okay?"

I force a nod, already reaching to shut down the computer. "Didn't sleep much."

"Well, you better find time to rest. You're gonna burn out, Ani. And trust me, you're way less fun when you're dead on your feet."

I offer her a ghost of a smile, one that probably doesn't reach my eyes.

"Are you working tonight?" she asks.

"Yeah."

She groans. "Booze and bullshit. You really know how to treat yourself."

"Living the dream."

"You want to go out after. Just a few drinks. You need a break."

I pause, fingers hovering over the keyboard. The offer is harmless, normal even. It's the kind of thing I should want. But the thought of sitting at a table surrounded by laughter and small talk makes my chest ache in a way I don't understand. I'm not built for normal.

"Rain check?" I say quietly.

She just nods, too used to it to be offended.

"Your loss. Catch you later, spooky girl." She disappears behind the stacks, humming something upbeat just to spite me.

I shut everything down, grab my bag, and head out.

It's colder than I expected. That kind of lingering cold that settles in your bones and makes you feel like the night's already claimed you. I shove my hands into my coat pockets and tug my hoodie closer, slipping my headphones on as I start walking toward the bar.

The streets are quiet despite it being a Saturday night. Just the distant hum of traffic and the soft click of my boots on the pavement. I keep my head down, and let the music drown out the rest. Or at least I try to.

Halfway there, I get that weird feeling that something's off. That tight, crawling sensation at the base of my neck, like someone's watching me.

I don't stop walking, but my body goes rigid. Every hair on my arms lifts, my pulse climbing a little too fast. I glance over my shoulder casually—but there's nothing there. Just empty sidewalk and flickering street lamps.

Still, I pause the music. Just in case. But I still don't see anyone.

I pick up the pace telling myself it's just nerves and exhaustion. That my head's playing games after the dream, after the power outage, and that knock on the window that I still haven't explained away.

Still—my fingers curl tighter around the pepper spray in my pocket until I reach the bar.

The second I step inside, the noise hits like a wave. It's loud and overwhelming, and smells like cheap cologne, spilled beer, and regret.

My kind of crowd.

Sarah's already behind the bar when I walk in, hair piled on her head in a way that somehow makes her look both adorable and unbothered. She tosses a bar rag at me before I've even clocked in.

"You look like hell," she says, grinning.

"You smell like gin and disappointment." I grin back.

"Aw, babe. You missed me."

"Only because you owe me twenty bucks from last week."

She rolls her eyes, but there's warmth behind it. This is our thing—banter first, breakdowns later.

I slide behind the bar, falling into a rhythm. Wiping counters, pouring drinks, and flashing just enough of a smile to keep the grabby ones from escalating.

My phone buzzes, but I ignore it. It's probably Sloane again—trying to rope me into drinks, karaoke, or some other extrovert-coded nonsense I'm definitely not emotionally equipped for.

Sarah catches the movement out of the corner of her eye and arches a brow like she's about to start shit.

"Ooooh. Who are you texting?" she teases, leaning in with her drink tray like this is a gossip emergency.

"Did you meet someone and not tell me? Rude."

I snort. "It's Sloane."

"Of course it is. You know she's gonna show up if you keep ghosting her, right?"

"Let her. I've got barstools and sarcasm. I'll survive."

She grins, that wicked sister energy in full force. "You're so emotionally stunted, it's kind of impressive."

"Thanks. It's my coping skill of choice."

She laughs and wanders off to take an order like we didn't just have a full-blown therapy session in under thirty seconds.

The phone buzzes again.

And again.

Then once more—this time with the kind of urgency that feels personal. Whoever it is, clearly knows I'm trying to pretend it doesn't exist.

I sigh, wiping my hands on a bar towel before sliding my phone from my apron pocket.

Unknown Number: You look sinful tonight
in black.

My stomach drops.

I glance down at my outfit like it might've changed in the last ten seconds. I'm wearing a black tank top, jeans, and my usual boots. Nothing special. Nothing new. Nothing that screams sinful.

Unknown Number: Tell me, love. Did you
wear it for me?

My gaze lifts slowly, sweeping the room.

It's packed—shoulder to shoulder—but the shadows beyond the bar are too thick to make out anyone in particular. Just silhouettes and noise. A blur of bodies that all start to look the same.

I delete the message, and slip my phone back in my pocket, ignoring the spike in my blood pressure.

It's not the first time some drunk loser tried to get clever. But when it pings again—an hour later—I flinch.

Unknown Number: Keep ignoring me. See
what happens.

I tell myself it's a joke.

Just some regular playing games—someone who caught my name and decided to push. It happens. I've seen worse.

I'm behind the bar, rinsing glasses, ignoring the sticky feeling of sweat clinging to the back of my neck when Sarah slides in beside me, snagging a half-full beer glass and wrinkling her nose.

"Why do they always leave a quarter inch of warm foam, that's disgusting."

"Because men don't finish things they start."

I say it without looking up, and she cackles.

"You good?" she asks after a beat, her voice dipping into something gentler.

I pause, long enough to think, then shrug. "Yeah. Just tired."

She doesn't believe me. I can feel it in the way she lingers for a second too long before grabbing another glass. But she lets it go.

That's the thing about Sarah. She knows when to push and when to wait until I'm ready to fall apart on my own schedule.

My phone buzzes again, but I don't check it right away. I just stare at the glass in my hand and wonder which idiot I pissed off this time.

And then I feel it.

The air shifts.

Not dramatically—just enough to send a ripple through the room. A change in the rhythm. Every instinct I've got sits up and takes notice.

I don't even have to look. My body knows before my brain catches up.

Tattooed Man.

He doesn't come to the bar, he doesn't even look at me, or say a damn word. He just heads straight for a table in the back.

The darkest corner. His corner.

I grit my teeth and keep drying the same glass I've already wiped twice. I shouldn't care. One library hookup doesn't make us Facebook official.

It was one time.

One very specific, toe-curling, ladder-climbing time. But still.

If he wants to ghost me after that, that's fine. Perfect, even. Explains why I haven't seen him since.

No big deal.

"Uh... Ani?"

Sarah's voice cuts through my mental murder list as she slides up next to me, pretending to organize straws. "Tell me I'm not hallucinating that tall, tattooed Sex God who just walked in."

I don't answer. Mostly because I'm still glaring daggers at his stupid, unfairly beautiful face.

Sarah follows my line of sight. "Ohhhh," she says slowly, lips curling into a grin. "So that's your problem."

"He's not my anything."

"Mmhmm. You're drying that glass like it owes you child support."

I slam it down a little too hard on the towel.

"It does."

Before she can press, a blonde saunters into the scene like she's walking in slow motion. She's got legs for days, and tits that defy gravity and the limits of spandex. She slides into the seat across from him with the kind of confidence that says she already knows what flavor his dick is.

She smiles, and that's when the burn hits my chest.

That irrational, blood-boiling kind of anger that makes you want to break something. Or someone. My fingers start to curl around the edge of the counter.

Sarah whistles low. "Damn. You okay, or do I need to start prepping bail money?"

"Fine," I snap.

Totally fine. Perfectly, irrationally fine.

Sarah narrows her eyes like she knows better.

"Want me to drop a drink on her by accident?"

"Tempting."

She pats my shoulder. "Say the word. I'm bored and clumsy."

I force a smile, but the ache in my chest is very real. Shoving out from behind the counter, every step toward his table sends a pulsing heat I refuse to name through me. I'm not mad. I'm not even jealous. I'm just... concerned that he might be wasting valuable oxygen.

The blonde across from him leans in, laughing at something he didn't even say—because of course she does.

I stop at the edge of the table, arms crossed, not bothering to fake politeness.

"What do you want to drink?"

The girl startles, blinking up at me with wide eyes. "Um, I'll have a—"

"Didn't ask you."

I turn to him, but he doesn't look surprised. If anything, he looks like he's enjoying himself.

The smug bastard.

"Well?"

His eyes drag up slowly, unapologetically—like he's savoring this. "Whatever you're serving, sweetheart."

The nickname hits like a slap. I grit my teeth, pen pressing so hard into the pad I'm surprised it doesn't snap.

"Hope you like bitter."

His smirk deepens. "Only when it bites back."

Oh for fuck's sake. Of course he'd say that and look like sex while doing it.

I ignore the heat creeping up my neck.

I'm not going to let him get to me. Not this time.

"Cute," I say tightly. "Is that what you're into? Girls who bat their lashes and hang on your every word?"

He shrugs like he's not actively lighting my spine on fire.

"Depends. They don't usually growl at me while taking my order, but I'm open-minded."

The blonde glances between us like she's just realized she walked into the wrong scene of a movie and is two seconds from being written out.

I glance at her. "You might wanna find another table."

She blinks, taken aback. "Excuse me?"

I tilt my head, slow and pointed. "He's already had his dessert."

She makes a little scoffing noise and turns to him again, like he's going to defend her.

He doesn't.

He just tips his head, dragging his dark eyes down my body with maddening patience.

"Careful, dear. Keep acting like that and I might have to find the closest ladder."

My entire body locks up, heat flashing under my skin like a match to gasoline. I won't give him the satisfaction. But fuck, my pulse is already thudding like it remembers exactly what happened the last time I was on a ladder with him between my thighs.

I walk away before I say something I can't take back, and he doesn't stop me. But I feel his stare like a brand between my shoulder blades as I duck behind the bar, grabbing the same glass I've cleaned three times just for something to do with my hands.

When I finally do glance up—when I can't help myself—he's leaned back in the booth, arms spread across the top of it like he owns the entire damn room. His legs are stretched out and he has that same unreadable expression on his face. But it's his eyes that get me.

He's looking at me like he's waiting for something.

I drop my gaze focusing on the glass in my hand and the way my fingers won't stop twitching.

Goddamn it.

I'm annoyed. I'm spiraling. And I hate that the only thing grounding me right now is a cheap tumbler and a slow-building rage I'm trying to swallow down with it.

"You only clench your jaw like that when you're holding back something violent."

The voice comes from behind me—low and smug, and entirely too close.

I jerk, nearly dropping the glass, because I didn't even hear him, I didn't see him leave the table.

He steps around the bar like we haven't been dancing on a knife's edge since the moment we met.

I stare at him, keeping my jaw tight.

"Jesus. You move like a fucking ghost."

He shrugs, unbothered.

"You looked like you were about to commit a felony. Figured I'd come check before you shattered something over someone's head."

"Tempting," I mutter. "But I have bills to pay."

He leans in, hands braced on the bar, and suddenly his presence is a weight. I hate how my thighs press together on instinct whenever he's close.

"Spit it out," he murmurs. "Whatever it is. You'll feel better."

I want to grab him by the collar and demand to know what the hell that was—the look, the blonde, the absolute radio silence since the last time he touched me like I was something he'd kill for.

But I don't.

Because he's too close, and my chest is too tight. And because I'm not sure what would come out if I actually do.

Instead, I force a bitter smile.

"I'm fine."

His eyes darken.

"You're a shit liar."

"Excuse me?" I snap.

He doesn't flinch. He just lifts a brow, calm as ever.

"You've already taken six steps," he murmurs. "That's usually when you turn around and start swinging."

My stomach twists.

Because—what the fuck?

I freeze, fingers tightening around the glass in my hand like that's going to steady me. That's the most unsettling thing anyone's ever said to me.

How the hell would he know that?

I stare at him, blinking like an idiot, because now I'm replaying it in my head.

He's still watching me with that maddening stillness like he's not just in my head—he's rearranging the fucking furniture.

He shrugs one shoulder, like he's commenting on the weather.

"You did it at the library. You do it here, too. Three steps, sharp turn, back again. Always in threes."

Always in threes.

My throat goes dry, and my blood goes cold.

I never even realized I did it that consistently until he said it out loud. And that's what rattles me. Not the fact that he noticed—but how fast he picked up on it.

"Some people count sheep. I pace. Congrats," I snap, tossing the rag on the counter and reaching for another glass, pretending like I'm not suddenly hyper aware of every move I make.

"Didn't say it was a bad thing," he murmurs. His voice sounds like dark velvet over broken glass. "Just interesting."

Interesting.

I glare at him across the counter. "You always psychoanalyze your bartenders?"

His lips twitch into something that might be a smile—but not the kind that reaches his eyes. It's darker than that. Sharper.

Then, in that low, deliberate voice that crawls under my skin like smoke through a cracked window, he says, "You've cleaned that glass for two minutes, clenching your jaw. You've got something to say. Spit it out."

My spine straightens before I can stop it. Of course he's clocking my every move.

I cross my arms, keeping my expression cool—detached—while my insides churn.

"What," I shoot back, "you keeping a stopwatch on me now?"

He just leans forward, elbows resting on the bar like he's getting comfortable, and ready to watch me come undone.

"You were ready to go for the throat over a blonde with too much perfume," he says. "Don't tell me you've run out of energy now."

My mouth opens. Then shuts. Because I have nothing. Nothing that won't sound like an admission.

He's not wrong. And he fucking knows it.

The glass in my hand creaks like it might shatter. Which,

honestly, would be preferable to letting him see how much he's getting under my skin.

"You don't know shit about me," I mutter.

But it's weak. Even I can hear it. And from the slight tilt of his mouth, he does too.

"I know how you look at me when you think I'm not watching."

My pulse stutters.

And now I'm the one gripping the edge of the bar, hoping it holds me up while I figure out how to survive this conversation without either jumping him or throwing something.

6

Ani

The street's too quiet. That should've been my first red flag.

I knew I should've called an Uber.

Hell, I should've taken the main road, like any normal person with a functioning survival instinct.

But I didn't. Because I'm an idiot.

I like pretending I'm not afraid anymore. Like the old me—the one who flinches at shadows and second-guesses every footstep—doesn't still live in the back of my head.

Spoiler...she does.

My boots hit the pavement, each step echoing too loud off the brick and concrete. My keys are wedged between my fingers, jutting out like teeth. I used to joke about it—telling Sarah I'm fine walking home because I was basically Wolverine.

It's somehow less funny when your heart's pounding in your throat.

Something shifts in the alley to my left. A shadow breaks off the wall like smoke, but I don't stop walking.

"You always walk home alone this late, sweetheart?"

That voice. Smooth as silk, but sharp as a goddamn razor.

Tattoo man.

I don't answer right away, instead I just turn slowly, letting him step fully into the light.

He looks like every crime I haven't committed yet and all the ones I already regret. His sleeves are shoved up over his beautiful tattooed forearms, and the ink at his throat coils like it might bite. That black stare eats me alive without asking permission. His jaw ticks once, but his shoulders stay loose—like a predator too bored to rush the kill.

"Didn't realize we were playing stalker now," I mutter, trying to ignore the skip in my pulse and the heat pooling low in my stomach.

My body clearly isn't getting any of the memo's when it comes to this man.

His smile is laced with something darker than amusement. "Not stalking. Walking."

His voice dips lower, like it's meant to curl straight between my thighs.

"Figured I'd be nice and keep you safe on my way. Call it a favor."

He pauses, dragging his eyes down the length of me with that same cold calculation he always hides behind.

"Not everyone you let close has your best interests, sweetheart."

That hits harder than it should. My stomach tightens, jaw twitching. What the hell does he think he knows?

"And what are you protecting me from, exactly?"

His smile drops like a blade. "Everything that wants to own you."

Some small, fucked-up part of me wishes he meant himself. I should roll my eyes, and throw a line over my shoulder, or veer off in the opposite direction and pretend like this doesn't affect me. But I don't move.

"What are you doing here?" I ask instead, my voice sharp

enough to slice through the chill climbing my spine. It's instinct—mask the shiver, bury the reaction, pretend I'm unaffected.

His hands stay in his pockets, but the way he steps closer feels like a threat.

"Same reason you're still standing here."

I blink, heat crawling up the back of my neck. "You don't even know me."

His gaze sweeps over my face like he's dissecting me cell by cell—filing away every twitch, every breath, every lie I think I've hidden.

"I know enough."

That shouldn't make my knees loosen or my pulse stutter like a faulty wire. But it does.

God, I hate how still he is. Like nothing I say can touch him. It feels like he's always five moves ahead and doesn't even care if I catch up.

And yeah, that does something to me, but it mostly pisses me off. Like who the fuck is this man?

This gorgeous, cocky, too-quiet, infuriating man with a stare that feels like a loaded gun and a mouth I want to both slap and sit on.

I want to demand answers, but all I can do is stand here, trying not to tremble, while my brain screams run—and my body whispers closer.

"Is that what you do?" I ask, crossing my arms to keep from fidgeting. "Follow women around and say cryptic shit to feel mysterious?"

That almost-smile ghosts across his face, and it's unfairly devastating.

"Only the ones who pretend they're not looking over their shoulder."

My heart misses a beat.

"Maybe I just don't like being followed."

He tilts his head. "You'd rather be alone in the dark?"

"I've handled worse."

His eyes gleam, catching the halo of the streetlamp behind me. That smile fades, just enough to show what's underneath.

"I don't doubt it."

I swallow the lump that rises in my throat, hating how that almost sounds like a compliment. Part of me wonders how much he thinks he knows. Because the truth is—I still don't know his name, and yet, somehow, he feels like a secret I've already told.

"You got a name, shadow?" I ask, not even pretending to hide the edge in my voice.

"No."

Then—he smirks. Like that one-word answer is a fucking mic drop.

Which, unfortunately, it is.

Goddammit.

My apartment's close, so I start walking again, only I don't want him to know where I live, so my steps are slow.

"You always this twitchy when someone walks you home, or am I just special?"

I glance at him over my shoulder, one brow arched. "You're a guy in a hoodie following me down a dark street. Forgive me if I don't feel like swooning."

He chuckles under his breath. "Swooning would be dramatic. I was aiming for mildly flustered."

"You'll be aiming for a black eye if you keep talking."

That earns a grin. One of those slow, crooked ones that makes it way too easy to forget how dangerous he feels. Lord, the things I would let this man do to me.

"Didn't realize threats were your love language."

I face forward, ignoring the heat crawling up my neck. "They're my everything language."

His boots crunch against the gravel as he steps closer. "That explains a lot."

"What's that supposed to mean?"

"Just that you're kind of cute when you're hostile."

I stop walking.

"Cute?" My voice could slice through concrete. "You're the one following me home."

His head tilts slightly, the corner of his mouth twitching into something that should not be legal.

"Is that what this is? Following?"

"You're behind me, aren't you?"

He steps forward. "Not anymore."

My breath catches—traitor—but I don't flinch. I keep my chin up, boots planted. "Don't get too comfortable," I mutter. "I'm just too tired to argue."

He smirks, dragging his eyes over me like he already knows what color I taste like.

"Whatever helps you sleep at night, sweetheart."

God, I want to slap him... and kiss him.

My stomach twists as we cross the street, and I realize I'm doing something stupid—memorizing the sound of his footsteps beside mine. The way his shoulder almost brushes mine. The heat rolling off him in waves. I tell myself it's just exhaustion, not the way his presence makes everything else feel muted. Like the world turns down when he gets close.

I hate it.

I slow my steps in front of a different building, like this is where I live. I'll let him think it, because the last thing I want is him knowing which door is actually mine.

He doesn't need to know which window stays lit too late. Which one creaks when you push it open. I don't need him tracing my patterns. I don't need anyone that close.

I stop at the stoop, shift my weight, and school the tension out of my shoulders like it's something I can exhale.

"Well, this is me," I say casually.

It's not. But he doesn't need to know that.

I glance at him from the corner of my eye—and he's not looking at the door, he's looking at me. Like he sees right through my lies.

Of course he fucking does.

"I'm good from here," I mutter, turning just enough to throw him a look that's more bark than bite. "Unless you plan on checking under the bed for monsters too."

His brow arches. "Wouldn't be the first time I've found something hiding under a bed."

My stomach twists. I can't tell if it's the threat buried in his tone—or the fact that I wouldn't mind if he crawled in with me.

The image alone is dangerous.

Him. My bed. The things he'd do once he got there.

I blink hard, trying to shake it off. "Do you always make breaking and entering sound so sexy?"

It's out before I have the chance to filter my thoughts.

His mouth curves, slow and lethal. "So you think I'm sexy?"

Why do I have to open my big fat mouth?

The sidewalk narrows where the streetlights flicker, casting a golden glow that makes everything look too intimate.

I stop walking. My eyes flick up to meet his, sharp and searching. "You gonna tell me your name?"

He studies me like he's deciding whether I've earned it. That quiet stillness he wears like a second skin settles deeper into his posture—solid and unreadable.

Then, with a voice like gravel and gasoline he says, "Why? You planning on screaming it?"

I don't give him the satisfaction of reacting, even though my thighs clench and my lungs burn, knowing damn well I'm drenched.

"You ask a lot of questions for someone who knows how to follow a girl home," I say, flipping it, letting the fire in my chest bleed into my voice.

He steps closer, with no warning, and no hesitation. His body brushes against mine and my back meets the cold, unforgiving brick of the alley wall.

"Your turn," he murmurs.

I blink, dazed. "What?"

"Your name."

"Luna," I lie, forcing my spine to stay straight.

His head tilts. Shit. He knows I'm lying. There's no way he could know my name. I don't wear a name tag at the bar for a reason. And when my boss makes me, it's new every time.

He doesn't call me out on it, though. He just leans in, until his mouth is at my ear, and I can feel the heat of him everywhere.

"Pretty name," he murmurs. "Shame it's not yours."

My throat tightens, but I don't crack.

"You gonna prove that?"

He doesn't move at first—he doesn't need to. He just watches me with that unreadable gaze, like he already knows how this ends. Then his hands slide to my hips, fingers curling tight, and he pulls.

Now I'm flush against him—chest to chest and my mouth starts to water.

"Sweetheart, I don't have to prove shit." His gaze drops to my mouth, then drags back up. "I decide when you break."

His thigh slides between mine, pressing up, pinning me to the wall as his mouth descends—hovering, grazing my throat, his breath teasing every inch like he's already claimed it.

"You like this," he says against my skin. "This game. Lying to me."

"I don't—"

I do.

He nips the underside of my jaw, enough to make me gasp. His hands lock on my hips, grinding me against his thigh with just enough pressure to make my brain short out.

"You do," he growls. "And if I pushed my fingers inside you right now, you'd be dripping, wouldn't you?"

He drags his nose along my cheek like he's savoring me, then presses his mouth to the shell of my ear.

"Say it."

"I'm not—"

"Say it."

My hands curl into his hoodie. I want to shove him away, but I also want to pull him closer. Fuck. I don't know what I want because my brain isn't firing on all cylinders right now. It's obvious what my body wants, though.

I don't say anything, because his thigh presses harder, and his mouth trails lower, while his hand grips the back of my neck like he owns me.

"You can keep lying to yourself, *Luna*," he breathes, dragging the name out like a sin, "but your body says otherwise."

His lips crush mine, punishing and filthy and hot enough to make my knees give out. And I kiss him back like I'm starving.

Just when I start to lose myself in it, he pulls away, like he knew the exact second to leave me breathless.

Motherfucker.

I scoff, turning my back on him before I do something stupid like ask for more. *Or climb him like a tree.*

"You're not going to invite me in?"

I glance over my shoulder, hoping my glare is sharp enough to cut glass. "Try breaking into my place and I'll show you how friendly I can be with a kitchen knife."

That mouth twitches again. "Noted."

He just stands there, watching me like he knows just how badly my body wants to invite him in.

"I'm going inside now," I say—more for my own benefit than his. Maybe if I say it out loud, I won't hesitate.

I turn the corner behind the building, each step echoing louder than the last. My pulse hasn't slowed, it's still thudding somewhere between my throat and my ribs, quick and uneven. I tell myself it's adrenaline, or maybe just nerves.

I glance over my shoulder, but he's not there.

The space feels colder without him in it, which is insane. The man's basically a walking threat in a hoodie, but there's a weird comfort in knowing exactly where he is—even if it's two feet behind you with a smirk and a comment that makes your skin flush and crawl at the same time.

I expected him to be there. Leaning against the lamppost. Waiting for me to change my mind. But the shadows are empty and the street's deserted.

Good.

Because I might've murdered him if he caught me sneaking past my fake address like a damn raccoon at midnight.

I cut through the alley, making a sharp turn toward the next building over—my building. The real one. Still a dump, just with a slightly less dramatic porch light. My feet are moving faster than I want to admit, boots hitting the pavement with the kind of urgency I refuse to name. Not panic, obviously. Just...practical fear.

God, I'm a disaster.

By the time I make it through the stairwell, my hand trembles against the railing and I have to tell myself it's the cold. Not the high voltage of adrenaline and hormones still coursing through my veins.

It certainly has nothing to do with the tattooed God of a man that seems to be lurking everywhere.

I don't stop until I'm inside my apartment—deadbolt turned, and every lock engaged like it's some kind of holy ritual. Only then do I let myself breathe. I let my back hit the door with a soft thud, like maybe that'll keep him out of my head too.

At least I can cling to one win tonight.

He bought it. *I think.*

Maybe I should've gone into theater instead of hiding from the wreckage of my own life and calling it survival.

The air inside is still and stale, but I don't move. Not right away. I just stand there, letting the silence settle over me like dust.

I'm so tired. Not just physically, but in that bone-deep, soul-frayed kind of way. The kind of tired that wraps around your spine and whispers that you'll never actually be safe.

I glance at my phone, tempted to call Sarah and tell her I survived another round of emotional whiplash, maybe send her a selfie with the caption "Still hot, still haunted."

She'd text back something like "Main character shit," and I'd pretend it helped.

But I don't, because if I do, I'll unravel. And right now, I need to stay upright.

I drag myself toward the kitchen, flipping on the light—only to remember it still doesn't work.

The bulb blew yesterday. I meant to fix it, then got distracted by trauma and a stranger with God-tier cheekbones.

Figures.

The fridge groans when I pull it open, the dim yellow bulb inside flickering weakly like even it's tired of my bullshit.

There's half a bottle of cheap wine, and a container of takeout I'm not brave enough to open. But there's also a sleeve of cookies, two eggs, and a pack of shredded cheese. I sigh and shut the door again.

Good thing I'm not hungry.

I bend over taking off my boots, and they hit the floor near the door with a dull thud. I toss my keys onto the counter and peel off my jacket, tossing it onto the back of a chair I never sit in. The apartment's still freezing, but I'm sweating. Nerves are weird like that—twisting your body into knots while your brain plays games with things that haven't even happened yet.

I cross the room and flop onto the couch, and it groans beneath me like it's just as tired as I am.

I still can't relax. I press my fingertips to my temples, squeezing my eyes shut. God, what the hell is wrong with me?

I don't even know his name. And yet, I can feel his voice in my bloodstream like a drug I didn't mean to take.

"You're not going to invite me in?"

Fuck off, is what I should've said. Go ruin someone else's night.

But of course, I didn't, because part of me wanted to let him in, but that's the part I don't trust.

The thought barely settles before I reach for my phone with fingers that feel too shaky to pretend anymore. My chest's too tight, and I don't even wait to second-guess it this time.

I scroll until I find her name, which isn't hard because she's the only person on my favorites list.

It rings twice before she answers.

"Ani Banani. Please tell me you're calling to say you finally got laid."

I groan. "Sarah—"

"That's not a no."

I can hear her sheets rustling, her smile practically audible.

"I don't know what I'm doing," I mutter, my voice cracking around the edges.

Sarah sobers a little. "Okay, talk to me. What happened? Are you okay?"

"I let him walk me home."

A pause. Then, sharper. "Him him?"

"The tattooed one," I admit. "Library ladder. Mouth of sin. Probably has a body count."

"Oh, for fuck's sake, Ani. Tell me you at least climbed him like a jungle gym before running."

I pinch the bridge of my nose. "No climbing. Just tension. A lot of staring. And a deeply questionable need for an orgasm the second I shut my door."

Sarah hums like she's taste-testing a dessert. "That's foreplay, sweetheart. Your brain just hasn't caught up yet."

I sink lower into the couch. "I pretended to go into someone else's apartment so he wouldn't know which door was mine."

"...but you wanted him to know, didn't you?"

I exhale. "Yeah. And that's what scares me. Because I don't trust the part of me that wanted him to come in, obviously."

She doesn't hesitate. "Ani. That part of you is called your clit, and she's been through some shit. Let her have something nice."

I laugh, half-hysterical. "I don't even know his name."

She gasps like it's a turn-on. "Even hotter. Anonymous dick with a potential criminal record? That's vintage you."

"Oh my God."

"You love a good red flag," she continues. "And baby, this one sounds like he'd fuck you up against a bookshelf and then read you poetry after."

I let my head drop back with a dull thud. "What about Frank?"

She snorts. "Ew. What about him?"

"I don't know. He's..." I trail off. "Present. Sometimes."

"Present like a ghost haunting your uterus?"

"Sarah."

"No, really. Are we emotionally attached to Frank or just too tired to delete his contact?"

I sigh. "I think it's guilt. Or history. Or trauma. Pick your poison."

She softens. "Okay. That's valid. But maybe don't chain yourself to a memory just because it showed up in a nice suit."

I go quiet, and she fills the silence. "Listen, I'm not saying Tattoo Man is The One. But if he makes you feel something other than dread and dry heaving? Babe, you owe it to your vagina to explore that vibe."

"I hate you."

"You love me. Now go eat something carby, masturbate to the memory of his mouth, and maybe—just maybe—text him something wildly inappropriate later."

I smile, despite myself. "Thanks."

"Always," she says. "Now go give that pussy the attention it deserves."

"I'll text you if anything happens."

"Good. And I mean anything, okay? Don't go all silent-film tragic heroine on me."

"Fine. I'll let you know if the world ends. Or if someone tries to marry me."

"Or if you get dicked into oblivion by Tall, Dark, and Dangerous. That counts too."

I snort. "Hot strangers, emotional sabotage, dick with consequences. Got it."

"Exactly," she says. "You know. Tuesday."

I laugh, curling under the blanket. "Noted."

7

"You can learn a lot from someone's whispers."
(Especially if they think they're alone)

Tattoo Man

I knew she was going to lie the second her boots slowed in front of the wrong building.

The pause was too rehearsed, like I haven't spent the last week watching every fucking move she makes.

She didn't even flinch, she just marched herself up to the shittiest complex on the block and stood there like it belonged to her.

She clearly wanted me to just believe it and walk off, disappearing into the dark. I'm already wound so fucking tight with the urge to take her apart.

I waited two blocks away, with my hands in my pockets while she looped behind the building. She probably thought she was clever, and didn't look back. Not once.

She thinks she's careful.

She's not.

Her window's dark now. But I know which one it is. Even though I know she locked the door behind her, I could pick it in five seconds flat.

Locks are for amateurs and I'm not some voyeur with a hard-on and a half-baked fantasy.

I'm worse.

I'm the kind of man who already knows how she tastes. Who's

already had her under him. Shaking and breathless. And if she thinks that was the end of it—she's out of her fucking mind.

I've had her on my tongue, felt her body tremble, clawing for control she didn't have. And fuck me, something broke in me the second she came.

She's not just pretty. She's beautiful—in that don't-look-too-close-or-you'll-bleed kind of way. All jagged edges and fire wrapped in five feet of fight, and she's nothing like I would've expected. That long hair—half white, half black—should look ridiculous, yet it doesn't. It fits her like the chaos she pretends she doesn't carry.

She dresses like she's going to war. Every piece of fabric is armor. Every layer, a challenge. I'd peel her like a fucking fruit, until there's nothing left but the soft center she doesn't let anyone touch.

The tattoos down her arms. The smudged eyeliner she never fixes. That fucking mouth—always a smart ass comment just waiting to come out. She walks like she's got brass knuckles braided into her DNA. Everything in me wants to break every rule she's made for herself just to see what it takes to keep her.

She's the kind of beautiful men ruin themselves over trying to tame. And she let me close. That was her first mistake.

The kiss wasn't about heat, it was about timing. Her phone slid right out of her pocket like it belonged to me.

Now it does.

I'm two buildings down, posted in the shadows between a rusted fire escape and a vending machine that hasn't worked since the city still had hope. It smells like piss, fried oil and rain-soaked concrete—but I don't care. Comfort isn't why I'm here.

She is.

Her phone's still warm in my hand, but it's locked. I huff a dark laugh through my nose. Cute. Like that's going to stop me.

Nothing does. Not when I want something. And I want everything.

Her texts. Her location. Her contacts. Her schedule. Her past, her patterns—her fucking blood type if it comes to that. I want the world she hides when she thinks no one's watching.

Installing the tracker is easy. Almost too easy. She'll never know it's there. She'll keep moving through her little routines, completely unaware that I can see her.

I lean back against the wall, adjusting the hard-on that's been testing the seam of my jeans ever since I pinned her against that library ladder and made her forget her own name.

I've already decided—she's mine.

The taste of her is still on my tongue and I don't want to forget it anytime soon. I want it seared into me.

She still thinks she has the upper hand here, but she doesn't even know she's already lost.

I close my eyes, slowing my breathing. Not because I need calm, but because I need control. If I let myself slip for even a second, I'll be in her room so fast, dragging her skirt up and licking her open again just to hear that wrecked little gasp she tried so desperately to swallow.

Her lights have been out for twenty-seven minutes. No movement. No pacing. Which means she's asleep. And when she sleeps, she sleeps hard.

Just for a second, something tugs at the edge of my focus. A hairline fracture in the pattern I've already memorized.

She doesn't stray. Every movement, every stop—down to her coffee order—is consistent. Predictable. But not like most people.

It's too precise. Almost like she's going through the motions and trying too hard to look normal. I've seen it before—people trying too hard to look like they've got nothing to hide. They overcompensate on the surface... And fuck up the parts that matter.

So maybe she's not just some innocent bartender with soft eyes and trust issues. Maybe she's playing me. And maybe she's lying about how broken she is.

An hour passes before I move.

The fire escape groans under my boots, metal whispering my presence to the night like it wants to be caught. I test the window, and it's unlocked.

Stupid girl.

I slip inside soundlessly.

The apartment smells like her. Lavender and coffee, edged with something wild and lived-in. It hits me in the chest harder than I expected.

There's a knife on the table, and her boots are kicked off sideways, one barely hanging off the rug, like she didn't have the energy to finish the job. She's draped across the couch like the day tore her in half and left the rest behind.

She has one arm over her stomach, and the other curled toward her face, twitching slightly.

I slide her phone onto the counter—right next to a chipped mug and a stack of takeout menus covered in her messy handwriting.

My gaze sweeps the room—books are stacked everywhere, and a half-empty water glass sits on the table. She seems like the type of girl who reads until her eyes bleed. Probably to drown out her own thoughts.

It fits her.

I start to leave, but then I hear her.

"Get off me... please don't..."

My body goes still. Every muscle locks, and every instinct that's ever made me a killer comes roaring to the surface.

I turn.

She's still asleep, but barely. She's breathing ragged, and her lips are parted. Her legs kick once, tangled in the blanket.

Her voice breaks again.

"Please..."

The word slices clean through me—soaked in fear. Half-formed through sleep, but there's nothing uncertain about the way it lands. It's a plea pulled from bone-deep memory, not imagination.

My hand hovers near the door, but I don't move.

She shifts on the couch, curled in tighter now, her knees draw up like she's trying to disappear. Her fingers twitch. Her jaw clenches as she takes another breath, and there's another broken whimper.

"Don't... not again..."

My jaw locks, hard. I don't even notice I'm grinding my teeth until the ache hits. *What is going on?*

She's dreaming. But this isn't just a bad dream, this is a memory with teeth. I take a single step back, eyes locked on her. Her face is half-buried in the couch cushions now, and there's just enough moonlight to catch the sweat at her temple.

Fuck.

She looks small.

She looks nothing like the sharp-tongued brat who throws sarcasm like knives and acts like the world owes her a reason to keep breathing.

Right now, she looks like someone who knows exactly what it's like to be prey. To be hunted. Her mask is off, even if she doesn't know it. And I don't want to look at her like this.

My fingers twitch again, as I curl them into a fist.

Then—so soft I almost miss it—"Don't let him take me..."

My chest goes still.

What the fuck happened to you?

I stare at her for too long. That raw sound of fear echoing in my head like a goddamn bell I can't unring.

And who the fuck is *him?*

Whoever it is, I want to meet him in a dark room with no cameras and the time to make it count.

My gaze drags down her body, taking in the shape of her, the mess of her hair sticking to her cheek, her bare leg curled up under her. She shifts again, her arm slipping down, and that's when I see it—a faint, jagged, scar running along the inside of her forearm.

My stare lingers on it, but I make myself move. My footsteps are silent as I back toward the window.

My pulse is still thundering in my ears when I slip outside, closing the pane behind me like I wasn't just standing in her space with one hand on her fucking secrets.

Back in my car, I sit for a second just breathing. But her voice keeps playing on a loop in my head.

Don't let him take me...

She's been through some shit, that much is obvious.

I need to get my head back in the game, whatever shit she's tangled in, isn't what I need to focus on right now.

I drive back to my place without even remembering the streets I turned on. My knuckles are white on the wheel the entire way. When I get inside, I don't even bother turning on the lights. I slam the door behind me, throwing the phone on the table, and drag my hoodie off like it's suffocating me.

My cock is already hard again.

The worst part wasn't hearing her beg. It's that I fucking liked it.

And if I had it my way, the only name she'd ever cry out in the dark would be mine—wrecked and trembling, the way she was in that library.

That voice.

That mouth.

That bratty, razor-edged attitude that makes me want to split her open just to see what she's hiding underneath.

I drag a hand over my jaw as I step into the bedroom, but I don't bother with the lights.

She's seared into me now. Every fucking nerve ending is tuned to her.

She's a walking contradiction—porcelain wrapped in warning labels, and soft curves strapped into combat boots. She's built like a problem and dressed for the fallout.

Every time I've seen her, she's in all black everything, like she's been at war with the world and shows up to every battle already dressed for the funeral.

Every step she takes is a challenge. Every smile dares you to try and tame her.

And fuck me—I hope someone tries, so I can watch them bleed.

She's small, stubborn, and unapologetically stunning. She's the kind of girl who doesn't ask for attention—she commands it.

And maybe I like the sharp edge of that. Maybe I want to bleed for it.

She's not just pretty. She's fucking dangerous. If it's a reaction she wants, I'll give her a reckoning.

I drop onto the edge of the bed, my jaw is locked, and blood is pounding through my veins like it's got nowhere else to go.

My fist wraps around my cock, already pulsing with every fucked-up thought she's burned into me.

That voice. That bratty, breathy edge that lives in my skull now. Sharp and soft and soaked in attitude.

My eyes slam shut and there she is. Mouth open. Head back. Thighs shaking.

Dripping for me.

That look on her face when she came... fuck, I'll never forget it. Like she didn't know whether to scream or cry. It was like her body finally figured out who it belonged to. I picture her on her knees— lips parted, chin tilted up, and those eyes daring me to ruin her like she doesn't already fucking know I would.

All I can see is that filthy mouth wrapped around my cock, while I hold her jaw open and fuck her until the only sounds she makes are the ones I give her.

Just tears caught in her lashes and spit dripping down her chin and the sound of her choking around me like it's the only thing she knows how to do.

It's not even the image that unravels me. It's the feeling. It's the way she looked at me after—like maybe she wasn't scared.

She wanted more.

I stroke harder, and my breathing turns sharp and ragged, my jaw locks as I chase the edge of something I'll never fucking reach. Not like this.

Not without her bent over and begging, with her voice cracking on my name while I fuck her until the only thing she remembers is who she belongs to.

It hits like a freight train—dark and vicious—and I come with a low, guttural sound that barely makes it past my teeth.

But even then... it's not enough. Because it's not her.

It's not that soaked cunt wrapped around my cock while she claws at my shoulders, asking me to ruin her.

I sit still, breathing like I just went twelve rounds in the cage. My hand is still twitching from the grip, and now my thoughts are a noose around my own fucking neck. I reach for the towel, wipe the mess off like it's going to make me feel less like a monster, and drop back against the mattress, my spine sinking into cold sheets that feel emptier than they should.

This wasn't supposed to happen.

The library should've been the end of it.

But it's not just the way she moaned, or the sound of her breath hitching when I bit her thigh, or how soaked she was from a few filthy words murmured like a promise. It's the way she fucking flinched. The way her mask cracked when she thought I couldn't see her breaking underneath it.

I want the tears and the sass. The fight and the surrender. I want every piece of her she's still trying to hide. I drag a hand over my face, then reach for my phone.

My thumb hovers over one contact.

It rings twice.

"I was wondering when I'd hear from you."

The voice on the other end is amused, and too fucking smug for someone who's still breathing because I haven't changed my mind yet.

"Yeah," I say, voice flat. "I've got a favor."

A pause. Then a soft, knowing laugh. "Aren't those supposed to go both ways?"

I lean forward, my jaw is clenched so tight it clicks. "I need eyes on someone. Quiet ones. I want routes. Patterns. Who they talk to, who talks back, and what changes when they think no one's watching."

Another beat of silence. "You're being cagey. Even for you."

"Just do it."

My tone drops. "And if anyone catches wind you're looking, I'll make it your last favor."

That earns a low whistle. "Still charming as ever. Alright. Send what you've got."

I don't say thank you, or goodbye, I just end the call and stare at the wall like it might bleed answers.

8

"If he offers you something wrapped in a bow…" (Always check for the knife behind his back)

Ani

I'm running on fumes. The kind that don't explode right away, just burn slow and spiteful, waiting to choke you out when you least expect it.

The bar's a mess tonight—too many laughs, too many glass clinks ricocheting off my skull, and the bass thudding against my ribs like a second heartbeat I never fucking asked for is making my head pound. I move on autopilot. Pour. Smile. Don't stab anyone. Repeat.

I toss out some sarcasm to the regulars like breadcrumbs, keeping them fed so they don't look too close. God forbid someone realizes I'm not actually here, just a glorified ghost with a liquor license and unresolved trauma.

The truth is, I haven't slept. Not really. Not since the nightmares started clawing through whatever peace I had left.

Every time I close my eyes, my brain thinks it's hilarious to rerun the worst parts of my subconscious like it's hosting a film festival. Flashes of blood, a crash, a scream that tastes like mine but might not be. Then I wake up soaked in sweat and half a second from vomiting.

Fun.

And of course—guess who hasn't come back.

Tattoo Man.

Library philosopher. Whiskey menace. Whatever.

I keep telling myself that's a good thing. No more brooding eyes or cocky smirks that see too much. No more subtle touches that make me forget why I built all these walls in the first place.

Still...every time the door creaks open, I look.

I wish I could stop thinking about him, but my body wants something it shouldn't. Clearly I'm a glutton for punishment and bad decisions wrapped in tattoos and self-control issues. So instead, I've been forcing my brain to focus on something safer. Something mine.

My bookshop.

I haven't said it out loud to anyone yet, because saying it makes it real and real things get ruined. But I've got tomorrow night off, and if the universe doesn't implode in the next twenty-four hours, I'm going to check out a few locations with Sarah.

It feels far away, like this isn't for people like me kind of far.

Still, it's the only thing that keeps me from unraveling when the silence gets too sharp.

My phone buzzes beneath the bar, but I don't have to check to know who it is. The stupid unknown number that's been sending me messages for a few weeks now.

I ignore it. Just like the last three. Even though my stomach knots in that too-familiar way, like it's bracing for something I haven't figured out yet.

It could be Sloane. Or Sarah. Or some drunk asshole playing games.

I don't want to know.

A sharp crack cuts through the bar—someone slamming a pool stick like they just lost their pride and I flinch harder than I should.

I take a breath, rolling my shoulders.

I've got shit to do and falling apart during happy hour isn't on the menu.

I'm behind the counter drying glasses that probably weren't even dirty, when I glance up—and there he is.

Frank.

Parked in the corner like he owns it, with one arm draped over the back of the booth, and a drink already in front of him.

I didn't even see him come in.

Must've been one of the new girls who served him. He's just smooth enough to make you doubt yourself.

His eyes find me instantly. No nod. Just that slow, deliberate once-over like he's re-memorizing every inch of me like I'm a fucking painting he commissioned.

I walk over anyway. Hips swaying a little too much on purpose —because if I'm going to play this game, I'm going to win by being petty.

His grin deepens.

"You always this happy to see me?" he asks, like we're picking up mid-conversation.

I glance down, and there's a black box on the table tied with a sleek ribbon. The kind of box that screams money and manipulation.

"Are you always this dramatic?" I flick the ribbon with one finger. "Showing up out of nowhere with a mystery box like it's Valentine's Day."

He shrugs, all ease. This man must think the world bends to his timing.

"And yet... you're still standing here. Looking at me like I'm exactly what you've been waiting for."

It takes everything in me not to roll my eyes, but I don't give him the satisfaction.

"I was just in the neighborhood," he says, casually as he lifts his glass to his lips. "Thought I'd stop by. Make sure you haven't forgotten about me."

I arch a brow. "That sounds like a you problem."

His smile flashes—all teeth. But there's something behind it now. Something darker. Something that didn't used to be there.

He gestures toward the box like it's a goddamn centerpiece. "You gonna open it, or just keep admiring the bow?"

I flick my gaze between it and his smug face.

"Haven't decided if it's for me... or if I'm just the lucky bartender you're using to hand it off to your actual date."

His grin doesn't falter. If anything, it sharpens.

"If it was for someone else, sweetheart..." He leans forward, voice lower now—quieter, but designed to crawl straight under my skin. "You wouldn't be the one still standing here."

My eyes drop to the box and I stare at it like it might grow teeth.

"Is it gonna explode?"

He laughs. That smug, low kind of laugh that always means trouble. He's never bought me a gift before. It's only been dinner and flirting this whole time. *What is he up to now?*

"Only if you ask nicely."

I sit, dropping into the booth across from him like it's a power move instead of a surrender.

I unwrap the ribbon without looking at him—just to spite the way I can feel his eyes dragging over my every move.

The box creaks open and it's a bracelet. I can tell just by the box that its designer—matte black, gold lettering I don't recognize but probably should. The bracelet inside catches the bar light and glitters, with a thin platinum chain and a single diamond at the center.

It's beautiful.

Which makes me hate it more, because he's never been this persistent. Hell, I don't even wear jewelry.

But that's the thing about men like him. They don't need permission to decide who you are. They just dress you up like you already belong to them.

I close the lid politely, but not fast enough to be rude.

"Cute," I say. "But unnecessary."

His gaze sharpens a fraction. "It made me think of you when I was out of town."

I lean back, arms crossed, letting one leg slide out under the table.

"I wear boots and sarcasm, Frank. Not diamonds, but thank you." I pause, then arch a brow. "You think a gift's gonna make me swoon?"

His mouth curves. "I think you've already started to."

I scoff, but my pulse betrays me. It always does with men like Frank—I know he's the kind of guy who watches for tells, and feeds off my reactions.

"You're cocky for someone who comes and goes without warning."

He tilts his head, eyes narrowing slightly. "I told you I was leaving town."

"I don't care where you are."

He leans forward, elbows on the table, voice dipping lower—sharpened into something that could draw blood.

"Then why haven't you told me to fuck off for good?"

Because you make me feel like I'm being watched even when you're not here. Because a part of me still wonders what it would feel like to let you win.

But I smirk instead. "Because telling you to fuck off would mean I cared enough to finish the sentence."

His gaze drags over me—trying to memorize the shape of my defiance.

"You do. You just don't like admitting it."

"And you like hearing yourself talk."

He laughs, rich and dark. "You've missed me."

"I've missed my peace and quiet."

Frank finishes his drink in one swallow, the glass clinking softly as he sets it down. That charming mask—danger wrapped in good tailoring—slides perfectly back into place.

"Are you free tomorrow?"

"No."

"You didn't even check your schedule."

"I didn't need to."

That smile of his doesn't falter—but his jaw ticks.

I turn my back before he can see the satisfaction curl across my mouth, but I feel his stare press between my shoulder blades like a brand. He doesn't leave for the rest of the night. He just sits there, drinking his water like the bar exists because he allows it to.

It's not until close that he moves again, sliding up to the bar while I'm stacking glasses and wiping counters like I didn't just spend the past hour pretending I couldn't feel his eyes crawling across my skin.

"One more before I hit the road?"

I glance at the clock. "You driving?"

"Wouldn't be drinking if I was." His smirk ticks up a notch. "Just figured I'd keep your pretty face company."

I snort, grabbing a clean glass anyway. "You must be really bored."

"Only with everyone else."

He laughs, soft and smug, like this is a game and he's always three moves ahead.

"Can't blame a man for trying."

I set the drink down harder than I need to, watching the amber swirl. "Are you staying until we kick you out?"

He shrugs, taking a long, unbothered sip. "Wouldn't be the first time I've closed down a place with you."

"You mean sat in the corner until I told you to leave?"

He grins. "Semantics."

Across the bar, the new girl throws me a look, mouthing everything okay? I nod once. It's not a lie, but it's not the truth either.

Where's Sarah when I need her? She would've clocked this whole thing five minutes ago and started dry-running his obituary.

It's always like this. It's been this way since that night in the alley. He's always been flirty, so it doesn't really bother me.

I start counting the till and wiping the last stubborn ring of grime off the bar. He stands slow and unrushed, with that same air of entitlement he always wears.

"Come on, Ani. Let me give you a ride."

I grab my bag without looking at him. "My Uber's already on the way."

He doesn't answer right away.

"You sure?" he asks. Voice dipping just enough in something that doesn't quite match the charm.

"Positive." I tap the side of my phone like it's proof. It's a lie. I was going to walk, but I'll be damned if I owe him anything. I'm not giving him any ideas.

The second he steps out the door, I sigh and finally order the damn car. The price climbs with every passing second, mocking me.

The bright side is, at least I don't have to walk home. My feet will thank me—my pride, maybe not so much.

I finish locking the door behind me, sliding the key into place with a satisfying click. The alley beside the bar is quiet, lit only by the flickering lights overhead. I shove my hands into my jacket pockets, bracing for the chill that always creeps in after close—only to freeze halfway through the motion.

Frank's standing there like he's been waiting for me.

He has one foot propped against the wall, with his hands tucked into his coat and that same cocky half-smile plastered across his face.

"You really should let me drive you home," he says smoothly, pushing off the wall and stepping toward me.

I take a small step back, not because I'm afraid, but because his presence always feels like a little too much. Like standing too close to a fire. You don't know if you're warming up or about to get burned.

"My Uber's almost here." I shrug, forcing my voice to stay light. "Besides, I don't make a habit of getting into cars with strange men."

"Strange?" His smile tilts, not quite a smirk, but not super friendly either. "Ani, we've been seeing each other for months. Come on."

Fuck. I was afraid of this. Why can't men just let things be the way they are and be okay with being friend zoned.

If we're dating then what I did in the library... No, I'm not going there. I've always been clear with Frank about my feelings.

His gaze drags over me, and he smiles. "Why are you still pretending this is some cat-and-mouse thing? You're not hard to get —you're just scared to want it."

I scoff, but before I can come up with something snarky, he moves closer.

My back hits the wall with a soft thud as his hand braces beside my head, his body angled just enough to keep me boxed in without ever touching me.

"I know you're stubborn," he murmurs, voice dipping low. "But isn't it exhausting pretending you don't want this."

His mouth dips—hovering near mine. Just close enough that I can feel his breath, and taste the mix of whiskey and smoke still clinging to him.

My heart starts racing and every nerve is on alert, even as my brain screams *bad idea* like it's the only word left in the English language.

I hate how controlled he is. I also hate how every move he makes is calculated and carefully timed, like he's playing a long game I haven't been given the rules to. I don't even know what to think anymore.

"Frank—" I start, tone sharp.

But then he kisses me.

Not rough. Not demanding. Just soft. Intentional. A brush of lips that lingers a beat too long to be casual.

It's the kind of kiss designed to disarm. Like if he plays it just right, I'll fold before I even realize I'm doing it.

And maybe I would've. If I didn't know better. If I wasn't already haunted by another mouth.

Before anything more can happen, a sharp honk slices through the night. The Uber. *Thank God.* We both glance toward it, headlights cutting across the brick wall.

Frank just leans back a fraction, with that smug, practiced smile sliding back into place, smooth as ever.

"I'll see you tomorrow, doll."

I don't answer. I'm not giving him the satisfaction. I really need to figure out what the hell I'm doing about the men in my life.

I push past him, gripping the car door handle like it's the only thing anchoring me to reality and slide in without looking back.

Because the truth is...yeah, he's good-looking. He's the kind of man girls ruin their lives for. But I'm not most girls.

And I've already been ruined once.

The last thing I need right now is a man. The only issue is—he's not the one I can't stop thinking about.

It's not his inked hands I want touching me. Not his voice curling under my skin and making it hard to breathe. It's not his stare that sees too much—stripping me bare like he already knows what I'm hiding.

Frank looks like the prize. But he feels like a fucking trap.

The Uber driver doesn't say a word as we pull away, and I don't look back. Not once. I just sit there—silently—watching the bar disappear behind me like a chapter I'm pretending not to reread in my head.

I'm too wired to breathe, and too tired to care. The kiss still lingers on my lips, and it feels like a mistake. *How did this happen?*

My mind drifts back to the first night I met Frank.

Thick, dark blood soaked through his shirt. His hand was pressed to his side like he was trying to hold himself together.

I remember freezing.

Not because I was afraid, but because of the way he looked at me. He was smiling through the pain. His knuckles were scraped, and his jaw was already bruised. He looked like he'd been jumped —or dragged behind a truck.

"You're supposed to look scared," he said, sounding all gravel and pain.

I wasn't scared of him, what could he possibly do in that state.

I dropped beside him and pressed my hands over his, trying to slow the bleeding. He winced and told me I didn't have to stay. But I did.

I thought it was the right thing to do, to at least stay until the ambulance came. He never passed out. Not once. He just stared at me with that same unnerving calm, like we were meeting under normal circumstances.

When the medics arrived, he still found the strength to smile at me and insisted I ride with him to the hospital. He said it was either that or bleed all over the EMT who looked like he might puke at the sight of a paper cut.

And for some goddamn reason—I went.

We talked the whole way there. Or rather—I talked. He listened. Mostly because I was afraid if I didn't keep him awake, he wouldn't make it. But maybe part of me just didn't want to leave him alone. Not like that. Not bleeding and half-smiling.

I couldn't have that on my conscience.

At the hospital, he told me saving his life meant we were connected now. It was some pretty fucked-up logic, but somehow he made it make sense. He asked me to stay until the doctor came. So I did.

When they told him it wasn't as bad as it looked—that he would just need a few stitches and a night under observation—he grinned like he'd won a bet.

He told me I was now his favorite person in the city.

I should've walked away right then. I should've let the ER

doors close behind me and left him as nothing more than a crazy night wrapped in gauze and smug gratitude.

But I have no self preservation skills.

The next day, he showed up at the bar. Not with flowers or some grand gesture—just a coffee. It was somehow my order, and he sat at the end of the bar like he belonged there and then it became a pattern.

A drink always waiting before I even clocked in. Dinner. And that slow, steady smile like he had all the time in the world for me.

Frank never pushed. Not really. That's the part that made it harder to see coming. He was all smooth lines and slow smiles. He never asked for more than I was willing to give—until suddenly, I'd given just enough to make it hard to pull away.

And now he shows up out of nowhere, flashing expensive jewelry and that same cocky look, like we're still writing the same story.

The bell over the library door jingles as someone leaves. The soft rustle of pages and the ancient air vent's low wheeze are the only sounds that remain.

I move through the stacks with purpose. Or at least, what I'm pretending is purpose—arms full of books I've already shelved once today. Maybe twice. I tell myself I'm just being thorough. Responsible, even.

The chair by the back window is empty. Again. Sunlight spills across the seat like a cosmic joke.

It's pathetic. I know it's pathetic.

I jam a book back into its spot a little too hard, wincing when the spine smacks the shelf loud enough to echo.

It's not like I wanted to see him. I just... noticed he hadn't been here. And okay, maybe I was actively looking. Maybe I took the long way around the return desk three separate times. Maybe I circled the philosophy section so many times I'm starting to feel like a creep in my own workplace. But apparently, the universe had other plans.

"You okay, or did Aristotle just finger your frontal lobe?"

I jump—hard. Spinning around like I've just been caught watching porn in a church.

Heat scorches up my neck, flushing my face so fast it makes me dizzy. I can feel the blush blooming across my cheeks like a goddamn crime scene, and of course—Sloane notices.

She leans against the end of the aisle, arms crossed, with one brow arched like she already knows what was going through my head.

She pops a piece of gum into her mouth—slow and dramatic—like this is just another Tuesday for her.

Which, honestly? It probably is.

A grin curls at her lips. "Wow. That bad, huh?"

I blink. "What?"

"That flush." She gestures toward my face. "You look like you were two seconds away from dry humping Fifty Shades and got caught."

I groan, dragging a hand down my face. "I was not—"

"Sure, sure," she cuts in, already laughing. "So... who were you hoping to run into over here? Or should I say... who were you trying to climb?"

I freeze.

Heat flashes up the back of my neck going straight into my ears, and I fumble the stack of books like she just tasered me in the uterus.

"I'm doing my job," I mutter, clutching the books tighter, suddenly fascinated by the nonfiction section.

"Uh-huh." Sloane leans against the shelf, one brow raised, her smirk is full of judgment and unholy delight. "Must be a riveting morning if you've alphabetized the same section four times."

"I'm not looking for anyone," I snap.

Instant regret.

Her grin stretches. "Didn't say you were."

I roll my eyes and shove the last book into place with a little too much force. "Do you ever—like—not talk?"

She taps her chin, pretending to be deep in thought. "Only when I'm asleep. Maybe. Honestly, I'd have to ask someone."

I hate how easy it is to smile around her. I also hate how she sees through every single mask I try to wear, and still chooses to show up like I'm worth the effort.

"You're the worst," I tell her, biting back a grin that she absolutely doesn't deserve.

She winks. "And yet, here I am. Saint fucking Sloane."

I snort, shaking my head. "Have I ever told you you've got a real gift for compliments?"

She leans on the edge of the cart, grinning. "One time in high school, I told a guy he had serial killer eyes. You'd think that'd be a dealbreaker, right? He asked me out the next day."

I blink. "Did you go?"

"Obviously," she deadpans. "I wasn't gonna let all that opportunity go to waste. I made him take me to Olive Garden. Unlimited breadsticks or bust."

A laugh escapes me before I can stop it. It feels... good. I almost forgot how easy it was to just be.

She nudges me with her elbow. "See? I'm good for something."

I open my mouth to agree—but something about the way she says it flicks a switch in my brain.

I'm good for something.

My smile falters. Just long enough that I have to look away, forcing a soft chuckle so she doesn't see.

"You, my friend, are deeply unwell," I say instead, going back to our usual playful as I shove the cart forward.

"All the time." She tosses her ponytail like it's a badge of honor. "But at least I'm consistent."

The rest of the shift drags. There's a lull around lunch that leaves too much time to think, and not enough distraction to keep my brain from spiraling.

I glance at the door every time the bell chimes telling myself I'm just hoping for something interesting. That I'm bored, and it's not him I'm waiting for.

God, I'm a mess.

By the time I clock out, I'm ready to call it a day and finally do what I actually wanted—go stare at buildings like I originally planned with Sarah. She was going to help me scope out a few spaces, something small with potential. Something that could actually be mine.

Some of that excitement starts to creep back in, bubbling just enough to remind me what hope feels like.

But fate, apparently, has other ideas. Because the second I step out from the break room, Frank's standing there. He's leaning near the front desk, hands in his pockets, black button-down rolled at the sleeves, and dark slacks hugging his frame.

His shirt's unbuttoned just enough to flash the edge of ink across his collarbone. The dark leather watch strapped to his wrist probably costs more than my rent, and the stubble lining his jaw is trimmed with obsessive precision.

He looks like a GQ cover boy with a secret body count and zero remorse. I don't hate it, but he's also not Tattoo man. *Where did that come from?*

He pushes off the counter with that lazy, crooked smile sliding into place like muscle memory.

"Hey," he says, casually, like we do this all the time. Like it's normal for him to pop up at my job looking like the human embodiment of a red flag with a Rolex.

I blink. "What... are you doing here?"

His grin deepens. "Picking you up for our date. I told you we were going."

My mouth opens. Then closes. Then opens again.

Brain fog's a bitch, but I know I didn't agree to that. I would've remembered agreeing to a date with the man who gives charming narcissism its own zip code.

"I—when did I agree to that?"

He shrugs. "You said you were off today. I figured I'd take you somewhere nice. You've been working too hard."

My mouth is halfway to saying no when I feel Sloane step up behind me, close enough that I feel her smile through the back of my skull.

"If you don't want him, I will," she whispers, giddy and completely useless.

I elbow her without looking. "You're not helping."

She backs off, humming something filthy under her breath. I make a mental note to bring that up later.

My eyes cut back to Frank—who's still watching us with that smug, unbothered expression of his.

"I didn't tell you I work here," I say, crossing my arms before I can stop them. The words come out sharper than I meant—but not sharp enough to regret. Not that I owe him anything.

The bar was one thing. But the library? This is mine. He doesn't know where I live either—and that's not an accident. Our entire relationship so far has been bar flirting, dinner, occasional texting, and him showing up with smug persistence like a handsome virus I haven't shaken yet.

Until recently, *"date"* wasn't even on the list. And now... here he is. Inside my library.

"You mentioned it." His tone's too light to be innocent.

I hadn't planned on seeing him today. I had plans—real ones with Sarah that were long overdue.

"Did I?" I ask, voice dry.

He shrugs, all charm. "You probably don't remember. We've talked about a lot."

And just like that, I feel like the asshole, because we *have* talked. There was that one night he sent me a meme at two a.m. about red flags and said it reminded him of me.

I told him to go fuck himself. But I laughed. Maybe I've been leading him on or maybe I just liked the attention, or the consistency. The idea of someone choosing me over and over—even if it's for the wrong reasons, makes me feel wanted on some fucked up level.

I glance at my phone. The map is still open with all the listings I planned to check out today. I was supposed to spend it chasing something that felt like mine. Not detouring into whatever the hell this is.

A small pang of guilt tugs in my chest. Sarah's going to be so pissed. She was going to be my designated hype girl, dressed in black with iced coffee and way too many unsolicited opinions about which places "gave off emotionally stable vibes."

I shoot her a text.

> Me: Change of plans. Raincheck on building-stalking. Blame GQ Barbie. Also… if I go missing, check his trunk first.

A beat later, the bubbles appear.

> Sarah: Excuse me?? YOU'RE ON A DATE?? With the man who looks like he bench presses trust issues?? I hate you. Go. Have. Fun. But text me the second he starts talking in riddles or offers you a diamond collar.

I snort under my breath and lock the screen. So much for not getting guilt-tripped into a date I never agreed to.

But he's here and he's... trying right? Sort of. This is the kind of attention most girls would kill for, so why do I feel so bothered by it?

Maybe this is what taking it slow looks like. What it's supposed to feel like.

The bracelet from last night is still sitting on my kitchen counter—unopened, and untouched, and suddenly I feel like a dick.

I sigh. "Fine. But I'm picking the music."

His smile is slow and infuriating. That self-satisfied kind of smug that says I never actually had a choice.

The doors slide open, releasing us into the thick, early-summer air. It clings to my skin like a warning, but I follow him to the curb anyway.

9

"If the room adjusts around him, leave."
(You're not on a date if he owns the building)

Ani

The music is too loud. It's pounding with the kind of bass that rattles your teeth and makes your brain feel like it's leaking out your ears.

I blink through the strobes, already regretting every life decision that led me here—starting with saying yes to a date without knowing where the hell he was taking me. Frank said dinner. Just dinner.

Which, fine. He delivered. It was a fancy place, with white linen tablecloths, and wine I couldn't pronounce. The glasses were so delicate I was afraid to breathe near them, and there were more forks than one human should ever need.

But this? This is sensory warfare dressed up as nightlife.

"I thought we were getting drinks," I shout over the bass, wincing as a strobe hits me dead in the retinas.

Frank leans in like this is the most natural thing in the world—his lips brushing the shell of my ear, and his voice oozes that slick charm. "We are. This just felt more... fun."

I glance around, taking in the crowd. Designer everything—outfits, cologne, watches. And yet no one bumps into Frank. The crowd moves around him like he's some kind of royalty. Or worse—like they owe him.

He orders for us without asking what I want and I hate that I'm not surprised. When he slides a drink across the high-top table like we're at a private tasting instead of a goddamn rave, he flashes that smile. "You good?"

I raise the glass, trying not to grimace as the music kicks up another level.

"I'd be better if I could hear myself think."

He just smirks and sips his drink, like this is exactly where he belongs.

I work at a nice bar, but this makes mine look like a dive on a bad night.

"I told you I'd take you out," he says, eyes flicking up from his glass. "I like to keep my promises."

I lift a brow. "That's what this is?"

His grin spreads. "Something like that."

A laugh pushes up—but I swallow it back. This whole night feels off. He's being too nice. He's trying a little too hard to impress me, more than usual. And I hate that a small, traitorous part of me notices.

This version of him looks like something you could fall for— right before it ruins you.

I sip my drink, while my eyes drift over the crowd—and for a second, I swear I see a man watching me, but he's gone the moment I blink.

I tell myself it's nothing.

That it's just the lights and the loud music messing with me, not something else slithering beneath my skin.

"I've missed this," Frank says suddenly, dragging my attention back to him. "Us."

"There is no us," I say, rolling my eyes with a smile I don't mean. "So what exactly is this supposed to be?"

His grin sharpens with that signature smirk.

"A beginning."

"A beginning," I echo, flat. "Is this the part where I trip into your arms and we slow dance in the middle of the club?"

He laughs, leaning in. His mouth is far too close to mine.

"We could. But I think we both know I'm not the dancing type."

No. He's the watch-you-from-the-corner-until-you-crack type. And right now, he's looking at me like I'm not just his date, and it's starting to make me uncomfortable.

I pull back, shaking my head. "This place is too loud. I feel like I'm yelling."

Frank doesn't argue. Just downs the rest of his drink in one practiced motion and stands, holding out a hand.

"Come on."

I hesitate.

His gaze flicks to mine.

"Just a quieter booth. Promise."

It's stupid that I even consider it. Stupider that I take his hand and follow him down the hallway.

The VIP section is quieter—but somehow worse. The music is a low, pulsing throb in the walls, and everything else is velvet curtains, dim lighting, and money that doesn't need to prove itself.

He leads me to a booth in the farthest corner, and I slide into the leather seat across from him, my fingers skim the edge of the table like I need something to ground me.

It's not lost on me that I'm here in combat boots, sheer black tights with one rip across the thigh that definitely wasn't there this morning, and a slip dress that walks the line between effort and accident.

My eyeliner's smudged, I don't have any lip gloss on, and I look exactly like someone who didn't know she was being taken somewhere with velvet ropes and VIP tags.

Everyone else in this room looks like a curated ad campaign.

Frank, of course, fits right in.

I glance down at my chipped nail polish and fight the urge to sink lower in the booth.

"Didn't know I was supposed to dress for the Met Gala," I mutter.

Frank grins, stretching one arm along the back of the booth. "You're perfect."

I snort. "You don't even know what I'm wearing under this sweater."

"I thought this was dinner and drinks," I say, sitting straighter. "Not amateur hour at the strip club."

He tilts his head with that same infuriating calm in his expression.

"It can be both."

I open my mouth, just to shut it again. Why the hell did I agree to this? Because I felt bad. Because he was bleeding in a fucking alley and I kept him from dying. Because brushing him off for months started to feel like more effort than just going to dinner.

I'm not the girl who waits around for a man to show up. Not even if he left me gasping in a library aisle.

"I didn't realize velvet booths were your thing," I say, waving a hand at the lush, shadowed corner we're tucked into.

He shrugs. "I like privacy." Then he smiles with that lazy grin of his. "Don't you?"

That earns a raised brow. "Privacy? From what, your fan club?"

Frank's eyes glint in the low light. "Jealousy looks good on you."

I laugh. But it's sharp and hollow. "That wasn't jealousy. That was secondhand embarrassment."

He chuckles, and for a second, I almost forget the weirdness. Almost forget the knot curling tighter in my stomach.

God, I hate how easy it is to laugh around him. How easily he slides back into the role like he never left. This night's just getting started and I already feel like it's going to end badly.

He leans back, one arm draped over the booth, legs spread

wide, radiating confidence in that smug, territorial way men do when they're trying to stake a claim without saying it out loud.

And it's working.

I feel like everyone who looks at him knows I'm the one he's here with—and that somehow makes me the possession instead of the problem.

The bartender appears without being called, she doesn't even glance at me. Just drops a drink at Frank's elbow like she was waiting for this moment to shine. "Let me know if you need anything else, *sir*." She says it like she's having sex and I can practically see drool coming out of her mouth.

Her eyes never flick to mine. Not once. Right. Because clearly I'm not the important one at this table.

Frank gives her a nod, like this happens all the time and that's when I start noticing the other things. The two men in suits who keep glancing over. The way one leans in and says something to the bouncer—who nods without question and disappears through a side door.

Frank doesn't seem to notice, which is the most unsettling part.

I watch how people glance toward him before doing anything. How the DJ gave him a head nod when we walked in. How someone brought him a drink before we even sat down.

I lean back slowly, crossing my legs as I study him from the corner of my eye. "So... tell me again how you found this place?"

He doesn't miss a beat. "A friend of mine owns it."

I arch a brow, lifting my drink to my lips just to have something to do. "Must be a fun friend."

He grins into his glass but doesn't answer right away—just takes a sip of his whiskey and lets the silence stretch.

"Don't know what you're talking about," he finally says, all smooth denial and sharp amusement.

Yeah, okay.

The DJ switches to something bass-heavy and obnoxious, vibrating through the floor and right into my spine. Frank leans in, his mouth brushes my ear like he's about to whisper something private—only a woman in stilettos cuts in, her dress barely covering her body. Her eyes are locked on Frank like she's hoping he'll remember her name.

"Frank," she purrs, breathy and lip-glossed. "I didn't know you were in town."

He doesn't even look at her when he answers.

"Just got back."

She giggles.

"Let me know if you need anything," she adds, dragging her fingers along the edge of the table before strutting away, swaying her hips, clearly hoping he's watching her.

I watch her go, then turn to him, deadpan. "You always bring your groupies on dates here or something?"

He smirks, staying infuriatingly calm. "Didn't realize this was a date. You called it that, not me."

"I said yes because you were annoying. I didn't realize I'd be sharing you with the cast of Love Island."

Frank laughs, but his hand slides along the back of the booth, brushing my shoulder.

"Are you jealous?"

"Of her?" I snort. "Please. Her heels were one wrong step away from a femur fracture."

He doesn't stop smiling. "I like you like this," he says finally. "Defensive. Sharp-tongued."

"I like me far away from overpriced vodka and mystery men," I mutter, leaning forward to place my empty glass on the table. "Which is exactly where I'll be if another one of your fan club girls tries to sit in my lap."

Frank chuckles—clearly amused. Then leans closer. "Relax. This place is safe."

"For you, maybe," I say, just loud enough for him to hear.

His eyes flicker. Then he reaches out, brushing a piece of hair behind my ear—his fingers linger a beat too long.

"This place is mine, doll. No one touches what's mine."

It echoes through my chest like a bell that was struck wrong. I can't tell if I'm flattered...Or fucking terrified.

His? I fucking knew something was up. Especially with the way people were acting around him.

And what the fuck did he mean by *no one touches what's mine?*

I lean back into the booth, as his words settle in my lungs like smoke. Around us, the bass throbs. Lights flash. People laugh and drink like nothing's wrong—like I didn't just hear something that could've been a flirtation... or a warning. Maybe both.

Frank's eyes scan the room, and just like that, the moment's gone.

He just sits there—arm slung over the back of the booth like he owns the fucking underworld. And I'm just the girl lucky enough to breathe in it.

That little flicker of unease spreads through my chest like a bruise. *What am I doing here?*

"I'm gonna hit the bathroom," I say, already sliding out of the booth before he can say something that makes me want to throat punch him—or worse, agree with him.

He doesn't stop me, he just nods once.

I push through the crowd fast—dodging the swaying bodies, sweat, and spilled drinks.

The hallway near the restrooms is quieter, but not by much. I lock the door behind me and grip the edge of the sink, trying to slow my breathing.

What the hell am I doing here?

It's not just the word *mine* that made my pulse spike. It's how he said it.

I turn on the faucet and splash water on my face.

"Get it together," I mutter at my reflection.

But the girl staring back at me looks pale. My eyeliner's smudged and my lips are pressed so tight they're practically color-less. I look like I'm about two seconds from bolting.

And then—I hear a soft thud behind me.

I jolt, heart in my throat, eyes snapping to the mirror, looking behind me, but the stalls are empty. It's just me and my own stupid panic in here.

"Cool," I whisper. "Let's just add bathroom jump-scares to the list of red flags tonight."

I step into the hallway, forcing myself to walk slowly, like I didn't just splash water on my face and talk myself out of crawling out the window.

When I round the corner, Frank's on his feet with one hand clenched into a fist, and the other fisted in the front of some guy's shirt—some guy who looks two seconds away from pissing himself.

His mouth is moving, but the music's too loud to catch the words. Doesn't matter. Whatever he's saying works, because the guy nods like his life depends on it—then stumbles backward and bolts for the exit like hell's on his heels.

Frank exhales, rolling his shoulders as he adjusts his sleeves. And then he sees me.

The grin he gives me is calm. It's the same grin he's worn all night, only it's a little off putting that he looks like he didn't just scare the soul out of someone.

He strolls back to the booth and I just stand there, pulse thudding, while something cold twisting beneath my ribs. Because for the first time since I met him... I wonder if maybe I don't actually know who the hell Frank really is.

"You good?" he asks casually.

I nod once and slide into the booth across from him. But something about Frank tonight feels... different. Sharper around the edges.

I don't have time to ask him about it before the waitress shows up. She still won't look at me as she drops another round of drinks off and vanishes.

Frank lifts his glass like nothing happened. "To finally getting that date."

I hesitate, then raise mine too—because not clinking glasses with a man who acts like he owns half the damn city seems like the kind of mistake that gets you a missing persons report.

I set my glass down slower than necessary, studying him. "Where'd you disappear to when you left town?" I ask.

"Business," he says. The same non-answer he always gives. His fingers curl around the rim of his glass like he's holding a secret— and enjoying every second of it.

I arch a brow. "That vague response is doing all the heavy lifting tonight, huh?"

His grin gets wider. "Are you asking because you care?"

I scoff, but it's a beat too late.

"I'm asking because people don't usually disappear for weeks."

He lowers his voice so I have to lean in just to hear him. "Didn't know you were keeping track."

"I wasn't."

He hums. "Could've fooled me."

I roll my eyes, settling back into the booth—only for his hand to land on my thigh under the table.

I go still.

"That wasn't a no," he murmurs, voice dipping low enough to send a chill down my spine. "You're curious. Finally."

I lift my drink, just to keep from saying something I'll regret—or worse, something honest. But he doesn't stop.

"I knew this date was a good idea," he adds, smiling. "One night out and you're already trying to peel back my layers."

"Don't flatter yourself," I mutter, ignoring the way my pulse skips when his thumb starts drawing lazy circles just above my knee.

He leans in, closer than necessary, cologne and danger bleeding into the air between us. "Too late, doll. I'm feeling very flattered right now."

His gaze drops to my mouth—when the waitress comes up asking if he wants anything else. Something like anger across his face at the interruption before he blinks it away. I take the out, straightening, and brush his hand off like it didn't short-circuit my common sense.

"So, hypothetically... if someone wanted to know what the hell you actually do for a living—where would she even start?"

His smile doesn't slip. Not even a crack. "You could start by asking what I like in a woman," he says smoothly. "But I think you already know."

God. He's insufferable.

I snort. "Right. Because that's definitely the first thing I want to know about a man who might be the mayor or something."

His eyes spark, but he just shrugs.

"I'm not the mayor," he says, brushing his thumb along the rim of his glass. "That would suggest someone else has a say in how things are run."

I blink. "Oh good. A man with a God complex. That's fresh."

He laughs, but underneath, it's all steel.

"Relax," he says, leaning in. "I work in investments. Management. That sort of thing."

I stare at him. "Vague as usual. Classic." I tip my head, keeping my voice flat. Can't have him think I care too much or it'll go to his head. "What kind of management? Clubs? Restaurants? Hitmen?"

He hums, tilting his head like he's deciding how to answer me.

"Let's just say I know how to keep people in line. And I'm very good at collecting what I'm owed."

Something cold skates across my spine. I blame the lighting and the bass vibrating under my boots like a second heartbeat. But deep down, I have a feeling it's none of those things.

"I'm still waiting for the part where this isn't a crime drama," I mutter, half into my drink.

Frank leans in closer, his fingers grazing my knee. "Come on, baby girl. You're smarter than that," he says, smooth enough to pour over ice. "You think I'd bring you somewhere like this if I knew you weren't safe?"

"Is that what this is?" I ask, tilting my head. "A safety demonstration?"

His grin widens. All teeth and no humor. "You haven't even seen what I'm capable of yet."

My stomach twists, because some dark, broken part of me wants to know. Just to see if he's bluffing. Just to see what kind of monster he thinks he is underneath the cologne and cufflinks.

The lights strobe across his face, painting him in flashes of red and blue. He looks carved out of something hard, and I'm about to push again—asking another question I won't get a real answer to—when he stands and holds out a hand.

"Come on."

I stare at it. "Why?"

His smile curls at the edges. "Because if you sit here any longer, you're going to start asking questions I'm not going to answer. Which will ruin our date."

I stand up, without taking his hand as we make our way down the hall. We stop at a side door near the back—one I didn't even realize was there, as he types something into a keypad, and the lock releases with a soft click.

"You got a panic room in there too?" I ask, arching a brow.

Frank chuckles as he pushes the door open. "Not yet. But I could be convinced."

How he managed to make that dirty, I'll never know.

Every nerve is buzzing, and my pulse is climbing for reasons I don't want to name. "That supposed to impress me?"

He steps in, crowding me back slowly until my spine hits the wall. His hands don't touch me, but his breath ghosts across my cheek, close enough to make me shiver.

"I don't need to impress you, doll," he murmurs. "You're still here."

My jaw clenches. "Because you're good at playing games."

His mouth curves. "I don't play games."

His hand lifts, and his fingertips brush along my jaw before sliding into my hair and tugging just enough to tip my head back. The move is slow and deliberate, like he's testing what I'll let him take.

I should push him off, and say something cutting. But instead—I let him. For what reason I'll never know.

"You think I don't know what this is?" I whisper. "You think I haven't seen men like you before?"

His mouth lowers to my throat, the words a hot promise against my skin. "No, doll. You haven't."

His tongue flicks over my pulse point, and I swear my knees almost buckle, but not for the reason you'd think. "Frank—"

"I've been patient," he says, voice dropping to something darker, more possessive. "Too fucking patient. You wanna pretend you don't feel it? Fine. But don't lie to me about what this is. Don't lie to yourself."

His hand slides under my jaw again, thumb brushing my lower lip, and I hate that my mouth parts instinctively.

He leans in closer—so close I can't think—his lips brush mine, with a feather-light touch. He kisses me slowly, like he's finally staking a claim he thinks he's earned and when he finally pulls back, he's breathing like he's the one who just got wrecked.

"You should go home," he says roughly. "Before I stop pretending I can be good for you."

What does he mean pretend? I arch a brow, as he steps back just enough to break the contact.

The air between us still hums but I force my voice steady. "I didn't ask you to do anything," I say coolly. "That's your fantasy, not mine."

His mouth curves, but it's not a smile. It's something sharper. "Is that right?" he murmurs.

I nod once, holding his gaze. "You think one kiss means I'm yours? That I'm gonna fall into your lap like every other girl in this place?"

His silence is louder than anything he could say.

"I'm not a fucking prize, Frank," I whisper. "And I sure as hell don't belong to anyone."

He watches me—still as stone—but there's a shift. A flicker of something darker in his eyes like he wasn't expecting me to bite back.

I reach for my bag, flipping my hair over my shoulder.

"Thanks for dinner," I say with a smirk that doesn't quite reach my eyes. I don't wait for a response, I just turn on my heel and start walking.

The club's too damn loud, the air heavy with perfume, sweat, and power games. My boots echo over the polished floor, head held high even though I can still feel the weight of his gaze burning a hole between my shoulder blades. I don't care, I just need to get out of here.

I aim for the side exit, the one I passed earlier by the VIP bar. But just as I reach for the handle, a body shifts in front of the door.

"Sorry love, can't exit here," he says, voice flat.

I blink, glancing past him like maybe he just means it's blocked.

"It was open earlier."

"Club's at capacity. Policy changed."

Policy changed? My jaw tightens. Yeah fucking right did the policy just all the sudden change. Maybe it did. How the hell would I know?

The door's so close I could spit on it and this guy's acting like I'm trying to breach the Pentagon. I glance over my shoulder, and the hairs on the back of my neck spike before I even see Frank. *Of course.* He's moving slowly, slipping through the crowd like he's got all the time in the world.

I grit my teeth, turning back toward the door. "I'm good, really. Just need to get some air."

The security guy doesn't even blink. I don't hear Frank behind me until I feel him. His voice slides in like smoke.

"Change of heart, sweetheart?"

My body reacts before I can stop it. My spine stiffens and my jaw locks, as I clench my fists to keep from spinning around and slapping the smug off his face, or worse, letting him see I'm flustered.

I school my voice. "Tell your guard dog to move."

Frank steps closer and the scent of expensive cologne and something darker curls around me. "You didn't answer my question."

I whip around, nearly chest to chest with him now. "You really don't know when to back off, do you?"

He studies me like I'm a problem he already solved but likes watching me squirm anyway. Then he leans in, his mouth brushing just beneath my ear.

"If you wanted to leave," he murmurs, "you'd have gone through the main entrance. You came here to make a point. I let you."

I freeze.

My heart hammers against my ribs, part adrenaline, part rage, and part something I don't want to name.

"You're not afraid of me," he says, like it's a fact and not a warning. "But maybe you should be."

I don't turn around. I can't. My spine locks tight as every inch of my body screams to react, to run or lash out or something—but I don't. I just stare at the security guard, like this whole moment was designed to remind me who's in control.

"Just let me go," I whisper.

Frank exhales behind me. "You're not trapped."

Not physically. But he doesn't move, and neither do I. He's so close that I can feel his fingers brush mine, it's soft enough to seem like an accident, but firm enough to make it clear it wasn't.

"You say you want space, and then show up looking like that? In my club?" His chuckle is dark. "You're sending mixed messages, sweetheart."

I grit my teeth. "Maybe I just wanted the free drinks."

His voice dips lower. "Or maybe you wanted to see what would happen if you pushed me."

I spin, finally, shoving past him, shoulder clipping his chest. He lets me go, but I feel him smiling behind me.

My boots hit the sidewalk hard as I storm down the street. I'm already pulling out my phone to order an Uber when the screen lights up.

> Unknown Number: You're too pretty to walk home alone.

My pulse stutters and I stop walking. Another ping.

> Unknown Number: Don't worry. I'm watching. I won't let anything happen to you. You look amazing in black, but you'd look better in nothing but my collar.

I spin in place, scanning the street, the rooftops, the shadows that feel a little too heavy now—but there's nothing.

My fingers tighten around the phone, gripping it like a weapon I don't actually know how to use. I'm not stupid. I know what this is. I know what it means when someone says they're watching.

But I don't know who it is—and that makes it worse.

Could be Tattoo Man? Hell, who else would it be? He's already proven he's the possessive, controlling type. Tracking me wouldn't exactly be a stretch. Unless it's Sloane fucking with me.

God. Please let it be Sloane or Sarah.

My pulse kicks harder as I glance down the street again, then force myself to walk at a normal pace, with normal posture. Like I'm not two seconds from spiraling into a full-blown panic.

Two blocks later, a pair of headlights crest the hill and pull to a stop at the curb. My Uber. I double-check the plate, my heart still racing, before sliding in.

The driver's older, and has earbuds in. He's half-listening to a baseball game, but doesn't say a word as I slam the door and melt into the back seat, finally letting my shoulders drop.

I don't relax. Not really. Because the whole ride home, I can't stop thinking about that message. Who sent it? Who's watching me?

By the time we pull up to my place, I'm already scanning the windows, the fire escape, the roofline across the street.

Nothing.

But I don't let my guard down. Not even for a second. I don't look over my shoulder when I unlock the front door, but every hair on my arms stands straight up like something's breathing down my neck. I feel like I'm missing something.

Maybe I'm imagining it.

Probably.

Once I'm inside, I deadbolt the door, sliding the chain across, and I press my back against the wood like it might hold me up if I let it.

My phone buzzes again but I don't move. I just stare at the floor, then slowly, I drag the screen up.

Unknown Number: Sweet dreams.

I stare at the message until my vision blurs. *Sweet dreams?* Ew. Two words too many, but it's enough to make my skin crawl.

My thumb hovers over the screen, as my pulse skips. There's a thousand things I could say.

Who is this?

Fuck off.

Get a life...

But I don't send any of them because responding means something. It means engagement. And I've learned—especially the hard way—that sometimes silence is louder.

I toss the phone face-down on the counter, which ends up being way too loud in the silence. I pace once, then twice. Yanking the curtains tighter, checking the deadbolt, the chain, and the fire escape.

Again.

I splash water on my face, gripping the edge of the sink, and stare into the mirror like it might explain why I feel like I'm being watched from the inside out.

"You're fine," I whisper.

But I don't feel fine, I feel hunted. Which is exactly why I grab my phone and call Sarah.

She picks up on the second ring, and I don't even get a hello.

"Oh, look who finally remembered her emotionally neglected best friend exists. You better be calling to say you're dying. Or pregnant. Or both."

I collapse onto the couch, already bracing. "Define dying."

She exhales dramatically. "Okay, are we talking full-blown crisis or just regular-grade I made a terrible decision and now I need to trauma-dump at midnight?"

I rub my eyes. "I got another message."

The pause is instant.

"Mystery Pervert or Loverboy Frank?"

"Unknown number. Again. Just said... Sweet dreams."

I don't tell her about the other ones, because I don't want her to freak. She groans so loud I can hear her rearranging her blanket in protest. "Okay, nope. That's not flirty. That's Annabelle doll climbs out of the basement energy. Are you alone?"

I scan the windows again, double-checking the fire escape. "Everything's locked. I've done the perimeter sweep like three times, and I'm still convinced something's breathing in here that shouldn't be."

"If a demon made it past your sarcasm and trauma armor, we're all gonna die."

A weak laugh escapes. "You're not helping."

"Not trying to. You ditched me for a mob husband and now

you're being haunted by the Blair Witch via text. Karma's got range."

I groan. "It wasn't a date. It was—"

"A dick appointment wrapped in guilt and danger? Yeah, I know."

I wince, glancing toward the bedroom. "I thought I could handle it."

Sarah hums. "You can handle it. You just shouldn't have to. And maybe next time, you don't ghost your ride-or-die for a man who buys you diamonds and ominously claims real estate on your soul."

"That's oddly specific."

"So is that message. Sweet dreams? Ani. That's what killers say before putting a pillow over your face."

I laugh again, a little too high, but real.

She softens, just a little. "Was it Frank?"

"I don't think so," I say. "He doesn't sneak. He performs. And this... this feels like someone watching."

"Okay. Real talk?" she says. "Frank gives Godfather brunch vibes. But this sounds like someone who wants you scared. Which means they're probably scared of you."

"I wish that made me feel better."

"You want me to come over?"

I hesitate. "No. I'm okay. Just—needed to hear a voice that doesn't make me want to punch something."

"You sure?" she asks. "Because I've got wine, knives, and emotional availability in a horrifying leopard robe. I can be there in ten."

"I'm good. I swear."

"Okay, then here's your action plan... eat something, lock your doors—again—and sleep with your knife. But not *with* your knife. Save the knife play for someone hot."

I roll my eyes. "I wasn't gonna—"

"You were. I could hear it in your horny little silence."

"I hate you."

"You worship me. And you'd cry at my funeral."

"Only because you'd haunt me with your ghost boobs."

"Exactly." Her voice dips softer. "Babe... you really okay?"

I glance at the shadows and my heartbeat skips one beat too long.

"No," I whisper. "But I will be."

She exhales, gentle now. "Alright. Text me if anything moves, breathes, or whispers boo."

"Define boo?"

"Tall, tattooed, emotionally constipated, and currently starring in your late-night brain porn."

I hang up before she can keep going, then I kill the lights, sliding the knife under my pillow, and crawl into bed like it might keep the dark out.

IO

"Distractions get you killed."
(Unless you use them first.)

Tattoo Man

Tuesday mornings are predictable. The library opens at ten, and she usually shows up by nine-thirty with her earbuds in, and her keys clutched between her fingers like a weapon.

But today, she's late. Ten minutes. Then fifteen. And when she finally walks in—something's wrong. Even from this distance I can see it. Her shoulders are curled tighter than usual. She flinches when the return bin thuds shut, and she's glancing over her shoulder like she's expecting someone to be there.

It's subtle, but I notice because I don't just watch her—I study her. I've memorized the way she moves when she's calm, pissed off, amused, and even when she's pretending not to care. I know what her laugh sounds like when she thinks no one's listening. I know she bites her bottom lip when she's stalling, not nervous. I know the difference.

This—this is neither.

The same girl who launched a whiskey glass at a drunk's head last week without blinking is now clutching her bag like it's the only thing tethering her to gravity.

Something happened.

I shift, staying in the shadow at the far end of the aisle—right where I know the cameras blur out. I know it's a blind spot, I mapped them all weeks ago.

The tension in her limbs. The stiffness in her spine. The split-second pause when she reaches for a book and her hand trembles before she steadies it. Yeah, something for sure happened. I was busy last night, but had checked in a few times and she seemed fine.

What happened between then?

The fact that she's trying to hide it and trying to pretend she's fine, makes me want to grab her and demand answers. The sick part —the dark, violent part of me that I don't let out unless I have to— wants to find out who the fuck put that look in her eyes.

If someone's trying to take her apart, I'll make sure they don't live long enough to finish the job.

I should leave her the fuck alone, but I'm not going to. The moment she turns down the aisle, it's like the air shifts.

She doesn't see me at first—she's too busy pretending to be busy. She has books clutched tightly in her hands, and her fingers are flexing around the covers like she's holding onto sanity by a thread.

Her already cropped shirt rides up just enough when she stretches, revealing that infuriating strip of skin just beneath her tits, and it's a fucking invitation that has my dick hard in seconds.

I don't move. I just wait until she feels me. And I know the second she does. I see the way her steps slow, and her breath stutters. Her spine straightens as she turns her head. Her eyes find mine and just like that, her walls slam up. The mask she wears settles into place like a second skin.

But I already saw what was underneath. I saw the way her body reacted before her brain caught up and fuck, if that doesn't make me want to tear that mask off with my teeth.

I close the distance, slow enough for her to feel it, and she backs up. She can't go far—but it's just enough to hit the end of the shelf.

I cage her in with one hand braced above her head, the other grazing her hip, and I feel her body melt into my touch.

"You always this jumpy," I murmur, "or just when you know I'm about to ruin you?"

She glares up at me. "You're in my way."

"I know."

She plants her hand against my chest, like she might shove me off—but she doesn't. I almost laugh because it's a boundary I could break in half with one breath.

"Are you always this cocky," she fires back, "or just when you're creeping up on women like a damn stalker?"

She sounds like she's on edge, but I can feel her giving up. I smirk. "Don't pretend you didn't feel me before I touched you."

Her jaw clenches. "I should knee you in the balls. Maybe that'll teach you to sneak up on people."

"You won't."

"Wanna bet?"

My eyes drag down to where her fingers still rest against my sternum. "If you meant that, I'd already be on the floor."

She huffs, but she doesn't pull away. So I lean in—close enough that her breath stutters—and brush my lips against the shell of her ear, letting my voice drop to a lethal whisper.

"You smell like someone who isn't me."

She stiffens.

I don't need confirmation, I already know. But I want to hear it from her lips. I want her to say it, to admit it. So I can carve it into my ribs and let it fester there long enough to justify everything I'm about to do.

My hand dips lower, dragging along the waistband of her shorts, teasing in a way that makes her twitch against the shelf.

"Did he make you come?"

I ask it like I don't already know the answer. Like I haven't memorized the way her body moves when she lies.

She says nothing, but her silence tells me everything.

I slide my hand higher, slipping beneath her shirt like I've got all the time in the world. My fingers splay across her ribs, and her skin is hot and soft against my palm. At this point, I'm not sure I could stop if she asked me to.

"Tell me," I breathe, my mouth ghosting over her ear.

Her answer is barely a whisper. "No."

Just one word. But it hits like a detonator.

I grin. "Did he even try?"

Her breath hitches. Barely there—but it's all I need. I can feel her walls crumbling like they were never built to keep me out in the first place.

Her hand drops to my shoulder. "Please..." she breathes, like a warning. But her fingers curl into the fabric of my shirt instead of pushing me away.

I drop to my knees anyway and she gasps—caught between panic and heat, the kind of sound that drives me fucking insane.

Fuck, if she only knew what she does to me.

My hands slide up the backs of her thighs, slipping beneath those tiny fucking shorts. Her skin's warm, and she's trembling. I can tell she's trying to fight me and pull me closer at the same time.

I press a kiss to the inside of her knee, then bite the tender spot just above it—hard enough to make her jolt.

Mine.

She tenses when I push her legs apart. Her breath catches like she's about to say no, but she doesn't. She just stands there, fists clenching at her sides.

I wouldn't care if she tried to stop me anyway. I wouldn't. My mouth follows the path of my hands—dragging up inch by inch, slow as sin. I kiss every soft patch of skin I can reach, biting when I want to hear her gasp, sucking hard enough to make her whimper and when I finally slip a finger beneath her panties.

God, she's a fucking mess.

She's lucky those shorts aren't any tighter. If they were, I'd tear them off right here—bookshelves be damned.

"Fuck," I mutter. "So wet for me."

I trace slow, torturous circles, watching her come apart without a sound. I watch the way she grips the shelf like it's the only thing keeping her grounded, and how her knees almost buckle when I push two fingers in deep and curl them just right.

She's fighting it. Still pretending she has control, and I fucking love that. That's my girl.

"You're not thinking about him now, are you?"

She shakes her head, breathless. "No," she whispers.

I pull back just enough to look up at her, lips ghosting over her inner thigh.

"Say it."

"I'm not thinking about him."

I reward her with a filthy twist of my wrist. Her back hits the shelf, one hand slapping against the wood like she's trying to stay upright. I bite her inner thigh, just to hear what sound she'll make when I add a third finger.

She gasps like I punched the air out of her. God, she's perfect like this—wrecked and still pretending not to be. I can tell she's close. Her whole body tightens around my fingers, so I pull back.

She curses, throwing her head back.

"Not yet," I murmur. "You don't get to come until you tell me who you fucking belong to."

She's trembling—every inch of her—but she doesn't give in.

Good. I don't want her to hand it over. I want to take it. I want to tear it from her piece by piece until she says my name like it's the only one she's ever known.

I lean in, keeping my voice low as I brush her skin like a promise.

"Wonder if he ever gets to see you like this. Soaked and panting?"

My hand tightens on her waist.

"Shaking. Letting me take you apart like you were made for it. You act like you don't want it, but your body's fucking desperate."

I kiss my way back up her stomach, dragging the tension with me. When I stand, I make sure she feels all of me—how hard I am, and how much I'm holding back.

I need to be careful or she's going to end up naked on a pile of romance books.

My fingers trail up her chest, over the rise of her collarbone, circling the base of her throat, right over her pulse. It's beating like it knows I could end her.

I pause there, long enough to remind her—I decide how this goes. Then I kiss her, hard enough to make her forget the name of whoever's been trying to play in my fucking sandbox.

And when I finally let her breathe, I mutter against her lips, "You'll come when I say you can. Not a second before. Understand?"

She glares at me, ruined and furious. "I hate you."

I grin. She doesn't even hear the way her voice shakes or the way her body leans on mine for support.

"No," I murmur, kissing her again. "You want me. That's worse."

She's breathless and trembling against the shelf, glaring up at me like she'd stab me if her legs weren't jelly.

I almost wish she'd try. I'd pin her down and make her beg again—just to hear how fast hate turns to need.

I grip the backs of her thighs and lift, forcing her legs around my waist as I carry her the few steps to the table tucked behind the stacks—hidden from the main floor, but not far enough to be safe.

That's the point. I want her squirming. I want her thinking about every sound she makes.

Her eyes widen, and her hands fist in my hoodie like she's trying to hold onto something real while everything else inside her is slipping. I drop into the chair and bring her with me, dragging her down onto my lap with a grunt that's more growl than breath. Her ass lands right against my cock, and she tries to squirm—tries to push off me—but my hands lock around her hips, holding her still.

She doesn't get to run now.

"Don't," I warn, dragging my mouth up the side of her neck. "You grind on my cock like that, you take it. All of it. That's how this works."

"I didn't agree to anything," she snaps—but her voice is breathless and shaky. Her body clearly didn't get the fucking memo.

Her fingers dig into my shoulders and her nails bite like she's trying to anchor herself—or claw her way out of the need running through her. I can see the sweat beading at her temple.

I smirk. "You're on my cock, sweetheart. That's consent enough."

She opens her mouth to fire back—but I yank her tank top down instead, exposing her breasts and her nipples are ready pebbled and waiting for me.

Her protest dies on her tongue the second my mouth covers the hard buds. I drag my tongue across one nipple, then suck it into my mouth, grazing my teeth just enough to test her. She's going to learn to crave the pain I give her. My other hand slides into her shorts and she's soaked.

She hisses through her teeth, arching her spine like a bowstring as I thrust two fingers inside—deeper this time. Rougher. Twisting just right, and stroking the spot I know she loves. Her body jerks, and her breath cuts off. Her thighs clamp down like she's trying to trap me inside her as her pussy clenches around my fingers.

One hand flies out, bracing against the table behind her. I grab her tank and yank it lower so my mouth can get better access to her other breast, biting down just hard enough to leave a mark.

She gasps—too loud.

I clamp a hand over her mouth without even looking up.

"You want to come?" I growl. "Then stay fucking quiet."

She moans into my palm like it's the only thing keeping her tethered, grinding against my hand, and chasing the edge like she thinks I'll let her fall over.

She should know better.

I finger fuck her slow and deep—working her open, my wrist pulsing, holding her right at the edge.

"I told you," I murmur against her throat. My cock straining beneath her. "You don't come yet."

Her eyes blaze. She's glaring down at me, cheeks flushed as sweat glistens at her collarbone. Her mouth moves behind my hand in muffled curses, and probably threats.

She's begging, even if she doesn't know it yet.

Her muscles twitch, and her thighs are trembling. Her whole body's begging for release. But I don't let her come yet. I'm teaching her a lesson.

I ease off just enough to rip a whimper from her throat, and she looks at me with daggers in her eyes.

I hear footsteps seconds before she hears them. Her eyes snap open, panic crashing through her as the sound echoes down the aisle.

I start moving my fingers. Pumping them slowly while using my thumb to rub her swollen clit.

We're buried deep enough in the shadows that they won't see us, but she doesn't know that.

The table creaks as she tenses, her body at war with itself— wanting to come, needing to hide, and helpless to do either.

I press my fingers deeper, adding a third. My mouth covers her nipple again, teeth grazing enough to make her jerk and nearly cry out.

I clamp my hand tighter over her mouth.

Her breath is ragged. Her panic is delicious as adrenaline pours off her in waves, sharp and dizzying and my cock throbs against her thigh like it's tasting it too.

The footsteps pause and she freezes, whimpering into my palm, eyes pleading with me to stop.

I keep moving my fingers enough to make her twitch. Her eyes lock on mine—wild, and burning with fire and fury.

She wants to come.

She needs to.

I lean up, brushing her ear with my mouth. "You'll take it," I whisper, dragging my fingers over that spot that makes her shatter.

"Even if they stop right fucking here. You're going to fall apart in my lap and pray they don't hear you. Understand?"

She moans—crushed beneath my palm like she's choking on need.

The footsteps shift again. Closer this time. She shakes her head, eyes going wide as tears pool in her eyes—not sure if it's panic or how goddamn close she is.

Probably both.

Good. Let her fall apart afraid. Let her come with someone ten feet away and my hand between her legs, owning every second of it, because this isn't about sex. It's about surrender.

And I'm not stopping.

Not when her legs start trembling. Not when her lips part around a desperate whimper. Not even when she grabs at my arm like she might claw herself free just to breathe.

She's so fucking close.

My hand at her mouth shifts to her throat—just enough to hold her in place and remind her who she belongs to right now.

My other fingers press deeper inside her, curling with lethal precision.

I'm not giving her release, I'm carving it into her. Her back arches and I feel her walls clenching, and her heartbeat slamming against my palm. She's seconds away from unraveling, so I stop.

She bites her lip to keep from screaming. And then, with a shaky voice. "Please—"

It's wrecked and strangled and burning with shame. I almost groan from how hard my dick is. I want to feel her wet cunt choking me, but that's not what this is about.

"Not yet," I growl, and it nearly breaks her.

She thrashes against me, frantic now. If someone rounds that corner, I don't care. I won't stop.

I lean in. "I know you're close."

My fingers start moving again, slowly. I know I'm being cruel, but I don't care.

"Just hold on for me, sweetheart. You're doing so fucking good."

Her eyes crash into mine—wide, desperate, and furious. She shakes her head.

"I hate you," she chokes out, even as her thighs shake.

"I—fuck—hate you."

Her wet pussy throbs around my fingers like she's trying to break on them. I dip my head and bite the curve of her shoulder, and she spreads her thighs wider, offering herself up like she doesn't even realize it.

I pull out slowly, dragging wet fingers between her thighs, across that swollen, needy mess I just made of her.

"Don't look away," I whisper against her skin. "You feel that? Hm? Does he do this to you?"

She moans and shakes her head. Still I hold her there. Because this is what she gets. I slam three fingers back into her, hard enough to jolt her whole body.

My other hand fists in her hair, yanking her head back just enough to bare her throat. She gasps—half sob, half curse.

"Fuck you," she breathes.

I sink my teeth into her neck and growl, "Now. Come for me."

Her hands clutch at me like I'm her last salvation—but she fucking breaks. She comes hard and messy, choking on a sob she tries to bury in my shoulder, but it tears out of her anyway.

I want it burned into her memory—how loud she got for me. I want her to remember that no one else will ever pull that sound from her again.

They can try.

Her body goes limp while her thighs are still twitching, her breath is all hiccupped panic and overstimulation.

I let her fall forward, forehead pressed to my chest, my fingers still inside her. Still holding her open. Still owning every single piece of her.

She just breathes against my throat—shallow and uneven—her body still trying to decide if it survived what I just did to it. Her fingers twitch against my chest, the aftermath still pulsing through her like an aftershock.

She broke, and I should feel satisfied. But all I feel is this fucked-up need to keep her here. I didn't just get under her skin—she got under mine, too. I could sit here for hours just feeling the weight of her on me.

I don't rush her, because I want her to sit with it. I want her to feel every filthy thing I just did. Every sound I dragged out of her, and every inch I claimed like she was made for it.

Her breath finally stumbles out, and she shifts—barely—like she's remembering where we are.

I drag the pad of my thumb over the inside of her thigh and she tenses again and starts to push up.

I grip her hips before she can move. "Next time, you don't let anyone else put their hands on you."

She goes still like I struck a nerve. "I can't be this girl."

My grip tightens, but I let the silence stretch between us, my fingers curl around her waist, and my other hand is resting on her bare thigh. My dick is still hard as a fucking rock under her and I'm considering taking her right now.

She doesn't breathe for a second too long and I feel the war inside her rise again.

The one she'll never win.

Not against me.

When she finally pulls back—just enough to glare at me with a look that says she wants to claw her way out of her own skin. She climbs off my lap without a word, straightening her shorts with shaking hands, and grabs the book she'd dropped and starts to walk away and doesn't look back.

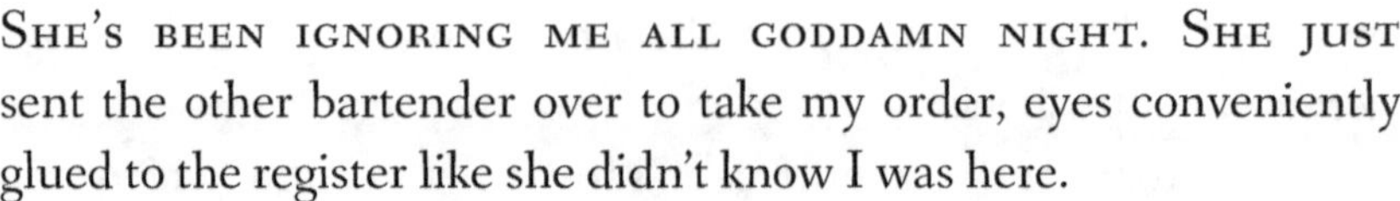

SHE'S BEEN IGNORING ME ALL GODDAMN NIGHT. SHE JUST sent the other bartender over to take my order, eyes conveniently glued to the register like she didn't know I was here.

Cute.

They're slammed, sure. But she's not that busy. Every time she walks past, she makes it a point not to look at me. Like I'm a ghost and if she pretends hard enough, I'll disappear.

It'd be infuriating if she didn't look so fucking good while doing it.

She's still in those cut-off shorts—the ink on her thigh poking out, and those goddamn boots on like she's ready to kill someone and look hot doing it. Her cropped tank clings to her chest, and every time she reaches for a bottle, it rides up just enough to show that sliver of skin I've already marked in my head.

I could sit here all night just watching her.

I don't get the chance to say anything because her friend has already clocked me.

The name tag says Sarah—and I've seen it before, blown-up on her phone screen in those late-night texts. The ones that always start with 'you okay' and end with 'want me to bury a body.'

Sarah slams a glass down in front of me like she's trying to rattle a corpse.

"You again," she says, one brow cocked, and her lips twisted in a knowing smirk. She's got the kind of attitude that doesn't ask permission—it announces itself. She's definitely trouble.

I glance at her. "Didn't order anything."

"Didn't ask," she says. "Consider it on the house. Or an offering. Depends on how weird you plan on getting tonight."

I lift the glass but don't drink. "You always this friendly with your customers?"

"Only the ones who eye-fuck my best friend from the back booth like it's a contact sport."

That gets my attention. I turn toward her fully now, but she doesn't back down.

"I don't know who you think I am," I murmur.

"No," she fires back, cutting me off. "I know exactly who you are. You're the one who shows up like clockwork, and makes my girl forget how to breathe."

I don't answer, instead I just lean back in the booth, watching her, letting the silence press between us like a blade.

She taps the edge of the table with one red-painted nail. "Look. I'm not saying I don't get it. She's hot, unavailable, and emotionally constipated. It's a whole thing. But if you hurt her..." She leans in, her smile going razor sharp. "I'll end you. And I'll make it look like an accident."

I blink once. "You done?"

"Not even close." She straightens, chin tilted like she's daring me to ask what she means. Then she jerks her head toward the bar. "You're welcome, stalker."

I take a slow sip of my drink, watching her over the rim. "She told you about me?"

She snorts. "Sweetheart, she didn't have to. I've seen that post-trauma glow. Plus, she came in looking like she got rearranged alphabetically."

I nearly choke on my whiskey.

She grins, unbothered. "Relax. I think it's romantic. In a feral, possible-felony kind of way."

I shake my head, biting back a laugh. I glance toward Ani, who's still pretending I don't exist with her tight jaw, and her long hair twisted up like she's trying not to think about the last time I had my hands in it.

Sarah follows my gaze, then leans in close, dropping the act just long enough for me to hear the warning in her voice. "Just so we're clear? I'm dead ass serious, I don't care how big and scary you think you are, I'll stab this straw through your eye and make the lobotomy look accidental."

Then she pats my arm like we're best friends, spins on her heel, and walks off like she owns the place.

I watch her go, knowing exactly what she is—trouble in red lipstick and loyalty sharp enough to cut. She's the kind of girl who'll smile at you while slipping the knife between your ribs if you hurt someone she loves. And right now, she's watching Ani like a hawk in eyeliner.

Good. Someone should be.

A flicker of movement catches my eye—Ani slips behind the bar again, her mouth is set in that sharp little line she wears when she's pretending she's fine. I can taste the edge of her unraveling like it's smoke on the back of my tongue. My dick takes it as an invitation and starts to press against my pants.

I barely notice the girl until she speaks.

"Hey there, stranger."

A voice cuts through the low thrum of the bar—too sweet, too rehearsed, and laced with too much perfume and the kind of confidence that wilts under rejection.

I ignore her, but she slides into the booth across from me anyway with her big smile, her too-tight dress, and cleavage shoved together like it's supposed to do the talking for her.

"You come here often?" she asks, biting her lip like it's supposed to be cute. "Because I'd definitely remember seeing you."

I lift my glass, taking a slow sip. I don't look at her, or say a word.

She laughs nervously. "That's cool. You don't have to talk. I can still suck you off in the bathroom though."

Jesus Christ.

I glance up then, finally meeting her eyes, and letting the silence stretch until it bites. Then I lean forward, resting my arms on the table.

"You always talk this much when a man's clearly not interested?"

Her mouth opens with some half-formed protest bubbling out, but I'm already looking past her—watching Ani disappear through the back door with a trash bag slung over her shoulder.

The girl blinks, stunned. "Excuse me?"

"No." I smile, sharp and unbothered. "Excuse yourself. Off my table."

She stands too fast, and the chair screeches. She mutters something that sounds like asshole as she stalks away.

II

Ani

Fuck him. I mean that in the throw-him-off-a-cliff-with-his-own-ego kind of way.

Fuck. Him.

He's the one who's ever wrecked me so thoroughly I'm still finding pieces of myself in places I didn't know were cracked. And then had the audacity to show up at my bar like he didn't say *'Don't let anyone else put their hands on you.'*

Right.

Real fucking rich, considering I caught him chatting it up with some giggling blonde with legs for days and a laugh that made me want to shatter a pint glass with my teeth.

I've spent the last hour refusing to look at him. Refusing to give him the satisfaction. I even sent Sarah to take his order like the petty bitch I am. And now I'm supposed to act like none of it happened?

Nope. Fuck this. I'm going home.

I shove past Sarah on my way to the back. "I'm going home. You good?"

She side-eyes me without looking up from the drink she's mixing. "Sure. I'll just close solo and pray I don't get murdered in the parking lot. Totally chill."

I roll my eyes. "I'll text you when I get home."

She glances up, pausing just long enough to smirk. "I'll tell Mr. Tall-Dark-and-Possessive to quit staring like he's auditioning for a restraining order."

"I'd rather tell him to choke."

She grins. "Kinky."

I flip her off, and grab the trash, heading for the alley before she can say something worse.

It's close enough to closing that she can handle the rest without me. The air outside smells like grease, sweat, and something vaguely sour, but it's better than inside, where the oxygen felt too thick and he felt too close.

I hurl the trash bag into the dumpster with unnecessary force, like it's going to magically make me feel less like I'm crawling out of my own skin.

Spoiler... it doesn't.

My boots echo off the bricks as I storm down the alley. Normally, I'd cut across the lot and down 7th. But tonight, my skin itches, and my instincts are too loud. And maybe—just maybe—I'm still pissed at the smug bastard inside, watching me like I'm his to fuck.

So I turn right instead. Screw routine, and screw him.

I'm halfway down the next block before I realize I'm still clenching my jaw, and replaying every stupid look he gave that girl.

God, I hate him.

The streetlight above me flickers before stuttering to life in a burst of sickly yellow that bathes the alley in rot. Every instinct I have goes rigid as I shift my bag on my shoulder.

I feel the itch at the base of my neck, and the weight of something off slithering down my spine, coiling around my ribs like it already knows how I'll scream.

I freeze mid-step as the air catches halfway up my throat and stays there.

I glance over my shoulder but don't see anything but cracked pavement, a rusted dumpster, and a strip of shadow that feels too still to trust. My fingers inch toward the pocket of my jacket, brushing the hilt of the blade I swore I'd never walk alone without again.

Something is very fucking wrong.

Two seconds too late, I feel a hand steel around my arm and I'm yanked sideways so fast the world spins. My back is slammed into the brick hard enough to rattle my teeth.

"Pretty little thing like you shouldn't walk alone," a voice sneers, hot and rancid against my skin.

The stench of him—sweat, smoke, and something sour hits me harder than the wall and I choke on it. Panic rises like acid in my throat.

I twist hard, elbow slicing through the air on instinct. It cracks against his cheekbone and the shock of it punches up my arm like a warning flare. He grunts, stumbling half a step back, but the bastard doesn't go down.

He doesn't let go either. That would be too easy.

No, he just fucking smiles, split lip and all. He's got blood in his teeth and he's looking at me with a crazy look in his eyes.

God, I've seen that look before. Nothing good can come from this.

He tightens his grip on my arm until I swear I hear something crack. His hand crushes over my mouth. "Told him I'd be able to find you easily," he growls.

Him?

Who the hell is he talking about?

I scream, but it doesn't make it past his palm. I dig my nails into his forearms, desperate for leverage, for something—anything—but he's already jamming a knee between my thighs, pressing all of his sick weight into me.

"You're gonna be a fun little bonus," he breathes, his other hand sliding to my throat, cutting off the air in jagged pulses. "No one said I couldn't have fun first."

My blood turns to ice. And then it fucking boils.

Because no. *Fuck no.*

I'm not some obedient little girl anymore. There's no fucking way I'm going down without a fight.

My lungs scream for air, and my vision dances at the edges—but I fumble to find my pocket and wrap my hand around the knife, and I twist just enough to get my arm loose and jam it up toward his face.

The blade slices across his cheek with a deep, satisfying gash that blooms red and trails down his jaw.

He rears back with a snarl, hand flying to the cut. The second of shock is all I need—I shove him off with everything I have. My knife falls to the ground, skidding across gravel, too far to reach.

"You fucking bitch!" He roars, yanking my arm and slamming me into the wall at a twisted angle—hard enough to make the joint tear free with a sickening pop.

Pain cracks through my shoulder like a gunshot and I don't even hear the scream—it's already lodged in my throat, splintering into a gasp that doesn't make it all the way out.

White-hot fire tears through my shoulder like my body's trying to rip itself in half. *Fuck that hurts.*

My arm dangles at my side, limp and wrong, as I try to breathe. Every inhale feels like there's glass in my ribs, and the only thing louder than the pain is the voice screaming inside my head.

I need to move but my body doesn't listen. His hand fists in my hair ripping my head up and my spine screams, but I don't make a sound.

"What I have planned is nothing. You'll wish for me, though, when he has you."

My stomach flips. *He?*

"Didn't say what shape you had to be in though."

The metallic click of his belt makes the world go still.

No no no—my good hand fumbles around, hoping for anything sharp, anything at all.

"You should've behaved," he growls, pinning me down. "I was going to make it quick. But now? I'm gonna make sure you remember me."

I see a flash in the dark, glinting once before pain explodes through my body. A tearing, blinding heat rips through my side—just beneath my ribs—and the breath flies out of me like I've been punched by lightning.

My mouth opens around a scream, but nothing comes. Just a raw, choked sound as the pain sears up my spine and makes the world tilt. For a second, I don't even understand. I'm just... burning.

Slick warmth spills down my hip. Wet and hot. I look down and see the knife.

He fucking stabbed me.

The ground tilts sideways as I stumble, my hand flies to my side like I can hold myself together with pressure alone. The shock is worse.

The sick bastard grins like it was foreplay as he leans in, and his breath—sour and rotted—grazes my cheek. "You should've been a good girl."

My hand scrambles to my side, slick with blood and panic, while my fingers fumble through shredded fabric, searching—until I feel it. Still lodged there.

I wrap my hand around the handle, gripping it tight and yank.

Pain detonates behind my ribs, and the scream tears out of me this time, but I don't stop. I drive the blade straight into his thigh, right above the knee and he howls, staggering.

His grip on me slips just enough, and for a second—a tiny, gasping second—I think I've won.

I don't see his boot coming before it collides with my ribs. All the air leaves my lungs in a strangled burst as I slam back against the ground. Stars explode behind my eyes, and something cracks deep in my chest and I can't tell if it's bone or just the last thread of hope I had left.

Everything hurts.

I can see the knife's still in his leg, and there's blood all over the pavement. My vision blurs, but I need to get up or I'm going to die here in the dark.

"Hey!"

That voice.

That fucking voice.

It crashes into me like the first breath after drowning. Familiar and furious. The man above me freezes. I see it in his eyes—the flicker of fear. Then a shadow barrels into him from the side, all force and vengeance.

He staggers, trying to recover. But he's already swinging again, fists landing with sickening, wet sounds—rage given form.

I don't know how long it's been or if he's still here, but I try to sit up—stupid, but I try. The moment my shoulder shifts, white heat flares through me, and a cry escapes before I can swallow it.

"Shit," a voice growls.

He drops to his knees beside me and I can feel him—his body heat, the sharp tension radiating off him in violent waves.

His voice slices through the dark, laced with ice. "You planning to bleed out here, or is this just your new way of getting attention?"

My whole body screams, pain pulsing from my shoulder like a siren, but somehow, I manage to lift my head.

"What's the matter?" I rasp. "Jealous someone else got to throw me around first?"

A muscle twitches in his jaw and under the dim streetlamp, I catch the flicker of his expression—he's furious. But the light blurs, and the last thing I see before it all fades is the hard set of his mouth... and something behind his eyes I can't name.

And then it all goes black.

THE FIRST THING I FEEL IS PAIN. HOT AND SHARP, LIKE someone injected fire straight into my shoulder. I try to move, turns out that's a bad idea. My body protests like it's been hit by a truck, as I try to crack one eye open.

This bed isn't mine.

The sheets are too smooth, and the mattress is too soft. The whole room smells like expensive cologne, smoke, and the kind of leather that probably has a criminal record.

I push myself up, or try to, with my good arm—barely making it onto one elbow before a fresh wave of nausea threatens to take over again. I don't puke. *Yet.* But I want to.

My mouth's a desert and my head is pounding like it's been used as a drum at a death metal concert.

The first thing I notice is that I'm not wearing my own shirt. The second thing... My arms in a sling.

I'm in a black oversized shirt that's definitely not mine. And, oh —great. No bra. Of course.

My vision's still a little hazy as I squint down at myself, trying not to spiral. *What the actual fuck.*

I scan the room, looking at floor-to-ceiling windows stretching across the far wall, revealing nothing but dense woods and darkness. No blinds. No curtains. Just glass and shadows and a big neon sign that reads remote murder cabin vibes.

The walls are black slate, broken up by built-in steel shelves that scream tactical more than decorative. If someone dropped in uninvited, I'd bet my life they'd be met with throwing knives and trauma.

There's a fireplace on the far side—it's sleek, with a matte black finish, but there's no mantle. Just fire and stone and silent fuck-you money.

What the hell does this man do for work? Crime lord? Sex dungeon interior designer?

There's no clutter and not a single photo or personal detail anywhere. And here I am—bleeding in the middle of it, in someone else's clothes.

On the nightstand, sitting dead center like it belongs there, is my knife. My boots are lined up neatly by the door like I'm some fucking guest in a five-star hostage situation.

Someone undressed me.

The memory hits like a freight train.

The alley. Blood. That man. My knife.

And Him.

The man with ink on his chest and a mouth that knows no mercy. Who kissed me like he wanted to ruin me and speaks in threats.

A shadow shifts in the hallway and the door opens. Speaking of the devil. He's shirtless.

And of course he's wearing the holy grail of thirst traps—gray sweatpants. They're slung so low on his hips that it looks like they're held up by arrogance alone. A towel hangs around his neck.

My brain? Gone. Offline.

Because fuck. His chest is carved from hunger and restraint— every cut and ridge is sculpted like some bored, horny god decided to personally design my downfall. Tattoos cover him like armor— thick black ink crawls across his chest and wraps down his arms like a dare. One sleeve is all blackout—solid and merciless, and the other's chaos. There's linework and weapons and symbols I don't understand but desperately want to. Script winds down to his knuckles, which is stupidly hot.

There's one sprawling across his chest and another trailing along his ribs, half-swallowed by shadow. I can't read them, but the second I spot them, my thighs clench like they've made up their own damn mind. I would lick every single one of those.

What the actual fuck is wrong with me?

He looks like someone took sex and violence, mixed it with gasoline, and poured it into the shape of a man I'm not supposed to want. And yet—yep. I want every goddamn inch of him on my tongue.

His arms are fucking massive. Don't even get me started on his veins, popping like a felony. I look a little lower, which isn't hard considering I'm basically eye level. That V that disappears into his sweats is criminal.

My mouth goes dry as heat pools low and fast and absolutely not invited.

This is a man built to fuck you up—emotionally, physically, and spiritually and I'm already halfway to falling apart and he hasn't said a single word.

My eyes drag down his chest again because I'm clearly trying to punish myself with the view.

I don't stop until I hit the waistband of those goddamn sweatpants, and even then, it's not because I want to. If I don't look away now, I'm going to spontaneously orgasm. I want to punch him in the throat for making me want him so damn much.

But I want to lick him first.

And that's a problem, because I'm laid out in his bed, bandaged and bruised, with my shoulder wrecked—and my first coherent thought when he walks in is how fucking hot he is and how much I want to impale myself on him.

I should be thinking about how he might've saved my life. I have no idea where I am—but I have a sneaking suspicion I'm in his house.

I should say something, but I can't. He looks like the kind of mistake I want to make on repeat until I forget why I ever tried to stop.

My pulse spikes when his eyes land on mine. *I sure as fuck hope he can't read minds.*

He stares for a beat, then clears his throat, nodding toward the glass of water on the nightstand.

"You're awake." His voice is smooth, yet rough.

Try not to sound too concerned about the fact that I nearly bled out in an alley while you were off charming blondes like it was your goddamn hobby.

I don't say that. So instead, I just stare at him, because what the fuck am I supposed to say?

"You look like shit," he adds, walking past the bed like he's not at all concerned that I'll lunge for the knife and stab him.

"Try not to bleed on the sheets. They're new."

My jaw locks. Every part of me screams, but I push myself up anyway. The pain lances down my side, ripping a sound from my throat I don't mean to make.

"You shouldn't be sitting up."

"No shit," I snap, gritting my teeth. "Thanks for the medical advice, Doctor Dick."

He exhales through his nose, but I see the corner of his mouth tilt, like he's trying not to laugh.

"Still got that mouth, I see."

"Still got that ego, I see." I pant through the pain, pressing my good hand into the mattress like it might anchor me. "Where the hell am I?"

"My house."

I keep my face neutral while my pulse decides to just trip over itself.

I glance around again, slower this time—like the walls might cough up a clue about who the hell this man actually is. I suspect he's not normal.

"Why?" I ask.

He shrugs.

Okay...because saving me from a back-alley murder attempt and peeling me out of my bloody clothes was just some casual Tuesday cardio. Like I'm the one being dramatic.

"You were bleeding," he says, keeping his voice maddeningly calm. "Didn't seem like you were in the mood to call an Uber."

"Oh, I don't know. You could've taken me to a hospital."

"Could've, yeah." His lips twitch. "But I wasn't in the mood for answering questions."

That shuts me up for exactly one beat. Because what the actual fuck. He drops into the chair across from the bed, arms draped over his knees like this is just some casual little chat. Still shirtless. Still smug. And still the exact kind of danger I should be running from— if I could run.

My gaze flicks to the tattoos again.

Mistake.

"What the fuck were you doing in that alley?"

I blink. "Taking out the trash and going home. What did it look like I was doing?"

"Alone?"

"Glad you were paying attention."

His jaw ticks. That cool, untouchable mask of his slips—just for a breath—before snapping back like it never moved.

"Are you always this reckless?"

"Are you always this obsessed?" I shoot back. "You've got a real problem with following me. You know that, right?"

He tilts his head like I'm amusing. "You were bleeding in the street."

"Yeah, and now I'm bleeding in a stranger's bed." I hiss the words. "That's not creepy at all."

"You're not bleeding anymore."

"And you're still a fucking asshole."

He leans back in the chair, smiling like he wants to carve his name into somewhere I'll never wash it off, then watches me like he's memorizing every twitch of my face just to use it against me later.

"You gonna tell me who that guy was?"

"Why? Are you jealous?" I smile—regretting it the second his expression changes.

His eyes go dark. "If I was," he says slowly, "he'd be dead already."

My breath catches, but I cover it with a smirk. "Charming."

He stands up and I flinch—just a little, barely more than a blink —but he sees it and freezes.

"I'm not gonna hurt you, Ani."

My stomach coils with the way he says my name.

Wait. *How does he know my name?*

I glare, breathing hard through the pain. "Forgive me if I don't take your word for it."

His jaw tightens. That faint tick again—like it wants to say something, but won't. And then he stalks closer and every instinct in my body screams run.

"You think I want to hurt you?"

I let out a bitter laugh. "No. I think you want to break me."

His mouth twitches—just barely. Like his mind went exactly where mine did.

"You're not that easy to break, sweetheart." He pauses. "But that doesn't mean I won't break what's left."

Jesus. Fuck.

I felt that one in my soul.

He stops beside the bed, towering over me, and the air shifts. I hate the way I have to tilt my chin to keep eye contact. I really hate the way my body just reacts to his every move.

And holy hell...

Up close, shirtless, and fresh out of the shower—he looks like war made of muscle.

Veins, abs, and that fucking V. I can't help but stare. What is a girl supposed to do? I'm not a nun. My eyes drag down his body like I've been drugged and the only symptom is thirst.

Yeah. I definitely have a head injury. That's my story and I'm sticking to it.

"You're staring," he chuckles.

"I'm concussed," I lie.

My gaze flicks—briefly—to the waistband of his sweats. Which is a *huge* mistake. Literally.

Fuck.

He sees it, *of course*, and that smile spreads like slow poison—smug, cruel, and fucking satisfied.

"Is that why your thighs keep clenching like you're trying to hold onto your last shred of dignity?"

Heat floods my face. "You're disgusting."

"And you're probably wet."

My pulse spikes with rage and...arousal. I don't know which one's louder. I just know my pussy's screaming.

"Fuck you."

He leans in bracing his hands on either side of the mattress, caging me in without even touching me. I can't breathe with his breath ghosting over my cheek. Not with his body that close and not with me being this fucked up.

"You'd let me."

His voice is all gravel and promises I'll regret in the morning, brushing against my ear like it has a goddamn vendetta.

My lips part, and God, I hate how badly I want him to close the distance. And honestly, he's not wrong. I'm soaked. I'm woman enough to know what I want, and right now, it's him.

My pulse flutters like I'm some wide-eyed idiot who's never been kissed—it's not like I'm not bruised and bandaged and still bleeding.

I'm pathetic.

His presence alone feels like I'm standing on the edge of a blade and begging it to slice deeper. Every inch of space he closes feels like a countdown I can't stop and a warning I refuse to listen to.

Despite everything—despite the pain, the blood, and the rage that still simmers under my skin—I want him.

Seriously, girl. What the actual fuck. Maybe try wanting, I don't know, an ice pack or a therapist next time.

I can feel the heat coming off his bare chest and the drag of his eyes over my skin like he's memorizing the parts of me I'm assuming he's already seen—because again, these clothes aren't mine.

Love that for me. Nothing says romance like medical trauma and unsolicited nudity.

His face is so close I can see the flecks of gold cutting through the dark in his eyes. They're sharp, and dangerous in a way. But beneath all that control, there's something darker. Something hungry. And it's locked onto me.

He's got serial killer eyes and I'm turned on. This is going great. I try to breathe through it, but my chest is tight, and my body is caught in the gravity of him, every inhale is shallow, every inch of space between us slowly shrinks like it doesn't matter anymore.

"Why did you bring me here?" I manage. "Needed a project?"

That flicker of dark amusement vanishes from his face, and his jaw clenches.

"I already told you—I didn't feel like explaining to the cops why some girl was half-dead in an alley."

"I didn't ask you to save me," I snap, but my voice breaks somewhere in the middle.

His eyes flash. "No. You were too busy getting the shit kicked out of you to ask."

I shift, dragging my elbow back against the mattress to sit up, just enough to put space between us. My shoulder screams in protest, and I hiss through clenched teeth, but he doesn't move to help me—he just watches with that cold, unreadable stare.

Cool. I'm bleeding, bruised, and getting emotionally steamrolled by an action-figure version of Satan. Living the dream.

Then, he slowly leans in again and the air tightens. "You still don't get it, do you?"

I lift my chin, forcing the words past the ache in my throat. "Enlighten me."

His fingers brush a piece of hair from my cheek but I feel it everywhere.

"You think this is about saving you?" His voice drops to something cold and lethal. "If I wanted you dead, sweetheart, you'd never have made it out of that alley."

My heart stumbles, and not in a sweet, swoony way. In a *what the hell is wrong with me* kind of way.

"But you didn't," I whisper.

His eyes drag to my mouth. "No," he says, roughly. "I don't."

The silence stretches way too loud for how close he is. Then his voice drops again, deeper this time. And it hits like a warning.

"Next time you walk out a back door alone, maybe think about what would've happened if I wasn't there."

I swallow and it burns all the way down. Oh great, now I've got shame and arousal mixing in my bloodstream. Fantastic. What a cocktail.

"Why did you follow me?" I ask.

"Don't flatter yourself."

Okay. Rude.

His hand drops, grazing the line of my waist—and it shoots a full-body tremor down my spine.

"You just have a talent for stepping into shit that doesn't concern you."

I shove at his chest, only my fingers just touch muscle and unfairness.

"Fuck you."

He catches my wrist like it's nothing and that smirk returns—sharp enough to cut bone.

"You're not ready for that," he murmurs. "You're recovering."

His thumb brushes the inside of my wrist like he knows what it's doing to me. Every touch is calculated. Every move he makes is intentional, even if he hasn't said it out loud.

"Then stop fucking touching me," I breathe—but my voice betrays me, coming out too breathless.

His eyes darken when they drop to my mouth, and his grip shifts—down my arm, across my waist—dragging the blanket with it. His fingers slide beneath the hem of my shirt.

"You want me to stop?" he asks. "Say the word."

My thighs press together like a reflex I can't control because there's no way in hell I'm stopping him. Not now. Not with his hands on me and the world spinning off its axis.

His hand drags lower across my ribs, settling at my hip like a brand, and I hiss. His eyes never leave mine.

"Didn't think so."

"Careful," I whisper, but it comes out like a dare. "If this is some fucked-up attempt to seduce me, you're gonna have to try harder."

His smile drops. "This is a warning."

The air splits like a crack of thunder and my pulse trips. Hard. Great. Nothing like a little light psychological terrorism with your post-trauma healing.

"You're playing a game you don't understand, sweetheart," he says. "You think this is about bruised pride or whatever the fuck happened between your legs back there, but it's not."

Oh, so we're going there.

My spine straightens despite the pain in my shoulder. It's throbbing, but it's nothing compared to the heat flaring in my chest at his tone.

"You keep showing up like I'm your problem," I rasp. "Pretty sure I didn't ask you to play bodyguard."

His smirk dies fast. "You didn't ask for a lot of things," he mutters. "Doesn't mean you don't need them."

Fuck him. That lands like a punch I didn't see coming.

"I'm not yours to protect," I snap, sharper now. But my voice breaks just enough to betray me. He grabs my chin with just enough pressure to remind me who's in control.

"You keep saying that," he mutters, each word dragging across my skin like a blade. "And yet, you keep looking at me like this."

Then his thumb brushes over my mouth, pulling my bottom lip down like he owns it.

"Go on," he whispers, "keep pretending you don't want me to finish what I started in that fucking library."

I breathe him in, trying not to break. Trying not to let my body answer before my mouth does. But it's too much. He's too much. And we both know it.

Seconds later, his hand drops away like he suddenly remembered himself, and touching me cost him something.

"Go shower," he growls, stepping back, suddenly angry. "I'll fix your bandages when you're done."

What the actual fuck is his deal?

He turns his back to me—running a hand through his hair, and his jaw so tight that he looks like he's fighting something I don't understand. And for a second, I'm not sure who's more dangerous. Me—or him.

I'm not doing this shit right now.

I swing my legs over the edge of the bed, and pain slices through my shoulder—but I push past it and plant my feet on the hardwood like I've still got a shred of dignity left to protect.

The bathroom is just as obnoxious as the rest of his house—dark tile, clean lines, and a rainfall shower that I absolutely don't have the energy to be jealous of right now.

Except I am, and I hate that, too.

The mirror mocks me the second I catch my reflection as I try to peel off my shirt. I wince as the fabric brushes the bruises already blooming across my ribs.

I've clearly never looked better.

I have a cracked lip, my ribs are painted in technicolor, and a shoulder that's pulsing like a fresh kill. One eye's already starting to bruise, and my cheekbone's pissed off and swollen. There's a cut near my hairline, and dried blood is crusted in my lashes like war paint I didn't ask for.

At least I can say I've looked worse. Yet, I'm not sure if that's comforting or just fucking sad.

I try to yank the shirt off one-handed by hooking my fingers under the hem and pulling it up, but it tugs against the bandage and I flinch, gritting my teeth.

I try again, but it catches on the tape across my ribs and I nearly choke on the sound that escapes me.

Goddammit.

I take a deep breath, trying not to throw up as I shift my weight, trying another angle, and—*fuck*. The pain in my side explodes again, and it's blinding. I sag forward, gasping, as my vision swims for a second.

I don't hear the knock, just the soft click of the door opening.

"Are you—"

"Out," I snap, whirling around.

The shirt falls back down as I turn, and that single motion costs me everything. Pain punches through my side, and my shoulder gives as I stagger, catching myself against the counter with a sharp cry.

He freezes in the doorway, looking at me like I'm the problem. His eyes sweep down—over my face, and the fresh blood soaking through the gauze, and now his shirt. He closes the door behind him without a word.

"I said out."

He just leans against the doorframe. But makes no move to leave. "You're bleeding again."

"Gold star." I shoot him a glare over my shoulder. "Maybe save the obvious for someone who gives a shit."

He crosses the bathroom in two strides, and his presence is enough to steal all the remaining air I have.

"I heard a noise," he says. "Thought you passed out again."

"You wish."

His gaze drags over me, lingering at the way I'm cradling my bad shoulder. "You can't even lift your arm."

"I'm managing." I lie through my teeth.

"Barely."

We lock eyes and there's something sharp in the silence. Yet, his expression is unreadable. I'm starting to realize that unreadable calm is not a comfort.

Then he speaks, and his voice is ice wrapped in velvet. "Let me help you take it off."

The words shouldn't send heat flooding under my skin, but they do.

"No."

Of course he doesn't listen. His hand grazes the edge of my shirt, and his fingers brush just above my hip bone.

I know what this is. It's a game. It's a calculated touch meant to see if I'll flinch or freeze or melt. I will do no such thing.

"I said no," I snap—but still don't move. My hands stay limp at my sides like they don't believe me either. His eyes don't leave mine. Not once.

He just stares as his fingers glide higher over skin that should be too bruised to feel anything. But it burns.

"You didn't say stop."

My breath stalls.

Then quieter—deadlier—his voice dips. "Hold still." And I do. *I fucking do.*

My body's already made the decision and left my brain out of the vote. And God, I hate how easily I obey. When did this sudden submissiveness happen?

I suck in a breath, but it's not from pain—it's how careful he is. He takes his time lifting the fabric over my head, easing it off my good arm—then slower, gentler—past the other.

The shirt hits the floor, and I can practically hear my pussy purring.

"Shower," he says, his voice rougher around the edges. "You smell like blood."

I roll my eyes. Anything to keep the heat in my chest from crawling up my throat.

"Glad you're so concerned."

He doesn't answer, instead, he steps past me, and reaches into the shower. The water crashes against the tile, as steam instantly starts to unfurl between us like smoke.

He's standing close enough that I could touch him if I leaned forward half an inch.

His jaw flexes. "I need to change your dressings after."

"Planning on watching me?" I snap, like I've still got teeth left to bare.

That cocky smirk of his returns, carved from sin. "Only if you beg."

Then he turns and walks out, door closing behind him with a soft, deliberate thud. Somehow, the silence he leaves behind is louder than anything he said.

12

"Never mistake mercy for weakness."
(Kindness doesn't mean they won't
gut you when it matters.)

Ani

The floor's cold beneath my feet by the time I find another shirt folded neatly on the counter—one I didn't see before I got in. It's so big, it hangs off one shoulder, swallowing me whole.

But it smells like him.

Thank God getting it on was a little easier than trying to take it off. I don't know if it's the bruises or the blood loss, but everything feels slow and a little muffled. It almost feels like I'm walking through smoke.

I step out of the bedroom and pause.

The hallway stretches in both directions, both long and quiet, lit only by the soft glow of recessed lights tucked into the baseboards. All I can see is wood, stone, and shadow. Everything smells like cedar and money. It's stunning.

And a little unsettling.

I have no idea where we are, but it's massive and silent. Almost peaceful. Every step I take echoes louder than it should, despite the fact that I'm barefoot.

Yeah. This definitely isn't the kind of place that hosts game nights. I'm brushing my fingers along a doorway I don't dare open, when I see another hallway branch off to the left, with floor-to-ceiling windows at the far end. All I see is black. I think it's safe to assume we're in the woods.

I don't know how far I walk, but eventually, the scent of burnt toast and coffee hit me. I can also hear something sizzling in a pan.

It smells like... normal. Which somehow makes it worse. I only follow it, because I'm starving, slightly concussed, and—let's be honest—I can't start the day without caffeine and maybe a little self-loathing.

And then I see him.

Fuck. Do I see him.

He's standing barefoot at the stove like some feral domestic hallucination of mine. Modesty isn't just dead, it's buried in the backyard and he's the one who pulled the trigger.

His tattoos are doing that thing—again—dragging my eyes right to them, like they've got their own gravitational pull. I really do try to look away.

I fail. Miserably.

Like honestly—does he own a shirt? Or is "half-naked and emotionally unavailable" just part of the control-freak aesthetic?

The sharp planes of his back flex as he stirs something in a cast iron pan, like he didn't just strip blood-soaked clothes off my body a few hours ago. And here I am—just standing in the doorway with a libido I can't kill.

I know I should say something.

Or move.

Or blink.

But I just watch him like a creep. A very thirsty, very broken creep.

There's a jagged scar just under his ribs—angry and uneven, whatever caused it didn't leave quietly. There's another one that rides his shoulder, it looks a little more faded but still just as deep.

I try to tell myself I don't care and I definitely don't want to ask. *Except I kind of do.*

"You're supposed to be in the shower."

His voice slices through the silence, making me jump, like he's known I was there the whole time.

"Sorry to disappoint."

He glances over his shoulder. And fuck. *That face.* That unreadable, detached calm he wears like armor—the kind of danger you crawl to instead of running from. My mind goes instantly to what it would feel like riding his face. Internally I groan, because I need to get my shit together.

"Sit down."

He turns back to the stove.

"You need to eat before I bandage your shoulder."

I don't move. "You always make breakfast for the girls you undress?"

"Only the ones who bleed all over my floor."

I don't think he could have sounded more unbothered if he tried. I almost laugh.

The ache in my body's worse now that the water's gone. My legs feel like glass and pride is the only thing keeping me upright, right now.

"You didn't even tell me your name."

He flips something in the pan like I'm just background noise. "Didn't know we were swapping life stories."

This mother—Okay. Nope. Not letting him get to me. I fold my arms, ignoring the tug in my shoulder.

"Figured I should know what to scream if you turn out to be a serial killer."

"You can scream whatever you want, sweetheart," he deadpans. "Doesn't mean I'll answer."

That earns him a glare.

"So... what? I keep calling you The Hot Tattoo Man forever?"

The second it's out of my mouth, I want to hurl myself out a window. *Oh my god.* Kill me. Right now. *Ughhh*

His smirk spreads. "You can call me God if it helps you sleep."

I roll my eyes so hard I might tear something.

"Jesus, you're insufferable."

"You bleeding out in my bed was the insufferable part."

He finally turns toward me, deciding I'm finally worth his full attention. Tattoos ripple across his chest and arms as he moves, and the ink is making me flush everywhere.

He sets a plate in front of me, and it's a breakfast burrito. Eggs, diced ham, and tater tots. It smells so good, it pisses me off.

"Eat," he says.

"What, no poison?"

"Didn't think you were worth the effort."

I raise a brow. "Charming."

God, he's such an asshole. And somehow it still sounds hot coming out of his mouth. Which probably says more about me than him. I don't love that. He's leaning against the counter with his arms crossed, and he looks like something I desperately wish I could climb right now. And of course his arms are doing that *thing*. I need to get my hormones under control before I start licking his arms.

"You want charm, try Tinder."

"Oh, I did," I deadpan. "He brought me to the woods and stitched me up after I got stabbed. Real romantic."

"Lucky you."

"I feel blessed. Truly."

His mouth twitches, but he doesn't smile. He just watches me with that unreadable calm—like he's already five moves ahead and I'm still figuring out the rules.

Yeah, well, fuck you.

"So?" I challenge, resting a hand on the back of the stool. "You gonna keep dodging the name thing, or should I just call you Dick?"

That earns a look. The slow drag of his eyes is making me feel like I'm being unwrapped sand discarded all at once.

"Call me whatever you want, dear," he says finally.

"God complex much?"

"Wouldn't need one if you knew how to behave."

The way he says that means he knows exactly what to say to make me fall apart. I grip the counter, knuckles whitening.

"You're seriously going to make me beg for your name?"

"You don't strike me as the type who begs."

He pins me with a look that hits like a chokehold, and the air disappears from my lungs, my brain short-circuits, and my thighs clench like the traitors they are. *Zero loyalty to my dignity.*

Jesus Christ. I'm feral. I need help. A priest. Possibly an exorcism.

And my pussy?

Of course she likes the guy who probably has a murder room in the basement. *Perfect. Love that for me.*

"Shame. You'd look good on your knees."

My pulse trips as he steps closer, he's now close enough that I feel that shift in the air.

"Steven," he says at last, unbothered. "But if you moan it, I won't stop you."

My mouth opens and closes. My brain is crashing under the weight of one stupid, filthy sentence that shouldn't do a damn thing to me. Yet, here we are, with my thighs clenched.

Get it together, slut! I should laugh in his face and remind him I've got a knife with his name on it. But my mouth won't cooperate either.

He turns back to the stove, totally calm and unbothered. It pisses me off that he can just wreck me with one line and walk away like it was nothing.

"Eat," he says again, calm as ever. "You'll need it."

I hesitate. "For what?"

The corner of his mouth twitches. "To survive the next time you decide to act like prey."

My grip tightens on the counter.

"Prey usually runs," I snap, rolling my eyes.

"They do." He sets the spatula down with deliberate care. "Right before they get caught."

I snort dryly and grab the plate—mostly to stop myself from throwing something at his perfectly smug face. *Okay, and I'm fucking starving. I'd eat anything at this point.*

His eyes stay on me as I take the first bite.

Oh my God. This is good. Like criminally good. It cuts through the nausea and reminds my stomach it's still alive. I chew, watching him like I still have the upper hand, even though we both know I don't.

"Not bad," I say, swallowing. "Could use more salt, maybe a little less serial killer."

"You talk a lot," he murmurs, "for someone who was shaking in my shirt twenty minutes ago."

My hand freezes mid-air and the flush that hits me isn't from embarrassment. It's rage. And maybe…that other thing I'm not fucking talking about.

"Excuse me?"

"You heard me."

I set the fork down, then push the plate just far enough away to make a point. My shoulder screams in protest, but I ignore it. So does my stomach. I try to ignore that too.

"And you're awfully confident," I bite out, "for a guy playing nurse in the woods with a half-dead girl he stripped without asking."

His eyes flick down, more intentionally this time, unwrapping me without moving a muscle.

"You weren't saying no."

"I was bleeding out!"

"Still are."

He steps toward me, and the air tightens like a vice. My lips part before I can stop them, and I don't even care how obvious it is.

His voice drops, low and loaded. "I'm not the one playing games, sweetheart. You are."

My pulse spikes in my throat, *and* between my thighs. The worst part is, I don't even know what the hell he's talking about. All I know is I'm standing here, wrecked and he sees all of it.

One hand lifts to my jaw as he tilts my chin up, our mouths are too close now. His grip is bruising, but his eyes don't leave mine.

"You like to provoke, don't you?"

His voice is quiet. Deadly. Like he's savoring every word. "Say shit you don't mean... just to see what I'll do."

I shift my hips a little, and his eyes flick down, devouring me.

"You're trembling."

"From hunger," I lie.

That smirk curls, and it's devastating.

"Yeah," he says, too smooth to trust, too dirty not to crave. "I can see that."

His thumb brushes my chin. One drag—down the column of my throat and I'm done for. I'm also soaked.

"You want me to ruin you?"

My thighs clench like they've made their own decisions. My mouth goes dry—ironic, considering how fucking wet I am. I should shut up and eat my food, and maybe try to cling to the last shred of dignity I haven't already bled out in front of him. But no. That would require impulse control. Or self-preservation. Or sanity. None of which I have at the moment.

"You couldn't."

The words slip out—bold and stupid, soaked in denial.

He exhales a low laugh and God—it's the kind of sound that should come with a fucking warning label. Because holy fuck.

"Sweetheart," his voice is like velvet, "you've got no idea what I could do to you."

Then—his palms come down beside me on the counter, caging me in. The heat of him wraps around me like a second skin.

"You really think you're ready for that?" His voice brushes my jaw like a promise I'm not sure I'll survive. "For me?"

God, yes. And also...absolutely not. I'm not built to survive whatever *that* look means. I can't move, I can't even breathe. My heart is racing and I want nothing more than everything he's offering.

"You couldn't handle me on your best day," he whispers.

I don't even get a chance to form a comeback before he pulls back. Just like that.

"Get up," he says.

I blink. Still in my lust haze. "What?"

"Counter. Now."

"Why—"

He doesn't wait. One arm hooks under my thighs, the other cradles my back—and suddenly I'm airborne.

"Hey—what the fu—"

He drops me onto the cold marble like I weigh nothing.

"Keep your mouth shut," he says, already turning away. "Unless you're gonna let me fuck that pretty little mouth of yours."

I mutter something that sounds like "fuck you" under my breath, but he's not listening. He pulls out a sleek black medical kit from the drawer—of course he has one—and sets it beside me like this is just another routine task. Then he pulls out a shot glass and pours some amber liquid into it and shoves it toward me.

"You're such a dick," I grumble, keeping my jaw tight. But I don't take it. I don't want to drink, let alone take a shot right now.

"And yet you're still dripping on my counter," he mutters back, calm as ever—snapping on a pair of black gloves like we're not both two seconds from spontaneous combustion. Then he slides the shot glass back toward me.

My stomach flips. My body burns. And my ego howls.

He opens the kit, and grabs a curved needle threading it with black surgical silk. He *would* know how to stitch skin and make it look hot.

"This is gonna hurt. So you're going to want that."

"You think I haven't felt worse?"

He pauses to look at me and fuck—his eyes. They are cold and unreadable, yet somehow still burning with heat.

"Good," he says, keeping his voice low. "Maybe now you'll remember who you're playing with."

I don't get any warning when he presses the alcohol-soaked gauze to the stab wound at my side—and I see stars. White-hot pain explodes through my ribs, and I clamp my teeth together so hard my jaw throbs. I actually hate needles. The familiar feeling of nausea creeps in at the sight of it, but I'm not going to give him the satisfaction knowing how much I hate this.

His hands stay steady as he gets to work. I can feel my body shaking and it feels like I can feel every goddamn nerve in my body screaming. I grip the edge of the marble hard enough my fingers go numb.

I don't cry. I don't flinch. And I don't fold. Because that's what he's waiting for, isn't it? To see if I break.

"Still with me?" he asks, not looking at my face.

I don't answer. Mainly because, if I open my mouth, I might throw up.

"Huh." He pauses. "So that's what it takes to shut you up. A little pain. Noted."

And he smiles. *Dick.*

My jaw locks tighter and it takes everything in me to just breathe through my nose. Hopefully that'll keep me from launching myself at him and stabbing him for once.

Tempting. But probably not wise considering he has a needle at my side.

I wouldn't even blink if he told me he's stitched up his own gunshot wounds in a motel bathroom before. The thought occurs to me to ask him if he's ever been shot, but I hold it in.

"You always this tough?" he asks, casual as hell, the tip of the needle hovering just above my skin. "Or just when you're bleeding all over someone else's kitchen?"

I'm starting to hyperventilate. I know I just need to hold still, but If I say one word, I'm either going to scream, sob, or start reciting all the ways I want to rearrange his face. And I'd rather not do that with him shirtless. But I'll take anything as a distraction right now.

He hums, tilting his head like he's inspecting damage.

"Let me guess," he murmurs, just as the first stitch pulls through. I almost black out right then. "You're the type who doesn't run. Doesn't ask for help. And you'd rather bleed out than admit you're hurt."

I flinch as he pulls the needle through, and now I want to kick myself. Grabbing the glass I throw it back, trying not to cough. Everything hurts.

"Mm," he hums. "Thought so."

The thread bites into my skin again, and it takes everything I've got to breathe through it without decking him. I glance down at him, at his perfect, infuriating calm hands. At the way he doesn't even blink while putting me back together like a broken fucking vase.

"Careful," I mutter, clenching my jaw. "You're starting to sound like you want to get to know me."

His hand stills for a second, but it's just long enough for me to notice.

"I don't need to know you," he says. "I've seen your type."

My spine straightens. "My type?"

He threads the next stitch, tight and clean, and it hurts like a bitch. But he still doesn't look at me. Luckily whatever was in that glass is helping enough to take the edge off.

"Tough girl. Smart mouth. Doesn't trust anyone, but still walks around acting like she's bulletproof."

Another pull of thread, and another flash of pain. But that one I feel in my chest. He's not done, he just keeps over analyzing me.

"The type that plays invincible until someone calls her bluff."

My fingers dig into the counter until my knuckles burn.

"You think that's what this is? A bluff?"

His lips twitch. "No." He looks up, "I think it's a defense mechanism."

That lands like a punch I didn't see coming. My mouth opens—then snaps shut.

Because he's right. How does he see it so easily? Am I really that predictable?

"Hit a nerve?" he asks, maddeningly calm.

I scoff, breathing through the tightness in my chest. "Fuck off."

I turn my head because I'm close to unraveling and I'm done being under a microscope. I'm so overstimulated on so many levels right now, it's not even funny. And I'd rather bleed out again than let him see me break.

"There she is."

The next stitch is much softer, which somehow makes it worse. I stare past him, looking at the far wall.

"You think you're clever," I mutter. "Like you've got me all figured out."

"I don't need to figure you out," he says. "You're already unraveling."

My jaw locks, and my throat tightens as I try to swallow the emotions clawing up my throat.

Fuck him.

I open my mouth just to shut it, again. "You ever..." I stop. Regretting it immediately.

His eyes flick up. Waiting. "What?"

"Never mind."

"No," he says, his tone is flat but firm. "Finish it."

My fingers twitch against the edge of the counter, but I still can't look at him.

"Do you ever feel like you're forgetting something important?" I whisper. "Like... your life looks like it's yours, and sounds like yours, but something's off."

He doesn't say anything, so I keep going.

"You know, like you're watching yourself from the outside. But nothing feels right, and no one else seems to notice." My throat tightens. "And the worst part is... it almost makes more sense that way."

He still says nothing. He just ties the last stitch, but doesn't move for a long beat. Then—"Every fucking day."

He strips off the gloves and tosses them into the sink, and starts washing his hands. Back to his usual untouchable, unreadable self.

I nod, swallowing down whatever the hell that was. I need to get out of here before I say anything else that resembles *feelings*.

"You hide it well," he says quietly. "But whatever you're running from..." A pause.

"Eventually, someone's going to catch on."

He grabs a clean towel and tosses it onto the counter beside me like an afterthought.

"You know where the bathroom is." His voice is back to what it always is—cold and distant. His mood swings are giving me whiplash.

"Try not to bleed on anything else."

Then he turns and walks away without so much as a glance back. I stay frozen, with my eyes locked on the broad set of his shoulders as he disappears down the hallway. And I'm still sitting here with my ribs stitched shut and my insides unraveling.

My ribs pull tight with every breath, the stitches sting, and the towel he tossed beside me is still clenched in my hands as I slide off the counter and drop into the nearest barstool like it'll anchor me somehow. It doesn't.

The silence stretches. I don't know how long I stay like this, with my bare skin against the cold leather of the stool, and my body aching, while my brain spirals.

What the fuck am I doing? How did I even get here, and what the fuck am I supposed to do now?

I'm in his kitchen—his territory—bloodstained and exhausted, trying to remember why I ever thought I had the upper hand. This man stripped me, stitched me, touched me like I was his... and walked away like I was irrelevant.

My eyes flick toward the hallway he disappeared down.

Am I supposed to wait?

No. Fuck that.

My brain feels scrambled—but I push to my feet and head down the same hallway he vanished into.

The floor's cold beneath my feet, and the house is silent. As soon as I reach the guest room, I close the door behind me, leaning against it longer than I should.

I catch my reflection in the mirror and don't recognize the girl staring back. My skin is bruised, my lips are cracked, and I'm still wearing a shirt that doesn't belong to me.

I glance toward the nightstand—and freeze. My bag.

Fuck. *Sarah.*

I snatch it up, digging for my phone like it's the only thing tethering me to what's left of normal. The screen lights up with unread messages.

> Sarah: Are you alive???

> Sarah: Bitch I'm gonna kill you

> Sarah: You disappear and now I'm googling what to do if your best friend gets kidnapped by a hot felon. You have 24 hours to contact me before I start to actually worry.

I huff out a breath that might be a laugh or a sob. It's hard to tell the difference right now.

Then I see the other texts.

Frank: It's been long enough. We're
having dinner. I need to talk to you.

Frank: I'll pick you up tonight. Wear
something I like.

My stomach flips. And not in a good way. More like a...crawl-out-of-your-skin kinda way. *Wear something I like.* How about you fuck off and I wear a paper bag.

I don't know what the hell kind of vibe I put out that men think they can just tell me what to do—but apparently I've got welcome mat energy, and I fucking hate it.

I stare at the screen, thumb hovering.

I should say no, I want to say no, but I know he'll just keep asking. Maybe I should just go, and we can actually talk.

Me: Fine. But only for dinner. I'll get my
own ride.

I hit send and immediately want to throw my phone across the room. Instead, I exhale, flipping to Sarah's name, and text her before she sends out a search party.

Me: I'm alive. Not kidnapped. Just
emotionally damaged and possibly
making stupid decisions.

Me: Can we meet for lunch later? I need...
a reset. And maybe a taser. I'll fill you in
then.

I toss the phone onto the bed and press the heels of my hands into my eyes until stars bloom behind my lids.

What the fuck am I doing? Seems to be the question of the century.

I head for the closet looking for anything I can wear out of here. I'm not about to leave in an oversized shirt.

There aren't many clothes, just a few black tees, sweats, and a hoodie. All his. I grab a pair of black sweats and a plain white tee that smells like cedar and clean linen—like him, which pisses me off more than it should.

I don't want to wear his clothes. But I'm also not walking around like a blood-soaked horror show, so here we are.

I pull them on slowly, and everything hurts. Bending, breathing, existing. My ribs scream with every movement. I somehow manage to get the shirt over my head, knot it at my waist, and pretend like I haven't just surrendered something vital.

I grab my phone from the nightstand and open the Uber app, I have no idea where I am—just that it's deep in the woods, and the house looks like it probably eats people for fun.

Still, I drop the pin and hit confirm, because I need to feel like I'm doing something.

I set the phone on the bed, screen-side up, watching the timer count down like it will keep me from losing it completely.

My hands are still curled into fists at my sides, when the screen lights up again.

Uber: Your driver will arrive in 2 minutes.

That was fast.

Good, it's not enough time to hunt him down or talk myself out of leaving.

I grab my bag and head for the door, my pulse hammering harder than it should. I'm not sure why, because I'm not staying in someone's house just because they stitched me up and made breakfast.

That's not how this works. That's not who I am.

The hallway is quiet, but I manage to find the front door on the first try without any awkward encounters. I sling the bag over my good shoulder and step outside into the cold morning air.

I stay on the stone path, scanning for headlights, when a sleek, black car rolls up the long driveway—I didn't double-check the name or look at the license plate, but it looks like the photo. Close enough.

The car stops just outside the gate and I hear a soft click as the back door unlocks. The driver steps out, opening my door for me. He's dressed in all black, but has a friendly expression on his face at least.

... Муравьевым ... к которым ...
... заключались как предл...
... которого желал позна...
... имет Сергея Мур...
... служения, касател...
... как о особенно умн...
... остаться в Киев...
... С Муравьевым Серг...
... приехал в полдень, в Усс...
... его бытности сих нес...
... которою я 6 месяцев не в...
... я участвовал ...
... были сочтены внимание следст...
... обществу, цель пребыва...
... предполагаемому тайному общ...

II.

... дозволение на арест
... 1826 года было послано отно-
... министрам, по имя Ермолова за

... прошу Ваше Вы-
... немедленно взять под арест
... Грибоедов со всеми прина...
... осторожность, чтобы
... и предать как оные...
... министром в Петербург...

... движение на ...
... выступил ...
22-го вечером, в
... Уклонскай
... в это время ...

13

"Don't interfere too soon."
(Watching them fall is half the fun.)

Ani

I stir the straw in my iced coffee like it personally offended me and Sarah's watching me like I'm an active crime scene. One she hasn't decided whether to report or cover up.

"You good?" she asks finally, tearing a piece off her croissant and popping it in her mouth.

I shrug, even though every muscle in my body feels like it's been steamrolled and sewn back together by a man with too many secrets and not enough shirts. "Define good."

Her brows lift as she gives me a once-over. "Alive? Semi-conscious? Not actively bleeding on the table?"

I snort. "Two out of three's not bad."

She leans back in her chair, sunglasses perched on her head like a halo she doesn't deserve. "You ignored me for over twenty-four hours, and you're covered in bruises. I was this close to storming whatever horror-movie basement you'd been dragged to with a shovel."

I glance down at my coffee. "Trust me, it felt like that. Just one with central air and a guy who thinks bedside manner means verbal warfare."

"Exactly. That's how dire the situation was. Bitch, don't do that to me again."

I let the corner of my mouth lift, but it fades fast. I really don't know what I'm doing or how I got here.

Sarah taps her nail on the side of her cup. "Ani."

"I'm fine."

"Don't lie to me."

I tear off a piece of my bagel. "I'm not lying," I murmur. "I'm just... not totally here yet."

She's quiet for a beat, then leans forward slightly. "Was it him?"

I know who she means. Not Frank. *Him.* Steven.

"Sort of."

"Ani—"

"I can't talk about it yet."

"Not an option," she says, taking a sip of her coffee. "You ghosted me and showed up looking like you got mauled by a sexy bear. So either you talk, or I start guessing—and you know I'm not shy."

I glare at her, but there's no heat behind it. I'm too tired, and frankly still too raw. "I don't even know where to start."

She shrugs. "Start with the part where you didn't die."

I exhale, leaning back in my chair, and stare at the chipped edge of the table, trying to decide how to start. "I got attacked."

"I see that."

"And he found me."

Her mouth tightens. "So the hot, tatted menace stitched you up like a psychopath-turned-doctor, and you still won't give me a name?"

"Steven." I mutter.

She whistles low. "Damn. I can't tell if I want to high-five you or call the cops."

"Same," I say, a dry laugh catching in my throat. "Honestly? I don't know what the hell I'm doing."

Sarah reaches across the table and steals a piece of my bagel. "One. Thank God you're alive. Two. Sounds like you're exactly where you're supposed to be."

We eat in silence for a beat when Sarah breaks the silence again. "Are you still seeing the other one tonight?"

I nod, stabbing my straw into the melting ice of my water. "He wants to take me to dinner."

"You gonna tell him to go fuck himself?"

"Eventually."

"Jesus." She leans forward, all playful sarcasm gone. "Just be careful, okay? I know you joke, but you've been off lately. And I don't trust Frank. I never did."

"Noted."

"And Babe?"

"Yeah?"

"I mean it," She says, pointing at me with her straw. "No more ghosting. If I don't hear from you by midnight, I'm calling the National Guard."

I shake my head, but there's warmth curling in my chest. "You're insane."

"And you look like shit, so we're even."

That's the thing about Sarah, she really would too. I know in a heartbeat she would murder someone for me and help hide the body. I really want to tell her the rest, but there's not enough time in the day. I'll tell her later when we have more time. Then maybe I can figure out what to do.

When we stand up to leave, she pulls me into a quick hug.

"You good?" she asks.

I nod, lying through my teeth. "Yeah."

She lets me go, but not before giving me a look that says she doesn't believe me for a second. "Text me. Or I swear to God, Ani—"

"Yeah, yeah. Hiking boots. National Guard. I got it."

We split at the corner, and as I head back toward my apartment, the weight of what's next starts pressing down on me.

I need to get my shit together, it's almost time to leave.

I know it's just dinner. That's all this is. But it's dinner with the man I used to think was safe. The man who smiles like he's harmless and holds secrets like weapons.

What's really getting to me—what I can't shake no matter how many times I try to logic my way through it—is that I don't know what's real anymore. The dreams are getting stronger. More vivid, and more intimate.

The only issue is, every time I reach for one, it slips through my fingers like smoke. It's like my brain is trying to protect me from something it knows I'm not ready to remember.

I stare at my reflection, trying to hide the evidence. The bruise on my cheekbone fades under layers of concealer, but it's still there if you know where to look.

The cut near my hairline disappears behind a twisted updo that looks effortless but took twenty minutes, a prayer, and a whole bottle of product. I'm a goddamn magician.

My shoulder throbs with every movement, and the bandages beneath my dress feel like sirens.

Still, I line my eyes, curl my lashes, and put on some dark red lipstick, the color I wear when I need to feel like I'm the one doing the devouring. Even if all I'm doing is smiling through my teeth.

The dress is just a simple black number that holds my ribs like armor. It dips at the collarbone, clings to my waist, and splits high enough to count as a distraction.

It's the kind of dress you wear when you want people to look—just not too close. Especially not at the way I flinch when I breathe too deep. I press a hand to my sternum and try to breathe through the tightness.

My phone buzzes again, breaking the silence. I expect it to be Frank with some smug confirmation, or how he wants to pick me up, but it's not.

> Unknown Number: I like when you pretend you're not scared, it makes it more interesting.

My stomach twists. I stare at the screen for a beat too long before snapping a screenshot and deleting the thread—like that'll make a difference.

The words are already stuck, buried under my skin, but I don't fucking have time for this right now.

I toss my phone in my bag and glance toward the window because some paranoid part of me needs to check. There's nothing but trees, and the apartments next door.

Still, I hesitate. Because whoever sent that text... knows too much.

I unlock my phone and open the Uber app like a normal person, doing normal things.

The driver's two minutes out. I watch the pin inch closer, then set the phone down on the counter and smooth my hands over my dress again, checking for anything that might give me away.

Frank said to meet at his club, but insisted we weren't staying. I grab my jacket from the hook as the Uber pulls up right on time, headlights slicing through the early evening. The driver steps out, all polite efficiency and harmless energy, and opens the door.

I nod, sliding into the backseat, and cross my legs like I'm not riding straight into a situation I already regret.

He tries to make small talk, asking if I'm having a good night. I give him a lie wrapped in a smile and toss the question back. My voice is fake, but polished. *I'm getting good at that.* The rest of the ride is smooth, and I spend most of it pretending not to watch the map. The closer we get to the club, the tighter my chest pulls.

By the time we glide up to the curb, I've already convinced myself this was my idea.

The car eases to a stop as I brace my palm against the seat and swing the door open a little too fast—pain slices through my shoulder and I freeze, clenching my jaw so tight it might crack. The movement yanked on still-healing muscle, and now it's screaming. *Deep breath Ani, we got this.*

The bouncer spots me before I'm even fully out of the car.

He's tall, built like a bulldozer in a suit, and gives me one long look before reaching for the velvet rope like he's unlocking a secret kingdom.

It's not even blocking anything. Just dangling there like a decorative suggestion. I've never understood how unclipping a piece of useless fabric became the universal symbol for wealth and exclusivity. But sure—I'll play along. In places like this, everything's about pretending.

I offer a tight, practiced smile.

The bouncer doesn't say anything to me, he just nods. One of those "I know who you are" nods. Or worse—"I know who you belong to."

Yeah. No.

Immediately fuck that.

My fingers twitch around the strap of my bag as I consider turning around and getting right back in the car.

"Evening," I mutter, sliding past the bouncer, but he doesn't reply, he just stares at me as I walk past.

I pause just past the entry, letting my eyes adjust. He said we wouldn't stay long, but from the second I stepped out of that car, everything about this screamed performance. The club smells like money, liquor, and desperation wrapped in designer cologne. There are bodies pressed into each other on the dance floor, moving to the bass like it's church.

I slip past a velvet curtain tucked just far enough to suggest privacy and there he is, sitting in a booth with his spine straight, and one arm draped casually over the backrest. He's laughing at something the man across from him said—but there's no joy in it. He looks pissed.

I'm close enough to hear him when he speaks, but barely. I've never seen Frank like this.

"...if he doesn't deliver, you know what to do." There's a pause. "I don't want excuses this time. I want blood."

Something cold runs the length of my spine. The man nods once, then Frank leans back like he didn't just order someone's death with the same tone most people use to order a drink.

He hasn't seen me yet. And for one breathless second—I get to see his mask slip.

When his eyes lift mid-sentence, and he sees me, everything shifts. The man across from him is still talking—something clipped and serious—but Frank doesn't even glance his way. Just lifts a hand, silencing him mid-word.

The man follows the gesture, turns, takes one look at me, and walks away without another word.

I don't move, because if I do, I might run.

Frank's gaze drags down my body, slow and possessive, like he's taking inventory of something that already belongs to him. I roll my eyes, and his mouth curves into that familiar, disarming smile—the one that used to make me feel safe.

Now it just makes me want to slap it off his face.

He stands—fluid, and polished. Every inch the man who gets what he wants.

"Ani," he says, all warmth and practiced charm. "You look..." His eyes sweep me again, slower this time. "Dangerous."

I tip my chin. "Yeah? So do you. Especially when you're ordering hits over whiskey."

His smile doesn't waver. Not even a twitch. If anything, it spreads into something cooler, more calculated.

"Come on," he says, waving it off like I accused him of stealing a parking spot. "It's not as serious as it sounds."

Not serious. Right. Totally casual.

I arch a brow. "You sure? Because it sounded pretty fucking serious from where I was standing."

He chuckles, and it grates on something buried deep in my spine.

"Business, baby. Sometimes people need reminding."

There's that word again. *Baby.*

A week ago, I might've laughed. I might've even let him. But I'm not the same girl he took to dinner last time. Not after what happened in the alley. Not after Steven. I still don't know what the fuck to do about him or whatever the hell is clawing at the back of my brain like it wants out. Ever since I met Steven, there's this side of me that I'm not sure what to do with.

Still, I smile, even though it's fake as hell. I still don't know where Frank and I stand anymore, but I'm inclined to think I need to stay single forever.

Frank extends a hand like the perfect gentleman. "Come on, baby. Our table's ready."

I hesitate, glaring at him. Only for a second, but I make sure he sees it. Something flickers in his eyes, like he's humoring me.

The music swells behind us, and his fingers brush the small of my back with just enough pressure to feel like possession.

"Is this your version of not staying?" I ask, looking around. "Because it looks a hell of a lot like staying to me."

His smile sharpens a fraction. "There's a difference between drinking here and dining here," he says smoothly. "I have a private table. You'll like it."

He doesn't give me a chance to answer before guiding me through the club. The second his fingers wrap around my bicep, I flinch. Pain jolts through my shoulder, but I don't say anything.

He must have noticed, because his grip loosens, and he adjusts his hand, moving it back to the small of my back.

He leans in close and his mouth brushes the shell of my ear. "Don't worry, I don't bite," he murmurs. "Until I want to."

He steers me past the velvet ropes toward a private booth tucked into the shadows, where a bottle of wine is already waiting. He's pulling out all the stops, it would seem.

Frank slides into the booth like he's settling into a throne, and nods for me to join him.

I move carefully, even though my shoulders still stiff from the strain of pretending I'm fine. The leather squeaks as I sit down, and I resist the urge to lean back too far—my ribs aren't up for the performance tonight. I definitely should've bailed.

He picks up the bottle and pours himself a glass first, then grabs the second glass sliding across the table before he lifts his own and holds it up.

"Let's toast."

I lift my glass, but I don't clink his. Instead I just take a sip. The wine's dark and expensive and does absolutely nothing to dull the buzz already building behind my eyes.

"What exactly are you trying to toast?" I ask, setting my glass down with a faint click.

His smile widens. "To us. To the future."

I study him. His words are casual, but there's something underneath. Something he isn't saying out loud. Frank is a really nice guy, and we've been doing this weird exchange since the moment I met him.

"I didn't realize *we* had one," I say lightly, tracing the rim of the glass with one finger.

He laughs at that, like I just said something adorable. "We do," he says smoothly. "You just don't see it yet."

I sit a little straighter, even though my ribs protest. "Frank—this isn't a relationship. We're not—"

He cuts me off with a wave of his hand. "Details, baby. All that matters is we're here now. Together."

I take another sip, letting it sit on my tongue like I'm someone who actually enjoys this shit, then set the glass down and lean back slightly. It's too sour—just like every other overpriced bottle men like him use to impress. But I still lift my chin and watch him over the rim like I'm impressed anyway. Because that's what this is, right?

"You know, you could've just asked me to dinner like a normal person."

Frank's smile twitches. "I tried that. You kept telling me no, remember?" He tilts his glass toward me in mock cheers. "I figured direct action might get better results."

"Direct action?" I echo, eyes narrowing. "Is that what we're calling this now?"

He laughs. Actually laughs. And somehow, it's worse than if he hadn't. "You always were dramatic."

"Right." I fold my arms. "Because that totally screams romance."

He leans in slightly, resting his forearm on the table, his voice is soft but full of bite. "If I wanted to scare you, Ani... you'd know."

My jaw clenches, but I don't let it show. Instead, I raise a brow. "Was that supposed to be comforting?"

Frank shrugs, calm as ever. "You're here, aren't you?"

"I'm here, because we're friends." I echo, matching his tone. "Doesn't mean I'm staying."

His gaze darkens—just a flicker, but enough to catch. "You will."

I let the silence stretch, then I smile. "So what is this then, Frank? A date? A business meeting? Another move on your weird little chessboard?"

He watches me like he's deciding which version of me he prefers. Then, without breaking eye contact, he picks up his glass, swirls the wine once, and says, "It's a reintroduction."

"To what?"

He lifts his eyes to mine. "To the life that's waiting for you."

I stare at him. I don't know what that means, but I already don't like the way it sounds. This is not going at all the way I anticipated.

I don't want to hurt his feelings, but this is what we do. He acts like we're dating, I keep telling him we aren't, and he never listens.

I tilt my head. "Is that the life you picked out for me, or do I get to participate in the decision-making?"

His mouth curves slowly. "Boundaries," he says, swirling the wine in his glass, "can be... flexible."

My throat tightens, but I don't blink.

"And what makes you think I'd ever bend them for you?"

Frank sets his glass down with a soft clink and leans in again with his elbows on the table now.

"You will," he says. "Because eventually, you'll stop pretending you don't feel it too."

My pulse skips. *Uhh this is exactly why I don't date.* "Feel what, exactly?" I ask, lifting my brows. "The overwhelming need to delete your number and block you?"

He laughs, like I'm being adorable again. "No," he says. "That pull between us. The inevitability of it."

I roll my eyes. "Wow. You should write fortune cookies. Real poetic shit, Frank."

His smile widens, but this time there's something else behind it. He doesn't blink when he says, "I'm not poetic, Doll. I'm persistent."

The table suddenly feels too small.

"I'm not interested in being worn down," I mutter, pushing my wine glass away.

His gaze sharpens. "Who said anything about wearing you down?" he replies. "I'm just waiting for you to come home."

I freeze.

Home?

My stomach twists, and my ribs throb in time with a memory I can't quite reach, and something in the back of my mind claws at the door like it's trying to get out.

I mask it with a smirk. "Look, Frank... you don't know—."

"I know enough." He cuts me off. A second later, his charm returns like a curtain dropping over a gun.

"That mouth of yours could get you in trouble someday."

The words settle over me like smoke, making it hard to breathe through. They're soft and smooth, but for some reason, every part of me recoils like he just pressed a knife to my throat and smiled. It's not the words themselves, but it's the way they land.

I know enough?

I shake it off and laugh. Because that's safer than asking what the hell he meant. I don't want him getting any more ideas.

"Frank," I say, draining the rest of my wine. "If you don't like what comes out of my mouth, you're more than welcome to stop asking me out."

He smirks. "Oh, I like it."

He leans in, putting his hand on my thigh. "Doesn't mean I won't punish it."

My stomach drops in that same nauseating way it does when you realize the ground beneath you isn't as solid as you thought. I need air.

"I'm gonna go freshen up," I say, already standing.

He doesn't stop me, he just smiles. "Don't keep me waiting too long."

I flash him a grin, rolling my eyes. "Wouldn't dream of it."

I weave through the club, and every step makes me all too aware of the ache still pulsing in my shoulder. The heels don't help, but I welcome the sting. It grounds me. It gives me something to focus on that isn't the slow, hot crawl of panic threading through my bloodstream.

The hallway to the restrooms is dim, lined with mirrors and backlit with warm gold that makes everything feel surreal. Pushing the bathroom door open, I lock it behind me, and press both palms to the edge of the marble sink.

My reflection looks like a stranger with painted lips, a perfect dress and heels to match.

But her eyes look too wide.

What am I doing? Frank's a good friend but I'm not sure I want it to go any further than that. I know I've kept him at a distance this whole time, but he's never really been this insistent either. Maybe he's run out of patience.

My phone buzzes in my clutch, scaring the shit out of me.

> Unknown Number: You wear fear well, baby girl. Just remember…some of us notice the things you try to hide.

My stomach flips so fast I nearly drop the damn thing. I read the message once. Then again. My thumb hovers over the screen like I'm about to toss it across the sink.

Baby girl? I swear I'm going to stab the next person to call me that.

I grip the edge of the marble and force myself to breathe. In. Out. In again. But my pulse is already spiking, sweat starts beading at the base of my spine. Someone's watching me.

I drag my hand down my face. It's too much. I'm so goddamn tired of not knowing what's real—of questioning every word, every glance, every "*coincidence*" that suddenly feels more like a trap. What if Frank's a decent man, and I'm just ruining it because I'm paranoid.

I take another breath, forcing my hands to stop shaking, and stare down at my phone.

Fuck this.

I type without thinking.

> Me: Then watch this, asshole.

I reapply my lipstick with the kind of precision I reserve for war paint, wiping the sweat from my collarbone, and square my shoulders.

I toss my phone back in my clutch and unlock the door, walking back toward the table like I own the whole damn floor. Because if someone wants to play this game with me...they should've picked a girl who didn't survive hell already.

I walk back into the club like I didn't just spend five full minutes in a bathroom having a mild existential crisis and talking myself out of throwing my phone into the toilet. The music hits me first—deep, pulsing bass vibrates beneath my heels like a second heartbeat.

I scan the room without trying to look like I'm scanning the room. *Just a girl in a dress trying not to have a panic attack. Nothing to see here.*

There's no new faces at our booth, no sketchy men hiding behind wine lists or plotting in corners. But the hair on the back of my neck won't settle. That hum beneath the skin—the one that says I'm being watched—it's still there.

My gaze sweeps again, slower this time. There's a man two booths down, half-sunk in shadow. Alone. He's not looking at me—technically. But the angle of his head, the way his glass is tilted just slightly in my direction... it's too casual to be casual.

A warning pings in my chest.

My heels click on the floor as I walk back with my chin up, even though my heart is loud in my throat. Frank's sprawled in the booth like he hasn't moved an inch, fingers tapping the side of his glass in that rhythmic, cocky way. But when I slide back into the booth, his eyes flick over me.

"You okay?" he asks.

I smile sweetly. "Peachy. Miss me?"

He doesn't answer right away. He just watches me like he's trying to decide if I'm joking.

I lean forward, resting my elbows lightly on the table, and tilt my head.

"You know," I murmur, "this whole night feels a little... curated."

Frank grins. "What can I say? I like giving you what you need."

I laugh. "Are you sure about that? 'Cause I'm starting to think you don't know what the hell that is."

Something flashes in his eyes—something that looks an awful lot like a flicker of frustration. But when he smiles again, it's smooth as ever. "I know more than you think, Doll."

I sit back, crossing my legs beneath the table, trying to ignore the ache in my ribs.

"You know," he says slowly, "this could all be easier."

I raise a brow. "Define easy."

He shrugs casually, as he swirls his wine. "We stop doing this whole... back-and-forth dance, and you could let me take care of you. Move in with me."

I blink. "Wait, I'm sorry. What?"

Frank smiles like it's obvious. "It's just a matter of time anyway."

My stomach twists.

"I didn't realize we were playing house," I say. My voice is light, but I can feel the way it tightens at the end. Like my body's rejecting the idea even before my brain finishes processing it.

"We're not," he says smoothly. "We're building something real. You just haven't caught up yet."

I laugh, or at least I hope that sounded like a laugh. "You really think that's how this works?"

"I know it is," he says, and the certainty in his voice makes my blood boil. "You don't have to believe it yet. You will."

Something in me stills.

"I'm not some doll you can dress up and keep on a shelf, Frank." Keeping my temper in check. "I don't do leashes."

He leans in, resting his hand on my thigh. "I don't want to—"

His phone buzzes, and he glances down but doesn't answer it. Instead, he slips a hand into his jacket and pulls out a black velvet box and my stomach drops.

"No," I say immediately, instinct flaring.

He smiles like I didn't say a damn word, then opens it. It's a necklace. A single dark emerald sits at the center of a small chain. It's elegant, and looks expensive, but it's also not really my style.

"A gift," he says. "For tonight."

I don't move. "Because you think this is going so well?"

He doesn't miss a beat, he takes the necklace out and closes the box with a soft, final click, setting it aside.

He's putting his arms around me before I can protest and I feel the brush of cool metal against my skin as he fastens the clasp at the back of my neck with steady fingers.

"There," he murmurs in my ear. "Perfect."

He watches me for a beat longer, then he stands.

"I need to make a call," he says. "Be right back."

I nod, waiting until he disappears behind one of the shadowed side halls. When I'm sure I'm alone, I exhale like I've been holding my breath for hours.

What the hell is happening?

A few weeks ago, Frank was just fine with our little exchange. He didn't complain about our friendship or try to pursue me. Now he's wanting to play house, dropping emeralds and acting like this is the part where I just give in and say yes.

The worst part is, it's working on some level because I keep showing up and I keep wondering if maybe this is better than feeling alone, and looking over my shoulder all the time.

Maybe some unhinged, masochistic corner of my brain thinks that's justice.

My phone buzzes—again—dragging me back before I spiral straight back into hell.

> Unknown Number: You looked this good
> the first time too.

What the fuck? My hand shakes as I type back.

> Me: Who the fuck are you?

I hit send before I can stop myself. Seconds pass before there's another buzz.

> Unknown Number: You'll remember. And when you do…

The message burns on the screen, and something inside me recoils. I type so fast, my fingers are shaking.

> Me: Tell me who you are, or crawl back into whatever sad little sewer you slithered out of. I'm not scared of creeps who play dress-up with burner phones. And if you think I'm the same girl you remember, try me.

> Unknown Number: Do you remember the look on his face when he handed you over?

> Me: You're disgusting. You don't know shit about me.

> Unknown Number: I know enough to be the reason you keep looking over your shoulder.

I almost hurl my phone across the room. Instead, I grip it tighter. "You want to scare me?" I mutter, clenching my teeth. "Pick a different girl."

> Me: I'm not scared of you. I have a boyfriend.

I almost laugh as I type it, because it couldn't be further from the truth. But my brain conjures Steven's face anyway.

I picture his tattooed arms, and that voice that sounds like violence.

If anyone could make a potential stalker second-guess themselves—it's him.

> Me: He's not exactly the understanding type. So if you come near me again, you better pray he doesn't find you first.

I hit send and just when I think I've finally scared this guy away, I get another message.

> Unknown Number: Cute. Pretend all you want. You'll remember who you belong to soon enough.

My jaw locks, and my pulse is thudding hard enough to drown out any leverage I thought I had. I read the message again. Every letter drags across my skin like it remembers where I've bled.

My thumb hovers above the screen, twitching to fire something back—something venom-laced, but I don't, because if I answer, I give them exactly what they want.

I lock the screen, sliding the phone into my clutch like I didn't just imagine hurling it through the goddamn mirror, and take one slow breath through my nose. *I'm fine.*

A shadow flickers near the hallway, and then Frank appears.

"Everything alright?" he asks, stepping closer.

I paste on a smile, but it doesn't reach my eyes. "Peachy," I say.

He reaches for my hand and I let him guide me out of the booth. I'm a live wire, ready to snap because someone out there knows more than they should.

If Frank thinks this night ends with me folded neatly into his world—he's about to know what disappointment tastes like.

The air outside the club is cooler now—damp with the bite of spilled liquor. It smells like perfume and sweat and the ghost of a fight that probably happened an hour ago.

I expect some sleek black car to be waiting at the curb with tinted windows, and the engine running, but instead, Frank leads me to the passenger side of his own car—a matte black coupe that looks like it was custom-built for egos and mid-life crises.

He opens the door for me, waiting until I'm settled in. His hand brushes my leg when he helps me pull the hem of my dress in so it doesn't catch in the door then walks around the car and gets in. He pulls out into the night like he owns the road too.

The silence stretches for a while, broken only by the hum of tires and whatever elevator music is slipping from the speakers. Nothing I'd ever pick—but of course, it fits him perfectly.

He doesn't say much at first, but when he finally glances over at me, it's with that same soft, dark smile that I can't decide if I like or not.

"Why do you always look like you're seconds from running?"

I raise a brow. "Maybe that's because I am."

He laughs, warm and deep like it actually touches something in him.

"I like that about you," he murmurs. "You don't give anything away."

I want to say he's wrong. That I give away too much. That I've been bleeding pieces of myself for months trying to figure out what the hell's broken in me. But I just smirk and look out the window.

"Don't romanticize it," I mutter. "It's called trauma."

He laughs again, and this time his hand drifts to my thigh, letting it sit there with his fingers pressing down softly.

"You look good in my car," he says, his eyes still on the road. "Bet you'll look even better in my house."

I turn my head, brows pulling in. "What?"

He smiles again. "I told you, it's inevitable. I'll give you 'til the end of the month. After that, we're done playing around."

And then we're pulling up to my house. The headlights flash across the parking lot of my apartment complex like a punch to the chest, and for a second, I forget what we were talking about.

Wait, I never told him where I lived. My jaw tightens and.. my mind stalls. *And what the hell does that even mean? Done playing around.*

I stare straight ahead, blinking hard, trying to process what he just said. I should ask, but the words get stuck in my throat, clinging to the edge of panic that never really left me.

It's the way he said it—so offhanded and casual, like it didn't mean anything. But I've seen what Frank looks like when he means something.

I open my mouth and close it. My hand hovers over the door handle, "I've never told you where I lived. How did you know I lived here?"

"You probably forgot, baby. You do realize we've been seeing each other for months."

He says it so easily, like I'm the one who must be confused. *Maybe I did forget.*

"You okay, Doll?" he asks. His tone is warmer now, sweet even. "You look like you're somewhere else."

I force a tight smile, grabbing the handle. "Long day."

He leans over slowly, but I don't move fast enough to stop him before he's grabbing my chin. His lips brush mine, and I just let it happen.

Because I'm tired. And he can be charming, sometimes. And because pretending someone wants me for something other than leverage feels better than nothing.

His hand slides to my upper thigh, fingers brushing over the fabric like he's memorizing the feel of me. And just as quickly, he pulls back—gone before I can react.

"Sleep well, baby," he smiles. "I'll see you when I get back from my trip."

I didn't even get dinner. What the fuck.

14

**"DON'T STEAL WHAT'S ALREADY YOURS.
MAKE THEM HAND IT TO YOU."
(PATIENCE IS A MOTHERFUCKER.)**

Steven

She sat on my counter in nothing but my shirt and an attitude, with her chin tilted up like she hadn't just been bleeding in the street. Still talking shit. Still challenging me like she didn't owe me her life. *Literally.* And then she left.

No goodbye. Not even an ounce of hesitation.

Good.

That's exactly how I wanted it to feel. Temporary and replaceable. *So why the fuck am I pissed?*

What's funny is, she really thought she could order a ride and slip out the door like she wasn't still wearing my shirt, smelling like me, and leaking cum all over her thighs.

Like I wouldn't notice.

I canceled her ride the second it popped up and replaced it with my own. The driver's one of mine—been with me for years. The car was already outside the gate before she even opened the app.

She thinks she's clever, that I don't see through the sharp tongue and that fake indifference. But I do. I see everything.

I see the way she fidgets when she's pretending to be still. The way her mouth tightens a split second before she lies. The way she flinches when someone touches her for too long, but doesn't flinch

243

at all when it's me. I want so badly to dick her down within an inch of her life.

She doesn't even realize she tells me everything without saying a word. And that makes me fucking insane.

She walks around like she's untouchable—when every step begs to be challenged. She was built to be bent, broken, and used. She pretends she's addicted to freedom, but the second someone grabs her by the throat and tells her to get on her knees, I'd bet every dollar I have she'd obey like it was instinct. And she'd love it.

Hell, she'd fucking thank you for it, then lie through her teeth and call it control. She plays the part too well. She knows exactly what she's doing—every movement, every glance, is designed to distract and to disarm.

I almost admire it.

Not many people are that self-aware. She clearly knows how to tilt her head just enough to bait a man without looking desperate. She knows to drop her voice when she's hiding something, and I'm not falling for that bullshit.

I happen to be in her area on business today, not the kind I talk about and not the kind that leaves paper trails. It's usually the kind that ends with someone bleeding or begging—or both. I'm wrapping up when the ping hits my phone.

She's home.

As soon as I round the corner on her street, my eyes scan for movement, and I see a car parked out front looking out of place. The engine's still running, so they aren't planning on staying long. It's the kind of car you don't drive unless you're trying to make a statement, and she's sitting right in the passenger seat.

I slow down, narrowing my eyes as I clock the whole scene in one breath.

Her body's angled toward him with her shoulder against the door like she's caged. I'm sure her legs are even crossed. That dress —black and skin-tight—hugs every curve like it was sewn onto her, making my dick instantly hard. She looks hot as fuck, she also looks like she's on defense.

He's leaning in, and I'm close enough to know his hand is sliding up her thigh, and she fucking lets him. Her body's stiff, but her eyes are drifting out the window, like she's somewhere else.

Interesting.

Rage slices through me like a fucking blade. My fists clench on instinct, and my jaw is locked so goddamn tight I could grind my molars to dust. I don't know what the fuck he said to her—and I don't care. It's already enough to make me want to burn this whole goddamn city to the ground.

I want to break his fucking fingers just for making her smile, whether it was real or not. I can't breathe without wanting to shove his face into the pavement and make damn sure he never steps into her space again.

One more fucking second and I swear to God, I'll end him.

She doesn't kiss him back, she just sits there, and it makes me want to put a bullet through his head. That should be my cue to walk the fuck away and let her keep playing house with a man who thinks a tailored suit and a fake smile earn him ownership.

But I don't move.

The way he touches her—it's not affection. It's control. It's a performance and she's letting it happen. She's sitting there like she didn't just cum on my tongue and dig her nails into my shoulders while screaming my fucking name.

It makes me want to drag her out of that car by the throat and remind her who's been inside her head since the second I touched her.

She fucking knows exactly what kind of man he is and what a man like that is always—always—waiting to take.

And yet, she stays.

She doesn't just stay, she plays along. Smiling when she's supposed to, keeping her voice light, and relaxed. Every inch of her screams confidence.

She's too fucking smart to be this stupid.

She's playing a game she doesn't understand. And whatever story she's telling herself to get through it—he's playing it better. He's two moves ahead and dragging her toward the checkmate she refuses to see coming and she's going to lose.

But that's not my fucking problem.

The passenger door swings open like nothing just happened and his hands weren't all over her. She steps out, and pretends she's not unraveling beneath his stare.

She could wear his ring, for all I care. Hell, she could wear his fucking name. But I know what her mouth sounds like when it's saying mine.

The next time she steps out of a car that doesn't belong to her, I won't be across the street. I'll be waiting at the fucking door.

An hour later, I'm still parked across the street with the engine off and the lights dead. Her shadow moves behind the curtain—outlined in that soft glow she always forgets to turn off. A beat later, the room goes dark.

I lean back in the seat, one hand wrapped around my phone, the other curled into a fist inside my coat pocket.

Waiting.

I pull up his number hitting call, it only rings once.

"You're late," his voice is rough, like he just woke up.

I stare at the building, and the windows that are still dark. "I need a trace," I say in the way that puts people on edge.

"Just find me the records. I want any movement, and all financials. Anything encrypted."

I hear him moving—then papers shifting, and tapping on a keyboard. "We talking foreign or domestic?"

"Both." I pause. "Start with offshore accounts, or anything tied to recent real estate shifts."

He whistles under his breath. "So we're pulling teeth this week. You know you're gonna have to give me more than that if you want this done fast. And it will cost you extra..."

My eyes narrow on the window again.

"Shut the fuck up." I don't bother softening it. "It's not the money you get off on, and we both know it. Just get it done."

A pause, then more tapping on his end. When I hear a muffled curse and what sounds like rustling paper or fabric. Either he's finally moving through files—or dragging himself upright like the dramatic bastard he is.

"Any flags I should know about?" he mutters.

"There shouldn't be."

I drag in a slow breath, eyes locked on the innocent person walking their dog.

"But if you find any, don't touch them. Just keep watching."

He hums. That thoughtful, slightly smug sound he makes when the job just got interesting.

"You think she's still a liability?"

I don't answer. Because that's the problem, I don't fucking know. The timelines don't line up, and ghosts I've buried are suddenly crawling back with new names and old scars.

"Focus on movement, and any incoming wires. Maybe look for gaps or mismatched timestamps."

"So, you think someone's hiding a transfer?" he asks, voice still dry—but I can hear it shift. He's intrigued now.

I glance out the window again, scanning the area.

"No," I murmur. "I think someone already did. I just want to know where they put the body."

That shuts him up. He knows exactly how deep this goes. He doesn't ask for context, he doesn't need to. He's been in my shadows long enough to recognize the cold edge of a buried truth when he hears it.

"Alright," he says, all business now. "I'll ping you when I get a hit."

Click.

I let the phone drop back into my lap, my eyes stay fixed on the apartment across the street. I've spent the next forty minutes staring at a window I have no business watching when my phone vibrates again. I open the file and my eyes narrow the second I catch the document header.

Property transaction.

Puerto Rico.

It looks like they tried to bury it under two LLCs and a trust account wrapped tight in enough legal tape to keep most eyes away. But Travis isn't most eyes. And no one hides shit like this unless they're trying to erase it entirely.

It's not the amount of the purchase that stops me. Surprisingly it's not even the purchase itself, it's the signature line that stops me.

Just a placeholder ID—nothing else. But the routing data doesn't match either. A mismatch that specific doesn't just happen by accident. Someone scrubbed the file and hoped no one would dig this deep.

A second buzz lights up the screen. Another file. Smaller this time.

The attachment is blurry, compressed to hell—like it's been scanned, re-scanned, and buried behind a dozen firewalls.

I zoom in.

The person in the photo's turned away, and their face is obscured. It looks like it could be heavily bruised, but then again, it's a shity photo, so it could be shadows. But those eyes...I know those eyes.

I stare at the screen for too long while that old, familiar rage curls low in my spine. Whatever this is, it's not business anymore.

The file is still open on my screen, burning a hole right through me. But that fucking timestamp. There's no way that's fake. *What are you up to?*

I take a slow breath, flexing my fingers like it'll calm the way my blood's starting to burn.

I can still see her in that fucking dress. That kiss. The way he touched her like he had a right to. He wouldn't even fucking know what to do with something that sharp.

It would seem like I've been too quiet and someone's gotten too comfortable.

I slide my thumb across the screen and open a thread I haven't used in a while. The last message I sent still has no response.

My jaw flexes, and for a moment, I wish I was there to savor the reaction.

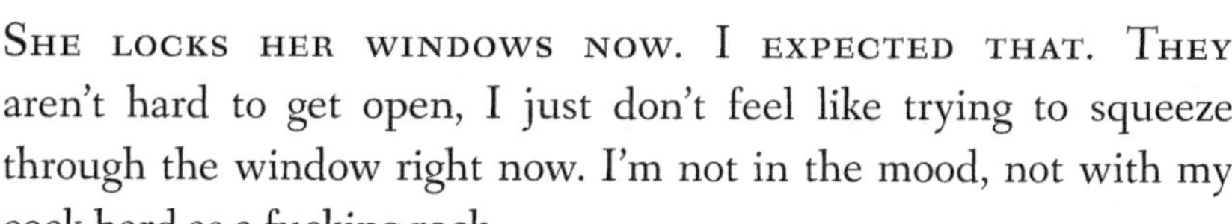

SHE LOCKS HER WINDOWS NOW. I EXPECTED THAT. THEY aren't hard to get open, I just don't feel like trying to squeeze through the window right now. I'm not in the mood, not with my cock hard as a fucking rock.

She deadbolted the door like it'll keep anything real out. Cute. She's cautious, smart, and maybe a little paranoid. I like that.

The lock's decent enough to slow someone down, but not enough to stop me. *It never is.* One shift of pressure, a flick of tempered steel, and I'm in. God, I'm good at this.

She doesn't even stir.

Inside, it's quiet, and the air carries a faint hint of something warm. Lavender, maybe or vanilla.

It smells like the girl who looks at men like she's daring them to try and fight, because she's clawing her way back from hell.

But the softness I see in her right now is a version of her I'm sure she doesn't let very many people see. She looks so peaceful, I almost want to disrupt it.

Only I don't move for a minute, I just stand here and listen to the faint hum of the fridge, and her breathing.

I move through the space without a sound, avoiding the places I already know creak. The place isn't that big, and she doesn't even lock her bedroom door, but she should.

Her breathing's uneven, and her lips are parted. One arm is tucked under the pillow, the other is curled protectively around her ribs like she's trying to hold herself together even in her sleep.

She's wearing the shirt she left my house in, and her whole hip is exposed, baring her whole leg where the blanket slipped, showing off a tattoo that I suddenly have the urge to lick.

Fuck.

I don't look away soon enough, and I feel the all too familiar ache pressing against the front of my pants. The violent timing couldn't be worse. My cock twitches like it wants to finish the job, but even the devil couldn't ruin her the way I plan to.

I should turn around, forget I was ever here, and let her keep pretending she's safe. But then I remember his hands on her while he kissed her mouth like it belonged to him.

My hands curl into fists.

My cock is still fucking hard, and all I can think about is what she'd sound like if I buried my fingers in her—if she'd wake up moaning my name, just like she did when she was bleeding on my kitchen counter.

I take a step closer to wake her up and find out, when she shifts and murmurs something under her breath. Her fingers twitch against the pillow, and her leg jerks. *"Don't touch me?"*

My spine locks, and my fingers flex at my sides.

What the fuck is she dreaming about now?

Her legs shift again, dragging the hem of the shirt higher, and I don't realize I've stepped closer until I feel the heat rolling off her skin. I'm right at the edge of the mattress now—close enough to catch the jerky rise and fall of her breath, and the shallow, panicked rhythm of a body trying to outrun something even while unconscious.

Her chest rises, and a sharp sound rips from her throat—choked and raw. It dies halfway out of her mouth, strangled by sleep and instinct. But it's enough to make me freeze in place as heat travels up the back of my neck. Her arm twitches against the pillow like she's trying to fight something off. Her head turns sharply and her lips move until they finally spit one broken word.

"Please."

I'm standing there, hard as a fucking rock, breathing through my teeth, watching her unravel. I don't even realize I'm touching her until I'm brushing a strand of hair back from her face. If I don't touch her, I might break something.

She twitches at the contact, and a soft whimper escapes her lips. "Figures. The first time you beg me, you don't even know you're doing it."

She stirs again, sighing as her body relaxes. I let my gaze drag over the bruises, the curve of her hip, the soft part of her inner thigh still exposed from where the blankets slipped. She's wrecked, and she's still the most fucking dangerous thing I've ever touched.

"Don't worry, sweetheart," I murmur. "It doesn't matter who took you before... they won't be the ones to keep you."

Her lips part on another breathless whimper, and my cock throbs.

There's a part of me—black and hollow—that wants to press a knee to the mattress, crawl over her and whisper into her ear until she says my name instead of his. She'd forget every hand that's ever touched her before mine.

But I don't.

I want her to wake up knowing I was here—and that I will be again.

She's breathing softly, as her chest rises slowly, like whatever chased her in that dream finally let go. But her fingers are still clenched in the pillowcase, and that does something to me I don't fucking like.

I turn away, walking back through her room like I haven't already memorized every inch of it. The soft rustle of my coat is the only sound as I pass the bathroom—then stop.

A pair of black lace looks like it was slung by the door like an afterthought. She must have peeled them off mid-step and kept walking, bare and unbothered. My filthy little liar.

I crouch down, lifting the soft scrap of fabric like it weighs more than it should and tuck them into my coat pocket. This isn't some fuckboy fantasy, this is about control. It's a reminder that she let me in. Even if she didn't mean to.

I step back into her room one last time, and she doesn't stir as I pull a notecard from my coat and set it on the nightstand—Impossible to miss.

She's under my skin—crawling deeper no matter how much I pretend she's not. Twisting her way into places I don't let anyone fucking near.

I reach into my coat pocket and pull out the black lace panties, looking at them like they have the answers I'm looking for.

She sat on my counter in these. She came in them. Now they're in my hand, and the scent of her still clings to them. I close my fist around the lace, feeling more frustrated than ever.

She's not just taken, she's claimed. He touches her like she's a fucking ornament on display. And she smiles for him and plays the part. Yet, I've had that same mouth open against mine. I've felt her break and go quiet. I know what she feels like when she gives in.

She can lie to him all she wants—hell, she can lie to herself all she wants, but her body isn't capable of knowing how to fake it for me and that's what matters.

The only problem is, she doesn't need someone like me. She needs someone safe. Someone normal. And I've never been any of those fucking things. I'm the thing you send when you want someone erased. The one you hire when pain needs a name. I was trained to vanish. To ruin and leave.

And yet—here I am, holding her ruined lace, with no intention of walking away.

I can feel my cock getting hard again. It's been hard since I watched her sleeping in my shirt, leg bare, and those fucking lips of hers parted. She doesn't even know what she does to me or how close I came to waking her up with my hands around her throat and her name between my teeth.

It's fucked. I know that.

She needs to remain at arms length, and she needs to stay scared of me.

My phone buzzes on the counter and I grab the device, checking the screen.

> Travis : Got something you're going to want to see. Sending now.

A second ping, and it's another file. Encrypted—of course. Layers buried under aliases and multiple offshore shell dumps meant to hide a money trail. This is the kind of mess these people specialize in. *The kind I used to clean up when I still took contracts.*

Only this one wasn't cleaned up well enough, because it took Travis all of two hours to crack the thing.

I open the file, expecting another shell property or another side account, but it's not. This isn't just a routine property transfer.

What the fuck?

What does Puerto Rico, and a private estate have to do with anything? It's hidden in plain sight with two dead board members and a sealed beneficiary file.There's no listed name and no signature. But the money trail doesn't lie. The last three tax payments are tied to a traceable account. An account that leads to a name I didn't expect.

Rivera.

The trail isn't perfect, it's filtered through several accounts that don't match. But it's enough to know where it didn't come from.

I scroll slower this time, thinking I had to have missed something. The next document he sends is a smaller file, half-corrupted, like it's been passed through too many hands. A bank log of a seven figure transfer.

There's no signature, but the route is familiar. It's one of the shells I flagged months ago. I scroll slower, then I see the name on the ledger.

DeLuca, F. C.

15

"The best predators don't strike."
(They make you beg to be caught)

Ani

I wake up choking on a scream I don't remember making. My sheets are soaked with sweat and twisted around my legs like I was wrestling demons in my sleep—and maybe I was. The nightmare lingers, slipping through my fingers no matter how hard I try to grab it.

I just remember bits of it. Blood. A scream. Another useless flash of an almost-memory that tells me nothing and leaves everything wrong behind.

My chest heaves, as I press the heels of my hands into my eyes and try not to scream again. It's like my brain's staging a horror movie on loop with no subtitles, and I'm supposed to guess the plot based on jump scares alone.

I'm so sick of having the same nightmare over and over again. There's so much I don't remember and it's so frustrating.

Cool air skates over my bare legs, and it takes me a second to realize I'm still in Steven's shirt from last night. *Whatever, it doesn't mean anything.*

I roll onto my back and stare at the ceiling, silently begging the universe to tell me what the hell is wrong with me. Frank's done everything right—he opens my doors, compliments me, and always pays the bill with a charming smile. He's already made himself comfortable as the main character of my life. I even let him kiss me in the car, because that's what you're supposed to do when a good guy takes you out.

But no matter how hard I try to want him, my mind always goes right back to someone else.

Someone I don't even know. Who looks at me like he already owns me.

God, I hate myself.

I sit up slowly, as I drag a hand through my tangled hair while I look around for my underwear. They're not on the floor, not draped over the chair, not tucked under the corner of the duvet where it would be if I'd undressed like a normal, functioning human being. I frown, scanning the room again, heartbeat ticking up despite how stupid it feels.

I swear I threw them off the side of the bed.

It was late. My head was a mess. I couldn't stop thinking about him and I told myself it was just to relieve some tension. By the time I'd slipped my hand between my thighs, I was too far gone to pretend it was anyone else.

I'd been soaked.

Disgusted with myself, I'd shoved the panties down my legs and tossed them off the bed like that could somehow separate me from the truth of it.

Now they're gone and I know I didn't get up to throw them out or tuck them into the laundry bin. I barely made it to sleep. Dizzy with guilt and something worse.

I throw my legs over the bed, and see a single white notecard, propped against the nightstand. I grab it, and turn it over. It's blank, there's nothing written on it.

My throat tightens as I throw the card onto the nightstand. The worst part isn't the fear. It's the way part of me reacts to the fear like it's a fucking love letter.

My phone buzzes behind me, and I flinch. When I turn, the

screen lights up, letting me know I have three unread messages. A few from the same unknown number and Sarah.

Unknown : Have fun last night? 😶

My stomach flips. I read it again. And again.

Unknown : That little black dress was stunning on you. You look even better out of it.

My skin crawls as I reach down and tug the hem lower, even though I'm alone.

Unknown : Your so-called boyfriend can't keep you safe.

It's not even the threat that gets me. It's the tone. That smug, mocking little twist in the words—like they're not just watching, but laughing.

I don't even hesitate this time. If he wants to play games, I'll give him a better one—one where he's not the only monster in the room.

Me: If you were really watching, you'd know I wasn't alone last night. So how about you fuck all the way off.

The silence after I hit send is loud. Like scream-into-a-pillow, check-the-door-locks-twice kind of loud. No typing bubbles. No dramatic three-dot pause. No retaliation that confirms I've poked the bear.

I don't know what I thought would happen. Another threat? A riddle in blood on the wall? A whisper through the vents? Instead all I get is—radio silence. And somehow, that's what gets under my skin. The nothingness.

I read the message from Sarah next.

Sarah: Please tell me you're alive… Or have you been arrested? Or are you in the middle of some kinky sex? If it's hot, then send pics.

I huff a laugh through my nose and shake my head, the tension bleeds off my shoulders enough to remember I'm still alive. Barely.

My chest is tight, but I try to breathe through it.

I count backwards, but the adrenaline won't fade. It just simmers, coiled under my skin like a fuse waiting for someone to light it. The floor is cold beneath my bare feet as I walk to the front door. *Just to check.*

I know I locked it. I remember the click. I remember flipping the deadbolt after I got in the house like I always do. I lean against the door with my eyes closed and my forehead pressed to the wood like I could keep everything out if I just held it shut.

My lungs are pulling in air too fast, my breathing is shallow and panicked, and I clamp a hand over my mouth because if I start screaming, I might not stop. All I want to do is cry lately. I'm fucking exhausted.

My eyes scan the apartment now—really scanning the shadows. Every creak of the building settles like a new threat in my bones. I don't even know what I'm looking for. Fingerprints? A message scrawled on the mirror in steam? Blood?

Something to prove I'm not crazy. Or something to confirm I am.

Everything feels like a lie. Every memory feels warped, but I don't trust a single thing—not the lock, not my instincts, and definitely not the people around me. Well except for Sarah.

Unfortunately life doesn't stop just because you're spiraling. If I don't get my ass in gear, I'll be late to the one place I actually feel safe.

I'm halfway through my granola bar when my phone buzzes again. *'I'm tired of this, grandpa!'*

My blood runs cold before I even unlock it, and I can feel it in my body, that hum of dread. I'm not even going to open it, but when I glance down I see what it says.

> Unknown : You think this is a fucking joke?

It slams into me harder than I expect, because I thought I was taking my power back. I thought the message I sent this morning made me untouchable—like maybe I had a little bit of control after all.

I refuse to let whoever this is know they got to me. I won't give them that satisfaction. Not now. Not ever. I lock the screen, dropping the phone face-down on the bench beside me, and pretend like my hands aren't still trembling.

I can hear Sloane laughing faintly from the front desk. Somewhere in the distance, someone wheels a cart across the tile. The library is humming with normalcy, but I'm frozen in the back room, drowning in static.

It buzzes again and I stare at it like it might explode. It's a stupid rectangle of glass and metal, and yet I'd rather be holding a grenade.

I reach for it with two fingers and flip it over. One new message. I know I should just ignore it, but I don't because I clearly hate myself. I really might need to just change my number at this point.

> Unknown: I'll fucking know if you let anyone touch what's mine.

The words slide straight down my spine. I stare at the screen, rereading them like they might shift into something less loaded. How can one random person cause this much stress?

The only person I know who talks like that is Steven. He's always had that edge, but this feels a little too unhinged to be Steven. *Right?*

Even when he was screwing with me, he never sounded this... unstable. *Ugh. I don't know anymore.*

My phone buzzes again with another message, and I almost drop my phone. No matter how many times I tell myself I'm not affected, it's starting to get to me. What if he found me?

> Unknown : If you think I don't know where you are at all times, you're not half as smart as you pretend to be...

A cold sweat breaks across my whole body, and I can't breathe.

I glance at the window, the door, at every corner of this goddamn room like maybe there's a camera pointed at my face, waiting for my reaction. I can't tell if I'm being watched or if my brain is breaking apart from the inside out.

I should call Sarah, or report it. But what would I even say? If it's not Steven—then who the hell is it? *Some part of me wishes it was Steven. And that thought scares me.*

I don't reply or throw the phone across the room, even though I want to. I just put it on silent and lock it again, shoving it into my pocket, then force my body to move. If I sit here for another second, I might drown in the static pouring through my brain.

I need to get up. Get over it. And get back to fucking work.

I repeat it like it's my daily mantra, grabbing a cart full of returns and shoving through the door like I've got somewhere to be.

I'm halfway through the third shelf when Sloane rounds the corner like a cat—probably holding a crystal in one hand and a coffee in the other. She watches me restack a few hardcovers, hopefully not noticing I've been holding them upside-down for the last five minutes. I really need to get my shit together.

"I'm fine," I say flatly.

She never wastes time with pleasantries. If she's quiet, she's reading me. Waiting for the best spot to dig her claws in and pull the truth out.

"Didn't ask," she says finally.

I slap another book into place like it owes me money, then instantly feel guilty about it.

"Good. Let's keep it that way."

"Mm." She crosses her arms and leans against the end of the shelf like she has all goddamn day. "You're spiraling."

I shoot her a look. "Wow. Did you get that from my aura, or the fact that I just shelved Hunger Games in nonfiction?"

She doesn't even smile. Tough crowd. "Ani, talk to me."

"No."

"Why not?"

"Because I don't want to, Sloane."

"That's not a reason. That's a defense mechanism."

I exhale sharply, ready to fire something snarky back—but I stop. Because suddenly my throat feels too tight, and my hands are shaking again.

She sees it too and her expression softens a little. So I give her something, because if I don't, I might actually scream. "Someone broke into my apartment. I think."

Her eyes lock on mine. "When?"

"Last night."

She waits for me to keep going.

"I got home, and everything looked normal, but then when I woke up, I could tell something was off. My..." I hesitate. "I'm pretty sure my underwear was gone and there was a card."

"A card?"

"Well, it was blank." My voice goes flat. "It was just... sitting there. I don't know. I don't remember it being there before, and I know it's not mine."

She freezes for a split second, but I catch the way her fingers pause mid-air, the slight narrowing of her eyes. Then it's gone. "So you found a blank piece of paper and probably did laundry?"

"That's not all," I mutter, "I'm getting texts."

I feel her body shift beside me. "What kind of texts?"

I slide a book into place. "The kind that makes your stomach crawl and your skin want to peel off."

"Do you know who it is?"

I pause, my hand hovering over the next book. "I thought I did," I admit. "Now I'm not so sure."

Sloane doesn't push. She's smart enough not to.

I glance sideways at her. "Don't say anything helpful or validating. I'm dangerously close to having a breakdown, and I'm still on the clock."

"I was going to say you look like shit."

That earns a small, humorless laugh from me. "Thanks?"

She's quiet again. "You need to be careful."

"Yeah. That's kind of the theme lately."

"I'm serious, Ani. Do you want to come stay at my house?"

"No."

I didn't mean it to come out that fast, but she just nods, brushing invisible lint from her sleeve, and says, "If you change your mind, I'm here."

Then she walks away like she didn't just pull a confession out of me with nothing but eye contact and a steady voice. I stare at the empty space she left behind, then slam the last book onto the shelf.

I'm not okay.

I know it. She knows it. And now the truth is sitting in the pit of my stomach like something rotten and I want to throw up.

I grab the cart, pushing it toward the end of the aisle, and detour straight to the break room like the shelves might collapse on top of me. The staff room is empty—thank God—and I sink into the hard plastic chair in the corner before my knees decide to give out.

I can still feel the words from the last text humming under my skin like a second heartbeat. *Touch what's mine.* It sounds a lot like something Steven would say, and I keep wanting it to be him. Because the alternative—that it's someone else entirely—terrifies me more than I want to admit.

Goddamn it.

One new message. Unknown number. *UGH!*

I open it and freeze. It's a photo. It's pretty blurry and grainy, but it's a photo of me, sitting on a couch with a couple other people I don't recognize. There's a man next to me—but his face is turned, half out of frame with a hand resting on my thigh.

My stomach drops straight through the floor because I don't remember this. I don't remember any of this. That kind of looks like my stupid ex, but I still don't remember this.

I zoom in, but it only makes it worse. My dress is wrinkled and my makeup's smeared.

Something's wrong with me.

The air punches out of my lungs and everything tilts. I think I'm going to throw up right here, in the middle of the break room.

Panic slams into me, fast and merciless, curling tight around my ribs like it's got claws.

What the fuck was that photo?

My fingers are shaking so bad I almost drop my phone, but I manage to hit the lock screen like that's going to stop the image from burrowing deeper inside me—behind my eyes, and in my veins. I can't unsee it.

Why the hell can't I remember?

My body can't decide what it's doing—my skin's cold, my blood's on fire, and my heart is jackhammering like it's trying to escape through my spine.

If I tell Sarah, she'll tell me to go to the cops. She'll tell me to file something official, and I can't. Not when I don't even know what I'd be filing. Not when I don't want to get into any personal details about what happened and why I'd be worried about the messages I keep getting.

The second they run my name, who knows what they'll find. Not to mention I don't want anyone finding me.

I'm very much aware that's how this works. You report a crime, and the system calls your monsters to come verify it.

So, no. I can't tell Sarah. Not yet. Maybe I'm over reacting. If it was that bad, I would tell her.

I chew the inside of my cheek until I taste metal. I'm spiraling now, and the only name in my mind is the last one that should be there, but it is.

He's the only other person who feels familiar, even though he might be a walking red flag wrapped in barbed wire and bad intentions, and I don't know what that says about me.

My thumb hovers, but the silence is pressing in like a body bag, and I don't want to be alone.

Me: Hey. You around?

I regret it the second it sends, but thirty seconds later, he replies.

Frank : Of course. Everything okay??

My throat tightens, because no. Nothing's okay.

Me: Just… having a day. Can I call?

Frank : I'll be free in ten. Hang in there, Doll.

I close my eyes and lean my head back against the wall, with my phone still clutched so tight in my hand my knuckles ache. Whoever's texting me just lit a match and I'm standing in gasoline.

It takes everything in me not to check the photo again. Not to zoom in and dissect every shadow, and every angle.

Frank : Still in a meeting. Give me a few?

I exhale. Not relief, exactly, but something less awful. At least I know he'll always respond, and that he'll always show up...even when I don't want him to.

Me: Yeah. It's fine. I'm actually feeling better.

Frank : Bad day? Or did something happen?

I chew the inside of my cheek, while my fingers hover over the screen. I should tell him. Maybe he'll say something useful. He seems like the kinda guy who might actually do something about it, if I needed him to.

Fuck, I don't know.

I don't know what the fuck I'm doing, or who the hell is messing with me, or how deep this rabbit hole goes—only that it's starting to feel like I've stepped into something I can't charm or claw my way out of.

Frank : I'll call you in five. Don't go anywhere.

I blink back the sting in my eyes and set the phone down carefully on the table like it's glass and wait. Five minutes stretch into seven. That turns into twenty and I start to wonder if he forgot, or maybe I imagined the concern. Then the screen lights up with an incoming call, I answer on the first ring.

"Hey," I say, barely above a whisper.

"Hi, sweetheart."

He says it like I'm the only thing he wants to hear today, but he always turns on the charm when he's talking to me.

"I'm sorry I made you wait," he adds. "Are you okay?"

"Yeah. I mean, no, but yeah. I'm fine."

"Right." I can hear the smile in his voice. "Can you tell me what happened?"

I sigh. *Well, here goes nothing.* "I just got sent a photo, but I don't remember it being taken."

His voice drops. "Oh, that's it? Do you want me to look into it?"

I blink. "Do you know how to do something like that?"

"Ani." There's something sharper under his tone now. "I'd do a hell of a lot more than that if someone's fucking with you. Just send me the photo."

The silence stretches. And then he quietly says, "I've got you."

Just when I wasn't sure if I was about to fall or jump, my throat tightens, but I don't say anything for a second.

"It's not a big deal," I murmur.

"I'll look into it."

I let out a breath I didn't realize I'd been holding. My eyes are still locked on the far wall, hoping it will keep me from unraveling.

"I'll be there at six," he says, calmly. "We'll figure it out. Together."

"Okay."

There's a beat of silence that's just long enough for the air to tighten and my pulse to pick up again.

"Do you trust me?" he asks.

The question cuts a little deeper than I expect it to.

I don't know. Do I?

"I think…"

That's all I can give him right now, and maybe it's more than I should.

"That's a start."

THE SECOND I STEP OUT OF THE LIBRARY, I SEE HIS CAR parked by the curb.

I cross the sidewalk slowly, one foot in front of the other with my bag slung over my shoulder. Every step drags, and I swear I can still feel the weight of that photo, burned into my brain like a brand.

He gets out before I even reach the passenger side, and waits by my door. All charm and polished—even I can admit he's a good looking man. I'm just not sure if I feel anything else.

"Hey, Doll."

He opens the door, and I slide in without a word. The leather seats are already warm and it smells like wealth and cologne.

"Rough day?"

I let out a short, brittle laugh. "Something like that."

It's always something like that, because if I say the truth out loud—what then? Someone slipped into my apartment, and left a note. Only the note was blank. Or maybe I could say the past is starting to feel less like a blur and more like a noose? No, I can't say any of that without sounding like I'm crazy.

He pulls away from the curb with one hand on the wheel, and the other on the armrest. Every part of him screams control.

"You wanna skip your shift at the bar?"

His tone is casual, but I can tell he doesn't want me to go. "I can call and tell them you're not coming."

I shake my head. "Can't afford it."

"I'll cover it."

Of course he'd say that. Because that's what men like him do, they throw money at the cracks and pretend it's glue.

"I can't afford that either," I mutter.

His jaw tics—barely—but he doesn't push.

"I just don't like the idea of you being alone," he says after a pause, like it costs him something to admit it. "Not after you told me that someone is practically stalking you."

Well I didn't exactly say I had a stalker. I don't look at him, instead I just let my eyes blur out the window as the streetlights smear past. What am I supposed to say? *Actually, I don't remember enough to know what the fuck's even going on.*

And, oh yeah, the only thing I'm sure of is the ache in my stomach every time my phone buzzes and I don't know if it's going to be a meme from Sarah or a death threat.

"You don't have to protect me," I say instead. "And I highly doubt it's a stalker."

Even if every part of me feels like it is, and he's probably right.

He snorts. "Sure I do. You're mine."

I am not going to even justify that with a response, so I just keep staring forward like he didn't just say that. God, what is it with men and claiming things they don't even understand?

The silence stretches between us, but he drops it, probably thinking my non answer is a confirmation. *Great.* Before I can correct him he interrupts.

"I have to leave for a bit."

I blink, turning my head, but his profile is carved in shadows, all clean lines and impossible calm.

"Where?"

"Work trip. I'll only be gone for a few weeks. I'm headed to the East coast."

Three weeks without him watching me and asking me out every day. Maybe that would be nice, but what if something happens when he's gone?

"I want you to come with me."

The words hit me like a left hook. *What the fuck?* I turn to him slowly, blinking like I must've heard him wrong.

"What?"

He doesn't flinch, if anything, he leans in, keeping his voice soft, like I'm a skittish horse.

"Just think about it," he says quickly, already laying the pitch out like a travel brochure. "It's not a big deal. I'll be working most of the time, but the place has a spa, private suites—you'd be safe, and out of the city. No more looking over your shoulder. You can just relax."

Safe.

God, men love using that word when they're the ones holding the key. I blink again, because I'm trying really fucking hard not to laugh. Or scream. Or throw the car door open and walk into traffic.

"Frank, I can't just leave for three weeks."

"Why not?"

Why not? Like my entire life isn't one missed shift away from collapse.

"Some of us have this thing called a job," I mutter.

He waves a hand like I'm the one being dramatic. "I'll pay whatever you'd lose. Call it a mental health break."

Yeah, I think. *Because nothing says healing like being trapped in a luxury suite with the one man I'm not sure I can trust.*

I shake my head. "I can't."

"Why not?"

This time his voice dips lower, and it's not a question anymore, it's a challenge.

I hesitate, because the truth is—I don't have a real reason. Not one I can say out loud anyway. Just a gut feeling that this isn't right. That going anywhere with him feels like handing over the last pieces of myself before I even know what they are. It wouldn't be fair to him if I jumped into this.

"I just... can't." I say finally. I should probably figure out how I feel before I tell him this isn't going anywhere.

He exhales hard through his nose. "You shouldn't be staying at your place," he says instead, flicking the turn signal as we merge onto another street.

"It's not safe. You know that."

"I changed the locks."

"Locks don't stop people who already know how to get in."

What's that supposed to mean? For the first time in minutes, I wonder who he's really trying to protect me from.

I glance at him, feeling a little unsettled. And yeah—a part of me can't help but wonder if maybe he's right, maybe being away would be safer.

But three weeks? With Frank?

There's no way in hell he'd keep his hands to himself and I'm not about to spend half a month dodging his idea of comfort while trying not to spiral into another situation I can't claw out of.

Yeah... no.

God, I think I'd rather take my chances with a stalker.

That thought alone slams the door shut. I'm not ready for that. And I'm definitely not ready for *him* like that.

"You want to pretend everything's fine, that's your choice. But when I get back from this trip, I want you out of that apartment."

My head whips toward him.

"Excuse me?"

"I'll help you find something safer. Something in your budget. I know a guy."

"Frank—"

"It's not up for debate."

The way he says it makes something deep in my gut twist hard. *Umm...*

"I'm not a problem you need to fix."

"You're not a problem," he says as we pull up to the curb. "I take very good care of what's mine."

He leans over and kisses my cheek like he's claiming the win. "I'll text you when I land."

16

"SILENCE WILL GET YOU FURTHER THAN SYMPATHY."
(ESPECIALLY WHEN THEY EXPECT BOTH)

Ani

Some nights, it hits the second I walk in. That itch under my skin feels like if one more thing goes wrong, I'm flipping a table and setting the bar on fire.

Tonight's one of those nights.

The second I step through the back door and into the low thrum of beer-slick floors and neon haze, I know I should've called in sick. But I didn't, because I'm a responsible adult with rage issues and poor coping skills. *And bills.*

Sarah's already mid-shout, barking orders at a guy who looks like he's two seconds from quitting. "Don't just stand there, mop it up before someone dies."

Another tray crashes near the pool tables and I flinch like it was aimed at me. My shift hasn't even started and I'm two minutes from an assault.

I shove past two regulars glued to the bar like barnacles, snatch a semi-clean towel, and start scrubbing the counter with enough force to take the finish off. If it had feelings, it'd file a restraining order

Sarah glances over from the taps with one brow raised. "You good, or are we about to have another bar fight?"

I don't look up. "I'm not not about to stab someone."

275

She smirks like she's proud of me. "There's my girl."

I keep wiping, trying not to spiral, but the walls feel too close, and my skin feels too tight. And I swear the ceiling's breathing down my neck. On the bright side, my tip jar's filling up, probably because I look like I'd bite someone if they touched me. Men are disgusting like that—mistaking venom for foreplay.

And then I see him. Sitting there in a black shirt, and built like sin, with that same unreadable face that makes you want to scream or sob, depending on the hour. He's just sitting there smirking at his phone.

I want to punch him. Maybe that's the feeling in my chest that lights the hell up the second I see him.

It has to be him. He has to be the one fucking with me. If it's not him, then I've officially lost my mind. And honestly, maybe that would be easier. Before I can think better of it, I'm across the bar.

"What the hell is your problem?" I hiss, slamming my palms flat on the counter like it's the only thing keeping me from launching across it.

"You're going to have to be more specific, dear."

Dear?

The way he says it is laced with condescension and it hits like a hot iron to the spine. I want to slap the smirk right off his face, then claw it off with my teeth.

My pulse is screaming, and my brain's glitching. All I can do is stare at him like I'm the only one who forgot we're not friends.

He looks like every bad decision I've ever fantasized about, poured into one perfect, infuriating man. God. Even his veins look like they could wreck me. My mind goes right to images of his big hands, and all the places I'd like them...

I snap. "You seriously have nothing better to do than play stalker on your off days?"

"If I wanted to watch you," he says, keeping voice low, "you wouldn't be standing here to ask me about it."

That voice—Jesus. It slides over my skin like smoke and settles between my legs like it pays rent. I hate how fast it happens too. How my body reacts like it's his problem to solve. Wait, what did he just say?

I blink, trying to keep my spine straight. "Was that supposed to scare me?"

"It's supposed to make you think."

"I'm not here for philosophy," I bite. "I'm here because you don't know how to stay the fuck out of my life."

He stares at me and the look in his eyes is lethal. "You think it's me."

It's not a question.

"Don't act like it's a reach," I say. "You've shown up out of nowhere. You've been in places I'm at. You've been circling me since day one like—like you're waiting for something."

There's that fucking smile again. I wish I wasn't paying such close attention to him, and wouldn't notice the way his shirt clings to every cut line of his chest. Or the way he smells—like cedar and violence. I also wish my thighs weren't currently pressed together right now.

"That's cute," he murmurs, eyes gleaming. "You think this is about you."

My jaw tightens.

"It's always going to be about me when I'm the one being followed."

His gaze sharpens. "You sure I'm the one following?"

I step in, close enough to feel the heat coming off him. My heart's pounding like a threat against my ribs, and it's getting harder to tell if I want to hit him or kiss him.

"Then what the hell are you doing here?"

He leans in, just enough to steal the air between us. "Watching."

"Why?"

His voice drops. "Because someone needs to."

I blink. That wasn't the answer I expected. But it's not a denial either. My pulse stumbles—just a beat—but I recover. *What's that supposed to mean?*

"Who else would send that photo?" I hiss. "Who else knows where I live? What I wear? Who I'm with?"

Something flickers behind his eyes. And for the first time, I think—fuck—maybe I'm actually onto something here. He straightens slowly, and it's fucking lethal because he towers over me.

"Must be someone close, then," his tone is smooth, but there's something behind it. "Someone you let in."

My jaw clamps shut. That lands too hard and way too close to the truth I don't want to admit. He's saying it like it's my fault someone crawled through the cracks and started pulling threads. *This is what I get for letting anyone in at all.*

I bite the inside of my cheek. Hard. Well, he can fuck right off. This isn't my fault.

"I didn't let anyone in," I snap. "They just... found a way."

He studies me in silence. It's the kind of still that says he's cataloguing every word I've ever said and storing it for later. Every fucking blink feels like a risk with him.

"So, because I look at you, and know what I'd do if I had you," he says, "you think I'm...?"

The air leaves my lungs in a rush. I try to recover but I fumble—my whole nervous system flares like it's on fire and he's the one holding the match. My skin is too tight and my throat is now too dry. Suddenly I'm back to picturing what he's capable of...in bed. *God, Ani, not now.*

"You don't even know me," I manage, though it sounds more like a dare than a defense.

"Don't I?"

His voice drops another octave, and my insides do that awful traitorous thing where they clench in all the wrong places.

"I know what perfume you wear when you want to be noticed. I know you chew the inside of your cheek when you're lying. I know you went on a date with a man who doesn't deserve to breathe your air—and I know you're still wearing the necklace he gave you like it means something."

My hand flies to my throat like a reflex. Fuck. Fuck. Fuck.

His mouth twitches.

"You do realize that made you sound exactly like a stalker, right?"

His smile is slow. "No. That's called paying attention, dear."

I roll my eyes so hard I almost see God, but it's just a cover. He leans in—elbows on the bar like he owns it—and his voice slithers under my skin.

"You were biting your nails when you thought no one was watching. But only when someone ordered gin. You hate gin. And the guy who orders it? Regular. You don't like him."

I blink. My pulse stutters. *What the hell is this, Dr. Phil?* But he's not done.

"You've checked your phone three times since I got here, but you haven't responded to anything. Which means you're dodging someone."

The silence between us locks up and all I can think is, he's been watching me longer than I even realized. *Maybe he is the stalker.* He leans back like nothing out of the ordinary just happened and he didn't just dissect me with surgical precision.

"That," he says smoothly, "is called observation. Not stalking."

My jaw tightens and heat crawls up my neck before I can shove it down. I hate that he's right about those things, and I really fucking hate that my pussy, for some deranged reason, loved every second of that like it was some kind of mating ritual.

Like yes, Daddy, thank you for noticing I flinch at gin orders.

I hate even more, that he sees things I didn't even know I was doing.

"I've got customers," I mutter, spinning on my heel.

I don't wait for a response before I shove through the swing gate and back to the taps, nearly elbowing some frat bro who smells like Axe and daddy issues.

"Two more whiskeys!" someone yells from table six.

"Then get off your ass and come get them," I snap.

He laughs like I'm joking. I'm not.

Sarah throws me a look, but I ignore it. My hands move on autopilot, but my head's somewhere else. If it's not Steven sending those texts...if it's not him who broke into my apartment and left that card...then who the hell is?

My stomach coils.

I should've gone with Frank.

I should've said yes, even though it would mean letting him play bodyguard in some overpriced hotel suite. Instead I'm here— still being watched and toyed with. I'm now questioning my own sanity instead of a man I should hate.

Steven might be dangerous, but if it's not him, and I was wrong, that means someone else out there is worse—and I don't know who they are or what the hell they want.

I wipe down the last sticky table and glance back toward the end of the bar, and yup, he's still there.

God, I hate him.

And goddamn it, he's hot.

I swipe a hand through my hair, muttering something under my breath I wouldn't want anyone to hear, and storm over like I'm not currently burning alive in my own skin.

He watches me approach—like I'm the only thing in the room worth watching and I slap my hand on the bar in front of him.

"You know, I've got a genius idea."

He lifts a brow. "Dangerous words coming from you."

"I want your phone."

He doesn't blink. "Oh, this should be good."

"You heard me." I lean in. "Unlock it. Give it to me."

He stays perfectly still. That mouth of his twitches like he might laugh—and I hate that part of me wants to know what he tastes like.

"You planning on finding something that will make you hate me? That's cute."

"I'm planning on calling myself," I bite. "From your phone. So I know once and for all if you're the one who's been texting me."

He leans back and looks more entertained than anything as he folds his arms across his chest. The way his shirt pulls tight over his biceps makes me want to drop to my knees and find out if he tastes as dangerous as he looks. *Fuck my life.*

Focus.

"So what," he says lazily, "you're just gonna cross-examine every guy who turns you on until one of them blinks?"

I should slap him. Or myself. One of us needs it.

"You're not that special."

He shrugs, smug as hell. "That makes one of us."

God, I hate him and the way his voice gets under my skin. *And between my legs. Ugh.*

"You realize this is more stalker behavior, right?" I try to sound pissed, but it comes out needy. "The shit you say, the—"

"Watching isn't stalking," he says smoothly. "We've been over this."

"Sounds like exactly what a stalker would say."

He chuckles. "And yet here you are, asking for my number."

My eyes narrow, and I'm seriously debating punching him. "I'm not asking for it. I'm verifying it."

"Right," he drawls. "Totally different."

Without blinking—he holds the phone out between us, with the screen already unlocked.

"Well?" his voice dips just enough to drag across my skin. "Go ahead. Call yourself."

I snatch it from his hand before I can second-guess myself. The phone is warm—still carrying the heat of his body—and the thought that hits me next is so uninvited, so stupidly feral, I nearly drop the thing.

It was just in his pocket.

Right next to—

No.

Absolutely not.

This is not the moment for a mental detour into dick territory. This is not the time to wonder how low that waistband sits, or if he's one of those guys who goes commando just to ruin lives. Or how big he is.

This is a who-the-fuck-is-threatening-me moment. A real-life danger moment.

Not a let's-imagine-what-he's-working-with-under-his-clothes moment.

I need therapy or celibacy. Or maybe a baseball bat and a rage room. Maybe all three.

I type in my number, and my fingers are sweaty. This is stupid. This is so fucking stupid. I have no idea why I'm so nervous.

I press call, and my phone—still face-down under the bar—starts to buzz.

I stare at it, flipping it over, and sure enough… it's not the one that's been haunting my screen.

My stomach dips, but I hang up and check the recent calls again just to be sure. It's not him and somehow, that's worse. Because that means someone else knows where I sleep, what I wear, and who I'm with. And I have no fucking clue who they are.

Which also means, I don't know what the hell I'm dealing with.

Steven hasn't moved. He just watches me with his arms folded, and those stupid unreadable eyes, like he's letting me choke on the weight of my own doubt. And suddenly, I feel stupid. Embarrassed.

"See?" he says, maddeningly calm. "Not me."

I hand the phone back without meeting his eyes, keeping my jaw locked tight. "You could have another number."

He takes it, totally unbothered. "I could. But if I wanted to scare you, Ani..." He leans forward, and his voice—God—his voice dips low and brushes the shell of my ear like a fucking confession. "I wouldn't use a burner. I'd show up. You'd know I was there because you'd be able to feel me."

My breath stutters.

Not because of what he says, but because I believe him.

Every word lands like a promise. No hesitation. No bluff. Just cold, hard certainty delivered in a voice built for temptation. *And it just turns me on more. I'm so fucked.*

"I don't play games," he murmurs. "I take what I want."

I laugh, sort of, but it comes out too high.

"Then maybe you should leave," I say tightly, "before you take something that isn't yours."

But my voice doesn't carry the punch I want it to. His eyes have already dropped—straight to my mouth—and I know that look. I've felt that look. That look knows things it shouldn't, like what I taste like when I forget myself, and what kind of sounds I make when I break.

He leans in just enough for the heat of him to skate across my skin— he smells like cedar and leather and whatever the hell lives between a loaded weapon and a fuck-you grin.

It's a scent I've already memorized and it's not helping the situation.

"I'd be careful if I were you." And just like that, he straightens to his full height.

Holy fuck.

I stare up at him and swear I can feel my common sense leaving the building like it's clocking out early to save itself.

My pulse is Wrecked.

My spine, Liquid.

And my dignity is holding on by a goddamn thread.

"I don't share," his voice is barely above a whisper, but it lands like a promise. "And I don't forget when something's mine."

Jesus.

How is my body this stupid? He opens his mouth and suddenly my ovaries are planning a hostile takeover. I step back because I have to. If I stay that close to him for any longer, I'll either hit him... or let him wreck me.

And knowing me, it'll be both. In that order. Then I'll probably want to hit him again. Just for making me feel this way.

"Newsflash," I breathe, trying to sound sharp. "I'm not yours."

That smile he gives me, nearly drops me to my knees. God, help me. That smile has no business looking that good on a man who talks like that and smells like sex and secrets.

"Not yet."

"I think you should go," I say, turning around because I'm too fucking overwhelmed to keep standing this close without combusting.

I toss a rag into the bucket and wash my hands at the sink, staring at myself in the mirror over the bar. I look tired. Not just end-of-shift tired—but trust-nobody, running-on-paranoia tired. My makeup's smudged, my hair's limp from sweat and stress, and my eyes...they look like they're waiting for something to go wrong. I dry my hands and grab my phone, seeing the text from earlier I never looked at.

You know what, fuck this. I'm going to block whoever the fuck this is.

My blood goes cold and somehow, it's worse than a threat—because whoever this is doesn't just want to scare me, they think they know me.

I block the number and shove the phone deep into my bag like that'll do something. *Like it won't still be there, waiting to gut me the second I look again.*

I know walking home right now is probably not one of my

brightest ideas. It's the kind of dumb-bitch decision that gets you turned into a headline, but it's late—or early, I guess—and the idea of standing under the bar's flickering lights waiting for a ride just sounds worse. I need to get as far away from him as possible.

I need air.

I told Frank I was fine, and I believed it when I said it, but now, out here on the sidewalk with nothing but the buzz of dying street-lamps and the occasional hiss of tires against wet pavement...I'm not so sure anymore.

There's no one around, and the only thing I can hear is my own footsteps and the sound of my breath trying not to turn jagged. My keys are laced between my fingers, poking out like dull little teeth. I don't know what I'd do if someone actually came at me—but at least I'd go down swinging.

I pass the corner where the street lights are always flickering and swear I feel someone watching me, but I don't turn around. Turning around means I think there's something there, and I'm not playing that game.

By the time I get to my apartment, I'm fumbling with my keys when my phone buzzes again.

> Franks : Leaving town early. Final offer—
> come with me. I'll keep you safe.

For a split second... I heavily consider it. I want to disappear. I want to feel safe. I want to stop thinking about shadows and text messages and cards left in my bedroom, but I know what going with Frank means.

> Me : I can't.

17

"Let them believe it's their idea."
(That's how you make them stay)

Ani

I officially have the next two weeks off work, which feels borderline illegal considering I haven't had a single day off since I moved here. I know I should use the time to figure some shit out—start looking at places, make a plan—but it's late, and I just got home from a double. My brain's mush.

I'll deal with it in the morning.

But the second I shut the door behind me, I know something's wrong. There's nothing louder than silence when you know you're not alone.

It's not obvious—no broken window, no door ajar, no horror-movie shadow in the hallway. But the air...is off.

I lock the deadbolt, then check it again just to be sure, and my fingers hover on the chain for a second too long, like that flimsy little piece of metal could hold back whatever's pressing against the edge of my sanity.

The lights flip on like normal, everything looks the same.

Mostly.

I drop my keys in the bowl, kicking off my boots—and freeze. The counter is too clean. Something is missing. I can't put my finger on what it is right now, but I'm certain something's gone.

I shake the thought, but my body doesn't buy it. The hairs on my arms stand up anyway. That old, familiar static crackles at the back of my neck, warning me that something's off, even if my brain wants to rationalize it.

I start checking rooms, but everything looks untouched. Nothing screams break-in. Nothing feels obviously disturbed, so why won't my heart slow down?

I circle back to the couch, lowering myself slowly, keeping my eyes locked on the door like I'm waiting for it to explode open.

Eventually, I must fall asleep, because I wake up to someone screaming my name. My eyes fly open and my pulse slams into my throat.

I click the lamp on in a flash and it floods the room with light—but there's no one there. Just shadows and silence. Except something is off. I feel it, heavy and humming just beneath the surface of the quiet.

I look over to grab the blanket I threw over the back of the couch before I left—only it's not there anymore. No, it's folded into a perfect square, sitting on the cushion next to me like a calling card.

My stomach lurches. I didn't fold that. I haven't even touched it. At least—I don't remember touching it.

God, did I?

No, I didn't.

So either I'm losing my mind... or someone was here *and* they were careful enough not to wake me. Am I crazy? Maybe I did fold it?

I'm up in seconds, grabbing a knife, and checking the door like it might give me a straight answer, but it's still locked and the chain is still firmly in place. I move fast now, trying not to panic, checking the cabinets, the closets, and even under the bed.

I check behind the shower curtain—because yeah, that's not exactly how I want to die. Naked and blinded with shampoo in my eyes... but there's nothing.

That's the part that scares me most.

I grab my phone off the counter, yanking the charger out of the wall like it personally betrayed me, and I have two missed calls. One from Sarah and the other from Frank. There's also a message from him, but I can't open it because if it's sweet, I'll let myself believe him again. And if it's annoying, I'll throw the phone through the fucking window.

Neither option ends well.

My thumb hovers over Sarah's name, knowing she's fast asleep like a normal person, but I tap it anyway. It rings once, then goes straight to voicemail.

I guess when you're unraveling at two in the goddamn morning, the universe makes damn sure you're alone for it.

I stare at the screen.

Steven's number is there from when I called myself earlier. As if I needed a reminder that he's now tangled in this mess too.

My hands are shaking. I don't want to need him, and I really don't want to owe him, but I also don't want to sit here wondering if I'm about to be the next dateline episode. I still don't type anything, because what the hell would I even say?

Hey, I think someone rearranged my shit while I was unconscious and now I'm spiraling—can you come be scarier than my stalker, please?

He also could be lying about the stalker thing. Yeah, no.

He'd probably laugh, then say something smug, unbearable and, infuriatingly, right. And I don't know what's worse—being alone... or being alone with him.

I toss my phone onto the couch like it's his fault I feel like this.

"I'm fine," I mutter to myself. "We're fine."

My legs feel like they're moving without me as I push up off the cushions. I head for the bedroom like it's a battlefield instead of the one place that I should feel safe. The lights are still off, and everything looks the same. Boring, even. The kind of boring I'd sell my soul to believe in right now.

I cross the room and step into the bathroom like I'm trying to prove a point. Maybe if I just go through the motions of getting ready for bed—brush my teeth, wash my face—I can convince myself I'm being dramatic. That my brain's just playing trauma Mad Libs again.

I flip on the light—my toothbrush is gone. It's not on the sink, not in the cup where I always leave it, and not on the counter. It's not even on the floor.

I turn slowly, dread crawling up my spine like a spider, and freeze in the doorway. My toothbrush is on my pillow. Placed dead center like someone wanted me to find it there.

My stomach flips, then nosedives.

Is this some kind of sick fucking joke?

That's not just someone messing with me. That's someone in my space, in my bedroom, in my head. I take one step back, then another, bumping into the wall and I am now one thousand percent certain that someone was for sure in my fucking apartment. They stood in my bedroom, they touched my stuff, and I don't realize I've started crying until a tear hits my collarbone.

My body betrays me in the worst way—ripping through the armor I've spent years welding shut, breaking past every defense I swore was unshakable. My feet are flying across the floor as I rush back into the living room, grabbing my phone off the couch like it's the only thing keeping me upright, and this time...I don't hesitate.

I call Sarah and it goes straight to fucking voicemail, again. Figures. She's probably asleep, drooling on her pillow like a well-adjusted adult with no one breaking into her apartment to rearrange her toothbrush.

I don't leave a message because the only thing I'd say is, *Hey, if I end up on a true crime podcast tomorrow, you have full permission to use a hot photo of me for the thumbnail.*

Nope. Can't do it.

My thumb hovers over Steven's name again, and just his name alone makes something in my chest tighten, like I'm about to make a deal I won't come back from. I stare at it for a breath. Then two. Then three.

Calling feels like too much, so I type a message instead—because it's safer to ask for help in words I can still delete.

> Me: If this is you, you win. I'm freaked the fuck out. If it's not you, then you're the only bastard I know who can deal with someone worse. What do I do?

I hit send before I can second-guess myself, but the second my thumb leaves the screen, my knees buckle. I slide to the floor, keeping my back against the couch, and my heart pounds in a rhythm that doesn't even feel like mine.

This isn't just some twisted prank anymore. Maybe it never was.

I stare at the screen, willing it to light up. Waiting for those little dots to show up and save me from whatever the fuck this is. But there's nothing. Just black glass and the sound of my own breathing, ragged and uneven. Tears are sliding down my cheeks, and my breathing picks up.

Of course he's not answering, it's the middle of the night. I'm sitting here, folded into myself on the floor like a child with a nightmare, clutching my phone like it's a lifeline instead of the evidence that I'm losing it.

I open my phone again, just to make sure the message sent. The silence starts pressing in, and I curl my knees to my chest and try to breathe, but my lungs are paper. The edges of the room tilt or maybe that's me. I can't tell anymore.

God, I'm tired of feeling like this.

I try to think—really think. To make my brain slow down long enough to separate reality from paranoia, from exhaustion, from whatever the hell this is spiraling into, but calm won't come. The more I chase it, the faster it slips through my fingers like water I was never meant to hold.

And then—without warning—I'm hit with something I don't have a name for.

There's a white wall, and someone's yelling. Maybe my name. Maybe not. It's muffled, like I'm underwater.

I squeeze my eyes shut hard enough to see stars, like pressure might push it all back where it came from. But it's too late. The memory doesn't play like a movie. It shreds its way out—jagged and violent—ripping through me with too much sensation and not enough shape.

There's so many fucking hands. Gripping and pulling. My legs are on cold tile, sticking to the floor. I can feel my pulse hammering and my throat closes just thinking about it. There's pressure in my chest again and I know that feeling, I've felt it before. I felt it that night.

I hear a man's voice cut through the fog. It's accented and unfamiliar, but not completely. It doesn't belong in the scene I remember, but now it's there like it's always been part of the story. *"It's already done. She's his problem now."*

I lurch forward as acid creeps up my throat, sharp and sudden, and I clamp a hand over my mouth before I ruin the floor.

I count backwards...*Five. Four. Three. Two*—I can't even make it to one before the breath shoves itself back into my lungs.

The pieces are snapping into place. Not clearly, not even all at once, but they're slow, ugly, and crooked. I suddenly understand why that photo—the one I pretend didn't have an effect on me— made my skin crawl the second I saw it. It's because the truth is ugly and it's getting harder to ignore. It's not just that I don't remember being in that photo, it's that somewhere—buried beneath the walls I've built and the memories I swore I'd burned—I do remember.

I've always remembered, I just didn't let myself know it. Now that it's here—rising like smoke I can't un-breathe—it's too much. My throat tightens and my chest squeezes like someone's yanked all the air out of the room and my hands won't stop shaking. I try to count again—to breathe—something. But all I can hear is that voice. All I can feel is that weight pressing down on me again like it never really left.

My phone buzzes, loud and jarring in the stillness, and I flinch so hard I nearly drop it. My heart slams into my ribs like it's trying to crack them open.

> Steven: You're not that easy to break, Ani. Don't start acting like it now.

> Get your shit together. Breathe. I assume you know enough to keep the door locked until I get there?

> I'm coming, so try not to look like you need me when I get there.

I stare at the screen, and I can practically hear his voice in my head—laced with that dangerous tone that makes you forget how to blink. He probably didn't even think twice after sending it, either. Just fired it off like a command and expected me to obey.

My jaw clenches, because somehow, in the span of a few sentences, he managed to make me feel like I'm both losing control and back in it.

I hate that it worked, but the second I read those words, my pulse slowed just enough that my lungs remembered how to move. My thoughts—still racing and messy—are locked onto one thing like a goddamn anchor.

Him.

And now I'm stuck in this fucked-up space between panic and something else entirely, because if he were here, I don't know if I'd scream at him or climb him.

I close my eyes leaning back against the couch, letting his voice live in my head for a second longer than I should. The audacity. Part of me wouldn't be surprised if the second I unlock the door, he'll be on the other side with blood on his hands and a calm expression on his face, like violence is just another chore he checked off on the way over.

My fingers are already moving before I know what I'm doing.

> Ani: Thanks for the pep talk, Daddy…Next time just send a Hallmark card.

I hit send, then roll my eyes. If I'm going to be this unhinged, I might as well commit.The second it delivers, I blink at the screen and sit back as a slow, delayed *oh fuck* rolls through me like thunder after lightning.

Shit.

I just realized how he's probably going to take that. *This is why we can't have nice things, Ani.*

"Smooth," I mutter under my breath, dragging my hands down my face. "Fucking genius."

I drop my phone on the coffee table like it might catch fire if I hold it any longer. I don't need to know what he's going to say in response, because I already know he's going to make it a thing.

I suddenly find myself biting back a laugh. It's too much or maybe it's just enough, because the silence in this apartment still feels wrong. My toothbrush is still sitting on my pillow like a fucking threat with a smile, so yeah, I'll let him come.

I'll let him storm in with that voice like a blade and those eyes that see too much. But if he thinks I'm going to fall apart in his arms and thank him for it, he really doesn't know who he's dealing with.

I stand up a little too fast, and start pacing again. I decide to head into my room to do something that feels like control—I need to change my clothes, and fix my hair. If he's really coming, I want to look like I chose to survive tonight, not like I barely managed it.

I yank open my dresser drawer and catch myself in the mirror above it. I look like someone who's already unraveling and trying too hard to pretend she's not. Yet, somehow, I know the second he walks through that door, he's going to see it. He's going to see the fear I've been wearing like perfume and there's part of me that doesn't know whether to fight him or collapse into whatever twisted safety he's offering.

One second I'm thinking about Steven, and the next I'm drowning in that memory on the floor again with my back against the couch and my knees pulled to my chest like they might hold something in.

There's a shift in the air a moment before Steven opens the door, and steps inside like he was summoned. Dressed in black, with his jacket unzipped enough to frame the danger beneath it. He moves like he's not here to ask if there's danger, he's here to find it—and kill it quietly.

His gaze sweeps the room once, cutting through the silence like a blade. Then it lands on me, still curled up on the floor.

"Let's go."

The words barely land before my brain starts short-circuiting. Go? Go where? Why the fuck does he have a key to my apartment, and why aren't we talking about that first?

I don't move, I can't. My feet stay rooted to the floor—maybe if I stand still long enough, this will all stop feeling so real. A hundred questions pile up like a traffic jam.

Where are we going? Why now? What the actual hell is happening? I didn't actually realize until just now, that I never told him where I lived. As far as I knew, he thought my apartment was the next complex over.

None of that makes it out of my mouth because deep down—under the panic and the defiance I keep duct-taped to my ribs—I already know the answer. And of fucking course, part of me feels safer for it. Even though he insists he's not the one stalking me.

I grab my bag like it might tether me to something real—something normal. But my fingers are half-numb and my body's already moving, already choosing to survive before my brain has time to come up with a reason not to.

He doesn't even look at me, he just turns and starts walking assuming I'll follow. *He's not wrong. I'm not staying here.*

I get up and do exactly that, following behind him. Keeping my mouth shut, despite the questions piling up.

I step outside and shut the door behind me, locking it fast—like that'll help. Steven says nothing as I catch up, I don't ask where we're going because it doesn't matter. The cold night air bites at my skin as we walk, my heartbeat finally slowing enough to register the silence between us.

I don't know what the fuck is going on anymore, or who to trust, but I'll deal with the part where I still don't know if Steven's the villain or the getaway car later.

18

Ani

The car's still running and so is my panic. *And my fucking libido, apparently.*

He glances over his shoulder to make sure I'm still there, then gets in without a word—like he already knows I'll follow.

I'm still standing on the curb, thighs pressed tight, fully aware this might be the worst decision I've ever made. And I get in anyway, because I need to know what those hands feel like when they're not choking out monsters—but pinning me down instead.

The car smells like him. Leather, smoke, and something darker. Something that shouldn't make my stomach flip but absolutely does. I'm wet just thinking about it, which is a turn of events I wasn't anticipating. One look from him can destroy every defense I've built. I want to crawl out of my own skin or right into his lap.

He pulls out onto the road. No questions. No music. Just his hand gripping the wheel and his eyes locked on the road like there's nothing in the world that can shake him. Which is hilarious, considering I feel like I'm barely held together by willpower and Aquaphor right now.

I shift in my seat, trying not to look at him, which ends up being an epic fail. He's all sharp angles and silent fury, his jaw is tight enough to crack bone. One hand grips the wheel like it's a neck he's thinking about snapping, and I can't stop staring at the way his forearm flexes, causing his veins to pop out like a roadmap to a bad decision I'd crawl into headfirst.

He's pissed and somehow, that only makes it worse. Because I should be scared, or at least cautious—but all I can think about is what those hands would feel like wrapped around my thighs instead of the steering wheel. I clearly have an imagination problem where I'm constantly visualizing what those hands could do.

I open my mouth to say something, only to close it again, because what am I supposed to ask...Where are we going? Also? Still not over the part where you somehow have a key to my apartment. That's not creepy at all. And... you don't get to storm in like that and act like this isn't a whole new level of fucked up. Because I don't even know if this is damage control or the next disaster.

I don't ask any of it because I'm not even sure he would answer. Not the way I want him to. Instead, I stare out the window and force my breathing to stay even.

Goddamn him.

After a few more blocks, I finally get enough courage to speak. The silence was starting to feel like a second skin I can't peel off.

"Is this normal for you?" I ask quietly, not looking at him. "Picking up strays and driving them someplace like you're not even curious what the story is?"

His knuckles flex around the steering wheel and I swear, the air in the car tightens with him. He doesn't answer. Not right away. He just keeps driving, like he's letting the question hang long enough for me to choke on it. And it's working. I'm starting to question everything—my sanity, my instincts, the fact that I texted a man I barely trust and then followed him into the dark like it was normal. Maybe I am the problem here.

I'll deal with that later—when I can fucking breathe. *And when I know I'll live to see tomorrow.*

I don't know if it's the car, the night, or the man behind the wheel, but it feels like I'm suffocating without anyone touching me. My fingers dig into my thighs enough to feel something that reminds me I'm still alive.

When he finally speaks, his voice is low. "You think I do this often?"

I blink, turning my head toward him, unsure if I heard him right.

Yeah, well. You didn't have to come get me. The fucking audacity on this man, like I'm the one projecting.

My laugh is dry, "You're avoiding the question."

He glances at me, and the look he's giving me knocks the air out of my lungs without even touching me.

"Maybe," he says. "Or maybe I just think you're smart enough to figure it out."

God, I hate him.

I hate that I-see-right-through-you energy that makes me feel more naked than I've ever been. I open my mouth ready to snap something back, but once again the words don't come because the truth is—I don't want an answer.

Whatever this is—whatever he is—it doesn't come with explanations. It comes with tension, and silence, and a storm in the shape of a man who keeps showing up right when I'm about to break. *I just haven't decided if that's a coincidence*

I also hate that I feel safer with him than I do in my own fucking apartment, so I turn back to the window and let him drive.

"I can feel you thinking," I mutter, crossing my arms and leaning my forehead against the glass.

"I've got nothing to hide."

I bark a humorless laugh. "Oh, that's rich. Coming from the man who somehow got into my apartment and dragged me into the night without so much as a where-the-fuck-are-we-going."

"You didn't ask."

"You wouldn't have answered."

"That didn't stop you from following."

My head snaps toward him, heat flares under my skin like a fuse was lit. "I didn't exactly have a lot of options."

"You really think I didn't notice?" he says, keeping his voice low and calm. But it lands like he's twisting a knife, just to see how deep it'll go.

I glance over. "Notice what?"

"The way you flinch—and still don't pull away. The necklace you won't take off. The look you get when someone puts their hands on you."

My stomach drops.

What the fuck? That hits lower than I want to admit. I'm starting to think I shouldn't have called him.

"You don't know what the fuck you're talking about," I snap. But my voice sounds thinner than I want it to.

He lets out a quiet sound—half exhale, half something crueler. "I know enough."

"Fuck you," I whisper, but there's no power behind it.

His mouth tilts just slightly. "Not yet," he says.

My thighs clench before I can stop them, like my body's already imagining exactly what that would feel like. I swallow hard, and I can feel my breath getting more uneven, and I hate how fast I go from furious to needing something violent with his name on it.

"Jesus," I breathe. "Do you even hear yourself?"

He doesn't answer.

"You're pissed at me and I don't even know why." My voice sharpens. "You keep looking at me like I've done something I owe you an apology for, and honestly I'm sick of it."

Still nothing. And that pisses me off more than anything else.

"You think I wanted this?" I snap. "You think I like being watched? Followed? Having to ask for help from someone who looks at me like I'm about to ruin his whole week on purpose?"

He glances at me—just enough to catch the fury in my eyes, but not enough to flinch from it.

"You called me," he says.

"I didn't want to."

"But you did."

His words land like a slap I want to lean into and my jaw tightens and so do my thighs. Because underneath all the rage and deflection, there's a part of me—rotten and starving—that doesn't want safety or softness.

It wants him.

I can't even look at him right now without wondering how his body would feel wrapped around mine.

"No one forced you into the car."

My head whips toward him, pulse spiking. "Are you fucking serious right now?"

His jaw ticks. "You walked out that door. You followed me. So don't pretend you didn't choose this."

I want to scream. I want to tell him that choosing something doesn't make it safe. That needing someone doesn't make them good. That fear and desire—sometimes taste the same. One burns. The other cuts. But either way, you bleed.

But I don't say any of that.

My thighs are clenched so tight that I can feel the slick heat between them like a confession I didn't agree to give. And no matter how hard I pretend otherwise, some sick, wrecked part of me wants to see what he'll do if I keep pushing him.

I don't answer, because if I do, it's going to be a moan. So I keep looking out the window, pretending the trees are more interesting than the heat pooling in my core, and pretend I don't feel him watching me, cataloging every breath, every shift, and every goddamn betrayal of my body. Everything is happening so fast, and I think I'm going to be sick.

"Pull over," I say.

It's barely a whisper, but I watch as his knuckles flex on the wheel, knowing he heard me. He yanks the wheel hard and pulls us off the road, tires grinding against gravel until we're swallowed by trees and shadows.

The second the car stops, I'm out, slamming the door behind me like that'll shove the fire back where it belongs—in my chest, not between my legs.

I hear his door open, then shut. He just moves—all quiet fury and lethal calm—stalking toward me like I'm the prey stupid enough to come too close to the cage. I back up fast, but not fast enough. My spine hits the hood of the car—and I curse under my breath.

His hand lifts slowly and his fingers brush my jaw, tilting my chin up. "You don't give the orders," he murmurs. "But you're so damn good at begging without even realizing it."

My body's betraying me—wet heat pools between my thighs like he dragged it out of me just by breathing in my direction.

"I didn't beg," I snap, but my voice is shaking.

He smiles. "Not yet."

His fingers trail down the column of my throat, pausing right over my pulse. I'm practically panting as his thumb presses just enough to make me want more. My knees nearly buckle, and it's not from fear—it's the promise of losing control.

"Go ahead," he whispers. "Tell me to stop."

I can't. Because I don't want him to.

His hand slides lower, brushing the edge of my hoodie, daring me to stop him. "Tell me to go back to the car."

My fingers curl into the fabric at my sides, knowing I should do something. Instead, I arch toward him like a fucking masochist.

His other hand fists in my hair, yanking enough to make me gasp, exposing my throat.

"You won't say it," he growls. "Because you want this."

"I hate you," I hiss. I also hate that I don't want him to stop.

"Good." His voice is dangerous. Addictive.

He leans in, dragging his tongue up the line of my cheek. "Then you'll really hate what I do to you next."

His teeth catch the skin beneath my ear and I moan—loud and

feral—the sound echoes through the trees like it belongs to someone else. My nervous system is too shot to care right now.

One hand grips my throat, and the other slips under my hoodie, grabbing my waist, and yanking me against him. His thigh pushes between mine, and I grind down without even thinking. His voice rumbles against my skin, deadly and smug.

"You're going to crawl for it."

"Over your dead body," I whisper, already knowing it's a lie. I've thought about it more times than I care to admit.

"Then you're going to beg."

His words drip down my spine like sin, curling into the heat already pooling low in my stomach. My hips grind down again shamelessly before I can stop myself—searching for friction. Anything to anchor me in the chaos he created.

He pulls back just enough for the cold night air to hit the space where his thigh just was, and the absence punches through me like a punishment. I whimper as the heat of him vanishes and my skin misses it—aches for it—before my mind can even catch up.

Apparently the slight shift in my hips is all the permission he needed to tighten his grip around my throat.

"God, look at you," his voice sounds like gravel. "You can't even stop yourself."

My cheeks burn. But another slick wave of heat shoots between my legs. I bare my teeth. "Fuck you."

His lips brush mine, but he doesn't kiss me. And somehow, that ruins me more.

"You keep saying that like it's not already happening," he breathes.

Then he lets go, and I suck in a shaky breath like it might save me from drowning in him.

"You want it here?" he whispers. "Out in the fucking woods like a filthy little slut?"

My knees go soft, buckling under the weight of everything I'm feeling—shame, want, and the ugly ache of needing someone I'm supposed to hate. But I lock them down, forcing them to stay put.

"I'd rather choke on pine needles."

His smirk could kill a girl. "You already sound like you're choking."

He's barely touching me and I'm soaked. I wouldn't be surprised if there was a wet spot on his leg. My breath is wrecked. And my mind is static—white noise, heat, and him.

"Christ," he mutters. "I'll bet you're soaked through your panties, and I haven't even put my fingers inside you."

I flinch like he just slapped me, but don't move. I desperately want him to find out.

"You keep talking like you hate me," he adds. How his voice is calm, cruel, and devastatingly soft at the same time, I'll never know. "But your pussy's begging louder than your mouth ever could."

I snap my head up, feeling the fire in my chest and shame in my throat, but he's already walking back toward the car, tossing over his shoulder— "Get in the car, Ani."

He says it like he doesn't care if I do or not—which makes my blood boil. So I don't move. I stay planted right where he left me, arms crossed, and my thighs trembling.

He doesn't say a word, he just slams the car door and in three heartbeats, he's in front of me again—closer this time.

"You want to play games?" he says, eyes darkening. "Fine."

His hand shoots out, grabbing my hoodie again—and this time, he doesn't stop short. He shoves me back—hard—into the side of the car with a thud that knocks the breath out of me. His body follows, pressing into mine, so I have nowhere to go.

And fuck—he's hard.

That thick length grinds right against my core, and it's enough to make my thighs clench and my brain stutter. Oh God, I want him so bad.

"You want to be a brat?" he murmurs, sounding like he's

seconds away from losing control. "Then don't pretend you don't want me to wreck you on this fucking hood."

"I didn't ask for anything," I spit but my voice wobbles. Even I can hear how shaky it is. He drops his hand to my waist, and his fingers dig into my hips as he grinds against me and I moan.

I fucking moan.

He leans in, lips grazing my jaw. "No. You didn't."

His grip tightens, and he presses his cock harder against my cunt, and my body leans into him. "But your body's been begging since the second I picked you up."

I suck in a breath, and I can't move. I honestly don't want to, even if I could. He stays there for one long, pulsing beat. I'm unraveling by the second.

"Last chance," he whispers. "Get in the car."

He pulls back, and starts walking back to the car. "Or I bend you over it."

Every nerve in my body is screaming. I'm wet, wild, and desperately wanting to be wrecked and he knows it.

So I do the only thing that makes sense in the chaos flooding my chest. I move, but not toward the car. I spin on my heel and storm straight into the woods. All I can hear are the branches snapping beneath my boots as cold air claws at my skin.

I don't know where I'm going. I just know I can't breathe next to him. I can't think with his cock pressed against me and his voice in my ear, telling me what I should or shouldn't do.

"Ani."

I hear him yell, but I don't care. I keep walking.

"Don't you dare."

I ignore him—because if I stop now, I'll do something worse than run. I'll let him wreck me right here in the dark. And I won't even pretend to hate it.

So I go deeper into the trees while my heart pounds like a warning siren, each beat echoing in places I didn't give it permission to reach. My legs are shaking. My chest is tight and my skin still burns from the way he touched me.

His voice slices through the dark like a fucking blade. I spin, but I can't see him. Branches creak, and something shifts to my left. Where the hell is he? Where did he go?

"You done throwing your little tantrum?"

It comes from behind me, closer now. I spin around, but still don't see him.

"You think I'm gonna chase you down like some idiot with a savior complex?"

I can't breathe, I can't see, and God help me—I'm so fucking turned on, it's embarrassing.

My hands curl into fists, because if I don't do something, I'll come undone just from the sound of his voice in the dark.

"I didn't ask you to follow me!" I yell, spinning again. But it comes out breathless and wrecked.

"No," he snaps, closing the distance like a goddamn storm. His voice crashes through the trees behind me, and then suddenly—he's in front of me again.

"But you knew I would."

His hand grabs my chin, rough and claiming, tilting my face up until there's nowhere to look but him.

"You don't get to run from this," he growls. "Not when your thighs are shaking. Not when your cunt's still soaked. Not when you walked out that door because you wanted me to fucking take you."

I gasp—sharp and involuntary—because fuck him and his goddamn audacity. My brain's still scrambling for a comeback, something vicious and lethal, but my pulse is pounding in places that make it hard to think. He's right. I want him so fucking much, it's hard to think.

My pussy absolutely wants this, but before I can run or decide if I want to drop to my knees and make him earn it—he slams me back against the nearest tree. The bark bites through my clothes, and he's all heat and fury and sex, pressing into me like he wants to brand every inch of my skin with his name.

Then his hand catches both of mine and pins them above my head—hard.

I gasp again, but this time I'm not sure if it's fear or foreplay.

His other hand drags down my side, over the curve of my waist and suddenly I'm all too aware of his cock pressing between my thighs, grinding against my core, thick and hard and furious, like he's daring me to pretend I don't want it.

"You can hate me all you want," he growls. His voice sounds like smoke and hellfire against my ear. "You can run your mouth and throw your tantrums all you want, pretending you're still some good little girl."

His hips roll forward, grinding against me—and God—I moan. The way my body just fucking gives, like it's not even mine anymore is something I'll have to look into later.

"But I know what you are," he murmurs, dark and low. "You're a fucking slut."

I freeze.

That word cracks something open. Something I should recoil from—but don't. Because the way he says it sounds like a claim.

"A spoiled little whore."

It slides under my skin like it was always meant to live there. What the fuck does it say about me that I want him to say it again?

I'm sick.

Feral.

Whatever the word is for a girl who never stood a chance the second someone saw the monster in her and decided to worship it. That's me.

His hand drops between us, pressing hard, right where I'm soaked. A sharp, humiliating gasp leaves me.

"You're soaked for me, sweetheart and you know it."

And fuck me. I do.

I bite my lip so hard it stings. My head's spinning and no

amount of pressing my thighs together is going to save me. It only makes it worse. I can feel the wet fabric clinging to my skin, and I know he's right.

I roll my eyes. "Great. Add that to your list of delusions—right under the idea that I'd ever crawl for you."

He drags his mouth along the curve of my jaw. "You fight so pretty." He keeps his voice low. "You don't even know your cunt's begging to get used."

I gasp, a sharp, involuntary sound, and his grip on my wrists tightens just enough to make me ache even more than I already am. I try to relieve some of the tension by arching my back, but it just presses me into him more.

"You're not going to run again," he growls. "You're going to stand there, just like this, and remember exactly how fucking wet you got for me."

His free hand skims down my side, grazing my breasts. "But I'm not going to let you come," he adds. "Not until I say."

A whimper escapes my throat—humiliation, heat, and desperation. You name it, and I'm currently experiencing it. He's right, I'm a needy slut right now. All I can think about is getting off. I can't even think straight.

Then, just when I think I'm about to come undone—he lets go. Leaving me breathless and soaked with nothing but bark at my back and fire between my legs.

"Now, get in the car."

My panties are fucking ruined and I'm two seconds away from falling to my knees and begging.

His eyes narrow. "Now."

I stare at him. At his mouth. At the cock still hard beneath his jeans.

"God," I mutter, trying to keep my voice from cracking, "you're obsessed with hearing yourself talk."

His jaw ticks but he doesn't move.

Neither do I.

If I move first, he wins. If he moves, I don't trust myself not to crawl to him and make a bigger mess than I already am. So I do the only thing that gives me back any ounce of control—I shove past him.

My shoulder clips his—intentionally. Every step I take is tight and rigid, while I try to outpace the ache in my chest and the humiliation curdling in my gut.

I yank open the car door, throwing myself into the passenger seat, and slam it shut like I'm the one with the power here.

The engine growls to life, and gravel spits behind us like we're being chased. I cross my arms tight across my chest, fingers digging into skin that still feels too hot, but I stay quiet.

I stare out the window like it's a portal to another life. One where I still had dignity and my body didn't betray me every time he looked in my general direction.

At least I forgot about the whole someone broke into my apartment thing for a minute. So, there's that.

19

"Some rooms aren't meant to be entered."
(Especially if the door was already open.)

Ani

The road winds tighter the higher we climb, trees crowding in like they know where we're headed. When the car finally slows, gravel crunches beneath the tires, and my stomach does the kind of slow roll that usually comes with regret—or foreplay.

"You aren't taking me to a hotel?" I mutter under my breath.

Steven doesn't even look at me. "Do I look like someone who books hotel rooms?" he says. "If you wanted a hotel, you wouldn't have called me."

That shuts me up. This—him—was never going to be safe. It was never going to be soft. I guess in some way, he's not wrong about that either.

The car rolls to a stop, and for a second, neither of us moves. The house looms ahead, all stone and shadow.

He gets out and doesn't wait for me. By the time I slam my door and follow him up the stairs, he's already unlocking the front door and pushing it open.

Heat spills out and I hover in the doorway, pulse hammering.

He glances over his shoulder. "Inside."

I step in and close the door behind me, the soft click echoes like a decision I can't take back. He tosses his keys on the table and shrugs out of his jacket, but I don't move.

"Do you want me in the room I was in before?" I ask, pretending I didn't just come apart in the woods and still want him.

His mouth twitches into one of those half-smiles that never quite reaches his eyes.

"You're not here to sleep."

My breath stutters. "Excuse me?"

He turns then. Eyes dragging down the length of me—slow and unapologetic.

"You wanted safe?" His voice is low. "Then you should've called someone else."

I open my mouth—ready to say something to claw back some power—but he takes a step forward, and I back up on instinct.

He doesn't stop.

Another step. Then another. Until my spine hits the wall and the firelight dances over his face like it knows exactly what he came here to do. His hand braces beside my head. God, it's embarrassing how much I want to close the distance between us.

"I'm not going to be gentle," he says, deliberately. A warning and a promise wrapped in smoke.

My breath hitches.

"Then don't," I whisper. "Just get it over with."

His eyes flare.

"Not how this works."

Then he leans in, his mouth brushing my ear. "You don't get to come apart unless I let you."

His hand finds my throat again, like he knows I'll bolt if he doesn't hold me still.

"Take off your hoodie," he says.

I don't move and he smiles. Fuck me, that smile.

"Or I can always do it for you."

I freeze long enough to feel the weight of that quiet threat in his voice. It has no business turning me on the way it does. He steps forward, and for a second, I'm positive he's going to rip it off me. *Oh my God, yes. Please touch me again.*

That snaps me out of those thoughts real fast, and my fingers finally move. I slowly pull it off, despite how shaky my hands are. I'm doing my best to act like I'm unaffected while my skin is humming. His eyes track every inch I reveal like he's already undressing the rest.

When I shrug it off, his hand brushes mine—and fuck, I flinch like I've been lit on fire. That's what it feels like every time he touches me.

He takes it from me without a word and turns—walking upstairs like I didn't just short-circuit in his shadow.

What the hell just happened?

My legs still feel like Jell-O in a windstorm, and I'm just standing there in the glow of his fire like some confused hoe with my arms crossed like that's gonna hold me together. I shouldn't be this fucking wet for a man who talks to me like I'm some limited-time offer he hasn't decided on yet.

Then his voice floats down the hall. "Are you coming?"

The double meaning is not lost on me. *I wish I was, buddy.* God, I hate him. *No, I hate how much I want him.*

Every step down the hallway feels like I'm walking deeper into something I won't come back from. My brain is screaming, but my body is begging. Am I seriously going to let him fuck me right now? Just like that?

He's waiting at the end—leaning against the doorframe like he owns me, wearing that same unreadable expression on his face he always wears when he doesn't want me looking too close. He's clearly already made every decision, and I'm just here trying to catch up.

"Let me know if you need anything." He pushes the door open with one hand, like this didn't just shift the axis of my entire fucking world. His voice is calm, but dismissive. And I hate that I flinch.

I thought—I don't know. I thought this was headed in a different direction. I thought this was going to be feral and violent. When he said I wasn't here to sleep, and looked at me like he wanted to taste the bruises he put on me, I followed him down that hallway ready to burn.

Fuck, I was ready to let him wreck me, if that's what it would take to get him out of my head. I would've let him nail me into the mattress and erase every thought I've been trying not to have. Just so I could say I survived it.

But now he's just... offering guest services like this is a fucking Airbnb.

How he can whisper filth into my ear while I moan into his throat like a goddamn whore, then toss me a throwaway line like I'm one of a dozen girls who've been here before—it's infuriating. And humiliating.

I swallow hard. "I won't need anything." Then shove the door shut—loud—and right in his smug, perfect face.

I stand there, unmoving with my jaw clenched and my chest heaving. Then lock it for good measure because the real danger clearly isn't him.

It's me.

Which—now that I think about it—is fucking pointless. If he wanted to get in here, he obviously could. Since it's his house and all.

The room hasn't changed since the last time I stayed here. Same clean sheets. Same worn book on the nightstand I never touched. Same walls I stared at while he slept in the other room, like some phantom who only ever shows up just to disappear again.

I peel off my leggings, flinging them across the room, and climb into bed in nothing but my cropped tee and underwear. I yank the blanket up like it might smother everything I'm feeling. *It doesn't, unfortunately, but a girl can dream.*

My body still feels him. My hand drifts up to my throat, where his was, and I shift under the blanket, squeezing my eyes shut, hoping that'll help.

Spoiler alert— it doesn't. I'm still throbbing and instantly wet. Again.

All just from remembering how his cock was grinding into me —how hard he was, how close, how goddamn smug. Fuck, I'm in trouble.

Awesome. Love that for me.

I'd take care of it myself, but he's in the other room—and I'm not about to rub one out over a man who devoured me like he wanted to ruin my life and then told me to *"let him know if I needed anything."* Yeah. I need dick. But sure, I'll settle for your throw blanket.

I might as well tattoo deeply unwell across my forehead and call it a fucking day.

Sleep doesn't come, just the past 24 hours, banging around in my head, along with the memories I keep having.

"It's already done. She's his now."

My stomach knots so hard it starts to hurt. I press the heel of my palm to my chest like I can hold the crack together. I bet if I just apply enough pressure, I'll forget all about it and fall asleep.

But the memories don't stop. Everything comes in flashes. Pressure across my ribs. A laugh that didn't sound like laughter.

I flip over, shoving the blanket off. The sheets are too hot and they're clinging to my skin like static. I swing my legs over the side of the bed and sit there with my elbows digging into my knees. I put my head in my hands like I'm trying to physically hold it all in place. I can't fall apart. Not here.

I blink—just once—and I'm not in the room anymore.

I'm back on cold tile with my cheek pressed against linoleum. My ribs are screaming, and I can feel my fingers sliding in something wet.

"Get her in the car."

Something crashes. Glass? Metal? I can't tell. A door opens and all I remember are the boots, then the hands. There were so many hands. One squeezing too hard on my thigh, and another grabbing my ass. My mouth opens to scream but—nothing comes out. Just silence thick enough to choke on.

I'm upright and off the mattress so fast it's like I'm trying to outrun my own skin. My knees almost buckle, but I catch the wall just in time.

Breathe.

If I stay vertical long enough, the rest of me will catch up I'm sure of it.

"Great," I mutter to no one, "love a good midnight PTSD sprint."

I stumble into the bathroom and flick the light on looking like I haven't slept all year. Dark circles, dead eyes, and secrets lining every bone.

I grip the sink, knuckles white. My vision flickers and suddenly the lights feel too bright. My hair's stuck to my face and there's blood dried under my nails, but I don't remember bleeding. There's a duffel bag on a bed that I don't remember packing.

I blink, and I'm back in the bathroom. Just me. No weird smelling room, or grabby hands. Except—I remember something.

A bracelet.

Thin leather—dark brown, worn soft at the edges from years of never taking it off. I remember the way it wrapped twice around my wrist. I remember the frayed thread I used to twist when I was nervous.

I never took that thing off. Not once.

Except... it's not on my wrist now. And that's what makes my stomach twist. So where the hell is it?

Thanks for the free trauma amnesia, I guess. Five stars. Would dissociate again.

I sit down hard on the edge of the bed, and my stomach is flipping like I missed a step. Part of me knows exactly what this means

—but I refuse to think it through. I don't need the answer. I don't want it.

I rub at my wrist. Hard. Like I can scrub off the phantom weight that's suddenly driving me insane. I grab my hoodie, yank it over my head, and I'm out the door before I can talk myself out of it.

I'm not looking for him. I'm not looking for anything, really. But the second I crack open the door, I know I'm lying.

The house is quiet, and for once, I hope he's asleep. He doesn't need to know I'm tiptoeing through his hallways in a hoodie and underwear like some ghost with a grudge.

The floors are cold under my feet, every step threatens to wake the dead—or worse, Steven. The hallway forks, and I decide to take the left instead of the right because knowing my luck, his room is probably down that way, and I don't have a death wish. Yet.

I'd rather snoop first. Get a lay of the land before I accidentally summon the demon I'm crashing with.

The air shifts the second I pass the stairwell—heavy and charged. A shiver skates down my spine and for a second, I swear I'm being watched but I chalk it up to nerves. And trauma.

And my deeply toxic tendency to snoop through emotionally unavailable men's houses like I'm not one bad night away from a full psychotic break.

The living room opens up ahead, and the firelight is casting long shadows across the furniture. I pause near the back of the couch, half-expecting to find him draped over it—shirtless, ridiculously broody, maybe a knife glinting in one hand and a glass of whiskey in the other.

Peak dark romance monster behavior.

But no. Just shadows.

I creep a little farther in, flicking my eyes toward the kitchen as I pass. It's dark, thank God. Which means there's no way in hell I'm flipping on a light—not with all these windows.

I lean over the back of the couch, making sure he's not at the other end—because God forbid I admit I'm just snooping like a nosy little gremlin hunting for red flags. My hair falls forward, and cold air slaps my ass like a reminder I'm not wearing pants.

Whatever, I don't care. If a girl sneaks around a psychopath's house and no one sees her ass, did it even happen?

I straighten, still wired, still nosy, and I keep moving. I feel the hair on the back of my neck stand, and I have that feeling again. I look around, but no one's there. There is however, a door tucked behind the main room that's slightly open, with a soft orange glow, like there's a fireplace inside there too. I'm not sure if it's an invitation or a trap.

I pause. Then sigh.

"I'm absolutely going to open this and regret it," I whisper to myself. "Honestly, if this ends in murder or orgasm, I probably deserve both. Just saying."

I push the door open and it creaks.

Of course it does. Shit.

Why wouldn't his office door sound like the start of a murder documentary.

Everything inside is stupid perfect. It smells like smoke and cedar—and something darker. It smells like him, and it's making my mouth water. It's the scent that still clings to my skin, right where he pressed his cock into me. But, I'm going to try not to think about that.

There's a fire flickering low on the far wall that's built into the stone like some cozy, masculine wet dream. Unless you're barefoot and spiraling in your maybe-stalker's house with no pants on. Then it feels less sexy and more like a potential crime scene.

"Cool," I mutter. "Of course he leaves fake flames going like this place doubles as a villain lair slash sex dungeon." Then, quieter, because if I'm going to talk to myself, I probably should whisper.

"I bet Frank's into that shit too—mood lighting while he fucks your throat and tells you you're lucky."

Ew.

The room is immaculate. There are books lined up like they're scared to disappoint him. His desk is spotless, there's not even a rogue paperclip to betray he's human.

It should scare me. Instead, it makes me want to throw something and make a mess.

Who the hell is this guy?

He's either a psychopath or a Pinterest board with a God complex—and somehow, I'm still wet for him. I still want him to follow through with every dark threat that's come from that filthy mouth of his.

Who just shows up, wrecks my nervous system, and walks off like he didn't just burn my sanity to the ground? Now I'm standing in the middle of his perfect, silent office—in my underwear—looking for proof he's not just hot and damaged.

He's dangerous.

I wave halfheartedly at the fake fireplace like it's to blame. "Yeah, okay. Definitely not something I need to be unpacking right now."

I move toward the desk. "I'm already trespassing. What's a little felony between strangers?"

When I reach for the drawer, I brace myself—for a booby trap, for disappointment, maybe both. The drawer slides open with a soft click—and something growls behind me.

I spin too fast, slipping a little. My heart is in my throat, and I practically trip over the chair.

"Oh my fuck—"

Before I can launch a book at the intruder or leap onto the desk like a cartoon damsel, the beast lunges—and stops inches from me.

It's massive—black fur and panting like it just ran a marathon straight out of hell. Its eyes are warm and brown and locked on mine like I owe someone money, or maybe an explanation. Its paws are the size of my face, and yet somehow, we just stare at each other like we're both trying to figure out who the hell let me in.

Then, without a sound, it steps forward and shoves its whole damn face into my stomach, sniffing like I'm a favorite drug.

"Oh my god," I breathe. "You're precious."

I drop to my knees like this isn't enemy territory. I'm going to just pretend I didn't almost shit myself two seconds ago.

It licks my face and I laugh. Actually laugh.

"You are so lucky I didn't kick you across the room," I whisper, ruffling its stupid, velvety ears. "What are you even doing here, huh? You guarding secrets or just here to emotionally disarm intruders?"

The massive dog leans into my hands like its waited all its life for this moment and my chest softens. Everything inside me softens. Because animals don't lie. Animals also don't touch you without permission or hold your wrists against trees or walk away like you're not falling apart.

I scratch its neck and find a collar.

Bernadette.

"Well, B," I whisper, forehead pressed against her stupidly soft head, "you have no idea how close you came to being traumatized by a girl who's three mental breakdowns past stable."

I scratch behind her ears and feel her whole body melt. Which is rich, considering I just tried to mentally file her under "bite risk" and "possible hellhound."

Jesus. She's a she. And here I thought she was a boy. Apparently I just assume anything dangerous and silent must be male. Sorry, B. My bad. Girl power. God, I really need to sleep—or scream into a void. I wrap my arms around her, sinking into fur. At least she doesn't look at me like I'm a ticking time bomb.

I pull back just enough to cradle her face in my hands and in my best dog mom voice, I coo, "Does he treat you okay? Blink twice if you're in a hostage situation."

She licks my nose.

"Shit. He's got you brainwashed already, huh?"

I scratch behind her ears, shaking my head. "It's fine. I'll steal you. I'll file a custody suit. I'll change my name to Luna and we'll move to a tropical beach somewhere."

She huffs like she's in on the joke, tail thudding once against the floor like a lazy stamp of approval. Of course she gets it. Honestly, if I were a giant shadow-beast living in a house with a part-time psychopath, I'd imprint on the first emotionally unstable woman who didn't scream too.

God, she probably sees right through me. Dogs always do.

"You wanna come with me?" I whisper. "I'm about to commit some kind of crime. Light breaking and entering, mild felony... emotional damage guaranteed. You in?"

B tilts her head, like she's analyzing me with expert precision. Her tail gives a twitch, like she's decided I'm not a threat, and she licks me again.

"Ride or die," I mutter. "Knew I could count on you."

I stand, and she follows like she's always been mine as we move toward the desk.

"You know where he hides the good shit?" I mutter to her. "A folder labeled Girls Who Forget the Wrong Things and Open the Wrong Doors would really streamline this existential crisis."

I yank the drawer the rest of the way open, bracing for... I don't know. Knives? Fake passports? A laminated collection of restraining orders? Something that screams I'm dangerous, run faster. But no. Just paper. Boring.

Until I spot an envelope shoved in the back like someone tried to forget it—but couldn't quite let it go. Which means it's either a confession or porn.

I glance at Bern. "If I vanish under mysterious circumstances, please inform Sarah I was trying to mind my business and failed spectacularly."

I pull it free and flip it open.

Not porn.

Not even close.

It's a bunch of faded, old photos. The first one's of a girl, who can't be any older than eighteen, with dirty blonde hair, big eyes, and smiling like it still meant something. She's standing in front of a run-down building—somewhere hot, maybe. Her cheeks are flushed. Her arms are wrapped around a dog, and there's a man behind her, but he's turned away. Something about the way he stands—arms crossed, half in shadow—makes my stomach twist.

I flip to the next photo, then another. She's in all of them. Laughing. Playing. Asleep in a chair with a book drooped in her lap. One shows her with a scraped knee and someone's sweatshirt wrapped around her shoulders like armor.

I pause on the last one, on the back, there's a note in small, neat handwriting.

"*L. 12th birthday.*"

I freeze.

I don't know who she is, but I know whoever this girl was... he's keeping her for a reason. *Maybe it's his daughter? I don't even know how old he is.*

I stare down at the photo in my hand a second longer than I should. Long enough to feel something catch behind my ribs and stay there—sharp and stupid and real. My throat goes tight, and I swallow hard. This isn't even about me. It's not supposed to hurt, but it does. More than I'll ever admit out loud. More than I'll admit to myself if I can help it.

This isn't the kind of darkness I was prepared to find.

I came looking for red flags, skeletons, and a reason to run. Not... this. Not whatever this ache is behind my chest that feels too close to grief.

I slide the photos back into the envelope, fingers clumsy now, like I'm suddenly aware of how much I shouldn't be touching any of it. I shove it into the drawer like maybe that'll undo the violation, and yet...part of me still wants to know why it's here.

Who is she? Why does he have all of these?

I close the drawer slowly this time, careful not to make a sound, like being gentle will erase how careless I've been. When I turn, Bernadette's flopped in the doorway like she's been guarding me the whole time.

"Great," I mutter. "Now I've emotionally trespassed and made myself sad. Love that for me."

She pants quietly in response, her tail thudding once like she agrees but doesn't judge.

"Yeah, yeah. Don't look at me like that. You're the one who let me snoop."

I scratch her head once, then pad barefoot back toward the stairs. Everything feels quieter now. Heavier. Like the whole house knows what I just did and is waiting for me to sit with it.

My adrenaline's gone, along with the curiosity, too. By the time I get back to the guest room, I swear I can still feel the weight of that drawer in my palm, and I want to cry. I crawl back into bed and pull the blanket tight, trying to focus on the firelight leaking under the crack of the door.

I don't know how long I lay there for—five minutes? Twenty?

Time's slippery when your stomach's full of guilt and your head's packed with someone else's ghosts.

Then I hear footsteps getting closer to the door. The knob shifts and the door creaks open an inch. And there he is, bare chest, with low-slung sweatpants clinging to his hips like gravity's got a personal grudge against me.

His muscles are cut and cruel, like someone carved him out of control and violence and left the mercy out on purpose. His tattoos snake down one arm and curl over his ribs—ink and shadow dressed up as art, flickering with the firelight behind him. And his eyes— those fucking eyes—are locked on mine.

He looks like he's trying to decide whether to drag me to hell or let me keep thinking I'm not already there. He just stands there in the doorway like a goddamn warning, carved out of restraint and barely leashed fury.

And at that moment, I knew.

He knows.

I sit up halfway, throat dry, heartbeat in my ears. Ready to... I don't even know.

Apologize? Explain? Lie?

I meet his gaze and try not to flinch. After a beat, his voice cuts through the silence. "Stay out of my fucking office."

The door shuts—but he might as well have slammed it. I let out a breath I didn't even realize I was holding, but I don't move. I just stare at the crack under the door, hoping he doesn't come back.

20

"YOU DON'T HAVE TO KEEP SOMEONE TO RUIN THEM"
(YOU JUST HAVE TO TOUCH THEM THE RIGHT WAY)

Ani

I could blame it on the fact that I'm tired. Or half-dressed. Or that he's terrifyingly hot and just caught me elbow-deep in the graveyard of his past. But none of those excuses fix the fact that I crossed a line. *And I didn't even find what I was looking for.*

I swing my legs out from under the blanket, pad over to the door, and lock it.

Knowing full well that it wouldn't stop him, but it makes me feel like I have some kind of choice left.

I crawl back into bed, dragging the blanket around my shoulders like it can shield me from myself, and curl onto my side.

It's pathetic, I know. But the guilt hits harder than I expected. I wasn't looking for connection, I was supposed to find proof. Red flags. A knife. Anything to confirm that I'm still the girl who can't trust anyone.

But instead... I found her.

The girl with the scraped knee and the sweatshirt too big for her body. The soft smile, and the kind of happiness that doesn't last.

I roll onto my back and stare at the ceiling like it owes me answers. Why this—of all things—hurts.

It feels like I touched something fragile, and now it's bleeding in my hands. And maybe for the first time since I ran... I don't feel like a problem to be fixed. I just feel wrong.

That note—scrawled on the back of one of the photos. *"First smile in months."* Wrecked me because it made him real. Not just the monster in my head, but someone who held on to her smile like it meant something. Like it still does. And I hate that I care.

I press my fingers to my mouth and squeeze my eyes shut until they burn. One tear, that's it. That's all I'm allowing. I wipe it away before it even dares to slide down my cheek.

"God, I'm such a mess," I whisper to the dark. "I'm gonna need a whole new trauma just to cancel this one out."

From the other side of the door, I hear a sigh.

Bernadette.

I drag myself up and unlock the door before I can talk myself out of it and she trots in like she's been waiting all night for the cue.

"Hey, menace," I mumble.

She doesn't hesitate—just leaps onto the bed with the grace of a linebacker and drops her head across the bed like she's claiming me.

"I didn't say you could," I mutter. But I don't move her, because the truth is, it's exactly what I needed. I crawl back under the blanket, her body warm and heavy against mine, and I fall asleep.

THE LIGHT STREAMING THROUGH THE WINDOW IS BLINDING. Which is great, considering I'm pretty sure I've just woken up from a coma.

I blink, once. Twice. My head feels like it's filled with packing peanuts, and my body aches in a way that has nothing to do with sex and everything to do with overfeeling.

I shove the blanket off and swing my legs over the side of the bed, squinting around the room like it personally wronged me. Bernadette is still sprawled across the floor like a bodyguard with zero ambition.

I grab my bag from where I dropped it last night, and start rummaging like a raccoon who just found a locked trash can. Wallet. Keys. Lip balm. A crumpled receipt from a gas station chicken nugget crime I never should've committed. Where the fuck is—ah. My phone.

Dead, of course.

I plug it in at the wall and sit there cross-legged, blinking against the harsh light while it boots up like it's doing me a favor. The screen finally flickers to life.

3:13 p.m.

I stare at it like it's lying to me.

"Nope," I mutter. "Absolutely not. That can't be right."

Bernadette yawns like she agrees, and I scrub my hands over my face. I've never slept this long in my life. Not even during the lowest points. Not even after... everything. Though back then, it was mostly fear that kept me from sleeping too long. Dragging a hand through my hair, I groan, of course the one time I emotionally break down and accidentally form a trauma bond with a dog, I crash for fourteen hours straight like it's a personality trait.

At least I have the next few days off. Which was supposed to mean apartment hunting. Maybe even checking out that bookshop space I still haven't admitted I probably can't afford. But instead, I'm here, in Steven's house, with his tattooed abs burned into the back of my skull like a crime I didn't mean to witness.

I finally open my phone. Four missed calls—one from Sloane, three from Sarah, and a handful of texts from Frank.

The most recent one is from this morning.

> Frank: You okay? Haven't heard from you. Wish you came with, but if you need anything, you know I'll take care of it.

I stare at the screen, and my stomach curls like it knows something I don't. Frank's always good at saying the right thing. Charming. Polished. Perfectly timed concern that reads like affection until you look a little closer. Or at least until the words start to feel like velvet ropes—soft, but wrapped around your throat before you even realize you're being tied up.

I don't answer. Instead, I scroll through the missed calls from Sarah—no voicemail, but she did leave a text.

> Sarah: Hey—where the hell did you go?
> Can you call me when you come back
> from the dead!

I almost smile. Instead, I toss the phone on the bed and scrub a hand through my hair like that'll fix anything. I should text Frank back, but I'm not going to right now. I definitely shouldn't be in this house with a man who terrifies me and makes my thighs ache every time I think about what happened in the woods. But here I am.

Barefoot. Hungover on trauma. And fighting off a feral crush like it's not actively ruining me.

I pick the phone back up, thumbs already moving before I can second-guess it.

> Me: Not dead. Just emotionally bankrupt.
> Will explain over coffee if I don't set
> myself on fire first.

Her typing bubbles pop up instantly.

> Sarah: Oh thank GOD. I thought maybe
> Frank locked you in a basement or Steven
> turned out to be a cult leader with a thing
> for knives. ***Wait. Is that still on the table?***

Me: Honestly? If he is, I'm ready to drink the Kool-Aid and let him carve his name into me. This man had me moaning and crying on his floor in the same 12-hour window. I'm not okay.

Sarah: OH MY GOD. WHAT. Who are you? Where are you? Are you safe or just dickmatized? Because one of those is fixable and one is how cults start.

Me: I think I'm both. Also there's a dog now. Bernadette. I think she imprinted on me. So I'm emotionally adopted and slightly possessed.

Sarah: You're clearly not okay. But like in a way that's really on brand for you. Call me before he tattoos his initials on your soul.

I laugh, putting my phone back on the bed and drag myself out of the room, wearing nothing but a T-shirt I found in the closet and the same leggings I left my apartment in. I need food more than I need a reality check.

The hallway opens into the kitchen, and I brace myself to see him there—towering, shirtless, and brooding over a cup of coffee like a warning carved out of stone. That whole tattooed menace with a morning voice that ruins lives energy.

But he's not there. The kitchen is empty.

Relief floods me, followed immediately by the kind of gnawing, unholy hunger that makes me want to bite the damn countertop. So, I start rifling through cabinets, expecting to find something unhealthy. A cookie, chips, a singular sad granola bar, anything. Only I find nothing. Just organized jars and alphabetized spices like this man is one spreadsheet away from villainy.

"What the hell is this?" I mutter, yanking open the fridge and stop.

There are... meals. Like actual, perfectly prepped, macro-balanced, muscle-god meals.

"Who is this guy?"

I'm not going to complain. It explains the abs and the brutal cut of his body. My thighs clench without permission, just thinking about it. Heat blooms low and deep like my body's staging a mutiny. Everything inside me tingles, traitorous and insatiable. I've never in my life met a man who brings out this type of reaction in my body, and I'm not sure if I should be excited or scared.

"Nope," I mutter, closing the fridge so hard it thuds. "We are not doing this."

I pause, and reopen it. I should make toast, or eggs, maybe something low-effort and morally neutral. Something that doesn't taste like I've taken a bite out of his perfect, secretive, probably-murdery life. But then again—he's not here. And I'm starving.

"Where the hell is he anyway?" I mutter, glancing over my shoulder. No Bernadette either, but there's just enough silence to choke on.

Before I can think better of it, I yank a container from the fridge and pop it in the microwave, stabbing the buttons like it's personal. "I'm eating this. And I'm not sorry."

Still no sign of Steven.

I glance around the kitchen, then back at the couch like it might judge me. It feels wrong, making myself at home in a place that isn't mine—in a house that belongs to a man who definitely knows how to make someone disappear without leaving a trace—but then again... I'm not going home right now, at least not until my landlord changes the locks.

Because home doesn't feel safe anymore. It feels like questions I'm not ready to ask. So, I might as well get comfortable, or fake it until I do.

It takes me three tries to figure out the remote—because obviously nothing in this house is user-friendly unless it's shirtless and brooding—and I finally land on Netflix. Once I find Harry Potter, it's game over.

Comfort food. Comfort movie. Emotional band-aid applied with duct tape and denial. *Check.*

I curl up on the couch with the container balanced in my lap, the first bite slides into my mouth like temptation and salvation had a baby. I barely register how good it is at first—because Harry just found the letter in the cupboard, and goddammit, I always forget how much this part wrecks me. That look on his face. The quiet kind of hope. Like maybe magic can still crack through the misery if you wait long enough.

I pause, with the fork halfway to my mouth, completely sucked in. Warmth stings the backs of my eyes, or maybe it's the food. Or exhaustion. Or that dangerous little part of me that still wishes I had a letter waiting somewhere for me too.

I blink and shovel in another bite like I can outrun nostalgia with protein and well-seasoned chicken.

I moan. "Oh my god. He cooks like this and has tattoos? What kind of unfair, walking orgasm-ass bullshit is that?"

I'm mid-bite when Bernadette bumps my elbow like the furry traitor she is, and the fork tips, sending food splattering across the cushion.

"Shit." I stare at the mess. Then at her. "Hurry. Eat it."

She just stares at me, stone-cold.

"Look, just eat it so it doesn't look like I spilled food on the couch, that I'm probably not supposed to be eating on. You know him, he's clearly a clean freak. Didn't you see the fridge? The man's unhinged."

Bern blinks once, then casually turns and trots off like she wants no part in my felony-level upholstery disaster.

"Seriously?" I hiss after her. "You were supposed to be my accomplice."

And then I hear a cough.

I freeze. Every cell in my body goes still like I'm prey who just realized the predator is watching. I turn slowly—because of course he's there, leaning in the doorway with his arms crossed. His dark eyes are loaded with something that looks way too much like amusement for my pride to survive.

"You know you're eating on my couch, right?"

"Yeah, but... in my defense, I'm also starving. And emotionally fragile." I don't even mean to say it out loud. But it slips out, coated in sugar and deflection.

His brow lifts. "You want me to get you a tray? Or a bib?"

I whip around, fork still in my hand like it's a weapon. "Wow. Do you flirt with all your houseguests by implying they're messy toddlers, or do I just bring out your inner asshole?"

His smirk deepens like he's proud of himself, and it makes something flutter and twist in my gut.

I actually laugh—a real one this time. It slips out before I can stop it. A look flashes across his face and that's the part that scares me more than anything. I feel almost... Okay. Like maybe being here—being seen—doesn't feel as wrong as it should.

He pushes off the doorframe and walks into the kitchen like he owns it, which, okay, fine, he does—but still. I didn't hear him come in, which means he could've been watching me this whole time.

"Where did you even come from?" I ask, needing the subject change like oxygen.

He pulls out a different container and pops it in the microwave.

"And why'd you let me sleep all day?" I ask, even though the answer probably won't matter. "What if I had to work?"

He shrugs. "You didn't."

I start to stand—some half-formed attempt to clean up or act like I'm not making myself at home in a stranger's house. But before I can fully rise, his voice cuts in.

"Sit. Stay there, and eat."

I freeze. Then slowly sink back down onto the couch, heart thudding way too hard for a man who just told me to keep eating. He nods toward the container like that's the end of the conversation

—and maybe it is, because I don't argue. I look down at the food and take another slow bite. I will not let him intimidate me. *Clearly.*

Apparently, that's who I am now—a girl who listens when told to stay. But honestly? I'm not even mad about it. Hagrid's about to kick the door down, and I'm two bites deep and too emotionally compromised to pretend otherwise. I tuck one leg under me, shove in another forkful, and try not to let it mean anything. This is probably the first meal I've had in days that didn't taste like cardboard.

The food is actually... incredible. Like five-star, perfectly seasoned, totally-unfair, amazing. And of course it is, because why wouldn't the emotionally unavailable sex god I'm currently crashing with also moonlight as a gourmet chef?

"Dangerous and domestic," I mutter under my breath. "Should be fucking illegal."

Bernadette—who ditched me the second Steven walked in, probably to avoid being caught eating couch-spilled contraband—reappears. She pads over, tail flicking with zero shame, and flops down beside me like she didn't betray me at all.

I side-eye her, but she blinks up at me, innocent as hell.

"Oh, now you show up?" I mutter, scratching behind her ear. "Just in time. Real supportive, B."

She huffs, settling in like she's ready for the show.

"Traitor," I murmur, still petting her. "You belong to me now. Hope you're ready for codependency and emotional damage."

I glance up, fork halfway to my mouth, just as Steven walks back into the kitchen—barefoot, and holding a container. He doesn't look at me, he just sits down and starts eating like it's the most normal thing in the world.

I clear my throat, because of course I can't help myself. "So when'd you get a dog?"

No answer. Just chewing. Like silence is his love language and I'm supposed to translate it.

"She wasn't here the first time I came over."

His eyes finally flick to mine, but the corner of his mouth doesn't even twitch.

"Neither were you."

My brows lift before I can stop them. "Wow. That's the line we're going with?"

He shrugs. Completely unfazed—like he didn't just fry my central nervous system with a truth I don't want to unpack.

"She came with the house," he says after a beat. "Previous owners left her."

I blink. "You're kidding."

"Dead serious."

I glance down at Bernadette, who's smugly sprawled across my lap like she owns the whole couch. She gives me a slow blink like *yeah, and what about it.*

"So what—you just inherited a dog?" I gesture toward her with my fork. "Like a tax write-off?"

"She stayed."

I pause. "She chose to stay? With you?"

That earns the tiniest twitch of his mouth. "She's smarter than most people I know."

He's still looking at me when he says it. Like he knows exactly what he's doing. Something flips in my stomach, low and hot, and I hate how fast I feel it. I stab another bite—sharper than necessary—and chew like that'll help me to *not* feel how turned on I'm getting over literally nothing.

Nope, not doing this right now.

"Of course she stayed," I mutter. "You probably grunted twice and opened a can of tuna and she was like, 'yeah, I could build a life here.'"

He tilts his head slightly. "Jealous?"

"Of the dog?"

I don't even know why I ask. My brain says no, but my body's already halfway into writing vows while his eyes drag over me.

"Of anyone who gets to sleep next to me without biting first."

My fork freezes mid-air and my brain short-circuits.

"You did not just say that."

He doesn't even blink. Just sits there—arms stretched across the back of the couch with his legs spread like he owns the oxygen between us. "You asked."

"No, I made a sarcastic comment. You turned it into a scene from a low-budget porno."

His gaze slides down my body like he's mapping it out and my thighs clench before I can stop them.

"Still hungry?" he murmurs, like it's not a question.

He's close enough that I can smell his skin—he's the worst kind of temptation—and my brain forgets how to function.

"That depends," I say carefully. "You offering dessert or just judgment?"

He gives me the kind of smile that undoes girls who should know better. And I'm not sure that I do. Ignoring it, I shovel a bite into my mouth just to avoid making a sound I can't take back.

21

"THE ONES WHO BREAK YOU DON'T ALWAYS RAISE
THEIR VOICE."
(PAY ATTENTION)

Steven

She's on my couch, wrapped in my blanket, eating my food, and watching my screen like she belongs here.

That should have pissed me off. It should've switched something cold and clean in my head—like it always used to.

I don't know when, or even how, but this reckless, infuriating girl started slipping under my skin like a habit I didn't remember picking up. She was a problem I should've solved with silence or violence. Something easy. Permanent. Instead, I want to bend her over the fucking kitchen counter and remind her who she belongs to—who she's always belonged to—even if she doesn't know it yet.

I'm standing here like a fucking ghost in my own house, listening to her talk to the dog like it's her therapist. She just walked in, peeled back a part of my life I've kept buried six feet deep—and didn't flinch. Worse—she looked at the photos like it meant something.

I could see it on her face, it was almost like she recognized the kind of pain that settles into your bones and makes a home.

I should be angry, but all I feel is this slow, gnawing heat in my chest and this need to claim her so hard she never questions where she belongs again.

As if seeing that hoodie ride up wasn't already handing me the perfect, filthy view of the ass last night. I wanted to leave her bruised and shaking, but it took everything in me not to shove her face-first into the cushions, rip that hoodie up over her hips, and fuck every last Frank-soaked delusion out of her reckless, pretty mouth.

Even now, it's taking every last ounce of control I have not to drag her to the floor, shove my hand between those trembling thighs, and show her what happens to girls who forget which monsters they're supposed to fear.

When she didn't wake up this morning, I stayed in the office, making calls I needed to make, and kept the plan moving. But I saw her on the cameras—barefoot, half-conscious, and wandering into my kitchen like a girl who's never been fed properly.

It was infuriating. *And fucking adorable.*

The second she opened the fridge and saw my prepped meals, her whole body slumped—like she didn't know whether to be turned on or betrayed. Her mouth would say betrayal, but her thighs would argue otherwise.

I glance over, and there she is—curled up on my couch like it's her throne. She's barefoot, and probably braless, wrapped in my blanket like she fucking belongs there.

She lifts the fork to her mouth and hums when the bite hits— like it slipped out before she could swallow it. And fuck me, my cock doesn't care if she's moaning over chicken or choking on it. It hears the sound and gets possessive.

I dry my hands, and my fingers tighten in the towel until the bones crack. She's not supposed to be here. Not like this. Not with Frank's chain still dangling from her throat like she chose it.

I shove the sound down. The one that's been clawing at the back of my throat since the second she walked into this house and made it feel like something I could lose.

I toss the towel on the counter and step forward. Her shoulders tense, and her thighs shift like they're already bracing for something. She feels me. Even when I haven't touched her.

And when I finally stop in front of her with my arms crossed and my shadow falling across her like it's got a mind of its own—she lifts her head.

Those fucking eyes. That mouth. And that wild hair looks like she just got fucked all night, is making it really hard to stay on track. My shirt's hitched up over her thighs, and the neckline is slipping just enough to flash the chain at her throat—Frank's chain. Still sitting there like a goddamn claim he didn't earn. Does she not realize how close she is to having it ripped off and replaced with something that screams mine.

The plate's still in her lap, clutched like a weapon she doesn't know how to use, and she looks up at me like I might ruin her. And all I can think is—you already are.

"You comfortable yet?" I murmur.

Her brow lifts like she's deciding whether to flip me off or pretend she's unaffected. She shovels another bite into her mouth instead, all brat and no self-preservation, chewing slow, like it's a challenge. *New fantasy unlocked. Watching her eat is like a wet dream.*

I tilt my head slightly, because if she thinks I can't see the way her legs keep pressing tighter, or the way her chest hitches every time I get too close—she's wrong.

I'm a trained killer. I notice everything.

Including the way her breathing stutters—shallow, and quick. I watch a flush creep up her throat, and I'd put money on the way her nipples are probably drawn tight under my shirt. She's trying to hide a reaction she doesn't even know how to understand.

She has no idea what it's doing to me or what she looks like, curled up here like she belongs to me. That mouth was made to say my name.

I lean down, forcing her to tip her chin up to keep my gaze. Good. I want her off-balance.

"Do you always make yourself at home in a man's house," I

murmur, my voice low enough to scrape, "or just the ones who haven't fucked you yet?"

She chokes. Beautifully.

The fork hits the plate with a sharp clang as her spine jolts, fire snapping in her eyes like she wants to claw my face off.

There she is.

Her temper flares as she straightens her spine in that silent challenge I've come to crave. That bratty mouth is already forming a comeback she doesn't have the teeth to finish. I love feisty Ani, once she's not mad, I'll have to find more reasons to piss her off again.

"What the hell is wrong with you?" she snaps, lifting her chin in that stubborn way that makes me want to ruin her composure all over again.

"Don't pout, sweetheart," I murmur, my gaze dragging across the flush blooming down her throat. "You started this."

She opens her mouth to spit something back—fire and venom, probably—but I cut her off before she gets the first syllable out.

I curl my fingers around the edge of the couch, right next to her thigh—close enough to crowd, but not enough to touch. She has to feel the heat pouring off me, but she keeps pretending she doesn't. I love that she keeps pretending I don't make her nervous.

I lower my voice, "You think I didn't see you last night? Bent over my couch, legs spread, with your ass bare, mouthing off about Frank like you forgot where you were?"

She freezes.

And fuck if that doesn't make my cock throb behind my sweats. I lean in close enough to smell the fear and the want fighting for space on her skin.

"Keep running that pretty mouth, pretty girl and I'll make sure you remember exactly who you're begging for next time you spread your legs."

Her whole body goes still. Except for her thighs, they clench.

Hard. And I feel it like a punch to the gut. She wants it. She might hate that she wants it, but she still wants it.

I straighten slowly, letting the silence between us coil tighter, until it feels like I'm breathing her in. She glares up at me like she'd rather claw my eyes out than admit what her body's screaming for. But I see the way her pulse ticks at her throat, and the way her breath catches. She's one push away from snapping. *She wants me to be the one to do it.*

Good. I want the fight. I want the bite. I want her so fucking ruined, so raw and wrecked, she forgets who she thought she belonged to. Forgets his name. Forgets her own. Forgets everything except the way I make her break.

She shoves the plate off her lap, setting it on the table so hard, it sounds like her composure shattering. Then she stands—chest rising, and her feet planted like she thinks she's still got something to defend.

"You think you know everything, don't you?" she snaps, fire flashing behind her eyes.

I smile. "I know enough."

"You don't know shit," she bites, voice rising. "You don't know what he makes me feel—"

She cuts herself off.

Too late. I see the crack in her armor. The shake in her voice. The flicker of fear when she realizes the leash around her throat might not belong to who she thinks it does.

She thinks she's hiding it—covering the fracture with rage and fake indifference like I haven't made a living out of spotting the weak point before I strike.

I tilt my head, the answer already written across her face and she gives me another one without even realizing it. That pause. That silence. That twitch in her fingers when she flinches away from the truth.

Frank has his hooks in her. I knew that. But now I know where, and now I know how to cut deeper.

She backpedals. Trying to pull the mask back on while I peel it off with nothing but proximity. I move in, close enough to cage her, and her spine meets the wall.

I brace one hand beside her head and lean in until I can feel the lie on her tongue.

"You want to finish that sentence, Dear?"

I keep my voice low, designed to get under her skin. And it works—because her breathing goes ragged, and her chest continues to rise too fast. She's unraveling and I'm cataloging every twitch, every shift, every goddamn stutter of her pulse.

If I touched her right now, I know exactly what I'd find—she'd be so fucking wet for me.

He might have her, but I'm the one who can make her forget.

I don't need to chase her. I just need to wait for the moment she begs to be caught and by the looks of it, she's not far off.

Her tongue flicks across her bottom lip, and my cock throbs so hard it's fucking painful. I can feel my balls tightening at the thought of being buried in her.

"You gonna tell me?" I say, dragging my gaze down her face, noting the frantic flutter of her pulse. "Or do you want me to make you talk?"

She glares up at me—and fuck, she's beautiful like this.

"You think I'm scared of you?" she spits.

"No." I step in closer, keeping my voice low and deadly. "You're scared of yourself."

She inhales sharply, but keeps her lips pressed tight. I can see violence in her eyes, before she tries covering it up.

"You're scared you'll like it," I say in her ear, letting the words sink into her skin. "Scared you'd crawl for it."

Her fingers twitch at her sides, and I just know her nails are curling like she's fighting the urge to either touch me or claw me open, so I lean in—close enough to feel her breath, to see if she'll flinch.

She doesn't.

Stubborn little brat.

She's stands there in nothing but leggings, my shirt, and that fucking chain she's too scared—or too stupid—to take off. Still pretending she's not already mine. That will make breaking her so much sweeter.

"You gonna hit me, sweetheart?" I murmur against her mouth, close enough she can taste the threat in the air between us.

"Maybe," she breathes back.

I smile because if she thinks she can start a fire and not burn for it, she's wrong. I'd love to see her try though.

"You can try," I say. "But we both know you're not gonna lift a finger."

Her body tenses—trembling with the effort it takes not to break first. I want her sobbing into my palm while I wreck every fucking inch of that smart, reckless mouth. I lift my hand and drag the back of my knuckles lightly down her cheek, just enough to make her shiver.

"You want to be a brat?" I murmur. "You want to pretend you don't already know how this ends?"

Her chest rises sharply against mine, but I don't miss the way her nipples pebble beneath the thin fabric of my shirt—and how her thighs shift, squeezing together like she can smother the heat building between them. She might walk back to him when this is over, but she'll be dripping my cum down her thighs—and he'll know he's getting nothing but my leftovers.

"You can run your mouth all you want," I say, trailing my fingers down to the chain around her throat. I hook a finger under it, feeling her pulse hammering against the delicate skin there.

"But we both know you're two dirty words away from begging me to ruin you."

She gasps, and it's the prettiest fucking sound I've ever heard.

"You're disgusting," she spits, but her voice cracks.

I chuckle. "You haven't even seen disgusting yet," I rasp. "But keep talking. Keep lying to yourself. See how long you last before you're on your knees, cum dripping down your thighs, begging for the monster you swore you hated."

Her face flames with fury and want. All tangled together into something messy and broken and perfect. I step even closer, pressing her back harder into the wall, making sure she feels the thick, hard length of me against her stomach.

It only takes a second before she arches against me—the moment she tips her chin up like she's daring me to do it—I almost lose it. Her breath stutters against my chest, and her body goes stiff with something I'm sure she doesn't want to name.

Good.

I hope it eats her alive, because I'm done playing nice. I'm done pretending I don't want to ruin her. And she'd love every fucking second of it.

My hand slides lower, still holding the chain. I drag the metal slowly along her throat and I feel her breath catch like a fucking prayer.

"Open that filthy mouth," I rasp, my knuckles grazing her pulse. "Give me a reason to break you faster."

Because I will. And she'll thank me for it—whether it's through tears or bitten-off moans. She'd look so fucking beautiful with my cock down her throat, tears streaming from her eyes. *Fuck.* I want to do things to this woman even the devil would whisper about.

Her eyes flash, and there she is. The girl who doesn't know how to quit, even when her body's already halfway mine.

"In your fucking dreams. You can eat shit," she fires back, sharper this time. But it only makes my cock harder. I love it when my girl bites.

I lean in, brushing my nose along the curve of her jaw, breathing her in like a death sentence I've already written.

"Yet you still haven't told me to stop," I murmur, my voice low and filthy.

She jerks in my grip, and I know she's fucking drenched.

"Has Frank ever made you this wet without even touching your pussy?" I growl, savoring the way she flinches.

She makes a sound that's part rage, part humiliation—and shoves at my chest. I let her pretend she has a choice, then I grab her wrists and slam them over her head, pinning her to the wall in one brutal move. She gasps, her body arching trying to get out of my grip, making her tits press against my chest. Her whole body trembles under the weight of everything she's trying not to feel.

"Keep fighting," I rasp, grinding my cock against her stomach. "I like it when you lie to yourself."

"Go to hell," she breathes, voice frayed and trembling.

"Only if you're on your knees when I get there, sweetheart."

Her eyes widen with fury, fear, and want—bleeding together so fast she can't hide it.

Having an idea, I let her wrists go and step back. "On your knees."

She doesn't move though, of course she fucking doesn't. That's my girl. She just stares at me like I've lost my goddamn mind. And then—she laughs. The kind of laugh that tastes like gasoline right before the world catches fire.

"You really think I'm gonna crawl for you?" she flips her hair like she's not already halfway wrecked.

"Is that how it works in your sadistic little fever dream? You bark, I beg?"

She steps toward me with her chin up, and her mouth twisted in that perfect fucking snarl. She's so fucking hot when she thinks she's the one holding the leash. I just might let her hold onto it for a few more seconds.

"You must've mistaken me for one of your other girls," she sneers. "The ones who moan when you tell them to heel."

I smile.

She's exactly where I want her. All fire and venom and fucking delusion. And I want every second of her fight. Because once she breaks—she's not getting back up without my hands on her throat and my name in her mouth.

I step back into her space, crowding her until her back hits the wall again, with a soft thud.

"They beg with their mouths. You do it with your cunt."

Her nostrils flare when I fist the hem of her shirt and shove it over her hips. I'm about to lose what control I have left.

She slaps my hand away, and I grip the front of her throat, "You gonna slap me again?" I murmur. "Kick me? Scream?"

She doesn't speak so I drop my voice lower, filthy enough to brand her. "Or are you gonna be a good little bitch and crawl?"

She jerks her chin back and fire flashes in her eyes. "Try me."

She's still fighting. Still lying to herself with every breath. But the tremble in her hands and the flush on her chest isn't fear. It's surrender trying to claw its way out, she just hasn't figured out who she's giving it to yet.

I grin. "Oh I plan to, on every surface in this house."

Her hands fist again. She's flushed, and I'd bet my life she's so fucking wet for me. I can see it in the way she bites her lip.

I close the distance in one brutal step, my fingers threading through her hair like a snare, while my other hand finds her throat again, pressing just enough to promise what I'll take if she keeps testing me.

Her hands fly up to grab my wrist, and her nails dig into my skin. I feel her panic, her pride, and her need all pulsing against my hand but she doesn't say stop.

"You think this is a game?" I growl, keeping my face inches from hers. The air between us hums, and it's suffocating. "You think running that bratty mouth makes you brave?"

Her eyes are glassed over, shimmering with tears she's too fucking stubborn to let fall. She blinks like if she fights long enough, she won't come apart in front of me, But I've already carved my name into whatever's cracking inside her.

She's trying so fucking hard not to break—and I love that I'm the one making her. I press into her harder against the wall, my grip tightening around her throat and her knees tremble.

"Let me teach you how this works, sweetheart," I rasp. "You don't get to fight and stomp and scream and think there's no cost. You mouth off? You pay for it."

She makes a sound—gutted and raw. Part want. Part fear. And all fucking mine.

I lean in, dragging my mouth over hers and catch her bottom lip between my teeth and I bite enough to make her gasp. I swallow it, like her breath is mine to fucking own.

Her fists land against my chest—more instinct than intent—but her fingers twist in my shirt like she doesn't know if she's fighting or clinging. She moans into my mouth rubbing that sweet pussy on me.

I deepen the kiss, devouring her, grinding my cock against her stomach so she feels exactly what she's done to me. How hard, how furious, and how far past the point of patience I am.

I pull back just enough to growl against her lips. "You think being loud makes you powerful?"

Her breath stutters like her body's unraveling before she's ready to admit it, but she stays quiet. And I fucking love how her body begs to be used and she moans like she hates how much she needs it.

"You want power?" I rasp, sliding my hand beneath the hem of the shirt she's still fucking wearing. My fingertips skate over hot, trembling skin. "You're looking at it."

I drag my hand higher— over her ribs, until I've got one perfect, aching breast in my palm. I squeeze hard enough to make her gasp and arch off the wall.

She's fucking perfect. Every part of her. From the way she shakes to the way she fights it—her body already knows it belongs to me.

"You're gonna beg," I whisper into her mouth. "And you're gonna thank me for it."

She shudders as her nails bite into my chest, fisting tighter in my shirt like she's bracing for impact—or chasing it.

I can tell how needy she is, so I shove my thigh between hers, spreading her open until she's straddling the pressure.

"Ride it," I order. "Show me how bad you want it."

Her eyes snap open—furious and burning—but her hips twitch like they've made the decision for her.

"Fuck you," she breathes, but she's already grinding against my thigh in tiny, frantic circles—like her cunt's too desperate to wait for permission. There it is. That war between pride and need.

"That's it, good girl." I rasp, dragging my mouth along her jaw, her throat, the shell of her ear. "Keep lying with your mouth. Your body's already mine."

She makes a sound—somewhere between a sob and a snarl—and her hips jerk, chasing the friction. Holy shit she's so hot when she does that.

"You gonna come like this, pretty girl?" I growl, voice rough with hunger. "Grinding like a fucking bitch in heat?"

Her nails rake down my chest, but it only makes my cock throb harder. I could fuck her right here, right now, and she'd take it. She'd beg for it. But not yet.

"Fuck you," she says again, but it lands more like a whisper. She's wrecked and barely holding it together. She's so close to breaking, I can taste it.

And when she does, she's not coming back from it.

I grab her chin roughly, forcing her to look at me. Her pupils are blown wide and her lips are parted and trembling.

"Please..." she begs.

"So needy," I murmur, dragging my thumb over her bottom lip. "You gonna fall apart already, sweetheart? We've barely started."

I crush my mouth to hers and this time, she doesn't fight it. She's kissing me back and it's not soft. It's desperate and messy.

Fuck, I've been waiting for this. I've been waiting for her to stop pretending, and surrender.

I drag my hands down her sides, drinking in every move she makes, memorizing the way her body gives up faster than her mouth ever could.

When I find her tits this time, I don't waste a second. I roll one nipple between my fingers, then slap the side of her breast hard enough to make her gasp. Her whole body bucks, wild and out of control. *Exactly how I like her.*

"There she is," I rasp against her ear. "There's my filthy little slut."

She shakes her head, but she's not denying it. Not really. Her back arches, pressing those perfect tits into my hands like she wants to be punished for it. I pinch harder and she cries out—a strangled, broken sound that makes my cock throb against her.

I slide my hand between her thighs, pressing the soaked cotton tight against her pussy. She's moaning—loud and needy—as she grinds into my palm before she can stop herself.

I press harder, drawing slow, torturous circles right over her clit with my thumb. It's not enough to let her fall over the edge, but just enough to keep her starving for it. She's panting now, and practically whimpers into my mouth.

"Patience," I growl, dragging my lips along her jaw. "You want it? Earn it."

She chokes on a sob, her nails sinking into my shirt like she's trying to anchor herself before she shatters.

"Beg me. Tell me how fucking desperate you are."

Her head thrashes. "No—" she gasps. "I won't—"

I slap my hand over her drenched little cunt and she jerks, gasping like she wasn't ready for how fucking good it feels to be put in her place. Her sob rips against my chest, wrecked and filthy..

"Say it," I growl again, lower this time. A command meant to wreck her.

And then it breaks—her last defense. That pretty silence she's been hiding behind like it could save her.

"Please," she chokes out. Barely audible. Ruined.

I smile into her hair. "There's my good girl."

I pull back just enough to look at her—and fuck, she's everything. Red-cheeked, glassy-eyed, soaked through, and trembling like she doesn't know whether to beg for more or run for her fucking life.

I curl one hand into her hair and force her head back. I want her to look at me while she falls apart.

"Look at you," I rasp. "So fucking beautiful when you break for me."

Her breath hitches, but she doesn't stop grinding. Her body's not hers anymore—it's mine. She's running on instinct at this point, chasing friction.

Leaning down, I drag my mouth across her jaw, then down the column of her throat. Breathing her in like a man starving for violence and sex and her.

"You want to come so bad it hurts, don't you, sweetheart?" I whisper. "You want to come on my leg like the filthy little slut you are."

She whimpers, nodding. Her entire body is trembling with need, so I shift—just enough to give her the pressure she's chasing. Just enough to make her crazy.

Her head drops, and her eyes roll back.

"That's it," I murmur, dragging the words out like a threat. "Use me. Rub your filthy little cunt all over me."

She moans as I tighten my grip on her hair and yank her head back again, forcing her to look at me. To see what she's become, what I've made her.

"Look at you—dripping and chasing your release like a bitch in heat."

Her eyes are glassy, pupils blown wide, as her mouth opens in a silent cry. She's so close I can feel it. I feel her body locking up, shaking against me.

I drag my other hand up the inside of her thigh, slow and taunting, teasing just shy of where she needs me most.

She whines, actually fucking whines, and it's the sweetest, filthiest sound I've ever heard.

"You want it?" I growl.

She nods, again but it's not enough. Not for me.

I fist her hair tighter, forcing her chin up, my mouth brushing hers but not giving her the kiss she's starving for.

"Then beg," I snarl. "On your knees or you get nothing."

For a long, brutal heartbeat, we just breathe the same suffocating air. I cock my head, smiling.

"Or maybe you'd rather crawl for Frank," I murmur, voice dripping with cruelty. "Bet he'd let you come like a good little whore."

Her whole body jerks like I hit a nerve. As soon as her eyes snap to mine, I can see how fucking hurt she is, it punches the breath out of my lungs. She doesn't even try to hide it.

"He's never touched me." The words rip out of her without permission, and it's too honest to be calculated.

Fuck me, they hit harder than they should. For half a second, everything in me short-circuits. *I'll store that away for later*

All thought, logic and restraint. Gone.

My brain fractures and snaps into something sharp and fucking lethal. I don't move, because if I do, I'll ruin her. She's not ready for that.

I grab her—hard—lifting her off the floor, causing her to yelp. Her arms go flying around my shoulders and her legs lock tight around my waist.

I smile against her throat as I carry her backward and slam her into the nearest wall. The sound of her gasp is heaven as I grind my cock between her legs—pressing against the soaked seam of her leggings, right where she needs it.

She moans—loud—and digs her nails into my back, desperate little claws that do nothing but fuel me. Her mouth crashes into mine and she devours me like it's the only way she knows how to breathe.

She's tearing at my lips like she's furious I'm still breathing and not inside her yet. Her tongue drags over mine, messy and violent. There's no rhythm, just raw fucking need.

Fuck, it makes my cock throb so hard I almost lose my patience and take her right here. I grab a fistful of her ass and yank her tighter against me, letting her work herself up again.

I pull back just enough to see her face—dazed with need—and clamp my hand around the back of her neck, forcing her to look at me.

"You want it that bad, sweetheart?" I rasp against her swollen mouth. "You wanna come all over my cock?"

I drag my tongue over her jaw, down her throat, biting hard enough to make her sob. I squeeze her ass, grinding her down onto my cock, dragging another broken sound from her lips.

"Keep grinding, pretty girl, keep soaking me. But you don't get to come until you're on the floor, crawling and showing me who you really belong to."

I murmur it against her ear as my fingers slide down and find her clit. I circle it once and tighten my grip on her ass.

"Feel that?" I whisper, pressing harder—with just enough pressure to make her hips jerk. Then I ease off.

"I'm gonna bend you over this fucking couch and make you wish you had, then."

Her whole body goes stiff and I loosen my grip and set her down, letting her feet hit the floor like I'm giving her a choice. But we both know I'm not.

Let her feel the loss of my body. Let her decide if her pride is worth the ache between her thighs.

"You gonna crawl?" I ask. "Or you wanna find out what happens when you don't?"

Her eyes burn into mine, full of a fury she can't weaponize anymore.

I see it in her eyes—she's scared. And she should be. She stares up at me, breathing like she just ran a marathon, chest rising too fast, as her fists clench and release at her sides, over and over—like she's trying to decide how bad she wants me. How much she's willing to give up to have it.

My little brat is so fucking perfect.

I step forward, slowly, looming over her—dragging my knuckles along the chain still locked around her throat.

"You should be afraid," I murmur, keeping my voice low. "Because I'm not Frank. I'm not gonna pretend you're anything but a pretty little mess begging to be broken."

She glares at me with wet eyes, and unsteady legs, like she wants to scream. Let her feel it, let her burn. It'll make it sweeter when she falls.

"You think you scare me?" she spits. "You're just another asshole with a god complex."

I smile, stepping back to give her space—like it's a gift. She still doesn't move, and I'm watching her now, wondering just how stubborn she really is and how far she'll take this.

"Get the *fuck* on your knees, Ani."

She probably thinks I'll let her keep pushing and knows what's coming, but I'm not fucking playing anymore.

She hesitates, and that war behind her eyes is so loud I can taste it. I can see the pride, the need, and the shame.

Then, in one breath, she sinks to her knees.

Fuck me.

She stays there, with her hands loose at her sides, waiting for me to step forward, to grab her hair and shove my cock down her throat like that's all this is.

But I just stand there and stare at her, letting her sit in it.

God, the way she's looking up at me right now with her lips parted, and her eyes full of something she doesn't even know how to name—it does something to me I don't want to fucking admit.

She's not supposed to look like that when she kneels. Not when I thought she already belonged to someone else. I want to hate her for it. I *need* to, but she's down there now, looking up at me like she'd do anything I told her to—and all I can think is how fucking right it looks.

I smile and take a slow step back, then turn and walk toward the chair across the room, dropping into it like a fucking king. Right now, I own her. Even if she's too stubborn to admit it yet.

My cock throbs behind my sweats, hard enough to hurt. I can't even remember the last time I had blue balls this bad. But I'm nowhere near done with her yet. Not even fucking close.

She starts to rise—like maybe that was it.

"Stop."

Her body freezes mid-movement, head snapping up to look at me, with her eyes wide. She's a quick learner. *Good girl.*

I sit forward, elbows braced on my knees, staring her down with every ounce of dominance she deserves to choke on.

"Take off that fucking necklace," I growl. "Or you don't move another inch."

She stiffens, and I watch it hit her. That chain around her pretty throat—Frank's chain, still clings to her skin like some kind of brand. Not fucking happening, not while she's kneeling in front of me. Especially not while she's soaking through her leggings just from the sound of my voice.

She hesitates.

I lean in closer, dropping my voice into something darker, and dangerous enough to make her whole body stall.

"Make your choice, pretty girl."

Her eyes flick to mine in a glare.

"You can keep his collar..." I hold her gaze. "...or you can crawl."

She doesn't move at first, not even to breathe. And then—slowly—her hand lifts to her throat, undoing the clasp, and the necklace slips free. She's looking right at me when she lets it fall to the floor with a soft clink.

"Happy now?" she snaps, her voice cracking at the edges.

I try and fail to hide my smirk. She's still fighting, but it's useless—and we both know it.

"Now crawl."

"I'm not crawling for you," she mutters, defiance hanging by a thread.

That bratty mouth of hers opens like she might argue again—but the words don't come. They die on her tongue, along with whatever pride she was still clinging to with the look I give her.

Whatever storm's unraveling in her head, she doesn't say a word. She just drops and starts to crawl. Every inch of her screams rebellion, but her body screams want.

At first, she moves like she's unsure. Her spine's stiff—like every inch forward is some kind of personal protest. She's moving like it's beneath her and she's making a statement with every inch. The fight doesn't vanish—it just turns inward with a quiet surrender. A raw, reluctant offering.

And fuck, if watching her break like this isn't the most beautiful thing I've ever seen in my whole Goddamn life.

I wait until she's right in front of me—kneeling between my feet before I lean forward enough for her to feel the weight of my voice against her skin.

"You ready to be fucked?" I murmur against her mouth. "A dripping, desperate slut who had to be broken just to remember how to fucking breathe."

Her breath stutters, but she nods.

"Use your words."

"Yes," she whispers. "Please."

I grab her by the hair and yank her head up—forcing her to look at me. Her wide eyes show hesitation already written all over her face.

"Use your words," I growl. "Tell me what you want."

She freezes—just for a second. And that second is all I fucking need. I shove her back hard, slamming her into the carpet with a roughness she doesn't even fight.

My knees land between her legs as I tear her shirt up to her waist and drag her leggings down in one motion.

She gasps.

And fuck—she's bare. No panties. Just her soaked, swollen clit. Her pussy is flushed and dripping like she's been waiting for this since the second I walked in.

I slap her cunt and she jolts, moaning. I lean in, breathing against her ear.

"You wanted control, didn't you?" I rasp. "Wanted someone to see what a filthy little mess you are—" I drag my fingers through her wet cunt. "—and take it anyway."

She nods frantically, tears pricking at the corners of her eyes as I drag two fingers through her slit, and her whole body arches.

"I'm gonna make you come so hard you forget how to speak," I snarl. "And then I'm gonna do it again. And again. Until you forget what it felt like to belong to anyone but me."

I shove my fingers deep, curling them just right, and a scream tears out of her throat—raw and wet and fucking feral. I drag my thumb over her clit, circling with the kind of ruthless precision that feels more like a warning than relief. The second her legs start to shake and her mouth falls open, she's already begging, and clawing at the floor like she doesn't care if she comes or fucking dies, as long as it's for me.

"Please—fuck, Steven—please, I can't—"

"Yes, you can," I growl, curling my fingers deeper, playing with that spot that makes her forget why she ever tried to fight me. My thumb rolls tight circles over her clit, not giving her a second to think, to breathe, or even to hide.

Her whole body locks up, every muscle taut. I keep dragging every ounce of sensation out of her until she's panting and writhing under my hand.

"You're gonna come for me," I bite out, right against her jaw, "and you're gonna fucking thank me while you do it."

She sobs, her thighs are quivering, and her hips rock helplessly into every thrust of my hand.

"Say it."

She claws at the rug, her voice breaking on every syllable.

"Th-thank you—fuck."

And then she shatters. Right there on the floor. Her spine bows like I've strung her up tight and snapped the cord as her pussy clenches around my fingers, dripping all over my hand as her cry splits the silence in half.

I don't stop.

I keep fucking her through it—dragging the orgasm out until she's gasping and coming so hard her whole body sings for me.

I just watch her fall apart like it's my fucking religion. And god help me—because I've never believed in anything more than the way this girl comes when I make her.

22

Ani

What the fuck did I just do?

My thighs are still shaking and my breath catches on every uneven inhale.

I feel hollowed out and rewired—like something vital was yanked from me and replaced with heat. I came all over him.

After crawling.

I should feel ashamed, or something. But all I feel is this white-hot static in my chest that won't burn out. I've never been so turned on in my fucking life.

What the hell is wrong with me? Why did I do that? *Why did I like it?*

I try to pull away. To reclaim some sliver of control, but I don't get far—because his hand is still between my legs.

His fingers drag through my slick folds again—slower this time—and my whole body jolts. Every nerve lights up, too raw to hide. He's not teasing me anymore—he's reminding me who I belong to. Every pass of his fingers reignites the heat and the need. And I can't stop shaking.

"Look at you. Still fucking open for me."

His breath skates across my jaw, and it's a threat disguised as worship.

And fuck me—I want it. I want him so bad. At this point, I'd do whatever he asked me to.

My pride screams at me to look away, to claw my way back to whatever scraps of dignity I have left and get up, but my body doesn't move.

I'm still open for him, because I need him to keep going. I'm so wrecked I could cry.

And God, I hate how much I need him right now.

I open my mouth to snap back—because I need to fight like I still have something left to protect. But then he does something unforgivable. He pulls his fingers out and for one, fleeting, horrifying second—I think it's over.

Then his hands are on me again—hauling me up off the floor like I don't weigh a fucking thing. My back's still slick with sweat, and my thighs are trembling from the aftershocks, but he doesn't give me a second to recover.

He drops to his knees between mine.

"Spread your legs," he says.

I don't move fast enough, so he does it for me. He puts one hand on each thigh and pushes me open again.

"Fuck," he breathes. "You don't even know what you do to me, do you?"

But before I can shake my head, or even react, he's eating me like he's punishing me for making him want it this bad. His hands clamp around my thighs, holding me still while his mouth works every inch—licking, sucking, and fucking me with his tongue until I'm shaking all over again.

"Oh God—please—"

"Say his name again," he growls, dragging his fingers through my soaked slit and thrusting them deep, "and I'll make you choke on mine until you remember who answers your prayers."

He devours me like he's starving and I'm the last thing worth tasting. When he finally pulls back—his lips are wet, and his eyes are fucking glowing. He doesn't even give me a chance to breathe—

just grabs me, spins me around, and bends me over the couch, yanking me back onto my knees like I'm nothing but a body for him to throw around.

And it's fucking hot.

There's no warning before I feel the thick, hot drag of him between my soaked lips—slow and punishing—coating himself in everything he just wrung out of me.

"You wanted control," he growls, as his thick tip presses right where I'm still aching. "You begged for it. Crawled for it."

He pushes forward just enough to make me jolt—and my arms give out.

"And now you're gonna take it."

My scream tears through the room, and I'm wrecked. He's everywhere. Inside me. Over me. Around me.

And—oh my fucking god—he's huge.

I've never actually seen it yet, but it feels like he's splitting me in half. My head spins and I can't catch my breath. I can't even think straight.

I can't do anything *but* take it.

His cock stretches me wide, and for a second, I swear my soul leaves my body.

Part of me feels like I should feel used in a way. But the only thing I feel is full. I have this need for him that's a fucking addiction at this point.

His hand fists in my hair, yanking my head back until my spine bows tight and I'm gasping—pulsing around him, completely gone.

"Say it," he growls, against my ear.

When his hips snap forward with one merciless thrust, the air leaves my lungs in a shattered gasp. My mind is gone. Blank.

My body isn't mine anymore, it's his. Every inch. Every breath. Every fucking nerve ending. It all belongs to him.

And God help me—I love it.

I love the way he's ruining me. I love the stretch, the burn, the wet sound of his cock slamming into my cunt like it's always belonged there.

"Yours," I choke out.

The word rips from my throat like it hurts to give, but his growl that follows is feral. His grip shifts from my hair to the back of my neck, shoving me down, forcing me flat with my face pressing into the couch. My ass is still raised, and I'm still split wide open around him.

Still. Fucking. His.

And I don't want it to end.

"Good fucking girl."

My pussy clenches—greedy and desperate—just from those three words. Instantly soaking him, as it drips down my thighs like I've been starving for this all along. *Which, to be fair, I have.*

He slams into me again—hard—and I cry out, my face mashed into the couch, helpless under the weight of him. I love the way he uses me like I was made for it.

"Look at you," he snarls. "You wanted a god?"

His next thrust knocks the air out of me, and my vision blurs.

"You fucking got one."

I'm spiraling. And not just from his cock. From his voice, and the way he says it.

Okay, fine. I wanted it the whole time. I wanted the monster, the god. The faceless fucking storm I crawled to worship. Something inside me needed to be ruined, to be split in half by someone who wouldn't flinch when I broke.

And now that he's inside me—claiming me with every fucking thrust—there's no coming back from it. There's no pretending I didn't ask for this.

My body isn't mine anymore—just raw nerve endings and a pulse that beats for him.

Each thrust knocks a sound out of me I don't recognize—broken, and completely unhinged.

Another orgasm builds low in my spine, and it's impossible to hold back.

He owns me right now.

Body. Breath. Soul.

And I've never been wetter in my fucking life.

"Please," I gasp. My voice is gone, as my nails claw at the couch like I can hold on to something. But there's no holding on.

There's only him.

He pulls out—just long enough to slap the head of his cock against my clit.

I jerk, moaning. This shouldn't feel this good. I'm right there, strung up and shaking, one touch away from seeing stars. *Oh my God, where has this man been all my life?*

He thrusts back in—only deeper this time. More unforgiving. This man isn't just fucking me—he's claiming me. He's marking places no one's ever touched. Places I didn't even know I had.

And I feel it *everywhere.*

"Steven—please—" I gasp, drooling into the couch, not even trying to hide how wrecked I am. "I can't—I need—"

His hand wraps tight around my throat. "You wanna be my good girl, don't you?" he growls.

Fuck.

I nod, whimpering.

He just laughs, dark and so fucking satisfied. "That's what I thought."

When he pulls out again—just to the tip—and slams back in, I choke on a scream. Every thrust knocks the sound out of me and he talks me through it.

"You looked so fucking beautiful crawling for it."

Thrust.

"Begged so good."

Thrust.

"And now you're gonna wait."

My hips buck without permission, searching for more, but he just presses me down with his palm flat between my shoulder blades, pinning me like I'm nothing but a toy he's not finished with.

I'm slipping fast, and he knows it. I can feel my release coiling tighter and tighter, until it's all I can feel.

It's too much.

"Fuck—please—please, I swear—just let me—"

"Not yet."

His voice is totally unmoved. He's acting like he's got centuries to watch me come apart. The second he says it—my body stalls. The orgasm just hangs there. Every goddamn second he makes me wait pushes me closer to losing it and jumping him. I'm clenching around nothing, soaked and dripping, my clit throbs like it's screaming for mercy. And he just watches me suffer.

He pulls out again. And I cry.

Real, pathetic tears.

I feel so fucking empty without him inside me. I start to protest, but he grabs my hips—hard—dragging me back and flips me on my back.

He slowly kneels between my legs.

"You wanna come?" His voice is low as he wraps one hand around his length—stroking slowly, while he stares at me.

I nod.

I'm surprised I even could give him that much.

And then—Thank God—he slides back in. And this time, he doesn't stop. He fucks me like he's carving his name into my soul. My nails dig into his back and my pussy clenches like it's never letting him go.

I shatter.

I come with a scream that tears from my chest like violence—legs shaking, back arching, body convulsing around his cock like it was built for this.

And he doesn't stop.

He fucks me through it, through the aftershocks and overstimulation and wreckage, growling against my skin like a goddamn animal.

"That's it," he breathes, dragging his lips down my jaw, over my throat. "That's what I fucking wanted."

His hips slam forward one last time—deep and brutal—and he buries himself as a groan tears from his throat, thick, raw and possessive.

His cum floods into me as my body collapses beneath him. I feel completely braindead, yet so alive.

He grabs my jaw, tilting my face up to meet his, and his eyes are still wild and hungry.

"You crawl when I tell you to."

He pauses.

"You come when I say."

Then he leans in—lips brushing my cheek.

"And this pussy?" he murmurs, thrusting once. "This fucking pussy is mine now."

He stays like that for a moment. Buried inside me. Breath ragged against my skin. And then, just as he pulls out, his lips brush my cheek again.

"Good girl."

Fuck me, it almost sounds sweet. It shouldn't sound like that. I didn't realize I was such a whore for praise.

He stands and walks out of the room, while all I can do is stare up at the ceiling. My throat is raw, and every inch of me is flushed and aching.

My chest rises in erratic bursts, while my lungs drag in air like my body's trying to piece itself back together.

What the fuck just happened?

Why do I want him to come back? And why do I feel empty now that he's not touching me?

I try to close my legs, but I can't.

Everything hurts. My thighs are shaking and my pussy's still fluttering like it's waiting for round two.

I hear footsteps, but I don't sit up. He steps back into the room with a towel in hand, and something else I can't see.

He crouches beside me—like he didn't just fuck the soul out of my body. Too calm and too fucking unbothered for what he just did.

Then his voice slices through the silence. "Spread your legs."

I blink up at him—dazed, unsure if I heard him right. When I whimper, he chuckles. "Don't worry, I'm just cleaning you up, we've got all night."

Something in me is still on the fucking floor crawling and I'm waiting for him to tell me what to do next. I don't know what to do with this. With him. No one's ever wiped me off before and I don't know how to be touched like this. *Not after being ruined like that.*

Hell, he's still leaking out of me.

His gaze drops to the space between my thighs like he could hear my thoughts, and I see the heat flash through his eyes.

Fucking hell.

The second the wet towel brushes my inner thigh, and I jerk, hissing through my teeth, still too raw to handle the drag of cotton on oversensitive skin.

He wipes me slowly—collecting the mess he made with a gentleness that floors me.

"This... is mine."

His voice is gravel, and his eyes are still locked on the slick mess between my thighs. "And if anyone else so much as touches it—I'll carve your name into their skin before I kill them."

The air punches out of my lungs in one long, ragged breath. My mouth opens as heat, then confusion, then want, rip through my body all at once.

What the fuck is happening to me and when did I turn into someone that gets turned on by violence?

I swallow hard, praying my voice comes out steady.

"You're insane," I whisper—barely more than breath.

He leans in closer, with the same voice that pulled the crawl right out of me. "No, sweetheart."

Then he presses the towel harder, cruel in a way that makes my back arch as a moan slips out—earning me a smile from him.

"I'm just getting started."

He finishes cleaning me up then tosses the towel aside and stands with that cocky silence stretching between us again. He turns away without a word, but at the doorway, he pauses.

"Go pee," he says. "Then come back."

Come back?

Not leave or go to bed?

What the fuck am I supposed to do with that?

I feel tender in places I didn't even know could be touched but I move anyway. Because apparently—I do what he says now.

The bathroom is dim as moonlight spills across the tile like water. I don't look in the mirror, I don't need to. I already know what I'll see and we don't really need to go there right now.

I wash my hands like I can scrub the submission off my skin but it's in me now. Humming under the surface. And still—I hover at the door.

I could crawl into the guest bed and pretend none of this happened. Rebuild the walls, but I *want* to go back out there.

I walk down the hall and see him sitting on the edge of the couch, shirtless and leaning forward with his arms resting on his knees like he's deep in thought.

The soft flicker of the TV is the only light in the room—Harry Potter's still playing and I hover in the doorway. I should probably thank him for telling me to pee, but instead I open my mouth and let the brat speak first.

"So what, is this standard procedure after you fuck someone stupid?"

He stares at the floor—like the whole world lives between his feet and whatever's still dripping out of me. The silence stretches, making my stomach twist in that way I hate. *Okaayyy.*

I shift, awkwardly glancing at the screen—and a laugh slips out before I can stop it.

Ron's voice echoes across the room. *"Why spiders? Why couldn't it be 'follow the butterflies'?"*

I snort and instantly feel his stare. He's not watching the floor anymore, he's watching me. His dark eyes are so intense it steals the breath from my lungs. I blink. "What?"

His voice cuts through the quiet, soft enough to gut me.

"You don't laugh like that."

I scoff, trying to claw the moment back before it gets too close or too real. "Are you keeping a file on me now?" I ask, raising a brow.

He smiles. "Crawls. Orgasms. Emotional outbursts...what's next?"

I roll my eyes and cross the room, collapsing onto the opposite end of the couch. My body still aches, feeling stretched and sore in ways I don't want to think about. Okay, I actually do want to keep thinking about them.

I grab a throw pillow and wedge it between us like that'll do anything. Whatever's between us hums louder than the movie, and I'm getting wet all over again just thinking about it.

I'm doing everything in my power not to look at the man who made my body beg and now sits there—composed, and relaxed.

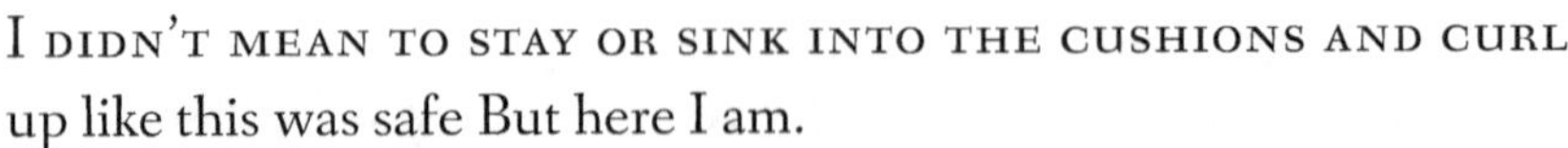

I DIDN'T MEAN TO STAY OR SINK INTO THE CUSHIONS AND CURL up like this was safe But here I am.

And apparently... so is he.

At some point, he shifted closer and his arms stretched across the back of the couch, close enough that I feel his warmth. It's taking everything in me not to lean toward it.

Sirius falls through the veil and I feel it hit—before it even happens. My chest is suddenly too tight and my eyes sting.

Harry screams and my throat does that awful, aching thing—like grief knows me too well to knock first.

I swipe at my cheek, fast, so he doesn't see anything. The last thing I need is...

"Jesus," he mutters. "You're crying over the dog-wizard?"

My head snaps toward him, face burning. Heat flashes behind my ribs, because of the audacity of this man right now.

"Fuck you," I spit, as my voice cracks.

He smirks, and it's just cocky enough to make me feel seen.

"He was the only family Harry had left," I say. Try to keep it light, but my voice cracks.

The smirk slips. "Didn't realize dead godfathers hit you that hard."

I grit my teeth, keeping my eyes on the screen like it's going to save me.

"They don't."

He tilts his head, watching me.

"Sure," he says after a beat. "You always tear up when guys fall through curtains?"

I glance at him through narrowed eyes and full defense mode. "You always act like you don't feel anything?"

That gets him. His jaw ticks—barely. He lets the silence settle in like it belongs there.

Then softer—"You've got that look."

My brow pulls tight. "What look?"

He shrugs one shoulder, all calm detachment, as if we're not standing on the edge of something neither of us can come back from.

"Like you've lost something you never got back."

The words land in a way that doesn't register until it's already too late. I don't even realize I've stopped breathing until my chest pulls tight and the air rushes out all at once.

The ache blooms behind my ribs—raw and familiar—and I feel the crack before I can pretend to brace for it.

I exhale hard, trying to push the air out fast enough, so that it'll blow the moment away with it before I lose it completely.

"Anyway." I fake a shrug, eyes back on the screen. "It's just a movie. Fictional wizard-dad dies. Big deal."

But the damage is done—and we both know it. He doesn't push, so I fill the silence, because God forbid I ever let one sit too long.

"I think it's the vanishing that gets me," I say, crossing my arms tighter. "One second, someone's in your corner—and the next? Gone."

Steven tilts his head, that unreadable stare narrowing. But he says nothing, so I keep going.

"Maybe I'm still bitter," I mutter, trying to laugh, but it cracks in my throat. "When I moved here, I didn't speak English. Not really."

I see him go still for two seconds before his body relaxes again.

"I was eight," I say quietly. "They stuck me in a class and just... left me. Just—sink or swim."

My fingers twist the hem of my shirt, anchoring me.

"I used to eat my lunch in the bathroom, because it was easier than trying to talk and explain why the words didn't come out right."

A breath pushes out of me—tight and bitter.

"There was this group of girls that called me Static. They'd tell me I made things awkward just by breathing."

I pause, clenching my jaw. That old burn flares in my throat, sharp and humiliating. Steven doesn't speak. But I feel the change in the air, in the way he watches me now—less predator, and more... something else.

"Then one day, this guy just sat next to me, he didn't say much, but he waited, and didn't flinch when I butchered a sentence."

A smile ghosts across my lips. "I think he said like four full sentences that whole week. But for the first time, someone listened and was just... there."

I blink at the screen just in time to watch Sirius fall.

"And then he moved away."

Steven blinks once. "So that's why the wizard-dog broke you."

I snort, eyes burning again. "Excuse you. He's an animagus. He also happens to be the only person who saw Harry. Who stayed. Who made him feel... less alone."

I glance at him.

"You'd cry too if your only person vanished into a curtain."

He just tilts his head giving me this look. My mind instantly goes to the photos I found in his office. The look he's giving me tells me he knows exactly what I'm talking about.

"So let me guess," he says finally. "You spent the next ten years perfecting your English and collecting emotional baggage."

I raise a brow. "No. I started lighting my Barbies on fire and learning how to fake smiles that don't invite questions."

His mouth twitches. "Therapy must love you."

"Therapy can't afford me," I shoot back.

There's a pause—just long enough for my brain to betray me. "My mom used to sing to me in Spanish. Only when she thought I was asleep though."

It comes out before I can stop it, like my mouth forgot we don't do that—don't share random things, but here we are.

"My grandma always said I had la tormenta in me. Too much storm and not enough silence."

He doesn't say anything—but the air shifts as the corner of his lips curl. And I fucking hate how much I notice it.

"And you've been in Denver since?"

I shake my head, casually. "No, I actually just moved here last year."

I glance back at the screen, like this whole conversation's background noise. "Honestly? I don't really remember the move. It was kind of a blur. But I just needed a change of scenery, you know?"

My thumb rubs over the seam of the blanket. "I was sick for a while—right after I got here. I kept having these weird dreams. Still do, but that's not important."

His eyes flick to mine at that—but he doesn't push. I pause, searching the edges of my memory.

Steven doesn't fill the space with reassurance like a normal person would. "I don't think it's normal to forget that much when you move."

Fuck.

Right. I probably shouldn't trauma-dump on the man who just rearranged my spine and threatened to brand me from the inside out.

I shrug, trying to play it off. "Guess I just wasn't paying attention."

It's a lie, but it's the safest one I've got. My thumb rubs at a spot on the blanket that isn't even there, chasing a memory I don't really want to catch.

The silence pulls tight between us. "So what came before Denver?"

"I lived on the coast," I murmur. "It's like there's this whole stretch of time I watched happen instead of living through it. Sometimes it feels like that life belonged to someone else."

He doesn't respond. But something in the way he's staring at me makes my skin prickle.

"What happened there?"

His voice is soft, but there's nothing gentle about it. The movie's over now, and the credits are rolling in silence. I feel raw and exposed. I also feel cornered, so I do the only thing I know how to do—snap back before I bleed too much.

"Wow," I mutter, pushing the blanket off my legs. "Didn't

realize I signed up for a therapy session. You moonlight as Dr. Phil, or is this just how you flirt?"

I can feel his jaw lock from across the couch.

"I ask a question, and you get defensive," he says flatly. "Interesting."

"Oh, sorry," I bite, standing up. "Was I supposed to sob into your lap and hand over my trauma like a good little patient?" I fold my arms, turning toward the kitchen. "I'm getting food."

23

"Sometimes the safest place is under watch."
(But only if the right eyes are on you.)

Ani

How is it that this man can make me wetter than a whore in church and ready to punch him in the face five seconds later? Something in my chest pulls tight, but I don't turn around. Not giving him the satisfaction.

I storm into the kitchen and start yanking open drawers like I belong here, even though I haven't got a damn clue where anything is. The first one's full of knives. Cool. That's comforting. I make a mental note of that, in case I need one later. The second drawer has a bunch of batteries and zip ties. Which is slightly alarming. The third just has a single loose rubber band and a pack of gum that expired two years ago.

I blink at it. "Jesus. What are you, a serial killer or a Boy Scout?"

Still no answer from behind me.

"Not even a protein bar or some cookies?" I mutter, slamming it shut. "What kind of maniac lives off rage and raw intimidation?"

I try to focus on finding food. I need something—*anything*—to do with my hands. I open the fridge and grab the first few things that look remotely edible—lunch meat, mustard, and a jar of what looks like pickles.

I mutter something half-feral under my breath as I toss the jar and the half-crushed bread onto the counter. I reach up—fast, too fast—and that's when it happens.

The cabinet above me swings open, and crack—"Son of a bitch."

My skull snaps back and the jar slips from my hand, hitting the floor with a wet, mocking splat. It's all over my foot, the floor, and the cabinet. The crime scene of my dignity.

I just blink at it, dazed. Maybe if I stare long enough, it'll take itself back. I can tell by the smell that they definitely weren't pickles. Not even close. "Is that... sauerkraut?" I mutter, wrinkling my nose.

I grab a paper towel swiping at the mess and somehow, I make it worse. Now everything's wet. *Perfect.*

I'm mid-wipe, muttering curses, when I feel him behind me. He steps into the kitchen, dragging his gaze over the splattered mess, then up to me and my flushed, mustard-footed mess.

"Of course you'd break something," he mutters.

That's it. Is he fucking kidding me?

I hurl the dirty paper towel at his chest without hesitation. "Go fuck yourself," I bite out. "With a butter knife."

It hits dead center and sticks—right over his chest. He looks down at it, then back up at me. No smile, not even a laugh.

Fuck.

Is he going to murder me for this? Is this it—the final straw, the moment I pushed too far?

And then—Fuck me. He grabs the hem of his shirt and peels it off in one slow, fluid motion. His muscles flex like the universe is punishing me on purpose, and tosses it onto the counter without a word.

Just like that—he's standing there. Shirtless. Giving me that look. That heavy, consuming look that sees right through everything I ever tried to hide. It's the same one he gave me when he made me crawl to him. And like the unhinged masochist I apparently am, I look lower.

The ink across his chest is impossible to ignore—and I can't help but trace the one that trails down his side, curving just beneath the waistband of his sweats.

My thighs clench before I can stop them, and I can feel my pulse throbbing between my legs.

Jesus.

I'm wet. Again.

Apparently, my body has zero survival instincts because the way he's standing there is worse than anything he could say.

Under his stare, I feel it all flooding back. The hunger. The surrender. The way I'd crawl again right now if he told me to. He takes one slow step forward, with his eyes locked on me like I'm the next thing he's going to devour.

I don't even know what I was going to say and all I can think is, *Goddamn it. He's going to wreck me again* and I'm going to let him. I clear my throat, eyes flicking back up to his face like I wasn't just eye-fucking him and all his tattoos.

"You planning to put a shirt on, or are we doing this whole... kitchen striptease thing now?"

It's meant to be sarcastic but it comes out breathless. His eyes narrow slightly, then he steps closer. I don't back away, even though I should. I'm fucked in the head, apparently.

He doesn't stop until he's right in front of me—close enough I can feel the heat coming off his bare skin. He leans in, and his mouth brushes the shell of my ear.

"You're the one who started stripping me, pretty girl."

My knees almost buckle as his fingers trail over my wrist. "You remember what happened last time you couldn't stop looking."

Of course I fucking remember. That will live rent free in my mind for life.

"You begged," he murmurs. "You crawled. And I broke you open with my fingers before I even let you have my cock."

I swear my pulse skips and I feel him everywhere.

"You want more?" he asks, deadly soft. "Keep looking at me like that."

And just like that, I'm trembling again. My whole body's humming, all too aware of every inch of his skin, and every slow breath between us. So I do the only thing I can do to shut it down.

I roll my eyes, scoffing through the burn in my throat. "God, you act like your dick has divine powers. Trust me, I've had better."

The second I say it, I know I've gone too far. It's a lie. A stupid, reckless, screaming lie. Because no one's ever touched me like he has. No one's ever looked at me like that—like they could tear me open with their hands and make me thank them for it.

He straightens and I can see that calm, cold mask slipping right into place—it's dangerous how in control he is.

"You didn't seem to mind when my cum was dripping down your thighs and you were moaning my name like it was salvation."

I go still, but he doesn't stop.

"You want the truth?" he says, cold enough to ruin me. "You looked wrecked. Your body already fucking knew it belonged to me. And you were so wet—" He leans in, eyes dark. "I could've buried my face between your legs and choked on it. I would've died happy, too."

My chest heaves—I can't tell if I want to slap him or crawl into his lap and make him say it again.

There is something seriously wrong with me.

No one should be allowed to talk to me like that, to say something that filthy and have my body light up like a christmas tree.

I swallow hard, trying to hold onto the anger, but it's slipping—drowning under the heat pooling between my legs.

"I guess it's easy to sound like God when you only fuck women who forget their standards."

His jaw flexes. But instead of biting back, he smiles. "Oh, sweetheart," he murmurs, taking a step toward me, "you didn't forget your standards. You just never had any."

I open my mouth to say something, but he cuts me off.

"You let me touch you the same day we met. You crawled for me like you had no self-respect left to give. Don't act like you're hard to break when you gave me everything without asking for a single fucking thing back."

The words hit like a punch to the chest and my throat burns, but I force the words through it.

"Right," I snap, eyes narrowing. "Because you're such a fucking prize. You think I didn't feel it?"

He doesn't answer. So I go for the throat.

"I know who you are now, Steven." His name tastes like venom. "I know exactly who I let crawl inside me."

His jaw ticks, but he still says nothing. The silence between us shatters and reconstructs a hundred different ways, all of them jagged.

"Or maybe you liked pretending I didn't know. Maybe that made it easier to treat me like a hole instead of a person you can't fucking stop wanting."

That hits somewhere deep, but he doesn't let it show. Not with his face. Just the way his whole body goes still.

"Careful, sweetheart." His voice is a low, lethal threat. "Keep talking like that and I'll remind you exactly how much you liked being used."

"Go to hell," I growl, pushing past him.

"Already there, *muñeca*. You just made it feel like home."

I stop. Dead in my tracks. The words bury themselves somewhere under my ribs and light the whole place on fire. *Why would he call me that?*

I turn slowly.

"Funny," I hiss, "you only ever seem to hate me when your cock's not inside me."

Something flickers in his eyes, but then he laughs. "Don't flatter yourself, baby. I've fucked a lot of girls who begged."

His next words come like a knife to the throat. "Difference is, they didn't crawl for me with someone else's fingerprints still on them."

Silence detonates between us and my stomach drops, but my blood turns electric.

"What the fuck did you just say?"

He steps closer, eyes black with something unreadable—something mean.

"You heard me. Maybe you should think a little harder about the men you spread your legs for. Starting with the one who owned you before I ever touched you."

He doesn't say his name but he doesn't need to. My heart slams against my ribs like it's trying to escape, and my face burns. My fists curl so tight my nails dig half-moons into my palms. And when I speak, my voice is shaking with fury.

"You don't get to talk about me like that," I whisper. "You don't get to use what you think you know as a weapon."

"I'm not wrong though, am I?" he growls, stepping in like he wants to drive the knife deeper. "I see it in your eyes every time he's near you. And worse—every time you look at me, like you're still trying to figure out who you belong to."

Are we fighting? Because I didn't come in here looking for one, but apparently all we do is fuck or fight—or both at the same time. I was just trying to breathe, and now I'm angry and exposed and staring at him like it's his fault I feel everything too loud.

"Go fuck yourself, Steven."

I turn around and don't stop walking, because if I do, I'll scream. Or hit him. Or worse—I'll stay. My feet carry me down the hall on instinct alone and my breath is caught somewhere between a sob and a snarl. I can't hear anything over my heartbeat. I shove the bedroom door open and slam it behind me like it might erase everything he just said.

You liked being used.

I suck in a breath that tastes like betrayal and every bad choice

I've ever made because it's not just the words—it's the way he said them.

I press my back to the door, keeping my fists clenched at my sides. My heart races as that heat rushes up my throat. I'm so fucking pissed, and humiliated that I let him see me like that. I sat there and let him pull me apart in ways no one ever has and now he's tossing it back in my face like it meant nothing.

Fuck that.

I spin, grabbing the nearest pillow, and hurl it across the room with a guttural scream that tears out of my throat like it's been waiting years to be heard. It slams into the wall with a soft thud and drops uselessly to the floor—like it's not carrying every broken thing I can't say out loud. Every scream I've swallowed. And every feeling I wasn't allowed to have.

I pace back and forth, but my breath's too loud, my blood's too hot, and I still feel his hands on my skin like a curse I can't scrub off.

I stop in front of the mirror—and wish I hadn't. My reflection looks unhinged, my hair's tangled, and my eyes are red and glassy with a rage I don't know where to bury. I hate this version of me. The one who still wants to be wanted.

There's a part of me that wants him to come after me, but I know he won't. Because that would require admitting something.

I grab my phone to call Sarah, my fingers still shaking as I open the screen. I need a distraction. Anything that isn't this hollow, clawing ache under my ribs. My vision's still blurry with tears I refuse to let fall, but I need to do something.

A new message from another Unknown number stares back at me. My stomach knots because I know I blocked the last one. So what the fuck is this?

I tap it open and it's a photo of me, taken from behind. I'm leaving my apartment—hood pulled up, hair a mess, and one hand white-knuckling my phone. It's grainy, and clearly taken from a distance. But it's me.

My blood turns to ice.

UNKNOWN: Still sleep with the light on and tuck your feet under the covers like you're hiding from monsters? They're coming anyway. You don't remember what happened, but I do.

My blood runs cold as I stare at the screen. *What the fuck does that mean?*

Even as I ask it, something shifts. A door creaks open inside me—one I boarded shut a long time ago and swore I'd never touch again. My throat tightens and suddenly, I'm not in Steven's house anymore. I'm somewhere else. I'm hiding in a room with the lights off. The floor is cold against my bare legs, and my knees are tucked to my chest. I can hear a man's voice—slurred and violent, while he screams. Something shatters, and the air's so thick with bleach I feel like I'm suffocating.

I'm under a sink, curled between a mop bucket and a jug of detergent, trying not to breathe. Someone's crying or maybe that's me.

And then— I'm back. Ripped out of the memory so hard I gasp. My hands are shaking, and I'm clutching my phone like it might explode.

My whole body's shaking and my vision's swimming.

I press a hand to my mouth, but the sob slips out anyway because whoever sent that message...they clearly know the part of me I've been trying to run away from. It has to be my ex. I don't think. I just move. I shove my phone into my pocket, grab the nearest hoodie off the floor, and head for the door. The second I step into the hallway, Bern starts barking.

"Shhh," I whisper harshly, glancing toward the living room. "Jesus, you're gonna give me away—"

I slip out the front door before I can think better of it. The night hits me like a slap—cold and sharp, and far too quiet.

Bern's still barking behind me as I move fast and low around the side of the cabin, cutting toward the tree line. I don't know where I'm going, I just know I need some space right now. Branches crunch underfoot and my breath fogs the air.

"Fuck this," I mutter under my breath, ducking under a low-hanging branch. "Fuck him. Fuck all of them."

I swipe at my face with my sleeve, still trying to get my breathing under control. That mother fucker, with his goddamn mouth and his accusations like knives. That photo. That message. Everything. I should've moved to Europe.

"Creep's probably watching from a goddamn bush somewhere," I spit, my voice getting louder. "Stalking me like I'm his. To do what? Erase? Control? Kill?"

My foot slips in the packed dirt and I catch myself against a tree, cursing again. I think I'm having a panic attack.

"God, and that smug bastard. Acting like he's the only one who's broken. Like I wanted any of this, I didn't give up my entire life for something I don't even remember!"

The wind gusts, cold and sharp across my face, but I keep going.

"I don't know who I was before."

The words scrape out. "I don't even know what the hell happened to make me leave. All I have is this pit in my stomach and a handful of dreams."

I pause, but it's too late to stop. Bernadette lets out a soft whine behind me, like she knows I'm unraveling. "I didn't ask for this." My voice is shaking as the burn hits my eyes. "Any of it."

I throw my hands out, pacing like the fury needs somewhere to land. "And now I'm just supposed to play house with some emotionally constipated psychopath while my past sends me hate mail from burner phones? Seriously? Fuck that."

I stop, my chest is heaving, and my hands won't stop shaking. I brace myself against the nearest tree.

"I'm not doing this. I didn't sign up for whatever the hell this is —I just wanted to disappear. I just wanted to breathe."

I press the heels of my hands into my eyes and whisper, "I just want to feel normal. I want to feel safe for five goddamn minutes."

That's when I hear it—a twig snapping behind me. I spin so fast my heart lodges in my throat. But I already know who it is. Steven steps out of the shadows like he's been there the whole time—watching, listening. His shirt's still off, and his eyes are locked on me like I'm both a threat and a tragedy he already fucking owns.

"You done?"

His voice is pure gravel—low and rough, dragging across my skin like it knows exactly where to hurt. A shiver rips down my spine and goosebumps flash across my arms, heat chasing them like static.

"Not even fucking close."

"Little late for a nature walk, don't you think?"

I glare at him, the adrenaline and fury in my chest coils tighter —like a fuse begging for a match.

"Move."

He doesn't. Instead, he tilts his head, narrowing his eyes like he's taking inventory of all the ways I'm coming undone.

"You planning to hike through the woods with just a hoodie and your trauma?"

My teeth clench. "Don't start with me right now."

His mouth twitches. "Do you always run when someone gets too close?"

My whole body stills. Not just from the words—but the way he says them. Like he's already dissected me and left the bones on the table.

I laugh. "No," I say, keeping my voice tight. "Sometimes I wait until they break something first."

My hands curl into fists at my sides and I hate how he gets under my skin without even trying. I fucking hate how my breath comes too fast, and my chest won't stop fucking heaving like I'm being chased.

I swallow hard and add, "Don't pretend like you haven't spent the last twenty-four hours proving I was right."

His eyes flick to the treeline, then back to me—unbothered. "I heard you," he says quietly. "Back there."

My stomach tightens and I stiffen. "Eavesdropping now? That your thing?"

"I don't need to eavesdrop when you're screaming at ghosts in the dark."

He takes another step, but I hold my ground. Only, it's harder now, with him this close—his body is all heat and shadows, but the scent of him is sharp against the cold air.

"You said something about playing house with a psychopath," he murmurs. "That supposed to be me?"

I lift my chin. "If the boot fits."

Another half-step and he's lowering his voice like it's a secret between us. "Or were you talking about the one you're really running from?"

My breath catches—just for a second—but it's enough. His eyes narrow, and his voice drops, quieter this time.

"You think I don't recognize it? That look in your eye when things get too close?" He stops in front of me. "I used to sleep with a gun under my pillow. Not because I was scared someone would come for me—but because I didn't trust myself not to get there first."

His gaze doesn't soften. If anything, it cuts deeper. "So don't talk to me about shutting down. I know what it's like to live in survival mode so long, peace starts to feel like a setup."

Something shifts in my chest. Maybe it's nothing, but maybe it's everything.

"You didn't bring your bag." His voice dips lower. "If you were really running... you wouldn't have left your shit in the house."

My throat tightens. "Maybe I wasn't thinking."

"No." He stops in front of me again, eyes pinned to mine like he's already dismantled the lie. "You were thinking too much. That's the problem."

His eyes search mine like he's sifting through rubble for the truth. "What happened before you got here, Ani?"

He's so close I can't breathe. And still—I lie.

"I don't remember." I say, forcing the words through trembling lips. He stares at me for a long moment.

Then soft and almost deadly. "You remember enough to be scared."

The words land like a punch to the gut, but I don't flinch. I refuse. Instead, I tilt my head, eyes burning into his like I might set him on fire.

"Yeah?" I whisper. "And what are you so scared of, Steven?"

That gets him. It's just the smallest flicker, but I see it. The vein in his neck pulses and his nostrils flare. That unreadable calm in his eyes ripples for half a second, like I found the wire he didn't want touched. I take a step toward him now, my voice is more controlled.

"You follow me. You watch me like I'm a weapon you're waiting to use—but you never tell me why. You don't ask. You don't trust. You just... hover. Like you're waiting for the part where I prove you right."

I pause, the cold air biting at my lips.

"So tell me, what is it exactly that you're waiting for me to do? Slip up? Bleed? Or just disappear, like everyone else you've ever touched?"

His eyes darken. But he doesn't answer. Because I hit something. And for the first time since I met him—he doesn't look like he's in control.

24

Steven

She thinks I don't know her patterns yet? I could find that girl in a blackout with nothing but the sound of her breath. I could map the rhythm of her panic in my fucking sleep. And somehow that's the part I can't stomach.

I shouldn't know her like this—shouldn't crave the sound of her unraveling. Fuck, I shouldn't feel my pulse shift every time she runs. But I do. And it's rotting something inside me I didn't think I had left.

She's twitchy, paranoid, and always calculating exits.

I see the tension in her jaw, and the way her eyes go flat like she's somewhere else. I see the way she wraps her arms tighter like she's trying to keep something in.

She's hiding something and I'm done waiting for crumbs. This was never about me. Which makes what I do next feel... inevitable.

I'm behind her before I even register the movement, hunger flares under my skin. When I grab her arm and yank her around, she gasps—but it's not fear in her eyes.

It's fury. Wild, sharp-edged fury that makes my cock twitch. I can also see the heat in her eyes, she wants me.

"Let go of me," she bites, shoving at my chest.

I pin her to the nearest tree, caging her in while one hand grips her hip and the other wraps around her wrist tight enough to feel her pulse.

"You done lying to me yet?" I growl against her jaw. "Or do I need to fuck the truth out of you too?"

Her chest heaves. "Fuck you."

I smirk, leaning in close enough to taste the anger shaking off her skin. "You already did, sweetheart."

My voice drops, "And if you wanted another round, all you had to do was ask."

I press in closer, and her back arches, and I can feel her tits pushing into me begging for my hands. I don't know if it's defiance or desire that's fueling her right now and I don't care.

"Tell me why you ran."

Her mouth opens, but no sound comes out, so I drag my hand down her thigh and squeeze.

"You gonna answer me?" my lips brush her ear. "Or should I remind you how loud you get when you beg?"

"Stop it," she whispers. But her hips tilt forward.

"Then talk."

She bites her lip—hard—and finally breaks. "I don't remember, okay?" she bursts out. "I don't fucking remember."

I go still.

"What do you mean, you don't remember," I echo, lower this time. Her eyes are wide and glassy in a way that tells me she's barely holding it together.

"I—I don't know," she stammers. "There's gaps. Nightmares. Things I can't explain."

My pulse kicks hard, there's now a dull throb at the base of my neck. Fuck.

She doesn't know.

She really doesn't know? I watch her carefully, masking everything. The urge to react, to speak, to tell her she's not crazy—that she's not wrong about the silence or the missing time. But I can't.

Not yet. Because if she doesn't remember... that changes everything.

It shifts the weight of the game I thought I was playing. She's sitting there unraveling in front of me, and all I can think about is how far this goes. It's not just an obsession anymore, this is something else.

I let the silence drag. Enough to prove I heard her. Not enough to admit it mattered. Because caring gets messy.

"What kind of nightmares?" I ask, carefully.

She exhales, "Hands. Strangers. My body not listening. Sometimes it feels like I'm screaming but nothing comes out. Sometimes I wake up and I'm already crying."

I clench my jaw so tight it aches. That would explain the things she says when she's sleeping. Now I'm burning—because for a moment I wanted to hurt her, to punish her for slipping away. But now I want to kill whoever put that look in her eyes.

She keeps going, oblivious to the storm tearing through me.

"I just—" She wipes her face with her sleeve. "Sometimes I get flashes of being dragged. Of motel lights. Of blood. And I never know if they're dreams or—" She cuts herself off, her voice cracking. "It doesn't matter."

It does. It matters more than anything. But I can't say that. Not when I'm this close to losing control. Not when the only thing I know how to do is take. Instead, I grab her chin, tilting her face toward me—rougher than I mean to. Her breath stutters, and fuck, that sound undoes something in me.

If she keeps talking, I'll say something I shouldn't and I can't afford that right now, so I slam my mouth down on hers.

It's not gentle. It's rage, heat, and punishment tangled into one. A feral, unspoken demand—because I need something I don't have the words for. I need to remind her exactly who owns every fucking inch of her body. That if I take her hard enough, maybe—just maybe—she'll stop slipping through my fingers.

I kiss her like I'm trying to win a war I already lost the second she looked at me.

She gasps, and I use it—swallowing her whole, pinning her against the tree like I'm staking a claim. My hands are already everywhere—fisting in her hoodie, yanking it up, dragging across bare skin and making her whimper.

"Steven—" she breathes.

"Shut up."

I hike her thigh up around my hip, pressing between her legs— and she moans, desperate and broken.

"You want something real?" I growl against her throat. "This is it. I already told you, you're mine."

Her nails dig into my back. She's shaking and angry and half out of her mind, but her body arches as her mouth finds mine again, like she's trying to punish me in her own way, for every question I asked.

I shove her pants down and rip open my own. When I push inside her, she screams.

It echoes through the trees like a warning as I slam into her again and again. My hands are tight on her hips as her back scrapes against the bark, her gasps are a broken prayer in the cold.

"You feel that?" I grind out. "That's what the truth tastes like, sweetheart."

"Fuck you," she chokes out. Her legs lock around me as her body begs. It's feral and messy. It's too much and not enough all at once. Her head falls back, and her mouth is open in a silent cry as I thrust harder, dragging her right back to the edge she swore she was done with. She clenches around me, slick and pulsing and fucking perfect—I lose whatever thread of control I had left.

My hand fists in her hair, yanking her head forward so she has to look at me when she comes.

"Look at me," I growl. "Let them fucking hear it."

She sobs—loud—and shatters all over me, her body is seizing like she's breaking open from the inside out. And I follow—driving deep with a growl ripping from my chest as I come inside her, hips slamming against hers like I'm trying to brand her from my cock alone.

I press my forehead to hers, breathing her in like the air might disappear if I don't take all of it now. Our exhales are ragged, tangled between us, and her skin burns against the cold bite of the night.

"If you ever let another man touch you again..." My thumb drags slowly over her bottom lip, still swollen from everything I've taken. "I swear, I'll fucking kill him."

She doesn't answer, but her mouth parts like she wants to. Her lashes are damp, and her pupils are still blown wide.

I lean in, lips grazing her ear. "I don't share. I don't forget. And I sure as fuck don't let go."

Then I slide out of her, watching the way her body flinches from the loss. Her breath catches, and she clutches at the space between us like she's still chasing that last wave.

Good. I wanted to ruin her for anyone else. The next time she thinks about leaving, she'll remember the way I claimed her. Even if she hates me for it. *Especially if she does.*

She tries to close her legs, but I stop her. My hand slides between them again, dragging through the slick mess I just fucked into her, smearing it everywhere. "You're mine." I whisper.

She jerks beneath my touch, trying to resist, but I don't let her. I bring my hand up slowly and press two fingers against her lips.

"Open."

She hesitates, but her lips pop open.

"Do you taste that?" I murmur, eyes locked on hers. "That's mine."

Her breath shudders as I push my fingers past her lips and she sucks in a sharp inhale through her nose as her lips close around them. Her tongue moves instinctively around my fingers, and fuck me, I almost lose it all over again.

"Good girl," I rasp, dragging my fingers back out and brushing her chin with my thumb. "Say it."

Her voice is wrecked and broken around the taste of us. "... yours."

The sound is a goddamn weapon and I will never let her forget who she belongs to.

I rest my forehead against hers for a beat, both of us breathing hard, the cold air cutting through the sweat between us. My blood's still boiling, but my head is already turning—calculating. Locking in on what I know, and what I don't.

"We're going back to the cabin," I say. "You're going to sit your ass on that couch, and you're going to talk."

I lean in, teeth grazing her jaw. "Or I'll drag the answers out of you another way."

I feel her shiver under my touch.

The walk back is quiet except for the crunch of the dirt and Bernadette's occasional bark in the distance. I stay close enough to catch her if she bolts again, not that she will.

Inside, the air is warm, and the dull flicker of another Harry Potter plays in the background. She doesn't speak as she collapses onto the couch, hoodie still half off, and her cheeks flushed. She sits like someone who's been hit by a truck and doesn't know if she lived or not.

I stay standing, watching her as she stares at the screen for a long time—eyes flicking toward it, but not seeing it.

"I don't know where to start," she says finally, her voice is small and raw.

"Try the beginning," I murmur.

"I don't remember the beginning."

She curls her knees up to her chest and hugs them. Her eyes are glued to the TV like she needs something to distract her.

"I remember... blood," she says slowly. "And voices. Someone was yelling. I was in a room, I think. A motel. I remember the wallpaper was peeling, and there was something in the sink. Or—"

She stops and swallows hard.

"I remember my ex slapping me. Hard."

My jaw flexes, but I say nothing.

"And then someone else came. I don't remember who. Just... that there were people with him. I remember being thrown in the back of a car." She blinks. "I think I kicked someone."

My pulse spikes, as I grit my teeth. "When?"

She shrugs. "I woke up somewhere else with new clothes and no idea where I was. I could tell I'd been drugged, so I panicked and ran. I found a bus stop, bought a ticket to Colorado with the cash in my pocket and never looked back."

I swallow the taste of rust in my mouth but stay standing. She's waiting for me to comfort her, share something back, maybe even meet her there, but I don't.

Because I fucking can't. If I open my mouth, I'll tell her too much.

So I stay quiet.

Every word she says is a breadcrumb, and I don't have the luxury of letting my feelings interfere—not if I want to get to the end of this. The movie continues to play, and I sit down beside her.

Her head tilts toward the screen, eyes half-lidded as the music swells—like something tragic just broke all over again. Then, slowly —without a word, without even looking at me—she leans sideways until her shoulder brushes mine.

At first, I think it's nothing, until she exhales. Her head drops gently against my arm, her body relaxing in increments, like it finally found a place safe enough to unravel.

She's asleep.

I don't fucking move. I can't even breathe. She just... folds into me like it's instinct. And it wrecks me in a way nothing ever has, because I didn't earn this, I don't deserve the trust that came with it.

Still—I sit there, for almost an hour, watching her chest rise and fall in steady rhythm. Her mouth is parted just enough to steal my attention, and her hairs a mess across her cheek. And all I can think is—how the fuck am I ever supposed to let this go now?

I move slowly, careful not to jolt her as I shift my arm under her legs and scoop her into my chest. She's weightless in a way that guts me—like she's been carrying so much for so long that even sleep can't anchor her.

Her head lolls against my shoulder, and for one fucked-up second, I let myself imagine this is normal. That she's mine in some quiet, unbroken way. I make it to the bedroom without a sound, easing her down onto the mattress and she stirs as the blanket slips over her legs.

"M'sorry," she mumbles, voice caught somewhere between sleep and storm.

I go still.

"What?"

Her lips part again, barely moving. "I didn't mean to ruin every-thing," she whispers. "I just wanted out."

Ruin everything...?

The words slice through me, and my pulse staggers. Something cracks deep in my chest.

Holy fuck.

What if I got it wrong? What if this whole time—this obsession, this twisted game—I've been chasing a ghost?

I back out of the room like I'm standing on a minefield, softly clicking as the door shuts. Then I'm heading straight to my office. My hands shake as I rip open the locked drawer and pull out the file I swore I understood. The one I've dissected, cross-referenced, and memorized. Now I flip it open and start from the beginning.

If what I'm thinking is true—if those dates are really missing—then everything I built this mission on is about to fucking implode.

I lean back in the chair, cracking my knuckles, as I stare down at the open file like it's mocking me. I've read it a hundred times and it still doesn't tell me what the hell happened to her or who she was before she stopped being her.

I pull my phone out of my pocket, and scroll to the only name I trust and he picks up on the third ring.

"Tell me this is about a body," he says by way of hello. "Because I'm elbows deep in a Sudoku puzzle and I'm starting to think the nine is lying to me."

"I need you to run something."

"You always need me to run something. I'm not your secretary. I want dental. PTO. Maybe a puppy."

"Travis."

"God, you're sexy when you're serious. Who is it?"

I don't answer right away and the silence stretches.

"I need everything, we missed something." I say. "Background. Employment. Education. Last name. Location history. All of it."

There's another pause, then his tone shifts. "Oooh. You've got your patented *I might murder someone but also might cuddle* voice on. I like it."

I pinch the bridge of my nose, trying not to snap. "There's something off. The records we pulled are too clean and too short."

"That sounds like half your exes."

"Travis."

"Alright, alright. Jesus. What are you not telling me?"

I don't answer. I've been watching all the wrong things. She hides it well, but not from me. I've seen enough people break to know what it looks like when someone's already halfway shattered before you ever touch them.

I lean back, jaw tight. "I don't think she knows who she is."

Travis lets out a low whistle. "You always find the fun ones."

"She remembers things that don't make any sense."

Travis exhales again, and this time it's different. No jokes left. No sarcasm. "Okay. Shit."

I lean forward, elbows braced on the desk, staring at her file like it's a loaded weapon. It's a smokescreen. Every time I dig, I find just enough to make me think I've reached the end. But I haven't. Not even close.

"Something happened before she got here. Something that made her disappear inside her own skin. I'm willing to bet he was involved."

A pause.

"You think she's one of his?"

I close my eyes and the silence that follows answers for me.

"Jesus, Steven."

I don't respond to that, and he pauses. "You need me to start from the beginning?"

"No," I say quietly. "I need you to start before the beginning."

He whistles again. "You're looking for a ghost." Another beat of silence, then, "You're in deep."

"Just find me the truth."

"I'll do what I can," he says. "But if I end up dead, you're giving the eulogy."

Click.

I stare at the file for another full minute before slowly closing it. Whatever he finds better not confirm what I already suspect. Because if she was never part of this—if she's innocent...then I've made a colossal fucking mistake.

I lean back in the chair, running both hands down my face, and I feel the pressure building in my skull like a countdown. The rage. The guilt. The fucking doubt. An hour later my phone's buzzing and I answer on the first ring.

"You're not gonna like this," Travis says—no sarcasm this time.

I sit forward. "What'd you find?"

"It's not what I found—it's what's missing. And before you say it, I know. I can't believe I didn't catch this sooner."

I say nothing, my pulse steady as my brain starts to calculate, waiting for him to elaborate.

"I ran her ID, birth certificate, and social. All of it checks out on the surface. But the timestamps are off. Backdated. Clean."

"You think it's fake?"

"It's sloppy work, actually. Someone rushed it. It looks like they needed her to exist on paper more than they needed her to disappear. You following?"

Barely. But the sick twist in my gut says yes.

"She ever mention where she grew up?"

I pause, jaw tight. "Just said she moved here from... somewhere."

"I cross-checked the birth certificate against hospital records in the state listed. No match. Whole thing's smoke. But..."

I sit up straighter. "But what?"

"I did find something older. School enrollment, elementary level. Facial recognition gives me an 89% match—same eyes, same jawline, even back then. It's her."

"And then?"

"And then nothing. Like the entire family vanished off the grid. But here's the thing—they didn't disappear."

"Meaning?"

"After they moved, the whole family started using a new last name. No court filing, no traceable paper trail. Just—new IDs. New address. New state."

I lean back slowly, watching the shadows shift across the wall.

"Her parents changed their identities?"

"Looks that way. And quietly too. No criminal flags, no obvious heat."

"And Ani?"

"Regular life. She had a job, an apartment, normal stuff. But then she quits her job out of nowhere. No digital trail. Just drops off for almost two years."

A cold breath drags down my spine.

"After that, she shows up in Colorado. Same face. Different last name with just enough paperwork to rent an apartment and get hired slinging drinks."

I stare at the file again like it might suddenly confess something.

"You think she remembers any of it?"

"I think she remembers enough to be dangerous. But not enough to connect the dots."

There's a beat of silence on the line. Then Travis exhales, "You starting to think she's not the collateral?"

I look toward the hallway at the soft glow under the door, the quiet reminder that she's still here, curled up in my bed.

"Fuck."

I drag a hand over my mouth as the truth settles like a blade between my ribs.

I've been treating her like she's just a piece on the board, but if Travis is right—if the missing years, the name change, the ghost trail all add up—then Ani didn't get caught in someone else's crossfire.

Which means I've been digging in the wrong place, watching the wrong angles, and she's been bleeding for it the entire time.

Goddamn it.

I'll have to pull back. Rework every angle. Rethink every move I've made since the moment I laid eyes on her. But more than that— I need to know who else knows.

There's more at play than I accounted for. Too many shadows. Too many missing pieces I didn't bother to chase—because I thought she was part of them.

"FUCK."

I slam my palm against the desk, wood rattling beneath the weight of it, and drag a hand down my face, jaw tight enough to crack.

I've been so goddamn focused on revenge I didn't see what was right in front of me.

25

Ani

I wake up to my phone buzzing violently against the nightstand like it's pissed I'm still alive. My first thought? Earthquake. Second thought? Sarah.

I groan, swiping blindly until I find the screen. "If this isn't about free alcohol or murder, I'm hanging up."

"You sound like you got hate-fucked by a lumberjack and left for dead."

I blink, sitting up slowly. My thighs ache, and my mouth tastes like sin. "Wow. Nailed it in one."

"Jesus. Was it him?"

I glance around the empty room and there's no evidence he ever existed outside my thighs. "Define him."

"Oh my god it was. Tattoo Dick finally put his mouth where his growls are."

"Sarah!"

"Don't Sarah me! I've been waiting for this feral man to rail the trauma out of you since you met him. Spill. Everything."

I rub my temple. "It was... a lot."

"Good a lot or needs-exorcism a lot?"

I fall back against the pillow. "Do I sound like someone who could walk in a straight line today?"

Sarah exhales like she's witnessing history. "I'm so proud of you. Did he growl?"

"He did worse."

She pauses. "I'm lighting a candle in your honor."

"Please don't. I'm already going to hell, I don't need your help decorating it."

"Did you make him breakfast? Is he naked next to you? Are you emotionally ruined?"

I glance at the untouched space beside me. "No, no, and shut up."

"Ah. The post-dick abandonment spiral. Iconic."

"Don't start."

"Oh, I'm not starting—I'm basking. Text me when you can sit without wincing. Love you, slut."

She hangs up before I can fire back. I lower the phone and just... stare at it. Like it might tell me something I'm too much of a coward to ask. My body's wrecked, my mind's fried, and my heart's somewhere under the floorboards trying not to be dramatic about it. I slept in his house, again. I let him break me open, and now I'm letting myself want something dangerous.

I don't know what I was expecting? Breakfast in bed and an apology for emotionally manhandling me into orgasmic submission?

God. I hate this. I hate that I feel everything and want more at the same time.

I shove the blanket back and swing my legs over the edge of the bed. The room feels hollow, like the aftermath of a storm and somehow, that makes it worse.

I know he's out there, somewhere in this house doing God knows what. I sit there for another second, trying to convince myself I'm not hoping to hear his voice or footsteps or anything that would tell me I didn't imagine the way he touched me last night. The way he looked at me like I was his to ruin—and he was already halfway done.

I drag myself out of bed, tugging his hoodie over my head while I pad barefoot down the hall.

"Bern?" I call. But I don't hear anything. I check the kitchen, the office, even the goddamn laundry room. I even peek into the bathroom like an idiot, like maybe he's just shaving in there, quiet as a ghost.

He's not.

There's no coffee mug on the counter to even indicate he was up this morning. My stomach tightens, and something about this doesn't feel right. I open the back door, squinting at the woods as the cold morning air rushes in. Still no sign of him or Bern. Just trees and silence and that low hum in my chest that always shows up when something's about to go wrong.

Well, okay. Fine. If he wants to vanish without a word and go dark without so much as a be right back—cool. I've been ghosted by better men than him, though I can't say I've been left in their house before. I should probably go home, but there's no way in hell I'm going back until I've had the locks changed, and the landlord still hasn't confirmed it's been done.

So, I make coffee that tastes like regret, take a bath that scalds the ache out of my muscles, and eat one of those prepped meals. Bern shows up at some point, and I even throw a ball for her, and we go on a walk in silence.

It's peaceful.

I keep telling myself I should enjoy it, that I should be grateful for the stillness. But even as I think it, I'm already reaching for my phone.

Didn't I block this shit? I open it anyway, heart thudding, dread pooling in my throat like something alive.

> UNKNOWN: Running only works if no one's chasing. You think you're hiding. But you keep leaving crumbs.

There's no photo this time, but it still punches the air out of my lungs. I block the number again. Throwing the phone on the couch like it burned me, only to hear the buzz of another text.

> Frank: Just wanted to say I miss you. Hope you're doing okay. I'll always make space for you, doll. Even if you're not ready yet.

Goddamnit.

Of course he's being sweet now. Soft, even. I don't know how he does this, but it works every time. I should ignore it—especially after everything. Especially after what I did.

I've been dodging Frank's advances for months, sidestepping every touch, brushing off every compliment, even pretending I wasn't leading him on. Telling him I just wasn't interested in dating anyone.

And yet here I am. Letting Steven crawl under my skin like he was always meant to be there. I don't even know what the fuck we are. Enemies? Addicts? Two feral things orbiting the same wound? Certainly not dating.

And what's worse is—I don't know what that makes me.

I stare at Frank's message for way too long before I finally start typing a reply.

> ME: Guess the universe knew I needed a breather. Hope everything's good on your end.

I hit send before I can talk myself out of it, then distract myself with Zillow. Again.

Scrolling through places I can't afford, chasing something—anything—that doesn't feel like it might cave in under the weight of my secrets.

I've been scrolling for what feels like hours, and I finally find something that just might work. It's a tiny studio on the outskirts of town, and it's available immediately. I text the number, asking to see it, and of course—it's open tomorrow at noon.

It feels like a plan. A win.

The sun is starting to set, and at this point I'm about to get an Uber to Sarah's. I'm so annoyed that I haven't seen or heard from Steven, that by the time the front door creaks open, my whole body goes tight.

I'm pissed that I'm so relieved. He walks in like nothing happened. All calm and casual, dropping his keys on the entry table as he shrugs out of his jacket like he didn't just disappear all day without a single word.

His eyes sweep the room, barely landing on me.

"You eat?" he asks.

I blink. Then scoff. "You ghost all day and that's your opener?"

He raises a brow, calm as ever—like I'm the one being dramatic. "You weren't bleeding. Figured you were fine."

Of course he did.

Steven drops into the armchair across from me, pulling his phone from his pocket like it's just another night, and we're a normal couple.

"You been here all day?" he asks, not looking up. What is this, small talk or some covert fucking interrogation?

"Was I supposed to do something else?" I mutter, eyes still on the screen. "You live in the middle of the woods. Not a lot of options."

I keep going, even though my pulse refuses to settle around him. "It was nice, actually. I did absolutely nothing, played with Bern, took a walk. Might actually start a cult out here if you leave me alone long enough."

Still no reaction. Just that quiet, unreadable stare like he's cataloging every shift in my voice.

I glance over at him, half-expecting the usual smart-ass remark. "I know I need to go home. I'll probably head back in the morning."

A beat of silence.

Then—"You can stay as long as you need."

I blink. That... wasn't what I expected. I nod slowly, trying to hide how thrown I am. "Thanks."

I'm already spiraling. Why is he being nice now? What changed? And why does it make my chest ache like I've been waiting for it all day and hating myself for wanting it?

I watched the clock all day, pretending I didn't hear every creak in this house wondering if it was him walking back in. And now that he's here, now that he's looking at me like I'm something he might not want to lose—I want to scream. Or kiss him. Or claw my way into his ribs just to prove I matter.

He leans forward, resting his elbows on his knees.

"You got plans tomorrow?"

I hesitate. "Maybe."

His eyes narrow. "Ani."

I cross my arms defensively before I even speak. "There's a rental listed just outside of town, so I booked a showing."

His whole body stills. "You what?"

I try to keep my tone breezy but it's shaky at best. "I'm not saying I'm going to jump on it, but—"

"You're not going."

I blink. "Excuse me?"

"You're not going," he repeats, with a final tone.

"Steven," I snap, standing. "You don't get to tell me where I can or can't go."

He stands, towering over me and every inch of him is coiled with control. His voice drops into something darker, more dangerous.

"I do when you've been acting like someone's watching you." His eyes narrow. "Jumping at shadows, checking your phone like it's a bomb. You want to lie to me, fine—but don't pretend something's not going on."

My mouth opens, but no sound comes out. He can't know about the messages I keep getting, but he acts like he does.

"You don't get to disappear and then show up playing house and telling me what to do." I snap.

"I'm trying to keep you safe."

I roll my eyes. "By keeping me locked in your house like a fucking pet?"

His voice drops to a low, dangerous tone. "You think I don't see what you're doing?"

"Oh, do tell," I snap, crossing my arms. "What exactly am I doing, Steven?"

"You're running."

I lift a brow. "From you?"

"From whatever the fuck happened to you that makes you look like you've seen a ghost every time there's a loud noise."

I freeze. He hit the nerve—and the bastard knows it.

"I'm done with this conversation," I mutter, brushing past him. "You don't get to tell me what to do."

His hand catches my wrist. "You can't run from this."

I yank free. "Watch me."

I storm past him, fury clawing up my spine, but I don't stop until I hit the kitchen.

Only then, when I'm alone, does it hit me. I rip open a cabinet like it owes me answers and yank out a box of mac and cheese like it personally betrayed me. I toss it on the counter a little too hard, but I don't care.

I'm halfway through fumbling with the burner when I hear the quiet creak of the floorboards behind me. His presence fills the room like a thundercloud—quiet, heavy, and charged with things that haven't been said.

I don't turn around when I mutter, "I'm fine."

"That's not how you boil water."

I whip around, glaring. "Jesus, what are you now, a chef?"

He nods at the stovetop. "You have to turn the burner on."

I blink down at it, and it's glowing. Just the wrong one. Fuck. I flip the right one and scowl. "Still doesn't mean I need help."

"I didn't say you did," he murmurs, stepping closer. "Just saying... you might burn the place down."

I huff a laugh. "Yeah, well. Wouldn't be the worst thing that's happened this week."

He stops a few feet away, arms crossed, watching me like I'm a puzzle he's halfway solved but doesn't quite believe yet.

"What?" I snap, grabbing the box and shaking it like that'll intimidate him.

"You can't keep pretending nothing's wrong."

"Says the man who disappears all day and then acts like I'm the problem."

"I didn't say you're the problem."

"You didn't have to," I mutter, dumping noodles into the pot even though the water isn't boiling yet.

A beat passes, and I barely hear him. "I don't want you to leave."

That stops me cold. My hand hovers over the box but I don't look at him, because if I do, I'll lose whatever hold I have left.

"Why?" I whisper. "Because you like fucking me?"

Silence.

"Because I don't like not knowing who's got their eyes on you when I'm not around."

I turn slowly, realizing just how close he is, and I hate how much I need him to be. My skin burns for contact, and my body leans toward his like it knows what I won't let myself say. But it's so much easier to turn that ache into anger.

If I let him in—if I admit I want him like this, I'll never survive what comes after.

"You don't get to act like this means something," I snap, stepping back like distance will help. "Not when you keep everything locked up like I'm the enemy."

His eyes flick down my body, slow and unapologetic. "Funny. You didn't seem to care what it meant when you were begging me to ruin you."

My breath catches, and rage flickers behind my ribs. "You think that gives you the right to own me?"

He steps forward. "No. Crawling to me did that."

His jaw flexes as his chest rises and we move at the same time. He reaches me just as I drop the box, hands tangling in my shirt, and our mouths crashing against each other.

There's nothing gentle about it. This kiss is a fucking detonation. It's weeks of circling each other like lit matches, waiting for something to burn. His hands are gripping my hair, and mine are clawing down his back like I'm trying to rip through skin just to feel something real.

He lifts me and slams me against the fridge, as my legs go around him. This time, when I gasp, it's not from fury—it's from the way he consumes me.

I'm tired of pretending I don't want this. He tastes like danger and ruin and I've never wanted anything more. Whatever this is—it's not safe, it's not smart, and it's already too late to turn around.

God help me.

His hand slides under my shirt, skimming my ribs, and his voice drops—wrecked against my mouth. "You don't get to crawl to me like you did and pretend you're not mine."

"I never said I wasn't," I pant. "I just never said I was, either."

His eyes are full of heat, and he growls. "Say it."

I shake my head, a crooked grin breaking across my lips. "Make me."

And he does.

This time—when he takes me, there's nothing holding either of us back. He grabs my jaw and kisses me like he wants to take the fight out of my mouth, he spins me around so fast I gasp. His hand finds the back of my neck, shoving me down until my elbows hit the cold stone countertop.

"Stay."

His body presses flush against my back and I've never wanted anything more than I want him right now. I could die and my life would be complete.

"Don't move unless you want me to punish you for it."

I let out a breathless, taunting laugh, just to test him. "Is that a threat or a promise?"

The sound he makes isn't human—it's feral. His hand fists in my hair, yanking my head back until I'm arching for him like something to be claimed, and I'm soaked, throbbing, and so fucking ready.

"You think this is funny?"

His voice is gravel and heat and every dark promise I should run from, but instead I want nothing more than for him to lose control.

"I could bend you over every surface in this goddamn cabin and it still wouldn't be enough. I'll ruin you until you forget what it felt like to not be mine."

Fuck—do I want that.

My breath snags as he yanks my sweats down to my knees in one brutal motion. Cold air suddenly hits my soaked skin, but I don't pull away. My hands brace the counter, and my knees almost buckle. I instinctively try to close my legs, but it's too late.

He hooks his fingers in the waistband of my panties—then rips. The sound tears through the air like a warning, and then they're gone—shredded, dangling from his fist like a trophy.

Before I can catch my breath, he grabs my jaw and shoves the ruined scrap between my lips, forcing it deep into my mouth.

"Go ahead, Mi cielo," he growls against my ear. "Taste yourself."

Mi cielo? I hate how it lands, it's too soft. That's not what we do, we fuck like we're trying to win. Does he know I speak spanish?

His grip tightens. "Tell me again how bad you don't want this."

I let out a muffled, strangled sound. My eyes are wide, and my thighs are shaking from how hard I'm trying not to melt into him.

God. I'm dripping, and my cunt clenches the second he

touches me. I bite down harder and glare up at him, pretending my body isn't already bowing to every brutal word he's said.

The way he talks and the filth that comes out of his mouth is every girl's wet dream. It's everything I've always wanted and never dared to ask for.

He smirks like he knows that too. If he keeps talking like that, I'm going to come without him even touching me.

He drops behind me like a man possessed, like the devil himself was starved and I'm the sin he was promised.

"Don't you dare hide from me now." His voice rumbles right against my core and I squirm. "Look at you. You're dripping."

His mouth is on me—in me—dragging his tongue through my slit like I'm the only thing he's ever fucking needed. He groans into me, like I'm feeding something starving and savage inside him.

My whole body jolts when his tongue flicks up to circle my clit —and I scream behind the panties in my mouth. I bite down hard, squeezing my eyes shut as my knees buckle. This isn't careful or sweet. This is a punishment.

I'm dripping down his chin while he groans like he fucking lives for this. And I can't stop it. My ass is pushing toward him for more and I can't stop the white-hot need pulsing low in my gut. I spit my panties out of my mouth. "Fuck—Steven—"

He doesn't answer, he just devours me. His nose is buried in my pussy like it's the only goddamn oxygen he needs. I writhe, moaning while one hand claws at the counter and the other slams against the wall for balance.

"God—please—"

He pulls back just long enough to growl, "You want to come on my tongue, or do I need to make you wait?"

I whimper. "Please—don't stop—"

"That's not an answer."

He sucks my clit hard, then slaps my ass. The crack of it echoes off the cabinets and I jolt forward with a cry.

"Use your words," he growls. "Or I'll leave you dripping and empty all fucking night."

My voice breaks free, ragged and wrecked. "Yes," I pant. "I want to come—Please, just don't stop."

He groans into my cunt then shoves two thick fingers inside me with no warning. Just a filthy, wet thrust that has me moaning as my body jerks against the counter.

"Fuck, you're so tight," he snarls. "So wet, I could drown in you."

Then he's curling his fingers just right—and my world fractures. I come screaming, and every nerve is thrashing. He doesn't stop. Just keeps eating and finger fucking me with ruthless precision. He's probably not going to stop until I'm spent and silent, shattered at his feet.

For the first time in my life, I want to be owned.

When I'm shaking—wrecked and sobbing into the marble—he stands, clamping one hand on my hip. The other snakes around my throat and yanks me up until my spine bows against his chest.

I feel him pulsing against my soaked pussy—and fuck me, I want him so bad. All of it. Every inch, every threat, every punishment he's been holding back.

"You wanted wild," he rasps against my ear. "You're about to fucking get it."

He kicks my feet wider, grabbing both my wrists and yanks them behind my back—pinning them in one rough hand. My chest slams back to the counter, cheek flattened to the cold marble, while my legs are spread open and shaking.

His free hand grips my ass, hard enough to bruise. Holding me like he's staking a fucking claim.

"Look at this fuckable little ass," he growls. "You were made for this. Made to take my cock with your face down and your body dripping like it's starving for me."

He leans in closer and I can feel his breath hot against my neck, the threat of his voice curling around every frayed nerve ending I've got. I can barely think straight.

"You think I was just gonna fuck your pussy and let the rest of you walk away?" he mutters darkly. "No dear, I'm taking all of you."

His palm spreads me open. Exposing everything. Making me feel so nervous, I start to sweat.

"I'm going to fuck this ass," he breathes. "Make you take every inch until you're sobbing—until you're begging to come with my cock so deep you forget your fucking name."

My breath stutters and I buck my hips. No fucking way am I about that. But I can't help the hunger that crashes through me at hearing him say it though. It's all I can do not to scream. I've never done that. Never even considered it. I for sure don't want to start now.

I bite down hard, trying to swallow the moan rising in my throat. The moment his fingers slide lower, brushing over that tight, forbidden part of me, my whole body jolts.

"Scared?" he taunts, keeping his voice low.

My pulse slams behind my ribs. *Yes, actually. I'm terrified.* I don't even know what I'd do if he—my thoughts cut off as his fingers return, slowly teasing.

"Relax," he murmurs, mouth brushing the shell of my ear. "I'm not gonna take it tonight."

Relief hits me hard... until his next words shatter it. "But I am going to play with it. Just enough to make your pussy clench for me."

I whimper as his slick fingers slide lower again, one hand still wrapped tight around my wrists, the other spreading me open like he's mapping out all the places I've hidden.

"I've got you," he breathes, as his fingers tease the place that makes my entire body go still. "You're safe. Even when I'm fucking ruining you."

Fuck.

That's what undoes me. Not the filth. Not the way my body's trembling. I'm soaked and stretched to the edge of breaking, but it's the truth in his voice. That brutal, terrifying certainty that he'll tear me apart—*and still be the one who puts me back together after.*

My throat tightens, but I exhale, loosening my jaw, the fight bleeding from my legs inch by inch.

"I trust you," I whisper. It's not a declaration. It's a surrender. I feel it when he hears me—I feel the shift in the way his body stills behind me.

His fingers drag through my wet pussy again—only deeper this time, slow and claiming.

"You want me to be gentle?" His cock presses against my entrance, thick and throbbing.

I shake my head.

"Then stop pretending you're not mine."

He presses deeper and his thumb still teases that forbidden edge, making my whole body shake.

"...you want out, you say the word. Otherwise? I'm not holding back."

A strangled sound claws out of my throat, but I still don't tell him to stop. Because I can't. My body's already gone rogue—arching like it doesn't care that I've never done this before.

"Steven—" His name slips out like a prayer and a warning.

Panic and arousal fuse, twisting into something feral. There's no denying how soaked I am for him. I'm so fucking close to begging for something I swore I'd never let anyone take.

"See that?" he growls. "That panic? That need? That's where I live, dear. Right in the space where you don't know if you want to run or beg."

He thrusts in slowly, like he's punishing me with his restraint, while his thumb presses down just enough to make every muscle in my body forget how to function.

"And tonight... you're staying."

He doesn't give me the satisfaction of being split wide the way I crave. Instead, he pauses there—just the thick head of his cock stretching me while his thumb keeps circling, tormenting me until I feel completely unhinged.

"Steven—" My voice breaks into part sob, part plea.

"Your cunt's trying to choke on my cock before I've even given it to you."

I let out a strangled sound, while my chest heaves against the counter. He still has my wrists pinned behind me in his grip. I don't know whether to scream, sob, or laugh—because everything feels too good. It's all too much. My brain can't keep up, and my body doesn't give a shit.

"You don't get to decide when I fuck you," he rasps. "You don't get to come just because you're desperate."

His hips pull back and I groan in protest. Instead of slamming into me—he drags the head through my slit again, soaking himself in my arousal, only to line up again and stop.

My thighs tremble as my pussy clenches around nothing.

"You crawl for me," he murmurs. "You beg. You fucking surrender." Then he pushes in—just the thick head—stretching me open, just enough to make my eyes slam shut and my breath catch.

His thumb presses deeper between my cheeks and I jolt, a broken moan tearing from my throat.

"That's it," he breathes, lips close to my ear. "Squirm. Fight it. I want to feel you come apart before I let you have it. I want you to know what it costs to be mine."

My breath comes in short, ragged bursts. I'm pinned and panting, dripping for him, shaking from how badly I need more. I want anything and everything this man is willing to give me.

"Please," I gasp, voice splintering. "Steven—please—"

He chuckles.

"You think that counts as begging?" he rasps. "Sweetheart, you haven't even fucking started."

"I need—fuck—I need to come," I pant, desperate now, pushing my ass back against him. "Please—"

He doesn't move. He doesn't even fucking budge.

"You think you've earned it?" he growls near my ear. "After the shit you pulled? After storming out like you don't belong to me?"

I sob. My body's on fire as actual tears run down my face. My cunt continues to clench around nothing, and honestly she's probably crying too.

"I'll be good," I whisper, breaking. "I swear—whatever you want—just please—please fuck me—"

"Not good enough."

His grip on my wrists loosens as he slides his hand up, catching me by the throat and dragging me upright against his chest.

"You wanna come?" he whispers. "Then say it."

I whimper, barely able to breathe. The teeter-totter between pleasure and pain tilts hard, and I'm not sure which side is winning. I think he asked me something—but all I can focus on is the way his grip tightens around my throat.

He slides it lower between the swell of my breasts. He cups one, then the other, rough palms scraping across sensitive skin before he rolls my nipples between his fingers until I gasp.

It keeps trailing lower, over my stomach, between my thighs—until it finds my clit. One touch, and I forget how to fucking breathe.

He starts to circle it devastatingly slow, while his cock still teases at my entrance, refusing to move.

"Say it, beautiful girl," he commands again. "That this perfect, filthy fucking body is mine to use. Mine to break. Mine to own."

My eyes slam shut. And I say it—wrecked, and breathless—but I say it. "I'm yours."

The second the words leave my mouth, he's inside me—one brutal, punishing thrust that rips the air from me.

"Yeah you are," he growls. "My perfect fucking brat."

He grabs my hips and drives into me again like he's claiming every inch and carving his name into my goddamn bones.

"You'll never let anyone else touch you here," his pace turns vicious. "Not your cunt. Not your ass. Not your fucking soul. You hear me?"

"Yes—yes—Steven, I—"

"Say it again, sweetheart." Another savage thrust.

"Yours," I sob. "Yours—all of it—fuck—"

My orgasm hits and I can feel him follow me right over the edge. I seize, knees giving out. I'd drop if he weren't still holding me —still fucking me through it like he owns every broken, burning piece I just gave up.

He leans over me, still buried deep, both of us wrecked and panting over the counter, but he hasn't let go. His lips brush the sensitive spot on my neck.

My body jolts. It should be too much—should terrify me—but instead, I feel myself getting turned on all over again, even when I can barely hold myself up.

God help me... I want that. I want him again.

Even now, with my sticky thighs, and lungs trying to reboot— I'd let him flip me over and ruin me again without question.

в собрании стихотворений, которое
вышло в октябре 1825 года. В кас...
смысле стрелял в Васильке. «чита...
в темнице? Суд об них, как имеют...
имеют важнейшее значение в ре...
рассуждения Пушкина, но в насто...
не входят исследование «намеренк»...
намерены были ни при чем о возник...
му стихотворению. Цензура не пропус...
нетронутые строфы распростра...
нетую известность, и после событий 14...
они в этому известно. В той пред...
Пушкин влагал в уста Шенье о тем...
и слова, которые подходили к совре...

Я знаю твоих силы гряда...
А славны... ...самовластие...

Все это было отнесено к восста...
А изображение состояния обще...
нялся попытки, погасшей изм...
стрелял того времени усмотр...

II.

...года Ваше дозволение на арест
... 1826 года было послано отно-
...Петербург, на имя Ермолова за...

...покорнейше прошу Ваше Вы-
...немедленно взять под арест
...со всеми пред...
...осторожность, чтобы...
...отослать как оные...
...курьером в Петербург...

...движение по...
...22-го вечером, в...
...генерал Удлонский...
...и это время в...

26

"IF THEY FEED YOU, PAY ATTENTION."
(IT MEANS THEY PLAN TO KEEP YOU.)

Ani

I shift, trying to stand and pull my sweats up, which apparently is a mistake. His hand snaps out and clamps around my hip like a fucking leash.

"No."

I freeze, turning to look at him. "What—?"

"You can stay like this." His voice is calm. Almost gentle. But there's nothing soft about it. "No pants. No panties. I want my cum dripping down your thighs while you eat."

My cheeks flame. The humiliation is instant, crashing into the raw aftershocks still pulsing through my core. "You're not serious."

He grabs my chin and forces my head back, eyes locking with mine. His stare is lethal.

"I've never been more serious."

I don't breathe for a full five seconds, and when he finally releases me and turns toward the fridge, I realize how hungry I am.

"Mac and cheese?" he mutters, opening the fridge and tossing ingredients on the counter. "Fucking hell. If I'd known you had the taste of a frat boy on house arrest, I would've let you starve."

I shoot him a look, too dazed to fire back properly. I'm still bare from the waist down, and still very much pulsing and flushed. I can feel his cum sliding slowly between my legs.

He glances over his shoulder and he's smiling.

"Stay there. I'll feed you."

My stomach flips.

A few minutes later, he sets a plate in front of me—grilled chicken, roasted sweet potatoes, and sautéed vegetables.

"You're such a weirdo," I mutter, dragging the plate closer with shaking fingers.

"If anyone's wrecking your insides tonight, it's gonna be me—not whatever powdered chemical shit that was."

I nearly choke on a bite. "Jesus. You're the one who had it."

He grins—smug and feral. "Eat."

I do. And when I finish, he doesn't say anything for a long moment—his dark eyes just watch me.

"Talk."

I blink. "About?"

"Do you want to come again tonight?" he asks, already standing, circling behind me. "Then you're gonna answer my questions."

His fingers graze my neck possessively. "You tell me something real... and I'll reward you."

I tense. "You're bribing me with orgasms?"

He leans down, lips brushing my ear as he smirks. "No. I'm training you to be honest."

A shiver rakes down my spine. I can't decide if I hate that... or want more of it.

"Well?" he murmurs, his hand trailing lower. "Start talking."

I scrape the last bite from my plate and push it away, standing slowly. I make a beeline for the couch and tug the throw blanket over my hips—like it'll somehow erase the fact that I'm still bare underneath.

He sinks down beside me with slow, predatory ease, draping one arm across the back of the couch, and the other is already under the blanket, resting on my thigh, drawing slow circles on my skin.

"Start talking," he murmurs again. "Something real."

I glare at the screen—Slughorn mumbling, Harry chasing shadows, but all of it blurs at the edges because he's doing that thing again with his fingers.

"I used to dream in Spanish," I say suddenly.

Steven doesn't move, but I feel him tense.

I swallow hard, but keep going. "When I was little. My mom always made me speak English, even in our house, but when I was alone—when I dreamed—it was Spanish. Still is sometimes."

Silence.

"I didn't even realize it until... Someone made fun of me for mumbling in my sleep. Said I sounded like I was casting a curse." A laugh slips out. "They weren't wrong."

His hand shifts, brushing slightly closer to my entrance. "Our house was always loud, and there was always someone yelling, playing salsa music or frying something with too much oil. My favorite part was in the mornings, the windows would fog up, and you could always smell rain in the air before it hit."

His touch stills on my thigh. "What else?"

I shift under his hand, pulse kicking. "You first. This isn't one sided."

He stares at me for a second, like he's deciding how much to give me. Then he speaks.

"Alright." He exhales through his nose. "There was a girl I grew up with. Not by blood—but she called me her brother. And I let her. Hell, I probably needed her just as much as she needed me."

His thumb moves once on my thigh, slow.

"I started working for her father, and the first job he sent me on, I thought I was supposed to be watching her. Keeping her safe. Thought it was a test." He huffs a breath. "Turns out she was there to watch me."

He pauses. "She made that real clear when she disarmed me five minutes in and told me my stance was shit."

He shakes his head once, like the memory still stings. "I was twenty-one, cocky as hell, and ready to prove something. She was seventeen and already better than most men I knew. Smarter, too. And meaner than hell when she had to be."

His expression shifts, hardening with something darker. I sit with it for a second, then glance down at where his hand rests on my thigh. "Let me guess. You were the reckless one?"

His mouth curves. "No. I was the weapon they kept on a leash until they wanted something dead."

A beat passes.

"Well." I exhale. "That took a turn."

I can't tell if he's joking or not, but what's alarming is my lack of reaction.

He huffs once, barely a breath of a laugh. "You asked."

"I did. And I'm regretting it a little now."

My voice sounds light, but my pulse's doing things I don't love. There's something razor-sharp behind his words—something old and buried so deep it scrapes when he tries to dig it up. He says it like a joke, but I have a feeling there's more to that story.

He leans in, eyes still on mine, and drops his voice to something quiet and lethal. "Then maybe it's your turn."

I should lie. Or dodge. Or throw something flirty and bratty back at him just to keep the balance. That's what I do—keep it so far from the truth that nobody thinks to look closer. But something about him in this moment makes the words slip out before I can stop them.

"I always wanted to open a bookstore," I murmur. "Nothing fancy. Just a tiny hole-in-the-wall shop with creaky floors and weird hours. Maybe a crooked bell over the door and a frenchie that bites everyone except me."

His hand doesn't stop, and I can feel the smile tugging at the edge of his voice when he finally responds.

"That's adorable," he drawls. "You? Curating romance novels and yelling at customers for dog-earing pages?"

I roll my eyes. "No yelling. Just strategic glaring."

He huffs a quiet laugh—and fuck, it shouldn't hit the way it does. It's low, and unexpected, almost like he forgot to keep it locked down. Something about that sound—how rare it is, how real—makes my chest pull tight. I feel like I just witnessed something I wasn't supposed to see. And I want to hear it again.

"Let me guess," he teases. "The shop's called something pretentious, like Mourning House."

I bark a laugh, cheeks flushing. "Wait, shut up. That's actually a good name."

He leans in slightly, while simultaneously grazing my clit. My breath stutters, but I don't pull away. A beat passes. Then another. When he speaks, his voice is different...quieter.

"You said something the other night." His tone's casually. "About how you don't remember getting here. To Denver. Is there anything else you can remember?"

I stiffen before I can stop myself. Why the hell would he ask me that and why the fuck does it matter? Despite the rising tide of questions and hesitation, I answer truthfully.

"No." A beat. "Maybe. There was a hallway and a couch I didn't recognize. I think... I think I was staying somewhere else. Just for a little while."

Another pause. Then his voice lowers, calm as ever. "Were you alone when you left?"

My stomach clenches. "I think so."

"You think?"

I glance at him, but his face gives me nothing. Just steady eyes pinning me in place.

"There was a lot of yelling," I whisper. "And I know I was bleeding... I just don't know where. My shoulder maybe or my face. I don't know—I just remember the taste of copper, and something warm dripping down my ear."

Steven's hand tenses on my leg. But I keep going. "I woke up in a motel, with my shirt on backwards, and my head was split in half, or at least it felt like it. My phone was gone and I had to get a new one."

A bitter breath leaves me. "Pretty sure that's when everything got fuzzy. Like my brain decided to slam the door shut and call it self-care."

He doesn't say anything right away. Then —"And you didn't go back?"

I huff a humorless laugh. "What, and leave a Yelp review? 'Two stars—terrible lighting, lots of blood, would not recommend.' Steven, it was a fucking crime scene. What the hell was I supposed to go back for?"

He stays quiet for another moment. "Did you ever tell anyone?"

I shake my head. "Not really. People get weird when you don't have a neat little trauma story, and your memories don't come in a straight line."

I glance over—and freeze.

There's something in his face. Just a flicker of rage in his eyes. He schools it fast, but I saw it.

"What?" I ask, voice sharper than I mean it to be.

His expression smooths out completely. "Nothing."

"Bullshit," I snap, sitting up straighter, yanking the blanket higher even though he's already touched every inch of me. "You just looked at me like—I don't know."

Steven leans back against the couch, elbow hooked over the backrest. Completely still. *Retreat mode activated.*

"You ever think maybe you don't want to know?" he says quietly.

My chest pulls tight, and by the look on his face, I'm not sure we're talking about me anymore. "What the hell does that mean?"

His eyes flicks to Harry and Dumbledore standing on the rocks beneath that spinning cave of cursed water. His jaw ticks again, but he still says nothing. I hate the silence. I also happen to hate the way he can read me like a book but locks his own pages shut.

"Jesus, why do I even talk to you," I mutter, standing up. "Every time I give you something real, you pull back like I'm the problem."

He stands too. "Because you *are* real. *That's* the problem."

I blink. For a second, I think I misheard him. "What the fuck does that mean?"

He closes the space between us in two steps—towering over me, still shirtless and completely unreadable. His eyes are locked onto mine like they're trying to bore straight through. But this time, when he touches me, it's different. He puts a hand on my jaw, fingers curled beneath my chin as he tilts my head up.

"You remember more than you think," he says in a whisper. "And someone out there is counting on that."

My stomach drops. A chill ghosts across my skin. "Steven—"

"Go to bed," he murmurs.

That's it. He turns, disappearing down the hall, leaving me standing there, heat still trapped in my chest and silence thick around me. A sound makes me jump—a single ping from my phone, that's in the other room.

I almost don't move, deciding to let it rot there. Whatever it is, whoever it is, I don't need it.

But my feet move anyway.

> UNKNOWN: Funny thing about ghosts. You can run from them, bury them, burn the evidence... But they always crawl back up when it's quiet. You know who you really belong to.

I stare at it. My blood is pounding, and my fingers refuse to move. It's vague, but not vague enough.

Are they at my apartment? Are they outside in the trees right now—watching?

My skin prickles as every instinct screams to move, to run and hide. I refuse to give them that.

I type a reply with fingers that feel like stone.

> ME: You don't scare me.

I move toward the hallway with my jaw locked and rage simmering beneath my ribs like a fuse.

If Steven wants to play cryptic, fine. But he doesn't get to shut down and leave me dangling.

Not after everything.

The door to his office is half-closed, but I push it open without knocking. He's sitting at his desk like he never left with that same controlled fury carved into the set of his shoulders, his fingers beneath his chin. His eyes look up the second I step inside and narrow.

"You shouldn't be in here."

"And yet," I mutter, crossing the threshold, "here I am."

The door shuts behind me with a soft click.

"You said something out there." I fold my arms, tightly across my chest. "About remembering more than I think. What did you mean?"

He just watches me like he's already calculated every possible way this conversation could go, and he's still three steps ahead. But I'm not leaving until I get something. Even if I have to burn the whole room down to get it.

He just shifts in his chair slightly—like he's not surprised I came in, only deciding how much rope to give me before I hang myself.

I step farther into the room. "You said I remember more than I think," I say again, slower this time. "So tell me what you think I'm forgetting."

Still nothing.

"You're really gonna sit there and act like you haven't been watching me unravel?" My voice cracks. "That I'm not walking around with fucking holes in my memory and nightmares that don't belong to me?"

His jaw ticks, and that's it. I snap.

"I'm obviously not the only one hiding shit," I step closer before

I can talk myself out of it. "So unless you plan on staying cryptic forever, maybe it's your turn to spill something real."

My eyes flick to the desk—papers, a pen, and one manila folder. "Starting with that," I add, already moving toward it.

"Don't," he warns.

I stop mid-step, heart pounding in my ears. "Why? What is it?" My voice drops. "Is it about me?"

He doesn't answer.

"You've been digging," I whisper.

He stands slowly, rising to his full height, and towers over me. Everything about him screams *don't push*, which only makes me want to push harder.

"Of course I have," he says coldly. "You think I let someone into my house without knowing who the fuck they are?"

I flinch before I can stop it. "I didn't ask to come here."

"No," he says, voice tightening. "But you didn't leave either."

"I tried—"

"Did you?"

His voice cuts like a blade. "Or did you crawl back because you wanted to?"

My throat clamps shut and I hate how fast he switches gears. I hate that I don't know how to answer.

"I don't know what I want," I say finally, feeling raw and wrecked. "But I'm done being the only one trying to figure out what the fuck is real."

His jaw ticks, as he tracks me like prey. But he doesn't move. So I close the distance, reaching for the edge of the folder waiting for him to stop me.

"Don't," he growls again.

I ignore him, running my fingers under the edge—

"Come here," he snaps.

I freeze.

Slowly lifting my gaze to his. His expression is unreadable, but there's heat there. Something darker sitting just beneath the surface.

"I'm not done asking questions," I say.

"I'm done reminding you who you're asking them to."

My hand hovers over the folder, fingers curled at the edge like peeling back one more inch might change everything.

"I said come here, Ani."

Somehow, the way he says it is worse than if he shouted it. There's something in his voice that slides straight under my skin and coils around every nerve. I step around the desk, heart hammering now, standing inches from him.

"Why am I here?" I whisper.

He doesn't answer, instead, his hand comes up and slides behind my neck, pulling me in until my breath catches.

"You're asking questions," he murmurs, "you already know the answers to."

"I don't," I whisper. "And that's what makes this worse."

He studies me while I stare up at him, his thumb stroking once at the nape of my neck. His expression doesn't change, but something in his body shifts. I can tell he's trying to rein something in—and he's not doing a great job of it.

"You know more than you think," he murmurs. "You just don't trust it yet."

A flicker of heat crawls up the back of my neck, slow and invasive, like the words know where to go before I do.

"And you do?" I ask, quieter than I mean to.

"I trust patterns," he says. "I trust instincts. And mine are rarely wrong."

My ribs lock around a breath I don't fully take. "So what are your instincts telling you about me?"

His eyes stay locked on mine. "That you're terrified of something," he says finally. "Something you haven't put words to yet. And that if I push too hard, you'll run—but if I don't push at all, you'll drown."

My throat goes tight. *This cannot be happening right now.*

"But that's the problem with you," he continues. His voice dips low enough to settle under my skin. "You never learned how to call for help. You just sink quieter."

And fuck him, because it hits too close, he didn't just pull a thread—he found the one holding me together and yanked, hard.

I want to laugh and tell him to go to hell, or throw up a wall and call it sass—but all I can do is stare. I've been carrying this sinking weight for so long, I stopped realizing it was heavy. Part of me still believes drowning quietly is safer than surfacing.

"And what does that make you?" I rasp. "The lifeguard?"

His mouth twitches with something meaner, and something sad. "No. Just the bastard watching from shore who got tired of waiting."

The silence stretches again, and my hand curls slightly against the desk behind me.

"You don't even know me," I whisper, voice cracking.

"I know how your whole body tenses when a floorboard creaks behind you. Like you're waiting to be dragged back somewhere you've already fought your way out of."

He moves closer, and his voice drops lower.

"I know you check your reflection twice—not to fix it, but to make sure no one's behind you. I know you sleep with your phone in your hand like it's a weapon. And I know the silence isn't peaceful for you. It's fucking loud."

My breath snags, and my chest tightens as he keeps going, like he's unraveling me stitch by fucking stitch. And I can't breathe.

Not because I'm scared—God, I wish that were it—but because he's cutting too close. Closer than anyone ever has. Closer than I want him to. He doesn't just ask, he knows. He's somehow already slipped past every defense I've got, and now he's just... taking inventory.

He's right though. I don't ask for help. I never have. I learned a long time ago that silence was safer than trust, that shrinking in on myself hurt less than being left bleeding with my heart hanging out. That if I kept my wounds quiet, maybe nobody would notice how deep they went.

But somehow, he noticed. And now I'm fucking suffocating under the weight of it. I'm not afraid of him, I'm afraid of how badly I want him to keep going. To see the whole bloody mess and not flinch. To look at me like I'm still worth claiming.

"I know you pretend not to care. That the sarcasm is armor, and the flirting's a distraction. But underneath it, you're just trying to figure out who the hell you were before someone turned you into a ghost with a fake name and a past you can't look at straight."

His hand grazes mine on the desk, barely touching me but it might as well be a spark to a fuse.

"And I know," he murmurs, "you'd rather bite your own tongue than admit you're scared. Because you think if you say it out loud... it makes it real."

I scoff, clenching my jaw. "Wow. You want a medal or something? Or just a participation trophy for psychoanalyzing the fucked-up girl you keep dragging back into your bed?"

His jaw ticks. That muscle in his cheek flexes like it's holding back something feral.

"Careful," he warns, with a razor-edge to his voice. "You're pushing."

"Good," I snap. "Because you're not some savior, Steven. You don't get to play protector just because you finally noticed I flinch. You don't get to look at me like I'm broken glass you're trying not to step on—when you're the one leaving fucking footprints."

The silence is charged. I know I shouldn't be pushing him, but I can't help it.

"What the fuck do you want, Ani?" he growls. "For me to lie? Pretend I don't see it? You want someone who'll keep their distance and let you spiral in peace?"

I open my mouth—then shut it again, keeping my jaw locked

tight. Because fuck him for being right. And fuck me for not knowing the answer.

"I want one thing that's real," I say, quieter now. "Just one. I want to know if I'm fucked up because someone made me that way... or if I'm just broken."

His eyes flash with something dark and dangerous.

"You're not broken."

"No?" I laugh, but it comes out bitter and raw. "Then why the hell do I keep choosing men who treat me like property? Like I'm supposed to bleed gratitude just for being seen?"

I can see that it hit him like a slap in the face. He leans forward slowly, but no less lethal.

"I don't treat you like property," he growls, each word edged in steel.

"No," I whisper. "You fuck me like you own me. Then vanish like you don't."

My pulse is a riot. His eyes flare—and there it is, the shift. The moment he stops pretending to be calm.

"You want to play that game?" he growls, voice dark and smoky as he grabs my jaw, forcing my face up to his. "You want to act like this doesn't mean anything? Like I don't already own every inch of you?"

I blink up at him, mouth curling into something jagged. "I think you like the chase. I think you like pretending I'm the one running."

His grip tightens—just enough to make me gasp. "You think I won't remind you?" he rasps. "That I won't drag you back and fuck the attitude out of you until you forget your own fucking name?"

I don't answer—not out loud. But my body does. My pulse surges, and my thighs clench like they know what's coming.

"I fucking warned you," he mutters, spinning me around and shoving me hard into the nearest wall. And I can feel him pressed into my back. "You push, I push back harder."

"Fucking do it then, Steven."

His hand fists in my hair, yanking my head back until his mouth is flush with my ear.

"You wanna bait the monster?" he growls. "Then don't cry when he breaks you."

My breath shatters as his palm presses flat between my shoulder blades, pinning me like prey. My shirt's halfway up, and the cold bite of the wall is shocking against my front.

"You think I haven't seen this act before?" he sneers. "The brat who talks shit so she doesn't have to admit she's desperate to be claimed?"

"I'm not—" I start, but his fingers slide between my thighs, dragging through the soaked heat there—and I choke on the lie.

"You're fucking soaked," he snarls. "Came in swinging, all attitude and fire—like you weren't already aching for me to shove you against the wall and ruin you again."

Two fingers push in—deep—and I gasp as my cheek scraps against the plaster as my knees buckle.

"Keep fighting. It won't change a thing." His voice drops. "You want to be used like a toy? I'll play rough. But we both know you're already mine—you're just too stubborn to admit how much you love being owned."

He thrusts his fingers harder, grinding his palm into my clit while I whimper—legs shaking, every inch of me unraveling against the wall.

I don't want to talk, I don't want his comfort right now, I want this. His control, his hands, and his fucking wreckage.

"That's it," he snarls. "Cry for me, sweetheart. Beg. Show me how much you hate this."

I whimper again—louder this time. Because I don't hate it. I crave it. I ache for it.

He drags his fingers out, smearing my arousal across my inner thigh like a brand. Then comes the low rasp of his zipper.

"You baited me," he growls, lining himself up. "Now you're gonna take every fucking inch like a good girl."

He slams in hard—and I scream. My body shatters against the wall, spine arching like he's splitting me in half. His hand wraps around my throat, holding me still while he fucks me with pure, punishing purpose.

"This what you wanted?" he grits out. "To see what happens when I stop holding back?"

"Yes," I say breathlessly.

He drags his cock out slowly before slamming it back in, hard enough to jolt my whole body.

"You'd rather be fucked like a toy than admit anything I said was right."

I arch my back trying to get closer, to feel him deeper. "Shut up."

"Hit a nerve there, dear?" He taunts. "Or are you just too busy coming undone to keep up the act?"

I whimper, the walls of my cunt fluttering around him, right at the edge—and then he pulls out. Completely. I let out a strangled cry, and my body's still trembling. God, why does he have to be right. Why do I hate that I'd still fucking crawl back for more.

"No," I breathe, hips grinding back instinctively, needing him closer. "Steven—"

"On your knees," he growls.

I turn, blinking up at him as he fists his cock in one hand, while it glistens with my slick.

"You want to drown instead of talk?" His hand tightens around the base of his cock. "Then open that pretty mouth and I'll fill it with something else."

I drop to my knees, palms braced against his thighs, lips already parting. I'm not thinking, or fighting. I just need this—need him— more than I need air.

He stares down at me, dark and unreadable. "Open your mouth."

I do. I tilt my head back and open my lips wide, breath stalling in my throat. And he spits straight into my mouth like he's marking what's his.

A sharp jolt shoots through my chest, ricocheting down to where my thighs clench so hard it aches. Because fuck, I wanted that. I wanted the filth, the control, the ownership. I want him to claim me so completely there's no room left to feel anything else but him.

"Look at you," he mutters, dragging his cock over my tongue. "Drooling for me. Desperate to erase the past."

And he's right. I am. I want this more than I want answers. More than I want the truth. I want to be ruined so thoroughly, there's no room left to remember what I was afraid of.

He feeds it to me slowly while I moan and gag and fucking take it.

"Deeper," he hisses, both hands in my hair now, controlling the rhythm. "Eyes on me. I want to see how beautiful you look, choking on me."

I look up—and his whole body jerks. Tears spill down my cheeks while spit drips off my chin, my throat works around every inch he gives me.

"Fuck—just like that," he snarls. "Keep going. That's it. So fucking messy—just how I like you."

My throat tightens, and I moan around him, licking and swallowing, giving him everything I have. His hips stutter—once. Then again. A raw sound punches out of him as he pulls back just far enough to slap the head of his cock against my cheek, groaning when I chase it with my tongue like I need it to breathe.

"You want it?" he rasps.

I nod, gasping. My thighs are clenching like I can pull him back in through will alone.

"Then beg for it."

"Please," I whisper, broken and breathless. "Please come in my mouth—I need it. I need to taste you—"

That's does it. That's what fucking wrecks him. He fists my

hair tighter, snarling something feral as his release hits. The growl that leaves his throat sounds like it's been buried for years—raw and guttural—as he spills down my throat with a curse so filthy it makes my toes curl.

I swallow everything, and eventually he pulls back slowly, still breathing hard, staring down at me like he's not sure what's worse— what he just did, or how much he liked it.

I drag the back of my hand across my mouth, cheeks flushed, lips swollen, and my knees aching. My body's still trembling from the edge he ripped away—and the fact that I want it again.

He leans down, grabbing my chin in one hand, and tilts my face up until our eyes lock.

"Remember what I told you," he says, keeping his voice low. "Orgasm for talking. Not lying."

Then he walks off—like he didn't just leave me ruined on the floor.

27

"SMILE WHILE YOU STRIKE THE MATCH."
(THEY WON'T SEE IT COMING)

Ani

"Jesus," I mumble. "Did you fight a bear out there or just beat the shit out of the trees?"

He looks wrecked—his hair's a mess, his shirt clings to his chest with sweat, and his knuckles are raw like he went the rounds with the forest and didn't win. His eyes flick up and they just look dark and cold. Whatever warmth cracked through last night is long gone—shoved back behind steel walls like it never happened.

I cross my arms over my chest, the oversized shirt suddenly feeling paper-thin. "Hey, you good?"

He doesn't answer. Just grabs a water bottle from the counter, cracking it open, and downs half of it in silence. His jaw ticks as he sets it down, staring at his phone.

"I don't make a habit of fucking the same mistake twice," he mutters—more to himself than to me.

I blink. "Wow. Charming."

He still won't meet my eyes. "I'm not in the mood to play games."

I snap, voice cracking as it claws up my chest. "Apparently I needed a reminder of how fast you can turn into a fucking prick."

He shrugs. No flare of guilt. No flicker of remorse. Just a careless roll of muscle and silence—like none of it meant shit. It's like I didn't have his cock buried inside me six hours ago while he whispered things that made me ache in places I didn't know I could *feel*.

Then he just walks away, disappearing down the hallway like I'm not even worth slamming a door over.

My breath burns in my lungs, trapped behind the scream I won't give him as I clench my fists at my side. I stalk to the counter, snatching the mug he made—still full, still steaming—and carry it to the bedroom like it'll keep me from doing something stupid like going after him.

Instead, I sit on the edge of the bed, clutching my phone like it owes me answers, staring at Frank's message.

> Frank: I'm starting to wonder if you're avoiding me. That wouldn't be smart, Ani. I'm not a man you ghost.

I don't have time for this. My stomach lurches as another text pops up from another unknown number. I'm about to throw it across the room and never look back.

> REALTOR - LITTLE RIDGE PROPERTIES: Hi Ani! Just confirming your 10:30 appointment to view the retail space at 15 Wisteria Street, near 5th. Looking forward to meeting you.

Shit—I forgot I even messaged her when I was spiraling and pretending like I had a future.

I stare at the screen like it's accusing me of something because I already know what I'm about to do. And I also know he's going to be pissed, but right now, I don't give a fuck.

If Steven wants to slam doors without slamming them, then fine. If he wants to act like I'm some inconvenience he didn't ask for, then let him. I've been dealing with men like him my entire life. Men want to control everything, but can't handle the consequences when they lose it. I'm not going to stick around and beg him to treat me like I matter.

I shove the last of my things into my bag—and tug my hoodie over my head with shaking hands and slip my shoes on, ignoring how my fingers fumble at the laces. I grab my phone, pull up Uber, and order the ride. Estimated time, ten minutes.

Perfect.

My hand hovers over Bernadette's soft fur as I crouch down in front of her. Her big brown eyes blink up at me like she knows, like somehow she's already picked up the scent of my spiral.

"I'll be back, okay?" I whisper, smoothing her ear back.

I don't actually know that, but it's easier than explaining why I suddenly can't breathe in this house anymore. Not like she cares anyway.

I step out onto the porch, because fuck him. If Steven's so worried about me staying put, maybe he should've thought about that before he decided to treat me like a fucking liability.

The wind slices through my hoodie, sharp and mean, and I tug it tighter around me, pacing the edge of the porch like it might settle the burn in my chest. Every breath tastes like smoke and pine.

Then I hear the gravel crunching under tires as a white Toyota rolls into view, with a woman behind the wheel who looks like she drinks herbal tea and apologizes to plants.

Thank God.

I yank the door open and slide into the backseat without a word. The synthetic scent of air freshener hits my nose like a slap, clashing with the pine still stuck in my hair. The engine hums, and we start down the winding mountain road—trees whipping past like a memory I didn't ask for as my phone buzzes again.

Sarah: Hey, I know you're probably
getting railed six ways from Sunday or
whatever, but any chance you could cover
a shift? Alex called out and I'm drowning
just thinking about it, and I miss you.
Don't ever take time off again…mmmkay
thanks.

I stare at the screen for a second, then glance out the window. The mountains are behind me now. My mind is replaying every moment. The silence, the secrets, the fucking whiplash of him.

But Sarah's message on my phone settles something in me. Work means normalcy, plus, she's not wrong. I haven't seen her for what feels like weeks.

Me: Yeah. Tell Alex I hope he chokes on
DayQuil.

I exhale, staring at the screen like it's some kind of anchor. I wasn't planning to stop at my place—I didn't exactly want a front-row seat to the ghost town of my own trauma—but I probably should change. I've been living in hoodies and Steven's tension for days, and if I'm going to walk into work and pretend I'm fine, I should at least look like a person.

The message from my landlord says everything's good to go and new keys are waiting in my box. So I give the driver a new address and have her drop me at my apartment. I tell her I'll be back in ten.

The building still looks the same as I climb the steps two at a time, keys jangling like guilt in my pocket as I reach the door.

Inside, it smells faintly like old coffee and whatever candle I left half-burned the last time I was here—something vanilla, maybe sandalwood. I head straight to my room and strip out of the clothes that still smell like him—cedar, sweat, and that faint trace of leather that's starting to feel like a bruise I can't wash off. I throw on jeans and a cropped sweater. Nothing fancy.

In the mirror, I catch a flash of some light bruising along my collarbone, and some faint fingertip shadows on my hip. I look away before the ache has time to register.

I water the plants next. The fiddle-leaf is dramatic as ever, slumping like it's personally offended I left. The succulents are somehow still kicking, which is hilarious, considering I can't remember the last time I touched them. It's dumb, but part of me clings to the idea that maybe keeping them alive means I haven't totally wrecked everything.

I wipe my hands on my jeans, grab my bag, and head back outside. I glance around the parking lot, only to find it empty. There's no white Toyota, and no rumble of tires waiting at the curb.

I frown and pull out my phone, opening the app. *Trip completed.* Thanks for riding with Susan.

What the hell? I told her I'd be right back. I curse under my breath and open the app again, thumb hovering over the Request Another Ride button and that's when the low purr of an engine creeps in from the corner of the block.

A sleek black car with the windows tinted slowly turns the corner, rolling to a stop in front of my building.

My stomach tightens, as my instincts flare—the driver's window rolls down. It's Frank.

His forearm drapes over the wheel, and his tattoos are stark against the leather interior. There's no smile. No wave. Just his dark unreadable eyes, fixed on me like I'm prey and he's deciding whether or not he's in the mood to hunt.

"Ani," he says smoothly. "Get in."

I blink. "What are you—how did you—I thought you—?"

He ignores all my questions, and keeps talking. "Didn't think I'd be back this early, but the deal closed sooner than expected. Lucky timing... for you."

I open my mouth and close it. Everything in me's still fried from Steven's mood swings. My nerves are worn and raw, and I'm exhausted.

"I'm good," I say quickly, gripping my phone tighter. "I was just ordering another—"

"I'll take you," he says, keeping his voice calm. "Where were you headed?"

I hesitate. "Just going to look at a place. And I've got work later."

His head tilts slightly, narrowing his eyes like he knows I'm leaving something out and doesn't care enough to call me on it.

Then his gaze drags down my body. "You look tired," he says flatly. "Rough night?"

My pulse skips.

"I'm fine." I swallow. "Frank, really. I don't need—"

"I didn't ask what you need, baby girl," he chuckles. "I asked where you were going."

It's a subtle warning wrapped in concern.

I shift my weight from one foot to the other, torn between flight and politeness. The whole scene feels off—like the street's too quiet, and the air's gotten thicker. But I'm too caught off guard to say no, and I don't want to be late. So I open the door and get in.

The leather's cold against the back of my thighs as I settle in, the door clicks shut behind me and I clasp my hands in my lap to keep them from fidgeting.

"Just downtown," I say lightly, forcing a shrug that feels too casual. "I'm meeting someone."

He says nothing, but watches me with one hand on the wheel, and the other tapping against the gearshift like he's keeping time with my heartbeat.

Then, finally, he smiles.

"Back to the grind already?" he murmurs. "Figured you'd want more time to rest after... everything."

My stomach curls, but I keep my tone bright. "Didn't realize I needed your permission to look at real estate."

His knuckles tighten on the wheel—barely, but just enough

that I catch it. A beat passes, then he lets out a soft chuckle, like I've said something funny.

"Of course not, Doll," he says smoothly. "Just seems a little soon, that's all. But you've always rushed into things, haven't you?"

It lands like a rock in my gut, but I smile anyway, keeping my eyes straight ahead, but my heart is pounding a little faster now. I'm sure he's pissed I haven't responded to any of his messages, but I just don't have it in me to care right now.

Outside, the neighborhood rolls by in a blur of pavement and porch lights, but everything feels... off. Like I've walked into the wrong version of my life, and left one threat in the woods and climbed right into another.

I press my palms against my thighs to ground myself, digging my nails in. It's just a ride and yet the silence in the car feels like it's waiting to devour me whole. By the time he pulls up to the curb in front of the shop, I'm already halfway out of the car.

"Thanks," I mutter, grabbing my tote bag from the floor without looking at him. I don't give him a chance to say anything before I close the door and walk up the steps, pretending I don't feel the weight of his eyes on my back. This isn't weird at all.

The bell above the door jingles as I step inside—and for a second, I just stand there and breathe, forgetting everything else.

It's perfect.

The light spills through the tall front windows, pooling across scuffed hardwood floors that whisper history with every crack. It smells like old paper and fresh potential.

Along one wall, there's a built-in—deep shelves that beg for color-coded chaos and curated displays. A back door leads to what's probably an office or a break room, I don't even care. I can already see it. My counter, my music, my shelves.

I'm halfway through rearranging the future in my head when the realtor clears her throat behind me, making me jump.

"Sorry," she says with a polite smile, clipboard tucked under one arm. "I didn't want to interrupt your moment. It's got a good vibe, doesn't it?"

"Yeah," I breathe. "It's perfect."

She hesitates, and that's when I know.

"There's already an offer on it," she says gently. "Came in this morning, about an hour ago. It's a cash offer, and it's above the asking price too, but there's always a chance it will fall through."

The floor doesn't drop out. Not exactly. It just... shifts. Tilts. Reminding me that I'm not allowed to have things that feel this easy.

I nod slowly. "Of course there is."

"You're still welcome to walk through," she offers, her voice dipped in that soft, practiced sympathy people use when they think you've just lost something important.

I nod, and walk the space like it still matters. I run my fingers along the exposed brick, pretending to measure the counter I'll never build. But my body's on autopilot.

The truth is, I'm not really here.

I'm stuck in every version of a future that crumbled before it even began, wondering if this is the universe's way of telling me to quit dreaming altogether.

The walk-through ends with a handshake I barely feel and a thank you I don't remember giving. I step back outside and pause just long enough to let the sunlight hit my face, to pretend it can warm anything still left in me.

That's when I see Frank still parked across the street with his window down.

Something cold coils in my gut. I square my shoulders, forcing my spine straight, and descend the steps with something sharp and wordless. If I wasn't in the mood before, I'm definitely not now.

I don't go to the passenger door, instead I walk straight to the window, stopping just shy of the open frame and plant my hand on the edge, leaning in until I'm in his space—close enough to see the glint in his eyes.

"You've got a real problem with the word no, you know that?"

Frank looks up slowly, his sunglasses pushed to the top of his head, exposing eyes that are too calm for the way my pulse is hammering.

"Get in the car, Ani."

"No." I cross my arms. "You waited out here the whole time like some kind of creep. I don't need a ride."

He shrugs. "Did you order a car?"

"I'm about to."

"Get in the car, sweetheart. You're making a scene."

My jaw tightens and I want to scream. I want to shove him, to throw my bag and tell him to fuck all the way off, but I don't. Because people *are* watching. And because part of me still doesn't know what he's capable of.

So I scoff, flip him off for good measure, and wrench the door open, slamming it behind me as I slide into the passenger seat.

"Good girl," he says without looking at me, shifting the car into drive. "Now was that so hard?"

The second those two words leave his mouth, they land differently. How can the same words make me feel invisible in one mouth—and completely claimed in the other?

"Fuck off."

His jaw ticks, just once. "Try that again, sweetheart."

I glare out the window, refusing to look at him. "Don't push me, Frank."

There's a pause. A thick, electric silence between us. Then— quiet, but deadly—"Don't forget who you're talking to?"

That does it. My breath catches, and my throat tightens with the tension between fear and fury. I don't respond. I can't. Not without giving him exactly what he wants.

Silence falls between us as we drive, and the only thing I hear is the tires humming against the pavement. I assume we're headed toward my apartment, so I don't think too much of it when he takes a left instead of a right. Then another turn. It's not until the third wrong street that I feel the cold twist at the base of my spine.

I turn in my seat slowly. "...You missed my turn."

He doesn't flinch or even look at me. "I figured we'd drive for a bit. Catch up. You've been quiet lately."

My heart starts thudding. "I said I was fine."

"I know," he says softly. "That's what worries me."

I stare at him, waiting for him to look at me again. When he finally does, he flashes that careful smile, the one that never quite reaches his eyes.

"Relax," he says. "I'm not going to hurt you."

Funny how that only makes it worse.

"You're not taking me home?" I whisper, mostly to myself. Because deep down, I already know the answer.

His smile widens slowly. "Of course I am, Ani. Just not the place you keep running back to."

And that's when it clicks. Something is wrong. Really wrong. He doesn't say another word when we pull up—just eases the car to a smooth stop in front of a house I've never seen before. It's set back behind a massive gate and hedges so thick you wouldn't even know there was a driveway unless you were specifically looking for it.

My pulse jumps, loud in my ears. The house is sleek, all sharp lines and privacy. Nothing about it is warm, and yet, it feels unmistakably his. Every inch of it.

Every warning bell inside me starts to ring and not softly as I try not to panic. "Where the hell are we?"

28

"IF THE OFFER FEELS PERFECT, ASK WHAT IT'LL COST."
(IT'S NEVER FREE. IT'S NEVER CLEAN.)

Ani

Frank kills the engine without answering, and the silence stretches. I stay frozen, watching him get out, then slam the door shut. I grip my phone tighter, staring straight ahead. Maybe if I don't move, I can pretend none of this is happening. Then the door is yanked open.

"Ani," he says, voice lower now. "Get out of the car."

I lift my chin defiantly. "Can you please just take me home?"

He exhales through his nose like he's counting to ten in a room full of triggers.

"You can either get out by yourself," he repeats, voice harder now, "or I throw you over my shoulder and take you inside."

That does it. I whip around, heat rising fast and furious. "Frank, I'm not in the mood and I'm not staying here."

He crouches slightly, one hand braced on the frame of the car—and everything about him shifts. The mask he's always wearing falls. Gone is the charming man with dinner reservations and polite smiles. This is something colder.

"I've waited long enough for you to get on board," he says quietly. "I gave you time, patience, and space. I bent over backwards trying to let you come to this on your own."

I stare at him. *What the fuck is he talking about?*

He clears his throat and the air gets smaller. "I'm done waiting."

"I—" I start, but he lifts a finger. That same fucking finger he used to brush hair behind my ear. A move that used to feel sweet. Now it feels loaded.

"You don't have to say yes," he says. "Just let it happen."

A slow freeze spreads through my limbs, because somewhere in that twisted logic, he actually believes this is going to work out. I guess I only have myself to blame for that, I like having him around, but I just don't think I want to date him.

"That's the thing about consent," he murmurs. "Sometimes silence speaks louder."

My mouth opens—but nothing comes out. I bolt upright in the seat, panic rising in my throat. "I'm not going inside with you."

"You are."

"Or what?"

He doesn't answer, instead, he just straightens slowly. He exhales and the mask slides back into place with a smile that doesn't quite reach his eyes.

"Jesus, Ani." He chuckles, like I've overreacted. Like this is all some lover's spat. "You really think I'd hurt you?"

I say nothing as he crouches more, bringing himself closer to my eye level, one hand braced on the car door.

"I brought you here to talk, baby. That's it." His tone softens. "You looked upset earlier. I thought maybe you could use a break. A breather. That little shop clearly didn't go the way you wanted it to."

I swallow hard, keeping my expression neutral.

He continues, coaxing. "Look, I'm sorry. I just... missed you. I've had a really long day. Come inside, have a drink, cool off. You don't have to stay long. I know you've got to work later."

His voice is all warm and confident as my heart hammers like a warning bell in my ribs, but I nod once and finally climb out.

"Good girl," he murmurs as I step past him.

It still doesn't hit the way it does when Steven says it. It lands flat, and I don't melt. I just follow him up the steps of a house I've never seen, telling myself over and over that it's fine.

The door creaks open, and I step into a space that's too clean. It's the kind of place that smells more like lemon polish and curated silence than real life. The walls are white, lined with expensive art. It's giving hotel lobby vibes in a mansion's skin. And somehow, that fits him.

"Kitchen's this way," Frank says, casually. "You want something to drink?"

I nod once. "Sure."

I perch on the edge of a barstool, when my phone buzzes in my pocket but I don't check it yet. It's probably another creepy text.

He sets the glass in front of me then leans against the counter with his arms folded. He watches me like he's trying to decide whether to play nice or press harder.

"I know you've had a rough couple of weeks," he says, his voice low and almost sympathetic. "And I'm not mad, love. I get it. You needed space. Time to think."

I grip the water glass tighter. I can't have another *feelings* conversation right now.

"I didn't mean to crowd you," he goes on, pushing off the counter to close the space between us. His hand lifts, brushing a piece of hair from my face like he does. "You're still getting used to everything. But I need you to understand something, okay?"

My throat tightens. Everything in me pulls back, because I don't want to lead him on even more.

"You don't have to pretend anymore," he whispers. "I know you don't remember everything. That's fine. I remember enough for both of us."

My stomach lurches. What does that mean, you remember enough for both of us? How did I even get into this mess? Sure, I might've led him on, but I never encouraged him to think I wanted to date.

His eyes narrow slightly, and his voice goes quieter. "You'll see. You'll realize I'm the only one who's been honest with you."

The room feels too small now. "I need to go soon. I have work."

He nods, like he understands, but he doesn't move. "Of course. I'll drive you," he says.

I push back from the barstool, forcing my voice to stay even. "I —I just need to use the bathroom."

"Down there," he says, gesturing down the hall. "Second door on the right."

I nod, turning too fast. As soon as I round the corner, I yank my phone out with shaking fingers, my pulse slamming in my throat.

There's another grainy photo attached, it's the outside of the bar. The exact back entrance I always use—the one without cameras. It's a photo of me and Sarah, mid-laugh. She's got her arm slung around my shoulder and my head's tipped back, mouth open. I don't need to know what the message says to know what the message is.

> UNKNOWN: If you show up tonight, I can't promise she'll make it home.
>
> I'm done waiting in the shadows.

My stomach twists as cold, paralyzing nausea floods me, slow and suffocating. I don't even realize I've braced both hands on the bathroom sink until my knuckles start to ache. My pulse is so loud it drowns everything else out as I check to make sure I locked the door.

I look like a girl who hasn't slept in days. A girl who's lived three lifetimes since yesterday, and maybe I have. I grip the sink edge and suck in a breath.

Get it together, Ani. You're smart. You're still breathing.

Glancing back down at my phone, I don't let myself cry. I don't let myself think.

I just type out a quick excuse to Sarah, fingers trembling as I hit send, and pray she doesn't ask too many questions. If anything happened to her...*No, I can't go there.*

> ME: Hey. I'm so sorry—I can't cover tonight. Something came up. I'll make it up to you, I swear.

> SARAH: Babe. You okay? Not judging, but if you're getting dicked down, just say that. AND It's fine. I'll figure it out. But you owe me greasy fries and deets next shift.

I look in the mirror again, I look like someone on the verge of unraveling and pretending not to notice.

"Get it together," I whisper, running cold water over my wrists like that'll magically stitch me back up. "It's fine. You're fine. End of story."

My fingers curl around the edge of the sink again, until my knuckles throb. I could text Steven... The thought barely finishes forming before I kill it.

No.

Fuck that.

I don't need saving. Not from him. Not from Frank. Not from anyone.

I'll stay here for the afternoon, keep my head down, then bail later. I'll say I'm sick, or tired, or just not up for it. Hell, it's not even a lie.

The truth is—my body still hurts from last night. Every inch of me aches, and not just from the sex, but from the emotional whiplash of being wanted, then discarded, then wanted again. My brain can't keep up. My chest is tight, and my thoughts are loud enough that I'm not even sure who I'm running from anymore.

Myself, maybe.

I dry my hands, swiping under my eyes with the cuff of my sleeve, and force a deep breath into lungs that barely expand, and head back downstairs.

Thank God Sarah will understand, and not question me if I don't respond to her text. I'm not going to tell Frank that though, I don't need him to have any more reasons why I should stay here and hang out with him.

He's still in the kitchen with his sleeves rolled up, and a pitcher of something bright and citrusy on the counter beside two plates. He looks up as I step into the room, with a smile already in place.

Frank's voice cuts through the quiet. "You okay?"

I nod. "Yeah. Just tired."

"You look like you didn't sleep much last night," he says gently. "Have you been eating?"

I blink slowly. Well, that's one way to say I look like shit. Every girl's dream compliment.

I glance up at him, and he's watching me now, not bothering to hide it. My fingers tighten on my phone, but I keep my mouth shut since I'm trying to get out of here in one piece.

"I was thinking," Frank says, his voice low and coaxing. "Do you want to grab dinner before your shift?"

I don't answer right away. Something about the way he says it gives me pause. I know I should say no. That I should stand up, say thank you for drinks, and walk the hell out of this house with whatever dignity I've got left. But my limbs feel heavy. Not dramatic like I'm about to collapse—just slow. *Probably means I should eat something, honestly.*

"If it's just dinner." I say—mostly to myself. But even as the words leave my mouth, a part of me knows he's not going to make it that simple.

He nods and gestures to the couch. "Sit a minute, won't you."

I hesitate—because I *am* tired. Hopefully I'm not sitting for too long, because I'm sure the second I let myself think about how easy it'd be to rest here, to just lean back for a moment—I'll be out.

But I sit anyway.

The couch gives beneath me, soft and warm like a fucking invitation. I fold my arms tight, trying to keep my nerves in check. I can't stop thinking about that text, but at least Sarah's safe for now. Frank moves quietly around the kitchen, stacking plates like we're some kind of couple and this is just a normal afternoon. When he returns, he's got a blanket in one hand. He doesn't ask—just drapes it across my lap with careful hands.

"Almost done." he murmurs, smoothing the edge of it. "Then we'll head out."

I blink up at him. *Head out?*

Right. Dinner.

For a second I think he might cancel, or let me off the hook and pretend this whole thing was never meant to happen. But instead— "You can shower if you want," He smiles. "Or we can head out now. Up to you."

Right. Because nothing screams casual like showering in a stranger's house without any of your own clothes, and your past breathing down your neck through unknown number texts. But I try not to let my face show any of that. "I didn't bring anything with me, I wasn't planning on showering."

He shrugs, like this isn't the most loaded moment of the day. "There's a clean towel in the bathroom, and a new toothbrush under the sink."

Then, like it's nothing, he adds, "And I left you something else for you. My assistant dropped it off last night."

His eyes catch mine. Waiting. "You can wear it if you want to."

I stare at him.

"Don't look so shocked," he says with a smirk. "I'm not a complete savage."

No, just the kind of man who makes you feel like you're slowly boiling while he keeps smiling and stirring the pot. Still, the thought of rinsing off is enough to make me nod. At least just so I can have a minute to myself, maybe check in with Sarah to see what I should do.

"Five minutes," I say, already pushing myself up from the couch.

"Take your time, doll," he calls after me. "We're in no rush."

By the time I reach the bathroom, I half-expect the mirror to fog just from how hot my skin feels right now. Why do I get the feeling that Frank is some closet weirdo with a foot fetish.

There's a soft gray towel on the rack, perfectly folded and a brand-new toothbrush sitting beside the sink. I turn and see a dress hanging on the back door. It's sleek, black and silky. And unmistakably my size.

My throat goes dry.

What kind of assistant drops something like this off without confirmation that I would be here? And what kind of man has a fucking outfit ready when he didn't even know if I was going to say yes? I guess that's what having money does. You just buy it anyway, assuming no one will tell you no.

I stare at it, heart thudding. *It's just a dress, Ani. Not a collar.*

I should text Steven. The thought hits hard, and I'm not even sure where that came from. I don't even know what I'd say. *Sorry I ghosted, just needed a breather and accidentally ended up at my almost-boyfriend's mystery mansion where everything feels like a fucking trap?*

I squeeze my eyes shut, and open the bathroom door slowly, half expecting something to be different.

The house is quiet as I make my way back downstairs, and I try not to hold my breath, but my chest is tight anyway.

I step into the kitchen and he's moving with casual precision, sliding something off the stove like we do this all the time. Calm as ever. Because apparently, I've decided today's theme is ignore the red flags and go to dinner.

Frank gives me a warm smile—one that makes my skin prickle despite how soft it looks—and sets his mug down. *I really need to take a vacation after this. A real one. I'm exhausted.*

His eyes drag over me in one long sweep and I can see the moment he notes the outfit choice. But he doesn't comment.

"Good," he says, grabbing his keys off the counter. "Let's go."

I blink. "Now?"

"Unless you want to change?"

The smile he gives me is soft. I glance down at my outfit, shrugging. I'm not wearing that dress, despite how cute it was. But saying that now feels like poking the bear with a toothpick and hoping he doesn't bite.

"What I have on is fine. Thank you, though."

He holds the door open for me, and I follow him to the car in silence. The moment we pull out of the driveway, my nerves start to hum, and I'm getting tired again. Thank God when this is over I can sleep and I don't actually have to go back to work. Even Frank isn't talking much. Just flipping through his phone.

"Where are we going?" I ask, trying to sound light.

"You'll see."

Classic. Totally not suspicious at all. When we pull through the gate and the sleek black car starts winding around the perimeter of a private airfield, everything hits me all at once. The hangar. The plane. The people waiting near the tarmac.

"What the hell," I mutter, sitting up straighter, and feeling light headed. "Frank... is that—"

He parks, cutting the engine, and glances over at me with a smile so smooth it could be carved from glass.

"I told you, baby girl, I was taking you somewhere nice."

I stare at the jet in disbelief. "For Dinner?"

His grin widens. "You deserve more than Taco Bell, Ani."

This is too much. Or he's just *that* guy that does this kind of shit last minute.

The tarmac heat bites through the afternoon breeze as we approach the jet. It's sleek—matte gray with tinted windows and two uniformed staff waiting by the steps. Frank nods at them like this is normal, not a fucking private plane dinner run.

"This is insane," I mutter, squinting toward the sky. My voice sounds far away.

Frank's hand grazes the small of my back as we climb the stairs, warm and steady—staying there longer than it should. I should pull away, but I don't. I lean into it, only because I'm so exhausted and this is somehow taking all the energy I have. Which should be my first red flag.

"Insane would've been taking you to Applebee's," he replies with a smile. "Come on."

Something about all of this feels like a set up, with wine and roses and leather-bound menus. I tell myself not to make it a thing. Not to panic. But the longer I stand there, the more I feel like I'm walking into something I won't know how to get out of. I need to just tell him the truth. I don't need to tell him about Steven by any means, but I need to come clean that we won't ever be more than friends.

I step onto the plane, and the interior is ridiculous—cream leather, glass dividers, and there's actual art hanging inside a plane. There's also a table set for two near the back, and a bottle of champagne already chilling in a silver bucket.

"Get comfortable," Frank says, loosening the cuffs of his shirt before rolling them up. "We'll be in Taos in under an hour."

Taos?

Jesus. He's flying me across state lines for dinner?

I settle into the plush seat near the window, forcing a neutral expression onto my face while my heartrate kicks up a notch. I take a sip of water, glancing out the window. Trying to focus on the ridiculousness of it all just long enough to distract myself from the obvious.

When the flight attendant passes by, brushing past with a tray of citrus-scented cloths and warm towels— it hits me like a punch to the sternum.

What is that smell?

My hands start to shake, so I press them to my thighs. My body lurches before my mind catches up.

"Are you alright?" Frank asks, appearing beside me with a glass in hand.

I nod too quickly. "Just motion sickness." I lie.

His eyes narrow slightly, but he doesn't push. He sets the glass down and adjusts the air vent above my head like he's the fucking doting boyfriend.

"We'll be there soon," he says, smoothing a hand along the top of my thigh. "And I promise—this place is worth it."

I force a smile, but my throat is closing, because for the first time in days, something broke through. Not just a flash or a whisper —but a feeling. A place.

And I don't know what scares me more—what I almost remembered…Or the man currently holding my knee like I'm his.

The windows reflect nothing but my own confused face, I have no memory of falling asleep again. No idea how long I've been out.

My phone vibrates—another call from an unknown number. I decline it without thinking, too tired to deal with one more goddamn thing.

A second later, it dings. Then again. And again. Three texts.

> Steven: Ani. Where the fuck are you.
>
> Steven: You have five minutes to answer or I will come find you.
>
> Steven: Don't make me tear this fucking state apart.

Shit.

Of course he'd threaten to track me down. God forbid I slip the leash for half a second without him yanking it tight like it's some kind of test I just failed. My grip tightens on the phone, while my jaw tightens at his audacity.

I know Frank's probably the safe choice. The guy who plays nice and doesn't growl when I breathe wrong.

So why do Steven's words land like a hit I wasn't bracing for? Why does every bone in my body go hot and hollow at the thought of him showing up? And why the hell do I suddenly want him to?

I shove myself upright, and the floor tilts a little, or maybe that's just the war inside my chest. My phone feels radioactive in my hand, like if I look too long, I'll say something I can't take back.

I type a reply.

Delete it, then type again. Then delete it. Again.

Everything I want to say is wrong, and everything I should say is a lie. It's not like he won't know. He'll for sure figure it out, somehow he always fucking does.

I can't have him coming here. I just need to break things off with Frank so this doesn't get messy.

I type out just enough to buy me some time, to keep him from blowing up the front door like some dark knight with a vendetta and a death wish.

I need space and I need to think. And I sure as hell can't do that with him breathing down my neck.

> Me: I'm fine. I need space before I drown in all the shit I'm feeling. I'll talk to you when I can think straight.

Frank steps out of the cockpit all relaxed charm and polished teeth. "Ready to go?"

I stand up, pulse flickering. "Frank, listen... this was really thoughtful, but I think we should go back."

His smile doesn't drop, but something behind it wavers—just enough to chill the air between us.

"And go where?" he asks softly. "To whoever's been keeping your attention lately?"

I freeze.

Fuck. There's no way he knows...right?

"You don't have to run every time things get hard, sweetheart," he murmurs, brushing his knuckles along my jaw. "I'm not your enemy."

But my heart's already pounding. Why is it that two people have said that to me in the last 48 hours?

He smiles—smooth as ever—and steps back, giving me space. Pretty sure that was him making it crystal fucking clear that he's been paying closer attention to me than I thought.

Walking down the steps in silence, I notice a black SUV waiting at the edge of the lot with the engine running.

Frank opens the door for me, but doesn't say a word as I slide into the leather seat and buckle in. My skin's still humming from something I can't name as he rounds the front of the car and climbs in beside me, casual as ever—like we didn't just spend the morning pretending this wasn't a power play.

Then—my phone vibrates and I jump, blinking down at it like it bit me.

UNKNOWN NUMBER: You're not safe with him.

29

Steven

I *don't make a habit of fucking the same mistake twice.* The words echo like gunfire in my skull.

I meant Frank. I meant everything I've done to get close enough to put that bastard in the ground. I meant the years I've wasted chasing ghosts through blood and shadows, only to find myself right back where I started.

But it didn't matter what I meant. Not when she looked at me like I'd just spit in her face. Not when her expression went from fury to disbelief—then to something that felt like fucking betrayal.

I was out tracking down a lead—one who liked to talk big until his face met the pavement. It took too long to get anything useful out of him, and when he finally cracked, all he said was, *"She gave him something that led him straight to you."* I was half-listening when she started talking to me, still hearing that line on repeat in my head.

I didn't just piss her off. I lost her.

I'm sitting at my desk with my elbows planted and my jaw clenched so tight it aches. The blinds are half-drawn and sunlight slices through the dust in sharp, perfect lines. I know where she's going, she said she had a showing at some place she was interested in.

So I let her go, even though I know I shouldn't have.

I should've followed her the second she walked out the front door with murder in her eyes, but I didn't. I was waiting for something I needed in my hands, before I made my next move. Something that could finally tie in the last piece of this whole fucked-up puzzle.

So I stayed.

And now—she's fucking gone.

I lean back in my chair and pull up the feed on my monitor. The camera outside her apartment flickers to life. She came home, changed clothes, watered the plants like it meant something to her, then she stood at the window for almost ten minutes, just... thinking. Then she left again, walking out like it was any other day.

Then—nothing.

I know she went to the listing.

But after that, nothing. No texts. No calls. No location ping. Not even the usual breadcrumb trail she leaves behind when she's pretending she's fine.

Just silence. Something's up. It's too clean to be an accident. I checked the tracker again, and sure enough, it's glitching. It's the same lag I noticed when she left her apartment. I thought it was a bad signal. Now I'm not so sure.

I was already halfway to the door—boots on, gun holstered, and my keys in hand—when my phone buzzed.

> Ani: I'll talk to you when I can think straight.

Like that would ever be a fucking option.

She thinks she needs space? I'm the only one who's kept her alive this long. If she's not running, then why the fuck does it feel like I'm chasing her all over again? She doesn't get to disappear behind her words like that and expect me to wait around. Not when I already know where this is headed.

She wants space? She'll get about five more minutes of it.

Then I'm coming.

And God help anyone standing in my way.

I force myself to stay still and wait, to breathe through the instinct screaming at me to burn the world down and drag her back with my bare hands.

That's why I sent Travis. Because if I chased her myself—I wouldn't stop. There isn't a line I wouldn't cross. I've never lost a mark, never lost control, but this isn't about vengeance anymore.

If Frank thinks he can put his hands on her—keep her—I open the drawer, fingers curling tight around the handle of the blade inside. *Let him fucking try.*

The cabinet slams shut louder than I mean, and Bern whines behind me. My phone's been silent for hours and I've already circled the cabin three times trying not to punch through the goddamn walls.

I cross the room, picking up her empty mug like it might hold a clue or explain why every second since she left feels like a fuse burning straight down to detonation.

Either way, someone's bleeding when I find her.

My phone buzzes. *Finally.*

Travis: Got eyes on her.

Travis: She's with him.

I grip the edge of the counter, hard enough to make the wood groan. She went to him?

No. *There's no fucking way.*

She wouldn't—but the silence on the line says everything I need to know. Of course she fucking did.

She ran straight to the devil the second she felt cornered. Right into the arms of the man I've been trying to bury for years.

I told her. I fucking told her not to leave. Not to trust anyone. Especially not him. I'd practically been screaming it at her.

I shove back from the counter, the chair clattering to the floor behind me and my vision narrows.

Me: Where?

Travis: Jet landed in Taos about ten min ago.

A bitter laugh escapes my throat, sharp and violent. I dig my knuckles into my temple because this shouldn't matter. Except it does, because she wasn't supposed to look at me like that, she wasn't supposed to let me in. Fuck, she wasn't supposed to crawl —and whimper—and say my fucking name like it meant something.

I should've stuck to the plan.

Instead, I let her get under my fucking skin—and now she's in the hands of the one man I came here to bury.

Me: If he touches her, the plan is out the window and I kill him.

Travis: Thought she was just leverage?

Me: She was.

Me: Until she wasn't.

Travis: Want me to move?

Me: No. I need you where you are.

Me: I'll handle it.

I'M ALREADY DRAGGING THE DUFFEL FROM BENEATH THE couch. It's my secondary kit—clean, fully loaded, and always ready to go.

Frank wants to play house? I'll burn the whole fucking estate to ash.

I toss the bag onto the counter and unzip it, taking inventory of every weapon. False IDs, glock, blades I haven't touched since Prague, and even some vials I swore I'd never use again.

But this isn't a hit.

It's a war.

> Travis: Dinner just started. Candlelight and everything.

My jaw ticks hard enough to crack.

> Me: Keep eyes on her. Do not engage.

> Travis: You think she went willingly?

> Me: Doesn't fucking matter.

I slam the door behind me and stalk to the car because if he thinks she'll forget what it felt like to crawl for me, come for me, and scream for me—he's more delusional than I gave him credit for.

She's mine.

Even if I have to remind her who she fucking belongs to.

I'm halfway to the car with the keys clenched in one hand, when my phone lights up again with an incoming call.

"What."

"You really don't have a tracker on her?"

I stop walking.

"What the fuck are you talking about?"

Travis laughs. "Don't tell me she's been practically living in your house and you didn't tag her."

I snort. "I tagged her the first night I followed her home." Then sharper— "I went through her phone while she was asleep. Set it up and scrubbed—."

Of course I fucking tagged her, she's been wired since day one.

Then it hits me. Not that she's tagged, but that I've been looking at the wrong shit. I only ever checked what mattered to me. To the mission, and to Frank. I flagged the messages that mentioned his name, scanned for keywords, patterns, and connections. Everything that would tie her to him.

I didn't look at anything else. I didn't think I had to because I was so fucking sure she was just collateral.

A low curse slips from my mouth as I hang up the phone, rage already boiling under my skin. I storm to the drawer and yank it open, pulling out the cloned copy of her phone.

I open the messaging app—this time, no filters. No search terms. No tunnel vision. It's all here.

Thread after thread of quiet fucking panic. Unsaved drafts. Notes she never sent. All the texts between her and Sarah. Deleted photos.

Then I see several messages from an unknown number.

"You still sleep with the light on. You're hiding from monsters. They're coming anyway. You don't remember what happened, but I do."

"You can play house all you want. But you know who you really belong to."

Rage slams through me and my vision goes white around the edges.

Fuck.

These messages aren't just from someone watching her. They're threats, and they're intentional. Personal. And I let her walk straight into Frank's arms thinking I was the biggest danger.

I drop into the chair at my desk, eyes locked on the glowing screen while my pulse hammers behind my teeth. The burn under my skin isn't anger anymore—it's fire.

Someone thinks she's theirs, and touched what's mine.

I pull up the tracking app and still can't get anything on where she's at. Either she found out it was there, or he did.

Fuck.

I don't care how many smiles he's fed her. How many silk sheets or lies or dresses he's tried to put her in. I'm going to carve the truth into his ribs. And when I drag her out of that gilded cage, she's going to remember what it means to belong to someone.

I slam my fist down and call Travis. He picks up on the second ring.

"Yes, dear."

My voice is ice. "I need eyes back on her. Now."

"She's still at the restaurant—same place she was ten minutes ago." He exhales. "You want me to move in?"

"No," I snap. "Stay the fuck where you are. Keep eyes on all three of them."

A pause.

"You think she's lying to you?"

"I think," I growl, "she's been lied to so many fucking times, she doesn't know what the truth is anymore."

All I hear is the typing he's doing in the background.

"He knows something." My fingers curl into a fist. "And if he lays one hand on her, I'll bury him next to the last man who thought he owned her."

Travis lets out a low whistle. "That bad?"

I don't answer. My eyes stay locked on the last message she got, glowing on the screen.

You know who you really belong to.

"She's been marked," I say finally. "Before any of this started."

"How does he tie into this?"

I exhale through my nose. "I think he's trying to finish what someone else started. Or maybe he doesn't even know the full story —maybe he's just a pawn. But if she's in his hands now, it means one of two things."

"And neither of them's good."

"Exactly."

There's a pause, and I can tell he's trying to be careful, "You think she's keeping it a secret?"

I rub the side of my jaw, eyes flicking across her screen again. The hidden messages, the silent spirals, the dreams she wrote down.

"And what happens if it's true?"

I grip the edge of the desk hard enough for my knuckles to turn white. "That depends on whether I get to her first."

"Steven—"

"I've let her believe too many lies," I snap. The words tear out of me. "I let her walk straight into the mouth of a fucking lion while I sat here watching. Waiting for what?"

My voice drops. "No more space. No more waiting. She wants to play house with a monster, fine. But I'm the one who knows what's hunting her. And I'm done playing nice."

There's a long silence on the line. The kind that feels like the calm before something shatters.

"Tell me where to be."

I sigh, rubbing my hand down my face. Knowing he's going to have his attention split. "Eyes on the restaurant."

"You sure you're in the right headspace for this?"

"No," I answer flatly. "But I'm the only one who knows how this ends."

And I've already made one mistake with her—I won't make it twice.

The house is too fucking quiet. The blanket she curled up in still sits crumpled on the couch, and her mug rests by the sink, half full and cold. I drag the knife from my duffel and slam it into the butcher block. The sound echoes through the room.

I don't do rage. Not like this. Not since I buried the last man who deserved it.

But Ani makes me forget the rules. She's in there now—to the bone. Threaded through the wreckage like she belongs there.

I sink into the chair I haven't used since the day I opened the file that led me here. Frank's name is still stamped across the top. I stare at it like a fucking bull seeing red, while I go over them again.

It's a list of shell companies, an inheritance tied to property in Puerto Rico with the name scratched out in every file except one.

I open my laptop and pull up the encrypted drive Travis sent over weeks ago. I'd skipped this file before because it all looked like the same shit we already had on him.

This time, I open the folder labeled REDACTED – R. INHERITANCE CLAIM.

And this time... I find something else. A document that looks like it's only half scanned, and burnt along the edges. It looks like a will. It's signed with a signature I've seen before—only once. There's also a surveillance photo, and standing next to Frank like a shadow from the past, is someone I recognize.

But it's the clause at the bottom of the page that stops me cold.

In the event of my passing, my estate shall pass to one A. R., my blood and only heir. No other claim shall override this.

I go still.

Everything in me locks down. It's a half-buried detail—one I brushed off because it didn't feel relevant.

My blood.

I sit back, piecing it all together. This isn't just some vague reference. This is a legal transfer of power. This isn't about Frank laundering money or manipulating girls anymore. This is about Frank having control.

Now I can't fucking breathe because if I'm right, then she's not just tangled in this, she's the center of it.

And she doesn't even know it.

Or she does and she's lying through her teeth while she sleeps in my bed, and moans my name while she's playing me.

I don't know which truth is worse.

I press my hands into the edge of the desk, trying to stay calm—but my knuckles are white and the only thing I can think about is her face, and the way she looked when she flinched in her sleep. The way she sounded when she whispered, *"Don't let him take me."*

Fuck.

She's mine. That's never changed—not since the first time I saw her. Flashing eyes, smart ass mouth, and that untouchable fire buried beneath all that fear. I wanted her then. I want her now. But if she's tied to this—if she's been protecting Frank— I don't know if I want to drag her home... or punish her for it.

She knows something. But does she know who he really is?

She sure as fuck doesn't know who I am. Because if she did—if she had any idea what I've done for less than what she's worth— She wouldn't have left my house. She wouldn't have gotten in his car. And she sure as fuck wouldn't be looking at another man like he could give her a future I haven't already decided for her.

I pace across the room, heat crawling up the back of my neck like a fuse begging to be lit. Every part of me is wired and crackling. I'm halfway to the door when my phone buzzes on the desk.

> Travis: You're gonna want to see this.

The file hits my inbox a second later. It's a timestamped image with surveillance footage with low res, and grainy as hell. But not so grainy that I can't make out the woman in it.

No. Fucking. Way.

My vision narrows and all I hear is static. I'd recognize that face anywhere, but it can't be her. It's not possible. But the longer I stare, the more certain I am.

She has the same dark eyes, the same slope of her mouth and the same defiant tilt to her jaw—like the whole world could fall and she'd dare it to land on her first.

My thoughts snap straight to that night, when all I could see was a gun pointed at her head. Her body dragged forward like a shield, and his voice behind her.

"One move and I paint the walls with her."

I'd never moved so fast in my life. Then there was the scream that's haunted my nights every day since. I came to with blood in my mouth and a hollow feeling in my chest that's never healed.

She was gone.

It was taken outside a building I already flagged once—a shell corp buried under layers of offshore money and fake tax IDs. It's one of his.

Which means this wasn't random. She wasn't spotted on the street out and about, this wasn't an accident.

Was she working? Was she complicit?

No. No fucking way. That's not her. That's not—but I don't know anymore because if she's been here this whole time...Why the hell didn't she say anything? Why disappear without a trace?Why let me believe it?

My hands curl into fists at my sides as my jaw locks, and my pulse pounds like a countdown I can't hear the end of.

None of this makes any sense. Unless—unless he's using her. Unless he found a way to keep her under his thumb. But even then —how the fuck has she stayed hidden this long? There's no fucking way she stayed willingly. I can't believe that.

I shut the file. I don't need more fucking questions, I need answers. Real ones. The kind that bleeds when you cut them open, and leave a trail.

I know exactly where to start. Picking up my phone again, I dial and he picks up on the first ring.

"Tell me you're packing a go-bag," he mutters.

"I'm not calling you to babysit," I snap.

"No?" A pause. "You sound like you're about to burn something down."

"I am."

"...Shit." I hear a rustle—probably him grabbing a pistol or sliding on his coat. "Talk to me."

I'm not sure I can say without losing control. If I open my mouth, I don't know what's going to come out.

"I've been looking in the wrong direction," I mutter. "I thought

Frank's interest in Ani was nothing more than a piece of ass he couldn't get out of his system, but it's more than that."

"She's connected?"

"She has to be. It's too clean. All the data points line up. How did we miss this?"

"And you're sure she doesn't know?"

"I don't think so." I grind my jaw. "But if she's been lying to me—"

"You gonna kill her?"

My blood goes cold.

"No," I say flatly. "But I'll make damn sure no one else touches her."

30

"Don't corner something feral."
(Unless you want it to bite)

Ani

I lean my head against the window, watching clouds blur past in streaks of white and gray. The hum of the engines fill the cabin, and it's almost soothing.

I woke up this morning alone in a hotel bed I didn't remember climbing into. My shoes were off, my makeup was smudged, and the dress I didn't agree to wear was folded on the chair across the room.

The sheets on the other side of the bed were undisturbed, but there was a note on the nightstand in that slanted, too-neat handwriting that said, *Flights at nine. Room service's on me. You looked beautiful last night.*

I don't remember last night after the first glass of wine. I remember ordering a steak, and laughing at something he said about fruit imported from a volcanic valley in Iceland. I remember his fingers brushing mine, and I remember smiling even though it didn't feel like mine.

He said nothing happened. We ate dinner, stayed up talking, and I was practically falling asleep at the table. He said I basically told him I didn't want to fly back that late, so he booked a suite just to make things easy.

At least... that's what he said.

When I questioned him about it, he sounded offended like I'd insulted him for asking.

He didn't do anything wrong. Not technically. He was charming. Generous. Warm in all the right ways. But that's the thing about people like Frank, the kind who always says the right thing—you don't realize you're bleeding until you look down and see the knife.

I shift in my seat, with my arms crossed, pulling my hoodie tighter around me. Still trying to ignore the fact that I don't remember agreeing to any of this. Not the room. Not the flight. And certainly not waking up feeling like someone pressed mute on half my memories.

I'm still trying to forget the way he looked at me this morning—when I came downstairs after the fastest shower of my life. Like I'd already said yes to more than breakfast.

There's a low clink of glass behind me—champagne, probably. I don't turn around. I just keep staring at the clouds and swallowing the weird twist in my gut. The croissant tasted like something I've had before. Or maybe that was just my brain playing tricks again.

There was a brief moment this morning when I saw a flash of something. A girl—barefoot on marble, and a voice yelling in a language I didn't recognize. And then it was gone.

I told myself it was nothing, but I haven't stopped thinking about it since.

The plane dips slightly, starting its descent and I exhale through my nose, willing my heart to slow. It's fine. It's just a weird day, I've had worse.

It's not like I'm locked in some gilded cage or—"Still with me, doll?"

His voice cuts through the hum behind me, and I blink up at him, heart beating hard against my ribs. I force a smile and nod like everything's fine.

I'm still pissed and he knows it. I found out over breakfast that Frank called the bar to excuse me from work—only to be told I wasn't scheduled. He laughed it off saying it worked out, that I clearly needed the break.

The fact that he went behind my back and figured out my schedule pisses me off. I know Sarah wouldn't do that, so I'll have to have a nice chat with the servers about that. Good thing I work tonight.

I turn back to the window before he can see what's written all over my face. Because if I don't, I might say something I can't take back.

He settles into the seat across from me. "We've got a big weekend ahead."

My stomach knots so hard it feels like it's trying to fold in on itself. *A big weekend?*

Funny—I don't remember agreeing to that, but I don't argue. Not up here.

So I smile. Or at least something that passes for it. I lean back in my seat and nod like I'm going along with it, even as my nails dig into the cuffs of my sleeves and my mind's already flipping through options for when we land.

By the time the wheels touch down, my jaw aches from how long I've been clenching it.

Frank's hand brushes my lower back as we exit the plane with the kind of touch that's supposed to feel safe, or make me feel special. Only it doesn't.

The ride is quiet as I watch the trees blur past the tinted window. Somewhere along the way, Frank starts talking about something to do with some meeting tomorrow at the club. His late dinner tonight, then something vague about property acquisitions and a new opportunity in the city.

I nod at all the right times, smiling once or twice, but my head is miles away. Something is trying to claw its way out of me, and the more I ignore it, the more it eats me alive.

"We'll stop at my place first," he says casually, like it's already been decided. "Then I'll drop you after."

I blink, turning toward him. "I have work."

"I know," he says, smiling just enough to make my pulse skip. "You'll make it. I'll be quick."

By the time we pull into the driveway, the sun is high overhead and I feel like I haven't slept in days. Frank opens the door for me before the driver even has the chance. He doesn't say anything, just offers his hand like he's the hero in some vintage romance. I don't take it, I'm too tired to pretend.

"You okay?" he asks, watching me a little too closely.

I nod. "I'm just tired."

His smile is warm and familiar, and it's the kind that used to work on me. The kind that might've worked again—if I hadn't already seen what it looks like when someone doesn't pretend to want you.

Frank's house is just as pristine as the last time, and just as suffocating.

"This won't take long," he says, unlocking the front door and guiding me inside like I wasn't here. "Just a quick meeting in the office. Then I'll drive you back so you can get ready for work."

I blink. "You said you'd take me straight home."

"And I will. In just a minute." He smiles over his shoulder. "Guest room's made up if you want to lie down. First door on the right, down the hall."

Lie down? Right, because this is so casual. So fucking normal.

"Take a nap if you need," he adds, already turning toward his office. "There's a phone charger on the nightstand."

Of course there is.

And just like that, he's gone.

I head down the hall, every step heavier than the last, and plug my phone in before even sitting down. No new messages. No missed calls. Which is a little weird. At least for Sarah.

I sit on the edge of the bed, staring at the screen like it's supposed to tell me what the hell I'm doing. My reflection stares back at me in the black glass and I hit Sarah's name, it rings once then goes straight to voicemail.

Rude!

I don't leave a message, I just stare at the screen like an idiot, wondering what the hell is wrong with me. Why I came, why I stayed. Why I keep lying to myself, and that this isn't exactly what it looks like?

Frank hasn't done anything wrong. Not technically. But there's just something about him that is starting to make me feel uneasy.

I don't know how long I sit there, picking at the skin around my thumbnail, before the thought hits me like a slap. I don't know why I'm sitting here, I want to leave.

How do you walk away without being rude when someone's been nothing but... good? Pushy lately, yeah. Intense in ways that feel like more than just interest. But still—he's been constant. I've known him since the night I rode with him in the back of the ambulance and he's done nothing but show up for me since. And now I'm here, in his house, staring out his window—and plotting how to sneak out without a goodbye.

What the hell is wrong with me?

The only reason I haven't left yet, is because I want to tell him we're not going anywhere. That I don't like him like that. That whatever this is, it needs to stop.

I grab my phone and shoot Sarah a quick text.

> Me: Are we hanging out at work tonight, or are we hanging out at your place?

The message sends, but there's a weird delay—just a spinning circle before the "delivered" finally pops up. It takes a full minute before my phone buzzes, which is unlike her.

> Sarah: My place tomorrow if you don't ghost me again • • You good? You kinda disappeared.

Perfect.

I move toward the window and part the curtain with two fingers, peeking out at the driveway. I can hear his voice from somewhere downstairs, so whatever *meeting* he was having, he's still not done.

Frank's voice drifts up again—probably on another call, planning another surprise like we're characters in a movie I never agreed to star in.

On my way out, I catch my reflection in the mirror. I look calm, but that's the lie. Under the surface, I'm vibrating. That brittle kind of tension that only shows up when something's about to snap.

I slip out of the room like a ghost with my phone gripped tight in my hand. My heart hammers in my throat as Frank's voice murmurs faintly from his office down the hall. I don't know why it suddenly feels like this. Like a trap wrapped in kindness. But it does.

I move toward the door with my breath shallow, as my fingers brush the handle.

"—she's useful," Frank says, keeping his voice low. He still has that edge of charm, but it's different now.

I freeze again as another male voice responds, "Useful doesn't mean reliable. You sure she's not going to bolt again?"

My lungs stop working.

Frank laughs. Not loudly, but it's enough to make my stomach twist.

"She's not going anywhere, she's too wrapped up in the story I gave her. She still thinks this is about us."

Us? Is he talking about me?

"I mean hell, she's a good girl when she's distracted. I've been patient long enough."

"You sure you're not getting soft?" The other voice says.

"I'm protecting my investment."

A numb, detached kind of horror that hits too fast to make sense, fills my body. A shiver runs down my spine.

Investment? What the actual fuck.

"You think she's worth all this?" the man asks.

Frank laughs again.

"She doesn't even know what she's worth." There's a pause. "Not after what happened in Cali. Hell, she barely remembers that night."

My blood turns to ice and the words hit me like a slap—sharp and sudden, and somehow...familiar? Every nerve in my body stills like I've been thrown underwater. The air is too thick. The silence is suddenly too loud.

But Frank just keeps going.

"The club is the cover, it'll have to work for now."

I don't know what the fuck I'm hearing, but I'm going to pretend he isn't talking about me like it's not the most brutal thing I've ever heard.

His voice picks up again, careless now. "This place was supposed to be about leverage. And she walked right back into it like the good girl I know she is."

The laugh that follows shatters something inside me. Then, like he's making sure the man on the other end really gets it—"Worst case," he says with that same damn calm, "I'll get what I need, same as the first time. She didn't remember it then, and she won't remember it now."

The words echo, but it's not the words that split me. It's the way he says them. And just like that—The smell hits me again. Bleach, cheap cologne, and blood. I'm back in that motel hallway and the fluorescent lights are flickering. The floor is sticky, and my legs are so weak.

Next thing I know, I feel hands on me and I see my ex's face, his dead eyes and a mouth full of apologies, but this time he's yelling.

"Let go of me—get the fuck off—" My own voice is screaming, and its cut off with a slap.

Then a man's voice. Cold and final.

"She's mine now. It's done."

All I see is a gold bracelet with a piece of paper in his hand as he hands whatever it is to my ex with a flash of teeth.

Everything's coming in so fast. I remember the sound of pen on paper, and some sort of deal being made. They shake on it, but what was it?

Then I'm bleeding and dizzy on the floor, in a room I don't recognize, trying to crawl. And someone says—"She won't remember anything. Just clean her up."

Then nothing.

I jolt out of it, and I'm right back in Frank's house, with my breath trapped in my throat. My hand is on the wall, and I don't even remember putting it there.

My fingers curl into a fist, and he's still in the other room talking like it's just another day.

My vision tunnels, but I don't hear the rest. I don't want to. I'm already backing away from the door, with my heart slamming so loud it feels like it's echoing in my ears. I think I'm going to be sick.

I stumble down the hallway and duck back into the guest room just long enough to catch my breath.

Fuck. Fuck. Fuck.

My chest's too tight, like my ribs are wrapped in barbed wire and the walls are pulsing in on me. I'm one blink away from either screaming or throwing up. Maybe both.

I promised myself I would never be that girl again. The one who waits. Who plays it safe. Who lets a man talk over her instincts until her silence becomes survival.

I don't know if he's talking about me or someone else, but I don't care.

Never again.

I would rather burn the fucking world down than let someone like Frank rewrite my story. Again.

I've played nice. I smiled and nodded while my body screamed.

I've folded small enough to fit inside someone else's fantasy, and I swore I'd never make myself that small again.

Now I get it. Now I fucking remember what this feels like. This rage. This itch beneath my skin. It's not fear anymore, it's the crackling static of something waking up inside me.

Something that was buried so deep, I forgot it had claws.

I move fast, heading out the door and down the hall. I don't let myself second-guess it, don't let my breath hitch or my heartbeat slow. I just move.

Outside, the air is cooler than I expected, biting at the edges of my sleeves as my feet hit the stone steps. The wind cuts across my cheeks, sharper than it should be, but I don't stop.

The gates shift open with a slow mechanical groan as I walk past, the second I'm through, I exhale like I've been holding my breath for days. I don't stop walking until I'm down the street and around the corner.

INSIDE, THE BAR'S ALREADY PRETTY BUSY. SARAH'S BEHIND the counter with her signature bun, two braids knotted through it like a spell that says fuck around and find out. She's mid-pour, flipping a bottle in one hand and jabbing the tap with the other, when a guy at the corner nearly wipes her out with an elbow.

She doesn't miss a beat—just glares at him and hisses, "Do that again and I'll wear your liver like a purse."

Then she sees me and her whole face lights up. "Oh, thank Christ. I was one crypto bro away from lighting a ceremonial fire and disappearing into the woods."

I let out a dry laugh and slide behind the bar, catching the apron she throws at me.

"You would've had to leave me a note," I mutter. "Or a blood trail."

"I was thinking smoke signal. Maybe a coded message in limes."

The second I'm in motion—stacking glasses, wiping down the counter, dodging elbows and pickup lines—the static in my head quiets just a little.

The next few hours blur as the rhythm takes over. I flirt just enough to double my tips and avoid every man who thinks a wink is a personality trait. And through it all, I keep checking the clock.

By ten-thirty, my shirt smells like citrus and regret, and Sarah slides up beside me with two shot glasses and a look that says spill or I swear to God, I'll hex your shampoo.

"You gonna tell me where the hell you've been," she says, handing me a shot, "or am I gonna have to summon the dead?"

I sigh. "Can I plead temporary insanity?"

"You can plead whatever you want. I still know you're full of shit."

We clink, then throw them back and it burns just enough to make me human again.

"Okay," I exhale. "Frank flew me to Taos for dinner."

Sarah's head jerks like I slapped her. "You what?"

"It was just for dinner," I say quickly, "but I stayed the night."

Her eyes narrow. "You stayed the night? Ani—"

"Nothing happened," I cut in. "At least, I don't think it did. I was exhausted. He said I practically passed out at the table and didn't want to put me back on the plane."

"Okay but... are we sure he didn't drug you, or did he just charm you into a blackout?"

"I don't know." My voice drops. "That's the part that's got me all twisted up."

She doesn't press. Just pins me with a look only your best friend can give you—the one that says I'm here even if I want to slap you.

"So, what about the tattooed sex god?" She asks eventually, sipping her drink like it's casual.

I blink. "Steven?"

"Unless there's someone else you haven't told me about. Then I'll be pissed and demand you tell me where mine is waiting. The one with the jawline carved by vengeance and a stare that could burn through kevlar. You know, that Steven."

My laugh comes out a little too fast, and too shaky. "Jesus."

Sarah just smirks. "What? I'm not blind. The man looks delicious in leather. I bet if you said the wrong thing during sex, he'd punish you and somehow make it your idea."

I snort into my glass. "That's not inaccurate."

"Please tell me he's mean."

"He's awful."

"Ugh, thank God."

I grin, but it slips too easily. "He's... intense. And dangerous. He watches me like I'm either his last meal or a threat to be neutralized. Sometimes both. And he's way too good at knowing when I'm about to lie."

Sarah hums. "Sounds feral."

"He is."

"But?" she prods.

I sigh, dragging my nail along the rim of my glass. "But I think I trust him more than I trust Frank."

Sarah blinks. "And yet... you flew out with Frank."

"Yeah," I murmur. "I know."

She doesn't say I told you so. She just leans her arm into mine, silent and solid in the way only she can be.

"Are you done with him?" she asks softly.

"I think I've been done," I sigh. "I just... didn't want to believe it. He makes everything sound so damn reasonable. Like I'm the one who forgot what I said and I'm always two steps behind a conversation I never agreed to."

"Yeah," she says. "That's called manipulation, babe."

Before I can reply, some guy stumbles up to the bar, waving a ten-dollar bill like it's a VIP pass and shouting over the music, "Can I get two Jäger—"

Sarah doesn't even break eye contact. "I'm catching up with my best friend, Devin," she says calmly, like she's explaining something to a small child. "You see that? You see the talking that's happening?" She gestures between us like she's conducting a ceremony. "That's sacred. That's girl code in action. You're on very thin fucking ice, my guy."

Devin falters and slowly lowers the bill. "Oh. Uh. Okay."

She narrows her eyes. "Do I look like a woman who's about to pour you Jäger, or do I look like a woman who's five seconds away from banning you from this bar forever?"

Devin backs away like she just threatened to key his soul. "It's cool. I'll come back later."

"You do that," she says sweetly, turning back to me. "Anyway, where were we? Right, murder crush. Has veins in his neck like Greek columns. What's that like?"

I stare at her, blinking. "Jesus."

"What?" She shrugs. "You don't interrupt girl talk about murder crushes. It's the law. I'll get it tattooed if I have to."

"You're insane."

"Unmedicated," she corrects. "And thriving."

I laugh into my drink. "You threatened a man over Jäger."

"I did. And I'd do it again." She smirks. "Also, Jäger? In this economy?"

I shake my head. "God, I missed you."

"Of course you did. I'm a delight. Now tell me more about Steven and the way he undresses you with his serial killer eyes," she says, resting her chin in her hand, and her eyes are practically glittering with dangerous curiosity.

I take a slow sip of my drink, but it doesn't help.

"He looks at me like he's already fucked me six different ways," I say finally, my voice low. "Like he's deciding whether to bend me over the counter or drag me into a dark alley and make me beg."

Sarah lets out an actual whimper. "Okay, ma'am. Continue."

"And it's not just the stare," I go on, eyes unfocused now, because the second I start thinking about it, it's game over. "It's the way he talks. Calm. Cool. Collected. But filthy. Like the devil would blush filthy."

Sarah raises a brow, fanning herself with a bar napkin like we're in church. "Is this safe for work?"

"No," I whisper. "It's not safe for anything. This man spit in my fucking mouth."

She gasps like I just confessed to arson. "Shut the actual fuck up."

"I crawled for him, Sarah," I hiss. "Like, willingly. On hands and knees."

Sarah slaps the bar again, eyes wide with reverent horror. "My last situationship didn't even make eye contact during sex and this man's got you crawling? You're living my literal wet dreams right now. I have FOMO. Look—I'm literally getting chills."

She sticks her arm in my face like that proves her point, and yeah, we both lose it.

"I don't even know who I am anymore. He looked at me and said, 'You don't get to come till I tell you,' and then railed me like vengeance had a dick."

She shrieks. "Is that even legal?!"

"It shouldn't be," I mutter. "He had my thighs shaking so bad I forgot my own name."

"Jesus Christ, Ani."

She presses a hand to her heart like she's witnessing a love story. "You're telling me your murder crush is a full-time Dom with God-tier dick and Olympic-level stamina?"

I nod slowly, "Like if Daddy issues came in six-foot-three and wore black."

She groans, forehead to the counter. "I want one. I want your ghost to haunt me and tell me bedtime stories about this man."

I sip my water. "He called me a *good girl* and I practically climaxed out of spite."

"I'm gonna need to lie down."

Someone tries to get our attention—some guy waving a credit card and mouthing vodka soda—and without missing a beat, Sarah flicks a death glare in his direction.

"Can't you see I'm in the middle of something with my emotional support whore? BACK UP."

The guy vanishes like he felt the wrath of a thousand ex-girlfriends.

I blink at her. "Yup, insane."

She shrugs. "You crawled, Ani. The friendship contract requires respect."

I roll my eyes so hard I'm surprised they don't pop out. "Okay, well, we're both still on the clock and I'm two tequila shots away from actually saying 'sir' out loud again, so let's not."

"God forbid." She grabs a stray lime wedge off the bar and tosses it into a trash can. "Back to work, slut."

We fall into motion with her taking a round of beers to table seven while I cash out a regular. It's mechanical and easy, the kind of rhythm you only build by bleeding side by side through summer rushes and blackout holiday weekends.

By the time I wipe down the last spill and pocket a folded twenty from a guy who thinks tipping makes him charming, my fingers are already twitching toward my back pocket.

I pull out my phone and check it, noting all the messages that currently give me immediate anxiety.

I glance over my shoulder toward Sarah, who's mid-sarcasm with Devin again.

UNKNOWN: So brave behind other people's doors. Let's see how brave you are alone.

FRANK: Could've sworn we had plans.
Let me know when you're off.

STEVEN: Ani. Pick up your fucking phone.

I haven't talked to Steven since I left his house. Since he said things I can't unhear, and I said things I can't take back.

But still—he's the one I want to respond to, and that's what makes this worse, because if I text Frank, I'm playing into whatever he's trying to spin. If I text Steven, I'm letting him back in.

And if I do nothing, I'm going to explode. My thumb hovers over Steven's name, but I just shove the phone into my pocket and keep working.

As for the unknown numbers, it's the same shit different day. So I do what I always do, and don't respond. I just sit there, spiraling with my fists clenched, so I don't do anything stupid.

"Yo." Sarah leans across the bar and snaps her fingers near my face. "You good, or are we planning a murder? Blink once for unalive."

I force a breath and shake my head. "Nah. Just tired."

Which is only partly true. I am tired—bone-deep, soul-level, emotionally dry-heaving tired—but mostly, I just need to get the hell out of here before I say something I can't take back. I can't involve her, it's not safe.

I clock out ten minutes early and tell Sarah I've got cramps, which is both a lie and not. She narrows her eyes like she knows, but lets it go. She just tells me to text her when I get home and reminds me not to crawl for any man unless he's buying us both brunch afterward.

I fake a laugh, shoving open the back door, and request the Uber before I hit the alley. By the time I'm outside it's already waiting.

The make and plates match the text, so I yank the door open, slide in, and slam it shut harder than I need to as the car starts moving.

31

Ani

I'm looking down at my phone, double-checking that I actually texted Sarah to apologize for bailing early. Nothing about tonight feels real, and if this driver takes one wrong turn, I'm tucking and rolling straight onto the pavement.

"Someone's dramatic tonight."

My blood freezes over and my head whips to the driver's seat. Steven's hands are relaxed on the wheel, with a smirk ghosting his mouth. His eyes are full of trouble in the rearview.

"You stole a car," I breathe, like that's the most offensive part.

"I borrowed it," he says smoothly. "From someone who won't be needing it for a while."

"You're stalking me."

He snorts. "You ordered the ride. I'm just punctual."

I glare at him through the mirror, but the car's already moving, and I know better than to open the door mid-drive. *Though I'm highly considering it.*

"I hate you," I mutter.

"Lie better."

The silence that follows isn't peaceful. The car slows to a stop and I'm already reaching for the handle when he adds, "You done being pissed? Or do I need to drag you upstairs and work it out of you?"

I slam the door without answering, knowing what it's going to cost me. I don't care. He follows close, but I don't wait. I storm up the steps, two at a time, keys shaking in my hand—but whether it's rage or adrenaline, I don't know. By the time I shove the door open, I'm breathing hard, and I'm wet. I head straight for the kitchen just to give myself something to do.

The lock clicks behind me. "You weren't answering your phone."

I don't turn around.

"Maybe because I didn't want to talk to you."

I hear him move behind me. "Where were you?"

"You don't get to ask me that," I snap, turning to face him. "And what, now you're going to show up and play watch dog."

I brush past him, heading straight for the sink, pretending I'm not seconds from combusting. The faucet creaks when I turn it on, I just need something to do with my hands before I use them for violence. Or worse—for begging.

I don't look at him when I speak.

"Are you always this invasive, or am I just your favorite little project?"

He doesn't say anything, but I feel him come up behind me. He's close enough that my spine straightens and my mouth goes dry.

"I don't owe you softness. I owe you *nothing*. But you're still mine."

And just like that, something sharp and traitorous cracks open in my chest. I hate how he crawls under my skin and settles there like he belongs. I almost forget why I was mad. *Almost.*

"I told you to stay away from him."

The switch flips. I spin to face him, "You don't get to tell me shit."

His jaw clenches. "You ran, Ani. Again."

And that's the one that hits too deep. He's not wrong there.

He pushes off the counter slowly, every inch of his movement is deliberate. "What did he say?"

I glare. "Why? So you can twist it into another half-truth?"

"I'm not the one keeping secrets."

"Oh, fuck you."

He steps closer as my back hits the edge of the sink and I brace both hands behind me like it'll hold me together. He smells like cold air and fury and something darker that makes my pussy tremble.

"Did he touch you?" Steven's voice drops.

"Jesus Christ, are you serious?"

His eyes are all heat and violence with that unreadable stillness he wears like a second skin.

"Did. He. Fucking. Touch. You."

My whole body flashes hot, then cold. My fists ball, while my pussy throbs for his attention. I shove at his chest—hard. "What difference does it make?"

It's a stupid question because we both know the answer.

His hand snaps up, catching my wrist before I can land another hit. He just holds me there like he's reminding me I'm not going anywhere unless he lets me. And fuck me, it should make me afraid. But all it does is make my thighs press together.

I can feel it. That slow, shameful throb building between my legs like I'm wired wrong. Or I'm just hardwired for him.

His voice is a threat all by itself. "Because if he did, he dies slower."

I laugh, but I get the feeling he's not joking. "Frank's not the only one playing games, I see."

His grip tightens enough to remind me he's still in control, even when I'm pretending I'm not about to melt in his palm.

"What did you hear?"

I should lie. Instead, I meet his eyes. "Why don't you tell me what you already know? Seems like you've got all the answers."

A slow breath leaves his chest like he's trying not to lose his temper. "You don't know what you're talking about."

His words wrap around my spine and squeeze. I hate that I lean closer without meaning to. I want more—more truth, more lies, more of him.

"Then say something, Steven. Anything. Just tell me something real."

He stares at me like I'm a problem he can't solve and he's one second from forcing the answer or burning the whole thing to the ground.

"I don't want to lie to you."

The words hit soft and I still feel them. Right in the part of me that keeps stupidly hoping he's not the villain I already know he is. I swallow hard, but it catches in my throat like a splinter.

"But you don't want to tell me the truth either."

Silence. Figures.

I rip my wrist free and spin, grabbing the first thing I can find—my mail. I whip it across the kitchen and it smacks the fridge before sliding pathetically to the floor.

That's when he moves. One second I'm alone, and the next his arm is banded around my waist—hard—dragging me back into his chest like I never had a choice. His other hand buries in my hair, pulling just enough to arch my spine, and my whole body betrays me—again. I'm wet, and strung so tight I could snap.

I twist in his grip, teeth bared. "Let me go—"

"You want to hate me?" he growls against my neck. "Good. Hate me."

Then his mouth is on my skin—biting me, and I melt for him. My body says yes even when my pride is screaming no. I'm so fucking pissed off and horny right now, I don't know what I want more. A fight or him.

"You want the truth?" His voice drops, and it's meant to wreck me. "I think about fucking you every time I close my eyes. I could spend the rest of my life inside you and it still wouldn't be enough.

I think about dragging you to your knees and making you forget why you ever said his name out loud."

He steps closer, crowding out my breath. "Not just until you forget him—until the only thing you know is me. My hands. My voice. My fucking name in your mouth."

I should move or something. But all I can do is stand there and burn. My legs buckle the second his hand starts to slide down, and his fingers slip beneath the waistband of my jeans like he's done it a thousand times in his head.

God help me—he's not the kind of man you survive. He's the kind you choose to drown in. And I'll happily do it.

"You're just too busy playing detective to realize you've already chosen me."

"I haven't—"

"You're home."

He spins me around and lifts me onto the counter as his mouth crashes into mine—and it's devastating. I taste metal and anger and everything I shouldn't want but do.

He tears my shirt off over my head.

"Still think you can lie to me?" he hisses, fingers trailing down my spine like a fucking promise of what's to come. I dig my nails into his chest—hard enough to leave marks. "Still think you're the one in control?"

His eyes flash with heat, then he drops to his knees. There's nothing reverent about it—no softness, no pause. Just hunger. That cold, ruthless obsession burning in his gaze as his hands yank my jeans down in one brutal motion.

He drags my panties down next, cursing under his breath like they dared to get between him and what's his. And before I can even take a breath—He's on me.

His mouth locks to my cunt licking through my slit until my knees start to buckle. Then he finds my clit. His tongue does sharp, filthy flicks that make my whole body seize.

"Steven—fuck—" I gasp, and my head falls back, while my fingers scramble to grab the edge of the counter behind me.

He moans into my pussy and I feel his arms hook around my thighs, dragging me closer until I can't do anything but take it. His tongue slides deeper, licking into me like he wants to memorize the shape of my cunt from the inside out.

"Please—"

"I want to bury myself so deep in you, you forget every man who ever touched you before me."

My breath stutters. "Then make me beg."

His eyes flash. *Challenge accepted.* His mouth slams back onto me with brutal precision—sucking, flicking, and savoring every inch. He devours me like he's starving and I'm the only thing left in the world.

My body starts to shake. Not just from how good it feels—but from the need. The pressure. The brutal, aching pull of falling apart. Every time his tongue drags through me, I feel myself break a little more. Every flick over my clit short-circuits my brain until I can't think—can't breathe—can't remember what the fuck I was even fighting for.

I'm panting.

I now have one leg thrown over his shoulder and his hand is locked around my thigh, holding me open, daring me to pull away.

I hold onto his hair for dear life, twitching my hips under his mouth as the orgasm builds faster. It feels violent and I know that if I let go, I won't come back.

And just when I'm there—right fucking there—He stops.

"Don't you fucking—"

"You want to come?" he rasps.

You have got to be fucking kidding me. So help me...

"Then get on your knees and show me who you belong to."

"Steven—"

"Get. On. Your. Fucking. Knees."

My knees hit the floor with a thud, and I look up just in time to see him towering over me, unbuckling his belt, eyes gone dark with something that isn't lust anymore.

It's possession.

I was going to obey. Swear to God. But damn if that wasn't the hottest fucking thing I've ever heard. My thighs clench. And all I can think is—Maybe I should push him a little more. Just to see what else he does when he snaps.

"You want honesty?" he says, pulling his cock out, thick and hard and already glistening. "You're going to suck me until your throat's raw, and then I'm going to fuck you so hard you forget why you're mad."

I moan as he fists my hair and forces my gaze up to meet his. He knows exactly how much I fucking want him right now, the bastard. His cock is throbbing just inches from my lips, and it takes everything in me not to stick my tongue out and lick it. "That's it," he growls, his voice sounds like gravel and gasoline. "Open that bratty mouth and take what you've been begging for."

My tongue parts my lips, and the second the tip of his cock brushes them, something inside me breaks. I want him in my mouth so bad my hands tremble where they grip his thighs. I want the weight of him heavy on my tongue. I want to be used. Owned. Erased. Until the only thing left in my head is his name and the taste of him on my tongue.

When he thrusts deeper, his cock hits the back of my throat and I moan, or try to, but it just sounds like a gag.

His hand twists in my hair, keeping me right where he wants me. "Good girl. Just like that. Fuck—that's my favorite sound."

I gag again, eyes watering instantly as his cock hits the back of my throat. My fingers claw at his thighs, while my nails dig into his muscle.

"That's it," he grunts, hand tightening in my hair. "You wanted this, didn't you?"

My throat tightens again, and I choke around him—nodding.

But I don't pull back. His voice wrecks me, I've never wanted anything more.

He fucks my mouth like it's his to use. My mascara burns as tears streak down my cheeks and drool coats my chin. I've never felt this owned and completely undone before. I feel so completely safe—in the most fucked up, feral way.

He snarls, dragging my mouth down harder, choking me.

"Look at you," he smiles. "So fucking pretty like this. Gagging like the little slut you are."

A whimper slips out as I clench, and the wet heat between my thighs drips lower—sliding down to my ankle like proof of how gone I am for him.

As if he can read my mind, he chuckles. "I bet you're so fucking wet from choking on my cock?" he hisses, thrusting deeper, his voice is pure control. "God, I knew you were filthy—but this?"

He groans as I gag again, spit dripping down my chin.

"You were made for this. Made to kneel for me with that pretty little mouth—and take every fucking inch like you were born for it."

My head spins as my lungs burn. And I don't care, because he's right. He owns my mouth. Every breath. Every gag. Every broken sound I try and fail to swallow.

He pulls out with a wet pop, wrapping his hand around his cock and stroking himself with brutal precision, and even as I'm left panting and drooling from the sudden emptiness—his fist tightens in my hair again, dragging my gaze up as he growls, "Stick out your tongue."

The command slices straight through me as I tilt my chin, opening my mouth. He strokes himself, keeping his eyes locked on me like I'm the altar and he's about to break—and when he does, it's with a guttural snarl as he spills across my tongue, hot and thick, branding my lips, my face, and every shattered piece of my soul like I already belong to him.

"Fuck," he growls, eyes fixed on the mess he's made of me,

watching it drip down my chin while his chest rises hard and fast, like the sight of me on my knees is undoing him all over again.

"You're such a good girl," he murmurs, voice rough with reverence and wreckage. "Taking it all."

My lashes flutter, as tears cling to what's left of my mascara. His praise hits me like a drug, sliding under my skin before I can stop it. It settles between my legs and stays there.

Good girl.

The words echo in my chest—ones I didn't even know I'd been starving to hear. And fuck me, I want to earn them again.

God. Who knew?

I'd take everything he wants to give me, I'd crawl to him again in a heartbeat if he asked me to. I'd let him use me like this a hundred more times if it meant hearing him call me that again.

My body is still trembling, lips parted and slick with the mess he left behind when his hand slides down, fingers curling beneath my jaw.

"Open."

I do, because there's no version of me that won't do what he says. Not anymore. Not after this. I belong to this moment. To him.

He drags his thumb across my lips, smearing his release, and pushes it between my teeth.

"Swallow it," he rasps, eyes locked on mine. "Every last drop."

I obey. How could I not?

My cheeks hollow around his thumb and the taste of him spreads across my tongue.

"Good fucking girl," he breathes. His voice is so low it's almost reverent.

And I melt for him.

His voice drops to a whisper. "Now bend over. I'm not fucking done with you yet."

My breath catches, and before I can blink, he's yanking me to my feet—turning me, pressing me down over the counter like he's staking a claim. This is obviously his favorite position. *You're not going to find me complaining about it either.*

The edge bites into my hips as my palms scramble for grip on the cold surface. It's just the right amount of pain and pleasure to keep me right on the edge.

"You're mine," he growls behind me.

And then slams into me. I scream and the sound ricochets through the kitchen as he fucks me like it's punishment.

The edge of the counter digs deeper with every thrust, but I barely feel it. All I can feel is him. All I can hear is the sound of his body slapping into mine like he's trying to fuck the air from my lungs.

"Is this what you needed? He whispers against my ear, one hand wrapping tight around my throat.

"Is this what gets you wet, pretty girl? Getting used like a toy."

I couldn't answer even if I wanted to, but my body answers for me. My back arches, and I push out my ass, right into his next thrust, and I clench around him like he's the only thing keeping me alive.

"I'm gonna fuck him out of you," he growls. His voice is coated in venom and heat. "Every place he touched you? I'm taking it back. With my cock. With my mouth. With my fucking name burned into your bones."

His grip on my throat tightens and a moan rips from my throat. He shoves deeper, grinding against the spot that makes me see stars.

"Say it," he hisses. "Tell me again who you belong to."

My mouth opens—then snaps shut. My brain's fried, legs shaking, and my lungs are barely working...But I still find the worst possible answer, because I want him wild.

"I belong to nobody," I whisper, chin tilted just enough to challenge him. Even now. Even when I'm one thrust away from blacking out. Because some feral part of me still wants to push.

His hand cracks against my ass, hard enough to rip a yelp from my throat, and before I can breathe, he's grabbing my wrists—yanking them behind my back, locking me in place.

"No, dear," he growls, fisting my hair and yanking until my back arches for him. I shift, trying to ease the pressure in my shoulders—but it's useless. He's everywhere. "You don't own yourself anymore. You gave that up the second you dropped to your knees."

And then he slams into me again—hard.

"You want to be ruined?" he growls. "Fucking say it."

"Ruin me," I gasp, and I mean it. I want him to obliterate every part of me that still flinches. I want him to erase me in every way possible, and bring me back to life, like only he can.

"You're being such a good girl," he growls, shifting his grip so one hand slides between my thighs. "You're dripping all over me like you're fucking addicted."

He circles my clit once and I nearly collapse.

"You hear that?" he murmurs against my ear. "That's what it sounds like when you belong to someone. When your cunt knows exactly who's inside it."

"Steven—God—"

"Don't you fucking dare," he snaps. "You don't pray to anyone else. Not when I'm inside you."

I moan, helpless and grinding against his hand as his thumb circles with cruel, perfect precision. I don't give a fuck how it happens, but I need to get off right fucking now.

"You gonna come for me, brat?" he growls, voice hot against my ear.

I nod, sobbing into his shoulder, unable to form a single coherent word.

"You gonna fall apart and thank me for it?"

"Steven—" I try, but he grabs my chin and yanks my head back, forcing me to meet his eyes.

"No," he snaps. "You don't get to lie to me and come in the same breath."

I flush with rage, and need. "I'm not lying—"

"Then why did you sneak out?" he snaps. "Why did you crawl back into his world after everything you felt in mine?"

"I didn't go back to him!"

His hand tightens.

"Didn't you?" he growls, as his nose brushes mine. "Or did you just let him pretend he still had a chance? Did you smile while he touched you, Ani? Did you let him think he could keep you?"

"No," I whisper, because I didn't. Not really. But I did lie and we both know it.

He drops his hands like touching me any longer might make him do something he's not ready to admit. He scrubs a palm over his jaw, then he steps back in, gripping my hips.

His control is hanging by a thread. "You want to come?"

I nod, breath ragged. "Yes. You know I fucking do."

"Then look me in the eye when you break for me. You'll fall apart on my cock with my name on your tongue and your soul fucking screaming for it."

His hand slides back down, and this time when he finds my clit, it's ruthless—fast and steady, dragging me toward the edge.

"Eyes on me." His voice is shredded and breathless. "I want to watch the exact second you stop pretending you ever belonged to anyone else."

I twist in his grip, because I'm there. "I'm gonna—"

"That's it," he snarls, driving into me. "Milk my cock and make it fucking count."

And I do. I come with a scream that sounds like it's been caged in my chest for years—loud, broken, and holy. My knees give out and I collapse against him, sobbing his name like a prayer.

He grabs my chin and kisses me like this is war—teeth, tongue, and all dominance—he fucks up into me with savage precision.

"You're mine," he growls into my mouth.

"Yours," I sob.

He lets go of my throat and yanks my head back, watching me come undone. "You'll never let another man inside you. You'll never even fucking look at anyone else."

32

"The first bite isn't the one that ruins you."
(It's the one you start craving.)

Ani

He leans against the counter with his arms crossed, staying dead silent as I take a bite.

"I want everything from you, Ani."

I blink. "Excuse me?"

"You heard me." He pushes off the counter and steps closer. "No more half-truths. No more deflections. I want it all—where you've been. What happened? What you remember. What you're hiding."

I laugh, but it's brittle. "What makes you think I'm hiding anything?"

His voice darkens. "Because you flinch like someone who's still bleeding. And because you look at me like you want to tell me everything—right before you run."

God. How does he see me like that?

The fork I'm holding just slips through my fingers like everything else I can't hold onto lately. I stare at it on the counter, my heartbeat is thick in my ears, because he's right, I want to deny it. I want to roll my eyes and shoot back something sarcastic enough to cover the ache that just cracked open in my chest. But I can't. Not when the truth is sitting in front of me, shirtless, intense, and so fucking undeniable it makes my bones ache.

Every time someone gets too close, or something starts to feel real, I feel myself slipping. I run. And here he is, seeing every bruised inch of me like I've already been exposed.

I finally look up. "I already told you, I don't remember everything, but I'm trying," I snap. "I've pretty much told you most of what I know. I know something bad happened, I know there were men involved, and I know I fought. I also know there's blood in my past that doesn't feel like it belongs to me."

He doesn't move.

"Frank?"

I hesitate. Then shrug my shoulders. "I don't think so, but maybe. There are pieces that I can't remember. Sounds. And someone saying I belonged to them."

My breath hitches on the last word.

And Steven... freezes. His whole body goes still.

"I don't remember who, besides my ex," I add, fast. The words tumble out like it might fix it. "But he said something when I was there, and I just—"

"Where is he now?"

I blink. "Frank? I don't know, I left when he was in the middle of a meeting."

Steven nods once, but it's a loaded nod. His expression is carved from stone, but I can see his control tightening around him like armor.

"Why do you care?" I whisper. "Is this about him?"

His jaw flexes. "Not anymore."

I suck in a breath. "And me?"

"You're mine," he says with no hesitation. "And I'll fucking kill him if he touches you again."

My body lights up like a live wire. I should tell him to calm down, but the way he says it does something to me I can't explain.

Lord, first it's a fucking praise kink—now it's a possession problem? What's next?

Maybe I'm just tired of being someone's pawn, and used like

I'm some pretty little piece of ass waiting to get sacrificed. Maybe what I really want... is to be someone's fucking obsession.

I glance over at Steven as I set the bowl down—and just like that, I'm not hungry anymore. At least not for food.

"That doesn't scare me."

His eyes lift to mine—calm in that dangerous, calculated way that makes my lungs forget what they're supposed to be doing.

"It should." He pauses, waiting. And then—"You know I'll burn everything down before I let him have you."

I can't help but giggle at his possessiveness, even though something tells me he's not joking.

His jaw ticks. Just once. And that's the only warning I get. The chair scrapes back, hard—then he's in front of me. Two strides and I'm yanked to my feet, his mouth crashing to mine like a punishment.

I moan into him, fisting his hoodie as he grabs the back of my thighs and lifts me effortlessly.

He carries me down the hall, his mouth dragging over my jaw and throat—until his teeth sink in hard enough to steal my breath. By the time the bathroom light flickers on, I'm already soaked.

"I heard it," he growls against my throat. "That wrecked little voice telling me you're mine while you were soaking my cock."

I can barely breathe. I want him—fuck, I want him to give me what I need—but he's taking his sweet-ass time, dragging it out like he knows I'll break for it.

"I meant it," I whisper.

He pulls back just enough to look at me—eyes black with possession.

"Good," he rasps.

And maybe that's the most dangerous thing I've admitted all week, because Steven isn't gentle. He's not soft. He's not safe. But he's real.

He peels my pants down slowly, and when he sees I'm not wearing anything underneath, he stills. His mouth twitches and those dark eyes drag over every inch of me like he's memorizing the mess I've already made.

"Fuck," he murmurs, voice thick. "No one else gets to see you like this. No one else gets to have this." He steps back, just enough to watch me squirm. "You were made for this. For me."

"Then shut up and prove it already," I tease.

That must have triggered something, because his hand closes around my throat enough to make my pulse spike and my breath catch.

I freeze—everything inside me clenches. My thighs. My chest. My jaw. *Fuck.* I've never wanted anything so badly in my life, and I just had him a few hours ago. It's starting to feel less like lust and more like madness. It can't be normal to want someone this much.

His thumb slides along my jaw, way too gentle for how hard he's still holding my neck—and the contrast sends a rush straight through me.

God, he's hot.

That hoodie's hanging open like he forgot to finish putting himself together—tattoos on full display, chest bare—and all I want to do is lick him. I'm still wrecked from earlier, and my body's already begging for more like it doesn't remember how to be satisfied. I don't even know what to do with that. I just know I want him. Again. Harder.

"You want proof? You'll be feeling it every time you try to walk."

My whole body reacts like he just reached inside and flipped a switch I can't turn off. God help me, I want to feel it. I want the ache.

I reach for the zipper of his hoodie and my fingers tremble as I drag the zipper down, inch by inch, exposing the inked lines of his chest and the sharp cut of muscle beneath. He doesn't move, he just stands there and lets me.

His hand leaves my throat, only to slide to the back of my neck. His fingers thread through my hair, tugging just enough to make me tilt my chin up for him. The other glides up my stomach. When he closes over my breast, I hiss—but I don't pull away. I lean into it, because that's what he does to me.

"You know what I see when I look at you like this?" he murmurs.

"A girl with questionable taste?" I breathe.

His thumb rolls over my nipple, slow and punishing. "I see someone who likes being owned." He dips his head, mouth brushing my ear. "And I haven't even started."

My knees threaten to give out, but I hold his gaze like I'm not falling apart.

"You ready?" he asks.

"Are you asking for permission now?" I shoot back.

His grip tightens, and he smirks. "Nah. Just giving you the chance to say thank you before I ruin you."

His eyes drop to my nipples, and that smirk—the dark, dangerous one—spreads slow across his mouth.

"Fuck, look at you," he says. "You love to act like you're in charge... until my hands are on you."

His hands slide up my sides, and I shiver—every inch of me strung tight with anticipation.

Then he's gone. Just for a second.

The shower knob turns behind me, and the sound alone sends heat flooding back through my body.

Steam starts to rise, curling around us, and I don't realize he's already moving again until I turn—and see him stepping back, fingers hooked in the waistband of his sweats. He drags them down without a word, and fuck—he's all muscle, all heat, all mine.

Oh. My. God.

Everything in me stops—thoughts, breath, pride. Gone.

He's naked.

It shouldn't hit this hard, but lord—he is gloriously, savagely naked. All hard lines and ink and muscle—sculpted by the Gods themselves. I'm pretty sure I'm drooling.

The second I step into the shower, the heat slams into me—coating my skin, making it impossible to tell if I'm sweating or already soaked for him again.

He leans in, skimming my collarbone with his mouth, and slowly trails lower. That grin he gives me, feels like a promise as he sinks to his knees in front of me, gripping my hips like he owns them. His tongue flicks out, licking a slow, devastating stripe from my navel to the underside of my breast, and I gasp—sharp and wrecked.

He doesn't stop. Not until I'm breathless and shaking, thighs sticky with want. Again.

His hands roam everywhere—up the backs of my thighs, over the curve of my ass, fingers spreading as he grabs me like he's staking a claim.

When he shifts forward and lifts one of my legs over his shoulder, I swear I black out for half a second. It's too much. Too good. Too filthy. And I want every goddamn second of it.

His hands glide between my legs, fingers slipping through my folds like he's memorized the exact way to make me fall apart. The second his thumb brushes over my clit, I jolt—twitching against his mouth as the hot water rains down over us. My hand flies to his shoulder—partly to keep from slipping, and partly because I just need to touch him.

Water pours over my back as the steam curls around us, and I swear I can feel myself dripping down my thigh. When he slides two fingers into me, curling them just right, and I gasp, grinding down on his hand.

"Still think you're in control?" he growls.

I shake my head, too far gone to speak. As much as I love pushing his buttons, tonight's not the night.

"I could keep you like this," he rasps near my pussy. "On your knees. On your back. Doesn't matter—as long as you remember who this fucking body belongs to."

I nod, still grinding. Still chasing that edge and I don't care what it costs me.

Then he pulls back.

"No—please—"

He reaches for the soap behind me, his fingers grazing my waist. "Turn around," he murmurs. "Let me wash you."

Water slides down my front as he lathers his hands, and suddenly, I have the urge to cover myself. Somehow, this feels more intimate than any of the filthy sex we've had so far. He runs his hands over my shoulders, arms, and the curve of my spine. He moves around me like he's got all the time in the world—every touch is slow, focused, and far too reverent for how wrecked I already am.

"Every inch of you is perfect," he rinses me. "Even the bruises I left. *Especially* those."

His palm glides over my ass, fingers lingering at the base of my spine. "You don't even know what you do to me," he murmurs. "You get like this—dripping and wrecked—and I swear to God, all I want to do is ruin you."

He's not just washing me. He's claiming me with his touch. With words. With patience I didn't know he had and I want to sob from how badly I want him to never stop.

"You'd let me," he whispers. "Wouldn't you?"

I nod. Because it's not even a question. It's a fact I've already surrendered to.

He grips my ass, spreading me just enough to make me gasp. He takes his time, lathering slow circles over the soft skin before moving between my thighs. And when his fingers drag over my pussy and brush my puckered hole like it's just another part of me he owns, my vision goes white at the edges. He's just washing me, but I'm trembling, wet, and seconds from coming undone.

By the time he finishes, I'm breathless—and he hasn't even fucked me yet. He shifts behind me, rising slowly, and the heat of his chest presses to my back. I shiver from the unbearable tension of his slick hands sliding down my hips like he's still deciding whether to stop or ruin me all over again. His fingers linger like a man caught between reverence and hunger. And I swear if he touches me again, I'll beg. I'll crawl. I'll do whatever the hell he asks.

I turn my head to look at him, and he looks like he's fighting the urge to bend me over and fuck me into the tile right now.

I reach for the soap because I need to touch him. After everything he's just done to me—every inch he worshiped—I want to see if he can survive being wanted the same way. If he can stand still while I trace every line of him, shaking with the effort not to fall apart.

My fingers are unsteady as I lather the soap, and the second my hands meet his chest, he goes still. He obviously doesn't know what to do with the soft parts of me I haven't offered until now.

He exhales, and clenches his jaw. "You don't have to."

But I do. God, I do.

I don't know if it's weird to say how beautiful he is, but UGH. Like, he's got to know how fucking hot he is.

I glance up, breathless. "You're kinda stupid hot, you know that?"

His eyes cut to mine, but I don't stop. I press closer, palms slick over ink and muscle. "Don't tell me what to do."

Hot water cascades over his shoulders, down the thick lines of his arms, across muscle that flexes under my touch like he's trying not to let go. I run my hands over his chest, watching the soap swirl and rinse away as I drag my palms over every inch of him I can reach.

I want to mark him with my mouth.

I want to taste him again.

I want to press my lips to every inch of skin he refuses to believe is worth worshiping. I trail my hands lower, over the cut of his abs, down to the sharp line of his hips—and the second I wrap my soapy fingers around the base of his cock, he grabs my wrist.

"Ani." His voice is strained—tight with restraint, and rough with warning. But underneath it, I hear the truth. He's not telling me to stop. He's telling me he's close to losing control.

I meet his eyes, but I don't let go. "Let me touch what's mine."

His jaw flexes, like he's trying to hold something in. His hands drop to his sides, and his fingers twitch. He's breathing is ragged, but he lets me. Fuck, the way he's looking at me now—like I'm the dangerous one—makes my stomach flip and my thighs squeeze tighter.

There's something addictive about watching him fall apart from something I'm doing. All that control, all that power—and I'm the one that can bring him to his knees. Yeah. That does something to me.

I stroke him, and his whole body shudders.

God. I could get drunk on this.

I keep going—washing him with slow, reverent strokes—dragging my fingertips over his thighs, behind his knees, along the curve of his ass. Every inch of him feels like something I wasn't supposed to have—but I'm taking it anyway.

When I reach his cock again, I stroke him harder, slick from the soap and water and the kind of need that won't burn out until it consumes us both. His hands fist at his sides.

"Ani." This time, it's a warning.

He lowers his forehead to mine, breathing hard, holding my face like he's memorizing the shape of it. And then he snaps. In one brutal motion, he's shoving me back against the tile, and lifts one of my legs around his hip.

"You want this?" he growls against my throat, slamming into me.

I cry out, and it echoes off the tile.

Jesus. I can feel him in my ribs.

His hand braces the back of my neck, holding me steady as he drives into me over and over again—grunting and breathing like he's seconds from blacking out. There's nothing more intoxicating than watching him lose control, and the monster stops pretending to be human.

"You make me lose my fucking mind," he growls, each brutal thrust branding the words into my skin. "You want to see what happens when I lose control? Then fucking feel what that costs—every inch, every second, until you forget how to breathe without me."

I claw at his back, nails scraping slick skin, as my head falls back against the wall as he pounds into me. I'm already close. Hell, I never really stopped being close.

When I come, it's not a climax—it's a fucking exorcism. I scream his name, my whole body seizing around him, trying to keep him buried inside me. I should be embarrassed. I should be mortified by the way I break apart for him—loud, messy, and wild—but all I can think is please don't stop.

I don't know where I end and he begins and I don't care. He owns me. And God help me, I fucking love it.

He follows—groaning my name, burying himself deep and staying there, like leaving me isn't even an option. For a moment, there's only the sound of water and the pounding of my heart.

His forehead rests against mine as we breathe together, still tangled and pressed against the wall and I'm genuinely surprised the water isn't freezing.

His hand slides to my waist, then he leans in and kisses my shoulder. "I'm still hungry."

I laugh—weak and dizzy. "God, you're disgusting."

"Not what you said five minutes ago." His smirk is lethal.

I roll my eyes, stepping out of the water, still catching my breath. "So what now?"

He runs a hand through his hair, flicking water from his fingers before reaching for a towel. "Now you tell me what you heard from Frank."

My whole body goes still.

Shit.

That isn't exactly what I had in mind. But okay. I wrap the towel around myself like it can shield me from what's coming next.

"What did he say, Ani?"

I hesitate. Grabbing a towel, curling it tight around my shoulders.

"He said..." My throat closes, but I force it out. "He said worst case, he lets me think I matter until he gets what he needs. That I didn't remember it the first time. And that I won't remember it now."

33

**"It's not the first time they touch
you that wrecks you."
(It's the times after that when you
know what it costs)**

Steven

She's curled against my chest, tucked into me like she belongs there. The world will come for us eventually—it always does—and when it does, it'll tear this to hell. But until then, she stays pressed to my side, one arm draped over my chest.

I watch her longer than I should. Long enough to map out every freckle on her shoulder, and every scar I didn't put there. She looks so calm and peaceful, it makes me want to stay. Makes me want to lie here and pretend that the storm clawing at the edge of my mind can wait until morning. For once, the world outside this room doesn't matter. But it can't. Because I don't leave loose ends.

A sharp buzz cuts through the quiet—my phone, vibrating somewhere in the kitchen. I don't want to move. Three seconds pass. Then five. And she still doesn't stir.

Slowly, I shift beneath her, careful not to wake her. I move like a man disarming a bomb with his bare hands. Her fingers twitch in her sleep, flexing once over my stomach—reaching for me even when her mind's somewhere else.

Christ.

I lean down and brush a loose strand of hair from her face,

tucking it behind her ear. Her breath stays steady, and she doesn't flinch, so I pull the blanket higher over her bare shoulders, covering what I've just spent hours uncovering.

She looks soft like this—peaceful in a way that guts me, and breakable in a way that makes me want to tear the world apart just to keep it from touching her.

My body moves on instinct, every muscle is coiled with purpose. Something colder is waking up in my chest again, something that doesn't sleep just because she is.

When I get to the kitchen, I grab the phone just as the screen lights up again and everything in me goes still.

> TRAVIS: Location just pinged off a secondary line he hasn't used in months. Sending coordinates now.

A second message follows with a dropped pin. It's an old warehouse near the outskirts of town. One I've been to before. I stare at the dot, and everything inside me coils tight.

Another text comes through.

> TRAVIS: Got visual confirmation. I think you should wait. I'm thirty minutes out.

I pace the kitchen, but everything inside me is chaos. Controlled only by habit. This was supposed to be clean. Simple. I was going to put him down with cold hands and a clear conscience, no loose ends.

But this isn't about revenge anymore.

It's about her.

The girl curled up in the other room with nothing but a blanket and my name still drying on her lips. The one who somehow fucking clawed her way into my veins without even trying. The same girl who let me wreck her without knowing who I really was.

I rake a hand through my hair, grabbing the phone from the

counter, and open the photo I've been staring at since this afternoon.

My eyes catch on the man next to her—and just like that, everything slows. I can make out enough to know something's wrong. If he's been holding onto her all these years as leverage—Then I just move up the timeline. He dies either way.

I don't even want to think about what it'll mean if she's there willingly. There's no way. But if I'm wrong—If he's got his claws deep enough to twist her loyalty, then I'll rip the truth out of whoever put her there. Even if I have to bury them all to do it.

I set the phone down, already moving for the jacket I threw on a kitchen chair. The one that's lined with tools most people don't believe still exist. I draw the silencer from one of my inner pockets and my hand steadies the second it touches steel. This is what I was made for.

I run through the entry points in my head—warehouse, north side, two guards minimum, rear door coded. There won't be a back exit for him and I won't need one for me.

I push through the door, stepping into the night without a sound. Her scent still clings to me—peach, sweat, and the wild ache of something I shouldn't have touched. I memorize it, then lock it down.

She's going to lose her shit when she wakes up and finds the bed cold. But if I move fast—if I'm smart—I'll be back before those lashes even lift. *At least that's the plan.*

The hallway's quiet, but I don't slow down. Every motion is second nature—etched into me like a scar. You don't lose that kind of control when it was the only thing that ever kept you alive.

I pull out my phone and start to type—something simple. Telling her I'm not gone, just handling something and I'll be back.

My thumb is still pressed to the screen when my boots hit the sidewalk. I'm too fucking distracted and too wrapped up in the echo of her voice whispering *'yours'* like it meant more than surrender, to notice the brush of pressure at the side of my neck. It doesn't register as a threat until it's already done.

Something's wrong.

And I'm already too late.

My vision tilts as my phone slips from my hand, skittering across the pavement with a hollow scrape. I lurch sideways, reaching for a lamppost that isn't fucking there and my knees hit asphalt a second later.

"Mother—fuck—"

My voice comes out slurred and distant. My muscles feel like they're firing in all the wrong directions. I reach for the blade under my jacket, fingers twitching for steel—but I'm too late.

A boot slams into my ribs, flipping me onto my back and pain flashes, but it's already fading—dulled by whatever cocktail they just pumped into my bloodstream.

The world tilts—fractured into sharp angles and smeared shadows, like reality can't decide what shape to take.

A figure steps into view, kneeling beside me, calm as hell.

"You're good," the man says, full of smug satisfaction. "But not untouchable."

Pain wakes me before the light does, throbbing along my jaw. Something warm and wet drips from the corner of my mouth—blood, likely mine.

The world seeps in piece by piece.

I can taste metal on my tongue, and I hear the buzz of a single overhead bulb. My wrists are bound behind the chair, and rope bites into my skin. My ankles are free, so either they got cocky...Or they don't know what I am.

That's their first mistake.

My vision is sluggish but sharpening. The floor's concrete, and it's cracked and wet beneath my boots. There's dust in the air, and I can hear a pipe dripping somewhere off to the left.

I'm in a basement.

What matters is—they brought me underground and they didn't kill me.

That's mistake number two.

I flex my fingers, and I can feel some slack in my left wrist. Not much, but it's enough. I test the friction, and I can feel the rope burn flare down my forearm, and my shoulders are screaming.

Fuck.

Whatever they used, was enough to put a man twice my size down. I breathe through my nose, slowing my breathing, cataloging everything through the haze.

The faint clicking in the wall to my right sounds like rats. I listen harder, but I don't hear any voices or footsteps. Which means they're either watching, or waiting for me to wake up. Which also means they want me alive.

They have no fucking idea what a mistake that is.

I rotate my neck and a sharp pain ricochets down my spine. My lip's busted, and my nose might be broken. My ribs—bruised at best. Whoever took me got sloppy.

Then it hits me.

Ani.

She's alone and unprotected. She doesn't even know I'm gone yet, but when she does—she'll leave. And if Frank finds her before I do, I'll rip his fucking throat out and paint the walls with what's left.

No. No fucking way. She won't leave, she's smarter than that. She's mine and I will kill every last person in this building if they've touched her.

I hear footsteps.

I stay limp, letting my head hang. *Let them think I'm weak.*

A figure steps in. Tall and broad, dressed in a cheap suit, and cologne that tries to hide the scent of smoke.

"You're awake," the man says.

I smirk. "Disappointed?"

He chuckles. "No. Just impressed. Thought we'd need a little longer with how much we gave you."

He circles me slowly, keeping just out of reach. I keep my eyes on him, but my focus is everywhere—walls, corners, the hum of ventilation, the temperature drop.

"You're lucky," he finally says. "Most men in your position don't get this far."

I smile, and I can feel the blood sliding down my chin. "That supposed to scare me?"

He paces again. "Most men in your position don't talk back, either."

I lift my head, inch by inch, until our eyes lock. My voice stays flat. "Most men aren't me."

He hesitates, just for a second. Then circles again, slower this time. Like he's trying to read me. "Keep talking. See how fast that mouth gets you buried."

I smile. Just enough to show the blood in my teeth. "You better bury me deep." I pause. "Because if I get up? I don't leave survivors."

I'm getting out of this room, and when I do, Hell's coming with me.

The thought alone coils tight in my chest, sharpening every fractured nerve as I watch him—closer this time. The way he moves. How he glances toward the door, which means someone promised backup if things go sideways.

His confidence is trained. I can smell the fear, buried under protocol and a borrowed sense of power. He's not built for blood.

He doesn't know it yet... but he's already dead.

"I'll talk to the man in charge," I jab, testing the rope again behind me. It's thick and twisted, but not reinforced. "Not the intern."

That earns a flicker at the corner of his mouth, but he doesn't take the bait. He's smart. *But not smart enough.*

"You don't get to make demands," he says, all bark and borrowed authority. "You're a message."

I smile, letting the blood on my lip smear. "Frank ever tell you how many messages I've buried?"

He blinks. Just one beat of hesitation and that's all I need. I dislocate my thumb with a crunch—*and fuck that hurt*—but I ride the pain. I've lived through worse and I don't have time to care at the moment. The rope gives and I rip my wrist free, driving my elbow up into his throat. His breath seizes in a wheeze as he stumbles backward, out cold.

The second one lunges from the doorway and I pivot, catching his momentum and looping the rope around his forearm mid-strike. I twist hard, dragging him off balance and slamming him into the wall so hard the crack of bone echoes through the room. He crumples, spitting blood on the floor.

I crouch over him, while my lungs claw for air. Blood drips from my knuckles, and my vision narrows slightly, but I don't let it pull my focus.

Not yet.

"You should've run," I growl, as I reach for him again.

I've got him in a chokehold, seconds from crushing his windpipe, when it hits. A sting at the base of my neck.

My body reacts before my brain catches up.

Fuck. *Not again.*

I rip the dart from my neck, my vision already tilting sideways while the floor shifts beneath me. This time it kicks in faster, since it's already in my system. My legs don't respond the way they should—as my muscle turns to dead weight, every step harder than the last.

My pulse slams against my skull, but I shove off the wall,

willing myself forward, sheer instinct dragging me three paces before my knees hit the concrete.

Hard.

Pain fractures through my shins, but it's distant. Drowned by the chemical fog bleeding into my veins.

A shadow moves. The silhouette sharpens as it steps into the light—and the second I hear the voice, I know.

"Hello, Steven."

My blood runs colder than the concrete beneath me.

No.

It can't be her.

That voice doesn't belong here. It belongs to a nightmare I buried in a different life—wrapped in fire and gunfire and the smell of burned skin.

"Get him tied back to that chair," she says, calm as ever. "And do it tighter this time. If he breaks out again, I'll cut your fucking hands off myself."

Leather boots scrape behind me as hands grab my shoulders, jerking me upright with the grace of a butcher lifting meat. The rope bites into my skin, tighter this time. I feel my blood throb beneath it.

She steps in closer, just enough for me to smell the faint trace of something floral under gun oil. Jasmine and violence.

I lift my head, muscles twitching with resistance, but the serum's already dragging me under. I can feel it. My thoughts fracture, and the only thing still sharp is her.

"Still hard to kill, I see."

I stare at her, unmoving. I couldn't respond if I wanted to. My body's failing, but my mind's screaming.

The last time I saw her, the world was burning—and she was at the center of it. There was blood all over her hands, and she was screaming.

My vision flickers.

The concrete bleeds into memory—blood pools in the cracks of the warehouse floor, bodies are slumped against rusted beams, the light flickers, and shadows crawl up the walls like they've never left.

"You should've stayed gone," I rasp, trying not to pass out. Every word drags like sandpaper being torn from my throat.

A soft, low chuckle follows, laced with something dark. "You should've stayed dead."

Then all I see is black.

I FIGHT TO LIFT MY HEAD, VISION SWIMMING. THE LIGHT above swings, casting her face in flickering shadow—and still, there's no mistaking her.

Time didn't soften her, it carved her into something cold. The girl I bled for is gone. What's standing in front of me now...isn't flesh and memory. It's a phantom draped in the face of the girl I should've saved.

"What did he promise you?" My tongue feels thick and dry. "Money? Power?"

"Closure," she says softly. "Funny how we both came for the same thing."

My gut twists.

"You were with him?"

"Still am."

Her voice is too calm for a girl who once clung to me with blood on her hands and terror in her eyes. It doesn't match the memory I've spent half a decade chasing. If she's really standing here, alive and colder than I ever remember—then either she's been broken into something I don't recognize...or I've been chasing a ghost that never needed saving.

And fuck, I don't know which is worse.

"You never understood, Steven. You thought you were the only one he broke. The only one who survived."

She crouches, putting her face inches from mine, and it's like staring down a barrel I used to trust.

"But I didn't survive," she murmurs. "I adapted."

Her arms were in front of her, tied at the wrists, trembling so hard I thought they'd snap. He leaned into her, saying something low against her ear—and even now, I can't stop hearing the silence that followed.

I lunged—then the gun went off.

She screamed. I saw her fall. I watched the blood bloom beneath her body. I thought she was gone.

I buried that night in the deepest part of me and let it rot there. And then I burned everything in my path trying to make him pay for it. I mourned her like a fool, but she was never a victim.

"You killed that part of me," she whispers, almost tender. Almost like she's grieving it. "The night you ran."

"I didn't run."

"You didn't stay either."

My jaw locks, the ropes biting deeper as I clench my fists. "Are you fucking kidding me right now?"

She straightens, smoothing her skirt like she's wrapping up a therapy session and not carving me open. "He taught me how fast love turns into leverage."

I almost laugh because nothing about this is funny. "Why now?" I ask. "Why bring me here?"

She tilts her head like she's weighing the truth. "Because you're circling something you don't understand. And he thinks you'll get to it before he does."

"What the fuck are you talking about?"

She smiles. "The girl."

My entire body goes still. "Ani?" I whisper.

She shrugs. "Is that what she calls herself?"

She's fucking with me. Or worse—she's not. And that's the

part that twists deeper. It confirms everything I've been thinking for weeks. But hearing it from her mouth is a different kind of poison.

"You don't touch her," I snarl, teeth bared.

She doesn't flinch. "I don't have to. Frank's already inside her head. You're just the decoy."

I jerk against the rope, and my vision flashes red with rage.

The decoy?

No. That's not possible.

It can't be. But the pieces are already shifting in my head, and they're too fucking clear.

I thought I was closing in. Every move felt like progress—like I had him. But it was a lie. He was never running. He was playing with me. Keeping me busy while he bled her dry.

She was the fucking bait. Fuck.

My pulse hammers against the rope, pounding in my ears like it already knows what's coming. I don't know exactly what I'm walking into—but I know it's worse than I imagined.

"She's not part of this," I grit out.

She leans in again, lips brushing the edge of my ear. "She's always been part of it," she whispers. Like I should've known all along.

I snap forward, headbutting her so hard the chair tips. Pain detonates through my skull, but I hear her stumble back with a grunt.

"Still got fight in you," she breathes, wiping blood from her lip.

I spit on the floor. "You have no idea."

But I'm outnumbered, still drugged, and the second guard is probably on his way back.

"Tell Frank he picked the wrong fucking girl," I growl.

She kneels beside me, slow and graceful like a predator, and drags her nail down my cheek. The sting is sharp, but it's not about pain. This is war after all.

"Tell Ani," she purrs, her voice dipped in something colder

than venom, "that the monster she's running from sleeps in her bed."

My whole body goes still. Rage pulses so hot behind my eyes I could fucking explode. I breathe through it, forcing my focus through the haze. She's trying to break me.

"What did he do to you?" I rasp.

Her smile fades. For the first time, something flickers in her expression—loss, maybe. Grief? But it's gone a second later, replaced by steel.

"He taught me how to survive."

34

Ani

The first thing I register is the silence. The kind that makes you feel like the world's holding its breath. Light filters through the blinds in weak strips, casting gold across the bed sheets. My body aches in places I can't name, my throat's dry, and my chest is doing that annoying thing again.

That fluttery, jittery, anxious-flirty thing that only happened after I fell asleep in Steven's arms. Which, obviously, was a terrible fucking idea. I should've known better. I don't sleep like that—haven't in years—and definitely not next to someone who could ruin me.

I stretch, dragging the blanket up over my bare chest and pressing my face into the pillow that smells like him—dark, woodsy, and sinful. *God. I'm so screwed.*

It's not until I roll toward the nightstand that I realize two things at once. Steven is gone, and there's a notecard on my nightstand. It's sitting right on top of my phone.

My breath stalls. The last time I found one of these, it was blank. Just a card without anything on it... I don't even know what it meant. Except maybe I do—because if this one is from him, does that mean so was the last one? I'm not even going to think about that right now. Looking down at this one, it has actual writing scrawled across it.

Don't go anywhere. I'll be back.
Don't make me come find you.
- S

My body reacts like he just whispered it against my skin. I can still feel his hand sliding between my thighs and his voice whispering filth into my ear. I hate that it makes me smile, I hate that my stomach flips, and I hate that my heart does this stupid kick thing like he carved his name into it when I wasn't looking.

I hate it because it means he got in. Past every wall I built, every don't-touch-me edge I sharpened just to survive. He got under my skin and he made it feel good. And now I can't scrub him out without bleeding.

He isn't sweet. He's war wrapped in sex and shadows. And yet this... this little gesture feels more intimate than all the ways he ruined me last night.

I swing my legs out of bed, the hardwood is cold against my bare feet. I'm still sore in places that remind me exactly how last night ended, and still too tangled up in the chaos to make sense of any of it.

I need caffeine.

And maybe a lobotomy.

I sit there for half a second longer than I should, staring at the note he left like it's supposed to explain anything.

I march to the bathroom and scrub my face like it personally offended me, throwing on the first semi-clean outfit I can find. A pair of black leggings, an oversized hoodie, and my favorite combat boots. The hoodie still smells faintly like him—like smoke and that stupid, expensive soap he uses that should not make my stomach flip the way it does.

I spray perfume on just to spite it. My phone's already buzzing with a message from Sarah.

Sarah : You up? Cuz I have donuts and possibly a crisis.

Perfect.

This is exactly the emotional energy I need.

I shoot her a quick reply—*On my way. Save me one with sprinkles or I'm keying your car*—then grab my bag, and head out.

The walk to Sarah's is short, maybe ten minutes, but it's enough to get my blood moving and knock some of the chaos out of my head. The morning's cold enough to make my fingers numb, and the air smells like wet concrete and dried leaves.

I keep my head down, just in case. I know he said not to leave, but it's just a few blocks, if he comes back before I do, I'm sure he'll call me. By the time I round the corner, I've half convinced myself that I'm fine. That none of this means anything. What happened with Steven was just adrenaline and trauma and maybe a little too much skin.

When she opens the door in fuzzy socks and a pineapple robe and pulls me into a hug that smells like vanilla and chaos, something tight in my chest loosens for the first time all day.

"Okay," she says, squinting at me like she already knows I'm lying. "What the hell happened to you?"

We end up on the couch ten minutes later, a donut box between us and her cat purring at our feet. The place smells like hazelnut coffee and a witchy Pinterest board come to life—with way too much vanilla and not enough sage.

Home.

"So," she says, biting into a maple bar like it personally wronged her, "are we starting with the murdery one or the emotionally unavailable one?"

I blink. "That's the same guy."

"Oh right. Sorry." She wipes her mouth with the back of her

hand and leans back dramatically. "Forgot we're in the 'handle your trauma solo' chapter."

I groan, flopping sideways into the cushions. "I didn't tell either of them anything."

"Steven included?" she asks, tone softer now, like she's not sure if she's treading on a landmine or sitting on it.

I hesitate, staring up at the ceiling like it might give me answers. "He knows something's off. But I didn't tell him everything, it didn't come up."

Sarah hums. "So you're just... raw-dogging the emotional fallout?"

I shoot her a look. "You're literally eating cheese puffs and donuts for breakfast. Don't come at me."

"I'm coping," she says, pointing one at me like a threat. "You're spiraling in silence, which is hot in theory, but in practice? Kind of a mental health nightmare."

I blink at her. "I'm not spiraling?"

"Hmm." She takes another bite. "Tough to say. You did crawl for him."

"Okay wow," I shove her knee. "Don't use that tone like you're not the bitch who fell in love with a guy who couldn't even spell 'affection' without autocorrect."

"That was one time. And to be fair, he had great arms."

"He was catfishing you from a prison phone, Sarah."

She shrugs. "Again. Great arms."

I laugh so hard I nearly choke on my coffee. A beat of quiet falls over us, and I can feel her watching me. She looks at me like she can't tell if I need comfort or chaos—and she's fully prepared to deliver either. That's what I love the most about her, she's not my ride or die for nothing.

"So," she says gently, "are you gonna tell Steven the truth?"

I shake my head, fingers curling tight around the mug. "I don't know. I think part of me wants to, but if I say it out loud, it makes everything real."

"You didn't *let* anything happen," she says, keeping her tone flat. "You survived."

I look at her, and for once, I don't make a joke. I just nod.

"Besides," she adds after taking a sip of her drink, "if Steven is even half as obsessed with you as he seems, he's probably already figured you out."

We fall into silence again. She stretches her legs out across mine and sighs. "Okay, now can we talk about my problem?"

"Oh god. What happened now?"

"Some guy on Tinder messaged me five times yesterday and somehow found my booktok account."

"Wait, what? No. No. We don't bridge apps. That's against the rules."

"He sent me a Goodreads link to a book I reviewed in 2019 and said, *'I bet you look good in glasses.'*"

I make a strangled noise. "That's not flirting. That's a threat."

"Right?? I don't even wear glasses anymore."

"So, what did you say?"

She smiles. "I sent him a picture of Pennywise holding a library card and said *'same energy.'*"

I wheeze. "I love you."

"Obviously."

I sink further into the couch, pulling the blanket over my lap. The sugar's kicking in, and the coffee's working. Thank God.

Even though everything is chaos—Steven, Frank, the truth I still haven't said—right now, in this tiny apartment with my best friends, her disaster of a dating life and her candle-induced asthma attack waiting to happen...I feel almost human again.

My phone buzzes on the coffee table, slicing through the moment. It's Frank. I don't even bother opening it. I can see the preview just fine. Another fake-sweet check-in, like he's worried. Probably followed by some vague apology that doesn't actually take responsibility, wrapped in charm and old memories and whatever script he thinks still works on me.

I delete it because I'm done pretending, done letting him talk in circles around my instincts, like I'm the one who's crazy for hearing the alarm bells. Something's wrong and it has been for a long time.

Last night, I chose Steven. *Okay, let's be honest. I think I chose him the first day in the library.*

I let him touch me. I let him see me. And I fell asleep with his arms around me like I wasn't still broken. Even if I don't know what it means yet, it matters.

I set the phone back down, exhaling once, and press my fingers to my temples.

Steven said no more lies, and I meant it when I agreed. I need to end things with Frank, for real this time.

I haven't even talked to Steven, not since last night, and that silence is starting to settle like a bruise. I bite the inside of my cheek, hard. I'm not going to spiral. I've done enough of that lately.

"Okay, you're doing that thing again," Sarah says, nudging my leg with her foot from the opposite end of the couch. "The one where your face goes full war-crime and I start wondering if I need to hide the knives."

I blink over at her. "Sorry. Just thinking."

"Right. That's the problem." She sets her coffee down, narrowing her eyes. "Did lover-boy disappear already? Or is he still lurking in the shadows, sharpening his cheekbones and planning your joint funeral?"

I snort, then shake my head. "Haven't heard from him."

Her expression softens. "And that's...not normal?"

"I don't know." I rub the back of my neck. "I mean, it's only been a few hours, and he's not exactly a good-morning-text kind of guy, but something feels...off."

"Off how? Like emotionally constipated and brooding, or ghosted-me-for-no-reason off?"

"Somewhere between both," I mutter. "With a sprinkle of emotionally unavailable and weirdly intense eye contact."

"Love that for you." She sighs, leaning back against the cushions. "But also, he does look at you like you hung the moon. So maybe give it a minute before you go full Scorpio death spiral."

"I'm an Aquarius."

"Same difference. You just alphabetize the knives before you use them."

I crack a smile—small, but real.

"Look," she says, shifting so she's facing me. "You don't have to know what you want from him yet. Or from Frank. Or from yourself. You're allowed to be in the middle of the mess."

"Thanks, therapist Barbie."

"Anytime, emotionally constipated Barbie." She grins, then taps her phone. "Now if we're done unpacking your man drama, there's something I need to tell you."

I raise an eyebrow. "Please tell me this isn't about the guy who offered to buy your feet pics and your air fryer."

She snorts, nearly choking on her coffee. "Oh my god—no. That guy was unhinged. He wanted to sniff my air fryer. Immediately blocked."

I laugh, the sound catching in my throat. "You attract the weirdest men. It's honestly impressive."

"Right?" She flops back dramatically against the couch, pulling her blanket up to her chin. "But no. This one's... different."

I narrow my eyes. "Different how? Like 'not a felon' different, or 'has a working shower head' different?"

Her face flushes, but she tries to play it off. I know that look. "You like him."

"No," she says too quickly. "I mean—yes. Kind of. Maybe. Shut up."

I grin. "Give me details or I'm telling your mom you still don't separate your lights and darks."

"Rude. And I do now—mostly." She tucks a piece of hair behind her ear and sighs. "It's nothing dramatic. He just...talks to me. Sends me memes. We joke about the dumbest shit. Yesterday he told me he'd die on the hill that shredded cheese tastes better than sliced, and honestly? I respect it."

"You're in love."

"I might be," she groans. "But don't ruin it. He hasn't asked for nudes or pitched a pyramid scheme yet, so I'm just trying to enjoy it while it lasts."

I lean back into the couch cushions, warmth settling in my chest despite everything else.

"Keeping my fingers crossed."

"Me too," she says softly. "Because if this one turns out to be another feet guy, I'm retiring from dating forever."

I smile, looking out the window, where the sky is starting to shift. For a second, it almost feels like the world might give us both a break.

"This is why I need you in my life," I murmur, nudging her knee with mine. "Don't go anywhere, okay? I'll find you. I love you that much."

She grins. "If you didn't chase me through the woods, you obviously don't really love me."

"Oh, I'll chase you," I say, deadly serious. "I'm not gonna fuck you, but I will throw a dildo at your fucking face, bitch."

She snorts water out her nose and nearly chokes. "Jesus Christ, Ani."

"You knew what this was when you signed up."

35

"THE DEADLIEST WOUNDS DON'T BLEED."
(BUT THEY RUIN EVERYTHING ANYWAY.)

Ani

Sloane isn't at the library when I get there, which is weird. She's never late. Not once in the entire year we've worked side-by-side—through blizzards, food poisoning, and that time she tried to "reconnect with her inner child" and wiped out on roller skates.

But now, her chair's empty, her name tag is still hanging on the staff board, and there's no text. No explanation. Just a weird, crawling sensation under my skin that won't quit.

People have lives, Ani. Not everything is an omen. Not everything is about you.

Still, I check the staff lounge twice. And the bathroom. And the alley behind the drop box.

Nothing.

I make it an hour and a half before she finally walks in—flushed and breathless, with her ponytail crooked and her cardigan buttoned wrong.

"Sorry," she says quickly, tossing her bag behind the desk. "I had...uh, a thing. You're good to take your break now though."

I blink at her. "You sure? I haven't finished shelving the new—"

"I've got it," she cuts in. "Seriously. You look like you need air. You've got that...I've-been-thinking-about-him-again face."

I open my mouth to argue, but she's already moving, grabbing the cart and heading for the stacks like she's on a mission.

Weird.

Sloane never volunteers to shelve. Ever. She once called it "the most spiritually deadening task in human history." And now she's humming under her breath and pretending not to glance at the front door every ten seconds.

I just watch as that uneasy prickle turns into a full-on internal itch.

"You okay?" I ask finally.

"Peachy," she says—a little too fast. Then she hesitates, glancing over her shoulder. "If anyone asks where I went, just say I had to make a deposit."

I blink. "What kind of deposit?"

"Doesn't matter. Just say it like you mean it."

"...Okay."

She grabs a book—putting it back upside down. Then pauses again. "And hey. If you ever find yourself somewhere that smells like my grandfather's cigars... don't sign anything."

"What the hell does that mean?"

She just gives me a small smile. "Just... promise me you'll remember."

"...Okay. Weird, but okay."

"And hey—text me before you leave."

"Even if you're still here?"

She nods, a little too eagerly. "Especially if I'm still here."

There's a beat of silence. She grabs another book. "People aren't always who you think they are, Ani. Just—remember that."

She flashes a smile, then disappears down the aisle labeled Historical Non-Fiction, humming some off-key lullaby that makes the hair on my neck stand up.

Something is definitely wrong.

It's almost time to leave when I realize I still haven't heard from him. The thought lands hard and sharp as I flip the last chair onto the table and wipe down the desk in slow, robotic circles. I don't want to spiral about it. He's told me I'm his more times than I can count. I know that doesn't mean we're in a relationship or whatever —but I thought I'd at least get a message. Something. Anything.

My fingers itch toward my phone, even though I know I shouldn't check again. I've already looked—twice.

Sloane's been acting weird all day. Not just distracted—jumpy. She made me reshelve an entire cart in the wrong section, then snapped at me when I corrected it. And now she's standing at the far end of the room, pretending to tidy up the archives, even though no one's been in there for days.

I glance at her, and she looks up too quickly.

"Hey," I call out. "I'm locking up."

She nods, but her smile doesn't reach her eyes. "Cool. I'll be out in a sec."

I don't buy it, but I don't have the bandwidth to dig. Not now. Not when my chest is already tight for reasons I can't name and my brain's playing ping-pong with worst-case scenarios.

I duck into the staff hallway, more out of habit than anything— just a quick breather before grabbing my bag.

My phone buzzes and I pull it out faster than I've done anything all day. My heart skips, praying for his name. Only, it's not from him. It's not a message, it's a photo. And the second I open it, my knees buckle against the side wall.

It's Steven.

He's slumped in a chair, head down, face bloodied, one arm is hanging like it's been pulled from the socket—and his shirt soaked through, and he looks...he looks dead.

No.

No, no, no.

I can't breathe.

My lungs seize up, and the phone shakes in my hands so violently I almost drop it. The edges of the hallway blur, and everything tilts. My body is frozen, but my thoughts are screaming.

Who sent this? Where is he? Why would someone—The photo burns itself into my vision. I need to—I don't fucking know. Call someone? Run? Scream until my lungs give out? My brain's short-circuiting, sparking and crashing in loops I can't get out of. I just know I need to move because standing here like this, shaking and useless while he's somewhere, tied up and bleeding—yeah, that's not an option.

I shove the phone into my pocket and whirl back toward the front of the library. Sloane's at the desk now, but I don't even look at her as I snatch my coat.

"I need to go," I say, breathless.

"You okay?" she asks, too fast. "Do you want me to—"

"I'm fine." I lie.

I don't remember grabbing my keys or texting Sarah. I barely remember pushing through the front door, except for the part where the air hits me like a punch and my body finally remembers how to breathe.

The image of Steven—bleeding, tied, broken—won't leave me alone.

I don't know what I'm walking into. But I know who might have answers and if this has anything to do with Frank—If the gut-deep wrongness I've been ignoring finally decided to show its teeth —then .

My fingers move before I can stop them, dialing Frank. He doesn't answer. The call cuts off on the first ring like the call was rejected. A second later, a message lights up the screen.

> FRANK: Busy at the club, baby. What's wrong?

My heart slams against my ribs because it doesn't make sense. Something about it is off. Since when does Frank pass on a chance to talk to me? But still—some panicked, scrambling part of me thinks maybe he can help. Maybe if I show him the picture. Maybe if I lie and say Steven's a friend, or my brother. Frank's always been protective when it suits him. Calculated, but territorial.

He wouldn't let someone hurt me... right? Not if he still thinks I'm his?

I don't know but I'll figure out the story when I get there. I just need him to look at it and tell me who the hell would send me something like that. And if he hesitates—Even for a second—I'll know.

Even as the words echo through my skull, I know I'm grasping at smoke. But it's a lie I need to believe—because the alternative is worse.

So I get in the Uber, heart racing like I've already made the wrong call, and I tell myself it's a smart move. I'll get help and play nice long enough to get answers. Then I'll deal with everything else.

The car slows and the club looms in front of me like a monument to every lie I've swallowed. Every choice I didn't get to make. Every time someone called me sweet or pretty or safe—then used me anyway.

It's dark.

No valet.

No cars.

No bass bleeding through the walls like usual. Just shadows clinging to the doorframe like a warning. The front entrance is shut tight and there's no flicker of security, no line of overdressed assholes checking their lipstick in the windows. Just silence and dead glass—reflecting nothing but me.

The driver glances back. "You want me to wait?"

"No," I say, though my voice sounds hollow. Like someone else's mouth is moving.

I step out and the door clicks shut behind me like the punchline to a joke I haven't caught up to yet. My boots echo across the pavement, every step feels too loud. Frank said he was here, and that he was busy. So where the fuck is everyone?

My fist curls around the handle before I even register the movement. Locked. *Of course it's fucking locked.*

I press my knuckles against the glass, leaning in, and cup my hands around my face to kill the glare. There's nothing behind the doors. No bartender. No bass line. No overpriced perfume bleeding through the vents. Just overturned chairs, dark bottles lining the shelves like trophies, and a bar stocked with lies.

No Frank.

Not even a shadow.

My chest tightens, as heat starts rising fast—curling through my throat like smoke before the fire. He told me he was here and that he was busy. So why does it look like this place hasn't seen a crowd in days?

The thought slams through me like a hit to the ribs, and suddenly everything inside me tips sideways.

My heart thunders, but it's not panic this time. It's rage.

He lied.

Not some casual omission, or a soft-edged sidestep or a clever half-truth—a flat-out, deliberate fucking lie.

I may not know where Steven is. I may not know who sent that photo or what the hell I'm about to walk into—but I know exactly what I feel.

Betrayal and fury.

They coil hot and sharp in my chest, winding tighter with every second I stand outside this empty fucking club, piecing together lies that should've never made it past me in the first place.

My phone buzzes in my hand, slicing through the static in my head like a blade to the spine.

I'm so goddamn sick of this game—sick of being dragged along by ghosts and threats that won't show their face. But my thumb moves anyway, already unlocking the screen.

This time it isn't a photo. It's a video. There's no caption. No message. Just grainy surveillance footage, frozen mid-frame. It has no timestamp, just static, shadows, and the promise of something worse.

A cold sweat breaks out across my shoulders, sliding down my spine as I tap it open. My pulse slams to a halt in my throat as my vision narrows until all I can see is the screen.

Please, God. Not again.

The video starts shaky—it looks like it's a security cam angle, maybe it's from a phone, but I know that jaw, that blood-smeared mouth. I know that body, tied to a chair and slumped like a puppet that's lost its strings.

Steven.

My heart lurches.

There's a voice from behind the camera. I can't see who it is, but there's enough movement in the shadows to know someone's there.

The camera angle tilts, catching the profile of Steven's bloodied face. He lifts his head slowly, like it takes effort just to move. One eye's already swelling shut, and his lip is split. He coughs once, and blood drips from his mouth.

Then he smirks. "She was a distraction. A means to an end." He spits blood to the floor. "Pretty easy one too. And when I'm done, I'll return her the same way you gave her to me... broken."

I stagger back, like the wind just got knocked out of me, and my body goes ice cold.

No.

"You think I haven't played this game before?" he spits. He looks up—directly at the camera, eyes like steel. "I've been after him since she disappeared."

Someone laughs, and the screen jolts.

And just before the video cuts out, Steven lifts his face one more time, eyes gleaming through the blood—sharp and defiant.

"Tell him I know who she is now."

The words land like a detonation. Then someone steps into

frame, and there's a blur of motion—an object raised, then a sickening crack. The screen jolts and everything goes black.

I sit there frozen, staring at my phone like it might start up again, maybe if I watched it again—I'd see something different. Hear something new.

Distraction.

Return her the same way you gave her to me.

Easy.

The words crawl into my skin like rot, and I can't scrub them out. I can't un-hear the way he said it, like I never mattered.

My hands are shaking, and my ears are ringing. My whole body feels like it's underwater, drowning in a betrayal I didn't see coming. And the worst part is—he looked right at the camera like he knew I'd see it.

My chest folds in on itself, ribs twisting like someone reached inside and snapped them for fun. God, was I always just a pawn? Was I so desperate to feel chosen that I didn't realize I was being passed around like leverage?

I can't breathe, and I don't even know who I'm mad at—Steven, Frank, or myself. Because somewhere in the middle of all this, I fell for him. And now I don't know if any of it was real.

Suddenly, none of it matters.

I don't give a fuck what that was, whatever it is, I see betrayal layered on top of betrayal—and I am so fucking done letting men decide what I'm worth.

They want to play games with fire?

Fine.

Let them fucking burn.

My hands won't stop shaking, but I don't slow down. I try the front doors again—locked. Every entrance is sealed up tight, but I know better. Frank has to be in there somewhere.

There's a side door I remember seeing when I was here last that was used by the staff. I don't even hesitate. I move like I've done this before—because in some ways, I have. Different hallway, different man, but same fucking fear.

It's locked—but security in this place has always been for show. Just enough to look intimidating, but not enough to stop someone who actually gives a damn. I pull a hairpin from my hair without thinking. Sarah taught me this trick once—half-drunk on a Tuesday, laughing too loud as she picked the lock on the jukebox just to skip to our song. I remember her saying, *"Everything opens if you want it bad enough."*

Turns out, she was right.

My chest seizes as I slide the pin into place, heart slamming with each shaky breath.

Then—*Click.*

The door gives, and I slip inside. It's pitch dark, and it feels like it's pressing against my skin. The air is stale with old smoke and the ghost of bass that used to shake these walls. I move slowly down the hallway, boots echoing too loud against the floor. Every overturned stool and silent bottle gleams under the emergency lights like a grave marker.

The hallway narrows as I push deeper into the back of the club, past the liquor closet and the half-busted utility door. The silence is suffocating.

When I reach his office, the door is open.

I pause, every instinct in me is screaming that something's off. But my feet move anyway, dragging me over the line like some part of me already knew I'd end up here.

The room is dark, lit only by a sliver of light cutting through the blinds. It lands in a pale stripe across the desk.

There's papers scattered like someone was in a hurry. Steven's name is on the first one. His real name. Full government file, sealed and stamped and tagged in a way that makes my stomach flip. There's photos clipped to the corner—grainy surveillance, maybe from weeks ago. Maybe longer. But it's him. In my apartment building, on the street outside the bar, in the library.

My stomach turns, but I keep flipping. Then I see another page, tucked halfway beneath the stack. I see my name in all caps. No middle initial, no address. Just a single word that feels like it's been branded onto the page. Above it is a Property Transfer Request.

I freeze.

The words don't compute at first. I stare like they're written in some other language—like if I just tilt the page or squint, it'll say something else.

It's a legal form, with my name, my date of birth, and a signature that's supposed to be mine—but isn't.

And there's more. Land deeds. Financial records. A fake ID tucked in the back with a photo of me I don't even remember taking.

What the actual fuck is all of this?

I can't breathe.

My knees nearly give out as I stare at the paper, rage crawling up my throat like smoke before the fire. My throat burns as I back away from the desk, chest cracking open around a scream I don't let out.

I find myself behind the bar, hands moving before I can stop them. I rip open the bottom cabinet like there's an answer buried in the sticky wood and spilled liquor. I don't even realize what I'm reaching for until my fingers close around it tucked between backup mixers and a half-empty bottle of gin that smells like regret —there it is.

Everclear.

Flammable as hell.

I pull it out with shaking hands, and something clicks into place.

From the second Steven walked into my life—stalking me, seducing me, crawling inside my skin like he belonged there—he knew.

He had to.

Frank couldn't pull off something like this alone. He needed someone like Steven. Someone who could get close to do lord knows what. That's what this was, wasn't it? He said he took care of things.

I was the package. The prize. The pretty little pawn passed between monsters. And maybe Steven wasn't supposed to fall for me—but that doesn't mean he didn't play his part. He got inside. He cracked me open. And now he's gone.

He knew what was coming.

That video wasn't a warning, it was a message.

God, how did I not see it?

My vision blurs and I blink hard, my knuckles are white around the neck of the bottle. He said he'd come back. He said no more lies. But if he meant it—why didn't he tell me the truth? Why didn't he warn me?

Heat roars in my chest like the match is already lit, and for once, I don't care, let it burn. If I'm going to be the girl they all pass around like property, then I'll be the one who scorches the kingdom down first.

I grab a rag and shove it halfway into the neck of the first bottle, then snatch another from the shelf. This one's top-shelf vodka, some ridiculous import wrapped in gold foil and ego. Frank always said he reserved it for clients who mattered.

Perfect.

That's all I've ever been to him, right? A pawn wrapped in lip gloss and trauma he thought he could mold into what? A trophy girlfriend?

Yeah, fuck that.

I move with precision and purpose, like I've done this before. Every time I've had to start over. Every time a man tried to own me. And tonight, I'm not starting over. I'm ending something.

The club's still dark, but I know every inch of it now. I know the curve of the bar where Frank liked to stand when he gave orders. I know the shadowed VIP booth he used like it was a pulpit.

I start at the entrance. The same one he walked me through like I was something to show off. My hand doesn't shake as I unscrew the cap and pour a steady line of Everclear straight down the glossy floor. From the front door where he first lied to me...to the booth where he kissed my wrist and told me I was safe. Then all over the edge of the stage.

Every step is deliberate.

Every drop is soaked in betrayal.

I move to the stage, climbing slowly as I pour another line of liquor along the edge. It drips down the wooden slats like blood. I coat the bar next. The counter. The floor. The velvet stools.

I don't stop.

Not when the bottle runs low. Not when the fumes sting my nose. Not even when the edges of my vision blur with all my feelings coming to the surface. I coat every inch in gasoline-flavored vengeance, baptizing it all in something truer than forgiveness—rage.

He treated this place like it was his kingdom, but it was mirrors and smoke and power disguised as charm. I was just some stupid pawn he paraded through it—dressed in promises.

I pull the matchbook from my pocket—lifted earlier from the emergency stash behind the register. It rests between my fingers for a beat, shaking slightly, then it flares to life.

"You should've killed me when you had the chance," I whisper into the dark, empty silence.

And then I drop it.

The fire catches fast—like it's been holding its breath, just waiting for the go-ahead. Flames snake along the trail I left, flickering toward the booths first. The velvet goes up in seconds, thick smoke poures off the fabric as heat swells around me. It devours every shadow, every lie Frank ever sold under dim lights and who knows whatever shady ass shit he was doing here.

The walls catch next, and the overhead bulbs burst like warning shots—sharp cracks of glass rain down like shattered promises. Behind the bar, bottles explode in a chain reaction, flinging ribbons of fire into the air like some twisted finale.

"You made me a monster. Now even the devil's afraid of me."

I turn, smoke curling around me—sliding over my shoulders like it's part of me now. My boots hit pavement with a finality that echoes in my chest. The scent of scorched velvet and burning liquor clings to my hoodie, my hair, my skin. It follows me down the block like a shadow I finally earned. And I don't look back.

I don't feel guilty. I feel awake, and alive. Which makes me feel a *little* guilty, considering I just committed arson.

The wind has teeth tonight, but I don't care. It bites at my cheeks, slices through the holes in my jeans—but nothing can touch the fire still crackling under my skin.

I don't even know where I'm going. Away from the lie Frank built. Away from the version of myself that sat and smiled through it.

I tug my sleeves down, trying to ground myself with the feel of fabric against my skin. But my hands won't stop shaking. I tell myself it's adrenaline—that it's just the come-down after everything. But it's not. It's him. It's everything.

Every step I took in that building was a scream I never let out. Every flame was a truth I buried just to survive.

The streetlights flicker above me, humming softly like they know something I don't. My brain's spiraling—Steven. The club. The message. That fucking video. It cuts deeper the longer it echoes.

God. I should've just gone home and called the police like a normal person.

I should've called Sarah, and curled up in my bed and waited this out like a sane person. But no—I had to go full feral. I had to light a match and pretend it would fix something.

So I keep walking. Fast. My feet are taking me somewhere—whether it's toward redemption or a fucking funeral. Honestly, I'm not sure I care which.

That's when I feel it.

A prickle at the base of my neck. Not the kind of chill that brushes past you, but the kind that sinks under your skin and settles in your spine.

I glance over my shoulder, heart thudding in my throat, but nothing. Just a quiet street, a stray breeze, and my own suffocating paranoia trying to crawl up my throat.

I shake it off and pick up the pace. I'm only a few blocks from home. If I can just make it to my door—get inside, take a shower, clear my head—

I'll be fine. I'll be better. I'll—

A car door slams and I freeze.

"Hey," a voice purrs, smooth and smug. "Need a ride?"

36

"FEAR ISN'T LOUD."
(IT WHISPERS RIGHT BEFORE YOU BLACK OUT)

Ani

My wrists ache. Which... yeah, sounds about right—considering they're zip-tied behind my back so tight it feels like the plastic is fused to bone. My head is pounding, my lips are wet and coppery, and every time I blink, the room spins.

There's too much silence, and I don't know where the fuck I am. I sure as fuck am not my apartment, and I know I'm not at Steven's place.

Panic claws up my throat.

I blink a few times as my vision clears just enough to catch the soft glow of light filtering through the window. At least I have a soft rug beneath me like this is some fucked-up slumber party. Except in this version, the host tied me up, backhanded me across the face, and called me a whore for letting someone else make me come.

Footsteps echo beyond the closed door. I test the zip ties, clenching my jaw, and bite back a hiss. *Okay, so those aren't coming off that easily. Noted.*

The door swings open, and Frank steps inside—only to stop short when he sees me still on the floor, lips swollen and cheek split.

For a second, something stupid flickers in my chest. Relief,

565

maybe. Some leftover, delusional part of me that still thinks he might've come to help. But then I see his face.

"Morning, sweetheart."

I smile, and I can feel the blood painting my teeth. "Aw. You're still here. I was hoping it was all a wet dream."

His jaw tightens. *Good. Let it piss him off.* He didn't even flinch at the sight of me like this. I don't know who hit me, but if he didn't put a stop to it, that means he let it happen.

"Stand up," he says.

"Can't," I shoot back, voice sweet and sour. "I'm allergic to bullshit."

He crosses the room in three strides and yanks me up by the arm like I'm not a person, just some object that stopped behaving the way he wanted. My shoulder screams in protest, but I don't give him the satisfaction. I let my head loll slightly to the side, limp enough to piss him off, but not enough to lose balance.

The second he gives me an opening, I'm taking it—and this time, I'm not pulling punches.

His fingers clamp around my jaw, rough and possessive, tilting my face. His gaze lingers on the split in my lip, and the bruising that I'm sure is already blooming across my cheek.

Then, without a word, he slices the zip ties from my wrists.

"You let him touch you."

"Touch me?" I fake a gasp. "Babe. He did more than touch. Want me to describe it? There was lots of tongue and at one point, I'm pretty sure I saw God."

The slap comes faster than I expect—but I don't flinch. And that's what really pisses him off.

"You've got some fucking nerve," he growls.

"I know." I grin, even as blood trickles down my chin. "It's my best feature."

He shoves me back hard, and I stumble, catching myself on the rug with one hand before I hit the floor completely. My palm scrapes against the carpet, rug burn blooming across my skin, but I don't make a sound.

He stalks toward the window like he needs space just to keep from murdering me.

Give me sixty seconds and I'll be the one dragging his body through the backyard with my boot print on his throat.

"You have no idea what you've done," he says quietly.

I blink up at him, all faux innocence. "Did I forget your birthday or something?"

His head turns slightly. "You think this is about a club?"

"Everything's about a club when you're a narcissist with a VIP complex."

His lips twitch, and it shouldn't hurt—but it does. Because even now, after everything, he still doesn't take me seriously. I was never a threat to him. Just a toy that got mouthy.

"You always had a smart mouth," he says.

"And you always had a God complex. We all have our shit, Frankie."

His eyes flash. "*Don't* call me that."

"Relax. It's not like anyone else calls you anything worth remembering."

His face doesn't change, but I see the twitch in his jaw, and for a second, it almost looks like he might laugh. But then something shifts. That crack in his mask goes still and he takes a single step forward. The shift in his energy is instant. I don't even have time to brace before he's on me.

His hand clamps around my throat, shoving me flat against the floor. My skull knocks the rug beneath me, and his body pins me like a weight I can't escape. Fingers dig into my neck until my breath stutters, until the room starts to spin. His breath ghosts my cheek—hot, sour, and entirely too close.

"I don't like sharing."

I look up at him, lips curled, fury burning through the lack of oxygen. "Then you better kill me now, because I'm not yours—and I never fucking was."

He leans closer, dragging his eyes down my face. "You've always been my favorite," he murmurs. "Even when you didn't know it."

I tilt my head slightly, keeping my voice soft. "Aww. And here I thought I was just the most useful."

A split-second pause. That's all I get before the air shifts. I know I should shut the fuck up. I know this is the part where girls go quiet—where they plead, where they lower their eyes and pray they'll be the exception to the rule.

But I'm not the exception. I never was.

If I'm going to die in this room, tied up and spit-shined—then I'm damn sure not going down quietly. But before I can savor the sting in his eyes, the door creaks behind him, and a new shadow steps into the room.

He's massive. Broad shoulders, neck like a tree trunk, and that vacant look guys get when they're built to break things, not think about them. He's also wearing too much cologne and not nearly enough IQ behind the eyes.

"Careful, Frank," I murmur, letting my eyes flick lazily to the guy still standing in the doorway. "Wouldn't want to make a scene in front of company."

There's a beat of silence that's just long enough for me to think. Maybe I pushed him too far. I really need to learn when to shut the fuck up.

The slap comes harder than the first. And that's saying something, considering the last one already made my ears ring.

This one feels personal.

The sound cracks through the room like a whip, sharp enough to sting the air itself. My head snaps sideways and pain rips through my jaw as copper floods my tongue.

God, I'm so fucking tired of bleeding for men who can't handle rejection.

For a second, all I see is white. And then he's got me by the hair, yanking so hard my knees almost give out. I suck in a breath through my teeth, but I don't cry out.

"You think mouthing off makes you brave?" he growls, his breath is rancid against my face. "You think just because I didn't break you when I had the chance, I won't do it now?"

I laugh. "Wasn't sure you had the balls," I rasp, dragging my gaze back to his. "Especially in front of an audience."

The man behind him clears his throat, shifting his weight like he doesn't want to get involved, but Frank doesn't let go.

"You want answers?" he hisses. "Start remembering. Because next time I lay my hands on you, sweetheart—it's not gonna be your cheek that bruises."

His grip finally loosens and I stumble back, breathing like I've just surfaced from drowning. But I don't cry, or scream. I just smile. *As if I'm going to let him know how much he got to me.*

Inside, though, I'm cracked open. There's this sharp, crawling feeling under my skin like everything I thought I understood just burned down and I'm standing in the ashes, still trying to pretend it's smoke and not fire. This isn't about temper or jealousy—this is control, and I'm the prize he thinks he owns.

My eyes dart without moving my head. The door is still cracked open behind them. Frank follows my glance, like a lion watching a rabbit twitch before it bolts.

"Don't bother," he says softly, and the threat under that one word slices clean, but I'm already moving.

I duck low, slamming my elbow into his ribs hard enough to hear the air leave him, and bolt for the door—only to get yanked back by the hood of my sweatshirt.

"Fuck—" My feet leave the ground as I crash into the wall, my breath knocking out of me in a wild gasp.

Frank's hand grips my jaw as he leans in, calmly. "I let you play pretend," he says, his voice filled with fury. "Let you run. Let you lie. I even let you fuck him."

He tilts his head like he's listening for the sound of my dignity shattering. "I can see him on you, doll." His thumb drags slowly down the side of my neck—taunting me.

"The bruises on your skin. That look in your eye like someone finally touched you and meant it." He leans in, dragging his tongue up the side of my face. "Don't insult me by pretending I don't know the difference between getting fucked and being claimed."

A pause, and then—"And if you want him breathing by tomorrow? I'd stop testing how far I'm willing to go."

My stomach lurches. No. No, no, no. He can't mean—my blood runs cold, but I don't react.

"I don't know what you're talking about." I whisper, and I hate how soft it sounds, but still trying to play it off.

Frank smirks. "You really thought he was different?" he asks, almost pitying. "Sweetheart... he's been lying to you since the first night you met him."

And just like that, the world tilts sideways. *No. No, that can't be right.* Every breath, every glance, every fucking whisper in the dark—None of it was real? He has to be lying.

My chest tightens, like my ribs are trying to fold in on themselves. Was I the game?

He steps back and starts pacing, he's clearly enjoying every second of this breakdown.

"Oh, he didn't tell you why he came here? What he was looking for?" He shrugs, casually. "He's not yours, Anianne. He's mine."

It slides under my skin before I can stop it, hooking into something tender. I laugh—sharp and breathless, but it sounds wrong in my own ears. "Bullshit."

"Believe what you want," he says with a shrug. "But you'll figure it out. Just like before."

Before? Before what?

Something stirs behind my ribs. But before I can ask, or rip the truth from his throat—he nods to the man behind him and turns toward the door.

"I'll give you some time," he calls back effortlessly. "Get your head on straight."

The lock clicks shut.

The silence after Frank leaves is a special kind of loud. It hums under my skin like a static that says he's not done.

I pace, because sitting still makes me feel caged—and if I stop moving, the panic might catch up.

My cheek still burns where his ring left a message I never asked for. I move toward the window and press my fingertips to the cold glass. Outside, it's just black sky and that one stubborn star I used to wish on like it was listening.

Did you think I wouldn't know the difference between someone fucking you and being claimed?

Steven did something to me. Not just touched me—he marked me. He got under my skin in a way that won't wash off.

But what the hell does Frank know? What does Steven know?

Fuck! I want to scream.

The two men in my life aren't who I thought they were and maybe they never were. Steven showed up like a storm I didn't see coming, and Frank slithered in wearing charm like armor. And somehow, I let both of them close. Now they're circling each other like wolves, and I'm just... in the middle.

How did I end up being something they both want for reasons I don't understand—and didn't agree to.

I keep trying to find solid ground, but every answer I get just tilts the world more sideways and all I have is more questions. The drugs in my system are making it hard to focus.

One second I'm breathing, and the next, I'm drowning.

I'm not in this room anymore. I'm small. Eight, maybe nine. It's hard to tell—time doesn't move right in this place. There's yelling, a man's voice cutting through the air like broken glass, and my mother's crying. Not the quiet kind either.

The whole room reeks, smelling like something sour, something that burns the back of my throat before I even breathe it in.

I'm holding a folder tight to my chest. It's thick and heavy. My arms are shaking, but I don't let go. There's a bunch of cash, crumpled papers, and a passport I'm not supposed to see.

My name is on it, and suddenly I know—whatever this is...I'm not coming back.

All I remember after that is a hand grabbing my arm, dragging me toward the door.

The voice in my ear is low and urgent, whispered in Spanish. "No mires atrás."

Don't look back.

My feet move before my brain does. Then it's all motion. A car. A plane. A hallway that won't end.

I can't hear anything past the sound of my heartbeat, pounding like a countdown I didn't start. My body's moving through time, through space, but my mind is frozen in that second—right where everything cracked open.

I snap out of it when I hear a man's voice in the hallway.

Shit. Frank.

The memory slips through my fingers like smoke as instinct takes over. I don't move. Not until the door creaks open and he steps inside with that same slow, smug ease he always wears.

He hums under his breath, strolling toward me. His fingers brush my jaw, soft enough to make my skin crawl. I tense and pull away. The thought of him touching me now, makes me sick.

"I told you," he murmurs, dragging his thumb over the split in my lip. "No one else touches what's mine."

The heat behind the words makes my stomach twist, bile licking the back of my throat. But I keep my voice light, because it's the only thing I've got left.

"And here I thought you were a businessman," I murmur. "Not a fucking caveman."

The slap comes faster than I expect—and sharp enough to blur the world for a second and paint stars behind my eyes. I bite down on the scream. All I can feel is the rage swelling beneath my skin.

I straighten slowly, licking the blood from my lip. Again.

That's what—number three? God, I'm getting really tired of this. At least it's only a slap. *Small favors.*

"Okay, Frankie," I mutter, trying to mask the panic that's creeping in. "I think the slapping's getting old."

His jaw twitches. Then he takes a step closer.

I smile. "Don't tell me that's what gets you hard."

I shouldn't say it. I know I shouldn't. But it's already out, and I'm running out of fucks to give.

I glance down—and sure enough, when I actually see it—I laugh. It's a sound that scrapes my throat raw and tastes like gasoline.

"You've gotta be kidding me," I giggle. "You hit me and now you're hard? Shit, maybe I've been giving you too much credit. I thought all those nice dates and big words meant you wanted something real. But no. Turns out all you really need is a girl who bleeds pretty, huh?"

Something cracks behind his eyes, and I see it too late.

He lunges—grabbing my arms, yanking me against him. My back slams into the nearest wall and he cages me there with his body. His breath is hot and wild against my face.

"You think this is funny?" he hisses.

"No," I say calmly, even though my breath is shaking. "I think it's a fucking horror story. And you're just pissed I stopped swooning long enough to notice."

His grip tightens.

"Oh, baby doll," he murmurs. "I paid for you."

The words don't register at first.

"I bought you," he says again, more force now. "Like a goddamn investment. I'm starting to think you're more trouble than the money was worth."

And just like that, the air gets knocked out of the room. My body goes still. My brain scrambles for understanding, but all I can do is blink. Because what the fuck did he just say?

"I knew you were too good to be true," he says, like he's admiring a painting. "All that fire. All that fight. You really thought the world was gonna let you keep it?"

He leans closer, and the smile on his face makes me want to puke.

"No, sweetheart. Girls like you don't get freedom. You get owned." His breath is hot against my ear, and I swear my soul tries to crawl out of my skin. "Girls like you are meant to be fucked into obedience."

My stomach flips so violently I have to bite my tongue so I don't gag. He pulls back just far enough to watch it land—to watch the truth carve me open.

"Don't look so surprised," he adds, cruel now. "You think I bought you for your winning personality?"

No, no, no, no. He's lying. He has to be lying.

Everything I couldn't remember suddenly has a shape. The shadow in the room. The voice in my ear. The hands that dragged me.

"What's the matter, sweetheart? Didn't realize all that freedom you've been pretending to have came with a price tag?"

I can't stop shaking. My mouth opens, then closes.

"I never—" My voice breaks. "I never agreed—"

He chuckles. "You didn't have to. The deal was sealed the second your ex decided you were worth more on paper than in his bed."

I stagger back like he hit me again. My hand finds the wall, and my legs don't feel real.

This can't be happening.

This whole time—this entire fucking time—I thought I escaped.

If he thinks he can keep me here after this, he's got another thing coming. I don't care if it takes fire, blood, or what's left of my sanity—I will burn my way out.

He grabs my jaw, squeezing until it aches. "You're mine, Anianne. You have been. Even before I bought you."

He releases me and starts pacing. "I gave your boyfriend a story," he says. "Paid him off to spin a little fairytale about the two of you moving off to paradise."

My stomach lurches.

"You don't remember that part, do you?" He taunts. "Don't worry. That's what happens when you get hit hard enough. It all gets a little fuzzy."

He's still talking—like this is a bedtime story and he's tucking me in with a fucking confession. He's so fucking deranged, he's acting like I'm supposed to feel grateful he cleaned up my past before wrapping a leash around my throat.

"You were supposed to go with him," he says, like we're swapping memories over coffee. "He was paid to deliver you. Nice and easy. A drop-off at the edge of town, nothing more."

He pauses—just long enough to let the next part hit harder.

"But you got mouthy and started asking questions. Then you tried to run." His smile is cold. "So we had to improvise and make other arrangements."

My throat dries up.

Other arrangements?

A spark flares in the back of my mind. I try to grab it, but it's no use.

"You—" I choke on the word. "What did you do?"

His smile turns razor sharp. "I made sure you landed exactly where I wanted you to."

The walls start to tilt.

"Your boyfriend handled the paperwork and the bruises." Frank's voice turns gleeful. "He fought for a bonus too, selfish bastard."

The blood drains from my face. I remember a fight, then being slapped. The floor. How cold it was, and the way his voice cracked when he said, '*She's your problem now.*'

Oh my God.

My legs go numb, but I don't fall.

"You should've seen yourself," Frank croons. "All scratched up, with blood on your lip, but still swinging like a little street rat. That's when I knew—I wasn't going to waste you. You were too much fun."

I take a step back, but there's nowhere to go. The room spins, and all I can hear is the sound of my own breath—sharp and ragged. And then I hear something else.

"Please. I don't want to go."

My body being dragged, the sting of bleach in my nose, and the reek of cheap cigarettes.

Frank's voice cuts through the memory like a serrated edge.

"I gave you everything," he says. "Let you work. Gave you space. Let you breathe a little. But you—you fucked it all up because you had to be a fucking slut."

My head snaps up so fast it makes me dizzy.

"I've been patient, Anianne." His smile doesn't reach his eyes. "But one thing I don't do is share."

He steps forward. "And I sure as fuck don't lose."

My body moves before my mind can catch up. I lunge, grabbing the lamp off the end table and hurling it with everything I have. It misses—shattering against the wall beside his head in a spectacular spray of glass.

"Don't come near me." My voice is shaking and so is my grip but I don't step back.

Rage coils in my gut, terror climbs up my spine, and bile rises in my throat—each one trying to claw its way out first, like there's not enough room for all three.

Frank's expression darkens. "You still don't get it, do you?"

I lift my chin, even though every part of my body is screaming. My lungs. My legs. That small, broken part of me that wants to disappear before he can say whatever comes next.

"I don't belong to you."

"You do, actually." His tone is calm. Almost gentle. And that's what makes it worse. He reaches into his jacket and tosses something at my feet. It flutters once, then lands face-up.

I stare at it, and in the photo there's a man holding a gun, and I can see Frank's face is blurred in the corner. I'm standing in a hallway, bleeding, and my eyes are wide and terrified.

I stop breathing.

My brain tries to reject it, telling me it's fake, or doctored somehow. I remember that hallway. I remember the blood. I remember being dragged like a fucking rag doll while men talked about me like I wasn't right there.

No. No, no, no.

The word *no* beats in my chest like a war drum, over and over, but I don't move. I just stand there—shaking and silent—because for the first time, I don't know if I'm going to survive this.

I don't know what's worse, the memories... or the fact that he's been sitting on them this whole time, pretending to be someone he wasn't. *What else did he lie about?* I feel used. I feel violated. And I feel so fucking stupid for not figuring it out sooner.

"This was supposed to be our new beginning," he murmurs, like he's reminiscing about a love story instead of a fucking crime scene. "But then *he* came in. Meddling prick thought he could outplay me."

My eyes snap to his face.

Frank smiles, but he ignores me. He crouches down and picks up the photo, brushing it off like it's a memory worth keeping.

"Don't worry, baby girl," he says softly. "He won't touch you again."

The words don't hit all at once. He's talking about Steven. My stomach flips, but I don't give Frank the satisfaction of reacting.

"Where is he?"

Frank's smile turns to a blade. "That depends," he says, tilting his head. "Are you ready to be mine again?"

I move before I think—pure instinct. I lunge like a cornered animal, but he's faster. His hand clamps around my wrist and squeezes. Pain flashes white behind my eyes. I choke on it, biting back a scream, but my knees give out when he yanks me forward and slams me into the wall.

"You've got one chance to make this right," he growls, breath hot on my skin.

I look him dead in the eye and spit in his face. His hand lashes out, and the slap, which honestly feels more like a punch lands with a sickening crack. Pain detonates across my cheekbone, and I drop like a stone. I hit the floor hard. My palm scrapes against the wood and beneath the pain, as rage coils straight through my bones.

"Oh, baby."

I don't move as he rushes over and falls to his knees beside me, breath ragged with false remorse.

"I didn't want to—fuck." His hand trembles as it reaches out. "You just... you push, Ani. You always push." Like it's my fault he keeps hitting me.

Warm fingers graze my shoulder and I flinch, the reaction automatic. He pauses. Not in guilt—he doesn't have the wiring for that —but like a man recalibrating a role he's played.

One hand smooths down my spine, slow and deliberate. The other hovers near my waist, suspended like he can't decide whether to touch me again... or snap me in half.

"You know how I get when you lie to me baby doll," he says softly. Like he's soothing a child. "It's your fault I have to be this way."

God. The audacity of this man could power a small country.

Then—like we're in a fucking rom-com—he helps me up gently. One arm braced beneath mine, the other cradling the back of my head. He wipes the blood from my lip with his thumb, so sweet it curdles.

His fingers rest on my jaw and when his mouth brushes my cheek, my stomach rolls. I almost throw up right on him. *Wouldn't that be the icing on the cake.*

"Get dressed," he murmurs, pressing a kiss to my forehead like a fucking brand. "We're leaving in an hour."

I straighten my spine and whatever warmth was left in me dies right there on the floor, bleeding out beside my pride as I go still.

"Leaving?"

He hums—casually like we're playing house and I didn't just hit the floor. "I've packed for you. You don't need any more of that black shit you wear."

I blink. "You packed... my things."

"Of course I did."

He smiles like this is a honeymoon and not a hostage situation. "I take care of what's mine."

My stomach turns, but I keep my face still. That's the game now. Just the dead calm that lives in the space between survival and something worse.

His fingers drag one last path down my cheek, slow and possessive, like he's branding me with touch. Then he steps back, grabbing his keys from his pocket.

"Oh, and Doll?"

I lift my chin, because even now—even cornered, and bloodied —I will never be small again.

He grins. That same terrifying, perfect politician grin. The one he wore when I thought he was just charming. Not a monster wrapped in silk and way too much cologne.

"Don't try to leave," he says, keeping his voice light. "You wouldn't want to ruin the progress we've made, now would you."

The door clicks shut behind him, and I hear the lock slide into place and I'm left standing in the wreckage of his psychotic episode, wondering how the hell I'm going to survive the next hour.

I wait until his footsteps fade, then I move straight to the corner. To the duffle bag he so generously "packed" for me.

The zipper groans, and when I pull it open—I wish I could say I was shocked. But instead, I just stand there, staring at a pile of delicate, barely-there lace that looks like it belongs in a bougie bachelor party gift basket, not my emergency escape plan.

Oh good. Lingerie. Nothing says you're being held hostage by a narcissist with a god complex like six thousand dollars of see-through silk.

I want to cry.

Instead, I pull out the top piece—a blood-red slip that screams power and fuck-you elegance. I'd wear this for Steven, easy. But for Frank? The thought makes me want to claw my own skin off and be done with it.

"Ah yes," I mutter. "The 'I may have bruises, but at least my nipples are festive' collection."

I dig deeper. *Shocking, more lace.* There's some strappy, bondage-adjacent thing I couldn't figure out how to wear sober—let alone while being emotionally waterboarded. I don't see any jeans, or shirts. There's no real clothes, and certainly nothing I actually own.

Just panties that could double as dental floss and a robe. He didn't grab my clothes, he replaced them. This is a fucking fantasy, and it's one I will *not* be participating in. I slam the bag shut and the zipper catches my finger and I hiss, pressing it to my lips.

Perfect. Love that. What's next—a papercut on a Bible? Razor burn in the shape of his initials? Maybe a corset that tightens every time I disobey. *Okay, maybe I'm taking it a little too far.*

I head for the bathroom desperate for space, for something that isn't him, but I stop cold in the doorway.

My reflection stares back—red cheek, makeup smudged like regret, lip split and eyes hollow. But none of that registers as I inch closer to get a better look. *As if that would help.*

Every strand on my head is darker than they've ever been.

No fucking way.

I lift a shaking hand to my head, threading my fingers through the pieces like maybe I'm wrong. Maybe this is just the lighting blurring my vision and my white side isn't just erased like it was never there.

He dyed my hair.

He touched me.

That mother fucker touched me while I was out.

My scalp starts to itch like his fingers are still there. Like, what the fuck? What was he doing? Parting strands and smearing color all over them while I laid there like a corpse in a salon chair?

I gag. My hand flies to my mouth, but it's too late. I'm already dry-heaving into the sink.

He's trying to erase me, one personality trait at a time.

Oh my God.

I clutch the edge of the counter, knuckles going white. The rage is back—sharp and volcanic.

"I will kill him," I whisper.

The words sound shaky, at best. I grip the sink harder, trying to hold onto something—anything—but my mind is unraveling faster than I can stitch it back together.

What does he want from me? I can't remember enough to piece it together. Just flashes. Smells. And that stupid, broken reel of memory keeps skipping.

And what about Steven?

Did he know? Was he part of it? Did he come to what, just finish the job?

I can't even think about him without tripping over the mess of my own feelings. And if I start thinking about my feelings for him— nope.

It's a straight shot to self-destruction. A full sprint toward heartbreak with a knife in my back and his name carved into the blade.

Oh God.

Sarah.

My heart lurches.

She'll come looking. She has to. She'll blow the whole fucking city up trying or at least raise enough hell to get someone's attention.

*Unless he already...*No. No. Don't go there.

Panic claws up my throat like it's trying to choke me from the inside. *Oh fuck. Oh fuck. Oh fuck.*

I slap the water on my face, trying to snap myself out of it, but all it does is remind me I'm still here. Still trapped. I press both palms to the counter and inhale, slowly.

Get it the fuck together.

If I want to make it out of here alive, I don't get the luxury of breaking down.

I lock eyes with my reflection again. "Well?" I whisper. "Got a plan, or just gonna keep bleeding until he fucks you into submission or kills you? Because that is *not* fucking happening."

I rub my arms, scanning the room like it's gonna cough up answers. Maybe somewhere between the overpriced decor and the scent of control, I'll find something more helpful than whatever advice they give the FBI's Most Gaslit Woman of the Year.

He's packed me away like a porcelain doll that he wants wrapped in lace and silence, ready to ship off to god knows where.

I may look like a doll, but I've got teeth. And if he thinks I'm playing dress-up in his psychosexual fairytale, he's about to learn what happens when you put a wolf in silk.

That's the spirit.

If he wants to play dirty, two can play at that game. I turn on my heel and head to the dresser. If he packed me a bag full of lingerie, maybe he stocked the drawers with something useful.

The top one creaks open like a horror movie cue, and my stomach flips. It's full of new clothes that all have the tags still on. It's just more outfits that scream 'trophy wife' and 'look how well-behaved she is now'.

Neutrals. Silk. Lace.

No black.

I try the second drawer and it's worse. It's all pajamas. Or at least his version of them—if you define sleepwear as slinky, see-through things a billionaire buys his mistress before flying home to his wife.

I hold one up and actually snort. It's sleeveless, translucent, and stitched together with enough bad intentions to make even a mannequin blush.

The third drawer makes my blood pressure spike.

Accessories.

Pearl hairpins. Silk scrunchies. A velvet choker that practically vibrates with the word obedient. I shut it fast enough to rattle the handles.

"Jesus, Frank. All this effort and not one bulletproof escape rope?"

I don't even realize I'm moving until I'm already storming into the bathroom. I start scanning the space like a crime scene investigator on caffeine.

If I find a perfume bottle labeled Stockholm Syndrome, I swear to God...instead, I find tampons. A toothbrush. And a brand-new razor.

As if a man who slaps me one minute and kisses my forehead the next gets to hand-select my shaving tools.

God forbid your hostage has stubble.

I hold it for a second—then toss it straight into the trash and it lands with a soft thunk. I stare at it like it might jump back out and crawl across the floor with a little bow on top. And then... I have an idea.

If he thinks he can just dye my hair—and erase everything that feels like me—then he doesn't get to keep any part of it.

If he wants a version of me he can mold, he's going to learn the hard way—I'll carve myself into something else first.

If I sit around doing nothing I'll have time to think, and then I'll remember the way Stevens's fingers brushed my jaw when he said I was his.

If I think, I'll spiral.

And right now, I can't afford to spiral. Not when I'm still a hostage, not when my memory is playing goddamn hopscotch.

God.

He was the only person who looked at me like I was a fucking storm and still chose to walk into it. He touched me like I was breakable and brutal at the same time and always kissed me like he was starving. *Do you know what that does to a girl?*

He took me apart like he already knew how to put me back together. And now, I don't even know where he is, or if he's alive.

My thoughts go straight to wondering if Frank was telling the truth? What if I was just leverage?

I want to laugh, but the sound gets lodged somewhere between my ribs and my rage. Because even if it's true—even if every look, every touch, every whispered *mine* was a lie—Steven didn't buy me.

Frank did.

And that alone tells me everything I need to know.

Whether Frank's lying or not, whether Steven's a monster or the only man who's ever touched me like I was real—I'm still here, locked in a fucking dollhouse. If I don't get out now...I might not get another shot.

I move fast. Checking under the bed, behind the dresser, in the closet, the windows, nothing.

I don't have my phone, but I do have an uncanny ability to lie to men who underestimate me.

37

"It's not the pain that gets you killed."
(It's the time it buys someone else.)

Steven

The room is too quiet. It's pressing in on my ears and now even my own breath sounds wrong. It's slow and not nearly as shallow as it should be considering I woke up in a pool of my own blood.

Again.

The light above me flickers. They've been drugging me—needle to the neck, needle to the thigh—until time turns to soup. But I'm pretty sure it's been at least three days—give or take a few hours.

The light shifted twice through the crack in the ceiling. The guard's only changed three times. Same footsteps. Same routine. Predictable fuckers. That's how people die.

They haven't brought in any food. Just water. Every second that passes is one more that she might be in his fucking hands.

My hands are still cuffed behind the chair, and my ankles are strapped to the legs—tighter this time. I guess they learned their lesson after I snapped the zip ties, broke one guard's windpipe and caved in the other's skull with a rusted pipe.

My ribs are bruised to hell. My face is split open and my right eye's swollen shut. I can still taste the blood in the back of my throat from when they broke my nose—again.

I've had worse. But I've never been this fucking angry.

I flex my wrists again as the cuffs bite into skin that's already flayed open. But it doesn't matter. Pain's a language I speak fluently. I try the same move I've used six times—twist, breathe, rotate my shoulder down and out—but the angle's wrong. The chair doesn't budge.

Fuck.

I close my eyes, and she's there. Burned into the backs of my eyelids like a brand I'll never get rid of. That smart fucking mouth, always running until I shut it the only way she really wanted. That sharp, wicked smile—half brat, half dare—begging me to lose control.

I see her crawling for me, chin tilted, eyes blazing like she knows I'll break her for it and wants it anyway. I hear that little whimper she makes when she's trying not to beg. The one that ruins me. The one I've been hearing every time the drugs wear off and I'm stuck in this body that won't fucking move.

I can still feel her. The heat of her cunt wrapped around me. The tremble in her thighs. The way her fingers clawed at my chest like she wanted to tear me open and live inside the wreckage. I see her flushed and breathless, whispering *mine* like she forgot it wasn't supposed to mean anything.

I think about how she looked at me that night on the cabin floor —like I was the only thing holding her together and the only thing tearing her apart. I didn't mean to care. I didn't even notice it happening until it was too fucking late.

I think about how I got here—drugged, bleeding, chained to a wall—wondering if she's okay. Wondering if he's hurt her. And for the first time in years, I'm not thinking about revenge or blood or the goddamn plan.

I'm thinking about her. And that's when the pain stops registering as pain. That's when it turns into something meaner.

She has no idea what he is. No clue what he's capable of. Hell —she doesn't even know who she is.

But I do.

I yank harder, and pain screams up my arm, white-hot and electric, but I don't stop. Blood slicks my wrist because of the cuffs that are currently rubbing my skin raw.

Let it fucking hurt. I need the pain. It's the only thing anchoring me to the present. If it hurts, I'm awake. If I'm awake, this is not some hallucination bleeding into my head like the nightmares that haunted me after the warehouse.

I should've called Travis back. Should've looked harder. Dug deeper. There were signs—and I fucking missed every single one of them because I was distracted.

Looking back, all the signs were there. The cracks in her voice. The way she flinched when she thought I wasn't watching. But I ignored all of it—too far gone, already drowning in the feel of her.

God, I was so fucking sure I had him.

And if Frank—

My head jerks up as the door opens. I straighten immediately, and the blood from my lip slides down my throat, but I try to keep my heartbeat level.

Frank steps into the room wearing dark slacks, and a tailored shirt with the sleeves rolled up. There's no visible weapon—but I know better. He always hides his teeth until it's too late. That smile curves over his mouth and he looks like a fucking psychopath.

"Stevie," he says, like we're catching up over drinks. He clucks his tongue. "You're not looking so great."

He starts to circle the chair like a shark scenting blood in the water.

"You're probably wondering how long it's been," he muses. "What you've missed. Who you've failed."

I keep my face blank, but my jaw locks tight enough to grind bone. Every second she's not in my arms is another second I'm counting in bullets.

"Don't worry," he says, stepping toward the table across from me. "I'm not going to kill you today."

He taps something on the table, and a screen flickers to life on the far wall. It's grainy at first. Then—

Fuck.

My chest caves in as Ani appears—standing dead center in the bedroom, her back to the camera. She's not moving much, but then she reaches for the robe.

No. I don't want to see this, yet I watch every second of it. Helpless. Bound. Breathing like I've been stabbed in the lungs while she shrugs out of her clothes.

My pulse claws at my throat as she steps into a red outfit, sliding one strap up her shoulder with a grace that makes me feel like I'm being gutted from the inside out. I know her. Whatever he's threatened her with offscreen was enough to get her to change, and it makes me sick. I've killed men for less than watching her like this.

Frank isn't watching the footage. He's watching me, smiling.

"I didn't think she'd wear it either," he says. "She held out, you know. For days. She's got fire, that one."

My body stays still because it has to. But inside—I'm burning.

"She looks so delicious," Frank adds, a little too casually and too fucking pleased with himself. "I'd even go as far to say she likes it here. Then again, she always did have a thing for powerful men."

I keep my expression locked down. But it costs me. Every second I don't look back at that screen costs me something I'll never get back.

I want to drag him across this room and beat the truth out of his teeth.

He watches me, waiting for any type of reaction or weakness, anything he can use. Then, with a flick of his wrist, the screen cuts to black.

"She'll be prettier when she cries," he says, light as air. "They always are. But I'll give it a few days. Soften her up. I'll enjoy breaking her a little slower."

Frank sighs and circles me again, and I can tell that he's pissed he's not getting the reaction he wanted.

"You know," he says, "I was going to kill you right away. Honestly, that was the plan all along. Drug you, bleed you out, and dump what's left." He leans in closer. "But then I thought... why not let you watch?"

I keep my eyes on the concrete. On the blood. On the bolts holding the chair in place.

"I think I'm going to let you sit here for a few more days. Give you a front-row seat. Maybe pipe in the audio when she begs. Maybe show you what she looks like when she finally calls me sir, and learns her place."

There's something that crosses his face—sharp and fleeting, but I catch it. Cold, barely-leashed frustration. The kind that comes from trying to tame something that refuses to break. He needs her alive. That's the problem. And it's written all over his face.

"She's going to learn to love the cage I give her." He steps back, brushing invisible dust off his cuff.

"You know what the best part is?" he says, pausing at the door. "She still thinks I bought her to fuck her."

He shrugs. "Sweet, isn't it? That little thread of hope she's still holding onto."

He pauses in the doorway, smile spreading slowly like he knows exactly what he just detonated.

I've never wanted to kill a man more than I do right now.

"Her grandfather wasn't just some rich old man in Puerto Rico. He ran half the criminal underworld from a cliffside villa with ocean views and a wine cellar full of severed fingers. Every drug route, every arms deal, every bribe and contract—they all went through him."

He lets that hang, like he's savoring the reveal.

"She doesn't just own a little money or a beach house. She owns it all." He leans in closer, voice barely a whisper. "She's the heir to a multi-billion dollar empire. Blood, land, and all the control. And the best part?" A cruel smirk curves his mouth. "She has no fucking idea who she really is or what she just inherited. What I will inherit."

He taps two fingers to his temple, looking smug.

My spine goes ice cold. I swear if this mother fucker keeps talking, I'm going to make him wish he was dead when I get my hands on him.

"And that, Steven, is why you're still breathing." He tilts his head, almost like he's explaining a simple math problem. "Because if she sees your dead body too soon, she won't cooperate as easily."

He straightens, brushing his knuckles along his jaw like he's admiring himself in a mirror. "Get some rest. You're going to need it for the finale."

The lock clicks behind him, and this time, the silence doesn't stretch. It settles. Heavy and final. Like a grave.

The words hit, but it's the way he says them—like he knows her. He thinks she's soft, he believes I'm nothing more than leverage to twist her into submission, but he has no idea. No idea who she is when she snaps. No idea what she'll do if he pushes her too far.

If she breaks—it won't be into pieces. It'll be into something worse. And I'll have to watch the girl I'm falling for burn the fucking world just to make the pain stop.

That's what he's not ready for. And that's the only reason I'm still alive.

I let my head fall back against the chair, eyes locked on the far corner—where the last camera blinked out three hours ago. I killed the first guard they sent in here with my fucking teeth.

I don't know if they replaced him, but it doesn't matter, they're sloppy now. I can feel it. They think I've cracked because that's what they always think when you bleed enough.

I hear two sets of footsteps, and I can tell one of them is dragging their feet. That's the one I'm going to kill first.

They always come at the same time. Every twelve hours. They

inject me with whatever cocktail Frank thinks will keep me compliant.

I won't be taking it today.

I shift in the chair as the cuffs bite deep, but the left side's loose enough that If I dislocate my thumb again, I can slip out. It'll hurt like hell, but I've walked through worse.

The door opens and they walk in laughing—loud and careless, like they've already forgotten where they are. One of them reeks of cheap liquor and cheaper intelligence.

Perfect.

The taller one steps closer and crouches, reaching for my jaw. His fingers are clumsy, fumbling for control, a needle trembling in his grip.

"Look at you," he mutters. "Big bad killer. Now you're just meat in a chair."

I smile.

It's subtle, but it's enough to make him hesitate. And that's all I need. My left hand jerks free with a wet snap—thumb dislocating as I twist the loosened cuff upward and slam the jagged metal straight into his throat. He chokes, gurgling, and drops the needle.

The second one lunges for the door, but he's too slow. I kick my legs forward, hard enough to break the tension in the ropes. The chair scrapes with me, dragging across the floor as I throw my weight sideways. Pain burns up my calves, but I don't stop. I ram the back leg of the chair straight into his shin and he howls.

I use the momentum to twist again, and crash to the ground with the first guy's body still tangled in mine. Something cracks— bone or metal, I don't know. Don't care. I'm already moving.

By the time I get my restraints off, one of them is out cold, and the other's twitching, half-conscious.

I wipe the blood from my cheek with the edge of his sleeve, then snap his neck without hesitation.

I work fast—because it's only a matter of time before someone checks the cameras and more of them come pouring in. I strip them both down, hands moving quickly searching their pockets, holsters, and boots. One's got a rusted butterfly knife—useless, but light. The other's carrying a compact Glock. I take both.

I pick up the security badge that's stuck to his chest, the plastic slick with sweat. The name reads M. Diaz—generic enough to be fake. Could be real. Doesn't matter.

I pocket it anyway.

The smaller guard had a comm that's still active, so I flick the channel to low, earpiece only, keeping the volume just loud enough to catch the static between garbled bursts of bored check-ins and caffeine complaints.

The hallway outside my room is dim, quiet, and smells like copper and bleach. I don't take the main path, I double back through a laundry chute, then through a boiler room. I've never been in this building before, but I know how compounds work. They always hide the good shit behind keycard doors and reinforced glass.

I follow the low hum of electronics until I find the security office. It's small and cramped, and there's barely enough room to stand. There's a desk, a chair, and a coffee cup still steaming like the guy just sat down. One man's at the console, headphones in, eyes locked on the monitors—completely fucking unaware.

I slide behind him and press the blade to his throat. "Not a sound," I whisper.

He freezes as I pull the headset off him.

"Where's Frank?"

He swallows. "He's—he's not here. He already left."

"Left for where?"

"I—I don't know. He left right after he came out of your room. Took two men and the Suburban."

I press the blade a little deeper, just enough to draw a line of blood. "Try again."

He stammers. "I—I swear. He doesn't tell us where. He just—he goes dark when he moves."

That part, I believe. He's a paranoid fucker who's really good at covering his tracks. But I'm sure his people always forget something. I scan the console, looking at the twelve screens.

"I want the access logs. Show me every device that pinged this network in the last twenty-four hours."

"I—I can't. I mean I'd have to—"

I pull out the Glock and put it against his temple. "You've got three seconds."

He fumbles a bit but manages to pull up a list—addresses, IPs, and device types. Most of it looks like junk. Just security panels, guard-issued tablets, and burner phones that rotate every day. But one of them stands out. It's a private line with an encrypted access tunnel—it has to be Frank's personal server.

"Can it reach external lines?" I ask.

The tech nods. "Yeah. But it's locked behind biometric—"

"Password?"

"I don't have—"

I slam his head into the console. Not hard enough to kill him—just enough to make sure he knows I could. Then I scan the desk. There's a thumb scanner, a backup keyboard, and what looks like the internal shell code running behind everything. Frank built it tight, but not tight enough.

I move to the side computer, find the back access point, and reroute through it using the admin override—the kind you only know exists if you've torn apart systems like this before. It takes a minute. Maybe less. Then I'm in.

"Travis. Open line. Emergency protocol black."

A prompt appears, then the chat opens.

[UNKNOWN]: THIS BETTER BE YOU.
[YOU]: IT'S ME.
[UNKNOWN]: HOW BAD?
[YOU]: I'M AMAZING. HE HAS HER.
[UNKNOWN]: YOU SURE?
[YOU]: SAME CAMERA RIG YOU FLAGGED LAST YEAR.
[UNKNOWN]: JESUS. OKAY. WHAT DO YOU HAVE?
[YOU]: HARD DRIVE. PERSONAL ACCESS FEEDS. LOOKS LIKE HE'S SETTING UP A TRANSFER.
[UNKNOWN]: FUCK.
[YOU]: PLAN?
[UNKNOWN]: MEET POINT BRAVO IN TWO HOURS. BRING THE DRIVE. DON'T DIE.

I kill the feed.

The tech is groaning now, dragging himself toward the radio like it'll save him.

"Wrong move," I mutter, and put a bullet in the base of his skull.

I grab the drive, the med kit, a burner pistol, and a black jacket hanging on the hook behind the door. My hands move without thought—muscle memory built on too many exits. But my mind's already ahead of me. I need to get to her before Frank puts a ring on her finger and calls it fate. *Or worse.*

I move through the corridor behind the server room keeping my footsteps silent. The hallway branches left toward what I'm assuming is the exit, and the one to the right goes toward what looks like a private office. I should keep moving. Time's running out, but something stops me.

That same sick, sharp instinct that's been twisting under my skin since the second she walked into my life. So I go right.

The door's locked, but it only takes a few seconds to bypass. I slip inside the small room, and the first thing I see is a wall of screens—feeds, reports, maps. Intel from across the country.

The second is a file left open on the desk. I flip it open and stop breathing. There are two faces that are burned into the back of my mind. My grip tightens until the paper curls, my pulse roaring in my ears.

"You fucking bastard," I whisper. "There's no fucking way."

I snap the file shut and shove it into my jacket, heart pounding like I'm already in the fallout. I take the back stairwell down to the garage and find one of Frank's men there—leaning against a pillar, smoking, and muttering into a comm.

It's the same bastard who spit on me during the first round of being beaten. He turns, and freezes. Recognition hits a second too late, but I move faster. My fist slams into his throat, the crunch is satisfying as he stumbles, reaching for his gun, but I'm already behind him. Glock pressed to his spine.

"On your knees," I say calmly. "Or I break them."

He drops.

"Please—"

I press the barrel to his chin.

"You want to know what the difference is between you and me?" I whisper.

He nods, shaking.

"I kill for a reason." I pull the trigger. Twice. One through the head, and one through the heart. Blood paints the pillar behind him and I drag the body to the center of the garage. Stripping off his shirt I carve two words into his chest with the same blade he used to cut my shoulder.

She's mine.

38

"Don't aim for the heart."
(Aim for what they'd die to protect)

Ani

The door swings open without a knock and I shoot to my feet, my pulse spikes so fast it makes my vision blur.

Frank walks in wearing a white button-down, with the sleeves rolled to his elbows, and his slacks are tailored to perfection.

"Anianne," he says, smiling. Drawing my name out like it means something to him.

His gaze drops to my hair. And I see the exact second it hits him. He stops mid-step and just like that, the mask cracks.

My long, dark hair is gone. What's left is a little choppy. I hacked it off with the razor I found in the bathroom. It barely brushes my jaw, and the ends are a little uneven, but I kinda like it.

"You changed it," he says. "I didn't give you permission to do that." The smile doesn't drop—but it sharpens. "You think cutting your hair makes you harder to control?"

His voice stays level, but there's a shadow curling behind it. "That hair wasn't yours to change, and you'll be punished for that."

He takes a step closer. "That hair was mine to look at. Mine to pull. And mine to bury my face in, when you learned how to behave."

I literally almost barf. Right there on the floor. I try to keep my mouth shut because I don't really want to be slapped again. He takes another step and the air is folding in on itself, thick with something hot and dangerous.

"You're still mine," he says. "Even if I have to rip you apart to prove it."

I keep my mouth shut, even though every cell in my body is screaming to throat-punch him and set the entire fucking house on fire. But I keep my face blank. Because if I flinch, he wins.

He suddenly glances around the room like he's here for a goddamn tour. "Anyway, thought I'd come check in," he says casually. "Make sure everything fits."

His eyes drop to the red lace that I covered up with a robe and tied shut.

"I didn't pick that one for no reason," he adds, looking me up and down, smiling like some pervert. "It's my favorite."

I snort, because there's no way I'm keeping my mouth shut through this bullshit.

"Are you always this desperate to see a woman in lingerie, or is that just why you had to buy one?"

He laughs like he's delighted I'm still fighting and he enjoys it more this way, but I see the twitch in his eye.

"Oh, sweetheart. I didn't buy you for your sass." He pauses for a beat. "But it's a fun bonus. For now."

He steps forward causing me to step back. His voice drops as he closes the distance.

"Careful," he murmurs. "I'd hate to restrain you again so soon."

I smile. "Try it."

For a moment, his expression cracks. Then he laughs. "You always were feisty."

He walks over to the table near the window as someone brings in a tray. He lifts the silver dome and reveals a steak, some mashed potatoes, and champagne.

I haven't eaten in... well, all day, and suddenly feel light-headed. Apparently being abducted, threatened, and handed a drawer full of crotchless lace takes more energy than I remembered.

My stomach growls loud enough to echo, and I roll my eyes, because of course my body would betray me right now. *Really?*

I eye the food suspiciously. It smells incredible, which only pisses me off more. He would make the meal a five-star plate while the room feels like a coffin with designer throw pillows.

"You thought of everything," I mutter, crossing my arms. "All that's missing is a tiara and a cyanide pill."

I look over and he's smug as usual, like he didn't orchestrate a whole goddamn hostage fantasy and cast himself as both captor and romantic lead.

I scowl. "I thought you said we were leaving."

He tilts his head slightly, and the look he gives me sends shivers down my spine. He looks like he's about to snap.

"I changed my mind," he says. "New plans."

"That fast, huh?" I raise an eyebrow. "So what—you're just gonna keep me here? Feed me? Dress me up like a sex doll until I forget what it smells like outside?"

His smile tightens a little more. "Dramatic much?"

"Delusional much?" I take a step forward, dropping my voice. "You don't get to just play house, Frank. You don't get to slap me around, lock me up, and then change your mind like we're rescheduling a lunch date."

He's still for a beat too long, then he throws his head back and laughs.

"You're right," he says, crossing to the table and setting down the silver lid with theatrical calm.

I blink. *Wait—what? I am?*

"I don't get to touch you. Or choose for you. Or make you mine." He lifts the champagne flute, holding it out like he's about to make a toast. "I already did."

I'm going to fucking kill him. I stare at the glass like it might explode, then I look at the food again.

I'm so fucking hungry I could cry, but what if it's poisoned? What if this is the test—wait me out, starve me down until I'm desperate enough to eat whatever they hand me... and it kills me. I hate that he thinks he's winning, and right now, with the way my stomach is growling, he is.

Fuck it.

I walk toward the table, picking up the knife, and slide into the seat like I'm the one in charge. I slowly cut the steak, never breaking eye contact. He watches me with a pleased look on his face, and yup, I still want to throat punch him. But I want to survive more.

"Don't get comfortable," I say before taking a bite.

"We'll start fresh tomorrow." He chuckles, setting down the champagne, and walks to the door. "And we'll deal with the hair. Actions have consequences, Anianne. You'll learn that soon enough."

The door clicks shut behind him and I'm left chewing a perfect piece of medium rare steak with murder in my heart and a knife still in my hand. I'm actually surprised he left me with a knife.

I'm not above eating the enemy's food. I'll take his dinner. I'll wear his lace. I'll swallow his champagne and smile while I plan how to gut him with the dessert fork. But if he so much as touches me, I'll do whatever I have to do.

I polish off the steak and leave the champagne untouched, cuz yuck. Then I sit back in the chair, staring at the empty plate wondering if I just played right into his hands.

I stand and start pacing. I need to figure out how to get out of here. And now. I'm now so familiar with this room that I know there's eight steps from the bed to the door, ten if I drag my feet.

I do it again, and again. Talking to myself the entire time, trying not to crawl out of my skin.

"Well, Ani," I mutter, dragging my hands through my hair, "you've really outdone yourself this time."

I glance around the room. Frank's version of luxury is all

marble and male fantasy. *Barf.* I check the camera in the corner again, and it's still blinking. "Hope the view was worth it, you sick fuck."

I check the whole bathroom for cameras, but don't find any. So they're either hidden, or there aren't any.

"We're going to survive this. And when we do... we're going to burn this place to the fucking ground too."

I wake up to the smell of coffee and clean linen and for a moment, I forget where I am. I don't remember falling asleep.

I look over to see a tray on the dresser and pull off the lid to find croissants, strawberries and some scrambled eggs. With a fucking mimosa. Because apparently I'm in captivity at the Ritz.

I roll my eyes.

"Oh good," I mutter, stretching. "Room service. Is this where the robe comes with a monogrammed collar and a bullet in my spine?"

The camera blinks, and I flip it off again. The door opens without any warning, startling me enough that I almost fall out of bed.

He's dressed like he's hosting another brunch instead of holding me hostage in his cream sweater, dark pants, and his sleeves casually pushed up.

"Good morning, Ani." His voice is warm. Back to the Frank I've known for months. The one who played prince charming, who brought me gifts, and flirted relentlessly with me at the bar.

I pull the blankets up slowly, trying to hide as much of me as I can. "Wow. The romantic breakfast tray. Did you get that idea from the same handbook that says to slap a woman before bed?"

His smile barely flickers. *I really should stop provoking him, but honestly, I just can't help it.*

"You must be starving," he says instead, stepping in like he owns the breath coming out of my mouth. "I thought we could eat together. Talk."

"Talk?" I echo, sliding my legs off the bed and planting my bare feet on the cold floor. "About what? Whether I prefer ropes or zip ties next time?"

He laughs. And for just a second—I almost see the man I once thought I liked. He gestures toward the tray. "You still like strawberries, right?"

I glare. "Cute. Did you look that up before or after you had me kidnapped?"

He takes a slow breath, and I can tell he's trying to stay calm. "You don't have to fight me, Ani. This can be easy."

I smile, but inside I'm picturing all the ways to stab him. "Easy?"

"You know, I've been patient," he whispers. "More patient than you deserve."

"That supposed to scare me?"

"No," he says, and the mask finally cracks. "But this should." He backhands the tray, and the food goes flying, crashing against the far wall.

I flinch as he steps closer, eyes dark now—real Frank in full fucking bloom.

"You want to talk back like a brat? Fine. But don't forget— you're here because I let you stay breathing."

My throat tightens. But I smile anyway. "Maybe you should just finish the job."

He grabs my face, and his fingers dig into my jaw hard enough to bruise.

"You still think you're tough, don't you?" he chuckles. "You think this is some power struggle?"

His breath is hot against my cheek now. "This is your life now, Ani. You are mine. And you will obey."

For one horrifying second, I see something unhinged in his eyes. He lets me go with a shove, and I stumble back.

He straightens his sleeves like nothing happened.

"We'll try again later," he says calmly. "I'm sure you'll be more... cooperative by then."

He leaves without another word and I realize something I should've known from the start. I underestimated him.

I pace for hours. Back and forth across the hardwood, bare feet slapping the floor in an uneven rhythm that makes my skin itch. There's no clock in the room and I don't have my phone. The only sense of time I have is the light outside.

I'm not afraid of him. At least, that's what I tell myself.

Again. And again. And again.

Somewhere between lap twenty-seven or fifty, I hear footsteps and I freeze near the closet. Because if I'm going to die, I'll do it standing. The door slams open and I know the second I see his face —he's done pretending.

Frank's jaw is tight, his hair slightly out of place. He looks like he's been running his hands through it. His eyes are black but he doesn't speak. He just shuts the door behind him and locks it.

Don't ask me how I know—call it gut instinct, survival reflex, whatever—but something happened. He's pissed, more than usual, and there's this edge to him now. Coiled tight, like he's trying not to snap. Like someone fucked up, and I'm about to be the one who pays for it.

He crosses the room in two strides. I don't have time to even flinch before his hand is around my throat, slamming me against the wall so hard the frame beside me falls and shatters.

The air leaves my lungs in a rush, and I'm clawing his arms as my airway closes.

"You don't get it do you?"

I try to speak, but it's just a rasp, and he tightens his grip.

"I tried to be gentle," he growls, vibrating with rage. "I tried to give you soft. Tried to give you a choice."

I blink as the back spots dance across my vision.

"But you didn't want soft, did you?" he snarls. "I see the bruises all over you."

He lets go and I collapse to the floor, coughing and gasping for air, hands on my knees as the room spins.

He paces, then turns, facing me again. "I gave you the chance to make this easy."

I lift my head, voice hoarse. "Yeah? And I gave you the chance to get a fucking hobby."

He grabs my arm and yanks me to my feet, throwing me onto the bed like I'm weightless. For half a second, I think he's going to climb on, and this is the moment I'm going to snap. But he doesn't. *Thank God.*

Instead, he just stands at the foot of the bed. Chest heaving, with his hands flexing at his sides.

"You'll remember this," he says quietly, almost to himself. "You'll remember how I had no choice."

Then he turns to the closet. His movements are calm now, calculated—like he's flipped the switch back to his favorite setting. He pulls out a floor-length black dress that looks like something you'd bury a mafia bride in, and tosses it on the bed beside me.

"You'll wear that tonight."

My voice is raw when I speak. "And if I don't?"

He smiles. And not in a charming way. "Then you'll wear bruises instead. And nothing else."

He moves toward the door, unlocking it with a click, and pauses. "You've got an hour to clean yourself up. Don't be late."

When I don't answer, he chuckles. "Wear the dress. Or don't," he adds. "Either way, I'm taking what's mine tonight."

Then he's gone.

Suddenly I can't breathe and every nerve in my body goes rigid.

I need to get the fuck out of here. Now. Before he decides he's going to act on that and doesn't need consent.

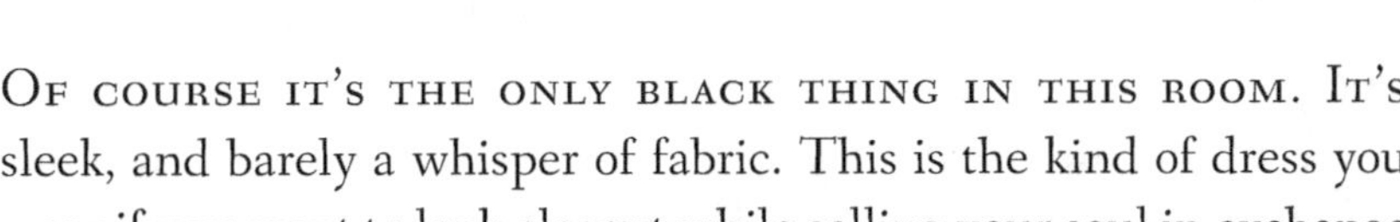

Of course it's the only black thing in this room. It's sleek, and barely a whisper of fabric. This is the kind of dress you wear if you want to look elegant while selling your soul in exchange for a yacht and a steady supply of imported champagne.

Which, coincidentally, is also what Frank smells like.

I hold it up between two fingers, it has thin straps, and a deep plunging neckline. There's also a slit up the side high enough to start a conversation. There's no way to wear this without being seen.

God, I hate him. How could I have ever been charmed by that fuck wad?

I toss the dress onto the bed and flop down beside it, flinging my arms dramatically overhead like I'm auditioning for the lead in Girl Who's Definitely Not Having a Mental Breakdown.

"Great," I mutter to the ceiling. "Look at me. Playing dress up for the man who's most likely going to kill me."

The camera blinks in the corner and I flip it off again. It's practically foreplay at this point, but I get up anyway because I'm not stupid. I know what happens if I don't.

I've seen enough Lifetime thrillers to know that if a lunatic tells you to wear a dress and you show up in sweats, you don't make it to the second act.

So I put it on. One leg, then the other. And the whole time I'm muttering to myself like I'm possessed.

"It's fine. This is normal. Totally normal to be dressing up for your kidnapper-slash-stalker."

The dress hugs my hips like it wants to apologize for everything my body's been through. *Yeah, well. I don't accept. The shitty thing is, I look fucking amazing.*

I reach for the perfume, spritzing my neck. I might as well smell good, especially if I'm about to die. I want to spray it in my palm and wipe it under my eye like war paint, but if I'm going to stab him, I need to be able to see.

"Dinner's at seven," I whisper mockingly to myself. "Don't be late."

I flip off the camera again for good measure, then I turn and start walking to the door. I'm pissed off, dressed like a sexy funeral ornament, and very much not in the mood to play house with the man who kidnapped me.

I look around for the clock that doesn't exist, then glance at the blinking red light in the corner that definitely does.

"Okay," I mutter, "I was told dinner was at seven."

I look at the door and roll my eyes. "Oh my God. How am I supposed to know when it's seven if I don't have a fucking clock. You dumb, fucking idiot."

I storm toward the door and rattle the knob.

"Heeellooo?" I shout, knocking so hard my fists hurt. "How am I supposed to be on time for dinner if you lock me in the fucking room?"

No answer.

Cool.

Love that for me.

I kick the bottom of the door lightly with my heel—not hard enough to hurt, obviously. But just enough to communicate that I'm this close to setting the curtains on fire out of sheer principle.

Finally, after another thirty seconds of me muttering to myself and threatening to scream, the lock clicks and the door swings open revealing some guy in black tactical casuals with the blandest face I've ever seen and a smile so polite it could be AI-generated.

"Right this way, miss."

Miss?

He says it like I'm not being held hostage by the world's most emotionally constipated narcissist. I look at him. Then the hallway. Then back at him.

"You gonna escort me with a taser or just vibes?" I ask sweetly.

He doesn't answer. Just gestures down the hallway like this is a job he didn't read the fine print on. I sigh, and step out.

"Lead the way, henchman number four," I mutter. "Let's go see what the king of daddy issues cooked up for dinner."

Not a single crack in his features. *Tough crowd.*

I trail behind my escort—Mr. Tactical Boredom—as my heels click against the floor. Of course Frank added heels to the goth barbie look.

I clear my throat. Loudly. But get no response from my escort.

"Do you guys get paid hourly," I ask, "or just in morally compromising bonuses and benefits?"

He just keeps walking.

I sigh. "Okay, cool, no talking. I get it. We must have similar childhoods."

I take a few more steps. Then I glance sideways, smiling sweetly. "So... does he make all his prisoners dress for dinner?"

That gets me a glance. Barely a flick of his eyes, but it's there. One tiny sliver of attention that almost resembles...pity?

Huh. I'll just tuck that away for later or I'll start crying.

That's the kind of look you give someone heading into a room they don't walk out of.

Can't wait.

I square my shoulders, lifting my chin, and follow him like I'm not already counting exits, shadow lines, and weapon potential. Frank might've picked the dress, but I still decide how the night ends.

When the door opens into a room that looks like it belongs in a magazine, I suddenly feel sick. There's candles lit on a table long enough to seat a small army of devoted followers—except there's only one person sitting at it.

Frank.

And he looks pissed.

I take one step in and feel the temperature drop ten degrees and my guard steps aside without a word. *Pussy.*

I must have a death wish, because I smile. That's what we do when we're about to get murdered in luxury eveningwear, right? *Fake it till you make it. Or until the champagne flute cracks across your face.*

"Wow," I say softly. "Romantic. You light all these candles yourself or did one of your minions get a promotion?"

He doesn't move.

Shit.

"You're late," he says.

I take a few steps forward, heels clicking like gunshots across the marble.

"My door was locked," I snap. "Kind of hard to be on time when your kidnapper forgets to include transportation in the fantasy."

He stands slowly and I swallow, but keep my head high. He rounds the table without breaking eye contact. This sure doesn't feel like dinner, it feels like a fucking execution.

"I gave you one rule," he says quietly. "One."

I know I shouldn't keep pushing him, but I have a sneaking suspicion he needs me alive. If I'm wrong, then at least I'm going out with a bang. Because over my dead body am I going to just sit here and take it.

"Right. Show up on time. Don't sass the psycho. Try the wine pairing."

He slaps me. Hard. My head jerks sideways, and the sting is instant. My vision whites out for half a second, but I don't fall.

I straighten slowly and I laugh because if I don't, I might cry. My face is starting to really hurt.

He grabs a fist full of my hair, yanking me forward until I'm inches from his face.

"You want to die here?" he growls. "You want to test how far I'm willing to go to break you?"

I grin through the pain, wondering just how far I'm toeing the line between tough and stupid.

He throws me into the chair at the table. Hard enough that the chair skids back an inch and almost tips over. He's breathing heavy now, and I can see that the vein in his temple is pulsing.

Good. Let him be mad. Mad men make mistakes.

He pours a glass of wine with a hand that's too steady for someone vibrating with rage.

"Drink," he says.

I take the glass, sipping as little as possible, then setting it down. He slams his fist onto the table so hard the glass jumps.

"I could've killed you the night I found you."

"But you didn't."

Silence.

He stares at me like he wants to set me on fire and fuck the ashes. Then he smiles and it's terrifying.

I just need to shut up, chew my food and nod like a good little captive, and pretend I'm one of those mafia wives on Instagram who decorates with gold skulls and thinks emotional abuse is romantic.

I take another sip before I can stop myself. Maybe I've been going about this all wrong. Maybe if I'm drunk, it won't suck as badly. Dangerous logic, I know—slippery slope, this captive shit. But it's easier than acknowledging the chill crawling up my spine like a warning I'm too fucking tired to listen to.

I pick at my plate. Across from me, Frank eats like we're at a fucking gala. Every bite is calculated. It's not just unsettling. It's unnerving in that quiet, crawling way that makes you want to scream just to prove you're still in your own body.

"You always eat like a serial killer?" I ask, stabbing a piece of asparagus.

He doesn't look up. "You always talk when you should shut your fucking mouth?"

Touché.

Yes, Ani. Shut the fuck up.

But my mouth keeps moving. Apparently, sarcasm isn't just my love language it's also my favorite weapon.

"Let me guess—now comes the tragic backstory and the part where I'm supposed to feel flattered?"

That gets his attention.

He sets his utensils down with deliberate calm, then wipes his mouth with his napkin. When he looks up, he's smiling.

"The alley," he says, like I'm supposed to follow his train of thought.

I freeze. The fork is still in my hand, halfway to my plate, but I can't move. My stomach twists—I have a feeling I'm not going to like this. His gaze sharpens like he can hear the question forming in my head.

"You thought that was a coincidence," he says, mocking me. "You thought you just... ran into me. Saved me."

He lets out a quiet laugh, and it's somehow worse than a scream. My grip tightens around the fork as he leans back in his chair, like he's settling in to relive his favorite story.

"I had to make it believable," he says. "It was the best I could come up with, in the time I had. Blood and just enough groaning to sound pitiful. The timing had to be perfect."

I blink. Once. Hard. "You... what?"

He just smiles, tilting his head. I wait for him to say more, to correct himself, to tell me I misheard.

My stomach drops. "You—" My voice falters. "You stabbed yourself?"

His smile sharpens, but he still doesn't answer. Silence stretches so long it turns into dread.

"You stabbed yourself," I repeat, quieter this time—more to myself than him. Like if I say it enough, it'll start making sense.

"I had to get your attention somehow." He shrugs. "Nothing

vital obviously. It was shallow enough to bleed, but deep enough to sell it. And your bleeding heart fucking fell for it."

He grins like I'm supposed to be impressed.

"You knelt down," he adds, voice turning soft and mocking all at once. "Touched me. Whispered, *'It's okay, I've got you.'* You looked so scared, and so sweet."

My stomach flips so violently it's like my body's rejecting the entire scene. I shove the plate away, my appetite suddenly gone.

"Are you seriously proud of that?" I snap, my voice tighter than I want it to be.

"Of course." He doesn't miss a beat. "It worked."

I stare at him while rage burns up my spine like acid. "You faked an attack. You hurt yourself. Just to get my attention."

He raises his glass in a slow, mocking toast. "To fate."

And for a second—I almost laugh. Because what the actual hell is this? A man stabbing himself to win me over? *The bar really is on the floor.*

"You're fucking insane."

He shrugs like I just complimented his tie. "You're just mad I fooled you."

He leans in, propping his elbows on the table, tapping two fingers to his temple. "That was just the day I stopped pretending."

And just like that—something breaks. All I can fucking think is that someone out there stabbed themselves just to get close to me. Beneath the jokes and the sarcasm I like to call a personality, I'm spiraling. Fast.

This man—this thing—just rewrote a memory I've been clinging to like a lifeline. The one night I thought that maybe I'd done something good. Something that made me feel like me. And now he's sitting there, smiling like he wants a thank-you card for weaponizing it.

I reach for my wine—not to drink it. Just to keep my hands busy.

He stabbed himself. For attention. Jesus.

All I did was kneel down and offer a stranger help. But in Frank's world that's apparently as good as a fucking proposal.

I lean forward, matching his intensity, refusing to blink. "You were background noise on my trauma playlist, Frank. I would've helped anyone. That doesn't make you special."

Then his hand shoots out, sweeping his plate, his glass, the entire goddamn centerpiece off the table. The sound of porcelain shattering rings out like gunfire.

I don't flinch, even though I want to. My body's screaming, my skin's crawling, and I feel like I might throw up right here in front of him. But I don't give him that. Because if I do—he wins. And I'd rather choke on my fear than let him taste it.

He stands slowly, chest rising and falling. One hand goes to the back of his neck as he tugs on the collar of his shirt like it's choking him and exhales.

He quickly composes himself. Then fixes me with a stare that should come with a body count.

"Get up," he says.

My heart stutters.

"Come here."

I don't move.

He takes a step around the table.

"Now."

I stand, not being able to stomach what will happen if I don't right now. I'm not actually trying to die tonight. My legs feel numb and my stomach turns to lead. I take one step, then another. I stop a few feet in front of him and he looks down at me like he wants to build a shrine and burn it down in the same breath.

He raises a hand and for the first time tonight...I think he might actually kill me.

My breath catches as every muscle in my body coils, preparing to take the hit. I brace for impact, but the strike doesn't come. He drops his hand, straightening his jacket and when he speaks, his voice is cold. Lethal.

"You're lucky I have to wait."

The words slide down my spine like ice water. *Wait? For what?*

"If I didn't need your signature... you would be in pieces on this floor."

My stomach lurches, but I don't move. He takes a slow step toward me, his presence swallowing mine. I want to take a step back, but I don't. Because prey runs, and I am not prey. Even if I feel like it.

He tilts his head, studying me. "I've killed men for less than what you said tonight," he murmurs.

His hand lifts again—not to hit me, but to trace a line down my cheek.

I go still. Paralyzed by the pressure of his thumb brushing under my eye.

"But your mouth..." he whispers, smiling now—tight and cruel. "Will be the death of you."

He leans down until his lips are just above my ear. "You think I'm cruel now?" he breathes. "You haven't seen what I do to women who forget their place."

The chill that runs through me this time is different. It's colder, deeper. And it buries itself in my bones.

"Go back to your room."

I blink. "What?"

"Now."

The rage is gone again, wiped clean beneath that same sharp control I've come to expect. I hesitate, a little too slowly for him I guess. He grabs my wrist and starts walking, dragging me toward the dining room door without another word.

He opens it, and shoves me through, slamming the door behind me. The sound ricochets down the hallway and I stumble back, heart hammering in my chest. My pulse pounds so loud it drowns out everything else. And for the first time in days, escape isn't what flashes through my mind.

Survival is.

39

"There's always a moment before the kill
when they trust you."
(That's the most intimate second you'll ever know)

Ani

I wake up like I've been hit by a truck. A velvet-lined, custom-upholstered, probably-stolen truck. But a truck, nonetheless.

This is why I don't drink, I tell myself.

My mouth is dry. My back aches. My eyes feel raw—swollen and crusted, like my body finally tapped out from crying sometime during the night.

Which... yeah. That tracks.

I'm on day... what? Four? Five? It's hard to say what day it is when there are no windows, no clocks, and no one acknowledging your existence unless it's time to play dress-up and eat under surveillance. Dinner's the only time anyone remembers I'm still breathing.

Until then, I sit. I wait. I rot. Repeat.

It's not bad really, I'm just a little more cracked than yesterday, a little quieter, and a little less me.

Five stars. Would recommend.

I close my eyes and my chest tightens like I'm being vacuum-sealed into my own ribcage.

I remember walking back in here, and by walking back here, I mean being escorted by sir-speaks-a-lot. Then I remember closing the door, and breaking. Completely. Silently. Crying myself to sleep seems to be part of my self-care routine at this point.

Some part of me must still think I can outsmart monsters. That if I'm funny enough, strong enough, or stubborn enough—I'll stay safe.

Jokes on me, I'm not safe. Not even close. Nothing feels real anymore, and as much as I want to believe I'm strong enough, I find myself slipping, wondering if I'll actually make it out of this.

My hands curl into the bedding as my fists tighten, like that's going to help. I should get up. Move. Scream. Set something on fire. *I'm going insane.*

Instead, I just lay here, staring at the ceiling like it might crack open and drop me into the void. A silent tear slips down my cheek.

The fact that he thinks I should be grateful for the things he does makes me want to throw up and find the nearest sharp object to stab him with. He found my knife, so now I get searched before and after I leave the room.

I almost want him to do whatever it is he keeps threatening, just so I know where the bottom is. At least then I can stop falling.

No.

Stop it.

You're Ani. You have teeth. You have fire. You have—

Nothing.

No phone. No allies. No plan.

Just a closet full of silk and a man who carved my freedom into a contract I've never seen.

I drag myself into a sitting position and the robe clings to my skin. I glance around the room, noting how nothing is different. *Except for me.*

This is the first morning I don't wake up with a plan. No escape route. No snide comebacks. No fantasy of stabbing him with a dessert fork and sprinting barefoot into the woods.

Just... silence.

I fold my arms over my stomach. *Is today going to be the day I break?* I sit there for a long time. Long enough to watch the light change across the floor. Long enough to start counting the scratches in the wood paneling under the window.

Sixteen.

At least none of them are mine.

I wonder if Sarah's sent out a search party yet. Sloane would probably assume I finally snapped and quit without telling anyone. She'd roll her eyes, call me a disaster, and cover my shift anyway.

Would anyone even call? Check my apartment? And what the fuck is happening to Steven? *Oh my God. Bern.*

The thought hits so fast I can't brace for it. My chest caves in as my throat tightens. I blink hard, once. Then again. And suddenly my eyes are burning.

Not now.

Not fucking now.

That slow, ugly swell of panic rises in my throat. Steven's gone and Bern's probably pacing the cabin, waiting for a door that won't open. *Oh my god, her last owners left her there. She's probably traumatized.* Another tear slips out.

No one's coming.

My hands shake as I press my palms to my eyes, willing the tears to stop. If I start crying again, I don't know if I'll stop this time.

I climb off the bed, which takes more effort than it should. My legs feel like they're filled with sand, and my stomach growls so loud I flinch.

You'd think a psychopath trying to court you with violence and wine would at least remember to feed you every day, but no.

Apparently, starvation is now part of the vibe.

I walk to the door and press my palm to it like it might suddenly open with the power of loneliness and carbs.

I knock once, then again.

"Heeey Silent Bob," I call out. "Any chance I could get a bagel and a therapy session? Maybe a cookie if you're feeling generous?"

Nothing.

Dick.

I crouch down and look through the crack of the door, and see a pair of shiny, black boots.

"Hey, Bootsy," I whisper. "Are you alive out there? Tap twice if you've got a conscience."

Still nothing.

I lean my head against the doorframe and sigh. I thought for sure I could break him by now, but no matter how much I try, he never even cracks a smile.

"God, you're not even going to pretend I'm a person, huh? Just... a body to lock up and parade around when he's feeling romantic."

I step back, flipping him off through the door.

"Cool. Super empowering."

I turn toward the window, and something catches my eye. I can see Frank walking over to his car. He's talking to someone but his posture is all business. He gets in the back seat, and the car pulls away.

I wait five minutes.

Then ten.

He doesn't come back.

I move to the closet, stripping out of the black dress like it's trying to eat me alive. I toss it into the corner without looking back and head for the bathroom.

He's gone. Which means it's finally safe to shower without imagining him standing just outside the door, about to burst in. There's no way in hell I'm getting naked while he's home. I'd rather marinate in my own anxiety.

Steam rises thick around me until I can barely breathe, but I don't care. I just stand there, letting the water hit me hard enough to sting. Maybe if I let it burn long enough, it'll scald the part of me that's starting to give up.

I tilt my head back and let the water pound against me until my fingers go numb and my skin turns blotchy. I need to figure out how to get out of here. I need a new plan. I don't know what he's going to do with me, and I really don't want to find out.

By the time I step out, the mirror is completely fogged. My skin's flushed pink and my hair's a mess, but I do feel a little better.

Honestly, right now, that counts as a win.

I wrap myself in a towel and pad back into the room, only to find something on the floor. It's not food, unfortunately. But it's a little piece of paper.

My pulse spikes.

I move quickly to go grab it, like if I don't hurry, it'll vanish.

It's just a piece of folded notebook paper. But the second I open it, the world shifts.

You're not alone.

I stare at it so long they start to blur from tears. Something I haven't let myself feel in days slips in.

Hope.

It's just a single sentence scratched on shitty paper, but it hits harder than every slap, every threat, or every hour of silence in this place.

This means someone sees me. Or it could be a trap, or worse, a joke. Maybe it's the final mindfuck from the man who makes me want to claw his eyes out.

Or it could be real.

I don't know which option scares me more.

My first instinct is to tear it up. Burn it. Pretend I never saw it. Hope is a luxury I can't afford right now, and I don't like the way it flutters in my chest like it's just been waiting for a reason to rise.

I glance at the camera, but it's not blinking right now. *Holy fuck.*

My heart's doing that staccato thing again as I walk to the corner of the room, crouching beside the desk. I pull a book to the side, and slide the note under the drawer. Just in case.

I don't want to think about what would happen if Frank found it.

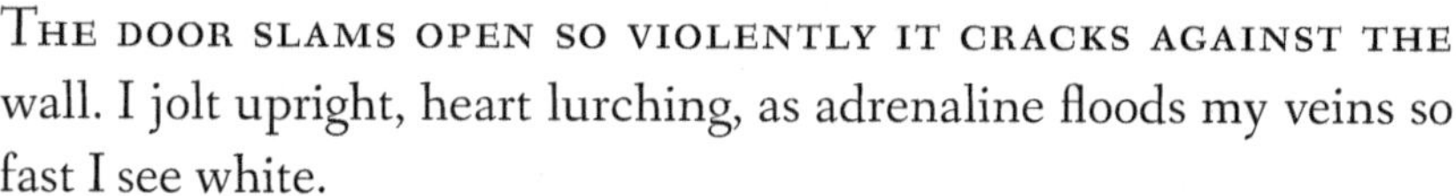

THE DOOR SLAMS OPEN SO VIOLENTLY IT CRACKS AGAINST THE wall. I jolt upright, heart lurching, as adrenaline floods my veins so fast I see white.

Frank stands in the doorway—looking wild and unhinged. His hair's a mess and his shirt's only half-buttoned. But it's his face that stops me cold. He looks... scared.

He storms toward me. "What did you do?"

I scoot back so fast, my spine hits the headboard.

"What—what are you talking about—?"

But he's not listening. And for the first time since this nightmare began, I'm scared.

"Don't play stupid," he spits.

My stomach drops because I have no clue what he's talking about. Unless he watched the cameras and found my little note? I could've sworn they weren't on. I run through every possible scenario that I think he might be talking about.

Fuck.

What did I do?

Frank grabs my arm—hard—rips me upright like I weigh nothing, and my towel slips to the floor and I'm suddenly naked in front of him.

He freezes for half a second and the look he gives me isn't just lust, it's hunger laced with loathing. Almost like he wants me and hates himself for it.

His hand slides to my throat and I freeze. Every muscle goes still because I don't know why he's here, unless it's time for dinner?

"You think I don't see it?" he growls. "The way you look at me. You think you're untouchable."

I try to move—just an inch, just enough to breathe—but he slams me back against the wall so hard my teeth rattle. And beneath the rage in his eyes, there's something else. Something darker.

"You know what I should do?" he whispers.

His eyes drag down my body, slowly. He smiles. "I should let my men have you."

The blood drains from my face.

He leans in close enough that his nose brushes mine, and my stomach twists. He can't be serious. No. No. No.

"See how much of a mouth you've got after the guards take their turn. A reward for having to put up with you."

He shrugs off a laugh. "Maybe then you'll remember your fucking place."

Tears sting my eyes and bite the inside of my cheek until I taste blood. I glare up at him. If he wants to see fear, he'll have to earn it.

He steps back, letting go of my throat—only to yank a fistful of my hair, dragging me forward.

"You've got five minutes to get dressed," he snaps. "Or you're getting on the plane like this."

Then he throws me back onto the bed and walks out the door.

I curl into myself, arms tight, heartbeat detonating in my chest. For the first time since he took me—I'm not sure I'm going to make it. My time is up.

He's going to take me out of this house, to God knows where, and the only thing worse than staying—is going.

My legs shake as I climb off the bed.

I need to get dressed, the last thing I want is for him to follow through with his threat and drag me out of here naked.

I stumble to the closet, flinging it open. Every option stares back at me like a threat. They're all dresses with slits so high they should come with a warning label.

I dig through it like salvation's hiding in the back somewhere and end up picking a dark green dress with long sleeves and a neckline that only dips a little. It hits mid-thigh and clings to everything I don't want anyone looking at, but it's going to have to do.

I just need to be covered.

Seconds later, there's a knock. Or rather, three sharp bangs. That's the only warning I get before the door swings open. And for one heart-stopping second, I brace for Frank.

But it's not him.

It's a new guard I haven't seen yet. This one's taller. Broader. He looks younger than the last one. He's grinning as his eyes crawl down my body like they've been waiting for this moment all day.

Ew.

"Eyes up, perv. You're not my type unless I lose a bet and go blind."

He snorts—and backhands me. Hard.

My head jerks to the side as blood goes flying out of my mouth. My cheek flashes white-hot, then settles into a burn. I look up, eyes watering but still locked on him.

"Oh, good," I rasp. "So you're not just a perv. You're predictable."

I don't even see Frank come in. One second the guard's stalking toward me, smiling like he's about to pounce, and the next—bang. Blood sprays the door, my face, the walls. It's everywhere.

A scream rips out of me before I even know I'm doing it—raw and automatic, torn straight from my throat as the shot rings out and the man drops like a sack of meat in front of me.

I flinch hard, scrambling back until I hit the wall, searching for anything solid to hold onto. My spine presses into cold plaster hoping it might swallow me whole. Frank steps through the doorway, gun still raised.

His eyes burn black, wild with something that doesn't look like rage—it looks worse. His chest heaves with slow, controlled breaths. He doesn't even glance at the body before he steps over it, turning the gun on me. Every cell in my body is vibrating, screaming for me to move, but I can't.

"What did I tell you," Frank says, eerily calm, "about letting people touch what's mine?"

My throat tightens. "It's not like I asked him to hit me."

Which was apparently the wrong thing to say.

He takes one step, then another—and that's all the warning I get. The calm drops and his mask shatters. In a flash, his fingers clamp around my wrist like a vice, twisting hard enough to make something pop. I cry out, stumbling forward, but he doesn't stop. His other hand slams across my face right where the guard just did, and I can feel blood drip down my face.

The room tilts as my knees hit the marble.

"You ungrateful little bitch," he snarls, yanking me back up by my arm like I'm a disobedient dog. "I give you everything—shelter, food, a fucking future—and this is how you repay me?"

I try to twist away, but he grips harder, dragging me in closer until I can smell the bourbon on his breath. His eyes are wild with unchecked rage—and he's gone. Whatever version of Frank that was there before is dead.

"You don't get to talk back. You don't get to fucking speak unless I say so."

He shoves me again. My back slams against the wall and the wind goes out of me.

"I don't need you to be healthy," he says, dropping to something dangerous. "I just need you breathing."

I bite the inside of my cheek, hard enough to split skin. Because if I don't—I'll scream.

His hand tightens again. Then he yanks. My shoulder jerks back with a sickening twist and I stumble as he drags me forward. I dig my heels into the floor, trying to brace against the wall, but it doesn't matter. He's stronger.

"Walk," he barks. "Or I'll make you crawl."

The floor blurs as he drags me out into the hall, still covered in the man's blood. My wrist is throbbing. My spine knocks into the edge of a side table hard enough to leave a bruise, but Frank doesn't stop. He steps right over the corpse like it's just an inconvenience, yanks the front door open, and drags me into the cold.

A black car is waiting at the curb and two men stand beside it in suits with their guns holstered. Their faces are blank, but they don't look at me. They don't look at the blood. They don't even glance at the body behind us. They just keep their eyes forward, stiff and silent. Obedient and dead in a different way.

Cowards.

Frank doesn't slow down. Just wrenches the back door open and shoves.

"Get in."

I hesitate.

His grip tightens on my wrist and he throws me into the car like I'm a rag doll. I hit the floor first, hip slamming hard, hair in my face, and my bloodied dress bunched around my waist.

I scramble to get up, choking on the need to scream. I pull my legs in, slide into the seat, and press my hand to the throbbing spot where his fingers were.

He gets in after me, suddenly calm again. The door slams shut, and the silence is worse than the yelling.

My wrist is already swelling and I can feel it throbbing with every heartbeat. I curl it into my lap and stare out the tinted window, biting the inside of my cheek until I taste copper again.

"You know what your problem is?" he mutters, causing me to jump.

I don't answer.

"You think you're untouchable," he goes on. "You think because I didn't break you the first time, I won't."

I shift, just enough to look at him.

"And you think hurting me will fix that?"

His smile is cold. Cruel. "No. But it'll make me feel better."

"Right. Because that's what this is all about. Your feelings."

He lunges, grabbing a fistful of my hair and slams my head sideways into the window with enough force to make the glass sing. Pain detonates behind my eyes, sharp and instant, as the taste of blood floods my mouth. My vision goes out in a violent flash, and I recoil hard, slamming into the door with a choked breath. One hand clutches the side of my skull while the other stays limp and useless in my lap.

I stay curled in the corner, trembling. My ribs tighten around my heart like a cage, and even through the fog of pain and fear, one thought digs in so deep it feels carved into my bones. *If I survive this... I will kill him.*

That's the last thing I remember before the pain kicks in, and everything goes dark.

I WAKE TO THE SOUND OF TURBULENCE AND THE PRESSURE shifting in my ears. A low ding cuts through the hum of engines, and cool air brushes against my skin.

I blink slowly.

Everything hurts. My head's pounding, my throat's dry, and it feels like I've been chewing on metal and regret.

It takes five full seconds before I register the leather seat beneath me. The seatbelt strapped tight across my hips, the blanket that's covering me, and the zip ties.

My arms are restrained beneath the fabric like I'm part of the luggage. I turn my head—and there he is. Scrolling his phone like this is a business trip and I'm just carry-on.

My mouth's too dry to form words at first. I try again, quieter this time. "Where are we?"

He doesn't answer. Doesn't even glance over. He just keeps

scrolling, perfectly at ease while my stomach flips and my pulse tries to claw its way out of my chest.

The plane dips and the floor tilts beneath me. I think I'm going to be sick. I press my head back against the seat and close my eyes. Maybe if I'm lucky, he'll think I'm unconscious. At this point, that might be the only card I've got left.

The hum of the engines deepens and I hear the landing gear drop with a metallic thunk that vibrates through the floor and straight into my spine. The cabin pressure shifts again, and my ears pop. My head throbs in response—thanks for that, by the way—but I don't move. I just sit here. Breathing slowly and counting every sound, every detail, every goddamn second—because it's the only control I have.

The zip ties around my wrists are a real buzz kill. The blanket is draped over me like an afterthought, and I can't even fix it. *Must be nice to underestimate me this much.*

Outside, through the slit in the shade, I catch a flicker of green. Palm trees, maybe?

I squeeze my eyes tighter as the wheels hit the ground hard. My body jerks in the seat and I risk the smallest peek through my lashes.

He's lounging across from me with one leg crossed over the other, phone to his ear, keeping his voice low. Whatever he's saying is hushed, but urgent.

We step off the plane into heat thick enough to chew. It clings to my skin instantly, wet and heavy, crawling into my lungs and settling there like smoke. It's not just hot—it's humid and familiar in a way that makes my stomach pitch sideways and my skin prickle with something close to dread.

Frank's hand clamps around my upper arm the second my foot hits the tarmac. Tighter than necessary.

As if I have anywhere left to run.

There's no sound beyond the echo of our footsteps and the hum of the engines cooling behind us. The runway is deserted, except for one sleek black car parked fifty feet ahead. There's two men standing guard beside it—suits, guns, and not a single blink between them.

There's nothing but heatwaves rising off the concrete and the blinding white glare of the sun reflecting off every surface. It hurts to look at—but I do anyway. Because then I see it.

Aeropuerto Internacional Fernando Luis Ribas Dominicci.

Puerto Rico.

My chest tightens. Something pulls at the base of my spine—deep and unexplainable.

What are we doing in Puerto Rico?

I haven't been back since I was a kid. Since my mother told me to stop asking questions and just keep packing. My heart starts pounding again, but it's not fear. Not really. It's something else.

"Keep your head down," Frank mutters.

His voice is cold again. All business. Back to his usual brand of narcissistic God complex—with his shoulders straight and that silent assumption that the world should part for him wherever he walks.

I do as I'm told. Only because my skull still hurts from the last time I didn't.

We reach the car, and the door swings open like it's been waiting. No one speaks.

Inside, the air conditioning hits like a slap—freezing and sterile. I fold my arms in my lap, as best I can with my wrists tied together, like that'll somehow help me stay calm, and I stare out the window trying not to freak out.

Bayamón.

The name flares in my mind like static—hot and foreign, yet familiar. I haven't said it out loud in years.

We drive for what feels like forever—through winding roads, sun-baked hills, and fields of tall grass. The trees start to thicken, and the world closes in. Jungle wraps around the car like it's trying to keep us out. Or maybe in.

The car turns off the main road. A long, curved driveway appears—lined with white stone pillars and palm trees so thick they block out the light. The gates open without a sound, and that's when it hits me.

I know this place. I don't know how, because I don't remember being here. But something inside me lurches—like a string pulled tight. My throat closes and my palms go damp.

I've been here before.

Frank leans over, and he's so close I can feel his breath on my skin. "You like it?" he asks. "It's mine."

He has to be wrong. Because even as he says it, the sunlight catches my eyes just right and something shifts. A flash of red. A dress. A woman's laugh floating through the air, warm and sweet. The sharp curl of perfume. Someone calling my name—in Spanish.

There's a hallway, covered in paintings. A man's deep laugh echoing off the stone, and the sound of a cane striking the tile. My head snaps back and I flinch so hard the seatbelt digs into my ribs.

What the hell is happening?

The car slows, pulling to a stop. Frank gets out, slamming the door shut behind him, but I don't move. I'm staring up at the house, and every inch of my body is screaming...*I've been here.*

One of the men opens my door and the heat hits me again. I don't move fast enough. A second later, Frank's back, yanking the door wider. He reaches in, grabbing me by the arm like I'm a ragdoll and not a whole, bruised, chronically sarcastic woman trying not to puke on the seats.

He doesn't say anything, just pulls me out, causing me to stumble, but catch myself.

The driveway's made of smooth stone, flanked by tropical flowers that look like they belong on a postcard and not in the nightmare version of House Hunters: Narco Edition.

The estate looms ahead—white, regal, and far too familiar. My feet already know the path and that scares the ever-loving shit out of me. Frank storms up the steps, talking to the guy who opened my door.

I mutter under my breath, "Careful. Wouldn't want to chip your ego on the stone."

He throws the front doors open with both hands and I cross the threshold behind him, and the air changes.

Literally.

There's a shift in pressure, a weight in the room that slams straight into my lungs.

The smell hits me next. It smells like cedar, citrus, and polished wood.

I stop just inside the doorway. Frozen. I am now one hundred percent sure I've been here before. Somewhere beneath the bruises and fear—my body remembers.

I've seen these walls before. The high ceilings. The sweeping staircase. The painting above the entry table—storm clouds over the ocean, with a ship caught mid-surge, bracing for impact.

I know that painting. My grandfather loved storms. He used to say they reminded him that the world could still surprise him. That not everything bows to power.

The second the memory surfaces, something cracks. I don't even realize I've stopped breathing until my chest aches. It's stupid, but it hits like a punch to the face. He used to say it with this crooked half-smile, like he knew something the rest of us didn't.

Frank steps in front of me and turns, arms outstretched. He looks like a fucking game show host at the gates of hell.

"Welcome home," he says, smiling like this is some kind of grand reveal and I've just won a trip to my own personal nightmare.

I blink. Hard.

"No," I whisper, mostly to myself, because saying it out loud feels like I might be able to undo the entire moment. "This isn't your home."

He tilts his head, a smile sharpening into that slow, precise, *I could break you without raising my voice* look he does so well.

"It is now."

But I'm not listening anymore. Behind him—down that hallway —I see something that shouldn't be there.

I see me. Tiny, barefoot, and darting around the corner in a red dress. Laughing. A deep voice calls after me in Spanish— *"Anianne, espera, mi amor... cuidado con la escalera..."*

And just like that, my knees almost give out.

It hits so fast I don't have time to brace. One second I'm upright, and the next—I'm swaying, body buckling under the weight of something I don't even understand yet.

Frank steps forward like he thinks he's going to catch me and I take a step back because I'd rather hit the floor on my own terms than let him touch me again.

His smile slips as I try to wrap my arms around myself, but can't. A new voice cuts in.

"Señor Calissi," the man says, with a thick accent. His tone is clipped and formal. "The lawyer is an hour out. He'll need the girl cleaned and dressed for confirmation."

Confirmation?

My stomach lurches. What the hell does that mean?

Frank reaches for me again, but this time I try to slap his hand away with more strength than I knew I had.

"You don't get to touch me," I say. But my pulse is rioting in my throat. "Not here."

His jaw tightens. But his control is slipping. I need to be careful.

He doesn't hit me. But he leans in, close enough that I can smell how much cologne he used this morning.

"I only need you long enough to say 'yes,'" he whispers. "After that... you're expendable."

40

"CONTROL ISN'T ABOUT WHO HAS THE GUN."
(IT'S ABOUT WHO MAKES THEM WANT
TO PULL THE TRIGGER)

Steven

"FUCK."

The word rips out of me, ricocheting off the walls like a warning shot. I'm already on my feet, pacing like a caged animal. Movement's the only thing keeping me from unraveling.

Across the room, Travis types like the devil's at the door, or in this case me. His fingers blur over the keyboard. He's a fucking machine running on caffeine and chaos. But it's still not fast enough.

None of it is.

I drag a hand down my face for the tenth time, but it doesn't help. My skin itches with the need to do something. To rip something apart.

The silence is a noose, and the waiting is nothing less than torture.

My pulse is in my ears, a war drum that won't fucking stop. Every breath feels like a countdown to the moment I lose what's left of my control.

She's gone.

I don't know where she is or what he's doing to her, and that's

635

the part that guts me. The not knowing. The silence. The thousand ways she could be hurting while I'm standing here doing nothing.

I see her in flashes—on the floor somewhere, covered in blood, still waiting for someone who never should've let her go.

My fists crack as I clench them harder. I pace the apartment like it's a cage, boots hitting the floor with purpose.

He took her.

He touched what's mine.

He was already dead the second I found out he was here. But now? Now I want him to beg for it.

I snap. "Say something."

He doesn't even pause. Then—finally— "Got her."

Everything in me goes still. "What?"

He shoves the laptop toward me. "Private airstrip. No manifests filed under Frank's name, but the tail number you gave me pinged. He's taking her to Puerto Rico."

I stare at the screen like it's trying to fuck with me. "Repeat that."

His voice drops, no smart-ass remark this time. "You heard me. She's en route. The jet left forty minutes ago. He's running her straight into the lion's den."

He pauses. "You've got an hour. Maybe less," he adds, eyes back on the data. "My contact says they're planning to move her into the system tonight. Once she's verified, it's done. Locked. You won't get near her."

"We're leaving," I snap, already crossing the room. "Tell them to fuel up."

Travis looks up—grim now, clenching his jaw. "They'll be expecting both of us. He knows you'll come. If I'm with you, they'll shut every door before you touch the ground."

"Then I go alone."

He doesn't argue. He just nods once. "Fucking hell."

Then—he stops. Eyes fixed on the screen. "Wait..."

I turn, walking back slowly. "What?"

Travis scrolls. Clicks. Clicks again. His fingers still, just long enough to hit enter. Then everything about him shifts.

"Holy shit," he mutters, turning the screen toward me. "So, uh... turns out there's a clause. Buried deep in the estate paperwork —like really deep. Took me three hours and an old decryption key to even get to it."

Steven's already glaring. "Spit it out."

"If the heir is alive, married, and physically present on the land, they become the primary controller of the estate. Everything gets locked to them. Assets, holdings, power of transfer—all of it. But here's the kicker."

He pauses. "The signature has to happen on the property. No remote access, no legal proxy, no workaround. It's old blood code shit. Written before digital records were even a thing."

Silence.

"That's why he hasn't killed her," I say quietly.

Travis nods. "Nope. He's just waiting for the wedding and the signature. Once she signs... it's over. It's all his."

My jaw tightens. "She doesn't even know what she's holding."

"No. But Frank does."

He pauses. "If deceased—or missing more than five years—it defaults to the spouse of record."

My vision narrows until there's nothing but blood. I don't care what I have to destroy—what I have to burn. I'll rip that fucking island apart brick by brick before I let him put his hands on her.

I glance over and he's staring at the screen so intensely, I almost expect the monitor to crack.

"Find what you can," I bark, grabbing my bag. "Send me everything else."

"Wait—" He exhales.

By the time he turns the screen, I'm already halfway to the door.

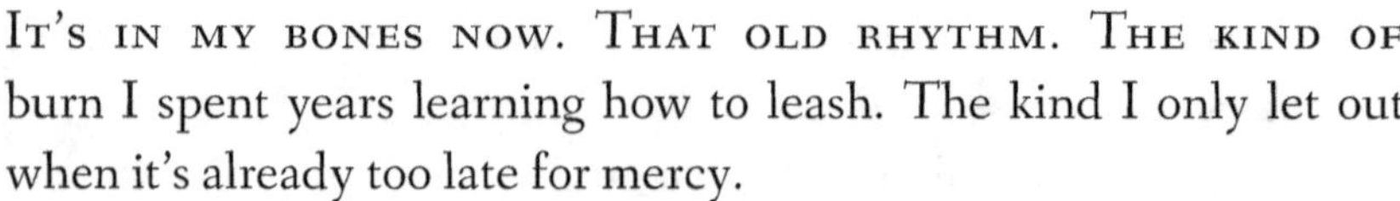

It's in my bones now. That old rhythm. The kind of burn I spent years learning how to leash. The kind I only let out when it's already too late for mercy.

But this isn't a mission. This is personal.

Someone touched her. Someone took her. Laid hands on her body. Tried to control her. I saw the bruises. Even in that short, pixelated clip Frank thought was enough to break me.

They don't get to walk away from that and keep breathing.

My phone buzzes and I answer without looking. "Talk."

"Her grandfather's name was Emilio Rivera," he says.

The name slams into me, it sounds so fucking familar.

Fuck.

I've heard it before. Whispered in the kind of circles I used to haunt—rooms full of power cloaked in shadows. Rivera was the kind of man people lowered their voice for because he didn't need a title. He already owned everything that mattered.

"Bayamón," I mutter, the name bitter on my tongue. "He ruled it like a goddamn king—kept everyone on a leash and made them thank him for the privilege."

"Not just ports," he mutters. "Land. Arms. Trade routes. Multiple offshore accounts under Rivera Holdings. He had his hand everywhere—political, military, global. Old-world power. The kind passed through bloodlines."

I stare out the window as the plane begins its descent. The island spreads beneath us in endless shades of green, veined with shadows that look too familiar.

"Tell me he's alive." I ask, already knowing the answer.

"Doubt it," he says. "Found some coded files. Internal chatter flagged a private alert three years ago. He was sick—but not that sick."

The tap of keys fills the silence between us.

"Here's the interesting part," he mutters. "Next of kin was listed as a son. On paper, it all looked clean. But I'm about to prove that document was forged."

My grip tightens around the phone. I don't speak yet. Just breathe through the static building behind my eyes. *How is this happening and how the fuck did I miss this?*

I shut my eyes. "You're telling me this whole thing—"

"Yup." He exhales hard, like he's been holding it in since the second I walked out that door. And suddenly it all clicks. Frank didn't just find her. He hunted her. Tracked her down and played the long game, waiting until he could own her on paper the way he already thought he did in his head.

"He needs her alive," I mutter, the words scraping my throat.

"Alive and obedient," he confirms. "Marriage gives him everything. As soon as she signs that form, the Rivera empire is his."

My chest goes tight. But it's what he says next that knocks the breath clean out of me.

"Hey, Steven."

He never calls me that. Not even on that evacuation mission. Not after the bloodbaths. Not even when I flatlined for 46 seconds in Morocco and came back pissed as hell the target got away. *It was only for 5 hours but still.* If he's saying my name now. It's bad.

"Just tell me," I breathe.

He clears his throat. "There's a private auction for offshore buyers only." He pauses. "It goes live tonight."

Motherfucker.

I go still. My body doesn't even register the turbulence. I'm past logic. Past forgiveness. I stare out the window, willing the clouds to part and show me where she is. Some sign. Anything. Because until I see her—until I touch her—I can't think about what the other options look like.

I know what she looks like when she's scared and trying not to be. I know how her breathing changes when she lies. I know the way her jaw ticks when she's swallowing a scream. And the idea that Frank might've seen that—might've touched her—

My fists tighten as something cracks in my chest and lodges under my ribs, too sharp to be rage, but too familiar to be anything but grief. I haven't cried since grade school. Not even when I lost everything. But this—the thought of losing her? I can't even fucking go there.

If I'm too late— if she's hurt, or he married her, I'll kill him. I'll take him apart piece by piece and make sure he knows exactly why. I'll burn his empire and salt the fucking earth with the ashes of everything he thought he owned.

"Hey." Travis's voice cuts in. I forgot I was still on the phone. "Don't go there, man." The silence stretches. "You lose your head, he wins."

I nod once, and hang up. He's right. Emotion makes you sloppy and I won't get to be sloppy. Not now. Not for her. Not when everything's on the line. This is what I like to call the calm before the reckoning.

The plane shudders on descent, and my phone buzzes in my palm again.

"I forwarded you everything I pulled so far—estate layout, floorplans, security grid, lawyer's name. And hey—I called in a few markers. Some friends of mine will be waiting when you land. Ex-military. Discharged dirty, but you can trust 'em."

I nod even though he can't see me. "How many?"

"Three."

It's going to have to be enough.

The plane touches down with a slow, hungry screech. The sound feels like a blade dragging across my spine.

I don't relax. Every second I'm on the ground is one more she's in his hands. One more second she might be hurt. Stripped. Branded. Married off like some pawn. I missed it because I let my dick get ahead of the mission.

I fucked up. I can't stop thinking about what it's going to cost me if I'm not fast enough.

The hangar doors creak open and the Puerto Rican heat slams into me. The sun's almost down, and trees swallow the sky.

And there—at the edge of the landing strip—is a beat-up black SUV. Three men lean against it like they've been here since the island was born.

They straighten when I approach. The one in front steps forward, holding out a hand.

"Cruz." he introduces himself. He's a big guy. Broad shoulders, tan skin, forearms thick with muscle. He's got three scars across his knuckle. The kind you only get in close-quarters work. "You're the guy who's gonna burn this place down for a girl, yeah?"

I don't take his hand at first. "She's not a girl," I say evenly. "She's mine."

He nods once, like that tells him everything he needs to know.

After a beat, I reach out to shake his hand. "Appreciate the help," I add. "Let's get this done."

"Good enough for me." He jerks his chin toward the truck. "We'll brief inside."

The vehicle smells like oil and cigarettes. The interior's stripped down, and is now filled with weapons, folded maps, old intel scrawled in sharpie across crinkled paper. If this were any other time, I would admire it.

The driver—Rico—is quiet. The other guy, lean build, older, with eyes like a hawk's name is Silva. The sniper.

Cruz turns in his seat. "Estate's up in Bayamón. Heavy canopy. Gated. Long drive. We scoped it this morning—the entry's clear for now, but they've got patrols. Cameras. Satellite coverage shows four exits, but we can't confirm what's active on the interior."

"Guards?"

"Ten, minimum, surround the perimeter. And if this Frank guy has half the pull your guy said—he's got people inside, too."

I nod, already expecting that.

"I say we wait. Hit it in the morning at shift change, we get two blind spots—front and rear. The easiest window is going to be at 5:45 AM. Sun's just up, guard swap happens at the gate, and staff rolls in around six."

He glances back at me like he just gave me a gift.

I meet his stare, dead calm. "No."

Rico glances up. "What?"

"I'm not waiting."

Cruz frowns. "We move now, we hit hard resistance. No blind spots. We don't know who's inside."

"I don't care."

I lean in closer, trying to keep my shit together. "I don't care if there's fifty men with guns and a fucking tank parked in the garden. She's in there. And I'm not leaving her for another goddamn hour."

My voice isn't raised, but it lands like a threat. Cruz opens his mouth like he's about to push back, then sees my face and thinks better of it. I'm not bluffing.

The only fucking thing I can think about right now is all noise —images of her skin banged up, all the fucked up shit Frank might be making her do. *Fuck.*

Silva nods once. "Then we move now. We do a shadow sweep, we'll find the quietest entry point. Breach and burn."

Maybe he's actually the one in charge. Wouldn't surprise me. He seems smart. Knows when to talk, when to move, when to shut the fuck up and listen.

That's the kind of man I want beside me when shit goes sideways in there. With Calissi you never know.

"There's two pressure sensors on the main gate. One under the west garden stones—probably old, but can't be too sure. East perimeter's got a blind spot if we cut the feed here." He taps the screen. "Ten yards inside the fence."

I nod. "We take the east. I want eyes on the master suite first."

"We can't use any aerial drones," Cruz mutters. "It'll trip perimeter detection."

"Don't need one," I say. "I know the layout."

They glance at me. I've studied every inch of that house in the last few hours. Memorized it. Every angle. Every line of sight. Every spot that might hold a camera—or her. If she's behind one of those windows, I'll find her. And if she's not? Then someone's going to bleed until I get an answer.

We load up in silence. This is the kind of quiet I trust.

Hang on, Dear. Just a little bit longer.

41

"Obsession makes you sloppy. Until it doesn't."
(Until it makes you lethal)

Ani

Getting ready was a blur. I spent most of it trying not to vomit, cry, or jump out a window. My brain short-circuited the second those two men showed up, all polite smiles and silent stares, saying they were here to "escort me to my room."

I thought they were going to drag me in by the hair. Strip me down. Pick out a dress and a necklace and maybe even a tiara while they held me down and told me to smile for the fucking photos.

Is this my life right now? Really?

A forced wedding, in a goddamn mansion. In Puerto Rico. To a man who probably killed my grandfather and keeps acting like I'm some lost little heiress who just needs a firm hand and a fitted suit to get her shit together.

Jesus.

How did I end up here?

I pace the length of the bedroom again, arms tight around my middle, ignoring the sting behind my eyes and the taste of acid crawling up my throat.

I mean, it's a beautiful room. Every detail screams wealth, and I hate it. The second I stepped inside, my heart stuttered with recognition.

I've been in this room before, lived here, slept here. How did I forget an entire life? An entire place?

And now it's being used as a prison.

I don't know what's worse—that I used to live here, or that I didn't even know it until my body remembered for me. Pretty sure it's the same damn furniture, too. Ten-year-old me probably loved it. Too bad current me is now getting dressed in it—for a wedding I didn't agree to, wearing a dress I didn't pick, for a man I wouldn't choose if the world was on fire.

I glance at the door. It's still locked. I checked. Twice.

The two men who brought me here didn't say a single word. Their posture was rigid, their guns clearly visible, and their energy screamed we're not here to chat. They were professional, cold, and efficient—no smiles, no warmth, just business.

I even tried to lighten the mood, making a sarcastic comment about whether this kidnapping package came with hair and makeup.

Neither of them reacted. Not a smile. Not a twitch. Just blank, polite professionalism—the kind that somehow felt more violating than being shoved inside.

Assholes.

They left without a word, shutting the door behind them like I was just a problem they'd successfully delivered. And now I'm alone. With a dress laid out on the bed like it's a gift instead of a fucking prison sentence, a pair of bone-colored heels that scream expensive hostage, and a full-length mirror that keeps showing me a version of myself I don't recognize.

I haven't even put the dress on yet. I've just been pacing back and forth across this bedroom that's somehow mine.

I keep trying to stay calm. Trying to think clearly. I've been freaking out in what I thought was a mature, adult way—meaning I bit the wooden bedpost once and seriously considered yeeting myself out the third-story window onto the decorative fountain below.

The dress is nice. Which makes me want to burn it more. Frank had it tailored to fit me perfectly, I'm sure. It's not even white—it's more bone than bridal, very fitting for a chic hostage aesthetic. I wish I could throw up on it.

I sit on the edge of the bed and breathe. I know—deep down—that once I sign those papers, I'm done. He won't need me anymore. Maybe he'll kill me. Maybe he'll keep me locked up, perfectly preserved in some psycho version of Stepford Wife prison.

Hell, I'd sign the papers right now if it meant I could go home. I don't even want any of this. I highly doubt he'd believe me if I tried telling him any of that though. I just want to sit on my couch, read a book, and eat stale popcorn. I just want to pretend none of this ever happened.

I don't want any of it.

And I sure as shit don't want him. But that's irrelevant, isn't it? Because what I want has nothing to do with it. He doesn't care if I love him or loathe him—just as long as I sign on the dotted line.

Have you ever looked at yourself and realized you're not inside your life anymore? You're just watching it—like a movie you didn't audition for—burning down behind a sheet of glass you can't break.

Yeah, that's me right now.

Hi. I'm Ani. But you might as well call me Alice, except this Wonderland doesn't have talking animals or tea—it has guards with guns and a dress that fits a little too well for comfort.

The knock at the door is soft. "Five minutes," someone says through the wood. "Be ready."

For what, exactly?

Surely he's not actually planning a wedding the same day we land. I mean—doesn't he need a florist? A schedule? Maybe a psych evaluation?

The footsteps outside are already retreating, leaving me alone once again with my thoughts. It's the kind of silence that sinks into your ribs and makes itself at home.

This is the part where I wish I could say something brave. Something clever. Something that sounds like survival. But the truth is, I don't feel brave. I feel tired. Shaky. Hollow in places that used to be sharp. My heart's thudding like it's trying to punch its way out of my ribs, and all I can think about is how fast everything unraveled.

I hate that I'm considering it. I hate that for one split second, I wonder if it would be easier to stop fighting. To just give in. To let them put the mask on me and pretend I belong here.

But I don't. And I never fucking will.

I clench my jaw, curling my hands into fists, and stand. Sure, maybe I don't remember everything yet, but I know this much, I'd rather walk straight into hell with my middle fingers up than stand here and pretend I'm not already burning.

Putting on the dress feels like surrender, and I hate that, but I do it anyway because what else am I going to do? Refuse and get slapped again? Yeah, no thanks. I'm too hot to have my cheek permanently dented from that fuckers hand.

My hands shake as I pull on the dress. It settles around me like it knows it doesn't belong—clinging to my skin, molding to every inch like smoke with claws. The shoes are worse. I hate heels. They're strappy, stiff, and tight in all the wrong places. These were clearly designed to look delicate while cutting off your circulation.

Which is perfect, all things considered.

There's no clock in this room either, but I know it's been at least five minutes. I sense the footsteps before I hear the boots coming down the hallway.

The bolt clicks and two new guards stand in the doorway. One gives a stiff nod. The other steps forward and extends a hand, like we're about to dance. I stare at it, trying my best to hold in the laugh that's coming up my throat. I try to walk right past, keeping my chin held high.

"Careful," I mutter as they fall in on either side of me. "Wouldn't want me tripping and signing the wrong name."

Neither of them reacts. *Tough crowd.*

They don't let me walk ahead—not really. One stays close at my back, the other half a step in front, boxing me in like I'm something fragile or dangerous.

We move past rooms I barely remember. I walk slowly, memorizing every step. Luckily I used to live here, so I'm sure I know where all the good hiding spots are, if I need them.

The main hall is cloaked in shadows. Literally. Only a few wall lamps are lit, like they're trying to conserve electricity—or add to the dramatics. Either way, it's too quiet.

I don't know what I expected. Maybe music. Champagne. An altar made of bones. Something appropriately theatrical for the horror of it all. I don't know, effort?

Instead, there's a man at the long table in a grey suit with wire-rim glasses and a neat stack of papers in front of him. No one says it, but I know who he is. At least I think it's safe to assume he's either the lawyer they were talking about earlier, or the one who's going to make all this official.

No one even looks at me when I walk in.

Frank stands off to the side, one hand around a glass of whiskey, with the smug calm of a man who thinks he's already won. He's not smiling, not exactly. It's worse than that—he's content, and he looks like he's already tasting the victory.

I stop at the edge of the table but I don't sit. Instead, I cross my arms on instinct.

He doesn't deserve to see me shake. He doesn't get the satisfaction of watching me fall apart. My body is vibrating with adrenaline, and a fear I refuse to name. My knees want to give out but I won't let them. So I hold still, staring him down.

"Sit," he says.

My feet stay planted, and every muscle in my body feels like it's waiting to snap. "What, no aisle? No music? You couldn't even spring for a flower girl?"

His jaw clenches and I can see the crack in his mask.

"I said sit."

"And I said no."

If I'm going down, it's going to be with a fight.

The man at the table—the priest, officiant, or whatever kind of legal parasite he is—finally looks up. His eyes flick between us, like he's just now realizing the bride might not be a willing participant. But does he say a word? No, of course not. He just blinks and waits, like paperwork matters more than consent.

If he signs that paper knowing what this is, he's just another coward cashing in on silence.

I smile, but there's no warmth in it. "Sorry. Didn't mean to interrupt your hostage ceremony. I just have a couple questions before we start."

Frank's nostrils flare with barely contained rage, dressed up in cufflinks and cologne, but I ignore him and take a single step to the left.

"First question," I say, keeping my tone steady, "does this become legally binding before or after you threaten to kill me if I say no?"

He sets the glass down, carefully eyeing me. He knows I'm up to something, I'm sure, but he makes no move to stop me. Yet.

"Second question," I continue, "should we ask him?" I nod toward the suited man. "Are you planning to lie for him? Sign off on a forced marriage and pretend it's consent?"

The man pales. His hand trembles just enough to make the pen twitch over the paper, looking between the two of us.

Frank takes one step toward me, but this time I don't flinch. I hold his stare, keeping my spine locked. I know what's coming. I must've always known, otherwise I wouldn't have run to Denver in the first place. But I'm done pretending.

This is a transaction signed in flesh and blood, and I'm the currency.

The silence stretches, letting the weight of it press into the walls until even the priest starts to squirm.

"Better get your money's worth, Frankie," I bite out. My voice is shaking with something that might be fear—or maybe it's just rage that finally found an edge sharp enough to cut. "Because once I sign that paper, you won't need me anymore. You'll get your empire. Your power. Your ego jerked off in ink."

His eye twitches.

"But let's not pretend you want a wife," I say, dropping my voice lower. "You want a puppet. And not even a willing one."

He moves so fast, I don't see him moving before the sound of his hand cracks across my face echoing like gunfire. My head whips sideways, and the floor rushes up before I can catch myself. My body hits the ground hard enough to make everything go quiet.

The taste of blood floods my mouth, and everything goes blurry for a second—long enough to register the priest frozen in place, looking between us.

I press my palms to the floor and shove myself upright, biting down on a gasp as the pain flares through my cheekbone. My lip's split, and I can taste blood, but I'm still breathing. Maybe if I push him just a little further, piss him off enough, he'll throw me back in that room and stall whatever sick plan he has for another day. The pain's worth it if it buys me time. If it gets me one inch closer to surviving this, I'll do it.

Frank moves so he's standing over me, breathing hard. His face isn't smug anymore—it's feral.

"You fucking bitch," he hisses.

I laugh—barely, because honestly, everything fucking hurts. I feel like I've been hit by a truck and then punted off a cliff for good measure. My body's screaming at me to shut up and survive, but instead, I lift my chin. Blood's in my mouth, and I spit it right between us—because, you know…

"Still think you're man enough to keep me?"

That's when he snaps. The second hit doesn't come from his hand, it comes from his boot. And it goes straight into my ribs.

Agony explodes through me, and it's brutal and all-consuming.

I can't breathe. I collapse onto my side, choking on air that won't come.

Okay. So maybe this wasn't my best plan. I figured he'd do what he always does—slap me around, throw a fit, maybe storm out and leave me ten minutes of oxygen. I didn't expect this. Not the silence. Not the shift in his eyes like I've finally pushed too far.

The guy in the suit finally speaks up—quiet, and a little unsure. There's hesitation in his voice, maybe even a flicker of fear, but it doesn't matter. Frank's rage steamrolls right over it like it never existed.

The third hit lands before the suited man can finish his sentence.

I don't even know where it lands this time—jaw, temple, maybe the back of my head—but wherever it is, it hits hard enough to rattle something loose and sends my vision sideways. The world tilts, and a wave of nausea crashes so hard it brings tears to my eyes. My ears won't stop ringing, and the metallic tang of blood stings the back of my throat. Somewhere in all the static—something clicks.

This was never about the contract. Hell, it's not even about business anymore. Or control. It's a punishment for talking back, for existing on my feet instead of on my knees, and being the one thing he can't seem to break without getting his hands bloody.

I curl around the pain, my body trying to protect itself on instinct, but I don't scream.

Even if it would help, even if it might make him stop—I won't give him the sound he wants.

A fist slams into my ribs—hard enough to crack something. I fold, gasping, but there's no time to catch my breath before his hand knots in my hair and jerks me back up. Another hit, this time to my stomach, and the floor lurches beneath me. I can't tell if I'm standing or falling as I let out a whimper. My knees buckle, but he's already got my arm, dragging me up like a ragdoll.

I brace for the next hit. My feet scramble for the ground, but I can barely stay upright. Everything tilts, and my vision is tunneling fast—Then he shakes me. Hard and violently.

"You will sign," he snarls, his spit hitting my cheek. "You will be mine. And you will fucking smile while you do it. Is that fucking clear?"

I blink hard, and feel the slow, sticky drag of blood sliding down my neck. My jaw throbs with every breath, and the taste of metal floods my mouth like I've been chewing on a fucking penny.

I mean it when I lift my chin. "Then fucking kill me, Frank. Because I'd rather bleed on your floor than smile while you think you own me."

His hand doesn't rear back this time like I think it will, instead, he reaches for his waistband and pulls out his gun.

"Sign it," his voice shakes with fury. "Or I'll put a bullet in you and make your corpse prettier than your attitude."

Oh fuck.

Good one, Ani. Real clever. Now what?

I just stare down the barrel letting the moment stretch—one long, broken heartbeat of knowing he might actually do it. But it never comes. Instead, he lowers the gun with a look in his eye that tells me the bullet is still coming—just not yet. Not before he wrings every last ounce of control from me.

He grabs me by the arm, clamping hard around the bruises already blooming under my skin, and then he yanks me toward him.

I stumble as my legs scream in protest and pain flares down my side. I let him drag me across the marble like some broken doll he thinks he owns, because maybe, if I make it to the end of this nightmare in one piece, he'll throw me in a room and lock the door and forget about me long enough for me to figure out how to burn this entire goddamn place down.

The officiant adjusts his tie and looks at us like he'd rather be anywhere else.

"Start," Frank orders.

The man hesitates. "Shouldn't we—"

"I said start."

The maybe-priest-maybe-lawyer blinks, like he's just realized he doesn't want to be in this room either. His eyes flick to me, then back to Frank. "Do you... do you want to begin with the—"

Frank cuts him off with a wave of his hand. "I don't give a fuck about vows. Skip to the end."

All I hear is the tick of a clock, and the faint ringing still buzzing in my ears. Across the table, the officiant's hand trembles as he flips the page again—like even the paper knows this is fucked.

"Please state your full name for the record," he says.

I don't answer and Frank's hand comes down on the table hard enough to rattle the pen. "Say it."

I lift my eyes to him slowly. My voice is a rasp when it comes out. "Anianne Rivera."

I hate every second of this. But nothing I've tried has worked. Fighting didn't work. Stalling didn't work. So now—I have to switch tactics. If all Frank wants is my signature and the house that comes with it, then there's a chance he'll be satisfied enough to lock me in a room and walk away. *That's what I'm counting on anyway.*

If he thinks I've given up, maybe he'll let his guard down. Maybe I'll get five minutes alone. I just have to stay standing long enough to survive this part. Then I'll find a way to burn it all down.

The man clears his throat and continues with a line of legal bullshit I barely register. Something about signatures and transfer of rights and full consent of mind and body. I could laugh. *Consent. That's rich.* I feel like the second I sign that document, something in me will splinter. But I don't exactly have a choice.

He'll take the paper, shake the man's hand, maybe even pour himself another drink. And I'll be carted upstairs like an afterthought—an inconvenience in heels—tossed into some gilded bedroom with blackout curtains and too much gold trim.

Maybe—if I'm lucky—he'll leave me there until morning.

I glance sideways, and that's when I see a single candle—

burning low on the dresser behind the table. I remember that candle. I remember lighting it once, a hundred years ago, before I knew what monsters smelled like when they smiled. And just like that, something cracks open inside me.

I was smaller then—my hands still unsteady, and my fingers were too clumsy to strike the match clean on the first try. The world around me was still soft in a way I didn't fully understand yet, like it hadn't decided to be cruel. It was my birthday. I remember the sound the match made, that sharp rasp followed by the hiss of flame catching. The air smelled faintly of sugar and smoke.

I didn't know what grief was yet. Not really. But I understood enough to know no one else was going to fix it. And maybe even then—at that age—I already knew no one was coming to save me. That if I ever wanted more, I'd have to go out and get it myself.

The memory hits like a flare and for one suspended moment, everything else drops away.

I blink once, taking a deep breath. The edges of the room blur, but the clarity inside me sharpens like a blade. My hand moves before I can second-guess it, reaching for the pen with a grip that feels too steady for what I'm about to do.

I wrap my fingers around it and in one quick, ruthless motion, I drive the tip straight into Frank's wrist.

He makes this awful sound—somewhere between a yell and a grunt—and stumbles back, blood already soaking through the cuff of his fancy-ass shirt.

The lawyer yelps like he just realized this isn't part of the script. Chairs scrape. Boots move. And then the guards are on me.

One of them yanks me back by the shoulders so hard my breath snaps out of my lungs. Pain blooms along my spine, but I don't stop watching Frank.

He lunges, and yeah—I knew this was coming. This is the price. But at least this time, it's mine to pay.

I'm shoved down, and someone pins my shoulders to the floor

while the pen is yanked from my grip with a twist so hard it jerks my shoulder, and I cry out.

Frank stands above me, his wrist stained dark now, blood soaking through the cuff, dripping past his knuckles. His hand twitches at his side as his lip curls.

"I gave you everything," he says crouching down beside me. "A second chance at a life you didn't earn. And this is what you give me in return?"

He looks at me and there's nothing there. No warmth, no love. Just pride and hunger dressed up like something close to affection—enough to fool someone who doesn't know better. At this point, I've lost count of how many times I've wanted to punch myself for ever thinking he had a soul.

"I didn't ask for a second chance," I whisper. "I didn't ask for you."

The guard holding me stiffens, but doesn't move.

Frank leans in closer, lowering his voice to something only I can hear. "You keep mistaking my generosity for weakness."

I meet his gaze, and I don't blink. "You should have killed me when you had the chance."

His expression changes and that's when I know I've won something, because he stands slowly, pressing his fingers into the blood at his wrist. Then turns to the officiant and motions lazily with the same stained hand.

"Do it."

"I—I can't," the man stammers. "She's not in a fit state. She's bleeding, and—"

"I said do it," Frank snaps.

The guards drag me back to the table with a fresh pen.

"Fine," I rasp. "I'll do it." They pause. Even Frank freezes for a half second before he recovers. I lean forward, calm as ever. "I'll sign," I say.

Frank frowns. "What?"

I smile, and something in my eye must make him second guess

himself, because he takes a step back. The lawyer looks confused and the guards glance at each other.

I laugh. "You knew who I was. You knew what I came from. But you thought all you had to do was buy me and wait for the crown." I take a step forward. "You never once thought about who I'd become once you did, did you?"

He blinks, and the guards shift a little closer.

"You don't own me, Frank. You bought a body, not a soul. And you're about to choke on the difference."

The table shakes as he slams his hand down. "Enough."

I shake off the guard with a force that surprises even me. Frank looks at me like I've lost my mind, and maybe I have.

"You want to talk about souls?" Frank laughs. "You think I give a fuck who you've become? You're a signature. A means to an end. You're a bloodline wrapped in tits and a tight little cunt. And I will use every inch of you until there's nothing left but what I need."

The guards shift again, but no one speaks. Even the man in the suit is frozen, caught somewhere between horror and denial.

Frank steps closer. "You're going to sign the papers. I'm going to collect what's mine. Then I'm going to fuck the fight out of you. Got it, bitch."

He says it with the kind of calm that sends a chill down my spine.

"I'll take you upstairs, dress torn, face bruised, and I'll show every one of my men what happens to a mouth that doesn't know when to shut." He smiles. "And then... I'll make you beg. For mercy. For silence. For death. And I'll deny you all three."

I can't breathe. I'm frozen in something colder than fear, something deeper than pain. It settles low in my stomach, like whatever's left of me is folding in on itself. And maybe it *is* rage, but not the loud kind.

I don't know what's going to happen next. But I do know one thing—I'm going to make his life a living hell. Every minute he keeps me here, every breath he takes thinking he's won, I'll be unraveling the seams.

He can either put a bullet in me or I'll find a way to burn this place down and walk out through the ashes. Either way, he'll wish he did kill me. Because once this is over—if I'm still breathing—I'll make sure he regrets ever learning my name.

Frank reaches down and pulls something from his belt. It's a switchblade. The click of it snaps through the room louder than anything he's said. He nods once and the guard behind me moves immediately.

Hands grab my arms—tight—and another slaps over my mouth before I can make a sound. Then I feel the cold metal at my throat.

Frank leans in, so close I can feel his breath as he whispers, "Sign."

The lawyer whimpers something about duress—but Frank doesn't flinch. "Sign it, and I might give you the night off," he says again, pressing the tip hard enough to break skin. I feel the sting and a bead of warmth sliding down my neck.

"I'll count to five."

The knife presses harder against my throat as I reach for the pen even though I don't want to. Every cell in my body screams at me not to. But this isn't about pride anymore, this is survival. And survival means biding your time.

My fingers curl around the pen and it shakes slightly in my grip, and for a second, I can't even see the page—only the shimmer of blood on Frank's wrist, the way his jaw ticks with triumph.

I sign my name and he lets go of me the second the ink hits the paper, and the knife drops from my throat like I'm suddenly not worth the effort.

He claps once. "There she is," he says. "My perfect little bride."

The priest stares at the paper like he's witnessing a war crime, but he signs it anyway. His hand shakes as he stamps the final seal.

"That's it?" I rasp. "It's done?"

"I'm never done," he says, stepping closer. "You think this was about paperwork?" His voice is low now, almost pleasant. "No, *princess*. This was about proof. I needed to own you legally before I broke you completely."

My stomach rolls as he leans in, brushing hair behind my ear. "You're not going back to a pretty bedroom. You're going downstairs."

I freeze. "What?"

Basement? What's in the basement? Oh God.

"The basement," he says. "Is soundproof. Steel door. One window. No lock on the inside."

I try to step back, but the guards are already moving. One grabs my arm again as Frank watches me with that same sick smile. The lawyer flinches. "That's not what we agreed—"

Frank rounds on him, keeping his voice deceptively calm. "Get out. Take your papers and your moral compass and get the fuck out of my house or I'll put a bullet in your head."

The man doesn't move fast enough. So Frank steps in close and drops his voice to something that makes even the air feel thinner. "Do I need to remind you what happens when people don't finish what I pay them to do?"

The priest's face drains of color but Frank doesn't blink. "The last man who didn't follow through paid the price." A long pause. "So did his wife, and his poor daughter."

The priest grabs the briefcase with shaking hands, nodding so fast it looks like a seizure. "I-I understand."

Frank smiles. "Good. Now get the fuck out before I change my mind about letting you live."

The guy doesn't wait—he scrambles, boots echoing down the hall. I jerk against the guard's grip, but it's no use. My limbs are shaking now, I need to think of something and quick.

Frank turns to the guards. "Strip her and make her remember who she belongs to."

My heart drops. Frank doesn't look at me when he says the next part. He looks at the men with their hands on me.

"And make sure you do it live," He pauses. "So they know what they're buying. And start the bidding at one million."

"No," I snarl, struggling harder. "You're not going to touch me. You're not—"

Frank grabs my chin in one brutal grip, tilting my face up toward his. "Oh, sweetheart. I already did. I touched your life. Your legacy. Your name." His voice drops into a whisper. "And now I'm going to take your body, too. Slowly."

I do the only thing I can think of—I bite him. Hard. Right on the hand still locked around my chin. I taste blood and keep going until someone yanks me off. Frank yells, stumbling back with his hand cradled to his chest.

"You bitch!" he roars.

The guard grabs my hair, yanking hard enough to rip a gasp from my throat. Then slams a knee into my stomach so hard I fold, all the air ripped out of my lungs in one ugly, choking sound. I hit the floor hard, pain bursting behind my eyes and I hear him bark the order through the haze.

"Throw her in the basement. No food. No water. Strip the dress. She doesn't deserve it."

Two guards move toward me. Grabbing me and dragging me like deadweight toward the hallway. Everything hurts, but I have to fight. I'm not going into that basement, or I'll never make it out.

The second they loosen their grip to readjust, I twist hard—slipping free for half a second, just enough to hurl myself toward the table. My hand closes around the candle and I don't think—I just throw it straight at the velvet drapes by the window. The flame hits, and for a second, nothing happens. Just this soft whoosh, like the room's holding its breath. Then it catches.

The curtains go up fast. One breath, maybe two—and then flames are racing up the velvet. Someone shouts behind me. One of the guards releases his grip and the other lunges, but I'm already moving—stumbling backward.

The heat pulses toward the ceiling. Smoke thickens, curling like black silk through the gold light. The velvet warps and peels as the flames lick higher with every second that passes.

42

"Truth always looks softer in candlelight."
(That's why it's the best time to lie.)

Ani

The room breaks apart around me. Shouts come from every direction as men burst through the door. Furniture crashes to the floor. The sharp, hollow crack of wood splitting somewhere off to my left. I hear the rush of footsteps scrambling over marble, as voices call for water, for anything that might stop this from turning into what it already is—ruin.

Beneath the chaos, I hear something else. Shouting erupts in the hall, then I hear a gunshot. One single crack that ricochets off the marble. Boots hammer against the tile, fast and closing in. More people are coming this way.

My breath catches as fight or flight kicks in and heat rushes down my spine. I'm about to run when a hand fists in my hair and yanks. Pain explodes across my scalp, sharp and blinding, ripping the air right out of my lungs.

The flames haven't even reached the other wall before a guard returns with a fire extinguisher. Another one yells something I can't make out, and there's a blur of motion, then smoke chokes the air. The curtains fall in a heavy, steaming collapse. And just like that, the fire is gone.

No.

I'm being drug backward—rougher this time, like now that I've shown them my teeth, they don't have to pretend I'm breakable.

My legs fold before I can stop them and I hit the floor hard and the guards don't bother lifting me this time. Frank stands a few feet away, his face a twisted mix of rage and amusement. His hair is messed up, his shirt half-untucked, but he's still smiling. He knows I've got nothing left.

And when I look around—at the wet floor, the burned drapes, the scattered papers—I know it too.

I lower my head, but I don't cry, I don't even know if I can. I sink somewhere deep. Somewhere hollow. Because if there's no escape through fire... then there's only one way out left. And right now, I don't know if I'm strong enough to take any more of it. My body is wrecked. My throat is raw. And my legs barely feel real beneath me.

Frank doesn't notice. He's still lost in his own rage, pacing and spitting fury while his hand clamps around my throat like he's trying to grind me into the floor with it. He's not even talking anymore—just snarling threats, half-formed words, violence bubbling through his teeth.

The door blows open. No warning, no dramatic speech—just a deafening crack of splintered wood. Steven walks in first. Calm and deadly like he's done this a thousand times. Two men file in behind him, all shadows and guns like they've been waiting for this moment. And just like that, the air shifts.

He doesn't yell when he enters. He doesn't even glance at the guards or at Frank—who's still got his hands around my throat like he owns me.

His eyes find mine and they don't waver. Not once.

And that's all it takes for something inside me to snap. A sound I don't recognize rips from somewhere deep, somewhere raw. I'm shaking, and sobbing without sound.

I don't care that I look wrecked. I don't care that I've lost every inch of dignity I had left. He's here.

He came.

Steven looks at me like the world could burn and he'd still walk through the ashes just to find me in the middle of it.

I was seconds away from giving up, from letting the silence swallow me whole.

But he came.

For the first time in what feels like forever, I feel like I can breathe. A single tear rolls down my cheek and my chest does something hideous—because the second our eyes lock, nothing else exists.

Just him. And the fury in his silence that promises he'll kill for me.

I see what looks like relief flash through his eyes. The sharp, desperate, possessive kind of relief that belongs to a man who's been living in hell—and just clawed his way out.

It's probably only seconds that pass, but they feel like hours. My chest barely rises. My lungs don't seem to know what to do. I just stare back at him, praying he doesn't disappear.

And then—he moves with something far more dangerous. Purpose. He takes one step, then it's chaos.

The first shot lands clean. A guard drops without so much as a sound. Another step. Another shot. Point. Pull. Drop. The world narrows and all I can do is watch.

It's not fear that keeps me still. It's not even the shock of the gunshots or the blood staining the floor.

It's him.

It's the way he walked straight into my ruin without flinching. I've never seen him like this before. A reckoning, shaped in flesh and vengeance, carved out of silence and rage. He doesn't speak. Doesn't shout commands or call attention to himself. Every step he takes screams louder than bullets.

I understand—somehow, through the fog in my head and the blood on my lips—I understand exactly what he is.

He's not here to save me. He's here to destroy anyone who tried to take me. And in that moment, I know without a shred of doubt that he would burn the world to the ground if it meant I was still standing on the other side of the fire.

He's covered in blood, his shirt's soaked in it. I've never seen him look so dangerous and so fucking delicious at the same time and I think that might be a sign I've fully lost it.

He's the kind of man you don't walk away from—you burn for him, or you don't come back at all.

God, he's beautiful.

His hair is damp with sweat, his jaw is tight, and he's breathing heavy, but it's his eyes that make him look like a God on a war path.

Steven sweeps the room with his gun still raised, eyes scanning like he's expecting another threat to rise from the shadows.

Whatever softness was in Steven a second ago, it disappears the second his eyes lock on Frank.

His entire body shifts into a cold, lethal stillness. Frank's got his arm locked around my ribs now, holding me like a shield. Like I'm the fucking insurance policy that's going to save his life.

But Steven doesn't raise the gun. He just tilts his head, and I can see him already measuring the distance between Frank's heart-beat and the floor.

And then he speaks—low, and terrifyingly calm. "Let her go."

Frank doesn't. Of course he doesn't. He's too arrogant and too stupid to realize Steven's not threatening him, he's deciding where to bury the body.

But I see it.

Steven steps forward, and Frank's lips part, like he's about to say something but Steven doesn't let him.

"I said, let her go."

He aims his gun, standing dead center in the room, blood still streaking down his face, breathing like he's holding every last ounce of violence inside and waiting for a reason to let it out.

And I can't stop staring at him. My body's still humming from the sight of him. From the way he moved. From the way he looked at me like I was his and nothing else mattered.

I should be afraid—Frank's arm is still locked around my throat, and Steven's here with blood on his face and a gun in his hand.

But I'm not. I know he won't shoot. Not if there's even a chance I could get caught in the crossfire.

God help me—I'm soaked by just the way he walked in and made murder look like devotion.

Frank wipes blood from his lip with the back of his hand, smiling through it like a villain who thinks he still has the upper hand.

"Touching," he says. "Really. You always did fall for the wrong things. First it was Lauren, now Ani? But at least you're consistent."

Steven doesn't flinch, but I do. My head snaps toward Frank. "What did you just say?"

His voice drips with smugness, like I'm just now catching up to the joke he's been laughing at for weeks. "He didn't tell you?"

Steven's jaw ticks and Frank moves us forward, even with the gun still trained on him. "Let me give you a little history lesson, sweetheart. The man you're looking at? He's not your savior. He's been watching you since before you ever met. Isn't that right?"

Steven shifts, his stance tightening as he keeps the gun trained on Frank without so much as a blink. The tension in his arm doesn't waver. Not even a tremor. And I don't know why he hasn't pulled the trigger yet. I can see it in Steven's jaw—how close he is to ending it. How much he wants to. But something's holding him back.

"He used to work for me," Frank says, almost fondly. "Until he got soft. Broke rank, and took something that didn't belong to him, making a call that wasn't his to make and thought he could disappear without consequence, so I found the one thing I knew would bring him back."

Steven looks at me—and for the briefest second, everything

inside him shifts. If I'm reading him right, it's like he's pleading for something I don't understand. And then it's gone.

"She meant everything to him, you know. He would've died for her. Hell, he did." He laughs. "He loved something that belonged to me. She always belonged to me."

"That's not true," Steven growls.

"No?" Frank asks, leaning in so his mouth brushes my ear. "Why do you think you caught his eye so fast, doll? Why do you think he was always there, always watching? He didn't fall for you, Ani. He used you. I made sure of it."

My breath catches as I look at Steven and for the first time... I'm not sure what I see.

"Is that true?" I whisper.

He doesn't move, but he doesn't look away either. His jaw ticks once, but before he can speak, the hallway door creaks open, and then she walks in. A tall, blonde woman. My pulse stops and my brain feels like it just tripped over itself trying to catch up. My vision tunnels, and I think I might pass out.

My brain trips over itself trying to make sense of what I'm seeing, like it's buffering reality in slow, broken chunks.

No. It can't be.

Frank smiles wider. "There she is, the woman of the hour."

Steven keeps his gun trained on Frank like it's an extension of his will. But one of the men flanking him lifts his weapon and points it straight at her.

My stomach drops and the whole room freezes in that single, suspended heartbeat.

"Lauren," Steven says, like the name burns on his tongue.

"Wait—What do you mean Lauren?" My voice cracks midword. I swallow, but my throat stays dry. "Don't you mean... Sloane?"

Her name barely makes it out, before my eyes start to blur, but I blink the unshed tears away.

Steven's chest rises and falls like his entire body is coiled around a decision he hasn't made yet. But it's not rage I feel coming off him, it's restraint. *What is going on and what the fuck is Sloane doing here?*

He doesn't lower his weapon and she doesn't blink. She just stands there, completely unbothered.

"Steven—" I twist toward him. "Don't shoot her. That's—she's —she's my friend."

He doesn't lower the gun and neither does the man pointing his right at her.

Sloane—Lauren—whoever she's pretending to be—just stands there. Watching me. I can't tell what's in her eyes, but I know what's in mine. Betrayal. Recognition. And the sinking, sick feeling that this whole story just cracked open wider than I ever wanted it to.

Steven's eyes cut to me—still black with rage, but now there's something else brewing underneath. Confusion.

"How the fuck do you know each other?" His voice is low, but it vibrates like a warning shot.

The woman doesn't flinch, she just tilts her head with the faintest trace of a smirk on her lips.

Steven takes a step toward her. "How are you not dead?"

She shrugs one shoulder, slow and infuriatingly casual. "Sorry to disappoint."

My pulse kicks hard in my throat. Nothing is making sense. Not her. Not Steven. Not the way Frank looks between them with smug satisfaction.

"That's the real reason he's here," Frank says, and his voice is smooth now. Confident even. "To finish what he started. Or die trying."

Okay, I'm starting to get pissed. I don't know if I'm going to laugh or cry, but I want to know what the fuck is going on. My head's spinning. There's something massive I'm not seeing here—and Steven's jaw clenches like he's seconds from snapping.

"What does any of this have to do with me?" I snap.

"Everything," Frank says, his voice sharp enough to cut glass. "You were the bait."

My breath catches. *Bait?*

"I only needed a signature. That's it. But when I found out Stevie here was snooping where he shouldn't be, I figured—why not kill two birds?" He doesn't turn—but I feel his grin as he shifts just enough to press his mouth near my ear, voice dripping with cruel satisfaction. "See, I paid your ex to sell you to me, but you were also an investment. I just needed to get you on his radar."

He nods toward Steven. "I needed time to get your grandfather out of the way. So I gave you a job to do—distract him. While I lured him in and made sure he stayed long enough for me to finally finish the job."

I think I'm going to be sick.

"You fell for him. Hook, line, and fuck-me eyes." His voice drops, and I don't know if I want to hear what's about to come out of his mouth. "The second he thought you were mine, I knew he'd use you. That's who he is. I would know, I trained him."

His smile is slow and smug, like he knows exactly where to hit —and fuck, it hits hard. It lands straight to the part of me I didn't realize I'd handed over.

No. That can't be true.

"He didn't come to save you," Frank goes on, chuckling. "He came to find me. You were just the shortcut."

"Shut your fucking mouth," Steven snarls. His voice is lethal, but I can barely hear it. My ears are ringing, and my eyes start to sting. I'm furious. Betrayed. Terrified. And so fucking confused, it's not even funny.

"Steven," I whisper.

Behind him, another man moves further into the room, keeping their weapon trained on Frank and Sloane. Or Lauren. Or whatever the hell her name is.

When he finally speaks, his voice softens—but his aim never wavers.

"Ani." His voice is rough now. He steps forward, one hand still raised, not in surrender—but something close. "Dear, look at me. Please."

Frank tightens his grip around my neck, "Not another step."

"Yes, I used you. That's the part he wants you to hear. That's the part I can't take back." His eyes flicker, behind me so fast I almost missed it. "I came for Frank, yes. I thought you were just leverage. I told myself you didn't matter."

I now feel like I want to puke. God, I feel stupid. Every look. Every touch. Every time I thought maybe this was real. Some part of me still wants to believe he gives a damn and that I wasn't just a convenient way to bleed the man who bought me. *Who also, turns out, didn't actually even want me like I thought either.*

"So I was just a job." I don't even mean for it to come out loud, but it does. "All of it. Just part of the plan?"

I don't cry. I'm too far past that.

"If Frank hadn't told me, would you have ever said a damn thing?"

Steven's jaw clenches. "No. Because I wanted to destroy him more than I wanted to save you. But now, there's no world where he walks away and you don't come with me." His voice is rough. "I told myself you were leverage. That none of it mattered." He shakes his head. "But it did. You did."

There's a blur of motion, and then I feel a shift in his balance, a sudden jolt—and Frank screams. A guy's already got him in some kind of brutal choke from behind, dragging him backward with a forearm locked across his neck and a knee jammed into the back of his thigh until it snaps.

Frank buckles, and when he does his grip on my throat slips just long enough for me to tear free. I gasp as I stumble forward—

but Steven pulls me against him. One hand curls around the back of my head, the other anchoring around my waist, and I melt into him before I can think better of it.

The world sways, and I still can't breathe, but I'm free. And he's looking at me with nothing but heat in his eyes.

He tilts his head, dropping his voice. "I didn't fall for you. I fucking drowned in you. And if you think I'm walking out of here without you—you haven't been paying attention."

Tears slide down my cheeks before I can stop them. I knew the risk. Knew what he was. And I still said yes. Still handed him the knife. Even when I knew better, even when I swore I wouldn't fall for a man who lies like it's love.

My throat burns. My heart cracks. And I realize—I'm not crying because he ruined me. I'm crying because I let him.

And then Frank's voice cuts through it all. "He's lying to you, that's what he does. It's all he knows how to do, Anianne. He's a killer."

Steven's eyes don't leave mine. There's something in them now —something raw and pleading beneath the fury. A silent question I don't know how to answer.

Slauren interrupts. "You can't trust him."

It lands like a slap and I jerk toward her, stumbling as I tear myself out of Steven's arms—nearly falling over.

It's like waking up from a trance. My skin's still buzzing where he touched me. My pulse still tuned to him like it forgot how to beat on its own.

"What the hell are you even doing here, Sloane? Why are you with him? What the fuck is going on?"

She smirks, shrugging one elegant shoulder like this isn't the end of the goddamn world. "He needed a reason to keep fighting."

But for the briefest second—so quick I almost miss it—something flickers behind her eyes. It's gone before I can name it, swallowed by the cold steel in her voice.

Steven's voice cuts through, and he's pissed. "Don't listen to her."

I look back at him again and his eyes... they're still on me. And I hate that I still feel it. That hollow ache. That pull.

After everything—after what he did, what he didn't say—I should want to spit in his face. But all I can do is stand here, wanting the monster who walked through hell for me.

He steps forward—just an inch—the veins down his arm flex where he grips the gun, and his eyes are darker than I've ever seen them. And fuck me, even now—after everything—I feel it. That slow ache in the pit of my stomach that would still crawl to him.

"You're mine," he says. "And I'm not leaving this room without you."

His words are the only thing anchoring me in this nightmare. And stupidly, I believe him. How did I end up in the middle of a live-action soap opera directed by Satan? Bleeding everywhere and trying really hard not to fall apart in front of the man who sold me, the man who made me feel safe just so I'd never see the knife coming, and the girl I thought was my friend but was apparently in on it the whole fucking time?

Not to mention there are guns pointed in every direction.

And what the fuck's up with Slauren. My friend? My fucking coworker! The woman I've had coffee with. Laughed with. Shared pieces of myself with, not realizing she was more tangled in this mess than I ever was.

My chest caves in so fast I almost miss the breath.

They're in love. They have to be. The way he looks at her. The way her voice cracked when she said he needed a reason to keep fighting.

Unless...

My ribs burn, but it's the bruises across my jaw that throb and I'm still tasting blood every time I swallow.

Steven turns on her then, and it's the first time I've ever seen his expression crack into something other than anger or control.

It's heartbreak.

"I've loved you since that first job together."

674

43

“IT’S NOT THE FIRST TIME THEY TOUCH YOU
THAT WRECKS YOU.”
(IT’S THE SECOND—WHEN YOU KNOW WHAT IT’LL COST.)

Ani

It shouldn’t hit this hard—but it does, because some pathetic part of me wanted to believe he’d only ever felt those things for me.

“I told you I’d always keep you safe. You were the only family I had left. And this is what you do?” His voice cracks.

She tilts her head, cool as ever. “Distractions get you killed.”

“You were my sister.”

The word hits so hard I almost miss it. *Wait.* Family? Sister?

My chest caves in, not from heartbreak but from sheer whiplash. My brain scrambles to reprocess everything that just happened. I feel like I’ve been sucker punched by the truth and somehow kissed at the same time.

He didn’t love her like that. He loved her like family.

Frank coughs, dragging in a breath like it hurts. But somehow, even half-conscious and wrecked, his voice still finds that smug, slithering edge. “You thought it was you?” He says it softly, but it lands exactly how he wanted it to. “Doll, she’s been his since long before you came along.”

My stomach hurts, and I would give anything to just sit down.

Steven takes a step toward me, dropping his voice into that low, sexy tone he uses—the kind that promises bloodshed and devotion in the same breath. *It clearly also says I have no problem killing for you. And smile while I do it.*

His eyes drag over me, and I see something shift behind his eyes.

"That all might be true," he says, "but I came here for you, pretty girl."

His hand grips my chin, and he rubs my jaw. "That hair suits you," he says, eyes dragging down like he's already imagined pulling it while I'm on my knees. "You look meaner and you finally stopped giving a fuck."

I swear I could come from his voice alone.

"It fucking turns me on." Steven mutters, so only I can hear him.

Then Frank pipes up, like he couldn't let us have the moment.

"Cute." His voice is hoarse. "You're still just some pathetic little orphan girl with a pretty face and a trauma kink he could twist into obedience."

It all happens too fast. He lunges without warning, driving his elbow into the nearest guard's face with a sickening crunch. I can hear the bone crack from here. The man staggers back, clutching his nose as blood pours between his fingers. Frank yanks a gun from his waistband, and the shot rings out before I even register the movement.

Frank screams, collapsing to the floor as blood pours from his thigh.

"You should be asking yourself why he never told you the truth," Frank grunts, spitting in our direction. "Why he let you walk into this blind."

Steven stalks forward and drives a punch straight into Frank's face. The sound of bones cracking fills the room.

His voice drops vibrating with restraint, then looks at me. "The only reason he isn't dead right now is for you."

Wait, me?

"The second you tell me you want him gone—he's gone." He says it like a vow.

Frank groans from the floor, fingers smeared with blood as he grips his thigh. But even now, he smirks through crimson teeth, like pain is just another game to him.

"Shut him up."

One of the men moves instantly, like he's been waiting all night to be unleashed. The butt of his rifle slams into Frank's temple with a sickening crack. Frank drops with a grunt. The man crouches beside him and presses a gun to his skull. He's coughing up blood on the floor, trying to sit up, and I open my mouth to say something, but Frank apparently has a death wish.

"You're no heir," he spits. "You're just a broken girl who got lucky."

Steven lifts the gun again, pointing it right at his head. I see that tick in his jaw. His restraint is splintering, cracking straight down the middle.

"You want me to kill him, beautiful? I'll do it. Right now. And I won't flinch." He tilts his head slightly, and I see heat flash in his eyes.

I don't know what it says about me, but I'm so turned on right now. But I turn, locking eyes with Frank.

"You know something, Frank?" I take a step forward. My body's screaming, and I think I might fall over, but I don't care. "I might be broken—but at least I didn't sell my soul just to sit at a table that still looks at you like the fucking help."

He jerks, but the man behind him pushes the gun further into his head.

"You thought you could own me?" My voice comes out a little wrecked—but steady. "Twist me up, turn me into your little puppet?"

I laugh—actually laugh. *Not so fun when the puppet cuts her own strings, huh?* Maybe it's madness or finally waking the hell up. But I could combust from how much rage is sitting in my chest.

"You thought you were building an empire." I step closer. "But all you were doing was digging your own fucking grave."

I take another step closer, enough to make my point, but not enough to be stupid. Out of the corner of my eye, I see Steven move too—like his body's already preparing to pounce if Frank moves.

"You're nothing but a scared little man with a crown made of ashes. And besides, you made me this way, and I'll be the one who burns your empire to the ground."

His eyes narrow—but something shifts behind them. Fear.

"You should've killed me when you had the chance," I whisper. "Now you'll die knowing I'll never think of you again."

My words hang in the air. Maybe I should feel guilty, but I don't. Not after everything.

"What now?" I ask, looking at Steven.

He steps forward like he thinks I'll bolt if he breathes wrong. But his eyes stay locked on mine.

"You're all I give a fuck about."

Another step.

"Say the word," he murmurs, so only I can hear him. "I'll end him before you even blink."

The world fractures. Or maybe it stills. I can't tell anymore. This man has been chasing vengeance for years from what it sounds like—dragging the ghost of his sister behind him—and still, he's standing here waiting for me.

Behind us, Frank laughs. A soft, ugly sound that cuts through everything, making my skin crawl.

"You two deserve each other," he spits, wiping blood from his mouth with the back of his hand. "A killer and a whore in a dress. Romantic."

Steven turns to him with the kind of patience that makes your skin crawl. But he still doesn't shoot. He's still giving me the choice —even now.

And then Frank shifts. That sick little smile stretches wider as he turns to Sloane, eyes gleaming.

"Do I need to remind you what's at stake?"

Sloane flinches like he slapped her. The temperature in the room drops five degrees. *What did he just say—*

Frank's smile turns serpentine. "Kill me and you'll never find Kody."

Steven's voice turns lethal. "Lauren—who the fuck is Kody?"

She's shaking, crying now. She lifts her hand—slowly—and the air around her crackles with a shift I can't name. She turns the gun toward me before I register what's happening. Her hand is trembling. And then—she shoots.

Frank screams as his knee explodes and he crumples backward onto the marble, howling.

"That was for Kody." Her voice is cracked.

I didn't see that coming.

Steven's men rush forward. One of them moving for Sloaren—while the other keeps his gun trained on her.

"Don't shoot!" Steven snaps, stepping in. His voice slices through the tension like a blade. He turns to her again, eyes wide.

"Who. Is. Kody?"

Slauren lowers the gun and whispers—"He's my son."

My heart stops. Literally. Like my brain can't compute the words she just said.

She has a son? Sloane has a kid?

My stomach twists violently and Steven just stares at her like everything he knew about her is slipping through his fingers. He looks like he might actually vomit.

"Why didn't you tell me?"

"Because I knew you'd come for him," she whispers. "Because I knew if you saw me, you'd try to fix it. And it's too late, Steven. You can't fix this."

Frank groans. Obnoxiously. He's laughing again even though he looks like he's bleeding out.

"God, this is beautiful," he slurs glaring at Steven. Then he says the one line that tilts the earth under my feet. "I should've killed the bitch and the kid when I had the chance."

Steven looks at me and something in my chest caves because I know what he's asking me with that look. That unreadable, aching look that says he'll do whatever I want him to do. That this final decision isn't his to make anymore—it's mine. He's holding the gun, but the trigger belongs to me.

He sees it written all over me—the way my lips part like I want to say something, but don't. My eyes sting, not from tears, but from the heat rising behind them. That slow, sharp burn crawling up my throat, boiling into something darker.

I meet his eyes and nod, letting out a breath I didn't even realize I was holding, and without a word, he turns to Frank, lifts the gun— And pulls the trigger.

The shot cracks like thunder—impossibly loud in the quiet room. I jump, even though I knew it was coming.

For a second, everything feels weightless. Frank's body drops. Just like that—it's over.

The silence that follows is too loud, and I don't breathe. I just stand there, staring at what's left of him. The blood fans out beneath his body like spilled ink across marble.

He's gone.

My chest rises and falls like it's waiting for the second act. The next horror. The next betrayal. I don't know how to stop bracing for impact—like my body still thinks the worst is coming. I think I'm in shock. And I genuinely don't know if I'm about to start sobbing or laughing.

Behind me, I hear Sloane. At first it's quiet—not even a sob, then something inside her finally snaps. She runs out of the room, covering her face, while emotion pours out of her—like it's been buried under her for years and finally clawed its way free.

I don't move—I don't even know which version of me is still breathing right now.

Steven looks at me like I'm the only goddamn thing tethering him to the floor. And something shifts behind his eyes, that lethal edge softens into something raw. I don't know if it's relief or regret, but whatever it is, it slices right through me.

I can't breathe.

I think—I finally think I understand what it means to choose your monster. Mine just murdered a man for me and I don't know if that makes me safer... or if it makes me his.

My hands are trembling and my heart is beating like it wants to run out of my chest and collapse on the floor beside me. When his hands finally land on me, I lean into him. Everything inside me is screaming, and he's the only thing that's ever been able to quiet it. I'm tense and trembling beneath the surface but the second he pulls me in, I come undone.

My chest caves against his, and I bury my face in the sweat and blood and smoke. It hits all at once. The pain. The fear. The fucking grief. Like my body finally got the memo that it survived. And now it doesn't know what to do with the pieces.

The first sob hits before I can stop it. Then another. And another. And suddenly I'm full-on falling apart and there's no getting it back under control.

My fingers bunch in his shirt, like if I let go I'll hit the floor. So I don't. I hold on. I press my face into him and just—let it happen. No more pretending I'm fine. No more acting like this didn't wreck me. I let it break me, right there in his arms.

His arms tighten around me like they were built to cage this kind of wreckage, and he holds me.

One of his hands slides into my hair while the other wraps tight around my waist, anchoring me. His mouth finds my ear, as he whispers the only three things I think I've ever really needed to hear.

"I've got you."

"It's over."

"You're safe."

When I finally lift my head, his eyes are already on me. He's looking at me like he'd burn the whole world down just to keep me breathing.

"You came," I whisper, the words slipping out before I can stop them.

His hand brushes his thumb across my cheek, wiping away a tear I didn't realize had fallen.

"There was never a world where I wouldn't."

And then—God help me—he smiles. That quiet, wrecked kind of smile that feels like it was built just for me.

"For the record?" he mutters, kissing the side of my head. "I know I was tied to a fucking chair, but I did say don't go anywhere." His arm tightens around me. "Didn't think I'd wake up in a basement while you were out burning down a goddamn club."

A stunned laugh tears out of my chest—half-choked, and just a little unhinged. "You're such an asshole."

He leans in, pressing his forehead to mine, his voice is low and maddeningly steady. "Yeah? Well, I love you too."

My heart flatlines.

"Steven..."

"I love you, Ani." He says it again—slower this time, like he wants me to hear every damn word.

His hands come up to cup my face, and my throat tightens like my body already knows what's coming.

"You're mine," he murmurs, kissing my cheek. "And I'm yours. And the second we get out of here, we're having a very long, very serious conversation about communication."

Then he kisses me—hard. All fire and frustration and every ounce of fury and devotion that's been building since the second we met. When he finally pulls back, his voice drops. "Starting with how you don't disappear without telling me where the fuck you're going. Ever again."

I blink at him, still breathless. "Did you seriously just threaten me with a feelings conversation?"

"Absolutely." He kisses me again. "You can cry, hit me, climb me—whatever you gotta do, but we're not doing this halfway shit anymore."

Anymore? So he's been all in this whole time... and I've been the one holding back?

His thumb drags across my bottom lip like he's memorizing the shape of it. "You and me, dear," he says, and his voice is doing that growly thing again. "It's murder-suicide do us part at this point."

The words shouldn't make my chest ache, my stomach flip or my pulse stutter. But they do. Because it's him. This is the language we speak—chaos, violence, and devotion stitched together with blood and bruises.

My throat tightens. God, I hate how much I need him.

"That sounds a lot like a proposal," I manage, even though my voice is barely there.

Steven grins—and it's all teeth. I'm so fucked. I'm also so in love it hurts to look at him.

"Good," he says, stepping closer until there's no space left. "Because I'm not letting you go."

His hands find my face again, steadying me. "You're it for me," he says, quieter now, but no less dangerous. "I don't care what we have to burn. I'll build a kingdom out of the ashes if that's what it takes to keep you."

And I believe him.

44

"Always make sure she knows she's loved."
(No matter what)

Ani

I don't remember much of the flight back. My mind was still trying to catch up to the fact that I was alive, and Frank was gone. That the war—at least this part of it—was over. I've replayed the last few days over and over in my mind so many times it's probably unhealthy.

Steven's lap wasn't exactly comfortable because every time the plane jolted, my ribs lit up like someone had punched me again. My hands wouldn't stop shaking unless his were on top of them, and even then, I could still feel the tremor, buried deep under my skin. But, it was better than the cold leather seats, and I wasn't moving.

Steven hadn't let me go since he found me in that room. I don't remember how long we stayed talking after he told me he loved me. It was long enough to realize we were suddenly alone and when we finally stepped out, everything looked the same, but it wasn't.

One of the guys Steven came with brought in a doctor. Some mystery man in scrubs with a black bag like we were in some back-alley mafia clinic.

He didn't say much, just started checking me over. I didn't argue. Didn't really have it in me.

Steven stood off to the side with his arms crossed, tracking every movement like he didn't trust anyone to breathe near me, let alone touch me. Which honestly, not the worst energy to have in the room when you're half-naked and bruised with a stranger stitching your face.

Nothing was broken—just bruises, cuts, and a lot of swelling. The doctor cleaned everything, bandaged me up, and walked out like I was already yesterday's problem.

We found Sloane—Lauren—whatever—halfway to the front door with a torn duffel bag and mascara streaked halfway down her face. She was sobbing and throwing things into a pile.

The shouting started almost immediately.

Steven was cold and furious, acting like he was trying not to lose it, and she screamed right back, saying things I didn't understand, and a few I did. Things about Frank, about the lies, about Kody, and all the ways she tried to protect the people she loved and all the ways it backfired. But in the end, Steven told her she was getting on the plane. And now— Here we are.

They've been talking the whole time, and I've only caught fragments of their conversation while I've been in and out of sleep. Just enough to thread together pieces of the story I didn't know I was missing.

She didn't meet Frank. Not really. He found her and raised her as his own, teaching her how to survive. But what he really did was —shape her into something useful, obedient, and dangerous.

She met Steven years later. He was seventeen—pissed off, and already halfway gone. Frank gave him a roof, a job, and a bed to crash in between bruises. Together, they figured it out from there. How to kill, how to lie, and how to hold on to each other when nobody else gave a shit.

When Steven asked her about the baby, she said it happened after a job. She'd come back to the house exhausted, and wanted to forget everything, just for one night. Steven was out on his own job, so he wasn't home. She'd been drinking when Frank showed up like he always did—uninvited, already drunk and already angry. But by the time she realized what was happening, it was already over. And a few weeks later... she found out she was pregnant.

When Frank found out, he locked her away, threatened her, and told her if she ever stepped out of line, she'd never see her son again. He's five now. He loves dinosaurs. Eats chicken nuggets like it's a food group, and refuses to brush his teeth without a fight.

She said she tried to run once. Frank showed her a photo of a body and told her it was Kody's. She didn't try again.

When the plane touches down, the night air feels heavier than it should—thick with all the shit we didn't say. Sloane walks toward a black car waiting near the curb, pulling the door open. She pauses, looking at me, then glances at Steven. "I'll come by in a few days," she says. "We've still got shit to deal with."

She nods to the driver. "Take me to the house."

Steven just nods, watching her go. And then she's gone—disappearing into the dark.

Without a word, he walks to our car, opening my door while I slide in, and he gets in behind me. The second I lean into him, he pulls me straight onto his lap. His arms wrap around me, and he buries his face in my neck, dragging in a slow breath. There are so many things I want to say, but I have no idea where to start.

Thank you? I love you? I know the world's on fire and I'm still bleeding, but if you so much as move your hand an inch lower, I swear I'm going to grind down on you and make everything a hell of a lot worse?

He's hard—pressed up against me like it doesn't matter that I'm still bruised and shaking. I know I shouldn't want it. Not right now. But I do. I want him so badly it hurts in a different place.

We pull into his driveway just after midnight. The porch lights are already on and Bern explodes out the front door before the car even fully stops. Her paws skid across the gravel, and for a second, I forget how much pain I'm in—right up until my leg gives out as I step out of the car.

She launches herself at me, and I drop to my knees. My face disappears into her fur, and just like that, I forget how to breathe.

"Hey, girl," I whisper, my voice already breaking. "You missed me, huh?"

I tried not to let myself think about her while I was gone. She's freaking out like it's just another day, and I didn't go missing. Somehow, that's what finally undoes me. "I missed you too," I breathe into her neck. "So much."

Steven doesn't say a word. He just stands a few feet back, watching—like he knows I need this and he's not going to take it from me.

I think I'm crying again. But honestly? I'm not sure I ever stopped.

He crouches in front of me—and that's the moment I break wide open. It's not the black in his gaze that wrecks me, it's the way he looks at me that has me melting, and forgetting my name.

He slides his arms around me, picking me up, and stands. He carries me inside, Bern trailing behind us, and sets me gently on the couch like I might break if he moves too fast. Then he crouches in front of me again, hand dragging down his face as he exhales.

"So," he says casually, "are we going to talk about the part where you committed arson, or the part where you almost married a mafia psychopath?"

My brain short-circuits and I laugh out loud. It escapes before I can stop it—this borderline hysterical noise that tumbles out of my ribcage. And of course, I cry harder.

"You're such a dick."

He shrugs. "Yeah. But I'm your dick."

"Jesus Christ."

"Not quite." He leans in. "But someone told me I have a God complex, if that helps."

And just like that, I forget how to breathe. I know he's joking—

but the truth's wrapped in every word. This man would gut the universe if it meant putting me back together. And if I think about it, that's what he's done since we met.

"You scared the shit out of me, Ani." His voice drops. "When I saw you in his house... when I realized he had you—" His jaw flexes like the memory physically hurts him to talk about. Then I see the rage flash through his eyes.

"I thought you were dead," I whisper, cutting him off.

"I was." He says it like it's no big deal. Which is exactly why it is. "Until I saw you."

I blink like that'll stop the tears, but I'm sobbing all over again.

He grabs my hands. "From the second I saw you," his eyes lock onto mine. "Even when I hated it. Even when I told myself you were just part of the job. You were the only thing I wanted that scared the shit out of me."

I wipe at my face, still falling apart. "You really picked a mess, huh?"

"I'm not asking for easy." His thumb drags over my knuckles. "I'm asking for real."

And just like that—I lose what little composure I had left. It pours out of me in quiet waves, shaking through my shoulders as I let my head fall forward until it rests against his.

"I hate how much I love you," I mutter.

"Too bad," he says quietly. "Because I decided you were mine on the ladder."

I laugh—but it's wet and ungraceful. "I'm a disaster."

He leans in, brushing his mouth against my jaw. "Still mine."

Then he kisses me. Nothing in the world could stop my pussy from being turned on right now. His lips are on mine and when he finally pulls back, he tucks a piece of hair behind my ear. "I meant what I said, we're gonna have to talk about your communication skills."

"Excuse me?"

"You disappeared without telling anyone where you were

going. You burned down a building and you walked into a mafia wedding with no backup—"

"I did have backup," I snap. "My rage and unresolved trauma came with me, thank you very much."

That criminal grin tugs at his mouth—the same one that ruined me before I even knew his name.

"I'm serious, Ani. As much as I want to fuck you right now—I need to know you're actually okay. We need to talk. With words."

"Wow. Feelings and accountability?" I arch a brow, trying to hide the way my heart's suddenly thudding. "You really are trying to wife me up."

He gives a short laugh, but it doesn't quite reach his eyes. His hands are still on me, like he's bracing for whatever I might throw at him next.

I roll my eyes. "Relax. You're doing great. Ten out of ten. Slightly traumatizing, but emotionally available, but you're my toxic little dreamboat."

The corner of his mouth lifts. "Keep talking like that, and I'll put you over my knee before we get to the talking part."

Don't tempt me with a good time.

Okay, I know he's right. We probably do need to talk. I sigh. "Okay. Fine. We'll talk."

I'm not ready to unravel just yet, so I tilt my head, keeping my tone light even though my pulse kicks up. "But I have one question first."

His eyes narrow, but he nods once.

"If you weren't the one sending me messages, who was?" I ask, crossing my arms.

He exhales through his nose. "I had it looked into. But we'll talk about it later."

My arms tighten around my chest. "That's not ominous or anything."

"Not now, Ani."

The words should piss me off more than they do, but he

chuckles under his breath, as he sits down, pulling me once again into his lap. "You want to talk now, or are you tired?"

I don't answer right away. I just go still against him, because I can feel it—that weight we've both been carrying since the second we stepped off the tarmac. *Do I want to talk, no. Should we, probably.*

I shift back slightly so I can see him. His arm tightens instinctively around my waist, like letting me move too far is a risk he's not willing to take.

His eyes flick down to mine, jaw flexing because he knows that I'm not going to let it go. "I had Travis run it."

"Who's Travis?"

He ignores my question and keeps talking. "I didn't want to drop it on you until I was sure."

"Well?" I blink. "Are you sure now?"

He looks at me with that look—that unreadable, too-calm stillness that usually comes right before someone bleeds.

"We'll get into it tomorrow," he mutters. "After you sleep and after I figure out how the fuck to say it all without making you hate me."

My chest tightens. "Is it really that bad?"

"Not everything," he says. "Some of it you deserve to know. Some of it you need to know. But yeah, parts of it are not going to be pleasant." His hand comes up, thumb dragging across the inside of my wrist. "You asked me once if I was the kind of man who lies."

"I remember."

"I don't lie. But I also didn't tell you everything."

"That's not exactly comforting...or a secret."

"I know."

Silence stretches out between us, thick and full of everything that's happened. I mean, could this man break my heart into a thousand pieces? Absolutely. But he makes me feel safe. A little frightened at times, sure, but I've never felt safer.

I know I should let it sit and give myself a second to process whatever the hell he means by *"some of it is bad."* But I can't. I'd rather just get it all out now.

"No," I say. "We're not doing this tomorrow."

His eyes darken and his arm tightens around my waist again. "Ani—"

"I'm fine." It comes out tighter than I expected. "I'm not dead."

His mouth opens, then closes again. His hand stills on my back. And for once, I don't fill the silence with a sarcastic jab or some emotionally-deflective punchline. I just sit there.

He exhales like I just knocked the wind out of him. "When I thought I lost you..." His voice cracks—just enough to break me. "Everything in me fractured."

My chest caves a little more.

"You don't get to say that and then make me wait till tomorrow," I whisper. "Talk."

He hesitates. Brushing his thumb along my arm like he's trying to ground both of us. "Frank planned to sell you the second you signed those papers, honey. You're the key to unlocking your grandfather's entire empire."

I go still. "...What?"

"You heard me."

There he goes, holding my entire world by the throat with three words and no apology.

"...My grandfathers what?"

His eyes don't move. "I'm not sugarcoating it for you, pretty girl. You're too damn strong for that, and we both know it. So I'm going to say it straight, and you're going to take it—because you can and you've already survived worse. Then we'll figure out the rest. Together."

He leans in close to my ear and his voice drops to something darker. "Maybe—if you're a good girl—I'll let you come. On my fingers first, then my tongue, and if you're still breathing after that... I'll fuck you so hard you forget your own name. Once your body's had a chance to recover, that is."

I like how he negotiates.

Heat floods my body, settling between my legs. My thighs clench together, desperate and aching, because I'm suddenly too fucking aware of where his hand sits on my waist.

There's tension crackling between us that's so goddamn thick I can taste it. And all I can think about is how this man just handed me my entire legacy like it was nothing—while gripping me like he plans to fuck the sanity right out of my body with the other hand.

And God help me, I want him to.

I swallow once and lean in close enough that my mouth nearly brushes his ear.

"Then talk," I whisper, then shift on his lap just to feel the thick length of him already hard beneath me. "Or do you want me to beg for it first, sir?"

He glances at me again, eyes a shade darker than before. "Your grandfather—Emilio Rivera—wasn't just a rich old man with property in Puerto Rico. He was one of the last remaining heads of a multi-generational crime network. Drugs. Weapons. Shipping ports. Offshore accounts. Government ties. The Rivera family is one of the oldest organized crime syndicates on the island."

My lungs seize and I stop breathing entirely.

"When he died," he says, quieter now. "The entire network went into lockdown. No one could touch the money or the land, and the people loyal to him refused to move. Not without blood."

And suddenly I'm five again. Sitting in the hallway while my parents whispered about Puerto Rico in Spanish, always looking over their shoulders. I used to think it was about pride. Or grief. Or some irreparable rift that families just bury instead of fix.

But this? This can't be real.

He watches me fall apart in silence.

"You're his heir, Ani. His only heir. The will—his whole legacy —it's tied to your blood. Frank found out. And he wanted it."

There's no way he's saying what I think he's saying.

I shake my head. "Why not just take it? I didn't know any of this. He could've just taken it and I never would've known any different."

"Because he couldn't," Steven says, choosing each word carefully. "Rivera's estate isn't like a normal inheritance. It wasn't just money or property. Everything your grandfather built—the land, the offshore accounts, the people loyal to him—was locked behind legal bullshit and bloodline clauses. Nothing could be transferred or touched unless it went to a direct descendant."

He pauses, watching my face like he's waiting for the pieces to snap together.

"He needed to be bound to you by marriage," he says. "Your signature was the last piece. You're the only one the Rivera estate would legally recognize."

My stomach twists. "So..."

Steven nods, clenching his jaw. "You were the key. The second your name hit that paper, Frank would've had access to everything. That's why he didn't just kill you. He had to own you. None of your men would listen to him without it."

My men? And that's when it sinks in. *Holy fuck.*

"I can't believe that fucker bought me."

Steven flinches. "Yeah. Your ex sold you out, and Frank paid him off. And when you ran... he sent people after you. Then planted himself into your life to get you back."

I press my hand to my stomach to keep from throwing up. I guess that explains why he was trying so hard to win me over. Funny how it never worked. Not really. There was always something off about him. I used to think it was because I didn't want to date, turns out, it was just him.

Steven shifts. "I didn't know. Not at first. I promise."

"But you knew something." I look up. "Didn't you?"

He nods once. "I thought you were with Frank, and I thought you were part of it. Until I didn't."

"You were going to kill him."

It's not a question, because after everything I've learned, Frank's days were already numbered.

His jaw ticks. "I was. That was the job. But then I saw you. And everything changed."

I look away, blinking hard, hoping it'll stop whatever the hell is building behind my eyes. I can feel myself getting wetter. Especially since Steven's hand is now on my thigh, and he's dragging his thumb in slow, lazy circles against my skin—each pass higher than the last. It's distracting in the worst possible way. My brain's trying to process bloodlines and betrayal, and my body's over here dripping like it got the wrong memo.

"You could've told me." I say, a little breathlessly.

"And you would've done what exactly? I didn't exactly know how and once I started falling for you..." He swallows. "The truth got harder to give."

I lean back trying to see his face, but his thumb is dangerously close to where I now desperately wish it was. "And the texts?"

"I told you I had Travis look into it," he says, while he's trying to distract me with his fingers. *And it's working*. His thumb is now dragging slow, lazy circles over my clit, and he has zero plans to stop. I try not to squirm, but it's hard to focus when every nerve in my body is leaning toward his hand.

"He hasn't gotten back to me yet," Steven mutters, like it's just a minor inconvenience. "We've both been a little... busy."

He's not wrong there. I don't even want to think about what would've happened if he didn't make it. That thought's been stuck on repeat. "And your guess?"

He leans in and his mouth brushes my ear. A shiver goes down my spine and straight to my core. He starts rubbing circles again, making it really hard to concentrate.

"My guess is, it has to be Frank. The timing lines up too clean. Whoever it was wasn't just trying to scare you—they were watching. Tracking your moves. They always showed up right before something went down."

My blood goes hot, but my skin goes ice cold. "And you didn't lead with that?"

His hand doesn't stop moving. If anything, it gets slower. Crueler. "I didn't want to dump more on you when you were already barely breathing."

I stare at him, long and hard and when I finally speak, my voice is quieter than I mean it to be. "And now?"

His thumb slows, deciding how much he wants to torture me, no doubt. All I can see is heat in his eyes as he exhales, sliding his hand away with a slow, deliberate drag that leaves me aching. His arm slips around my waist and pulls me closer and I can feel how hard he is. Suddenly I can't think of any more questions.

"Come on," he murmurs against my hair. "You're hurt. Running on fumes. And you can barely stand."

I hum into his chest, eyes fluttering. "Not true. I can definitely stand... just maybe not on my own."

"Exactly my point."

His hand slides down my spine as he leans back slightly, fingers tilting my chin until I'm looking at him. "We'll get you cleaned up, then you'll rest."

I blink up at him, caught somewhere between exhaustion and rebellion. And okay, maybe I want him to take control again.

So, I slide my palms up his chest, leaning in until my lips graze his. I whisper against the corner of his mouth—"Steven, if you don't get in that shower and fuck the trauma out of me, I swear to God I'll do it myself with your toothbrush."

His jaw locks, and I'll bet my life he's deciding whether to punish me or make me beg for it. That vein in his neck—the one I swear is wired to whatever control he has left, throbs like a promise.

"Ani—"

"Your toothbrush, Steven," I whisper against his jaw, lips barely brushing skin. "Soft bristles. No lube. Your call."

The sound he makes isn't human. *Holy fuck, how did I get this lucky?*

A growl rips straight from his chest like I just snapped the last thread of his control and I'm in his arms before I can blink. He turns toward the bathroom like a man on a mission.

"You're fucking insane," he mutters, laughing.

I bite his neck hard enough to make him grunt. "Keep talking shit and I'll come before we hit the tile."

He smiles. "Careful, dear. You forget who you're mouthing off to."

EPILOGUE

Ten weeks later.

Ani

Sarah was mad at me for weeks after I got back. She called every single day just to cry and cuss me out, reminding me —loudly—that she was still pissed I got kidnapped. That she could've lost me *and* didn't even get to shoot anyone over it.

Her words. Not mine.

Honestly, I think that last part might've been what bothered her the most.

"I'm serious," she sniffled on the phone, while I was curled up in Steven's lap and trying not to cry into his hoodie for the fifth time that day. "I thought you were dead. Do you get that? Like—actually dead. In a ditch. Or locked in some psycho's cage. Or—oh my God —*trafficked*. Do you even know what that does to a girl?!"

"I'm sorry," I whispered for the thirteenth time.

"I know," she sobbed. "I'm just so happy you're alive. But I'm still mad. And for the record, I knew Frank was a freak."

We didn't talk about the worst parts at first. But she sent me a care package with Sour Patch Kids, dry shampoo, and three new shades of black eyeliner, so I knew she got it.

When I finally did tell her the truth—about Frank, about Steven, about everything—I expected tears. Maybe yelling. Possibly a margarita to the face. Instead, she grabbed the tequila and poured herself three shots.

"Okay," she said after the third shot and one very suspicious egg roll. "I forgive you. Sort of."

I laughed. "What?"

"You're back, thank God. Now I'm over it."

"You've been mad at me for a month."

"Yeah, and I mourned you like a fucking widow—while rage-scrolling your TikTok and threatening to delete every ugly photo I have of you. That's how mad I was."

She stole my Sprite without breaking eye contact. "But also? I love you. Obviously. Now shut up, because I have tea." She paused just to be dramatic. "I think I'm in love with a man I've never met."

I choked on my drink. "I'm sorry?"

"I know. I know. Don't say it." She fanned herself dramatically, leaning back like it was a confessional. "But it's true. He's funny. He's smart. He gets me. And he's hot."

"You've actually seen this guy?"

She rolled her eyes. "Not technically. He FaceTimed me once, but he was wearing a ski mask. I heard his voice though—and I swear, Ani, it had daddy energy."

I snorted. "What does that even mean?"

"It means he probably looks like he drinks espresso in a three-piece suit and could ruin my life with one look. So obviously, I'm in love."

I blinked, because *what the actual fuck.* "Okay. I have, like, six follow-up questions—but let's start with the part where he wore a ski mask and you still got horny."

"Yes! Full blackout. No eye holes. Very mysterious." She nodded, dead serious. "Like Batman—if Batman had manners and a bigger dick."

I stared at her for a solid thirty seconds, because I genuinely didn't know whether to laugh, or stage an intervention.

This is what happens when you leave your best friend unsupervised with Wi-Fi and a vibrator.

"Sarah."

She blinked, all innocent. "What?"

"You're dating a voice?"

"Okay, first of all, don't kink-shame me. Second of all, I did a reverse image search of his profile pic and he passed the vibe check. Third, we're planning on meeting in person in a few weeks."

I couldn't help but stare at her like she'd lost it. "You're going to meet a stranger from the internet whose face you've never seen."

She grinned. "You dated a mafia wannabe and fell in love with an assassin. Let me have my little mystery man."

"Touché."

"I'm serious though. I have a good feeling about this. And you know me—I never have good feelings about men. They're usually the root cause of my migraines."

"Still could be," I muttered.

She laughed. "Not this one. He's... different. He actually asks questions about my life. *And* he doesn't send unsolicited dick pics or call me 'mami' like that guy from Tinder."

I ignored the fact that she said unsolicited.

"And you're sure he's not a catfish?"

She shrugged, but there's something soft in her expression. Something almost... hopeful. "If he is," she muttered, "he's way too emotionally intelligent for a catfish. Maybe he's a sea turtle. He has boundaries."

I couldn't do anything but laugh after that, but I did grab the tequila and get myself a round.

Sarah was in love with a masked man who types like he's hot. I was busy inheriting a criminal empire and pretending I knew what the fuck I was doing.

It's fine. We're fine.

I knew that look she had—wild-eyed, reckless, and a little

unhinged. I'd seen it in the mirror once. Right before everything went sideways.

These days, I've got backup accounts, burner phones, and apparently a reputation that makes grown men piss themselves. Which is hilarious, considering I didn't even want the job.

But for some reason, they only listen to me. No matter how many times I try to hand it off, the calls still come to me.

Some mornings, I still wake up wondering if I'll have to kill someone before breakfast. But I don't flinch at silence the way I used to—and the coffee's a hell of a lot better.

I do still sleep with a weapon, only it's not under my pillow anymore. It's next to me in bed. And he's 6'3", built like sin, and completely unhinged when it comes to me. So yeah. I'm good.

We got another dog somewhere in the middle of it all, and named him Ronald. *For obvious reasons.* He chews Steven's shoelaces and worships Bern like she runs the house. Which, to be fair, she does.

My relationship with Steven is obsessive and violent and louder than anything I've ever known, but it's real. And for once, it's mine.

I stretch, getting tangled up in the sheets as the sunlight filters through the window, making it the kind of morning that makes people want to journal or manifest or drink herbal tea.

Instead, I'm doom-scrolling for unsolved murders while wondering if there's any chicken and rice left in the fridge.

Steven's not here, unfortunately. Not that my pussy could handle round six right now. Pretty sure I didn't fall asleep—I passed out. A girl can only take so many orgasms before her soul starts leaving her body. And after getting edged within an inch of my sanity all night, I'm exhausted.

The man multitasks. Aggressively. And he always looks so fucking hot doing it. I want to unzip his skin and climb inside just so he takes me everywhere with him.

I can't complain—because whatever he's doing usually dictates what kind of mood he's in when he gets home. Which is exactly how last night happened.

I'm just about to get up and pour coffee when the knock comes. I freeze mid-stretch, and Bern lets out one warning bark from the end of the bed, like *how dare the world interrupt our soft era.* Ronald loses his shit on instinct—barking like a gremlin, feet scrambling against the comforter as he tries to figure out what we're mad about.

I pad barefoot to the door, tugging Steven's hoodie tighter around me—the black one with the bleach stain from last night when I impulsively bleached a chunk of my hair. Honestly, it's mine now. He just doesn't know it yet..

When I open the door, I freeze. *What the fuck?*

So many fucking boxes cover the porch and they're all addressed to me.

I bend down to grab the first one, and it's heavier than I expected. Now I'm mildly concerned I just picked up a bomb—but I don't stop. Curiosity outweighs whatever rational response I should probably be having, like calling Steven. Or, you know, just leaving them there.

So I start opening them, one by one, bracing for chaos. But nope—every damn box is full of books.

They're all first editions. Some are collector's copies that probably cost more than my old rent. A few I've loved since I was a kid, and some others I've never even heard of, but I can already tell I'm going to lose sleep over them.

It takes me a minute longer than it should to realize what I'm actually looking at.

And when it hits me, I'm already crying. These aren't just random books. They're all from my wishlist. Every single one.

Each box has a number written on the lid—1 through 27. And tucked just inside each one is a folded piece of parchment paper.

I open the first one, and it's blank. Second one? Also blank. Third—same. My hands are shaking, and my heart's doing something weird and traitorous in my chest, but I can't stop. *Am I missing part of the joke?*

And when I get to Box 11, it says, *"Until the very end."* I read it out loud and instantly regret it, because now I'm crying again.

Box 15 says: *"You are protected, in short, by your ability to love."*

And Box 20—*"Happiness can be found even in the darkest of times..."*

I whisper the rest without needing the paper. "...if one only remembers to turn on the light."

By then, I'm on the floor. Completely wrecked. Books everywhere, heart in pieces. He's probably smiling somewhere like the smug bastard he is, knowing I'd cry over this. And I've never loved him more than I do in this moment.

All the boxes are open, and I have my tears mostly under control—when I spot a smaller box I must've missed. The label says 9¾, and I swear I actually laugh through a sob.

I stare at it for a full thirty seconds before I can see enough to open it. Inside is a single book, with the quote taped to the top.

It's not Hogwarts, but it's yours.
You collect stories. I collect you.
So I built a place to keep both.

I turn and head straight for the bedroom to grab my phone, pulse picking up with every step. I'm already reaching for the nightstand—ready to call him—when my eyes catch on the card. I freeze for half a second. It's written in that same vicious scrawl I've grown to crave like oxygen.

Back hallway.
Third door.

*Try not to scream, you'll scare Ronald and he'll pee
again.*

My brows lift, but my thighs press together instinctively. Some feral part of me hopes he's waiting. I can feel myself getting wetter with every step, as I move down the hall. Past the guest room. Past his office. To the third door.

I open it—and forget how to breathe. It's not a guest room anymore, it's a library.

Floor-to-ceiling shelves wrap around the walls, already filled with books. There's a skylight above, and warm sunlight spills in like some kind of staged fantasy. But it's the ladder that gets me.

It's one of those sliding wooden ones—just like at the library.

My face goes hot instantly. The last time I was near one of these, he had his head between my legs and told me not to make a sound.

I shake the memory off and look up, spotting a book shoved at the very top—a black leather one with no title. I climb up to grab it, and the second I do, something slips out and flutters to the floor.

*You've got the house. The dogs. The guy. Now you've
got the room.
So next time I'm face-deep in my favorite little cunt,
I won't have to worry about being interrupted.
Enjoy your ladder, dear. I know I will.*

*P.S.—I'll be back before dinner.
PPS—Till murder-suicide do us part. I love you.
—S*

I cover my mouth, already blushing so hard it feels like my skin might melt off. I drop into the chair as tears stream down my cheeks, which feels wildly unfair, considering how fucking soaked I already am. My body doesn't know if it wants to keep crying or crawl into his lap and beg.

It still gets me sometimes that I'm here. That he's mine. That somehow, after everything, I crawled out of the fire and landed in a life that is actually pretty amazing.

It's mine. All of it.

And I don't even know what to do with that—except sit here, crying, soaked, and aching in this stupid chair I'm 90% sure he bought just to break me in later. He gives me everything I didn't think I could have... then fucks me like he's trying to erase the years I went without it.

The floor creaks behind me, and I turn—already knowing who it is. I know that walk like I know my own heartbeat. I would recognize it in a hurricane.

He steps inside, and my pussy clenches like it fucking recognizes him and knows exactly what he's about to do to it. One look and I'm ready to commit a whole list of felonies with his last name.

He's wearing a black shirt that's stretched across his chest, sleeves shoved to his elbows. His forearms are veined and flexed, tattoos on full display—and somehow the way he's just standing there makes me want to drop to my knees and ruin us both.

Then his eyes drop, and when they come back up, I catch it— that bulge in his jeans, thick and definitely getting harder. He's not even pretending to hide it.

My whole body clenches and I grip the note tighter, pressing my thighs together like that'll do a damn thing to help.

God, that look he gets when he knows he's wrecked me is my favorite flavor of fucked. His gaze drops to the note, then back up to my face—and it's a miracle I'm still standing.

He smirks, smug as hell. "You like it?"

I bite my lip. "The ladder or the threat of interruption while you devour me alive?"

"Yes." He chuckles.

I laugh through the tears. "You built me a library."

He steps closer, eyes never leaving mine. "You built me a life."

My chest does that stupid tight ache thing that makes me want to kiss him and punch him in the same breath. But before I can say anything, he reaches into his back pocket.

"I have one more surprise."

He pulls out a plain, silver key with a black tag attached to it.

My brows pinch. "What is that?"

He shrugs, like it's nothing. "A key. It goes to a building."

"What building?"

His mouth curves into the smile that ruins lives. "The one you wouldn't shut up about months ago."

My brain short-circuits. "The one that was already sold when I got there? Wait, how did you know about that?"

"Because I was the one who bought it."

My mouth opens. Nothing comes out because my brain's not functioning. I'm just standing there like a fucking idiot while my heart shatters.

"You bought it?" I whisper. "You bought me a fucking building?"

He leans in, kissing the side of my mouth. "Dreams are for the dead, pretty girl. You've got plans."

And now I'm crying again. How the hell are you supposed to breathe when the same man who wrecked you puts you back together—then builds you a library just to hand you the goddamn world?

You cry. You melt. And then you ride him into next week, thanking him—loudly. Bent over the desk. Up against the shelves. Maybe even on that stupid table by the front window, just to be dramatic.

He kisses me like he's starving—like it's been weeks, not hours.

And when I kiss him back, it's not because I'm broken. Or lost. Or looking to be saved.

It's because I finally stopped running.

For the first time in my life... I already have everything I need.

Him.